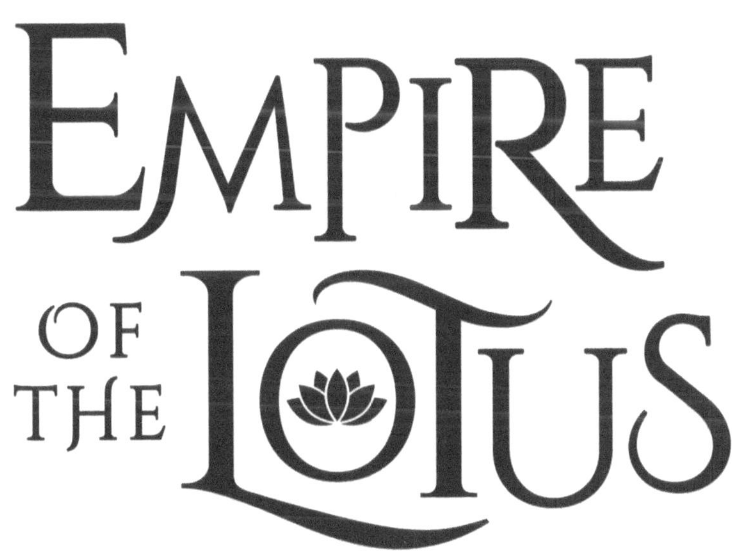

EMPIRE OF THE LOTUS

DOROTHY DREYER

Empire of the Lotus
Complete Series Collection

Copyright © 2021
Edited by Amy McNulty
Cover design by Covered by Nicole

Paperback ISBN: 978-1-952667-35-0
Casebound ISBN: 978-1-952667-36-7
Dustjacket Hardcover: 978-1-952667-37-4

Published April 2021 by Snowy Wings Publishing
PO Box 1035, Turner, OR 97392

Table of Contents

The legend goes …

The ancient deity Kashmeru knew only one true love—the Lotus empress Lakshmi, who in his eyes possessed all beauty and grace the universe could hold. Their hearts called to one another, a hold so strong that neither one could deny the bond. But Lakshmi knew that Kashmeru's spirit was not pure, for an evil dwelled within his soul, a wickedness so corrupt that it could destroy the universe.

And when she denied him her love, destroying the universe was the very thing he vowed to do.

Throughout the centuries, their reincarnations were drawn to one another, but the outcome was always the same: Lakshmi would never give Kashmeru her heart.

To put an end to his constant chase, the Empire of the Lotus defeated Kashmeru and sealed him in a tomb using mage powers, where he would remain trapped …

… until the Council of the Seven could secure the blood of the Lotus empress to set him free.

CRIMSON MAGE

BOOK ONE

ONE

Mayhara swore that if her ComLinq buzzed one more time, she'd hurl it through her computer monitor. Her fingers danced near the device, itching to grab it if it dared to make another sound. She inhaled deeply, cautioning herself to calm down.

Breathe in for four seconds. Hold for seven. Calmly exhale for eight.

She knew she wouldn't actually chuck the device; not only would she probably lose her job, but it would take forever to set up a new ComLinq, especially since she hadn't backed up her data for at least a month. Plus, it was unlike her to lose her cool like that. No. If Rajev had sent her another message, she would simply remove him from her contacts—which she should have done the moment she'd found out he'd logged into her bank account and transferred a thousand of her merits to his account. She didn't need to see another apology message or another excuse that he'd simply been borrowing the credit. She didn't believe him, and she couldn't trust him. No matter how many times he told her he loved her. Still, though she'd been quick to change her banking passwords, she hadn't yet blocked him from her Linq.

Breathe in for four seconds. Hold for seven. Calmly exhale for eight.

She was fooling herself if she thought she could actually hold her breath for seven seconds. Instead of the usual four-seven-eight, she opted for her more realistic four-five-six.

Cringing, she ignored the slight burn in her chest, refusing to believe it was heartache. Rajev wasn't worth it. It was probably just the curry she'd had for lunch. She took a sip of her bottled water and punched in the numbers for the next file she needed to process. She may have been down a thousand merits in her bank account, but she'd be damned if her stupid boyfriend—*ex-boyfriend*, actually—would cause her to fall behind in her work.

As the names and numbers on her screen began to blur in her vision, Mayhara took another slow, deep breath. She closed her eyes, calling upon the meditation technique she'd learned when she'd been training back at the mage academy—the very academy the government had all but forced her to forget about. She cringed at the heartbreaking memory of the academy's shutdown, the brutal invasion of the government forces, the outrageous law that announced that mages were now outlawed. The system that had stripped her of her identity. The only reason she was sitting at this desk doing government work rather than sitting in a prison camp starving to death was because she had agreed to give up chakra magic and become a pawn on the New Asian Administration's side of the law. And she had only done that to ensure the safety of her family.

Her fingers immediately went to the back of her neck, feeling the small scar that had been left when the government had implanted their blocking device. That was what they called it—a *blocking* device—but it didn't block mage powers at all. Instead, upon detecting mage powers being used, the device would send shockwaves of painful electricity to the implantee's nerve endings, causing enough pain that the mage would cease using their powers. When the mage stopped using those powers, the blocker would stop sending the shockwaves.

Cut it out. You've got work to do.

She opened her eyes and shook off the memory. There was nothing she could do about her old life now. She had no choice but to move forward. Darshana—her guru at the academy—had always taught her to hold on to positivity. To concentrate on any happy little thought she could find in her subconscious, anything that brought her even the smallest amount of joy. To think about that and only that for seventeen seconds. Doing so should bring a similar happy thought, and so on and so on, until the universe had no choice but to match that vibration and deliver something equally positive.

Darshana had said it could be as simple as enjoying the sound of rain or smiling at a cat licking its paw to clean its face.

She had a nice flat in the upper end of New Jaipur—one of the most sought-after places to live after the chaos of the East Asian Unification— she made a generous salary, and her two-year probationary job trial was almost complete, meaning she would soon secure an official position at the Citizen Census Processing Centre. All this at the age of nineteen; not every young woman in New United Asia was this lucky.

To hell with Rajev! She was better off without him.

"Hey, Mayha."

The voice from her office door pulled her out of her thoughts. She glanced up at Riya, who leaned against the door frame with her arms crossed over her tight sweater. Mayhara did her best to offer her friend a smile.

"Doing any better?" Riya leaned her head forward as she said it, lowering her voice. "Or do I have to kick you-know-who's ass?"

Mayhara appreciated that Riya knew not to spread the news about Rajev and his wrongdoings. The last thing she needed was rumors circulating about how naïve she was, especially before her promotion was finalized.

"I'm absolutely fine," she said, keeping her chin up. "That piece of scum isn't even worth a second of thought. I've got more important things to concentrate on. Why do you ask?"

"Because that 'piece of scum' keeps texting me to ask if you're getting his messages."

It took all Mayhara's energy to not roll her eyes. Instead, she focused her attention on her monitor. "Let him wonder."

Riya pushed herself off the doorframe, checking over her shoulder before approaching Mayhara's desk. "It's a shame. He was cute. I thought maybe you two would settle down together."

Mayhara almost laughed. Her relationship with Rajev had begun because they'd had something to commiserate over, namely missing their families. Except Rajev's family was in another country because of the business they ran, not because they were locked up in a prison camp. And that made it even more infuriating; he *knew* she was saving up to support her family once she'd be able to petition for their release. He knew how much she needed the credit, and he stole it anyway.

It was for the better that their relationship ended anyway. She had to put her family first. She shook her head at Riya. "I'm too young to settle down. Not in a serious, ready-for-marriage kind of way, at least."

"Right." Riya smoothed the material of her skirt. "I keep forgetting you're only nineteen. Feels like you've been here for ages."

Mayhara held back a sigh. The truth was, it felt like ages to her as well.

She'd been seized by the government when she'd been a mere seventeen, sacrificing everything to keep her family safe. Everything she'd ever known had been stolen from her: her scheduled training at the mage academy, her home, her parents, her sisters, her guru. Even her sense of self. In order to survive, she'd become what the government had wanted her to become.

A *ping* on her monitor snapped her out of her thoughts. Her nerves tensed for a moment, fearing that Rajev had found a way to hack into her work's server. Then she realized that rather than another message from Rajev, it was an interoffice notification.

"What is it?" Riya asked.

"Director Shei's secretary. Shei wants to see me."

Riya's eyes lit up. "Maybe she's promoting you early!"

Mayhara bit back a hopeful smile. "It could be anything." She stood and worried the collar of her blouse, making her way toward the door.

"Before you go…" Riya had a sheepish look on her face. "I need to ask you a favor."

"Sure, what is it?"

"Decon finally took the hint and asked me out."

"Came to his senses, did he?"

"Yeah. Thing is, I've been trying to figure out what to wear. And… you know that red dress you wore to last year's charity event?" Riya bit her lip.

"You want to borrow it?"

"Could I?"

Mayhara let out a small laugh, nodding her head. The only reason she owned the dress was because her boss had insisted she wear something appropriate. The charity event had had a strict dress code. "Of course. What time do you want to pick it up?"

"We're going to dinner at seven, so I'll need to come by… at the latest six? Five-thirty would be better."

"Oh. I'm not sure I'll be home by then." She rubbed at her arm, considering giving Riya the key code to her flat. Normally, she wouldn't have thought twice about it, but seeing as how the guy she had been in a relationship with had practically robbed her recently, she had a moment of doubt.

Riya flashed her a curious look. "Mayha?"

Mayhara shook her head, telling herself not to let Rajev's treacherous behavior affect all her decisions. "I'll linq you my key code if I'm not done by then."

Riya clasped her hands together, a huge smile plastered on her face. "Thank you, Mayha! You're the best. I promise I'll just be in and out. I just need the dress. It's going to make the evening so much better."

"Then I hope you have lots of fun." Mayhara shoved her Linq in her blazer pocket. "I better go before Shei pops a vein."

Mayhara made her way down the hall to the elevator, her heels clicking along the marble floor. The high-tech building's built-in sensors lit up her path as she maneuvered down the long hallway. When she reached the elevator, the doors opened without her having to push any buttons, the soft swish of it like a whisper, and the computer's voice welcomed her by name.

"Twenty-eight, please," Mayhara instructed.

The elevator doors closed smoothly. Director Shei's office was on the top floor of the twenty-eight-story building, so Mayhara had about a half a minute on the elevator to try to compose herself. If she got the promotion early, she might be able to petition to get her family out of the holding camp before the month was over. Her eyes brimmed with tears at the thought of being able to see her family again, to finally have them come live with her. She wouldn't be able to get them all out at once, but one-by-one, they'd be together again.

"Floor twenty-eight," the computer informed her.

As the elevator doors slid open, Mayhara blew out a calming breath and held her chin up. She couldn't show weakness or uncertainty. She had to come across as self-assured and confident.

Pai-han, Director Shei's secretary, stood as Mayhara approached, his form slender in his button-up white shirt and black slacks. He gave her a slight bow, which she returned, then gestured to a chair nearby.

"Director Shei will see you momentarily," Pai-han said. "Can I offer you some matcha?" His fingers hovered over the control pad on his desk, ready to click in an order.

Offering tea was a good sign. Mayhara's shoulders relaxed a bit. "No, thank you."

"Very well." He abandoned the control pad and gestured again to the chair. "Please have a seat."

She sat in the plush chair, clearing her throat. Though she felt impatient to find out why she was being called to the director's office, she was relieved to have a couple more minutes to compose herself. If she could just stop the sweat from forming at her temples, she might be all right.

Director Shei's office door opened, making Mayhara jolt upright. There was no chance to stop the sweating now.

Shiny silver buttons on a blue-grey, synthetic wool uniform—and an affixed badge sporting the New United Asia emblem—caught her eye. It was a law enforcement officer who'd stepped out of Shei's office, and Mayhara's brow furrowed. The officer turned to bow to Director Shei, who'd followed him out of her office, looking pristine and polished, her hair in a tight bun and her dress suit appearing freshly pressed.

The officer's eyes roamed toward Mayhara for a split second before reverting back to the director. "We'll be in touch," he said.

"Thank you, officer." She didn't smile or bow her head to him. She simply watched him leave for a moment before turning toward Mayhara. "Miss Guatama, you may enter my office now."

Mayhara stood and straightened her clothes, following her boss into the office. Inside, her eyes immediately went to the view of the city from Director Shei's panorama windows. It was incredible to see. The sun had started to set, spreading bursts of pink and orange through the sky and prompting the city buildings to darken into silhouettes. She had to stop herself from gaping at the sight and instead settled herself into the chair across from her boss's enormous desk. The feel of the cold leather brought back memories of herself at seventeen, sitting in the very same chair, being forced to choose between working for the government or being sent to a prison camp. She'd been terrified then, and somehow, her feelings in the present moment weren't that different.

"I hope I didn't tear you away from an important project," Director Shei said, straightening a stack of papers on her desk.

"No, Director." Mayhara fought to not fidget. "I was actually glad you called me to your office."

Shei raised a perfectly-plucked brow. "Oh? Why is that?"

Mayhara blanched. She found it hard to move her lips correctly.

Struggling to find her voice, she wiped her sweaty palms on her skirt and shook her head. "What I mean is… I'm always available for whatever you need."

"Hmm." Shei studied her for a moment and then leaned forward on her desk. "I have an important assignment for you. I hope you are diligent enough to attend to the task."

"Of course, Director."

Shei spoke slowly and concisely. "It seems the political unrest in the prison camps of Old Bombay is rising."

Director Shei pushed a button on the side of her desk, and the blinds on the windows began to lower. Sliding open one of her desk drawers, she pulled out a long cylinder tube. It was made of a shiny black material, and the ends were adorned with red tassels. Shei pushed a small silver button at one end of the tube, which omitted a beep. The tube opened, and Shei pulled out a scroll.

Mayhara inched forward in her seat as Shei unrolled the scroll over her desk. Shei spread her hand and dragged it along the electronic map of New United Asia. Bordered areas on the map lit up in bright blue lines on the electronic paper, and a series of red flashing dots were spread out in random spots. "These blue areas are the prison camps. The red you see are where accounts of rebellious behavior have been reported. At first the numbers were low, but the incidents are now climbing, and word is these radicals have formed a wide-spread band of mercenaries with the intention of waging war on the New Asian Administration."

"Is that why the Imperial Police were here? Are you being threatened?"

"It hasn't come to that, no. But the Imperial Police do want our assistance."

Mayhara hesitated. Something in her gut twisted. Though she couldn't claim to be of the same opinion as radicals, the people in those camps were her people. She narrowed her eyes at something on the map that caught her attention. "What are the black triangles?"

Shei seemed to tighten her jaw before offering the slightest of smiles. She rolled up the map and returned it to the cylinder. "Nothing to be concerned about. But the Imperial Police have been brainstorming ideas to deter the mercenaries and have come to us with one of their strategies."

"What do they need?"

"Leverage. The radicals must have families, close friends, people on the outside they associate with."

Mayhara swallowed hard. "Do the police mean to extort the radicals by threatening their families?"

Director Shei's expression became colder than usual. "It's not our business how the law deals with them. It's just our duty to assist them."

"H-How? What do you need me to do?"

"You work with the census records. I need you to track down the radicals' families."

"That could take the whole weekend."

"Do you have a problem with that?"

Mayhara was about to answer when she felt a vibration in her blazer pocket. Before logic could tell her to ignore it, she slipped out her Linq, low enough that Director Shei could not see, and glanced at the screen.

The Lotus is in danger. Meet me at the loop. 7 P.M. -GD

Mayhara blinked, unable to wrap her head around the message. She didn't recognize the number the message was from, but the mention of the "Lotus" and asking to meet at the "loop" meant it could only be one person. Especially with the initials GD.

Guru Darshana?

She hadn't heard from her guru since the school had been shut down. In fact, she doubted Darshana had ever had a ComLinq. It seemed unlikely she would have one now, but still...

The twisting in Mayhara's gut grew more intense, and her palms began to tingle. Her mage powers called out to her, and she then realized that it was why she'd started to feel pain. The device implanted in her neck was programmed to inflict pain if it sensed her powers being used. But this call for help was something the root of her being could not ignore. Her mage energy was naturally magnetized to her guru's beckon.

"Miss Guatama," Director Shei said, the authority in her voice almost palpable. "Please answer my question. Do you have a problem with my request?"

Mayhara squeezed her hands shut, trying to shut off the power. She opened her mouth, but no sound escaped.

Director Shei narrowed her eyes. "Do I have to remind you that the review for your official position with the government will be taking place soon? Your compliance in this assignment would do well to sway the board members in your favor."

And having that official position was what she needed to see her family again.

"No, Director Shei. I don't have a problem with it." Mayhara struggled to keep her hands shut. Her nails dug into her palms, making her want to wince. Still, she kept a straight face. "Of course I'll help."

"Very well." There was a hint of the smallest smile on the director's face. She rolled up the map and placed the scroll back in its tube. "Don't stay too late tonight. I'd prefer it if you were alert and at your best to work the entire day tomorrow."

Mayhara nodded absently.

"That will be all. Thank you for your service."

Mayhara stood and gave her boss a curt bow before leaving the office. She walked past Pai-han in a daze. It felt like forever before she reached the elevator. Once inside, she opened her hands. Small molecules of sparkling, crimson energy burst from her palms, clouding the elevator. Mayhara waved her hands around to clear the dust, ignoring the ache in her neck, and then whipped out her Linq to reread the message.

A cold shiver ran over her body. She winced as the pinpricks of pain shot through her. But the ComLinq message overwhelmed her more. The Lotus was in danger? How could that be possible? She hadn't even been aware the empress had been reborn.

TWO

*L*akshmi.

Naree opened her eyes. His voice caressed her like velvet. He was still with her. He'd never left.

"Kashmeru?"

Yes, my love. I'm waiting for you.

Naree turned her head, her cheek brushing against the silky pillow. This was not her bed. She could barely remember how she ended up in this apartment. All she knew was she was pulled here, as if some magical force had a hold of her heart and wouldn't let go until she followed where it led.

Lakshmi, I need you.

It wasn't the name she went by in this life, but it was her name once. Still. Deep inside of her, she was still Lakshmi.

"I can't," she said. "We can't be together. I should go home."

I am your home, my love.

"No." A tear escaped and slid down her cheek, for her heart did not agree with her words. She longed to be with him as much as he longed to be with her.

Come to me. I will show you.

She closed her eyes, letting the tears come.

THREE

Mayhara stayed off the well-lit city streets, and the black jeans and dark grey hoodie helped her blend into the shadows of the night. Getting to the underground station wasn't the tricky part, though. The tricky part would be catching the sub-train without anyone noticing her. But she had to take the risk; there was no other way of finding out if the message she'd received was really from her guru.

Before she'd ventured out into the dark of night, Mayhara had linqed Riya the key code to her flat and placed the dress she'd wanted to borrow near the front door so she wouldn't have to go searching for it. Her anxiousness about whether or not Riya would get in or if she'd remember to lock up once she left slowly dissipated the closer Mayhara got to the sub-train station. Instead, her thoughts were geared more toward why the Lotus empress might be in trouble, when the new empress had been reborn, and why Mayhara herself was being called to help.

She pulled her hood over her head as she got to the station and kept her shoulders hunched. Mages were outlawed, and though riding the sub-train wasn't an illegal act, she could run into trouble if anyone found out she was going to her old training academy.

Especially because it was located on the palace grounds.

She kept her head down until the sub-train pulled into the station, averting her gaze from the people on the platform and the passengers already on the train. Her shoulders remained hunched as she slipped into an empty seat. Her skin tingled, and she couldn't get past the feeling she was being watched. A guy in a black trench coat loitered by the train doors with his hands in his pockets. Fighting the acidic feeling in her stomach, she averted her eyes when he looked her way. She glanced at the route map on the sub-train monitor, noting that she needed to wait seven more stops before she reached her destination. It was something she actually had memorized, but counting down the stations somehow kept her calm.

The man lurking by the door shifted his position, leaning on the opposite side of the door frame and taking his Linq out of his pocket. She told herself not to be paranoid, that the man was probably not linqing anyone about her being on the train. As they approached the next station, it crossed her mind to get off, to see if he would follow her, but when the train pulled to a stop, the man exited and went on his way.

She let out a sigh of relief. The government was controlling, but she wasn't sure if they would go so far as to monitor her Linq messages. Of course, if they did, it was highly unlikely they would know what the "loop" was. Plus, if they were hell bent on keeping her away from finding out about the Lotus empress, they would be sure to have her followed. Yet everyone she'd been suspicious of on the train so far had departed.

Stop after stop, people exited the sub-train, much too concerned about finally getting home after a busy day to pay her any attention. The train ascended from its underground route to one above ground. They were out of the city now and traveling through the countryside on the outskirts. Her muscles loosened, and she began to relax in her seat, focusing instead on the scenery outside her window, even as dark as it was. It had been two years since she'd been to the palace. Two years since she'd been ripped out of the training academy on the palace grounds. She was both excited to see it again and fearful of the state it might be in after the Eradication soldiers had ambushed it.

One stop before hers, she was left alone on the train. She glanced around, spotting the security cameras and wondering if the train driver found it odd that she would be traveling so far. After all, there was nothing out here but the abandoned palace. She pulled her hood tighter over her head, hoping the cameras hadn't caught too much footage of her.

She stood as the train started to slow and headed toward the door. With her hands hidden in her jacket pockets, she exited the train and trudged toward the path that led to the palace.

Like a land of respite, the giant structure of the palace, which could be seen past the sturdy cast-iron fence standing sentry around the grounds, was surrounded by once-well-tended-to gardens, now abandoned and left to wither. There was apparent damage to the buildings that made up the different wings of the palace, but still it stood, holding strong like a sturdy skeleton whose flesh and guts had been beaten and ripped apart. Mayhara gasped as she drew closer, hardly remembering the piles of rubble and shards of broken stained glass littering the imperial property.

As she pushed open the unlocked gate, her heart felt heavy, as if it too had been partially demolished with the place she had once called home.

The fact that it was abandoned—and that no one seemed to be around for miles—made her think that the government had no further use for the palace, now that it was destroyed, and had left it untouched after the ambush.

Even in the darkness, Mayhara could make out the different areas of the palace: the guard stations, the mediation center, the jogging path for the students, the gazebo where they held special summer events, the zen statues, and fountains. She was glad not all of it was destroyed.

She made her way toward the palace entrance. The large double doors had been knocked down during the ambush, so there would be no problem getting in. Her heart raced with anticipation to see the familiar hall that had welcomed her so many years ago. The emptiness of the place surprised her; she had never seen the palace so vacant in all her years attending the mage academy. Though she spent more time in the classrooms and the training halls, the students of the academy frequented the palace on more occasions than she could name. Somehow, even empty, it felt as if it were filled with magic. Even the dust floating through the palace seemed to carry a magical element, as if it were still holding on to hope that the empire would be restored.

She checked the time on her Linq and pushed forward. The main hall led straight back, where she found the door that went out to the courtyard between the palace and the school. Weeds and debris covered the once-pristine sandstone path in the courtyard. The sound of her shoes crunching along through the dead leaves made her uneasy, as if she were disturbing a place of peace.

She passed a wooden bench under a tall Sakura tree, and her chest throbbed with the memory of spending free periods with her friends there. She wrapped an arm around her stomach, which roiled with the ache of being torn away from them all. She'd barely spoken any of their names since that day. Though it had been a time of anticipation—a period of time when the entire empire had waited for the reincarnation of the Lotus empress—

Mayhara and her friends had still been honored to be a part of the mage academy, training to defend the long-awaited empress, whenever she was fated to appear.

In front of the school, she took in the sight of the broken windows and overturned desks that had made their way out onto the lawn because of the attack. A shiver trembled through her as she fought the terror of the memory. She and her friends had been shocked. A few classmates and teachers had even died trying to fight back. If they had been prepared, perhaps they could have held their ground, but it had been an ambush— the Eradication, the government had called it—and they hadn't stood a chance.

They had all been detained, separated, and worst of all, they'd been confused. All Mayhara had known was that everyone she knew and loved was being threatened. The government had given her a choice, and in the end, she'd chosen to keep her family alive.

Tears brimmed in Mayhara's eyes. The memories that flooded back were like a tsunami of pain and sorrow. She shook her head, forcing the thoughts away. She was here for a reason, and she needed to hurry up and find out why. She needed to find out if the message she'd received was truly from her former guru.

She turned on her heel, facing away from the school building, and headed toward the combat field. Stone tiles were lined up in a circular pattern. This was where they'd done most of their mage training. Mayhara's palms grew hot just from being here.

She made her way to the center of the stones. Senses on high alert, she held her arms away from her body, palms down. For a moment, she hesitated, curious and a bit afraid that she'd been set up. Well, if she had, she would deal with it. There was no turning back now.

She closed her eyes and let her magic be free. A warm thrill spiraled through her, and she couldn't hold back the smile from finally feeling the exhilaration of allowing her mage powers to surface. Her blocker kicked in and sent electric pulses through her body. At first, she tensed up, letting out a groan from the pain. But she clenched her teeth together and pushed through the pain. She couldn't let that damned blocker stop her from finding out if her guru needed her help or if the Lotus empress had truly been reincarnated. What was a little pain compared to restoring peace to the world?

Okay, it was a bit more than a little pain. She squeezed her eyes shut and forced herself to fight through the pulsing ache in her veins.

Her hands grew hotter. She heard a shifting of stones.

Opening her eyes, she witnessed a sight she hadn't seen in years. A metal loop, eight feet in diameter, that lay within the pattern of the stones around her began to rotate. First in a circle around her until it sped up slightly and began to emit a red glow. And then one end of the loop lifted from the stones and into the air, the other end sinking into the earth, forming a vertical circle around her.

In the next moment, the stones around her seemed to drop into the ground, but they did so systematically, forming a spiral staircase that led downward beneath the surface of the ground. She smiled at the familiar sight, having at one time thought that she would never again be able to behold it. She waited until all the stones had shifted into place, and then she began her descent.

A feeling of nostalgia came over her as she descended into the dark underground chamber. Even running her hand along the railing brought back memories. As she reached the bottom of the staircase, she took in the sight of the huge training hall. The administration had not been aware of the space. It remained untouched. She felt relieved to know there was at least one place on the palace grounds the government hadn't decimated. The only sign of disturbance were small rocks and rubble that had fallen from the ceiling, evidently the fallout from the Eradication above-ground.

She took a few steps forward, scanning the area. The silence pushed in on her, and her palms began to tingle. Instinctively, she held them up, preparing herself.

"Darshana?"

From a dark corner of the space, a figure moved into the light. Mayhara's breath hitched as she realized it was not her guru, but some hooded man. His hoodie cast a shadow over his face, and she could barely make out his eyes.

I've been set up!

"Stop right there," she shouted, glowing crimson particles emanating from her palms, ready to do her bidding.

"You don't understand," the mysterious man said. He held up his hands.

Mayhara didn't have time to question whether he was about to unleash powers against her; she pushed her energy out.

Streams of rock-hard crimson particles flew through the air toward the man.

He ducked down to dodge them, rolled to the side, and then jumped up into a defensive position.

Mayhara charged at him, ready to hit him with another blast of crimson.

Instead of backing away, he swooped down, low to the ground, and knocked her off her feet.

She twisted as she fell, rolling to her side and pushing herself up. She swung her arm as if pitching a ball, and a glowing sphere of crimson coursed through the air. It hit him in the shoulder, knocking him down.

Not taking a chance that he would be down for long, Mayhara rushed toward him, palms up.

"Wait," came a voice from behind her.

Mayhara froze, nearly tripping as she skidded to a stop. Palms still up, she swiveled around to face the source of the voice.

"Darshana!"

The old woman raised a brow. "Long time, no annoying red dust."

Mayhara opened her mouth to respond, but the room spun in on her from shock. She stumbled backward, barely catching herself before she fell.

"Don't kill the boy, dear," Darshana said. "You need to listen to him."

FOUR

ayhara slowly lowered her hands. She felt the tingle of the glow fade to nothing by the time her hands reached her thighs.

With wide eyes, she took in the sight of her former guru. She hadn't changed much, save for a few more strands of grey hair. For someone nearing sixty—or was it seventy?—Darshana had an amazing complexion; she hardly had any wrinkles. Her form was petite, and though Mayhara had already been a head taller than her the last time they'd seen each other, she towered even higher over her now that Darshana had developed a slight hunch to her back.

Mayhara couldn't stop the smile spreading across her face. She quickly placed her feet together, made a fist with one hand, laid a flat palm over the fist with her other hand, and gave Darshana a respectful bow. As soon as she straightened back up, she ran toward her guru and threw her arms around her.

"Darshana, it feels like forever."

Darshana stroked the back of Mayhara's head once. "Time is but an illusion, my crimson petal."

Mayhara backed up, studying her guru in wonder. "What is happening? I'm so confused. I wasn't even sure that message was from you."

Darshana tucked her hands into her long, wide sleeves and nodded. "It was from me. We have come to a difficult circumstance, and the world needs your help."

"The world?" Mayhara shook her head. "But—Why me? And what does this guy have to do with it?"

The man cleared his throat, moving into the shaft of light that snuck through the cracks of the ceiling. He nonchalantly pulled his hood off his head.

Mayhara studied him, squinting her eyes. "Wait. I … I know you, don't I? I remember you from school. Jae-hyun?"

"I wondered when you would recognize me." He leaned forward, sticking his hands in his pockets. "But, please, it's just 'Jae.'"

"Jae. Right. You've… uh, filled out." As soon as Mayhara said it, she felt a hot blush spread across her cheeks.

Jae rubbed at his shoulder—the shoulder where she'd hit him with crimson energy, she realized. "Yeah, so have you."

As a flush crept across her cheeks, she turned her attention to Darshana. "Uh, so what's this all about?"

Jae took a deep breath and gave Darshana a look. Mayhara narrowed her eyes at her guru, her curiosity at its peak.

"It's about the Lotus empress. She's in danger."

"That's what your message said." Mayhara shook her head again, still not grasping the reality of the situation. "I didn't know she'd been reincarnated. We were all under the assumption the line had died out."

"Well, it didn't," Jae said, moving closer to them. "And I know this because the Lotus empress… is my sister."

Mayhara's jaw dropped slightly. "What? No." She didn't know why she'd blatantly called it out as if implying he was lying, but her mind couldn't process what he'd said. "How old is your sister?"

"She just turned eighteen."

"What?" Mayhara scoffed. "You want me to believe the Lotus empress has been alive for eighteen years and nobody knew about her?"

"Not exactly. Few knew—"

Mayhara cut him off as she pushed back her hair from her temples, her mind full of confusion. "But… But if your sister is the empress, and she's around our age, she would have been at school with us."

"When my parents found out about her, they feared for her life. They told no one. They hid the truth and kept her safe at home. They felt she was at risk because of the rumors about the Pishacha."

Mayhara's brow furrowed as she tried to remember how the legend went.

Darshana was the one to remind her. "Upon the one hundredth reincarnation of the Lotus empress, the dark god Kashmeru would send out his shadow army—Pishacha—to destroy the reborn empress, which in turn would bring about the collapse of the universe."

"So my parents kept her hidden," Jae said.

"But that's just an old made-up tale." Mayhara almost laughed. "Something we were told as children to scare us."

"It doesn't feel like a false threat when the possibility of a family member being killed hovers over you. Not to mention the world being destroyed. My parents didn't want to take any chances."

"And now they're looking for her," Mayhara guessed. "The Pishacha. They somehow found out."

"You could say that," Jae said, letting out a sigh. "Except it's a little more complicated."

"Complicated how?"

"Naree—my sister," Jae explained, "has been encumbered by the dark spirit of Kashmeru."

Mayhara blinked. "What do you mean? She's… possessed?"

"Not exactly." Jae seemed as if he were struggling to find the words.

Darshana spoke up. "Kashmeru has sent his spirit messenger, Bhutano, to collect her. Through Bhutano, Kashmeru's spirit is speaking into Naree's mind, seeking out the thousand-year-old soul of Lakshmi, the Lotus empress. He calls her to his tomb."

Mayhara shook her head. "Why?"

"He needs her blood," Jae said. "According to the legend, the empress's blood is needed to release the spell that keeps the whole of his spirit trapped in its tomb."

"If Kashmeru is successful in calling her to his tomb," Darshana said, "he will be born again and bring about the collapse of the universe."

"His messenger, Bhutano, is traveling in the body of a human he has possessed." Jae took a step forward. "He's taken her. And we have to track him down."

"She's been kidnapped?" Mayhara asked.

"You could say that. But it would appear she's gone with him willingly." Jae let out an indignant sigh, frustrated with the story himself. "Lakshmi's spirit dwells within Naree, and the connection Lakshmi has to Kashmeru is one of the most powerful bonds in history. Naree cannot help it—Lakshmi is drawn to him when she's called. It's as if she's under a spell."

"But I thought Lakshmi hated Kashmeru," Mayhara said.

"Yes and no." Darshana locked her hands behind her back and began to pace. "Kashmeru is Lakshmi's greatest love. And vice versa. They are, indeed, soul mates. But the evil and darkness that exists in Kashmeru's soul keeps them from being together. Lakshmi is pure light, pure and good energy, and that energy clashes with the darkness within Kashmeru. They cannot exist in the same plane. They each destroy one another. They are of a doomed love."

Mayhara could only stare at Darshana as she struggled to wrap her head around the information. "So Kashmeru is calling the empress to him to take her blood and be reborn."

"In order to destroy the world." Darshana nodded. "Yes."

"And you think that somehow I can help stop this?" Mayhara shook her head again. "Why? Why me?"

"Bhutano is very powerful," Darshana said. "There is no doubt he is collecting the Pishacha army to ensure the empress's journey to Kashmeru's tomb. A gathering of the elite mages is needed in order to stop them."

"But I'm not... I wasn't the top of my class."

"No." Darshana pressed her lips into a tight line for a moment. "But you are the most elite crimson mage who remains alive."

Mayhara blanched. "What? What happened to Fei Ling?"

Darshana lowered her head. "She was found dead just last week."

"No." Mayhara felt as if her heart stopped. Fei Ling had been her idol. She'd always worked hard to match the skill of Fei Ling's crimson mage energy. She put a hand on her chest, feeling the sad rhythm of her heart. "How did she die?"

"They think it was murder," Jae said. "But we haven't heard anything about the investigation going any further. It seems to have been buried behind other stories."

"Buried?"

"By the government, probably. They shut down our school without anyone blinking an eye. It shouldn't surprise you that they've got their hands in every business and organization in New United Asia, including the media."

Mayhara thought back on how their school had been shut down, how any pushback regarding the wait for the reincarnated Lotus empress had been quickly nipped in the bud. The public outcry had been swiftly silenced by arrests and new laws against mages. It was almost as if the government had taken their shot at being the greatest power in the land before anyone could stop them.

"What happened after the Eradication?" Mayhara asked. "What happened to the others? I lost track of everyone. And then I had no way of finding out."

"Most of the mages and their families were taken to prison camps, as I'm sure you know. Though some did as you did and gave in to the order."

"I don't see how it's much different," Jae said. "Being constantly monitored, forbidden from using your powers, told what to do and how to live … it's practically the same as being imprisoned."

"But I have a chance to get my family out," Mayhara said as a burning feeling covered the back of her neck. "It may take years, but I can get them out of there."

"Out of one prison and into another," Jae mumbled.

Aggravation tore at her. "What do you want from me? How do you expect me to help?"

Darshana wrinkled her brow and reached out, grabbing Mayhara by the wrist. She lifted her jacket sleeve and scowled. "Where's your wristband?"

Mayhara blinked. She had forgotten about her garnet stone wristband. All mages wore leather wristbands with corresponding stones that amplified their powers. Each stone was cleansed by a guru, cleared of all negative energy and made ready to be used for the purpose of helping in the protection of the Lotus empress. Because Mayhara wasn't allowed to use her power, she'd stopped wearing it. It was tucked away in a box in her apartment. The government didn't know about the wristbands, apparently, because they'd never demanded it from her.

"It's at my place," Mayhara said. "Why?"

"You're going to need it if you're going to be any help at all. We're going to need all the power we can harness. If there ever was a time to make sure you're wearing it, it's now."

Mayhara glanced at Jae, noticing his wristband. A sapphire stone caught the light, and she remembered he was a sapphire mage.

"I still don't understand how I'm supposed to help."

Darshana placed a gentle hand on her shoulder. "You know the prophecy of the legend?"

"I think so." Mayhara's brow wrinkled. "The Council of the Seven—the leading dark mages of the Pishacha. They want the blood of the Lotus empress to release Kashmeru."

"And you need to help stop that from happening," Darshana said.

"We need to find my sister and keep her from the Seven."

Mayhara's gaze darted between the two. "And that means going against my agreement with the government. That means breaking the law." It would mean her chance of getting her family out of the prison camp would disappear.

"Yes," Darshana said, her eyes locked on Mayhara. "But to save the world, it's our only hope."

FIVE

Every nerve in Naree's body burned. She wanted to run. But simultaneously, she needed to see Kashmeru. To be with him. It had been too long, and the bond between them had her buzzing with want.

He was like a drug. She knew it was wrong, that it would only lead to peril, but she could not resist him.

She followed the men—his army, the Pishacha—through the dark streets to the waiting car. She couldn't see their faces clearly because of the black mouth masks they wore. Only the one named Bruno had his face exposed for her to see.

Bruno opened the door for her and gave her a slight nod. She shivered, rubbing at her arms, before climbing into the back seat.

I'm waiting for you, Lakshmi.

She sniffed back her tears. "This is wrong," she whispered.

Come to me. You feel it in your heart. We need to be together.

The core of her body stirred. A hot, pulsing urge, centuries in the making. "I'm afraid," she said.

All will be as it should, my love.

Her skin prickled with ice. "No. I know what's inside you. Your vision of what should be is full of pain and sorrow. I cannot give myself to you."

Yet she was frozen in place. Unable to move. Unable to run.

Kashmeru beckoned, and it was fate that Lakshmi would answer.

SIX

ayhara hardly noticed anything during the train ride home. Her mind was ablur with everything she had just learned, and her chest felt heavy with the seriousness of the situation. Though her gaze touched upon the moonlit landscape, questions about the Lotus empress saturated her thoughts.

As did the unexpected news of Fei Ling's death.

She couldn't wrap her head around it. Fei Ling was someone she'd admired. Her skills in crimson power had been unparalleled compared to anyone else's in their school. And now she was dead. Murdered. All in some large-scheme plot to stop the empire from resurfacing.

She needed to calm down. She squeezed her eyes closed for a moment and thought of the mages. There were seven houses back at the academy, one for each type of mage. And each of the seven had a corresponding power. The mages were born with their specific power, and the academy's purpose had been to help them learn to control those powers.

Mayhara touched her bare wrist, thinking about her garnet wristband and remembering the houses.

Crimson mages: earth, stability, survival, security.
Copper mages: water, ice, pleasure, guilt.
Golden mages: fire, willpower, shame.
Emerald mages: air, wind, heart, love, grief.
Sapphire mages: throat, sound, truth, lies.
Amethyst mages: vision, sight, illusions, secrets.
Diamond mages: spirituality, emotion, virtue, integrity.

And the Lotus had all these powers. Every single one. Which made her both powerful and a target.

When she stepped off the train, her eyes went to the sky. Her gaze landed on the hazy streak that faintly smudged the panorama of stars. The Akutake comet was approaching. The newscasters had been mentioning it for over a year now. The celestial event was connected to the legend of Kashmeru and Lakshmi, but before knowing that the Lotus had been reborn, Mayhara hadn't paid much attention to it. Now, knowing the truth, Mayhara's skin grew icy cold. It was all falling into place, whether she was ready or not. With a shiver, she pulled her hood tighter over her head.

Before she knew it, she'd reached her apartment complex. It was quiet. Too quiet. Of course, it all could have been in Mayhara's mind. After all, one of the biggest lies she'd been led to believe had just been unraveled before her eyes.

The Lotus empress had been reborn, and she needed Mayhara's help.

When the elevator doors opened on her floor, the faint sound of her neighbor's televiewer gave her a sense of normalcy. Though she felt her world had been tipped on its head, it instilled a fraction of calm to know some things were still the same.

She reached her door and tapped her keycode into the lock pad. It beeped twice. Mayhara frowned. Normally, it would beep once, the lock light would switch from red to green, and her door would click open.

But the lock light remained red.

She rolled her eyes. She'd probably been so caught up in the events of the night that she'd punched in the wrong code.

She tapped the code in again, this time slowly, deliberately pressing each number of the code to be sure she didn't make a mistake. The device beeped once, and the light turned green. Mayhara let out a soft sigh of relief as the door clicked open.

She stepped inside, ready to remove her jacket, but she stopped short when her apartment lights didn't switch on. What was going on? First the lock pad and then the lights. *Probably a glitch in the electrical system,* she thought.

Resolving to do things the old-fashioned way, Mayhara felt for the wall near the front door, searching for the manual control panel. With a touch of her fingertip, the control panel lit up. She swiped the menu to the light settings and pressed the symbol for the living room. She squinted as the room lit up.

But when she turned around, she clapped a hand over her mouth and let a scream erupt into it.

Her heart leaped into a rhythm her mind couldn't keep up with.

Crumpled on the floor with a bullet wound in her head was Riya. The dress she had wanted to borrow sat in a wrinkled lump beside her. Riya's lifeless eyes were rolled back in her head, and her mouth was agape. Mayhara imagined the scream that was lost to the room—only to be heard by whoever had murdered her.

With a shuddered breath, Mayhara slowly moved closer to Riya's body. Her eyes shot back and forth between the puddle of blood where Riya's head rested and the rest of the room. Was she alone? Or had the killer remained behind to add Mayhara to their list of victims?

Barely able to breathe, she reached out to touch Riya's arm. Before she could even make contact, her eyes filled with tears and her skin crawled in fear.

Who did this? And why?

She wished mage power could heal. But maybe even healing wouldn't bring someone back to life. Wiping the tears from her cheeks, her mind raced with what she should do. Should she stay with Riya's body, or leave the apartment to call the police? As she struggled with the dilemma, a flash of something black and rectangular caught her eye. Without thinking, she reached for it. It was a plastic card, like a credit card, but there were no words or numbers on it. The only thing of significance on it was a thin horizontal line with a crescent moon on the upper right side. She flipped it over to find a computer chip. Was this Riya's, or had someone left it behind?

Mayhara stood and pulled out her Linq. She wasn't up for a visit from the authorities, but she had to report finding Riya's body.

As she swiped on her Linq, she heard a thump in her bedroom. Shockwaves of fear burst inside of her, causing her to back away from the sound. The back of her leg hit something—Riya's oversized bag, she realized. The collision caused her to stumble backward. Landing on her tailbone, she let out a muffled curse as her Linq and the mysterious card she found flew from her grasp.

Before she could retrieve her Linq, a figure moved from the darkness of her bedroom into the dim light of the living room. He was masked, dressed in black, and he moved toward Mayhara with a violent gait.

She scrambled to her feet, hardly able to catch her breath. Without thinking, she grabbed the lamp on the end table next to the couch and hurled it at the masked man. He blocked it with his arm, but it slowed him down.

Mayhara dove for her Linq, but the man pounced on her, grabbing her by the waist and twisting her away from the device. She screamed as her fingers dug into his hands in an attempt to pry him off of her. One of his hands loosened, but it was quickly repositioned onto the back of her neck. With a squeeze, the man sent Mayhara careening into the wall.

Black spots danced in her vision. Head spinning, Mayhara forced herself upright. Though she knew it would hurt, she called upon her mage powers and held her palms toward the man. Crimson particles formulated at the surface of her hands, and she quickly hurled a blast of crimson energy at the man. One ball of crimson caught him in the chest, pitching him back until he tripped over her coffee table. Mayhara shifted forward, ready to shoot another blast of crimson his way, but the man resurfaced with a shiny object in his hands.

Her breath stuck in her throat as she realized it was a taser pistol.

He fired the gun.

She tried to block the electrified bullet with her crimson particles, but the bullet was too fast. A searing pain cut across the outer side of her arm, causing her to cry out in agony. Her hand clasped over her wound, immediately slick with blood. But she couldn't feel the slug bullet, and there was an absence of electric shock—the bullet must have just grazed her.

The masked man had the barrel of the gun aimed at her as he stomped forward.

Mayhara couldn't breathe, backing up as if it would prevent the man from reaching her. Just then, a beep sounded, and the front door burst open. As two police officers barged into her apartment with weapons drawn, the masked man stopped in his tracks.

One moment, Mayhara was lifting her arms to show the police she was unarmed, and the next moment, she turned her head to find the masked man had disappeared.

The closer of the two officers aimed her gun at Mayhara, her eyes quickly darting to the unmoving form of Riya sprawled out on the floor.

"Don't move."

Though the pain from her wound was intense, Mayhara kept her arms up. "This is my apartment."

The second officer crouched down to inspect Riya. He placed two fingers on her neck. After a moment he let out a disheartened grunt, and then he pulled out a monitoring device and held it over her heart. He looked up at his fellow officer and shook his head. "She's dead."

The female officer set her mouth in a straight line and took a step closer to Mayhara. "Miss, put your hands behind your head and turn around."

"But I... but I found her like this. There's someone else here. He's broken in and attacked me."

Her hands were pulled down and drawn together. The next thing Mayhara felt was the cold steel of electro-cuffs locking onto her wrists.

"Wait. No. I didn't kill her," she pleaded.

"Save it, miss," the officer said. "You're under arrest."

Seven

Naree watched from the back of the parked car as Bruno met with a hooded man in the back alleyway. She couldn't hear their conversation, but she didn't miss the brown-paper bundle the hooded man handed Bruno. Bruno held out his Linq, as did the hooded man. Naree could almost make out the faint beeping of their devices as credits were transferred from Bruno's device to that of the hooded man's.

Bruno tucked the small package inside his trench coat and waited as the hooded man ducked his head and walked away into the night. When Bruno brought his Linq up to his ear, Naree used her powers to listen more clearly to what he was saying.

"Yes, Bhutano," Bruno said. "I've got it. Yes, she's still secure. I'll await further instructions."

Naree let out a shuddered breath and leaned back in her seat as Bruno came back to the car.

"What's in the package?" Naree asked once he was inside.

"You'll see soon enough."

His words weren't harsh, but they angered Naree. She knew this was part of the prophecy. Something that she must have lived through before, in her other lives, but she couldn't remember it all. Only bits and traces.

As they drove, she gazed out the window, her eyes finding the faint streak in the sky that played a part in her destiny.

She balled her hands into fists, frustrated with her fate, irritated with the magnetic pull Kashmeru had on her. Pissed at herself that she couldn't fight it.

She didn't want the prophecy to be fulfilled. She didn't want to be the reason the universe collapsed.

If only she could figure out how to resist him.

EIGHT

A loud bang thundering in her ears, Mayhara rolled hard against the side of the transport. She blinked, forcing herself to wake up from the electric-pulse-induced sleep the police had put her into. Her memory came back to her; she'd tried to get away as they'd dragged her out of her apartment, so they'd knocked her out with an electro-pulse to the neck. But she couldn't have been out long. She didn't live that far away from the station, and she was still in the transport.

She needed to move her hair out of her face, but her wrists were still cuffed behind her back. It took her a moment to adjust her position on the bench in the back of the van and focus her attention out the window.

City lights were scattered around them. They were downtown now. Close to the station.

The officer in the passenger seat turned his head and glared back at her through the laser-screen divider. "She's awake."

"Good," the driver—the female officer who'd cuffed her—said, sparing her a glance in the rearview mirror. "Didn't really feel like carrying her into the station."

Mayhara's throat felt dry. Her body still ached from the attack in her apartment, but she had to push her pain aside and concentrate on what she was going to say. They thought she'd killed Riya. She could only hope they'd believe her when she proclaimed her innocence.

"CL17 to base," the driver said aloud.

Something on the dashboard beeped. "This is base. Go ahead, CL17."

"10-19 with suspect in custody. We'll be up in a minute."

Outside the transporter windows, everything went dark. It took Mayhara a moment to realize they'd entered the parking garage under the police station.

She was jostled forward as the van came to a sudden stop. The transporter let out a ping as the engine shut off, and the officers exited the vehicle. Mayhara listened as their footsteps crunched along the gritty surface of the parking lot, and then a loud double beep alerted her that the back doors were about to open.

The female officer narrowed her eyes at her. Mayhara knew she was speculating whether or not she was going to give them a hard time. She decided to cooperate. It wouldn't help her case to put up a fight, innocent or not.

After scooting toward the door, the female officer took her by the arm to help her out of the van. With a firm grip, she led Mayhara away from the van as the other officer slammed the doors shut. The parking garage was full of police vans, and an elevator entrance could be seen at the far end of the garage.

As they made their way to the elevator, Mayhara tried to steady her breath. She wasn't sure if they would hook her up to a lie detector, but if her heart was racing, anything she said would be construed as a lie. She would have to calm down, and fast.

But calming down after finding her friend murdered in her apartment was impossible. *Poor Riya.* She had only wanted to borrow a dress. To go out with the guy she'd been pining over and maybe start a new chapter of her life. And now she was dead.

Who was the masked man, and had he killed Riya thinking she was Mayhara?

Mayhara swallowed hard, suddenly realizing that she had probably been the target. The news of Fei Ling's death came back to her.

You are the most elite crimson mage who remains alive, Darshana had said. Which meant it was most likely the Pishacha who'd killed Riya. The Pishacha were out to kill Mayhara.

I'm the elite crimson mage now, she thought. *I'm a target.*

She squinted against the bright, halogen lights of the station as they entered the building. As they passed through a maze of hallways, other officers of the Imperial Police cast her glances. She wanted to scream at all of them that she was innocent. That she was the target of a murderer. That there were real bad guys out there actually killing people, and the police should be dragging *them* in instead.

The female officer tugged on her arm as they stopped in front of a windowed door. The male officer opened it for them, and Mayhara was brought to a chair on one side of a black table. Her cuffs were unlocked, and the female officer glared at her a look as if daring her to make a run for it. Mayhara rubbed at her wrists and squirmed in her chair but remained where she was.

The male officer was the first to leave the room. Mayhara kept her eyes on the female officer, who was obviously convinced Mayhara was guilty.

"Sit tight," the officer said. "Our interrogation officer will be in shortly to talk with you. Until then, don't even think about going near that door."

Mayhara nodded sheepishly, her head swimming with how she was going to explain herself.

As the door shut behind the officer, Mayhara squeezed her eyes shut and raked her hands through her hair. What was she going to do? She wouldn't be able to explain her whereabouts before she'd come home to the apartment. If she told the Imperial police about the Lotus princess and her potential involvement, they'd probably send her off to a prison camp. No, she was going to have to be strategic in her answers without making it appear as if she was guilty of Riya's murder.

She took in the sight of the enormous mirror across from her. No doubt it was two-way glass with officers on the other side studying her. She wiped at her cheeks and kept her eyes on the table, practicing her guru's breathing techniques.

The door clicked open, and despite her determination to stay calm, Mayhara's heart hammered in her chest, and sweat formed at her temples.

"Good evening, Miss Guatama. I'm Chief Inspector Khapoor. I'm sure you know why we brought you in."

"My bets are on the dead body in my apartment." She flinched as soon as she said it, realizing how awful it sounded. Her adrenaline must have been doing a number on her attitude.

"Yes," Khapoor said, studying her face as he sat across from her. "Is there anything you'd like to say about that?"

"I didn't kill her. I swear. Riya is—was—my friend. I came home and found her there."

"Came home from where? And can anyone confirm your whereabouts?"

She kept a straight face. "I went for a walk. And no, no one saw me, and I didn't talk to anyone, so no one can confirm it, but I'm sure you can estimate the time of death and check the apartment building computer system for what time I came home."

"And how exactly did the victim get into your apartment before you?"

"I gave her my key code."

"Allegedly. We can ask the apartment manager to check the video feed from the hall." He glanced back at the big mirror and nodded, no doubt signaling for whoever was behind it to get the video feed. "But you could have entered the apartment with her, and following that theory, killed her. Then you could have left your apartment to use your key code and come back in, thinking it would throw off the investigation."

Her jaw dropped. "No. No, I found her there, dead on my floor. And she wasn't alone. There was someone else in the apartment. He came out of the bedroom and attacked me."

Khapoor took out a small notepad from his shirt pocket and flipped it open. He clicked open a pen and began jotting down notes. "I see. Can you describe this person?"

"He was masked, but about a half a head taller than me. I'm sorry. I didn't have much time to analyze him; he attacked me."

Khapoor continued writing. "And where was this perpetrator when our officers arrived?"

"I... I don't know. He disappeared."

Khapoor stopped writing and looked up at her. "Disappeared?"

"Y-Yes. One minute he was there, and the next minute he was gone."

Khapoor put down his pen and pinched the bridge of his nose. "Miss Guatama, are you currently under the influence of alcohol or drugs?"

"No. No, I'm not. Listen, I know it sounds crazy, but there was a man in my apartment. He attacked me. Look at my arm. He shot me with a taser-pistol. I'm sure he's the one who killed Riya."

With one raised bushy eyebrow, Khapoor took a two-second glance at the torn and singed material of Mayhara's sleeve.

"If someone shot a taser-pistol, there would be evidence of it in your apartment. A shell or a burn mark, if not the bullet itself—assuming it didn't penetrate you. It if did, it's a miracle you aren't in the hospital now instead of sitting here in interrogation."

A small ray of hope sparked in Mayhara's chest. "Yes, evidence. There must be something."

Khapoor closed his notebook and returned it to his pocket. "I'm sure you're not opposed to waiting here while we check out your story?"

Mayhara nodded. "Yeah, I'll wait."

"Did you want us to call anyone? A lawyer?"

She studied his face, wondering if the government would assign someone to her case who wouldn't really be on her side. All the lawyers were working for government. They had nothing to gain by taking her side. "No." Mayhara shook her head. "No one."

Chief Inspector Khapoor stood and gave Mayhara a solitary nod of his head before leaving the room. All Mayhara could do now was wait. Surely the officers would find a burn mark or the shell from the taser-bullet. Surely the video surveillance would show someone going into her apartment besides Riya before Mayhara had gotten back.

A shiver suddenly crept along Mayhara's skin. Her spark of hope was all at once extinguished into a puff of smoke. If the masked man could disappear without a trace, if he'd managed to leave her apartment without anyone seeing him, then it would be totally feasible that he could have gotten into her apartment without being detected as well. She wasn't being paranoid. This was real. And it scared her to the core.

NINE

They must have known the owners, Naree thought. Or the owners were also Pishacha. The other tables at the restaurant were unoccupied. They'd closed down the place for them so they could do this privately.

Bruno sat across from Naree, the journal he'd unwrapped from the brown-paper parcel lying between them, opened to a page scribbled with ancient ink. One of Bruno's men leaned forward on the table, playing with a pair of chopsticks.

"Anything?" Bruno asked.

Naree shook her head. She'd been staring at the sketch of a dagger on the withered page for almost an hour. Bruno had said she might get some insight from the drawing. Something that would help their mission.

But nothing came.

She didn't know whether to expect the memories of her last lives to come back to her all at once. But Bruno was convinced that the clues were there, lurking near the surface. He'd said Kashmeru had told him so. He'd said that Kashmeru promised him salvation if he helped his plight.

The bell above the door rang as one of Bruno's men entered. Bruno stood and buttoned his blazer, stepping out of their booth as the man approached.

"Did you take care of her?" Bruno asked in a low voice.

The man nodded and whispered something back to him. Naree wanted to use her powers to hear them better, but she knew it would upset Bruno. And Kashmeru. He was also watching and listening, after all.

Bruno's Linq chirped. He studied it for a moment, his brow raised. Reaching over the table, he closed the journal and grabbed his trench coat from his chair.

"We've got something," he said. "Come on. We need to go."

"Where are we going?" Naree asked.

"One of my guys found a lead. We need to go meet him and check it out. Maybe it will help spark some memory."

Naree tucked a strand of hair behind her ear. "It's late."

The corner of Bruno's mouth crept upward for a split second. "The end of the world is upon us, Your Highness. We haven't got a moment to spare."

TEN

It took all her meditation training and control techniques to not panic. Everything she had an impulse to do—bouncing her leg, biting her nails, folding her hands together—she decided against. She was paranoid that anything she did could be construed as guilty body language. Then again, remaining abnormally calm could be construed as suspicious, too. Not that it ultimately mattered. She had a feeling if the government or the Pishacha wanted to frame her, then that was exactly what they'd accomplish.

There was no clock in the interrogation room, so Mayhara could only assume she'd been waiting an hour before Chief Inspector Khapoor finally returned. His eyes met with Mayhara's for a moment before he cleared his throat and took the seat across from her.

Mayhara scooted forward in her chair, hoping he had something good to tell her.

"Miss Guatama, thank you for your patience," he said, but Mayhara could already tell from his tone that things were not going to go her way. "We had some officers check your apartment, as well as collect the video footage from the hall of your apartment building."

She held her breath.

"There was no sign of a taser-pistol being fired in your apartment. There were also no signs of a break in. The surveillance videos show your friend Riya entering your apartment at approximately 5:35 P.M. and you entering the apartment just ten minutes later."

"What? No. No, that's impossible." She felt as if a vise squeezed her heart and lungs and ribs. She could barely catch her breath. "I didn't get home until much later. It was at least 8 o'clock, probably later." Mayhara considered looking for her sub-train ticket to confirm the time, but then the officers would know about her traveling to the school. But maybe that would be the better option. Being charged with mage-related crimes would be better than being accused of murder, wouldn't it?

No. It didn't matter. She was obviously being set up. The video footage had been tampered with. Someone had forged the times on the recordings to make it look like she had been home earlier.

"What about the lock pad?" she asked in desperation.

Khapoor let out a sigh. "The computer monitoring system shows there were only two instances of your apartment door being opened. One at 5:35, and one at 5:45."

That's impossible.

Mayhara felt numb. She wasn't sure who had done it—the police, the government, the Pishacha—but whoever it was, she was being framed.

Her body began to shake. She squeezed her palms shut, trying to regain control.

"Miss Guatama, I'm afraid we're going to have to put you in a holding cell until we can officially transfer you to a prison camp."

"What? But don't I get a trial or something? Don't I get a chance to prove my innocence?"

"You can petition to have a trial and seek out council, but I have to warn you: nowadays, that can take months. It won't be denied to you, however. You just have to fill out the forms."

Mayhara was frozen. She wasn't sure if this was really happening or if she was suffering from a nightmare. All she had worked for, everything she had sacrificed, it all meant nothing. All of it, gone in one night. There would be no chance for her to save her family. And it would be too much to believe she would be joining them at the same camp. No. The government would ensure they would stay separated. She knew how the system worked.

"Miss Guatama," Khapoor said as he checked his watch. "I'm going to ask you to come with me now. There are two armed officers right outside this door who are going to escort you to the processing center. I do hope you will cooperate, so this can all go smoothly without any problems. We don't anticipate any problems, do we?"

Mayhara understood that the man was tired and didn't want her to put up a fight. Though Mayhara was just as exhausted, her body was hopped up on adrenaline. And fear.

She shook her head anyway.

Joining Khapoor in the hall, Mayhara felt as if she were walking in someone else's reality. She walked along in a trance, her eyes set on the back of the officer in front of her, the sounds reaching her ears muffled and the things she passed in the halls blurred.

In a daze, she followed the officer's instructions to place her hand on the info-tablet to record her fingerprints and access her data. She was then led to a holding cell at the back of the building until they could process her and move her to a prison camp. The officer said she should settle in for the night since the next transport wouldn't be until morning. Though she faced him, her gaze went right through him as he explained that the cell was electronically monitored and could detect if someone tried to tamper with the lock. She barely realized she nodded at him as she dropped her weight onto the bench against the wall.

At least she was alone. There was no one there to bother her, no one to ask her why she was there. No one to ask her questions she didn't really feel like answering.

What should I do? she thought. *Should I call someone?*

She didn't have her Linq. It had been lost in the scuffle at her apartment, and there was no telling if the police had seized it or not. If only there was a way to call Darshana without the police knowing who she was calling. If only someone out there was on her side.

Leaning her head back against the wall, she scolded herself for despairing so much. She brought to mind the positivity training Darshana had taught her.

She leaned her head back against the wall and tried to clear her mind. She had to call upon a happy thought. Even in this time of desperation, she had to find something that might bring her joy. She could hear voices in the distance, officers chatting with each other, doors being opened and closed with an electronic beep, the shuffling of feet. Squeezing her eyes shut, she tried to block it all out.

What do I have to be happy about? There must be something. As dire as things are…

Then a face came into her mind. Just this morning, on her way to work, a little girl had dropped her school books. Papers flew everywhere, scattered by the wind. Mayhara had been in a hurry, but she had stopped anyway.

She'd helped the little girl until everything she'd lost had been put back into her hands. And the little girl had smiled at Mayhara, a big, grateful, gap-toothed smile, and she'd said thank you and told Mayhara that she was nice.

Mayhara opened her eyes and smiled at the memory.

A figure came around the corner and into the holding cell area. His police uniform was pressed, and his buttons were shiny, but he kept his head down. He glanced over his shoulder, then approached the bars of the cell.

When he lifted his head, Mayhara gasped.

Jae lifted a finger to his lips to silence her as he pulled out his Linq from his pocket.

With a shuddered breath, Mayhara jumped from the bench and hurried to the bars. "What are you doing?" she whispered.

"Getting you out of here. Or did you pay for the weekend package?"

"It won't work. The whole cell is electronically monitored. I don't think you can even touch the bars without setting off some kind of sensor."

He huffed a quick laugh and attached a wire from his Linq into some port in the lock.

She narrowed her eyes, watching what he was doing. "You're a hacker."

"I prefer tech prodigy."

She scoffed.

"Who do you think talked Darshana into using a Linq?" he asked.

Something pricked her ears. "Someone's coming."

His device beeped quietly, and the cell doors slid open.

"Hurry," Jae said, grabbing her hand.

Instead of going the way he'd come in, they went farther down the hall, past the other cells.

"Do you know where you're going?" Mayhara asked.

Jae pulled out his Linq, checking the screen. A small glowing blue line showed a route through the building. "Just need to hack through a door or two."

Mayhara checked over her shoulder as they ran, cringing any time they had to stop so Jae could manipulate a locked door. If she hadn't been so anxious about getting caught, she might have been able to admire his smooth technique and clever know-how.

He brought her to a stairwell and began descending. "Just one floor to the exit, and we'll be out of the building," he said.

Her chest filled with hope. They might actually make it. Sure, she would be on the run. There was no way she could go back to work. The police and the Pishacha would be after her, and she would constantly be in fear of getting caught. But knowing she was one doorway away from escaping filled her with exhilaration.

Jae cracked the code for the final door and pulled her through it.

Suddenly, red lights flashed and an alarm sounded. Mayhara reached for her neck, a buzzing shock pricking the skin where her blocker was embedded.

Jae hardened his jaw and shook his head, pulling her along. "We're going to need to get that thing out of your neck. It's only a matter of time before they track you down. Come on."

He dragged her to a motorcycle and climbed on. She jumped behind him without so much as a question about a helmet. With chaos exploding around them, they raced out of the lot and into the cold chill of the night.

Naree leaned over the sink and stared at her reflection. The bathroom was private. Sure, the Pishacha stood guard outside, waiting for her to come out, but no one would be coming in. For a moment, she had a reprieve.

Lakshmi, I long to hold you again.

Naree swiped the back of her hand over her forehead, which was moist with sweat. Kashmeru's hold was getting stronger, and it was getting harder to resist his call. Any resistance was met with feverish chills, nausea, and a churning in the pit of her stomach. Though part of her still desired to flee, a deeper part of her, the core of her, was desperate to be with Kashmeru again.

Please come to me, my love.

"I'm doing everything you ask of me." Her voice was strained, hoarse with the threat of sobs.

Remember how good it feels to be together. Remember it, my love.

Naree felt a tightness in her chest. She squeezed her eyes shut, and visions filled her head.

Kashmeru stood before her in a courtyard. She could see a temple behind him, the white marble seeming to reach the skies. He was tall and handsome, and his golden-brown eyes twinkled as he held her gaze. He held out a hand, and she placed hers in it. His touch was electrifying. A shiver pulsed through her as he pulled her closer.

He leaned closer to her ear. The warm caress of his breath as he pledged his love made her gasp in pleasure. He kissed her neck, and she pressed herself into his chest. Everything else ceased to exist. It was just the two of them. Kashmeru and Lakshmi. They could live forever in each other's arms, without need for anything or anyone else.

She looked up at him, their eyes locking as she was about to accept his kiss.

But his eyes grew black. As dark as death.

She pulled away.

Naree opened her eyes, a stifled cry escaping her lips.

No, my love. It can be perfect between us if you just let me in.

She reached for her neck, the feel of his gentle lips lingering there as if it hadn't been almost a century ago. "I don't know if I can."

It is our destiny, Lakshmi. You cannot deny it. We belong together.

TWELVE

Wincing, Mayhara gingerly patted the gauzy patch on her neck.

"Don't mess with that too much," Jae said. "It won't completely erase the signal. It'll just throw them off. Blurs your location. They could eventually track you down if they get close enough."

"Sorry." Mayhara sheepishly put her hand down and slipped it between her knees. "Just stings like a bitch." She sat on the edge of an out-of-commission fountain at the academy.

Jae shot her a quick smirk before checking his Linq. He pressed his lips into a tight line and then tucked the device away. Mayhara knew he was trying not to show how frustrated he was, but she could feel it. She was just as frustrated. They had sent Darshana a message over an hour ago but still hadn't gotten a response.

"Do you really think it's safe here?" she asked.

He shrugged with one shoulder. "We're going to have to take our chances until we figure out what to do. But for now, it's probably the safest place in New India." He checked his Linq again. "Where is she?"

"I hope she's all right. Maybe she heard about the prison break and is keeping a low profile in case someone tries to follow her."

Jae nodded. "Yeah, makes sense. She's escaped them before, when they tried to arrest her after the Eradication. Well, if she doesn't write back in the next hour, we'll have to head out. Isn't safe to stay in one place, especially with that thing in your neck."

He walked toward her, his eyes on her neck, and Mayhara swore she could see the wheels turning in his mind from the look on his face.

"I can do it, you know," he said.

"What? Take it out? Did you go and get your medical degree in the last two years?"

"No, but my aunt is a vet."

"Um, occupation experience isn't linked via blood, you know? And, uh, I'm not exactly a dog."

"I spent a lot of time with her, stayed with her one summer. I hung around when she'd fix up the animals and stuff. I'm not saying I could perform organ surgery, but I'm pretty sure I'm adept enough to remove your blocker without hitting any major arteries."

Instinctively, Mayhara placed a hand over the patch.

A small laugh drifted from his lips. "I think you're just going to have to trust me. I've got some supplies at my apartment, though I'm a little leery about the police or the Pishacha tracking us down there."

She sat up a little straighter. "What about the nursing facilities?"

He narrowed his eyes and nodded slowly.

"I don't know what damage has been done to it," she said, "but I'm sure they couldn't have destroyed everything."

"It's worth a look. Let's go."

They headed for the East Quarter building where the nursing facilities had been located. Mayhara held on to the hope that the facilities hadn't been destroyed altogether. Not that she was looking forward to Jae cutting into her neck, but if there was a chance to throw the police off their scent, she knew they had to take it.

As she walked beside him, she noticed how square he kept his shoulders, how raised he kept his chin, and how his intense eyes seemed to take in everything in his sights. She felt as if he did more than just look at things; he really *saw* everything and understood what was there.

He gave her a sideward glance. "What?"

Ignoring the spread of heat to her cheeks, she asked, "So you didn't go back to Korea when the school closed?"

"I did. I wanted to help keep Naree safe, but our father started noticing strange things in our hometown. Like strangers lurking about and people asking questions. He told me to take her somewhere else, somewhere no one would suspect."

"You brought her to New India? Didn't you think that was like bringing the lamb to the lion's den?"

"Hide in plain sight. That's what they say."

They turned down the corridor, getting closer to the nursing facilities.

"Things were fine for a while, but then Naree started changing. She was acting like someone else and doing strange things. She kept disappearing, sneaking out at night. I decided to follow her and found out she was meeting up with some guy. I didn't recognize him, but I could tell he was bad news.

"I confronted her, told her she should be careful, but she told me I didn't understand. She would get a strange look on her face, as if she'd become someone I didn't recognize. She told me it was out of her control—it was fate.

"I didn't know what to do. Not only because I have this instinct to protect my little sister, but also because she's the Lotus empress. I mean, I can't just let the ruler of the Lotus empire go rogue into a dangerous city.

"I got worried. I called my parents to let them know my concerns, but she must have overheard me. She was gone the next day." He stopped in the hall. "We're here."

Mayhara watched as he opened the door to the nursing facilities, but her mind was fixated on everything he'd told her. She couldn't imagine not being able to control her own actions, to be drawn to a force so strong she couldn't resist it.

As they stepped into the room, the far-off sounds of sirens grew louder. It was probably instinct, but they both backed against the wall near the door, ears perked and bodies unmoving. Jae was so close, Mayhara breathed him in. She noted something minty in the soap he must have used, and something else—sandalwood?

His head was turned away from her, but his chest was practically pressed up to hers. As the sirens passed, he turned his face toward her, their eyes locking. It took a moment before Mayhara broke the trance and dropped her gaze. Jae cleared his throat and took a step back, swiveling to surveil the room.

Mayhara moved her hair back from her face, hoping her skin would get more cool air to evaporate the sweat that had formed on her temples. The room was only slightly dusty. It didn't appear as though the administration had bothered ransacking the room. It made Mayhara optimistic that they'd be able to find what they needed. As Jae searched a cabinet, Mayhara went toward a set of drawers on the far wall.

She went through two supply-filled drawers before Jae called out that he'd found a scalpel. In the third drawer, Mayhara found a suture kit.

"You might want to sit somewhere," he said.

Mayhara eyed the examination table and the chair next to the desk in the room. She hopped up on the exam table, figuring it would be better if her neck was closer to eye-level for Jae. Her muscles tensed as he came closer, though she was comforted with the fact that he'd found some disinfectant wipes to clean the scalpel and rub on her neck.

He got as close as he could and lifted his hands near her neck. She moved her hair out of the way and closed her eyes, her fingers grasping the edge of the table.

"Talk about something," she said. "So I don't have to think about this too much."

"Okay." He gently felt her neck, pressing the area, searching for exactly where the blocker was implanted.

She kept her eyes closed, so she wasn't aware of how close the scalpel was until she felt the ice-cold blade on her skin. She sucked in a breath, hoping he would say something more before he actually cut into her.

"When my parents first told me my sister was the Lotus empress, I didn't believe them," he said.

A searing pain stung her neck as he slowly made an incision. Her fingers tightened on the table's edge. "Why not?"

"I thought they just wanted me to be nice to her."

Mayhara almost laughed, but he pushed the blade deeper into her skin, widening the cut.

"I thought it was just a made-up story when I first heard it," she said, forcing her thoughts away from the pain. "A forbidden love between deities. It didn't make sense to me. I thought gods could do whatever they wanted."

"I wouldn't have believed it, either, but seeing the way my sister behaved… It's so unlike her. So either the legend is true, or my sister is under some heavy-duty hypnosis."

Mayhara felt as if he were ripping veins out of her neck. She hoped that wasn't the case. "Why aren't your parents here?"

"They wanted to come. I told them not to. They're not in the best of health, and they've already stressed themselves out to no end getting Naree this far. I promised them I'd take care of it. Not that they didn't argue with me."

The next thing she felt was a needle going through her skin and the sickening slide of thread. She scolded herself for thinking about it. "I wonder where Darshana is."

"That makes two of us."

"I wonder if she's written to my Linq. I dropped it back at my place during the attack. For all I know, it could be in the hands of the police."

"She'd most likely message my device, but we could check it out. We'll have to sneak in and out though. You probably want to pick up a few things anyway. Like your wristband."

"Good idea." She winced as he pressed something sticky upon her neck. "Are you done?"

She heard him chuckle. "You were very brave. I got it out. We're all good."

She cringed as she opened her eyes and took in the sight of bloody cotton on the table beside her. Off to the side was a blood-soaked piece of plastic embedded with tiny computer parts. Jae took a meshy patch, like the one he'd taped to her neck earlier, and wrapped it around the plastic and stuck it in his pocket.

"What do we do with that?" she asked.

"At first I thought we should destroy it, but then I figured we could drop it on a train or something and send the police on a wild goose chase."

Despite herself, she smiled. "I like that idea."

He rested his palms on the table and studied her face. "You okay?"

She resisted touching the bandage on her neck. "Yeah. I'm okay."

He nodded and took out his Linq.

"Anything?" she asked.

"Nope." He tucked it back in his pocket and sighed. "Hey, I want to show you something."

"Okay."

He took her hand to help her off the table. "Follow me."

They headed down a corridor behind the kitchens. Mayhara couldn't remember ever being down this way during her time at the school. She wondered how she could have missed it in all her years at the academy.

"I used to come down here sometimes," he said. "To think and stuff. You know, when everyone else was forming cliques and I was left out."

She gave him a curious look, not remembering him being purposely excluded from any group.

He shrugged. "It wasn't their fault. I guess I mostly kept to myself because of my parents. They were paranoid I'd become close enough friends with someone I'd tell their secret."

They arrived at a staircase that descended into an old stone corridor. He used his Linq to provide light. Pipes ran along the hall, and the farther they went, the more ancient the walls appeared. It was in that moment she realized she trusted Jae enough to let him lead her down some abandoned path under the school.

At the end of the hall was a double door made of withering wood. Instead of a wooden doorframe, it seemed to be surrounded by rock. Jae turned the iron knob on one side of the door and pushed it open. It let out a slow and ominous creak.

"That's not creepy," Mayhara mumbled.

Jae stepped inside, holding his Linq up high so Mayhara could see the room.

No, not a room. A cave.

"What is this?" she asked.

"I don't know. It's always been here. I think the school was built around it. Or, you know, on top of it. Come check this out."

He led her forward. Instead of a floor, there was hard rock and dirt at their feet. The walls and ceiling were all the components of an underground cavern. As they stepped toward the middle of the room, Mayhara noticed that the ground fell away in the center. When Jae repositioned his light, Mayhara could just make out an enormous structure in the center of the cave.

Squinting, she could see the outer surface of some kind of spiral edifice, like a humongous statue made of rock and crystal swirling in a vertical column that reached from the abyss below to the cavern ceiling. It was at least ten feet in diameter.

"What is it?"

"I don't know," Jae said, his voice quiet. "I never asked anyone because I wasn't supposed to be down here. It was different back then: lit up with a glow of swirling particles—I'm assuming mage elements. You can see the seven different sections." He pointed to the curves in the structure. "It was red at the bottom, then orange, yellow, green, blue, purple, and white at the top."

"The mage colors."

"The chakra colors connected to the mages, yes."

She stared at the enormous column in awe. "But it's not lit up anymore."

"I suspect the glow went out when the school shut down."

She paced a bit to the side, trying to see around the structure. "But what is it for?"

"That, I couldn't tell you."

It took a moment before she could tear her eyes away from it. "Do you think it has a significance in Kashmeru calling to Lakshmi?"

He smirked. "You read my mind."

"Maybe Darshana knows."

"I'm sure she'd be the one to ask. If we could just get ahold of her."

Thirteen

The place was crowded, filled with unsuspecting patrons, but Bruno took Naree to a section of the building only a few were allowed to enter. Bruno's man approached and handed him a file.

"Let's sit," Bruno said.

The two of them waited for Naree to take a seat, then joined her. A few of the Pishacha sat as well, and Naree caught a glimpse of their weapons as their leather jackets shifted away from their bodies.

Bruno opened the file so that Naree could see. There was a name and address along with a picture.

"You're sure this is our guy?" Bruno asked his man.

The man nodded. "That's him."

"Have you actually seen the dagger?"

"No," the man said. "But he has to have it."

Bruno studied the picture a moment longer, and then he slid it closer to Naree. "This is him."

Naree swallowed hard as she took in the man's face.

"I don't know if I—"

You must, my love.

Kashmeru's voice had her swallow back her words. Every syllable filled her with longing. His pull on her was growing stronger. It was getting harder and harder for her to fight it. Soon, she would be completely lost to his summoning.

This will bring us one step closer. Soon we will be reunited, and then we can pledge our love to one another, and all will be right in the world.

FOURTEEN

Though her anxiety was at its peak, Mayhara had to admit it was exhilarating sneaking to the sub-train platform and tossing her blocking device onto one of the trains. Of course, she could only admit this after the fact, when they were far from the scene and in the clear.

With the authorities most likely miles away, she and Jae headed to her apartment to grab her wristband and check if the police had confiscated her Linq. She also wanted to grab a bag of clothes. This would probably be the last time she'd ever be in her apartment, at least until they could rescue Naree, defeat the Pishacha, and prove her innocence.

Instead of going straight to her apartment, Jae had them take a detour to the surveillance room. He quelled Mayhara's fears about getting caught by explaining that nowadays everything was run by automatic settings, that computers, rather than actual people, kept an "eye" on things, lucky for him. It took him no time at all to override the cameras overseeing her hall and disengaging the monitoring of her lock pad.

Aside from worrying about being spotted by neighbors, their venture into her apartment went smoothly. Inside, Mayhara cringed at the state of her once-pristine apartment. She was a minimalist—not one to spend credits on material things while her family was locked away with nothing— but what she did have was strewn about her apartment as if a typhoon had blown through the small space.

At least Riya's body had been taken care of. Mayhara closed her eyes for a moment in reflection of her friend. She hadn't even had a chance to say goodbye, to have any closure from losing her. To apologize because Riya had died because of her.

The sound of Jae rifling through some things brought her back to the present.

"Looks like they got my Linq," she said.

"They're probably working on breaking into it to find out where you might have run off to."

"Maybe. But Darshana wasn't specific when she messaged me. She used words only I could interpret when she told me to meet her."

He nodded. "Smart. I may be able to clone it, get your information and apps for you. Then I can deactivate the one they have, make it a brick. But I need my laptop to do that."

"Sounds good. Thanks." Mayhara headed for her bedroom to find the box that held her wristband. As she entered the small room, she took a look around, and part of her mind was saying goodbye to her things as she touched them, feeling grateful for having had them and apologizing for not being able to take care of them anymore. It was a maddening thing to have so much one moment only to lose it the next, but what she was most dismayed about losing was her freedom.

But maybe Jae was right; she had never really been free after all.

She opened her dresser and moved her clothes out of the way to find the box. She pulled it out, running her hand over the smooth surface before opening it. When she took out the garnet wristband and slipped it on, it was as if she'd found a part of herself that had been missing.

After she'd replaced the empty box in the drawer, she quickly threw together a bag of clothes. As she rejoined Jae in the living room, something caught her eye from under her couch among papers and books that the police must have tossed on the floor. She bent down and picked it up, remembering seeing it after she found Riya's body.

It was the strange, cryptic plastic card. She flipped it over in her hand, searching for something she might have missed.

"What's that?" Jae asked.

"I found it next to Riya's body. I don't know if it was hers." She shifted uncomfortably. "Or if it belonged to the masked man who attacked me."

"Mind if I take a look? If it belonged to your attacker, and he's part of the Pishacha, then we might have a lead."

She handed him the card, which he studied intently.

"There's a chip on the back. I think my Linq can read it."

She stepped closer to him, peering around his arm as his device scanned the chip.

"All I get is an address," he said.

They exchanged a look.

"Should we check it out?" she asked.

"It's the only lead we've got."

When Jae brought the motorcycle to a stop, Mayhara stared at the building with its neon sign. A line of about fifty people dressed in tight, revealing clothes, waiting to be let in was snaked around the corner, and loud, thumping music vibrated through the air.

"A club?" Mayhara asked, still holding on to Jae's waist. "Are you sure this is the right address?"

"Yeah." Jae adjusted his grip on his handles. "You sure that wasn't Riya's card?"

"No way. This is so not her scene."

Jae shrugged. "Okay, let's find a place to park and check it out."

Jae leaned forward and drove the bike around the building to a full parking lot in the back. If he'd had a car, there would be no way he could have fit. He found space on a path near the back door, seemingly not concerned if he was allowed to park there or not.

Mayhara dismounted the bike and studied her clothes. "Well, this isn't going to do."

She grabbed her duffle bag that was strapped to the back of the motorcycle and rifled through it. Stripping off her hoodie to reveal a black tank top, she wrapped a choker around her neck—careful as she placed it over the bandage—and quickly tied her hair up in a messy bun. She then held up her hand. Small particles of crimson energy floated from her palm. The red dust settled, and Mayhara scooped it up with her finger. She then checked her reflection in Jae's motorcycle's mirror and smeared the red powder onto her lips, making a smacking sound with her mouth when she was finished.

"Better?" she asked.

Jae's mouth was agape as he looked her up and down. "That was so simple, yet so amazing."

She couldn't hold back her smile. "I'm just lucky I have my black jeans on. I hope they don't look as far as my shoes, though. They don't exactly scream 'club scene.'"

Jae gave her a crooked smile. "I'm sure you can figure out how to distract them from looking at your shoes."

She almost rolled her eyes at him, but he whipped out his Linq.

"It's Darshana," he said, his brow creased.

"Finally." Mayhara sidled up to him, trying to catch a glimpse of his screen. "What—none of that makes sense."

"It's code. Not that I haven't taken precautions, but she's being extra safe. She's lying low for a bit but tracking down the other mages."

Mayhara nodded. She wondered how many of the original elite mages were left. Knowing the crimson mage at the top of her class had been murdered caused her to believe the other mages were either in danger or already dead. She swallowed hard and stretched out her shoulders. She was going to have to be prepared for an attack. She couldn't let her guard down.

Jae shut down his screen.

"Wait," Mayhara said, placing her hand on his arm. "I need to know what your sister looks like. What if she's in there? I need to know who to look for."

"Good idea." He unlocked his Linq and opened a photo album, swiping until he found the picture he was looking for. "Here's one. This is from last year. Before Kashmeru found her."

He frowned as he added the last part. It took a lot for Mayhara to tear her gaze away from his sad eyes and examine the picture on his Linq instead.

In the picture, Jae had his arm around a beautiful, petite girl with bone-straight, light brown hair that cascaded down past her shoulders. They were both smiling, and they both had the same twinkle in their eyes. It looked like they had just shared a joke and captured the moment. Jae appeared relaxed and at peace. Naree looked like she was invincible.

"It's a good picture," Mayhara said softly, peering up at Jae.

His smile was small as he thanked her and tucked the Linq away. He gestured over his shoulder toward the club. "Let's see what we can find in there."

FIFTEEN

Mayhara's heart sank as they got to the end of the line. They could barely see the entrance from where they were standing, and at the slow pace the line was moving—if it was even moving at all—it was going to take forever to reach the door.

From the look on Jae's face, he was equally impatient. *Of course he is,* she thought to herself. *He desperately wants to find his sister.*

Suddenly, Jae stiffened. He moved closer to Mayhara, ducking his head down a little and shifting to face her. He lifted his arm as if scratching the hair at the top of his head. Looking past his bicep, Mayhara spotted the imperial police car that drove by the block. There were no sirens or flashing lights. Instinctively, Mayhara reached for her neck, running her fingers along the bandage. She had to remind herself that the blocking chip had been removed. It was halfway to New China by now.

As the patrol car continued on its way, Mayhara released a relieved breath. Jae checked over his shoulder to see the coast was clear, then let his arm fall as he stretched out his neck.

"All right," he said. "This is ridiculous. Maybe I could speed things along." He pulled out his Linq.

"How? What are you going to do?"

His eyes darted between her and his Linq for a moment, and then he swung an arm around her, pulling her closer.

When she shot him a questioning look, he leaned close to her ear. "Just trust me."

He held the Linq out at arm's length. The way they were standing, it appeared as if like they were simply taking a selfie. But the screen on his Linq showed one of the bouncers by the door. He was monitoring the line, his huge arms crossed over his muscular chest. In a matter of seconds, Jae zoomed in on the bouncer's face. His Linq captured his image.

Jae drew his Linq back and began pressing and swiping at it. Mayhara tried to see exactly what he was doing, but the angle was off. She only managed to catch a glimpse of a green square blinking over the bouncer's face and a file popping up.

Jae studied the words on his screen quickly, and then the corner of his mouth crept upward.

"Okay," he said, tucking his Linq away. "I've got it."

Jae took Mayhara's hand and stepped out of line.

"What are you doing?" she asked.

He pulled her along gently but quickly toward the door, and she had to move her feet to keep up. She made herself ignore the suspicious looks they were getting from the people they were passing in line.

When they got closer to the bouncer, Mayhara felt flustered. She wished Jae would have let her in on his plan.

The bouncer narrowed his eyes at them. He uncrossed his arms and stood akimbo.

"Line ends back there," the bouncer said.

"Freddy," Jae called out. "It's me, Rick."

The bouncer blinked, his eyes drifting over Jae's face as if trying to remember who he was. "Rick? I don't think—"

Jae leaned closer to him and lowered his voice. "You know, from the factory."

Freddy blanched for a moment, visibly swallowed, then checked over his shoulder to see if his colleague was listening. When he turned back to Jae, his expression had a hint of worry. "Keep it down, man."

"Yeah, yeah," Jae said, almost speaking out of one side of his mouth. "I got you, don't worry. Man, you think you can let us through? You know, as a favor? I had your back back at the factory, man. We all did."

Freddy looked back and forth between Jae and his colleague, the gears in his head clearly whirling. "Yeah, okay. You got it, man. But keep it down about back then, all right?"

"Of course, of course."

Freddy held his arm out to clear a way for Jae and Mayhara, then stepped forward and blocked the next people in line.

"VIP," he said to his colleague.

His colleague scanned their faces but didn't argue.

Jae held tight to Mayhara's hand as they squeezed past the people in line and into the entrance of the club. The music grew louder and the flashing neon lights pulsated faster. Streams of cold, white smoke blew turrets of clouds onto the floor as they passed the coat check and continued into the main chamber of the club.

It was hard to hear anything but thumping, and Jae had to repeat what he said before Mayhara could understand him.

"I *said*, 'Let's check by the bar,'" he said into her ear.

She simply nodded, not wanting to raise her voice.

A couple of young women dressed in what looked like streams of bandages wiggled in front of them, whooping and cheering and handing them tiny plastic cups of green liquid. Mayhara smiled and waved them away. Jae directed his focus over their heads, his eyes on the bar. He scanned the faces of the patrons, his frown deepening as he seemed to realize his sister was nowhere in sight.

"Let's ask the bartender," he said.

They shimmied to the bar and managed to squeeze between people.

"What can I get you?" the bartender asked.

Jae held out his Linq with the picture of Naree showing. "You seen this girl?"

The bartender raised a brow at him. "Maybe."

Jae pursed his lips and shook his head. "How much?"

The bartender opened a bottle of beer and handed it to the man next to Jae. Then he leaned closer. "Fifty."

Jae pressed a few buttons on his screen and held it out toward the bartender. The bartender touched the head of his Linq to the head of Jae's. The two devices let out beeps, and the men tucked their Linqs away.

"Yeah, I've seen her. She's in the VIP room." He pointed to a spiral stairway at the corner of the club.

"Any help getting up there?" Jae asked.

"Sorry, dude. It's gonna cost you more than fifty for that, and you'll have to speak to the boss, Bruno, to make that happen, and Bruno's off for the night. He's actually up there himself and asked not to be disturbed. Unless you've got an access card, but they are rare to come by. Good luck, though."

Jae nodded his thanks to the man and turned away from the bar.

"We're going up there?" Mayhara asked.

"We'll figure out a way."

She looked over his shoulder. Under the staircase, there was short hallway leading to a door. She could just make out the word ADMINISTRATION marked on the metal.

"I have an idea," she said. "That is, if you're as good a hacker as you seem."

"Tech prodigy."

She gave him a crooked smile. "There's a lock pad right outside the office door. Think you could break in?"

He followed her line of vision past the hoard of dancing bodies and narrowed his eyes. A smile slowly formed on his lips. "Yeah, I think I could." He glanced down at her. "We're going to have to do a little role-playing, though, so we don't get caught."

She held back a nervous laugh. "All right."

He placed a hand on the small of her back and steered her toward the office hall. Inching closer as they continued to walk, he bent his head until his mouth was right behind her ear. "Just warning you. We're going to have to get a little cozy."

The vibration of his voice on her skin caused goose bumps to erupt all over her body.

Get a grip, she told herself. *This is just for show.*

When they reached the hall, Mayhara looked up at Jae, not knowing what his plan might be.

Jae's eyes were on the lock pad. He pulled his Linq out of his pocket along with a short, black wire—the same one he'd used to crack the holding cell lock. "It'll take a moment to get the code, so we're going to have to make it look like we have a reason to be here. Even if that reason is—"

"To find a private place to make out?"

She bit back a laugh as his cheeks tinged with red.

"Yeah, uh…"

"Don't worry. I'm sure we can make it look convincing." Holding his arms, she positioned herself so her back was to the lock pad. There was just enough room for him to hook up his Linq. She took his head and directed it to her neck, giving him a view of the lock pad while making it appear to anyone who might come along that there was something else going on.

Playing her part, she ran her hands along his shoulders, every once in a while letting her fingers comb through the back of his hair. She kept her eyes on the end of the hall, making sure no one was coming, but a small part of her couldn't believe how amazing he smelled.

Behind her, the lock pad chirped, and the door clicked open.

Jae slowly lifted his head and slid his forehead against her temple. "Are we clear?"

She checked once more before meeting his eyes. "Yep."

He took her hand, glancing over his shoulder once before slipping in the door with her.

Mayhara tapped the control panel and pressed the button for the lights. The office was small, barely big enough for a desk, a bookcase, and a ratty-looking chair. Mayhara went over to the computer and found a metal box. Inside were plastic cards identical to the one she'd found in her apartment.

"The card I found," she said to Jae. "It's an access card."

Jae joined her, running his hand over a small machine standing next to metal box. "Okay, it's probably activated. Which means we need one more."

He hit a button on the keyboard, and the computer monitor came to life.

"You think you can get in?"

He scoffed. "Tech Prodigy 101."

She hovered over him as he sat in the chair and began typing away at the keyboard. She wasn't sure what he was doing, but windows were being opened on the screen and Jae started accessing files.

"Okay. Found it," he said. "Stick one of those cards in the reader."

She did what he'd asked, and as the machine made a buzzing sound, her eyes flitted over a few hanging pictures on the wall. One picture in particular caught her attention.

"Hey, check that out," she said.

Jae followed her gaze. "Is that the chief of police?"

"Yeah. With his arm around… Bruno, I'm guessing."

"No way." Jae seemed to go pale.

"You don't think that's him?"

"No, I do. It's just… that's him. That's the guy Naree's been seeing."

"Your sister's involved with Bruno? Wait, Darshana said the commander of the shadow army—"

"Bhutano," Jae said."

"Yes. Bhutano—that he's possessed a human body to lead the Lotus to Kashmeru's tomb. So Bruno is… Bhutano?"

Jae rubbed at his chin, glaring at the picture. "It makes sense. He and the police chief appear pretty chummy. Makes me even more convinced the imperial police are connected to the Pishacha. Assuming Bruno is being possessed by Bhutano."

"He's got to be. Right?"

"There's got to be a reason they brought Naree here. It has to have something to do with the Pishacha." Jae shook his head as he took the activated card out of the machine. "But I can't connect the dots yet. What are they waiting for? Why not just bring Naree to Kashmeru's tomb and bring him back to life?"

"There must be more to the story." Mayhara squinted at the picture. "Wait."

"What?"

"The guy on the other side of Bruno. I swear he's the officer I saw at my office. He had a meeting with the director."

Jae shook his head. "I think this whole thing involves more people than we think."

"Is there anything on the computer that might give us a clue?"

"I'm copying the files to my cloud. We can check them out on my Linq later when we're not in a compromised situation."

"We need to get a hold of Darshana, too. See what she knows."

"Yeah." He stood, holding up the access card. "But first, let's try to rescue my sister."

They switched off the computer and headed out of the office, checking to make sure no one was paying any attention. They kept close together for show and went straight for the staircase.

Before they reached it, someone caught Mayhara's wrist. She pivoted quickly, her eyes widening upon seeing who it was who'd grabbed her.

"Rajev?"

"Mayha, I didn't expect to see you here." Rajev's smile didn't reach his eyes. "I've been trying to get ahold of you. You haven't answered any of my messages."

Jae stepped closer to Mayhara, his shoulders squared. Rajev's insincere smile disappeared completely.

"I don't have time to talk to you, Rajev," said Mayhara. "In fact, it's probably better if we cut ties altogether."

"What? Baby—" He reached for her.

"I'm not your baby," Mayhara said, slapping his hand away. "You stole from me."

"Borrowed," he insisted. "I was going to pay you back, I swear."

"Really?" Jae asked.

Mayhara could just make out the blue glow on Jae's palm as he set his hand on Rajev's shoulder.

Rajev blanched. He made a futile attempt to back away from Jae, but something made him hesitate. Mayhara thought it might have something to do with Jae's powers.

"What were you really planning on doing?" Jae asked.

Rajev's brow crinkled. "I'm going to keep the credits. I had no intention of paying her back."

The color drained from Rajev's face.

Truth, Mayhara remembered. It was one of the powers of a sapphire mage.

Mayhara exhaled heavily through her nose. Instead of screaming at Rajev—which would have been her kneejerk reaction—she contained herself, just like Darshana had taught her. If Jae could use his powers on Rajev, so could she.

"Raj," she said, placing her hand on his other shoulder and feeling invigorated as her palm glowed red, "I hope this bothers you for a long time. Forever, in fact, so you never do it to anyone else, ever again."

She squeezed his shoulder, and Rajev's knees gave out. He crumpled to the floor, still conscious, but struggling to get his bearings.

Stability. Or rather the ability to manipulate it. One of the crimson mage's powers.

"Let's go," Mayhara said to Jae. "He's wasted enough of our time."

Mayhara wasn't sure it would work, but she put on an expression of confidence as she led the way up the spiral staircase. It only crossed her mind for a split second that Jae might be watching her backside as they climbed.

At the top of the staircase, behind a small table, sat a young woman with bright pink hair in high-set pigtails. She chewed her gum with her mouth open, and from the expression on her face, Mayhara gathered there were other places she'd rather be.

"Are you on the list?" the girl asked.

"We've got these." Jae held out the cards.

The woman seemed bored as she took the cards and slipped them, one at a time, into the reader machine on her table. The machine's green light lit for each card. "Yeah, okay."

She pressed a control panel at the table and the door to the VIP room opened. Mayhara gave Jae an apprehensive look before they stepped forward.

The room was long, with couches sectioning off small areas. It was only slightly less full than the chamber downstairs, but the music wasn't as loud. The lights in the VIP room ran on a slowly changing loop of light pink to deep purple to ocean blue and back again. Servers walked around with trays of drinks and small plastic cubes. Mayhara's guess was that the cubes held drugs in them, but she couldn't be sure.

A few of the patrons looked their way, but it wasn't until they reached the far end of the room that heads began to turn toward them with concern.

A young woman with long hair turned their way, following everyone's gaze. Mayhara gasped.

"That's her," she said.

"Naree!" Jae called out.

Naree stood, perplexed for a moment. Her eyes were like jewels. She stared at her brother. She was more beautiful in person than in the photo. She had an aura around her that was magical, and Mayhara couldn't help but be in awe of her presence.

Their view of her was quickly obscured by two tall men in black leather jackets and black mouth masks.

Jae set his jaw. "I'd like to speak with my sister."

One of the men pulled out a gun. "That's not going to happen."

Jae lifted his palms. Mayhara stiffened but readied herself.

The guys in the leather jackets drew their brows down and stepped forward. Behind them, one of the men beside Naree—Mayhara recognized him as Bruno from the picture in the office—grabbed her by the waist and led her quickly toward a rear door.

"Bruno?" Naree whispered.

"Let's go," he said, rushing her out the door.

The man with the gun aimed. Mayhara instinctively pushed out energy with her hands. Crimson particles shot out toward the gun just as the man moved to pull the trigger. The barrel was quickly jammed with red crystals, causing the gun to explode from the man's hand.

The second man lunged forward.

Jae grinded his teeth and raised his palm. Bright blue energy crystals began to form. Before he could generate enough sapphire particles to form an energy sphere, the two leather-jacket-clad men jumped him, one of them delivering a blow to his stomach.

Patrons around them were agitated and scared, some of them running for the main door of the VIP room to escape while others cowered beneath their tables.

Mayhara's blood grew hot with her mage powers. She shot off her crimson energy, hitting the nearest guy in the shoulder. He let out a yelp of pain as he was propelled backward, off of Jae. Without hesitating, Mayhara burst another crimson sphere at him, this one hitting him directly in the chest.

By this time, Jae had gained the upper hand on the other attacker, generating enough sapphire energy to hurl the man off of him and through the air. The man crashed into a table, his flailing legs knocking down a couple of chairs.

"Cover your ears," Jae said.

"What?" Mayhara asked, thrown by his request.

"Cover your ears!"

She did as he asked. As the two thugs struggled to get up, Jae clapped his hands together, his palms glowing blue. The air around his hands vibrated visibly, like a circular disruption in the space around them, expanding outward. It was coupled with a harsh ear-popping thrum. The two men screamed in agony, slapping their hands over their ears as they crumpled to the ground.

Sound, Mayhara remembered. Part of the sapphire mage's powers.

"Come on." Jae grabbed Mayhara's hand and ran for the rear door, clearly not bothered with whether or not the two attackers would get up again. "They can't be far."

The rear door opened into a narrow hallway. At the end of the hall was an emergency exit door swinging closed.

Jae and Mayhara ran for the door, and Jae's hand caught it right before it slammed shut. They found themselves at the top of a fire escape. Bruno must have known that opening the door wouldn't set off the alarm. Mayhara hurried to the edge of the railing just in time to see Bruno holding Naree by her shoulders. She couldn't hear what he was telling her, but they both looked up when Jae called, "Naree, wait!"

A black jeep racing through the back lot skidded to a stop beside Naree and Bruno. Jae and Mayhara raced down the metal steps of the fire escape, but by the time they reached ground level, the jeep raced off and Naree was gone.

Bruno faced Jae and Mayhara, reaching behind his back and under his jacket. He pulled out a long, black, metallic, stick-like object. There was a click when Bruno's thumb shifted, and the stick extended into a pole. When Bruno swung it, it made a low, hollow hum.

Jae grit his teeth and opened his palms, ready to defend himself—or attack. Mayhara followed suit and brought her crimson energy to her palms.

Bruno advanced, holding the pole in front of him with both hands. Jae put one foot forward as he formed an energy sphere and quickly shot it toward Bruno. Bruno twirled the pole. The air hummed with its rotation. When the sphere got close to Bruno, the pole somehow stopped and dispersed the energy particles, making them spark and crackle in the air as they disappeared.

Mayhara's eyes widened. By the look on Jae's face, she wasn't the only one surprised by the function of this weapon.

Mayhara's garnet glowed on her wristband. Her power amped up, she hurled crimson energy at Bruno, hoping her sphere could penetrate the pole's shield. But as crimson particles broke apart and spread, crackling into the air around them, she knew it was of no use.

Bruno smirked, knowing he had the upper hand.

But it was two against one; surely, they could sway the odds in their favor.

Bruno lunged forward, this time with the pole's end aimed at Jae. Jae crouched and spun to the side, avoiding the pole's impact, but Bruno swung the pole to the side, its metallic end catching Jae in the arm. The sound of ripping fabric resonated in the air at the same time as Jae's outcry of pain. He staggered back.

Mayhara whirled a crimson sphere at Bruno, putting a spin on it in hopes it would get past his weapon.

Bruno swung the pole but only caught part of Mayhara's sphere. A good portion of crimson energy hit Bruno on the side of his head, throwing him off-balance.

With an angry shout, Bruno advanced on Mayhara. She sidestepped the pole, turning and catching it in her hands as she thrust Bruno into a nearby car. Her palm glowed red, but Bruno whipped the pole out of her hands and swiped it down and to the side, catching her legs. She emitted just enough crimson energy to knock him off his feet as she fell. A clattering sound reached her ears. She thought it was Bruno's pole, but he still held it in his hands.

Suddenly, Jae was on top of him. Jae's face was red with fury. He grabbed Bruno around the neck and slammed him into the ground.

"Tell me where my sister's gone!"

At first Bruno was shocked from the impact of his head against the ground, but then his eyes narrowed, and an eerie smile spread over his face.

Jae pulled his arm back, his fist glowing, ready to throw a punch. Before he could, thick black smoke filled the space where Bruno had been lying. Jae fell forward, holding on to nothing.

The smoke cleared. Bruno had disappeared.

Mayhara's breath left her. She felt as if all the blood had drained from her brain. He was gone. Just like that. In a huge cloud of black smoke.

"Shit!" Jae dragged his hands over his face, his skin going red.

"What?" Mayhara shook her head. "How?"

Jae let out a guttural scream, pulling at his hair. Mayhara placed her hands on her cheeks, forcing herself to keep calm, to think logically.

She stretched her neck, looking up at the night sky. The hazy streak of the Akutake comet caught her eye.

No. She couldn't let their destiny unfold in such a way. She had to make sure they stood a chance.

"Wait." Mayhara straightened and rushed to the nearby car. She bent down and reached under it, remembering the clattering noise she'd heard during the fight. When she got to her feet, a small smile surfaced on her face. She held up Bruno's Linq. "We're not lost yet."

Sixteen

Naree's heart pounded in her throat. Her mind was clouded, and only one thought propelled her forward.

Kashmeru.

She couldn't resist him any longer. There was no reason for them to be apart. It was destiny.

The jeep sped down the highway, closer to their destination.

You know what you have to do.

She closed her eyes and nodded, having no choice but to do Kashmeru's bidding.

Bring me the dagger, and soon we will be together.

She opened her eyes, and suddenly a calm fell over her. She could do this. She would. For him. For her love. Nothing could keep them apart anymore. It was destiny. And she had no choice but to fulfill it.

Seventeen

Jae hissed through his teeth as Mayhara dabbed ointment onto the cut on his shoulder.

"Nearly done," she said softly, wrapping a bandage around the wound. She taped it off and packed up the first aid kit, stowing it on the shelf of Jae's small bathroom.

They'd gone to his apartment for recon after Bruno had disappeared. Jae wanted to read the files he'd copied from Bruno's computer as well as break into his Linq. Between the two sources, they hoped they could get a lead on where Naree might have been taken.

Jae stood, rotating his shoulder. With a wince, he pulled his shirt on. Mayhara found herself staring and quickly averted her gaze, turning to the sink to wash her hands.

"I forgot how invigorating it was," she said.

He tilted his head slightly, a look of bemusement on his face. "What?"

She wiped her hands off on the towel next to the sink, smiling at the sight of her wristband. "Using my powers without the pain."

The corner of his mouth inched upward. "Nothing quite like it."

"I mean, I probably shouldn't have used mage powers on Rajev." Darshana had always encouraged peace, emphasizing that mages should only use their powers in defense. "That was probably uncalled for."

Jae walked past her into the hall, continuing toward his living room. "You shouldn't feel bad about what you did to Rajev. If you ask me, he deserves a little destabilization."

She smirked. "I know. He's probably fine now, anyway. Even if it is with one thousand of my credits."

He stopped at the makeshift workstation his coffee table had become. "I can get them back for you."

"Yeah?"

"Of course. And if the authorities locked your accounts, I know a trick or two to unlock them and make it impossible to manipulate your records."

"You can do that?"

"No problem." He knelt in front of his laptop. "You need a little extra for the trouble?"

She laughed, resting her weight on the edge of his sofa. "Tempting, but no. Just what I earned fair and square."

"Mayhara, you work for the government. They don't deal with fair. You probably deserve ten times whatever they pay you. Minimum."

"Paid. Past tense. I'm pretty sure I've been fired at this point." She didn't want to think about her job. She bent her head, feeling disheartened. "I've been saving whatever I could for when I could get my family out of the prison camp. But I guess that's far from reality now."

Jae looked up at her with empathetic eyes, but he didn't say anything. She knew he couldn't promise her anything. Neither of them could know how this would turn out.

Feeling the need for distraction, she glanced around the room, her eyes landing on a Celadon vase engraved with a lotus. Beside it sat a Korean *Hoon-ro* incense burner, and hanging on the wall, staring back at her, was a *Hahoetal*—a Korean folk mask made of alder wood and used in dances and plays, but which were also regarded as good-luck talismans.

The seemingly intense stare of the mask made her shift in her seat. "What do you think happened to Bruno?" she asked.

Jae didn't look up at her, busy concentrating on breaking into Bruno's Linq. "If I had to guess, I'd say it's some kind of magic connected to Bhutano's spirit."

"Kashmeru's main henchman. Right. But, disappearing *with* Bruno's body? I wouldn't think a spirit needed one. Or maybe it's like a parasite and can't survive without a host."

"I don't know how it works. Just like you, this is my first rodeo. And someone forgot to tell us how to break in our chaps."

She stood, stretching out her back. "Yet another mystery we hope Darshana can explain."

As she was about to head to the window to check the street, a ping emanated from Jae's laptop.

"What's that?" she asked.

"I've set an alert so I can be notified if the media reports anything about the prison camps."

He opened a new window on his screen and turned up the volume.

"…centered around the possible uprising in the prison camps. One such extremist group came head to head with authorities at the Murwara prison today. While the imperial guards managed to get the attack under control, it wasn't without a few casualties. One guard and four prisoners lost their lives in the fight."

Jae looked up at Mayhara, concern etched in his features. "Is that where your family is?"

She slowly crossed her arms over her chest. "No. But it's only a matter of time. That's the third prison camp this has happened at. I don't know how these extremists are spreading through the system, but it terrifies me that my family will one day get caught in the crossfires."

"Something tells me your family knows to avoid the extremists," he said confidently. "Unless these extremists start camp-wide riots, your family should remain safe."

Mayhara's eyes were drawn back to Jae's monitor, where a picture of her was suddenly displayed on the news channel. Though she knew it was inevitable, it was still a shock to see herself on the screen.

"…has escaped from New Jaipur prison. We encourage all citizens to be on the lookout for the fugitive. Guatama is reported to be armed and dangerous. Anyone with information on her whereabouts should contact the imperial police immediately."

She looked down at her hands. Well, it wasn't exactly a lie. Her hands could be considered weapons. It didn't matter that she'd been taught to only use them to defend herself or to keep the Lotus empress safe. The authorities wouldn't care about that fact; she was a fugitive, and they would take her down at all costs.

Jae looked up at her. "I'm going to go ahead and say you're definitely fired."

She traced her garnet stone with a finger. "Now everyone will be keeping an eye out for me."

Jae rubbed the space under his bottom lip, studying her. "I've got a hat you can wear."

Despite the gravity of the situation, she let out a laugh. "You're a mastermind of disguises. Who knew?"

He stood, and for a moment Mayhara had forgotten how tall he was. She took a step back.

"But seriously," he said. "I've got some clothes here that belong to my sister. Some things she left the few times she crashed here—which was any time she needed to escape our overprotective parents."

He gestured for her to follow him as he made his way down the hall.

"I mean, I get it," she said. "That's a lot of pressure for her to have on her. And your parents. They were probably hard pressed to make sure no harm would come to her in any shape or form, and even if they were overprotective purely out of love, I imagine it can be suffocating."

Jae led her into the apartment's solitary bedroom—his bedroom—and opened up a drawer. He pulled out a pile of clothes and handed them to her. "Here are a few of her things. You can see what fits."

She stood there for a moment, staring at the clothes in her hands.

"What?" he asked.

"I don't know. It's just a little weird. Wearing the Lotus empress's clothes."

He smirked. "She's also just a girl, with normal thoughts and feelings, same as you. Don't let it get to you so much."

She nodded. "Yeah. Yeah, okay. Thanks."

He gave her a reassuring nod as he left the room. In the silence he left behind, Mayhara took in a deep breath and blew it out slowly. She smoothed her hand over the soft blouse on the top of the pile, trying to wrap her head around what her life had become.

When she had trained at the academy, she used to fantasize about what it would be like to serve the new Lotus empress. Having walked the corridors of the palace, it had been easy to imagine dressing in the imperial mage garb, her uniform of crimson and black always freshly ironed as the crimson mage cadets did their part to ensure peace in the palace and across the land. Of course, back then she'd always imagined being under the wing of Fei Ling, the elite crimson mage during her training years. Now Fei Ling was gone, the Lotus empress in the hands of the Pishacha, and Mayhara was on the run, wearing the Empress's clothes.

After she was dressed, she folded her clothes away neatly and set them on the corner of Jae's bamboo dresser. His bed—which sat low to the floor—was neat, but not made to perfection. She imagined his priorities lay more with finding his sister rather than making sure his place was pristine. For a split second, she had the urge to run her hands over his duvet to straighten it out. Instead, she cleared her thoughts and left his room.

She found him hunched over the equipment on the coffee table. A mug of steaming liquid sat next to his laptop. A short black cable ran from the laptop to Bruno's Linq. A program was opened showing a sequence of running numbers and letters. Mayhara guessed this was the software Jae used to hack into password-protected equipment.

"Any luck?" Mayhara asked.

"Getting closer," Jae answered. "I made us some tea." He gestured to the side table, where she spotted another mug.

"Thanks."

"Oh, and there's this." He handed her a Linq. "I got as far as the screen to connect it to your cloud. Go ahead and log in. It's untraceable, so you can download it onto there."

"You couldn't just hack into my cloud?" she teased.

"I only hack when I need to. I still respect your privacy."

She smiled at him. "Thank you. Believe me, I'm in a place where I could use a little feeling respected."

Next to her tea was a tiny plate with two *Ariselu*. She smiled, as she was fond of the sweet rice cakes. "Is this from the shop downstairs?"

"Yeah," he said, the hint of a smile touching his lips. "The kind old lady who owns the place took a liking to me. She rents me this place, which—as far as hidden apartments go— is a dream. And I help her out when she gets shipments in or needs help taking inventory."

"That's a nice setup."

"And her *Ariselu* are incredible."

Curiosity tugged at her. She took one of the cakes and indulged in a bite. "Oh, wow. Yeah, that's amazing."

She let him continue his work, enjoying the small moment of hot tea and sweet rice. She knew it wouldn't last long and was determined to take it all in while she could.

"I think I found something in the files I copied from Bruno's computer," Jae said. "It's a folder with names and addresses. But it's a long list. It'll take forever to go through. And there's another file here with some locations and maps."

"You think they have something to do with the Pishacha?"

"I wouldn't rule it out."

The ping from his laptop made Jae sit upright. "I'm in."

Mayhara set down her tea and moved to kneel beside him, her eyes darting around at all the names on the files he had open on the laptop. "Looks like the Census Information we keep track of at work. These locations are all over New United Asia. What's the connection? Who are these people?"

Jae's attention was on Bruno's phone. "I got into his messages. There's a name on a recent one. Jungkong Pi. Looks like they were trying to find this guy."

She inched forward toward the monitor. "There." She pointed at the name in the file. "Here's an address. Think we should check it out?" She waited as Jae typed the address into his Linq.

"Yeah," he said, getting to his feet. He held out a hand to help her up. "Let's go."

Jae grabbed a cloth beanie and a silk head scarf by the front door, handing the scarf to Mayhara. "You're probably going to want to hide your hair."

She nodded and wrapped the head scarf around her head, tucking the ends of her hair underneath it.

They left the apartment and descended the stairs that led to the *ariselu* shop. Jae placed his palms together and bowed to the shop owner, and he and Mayhara took the back door out to an alleyway. It was the same way through which they'd come, hidden and discreet. It explained how Jae was able to remain off the radar after he'd returned to New India from Korea.

Once they were out of the alleyway, they headed down the street, toward the rented garage where Jae kept his motorcycle. But halfway there,

Jae came to a sudden stop.

"What?" Mayhara asked "What is it?"

Jae pointed ahead of them. "Aren't those the guys from the club?"

Mayhara drew in a breath, recognizing the two men she and Jae had fought in the VIP room. They looked as if they were checking the shops and scrutinizing the passersby.

"Think they're looking for us?" Mayhara asked.

"Probably. Come on. We're going to have to get creative to get past them."

Jae led her across the street, the two of them keeping their heads down. Just as they slipped into a ramen noodle bar, causing the hanging bell on the door to ring, Mayhara glanced in the direction of the two men.

One of the men turned their way. His eyes widened and he yelled to his colleague.

Jae let out a curse as he put his hand on Mayhara's back and hurried her through the restaurant. The space between tables was tight, and in their rush, Mayhara's foot caught on the leg of one of the tables. She fell, and Jae nearly toppled over her. Waiters and cooks shouted at them, waving their arms around in anger, and then the bell above the door rang again as Bruno's men barged into the place.

Jae grabbed Mayhara's hand and tugged her to her feet. Mayhara's knee slammed into a chair, but she had no time to complain. They dashed for the back door, squeezing through it and slamming it shut.

Mayhara held a palm against the door and concentrated. Crimson particles rapidly generated from her hand, the energy spreading along the seam of the door and hardening. Once the door was sealed, she stepped back, hoping it would hold. She barely heard the pounding and shouts from the other side of the door over the hammering of her heart. But her crimson seal held.

"Let's go," Jae said, taking her hand and leading her down the back alley.

Mayhara fought off the pain in her knee, focusing instead on their trek to the garage. She just hoped they could reach Jae's motorcycle before Bruno's buddies could find them.

EIGHTEEN

Music played softly in the elevator as Naree made her way to the floor she'd been instructed to go to. She knew the apartment number. She knew what the man looked like.

There was only one more thing to do.

The elevator dinged as the doors opened, and Naree walked down the hall with confidence.

Soon she would be with her love. Soon she would feel his arms around her again, the soft feel of his lips on hers.

Soon, her destiny would be fulfilled.

She stopped in front of the door of her target and pressed the buzzer.

Only moments later, the man from the picture opened the door, gaping at her.

She wondered if he recognized her, but she couldn't be sure. There was no reason anyone would know who she was. She'd been hidden for so long. But perhaps those who secretly continued to work for the empire had spread the word about her existence.

"Can I help you?" the man asked.

"Yes," she said, stepping forward. "I believe you can."

NINETEEN

The address in Bruno's Linq led them to a high-rise apartment building in Kuchaman City. It had been a grueling two-hour ride. When Mayhara wasn't checking over her shoulder to make sure they weren't being followed, she was gritting her teeth against the roughness of the highway. The previous war had left it in ruins, and the administration had done close to nothing to renovate. Even when she and Jae dismounted the motorcycle, Mayhara couldn't shake the feel of the vibrating bike. It was as if the buzzing was alive in her bones.

The only respite Mayhara felt was that perhaps, with the distance between their current location and New Jaipur, the news of her escape hadn't traveled this far.

After removing his helmet, Jae slipped on a baseball cap and signaled to Mayhara to put her head scarf on. She obliged, tucking her hair into it, and then pulled up the collar of her jacket for added discretion.

The high-rise was a compendium of activity, brought about mostly from the shops and café on the ground floor. There were so many people coming in and going out of the main entry that Mayhara was sure they could blend in.

When Jae headed for the stairwell, Mayhara didn't question him. It was too easy to be caught in an elevator. A stairwell gave them more escape routes, though she wasn't too thrilled about the fourteen-story climb. At least it wasn't twenty—or more.

When they reached Jungkong Pi's floor, Jae tugged the bill of his cap down, his eyes drifting momentarily to the security camera mounted in the corner of the hall. They were counting on the high-rise running on the same automated security system as most buildings. It would be to their advantage if no one was constantly monitoring the halls. Still, they hadn't done anything yet to strike suspicion.

Mayhara pointed to the number plate outside the apartment they were looking for. "Fourteen twenty-two," she whispered. "You think she's here?"

Jae clenched his jaw. "I don't know, but if not, maybe this Jungkong guy can give us some information about where she went. And what she's up to."

Jae seemed to be holding his breath as he knocked on the door.

Mayhara kept her ears pricked, waiting for some sign that someone was home. All she could hear was Jae quietly letting out a curse before he knocked again.

"No one's home," Mayhara said after another minute of silence.

Jae glanced discretely at the security camera before pulling out his Linq. He was quick about hooking up his wire to it and attaching the other end of the cable to the lock pad on Jungkong Pi's door. In a matter of seconds, the lock pad's light turned green, and the door clicked open.

Jae went in first, and Mayhara instinctively checked over her shoulder before following him in. They looked around the living room, unable to find anything unusual. Mayhara turned toward the kitchen, and Jae signaled that he would check the bedroom.

Finding a pile of papers on the kitchen counter, Mayhara decided to rifle through them to see if she could find anything that might help them, but she barely touched the pile before Jae called her from the bedroom.

She didn't like the sound of his voice, and dread tore through her as she rushed to find him. It was as if she knew what to expect when she stepped into the bedroom. On the floor, on the opposite side of the bed, lay a bloody body.

Mayhara's knees almost gave out, but she caught herself on Jae's arm.

"Oh my God," she said. "Is that him?"

"I think so. Looks like he was stabbed."

Jae moved forward, and Mayhara swept her fingers under her head scarf, wiping sweat from her temples. Crouching on the floor, Jae inspected the area around the body.

"I don't see a weapon," he said. When he surveilled the room, something caught his attention, and he stood.

"What is it?" Mayhara asked.

"A laptop on the desk." Jae hurried over to it. "The camera is facing the room. There's a program on, recording everything. It's still running."

"Recording?" Mayhara made her way to his side. "Why?"

"I can't be sure. But let's see what happened here."

She leaned a bit closer as he tapped at the keys. In a matter of seconds, he brought up the video feed that had been recording. A man—the same man that lay on the floor, except very much alive—sat facing the screen.

"Hello, this is Jungkong Pi, one of the Sacred Keys. I'm attempting to send this message to the other Keys. If you find this before hearing from me, it means I've fled… or I'm dead. The Pishacha are coming. We must protect the daggers from the Council of the Seven. Kashmeru has the Lotus, and he—"

On the video, a door buzzer could be heard. Jungkong Pi disappeared from the camera, but before he'd left his room, he had switched the direction of the camera to face his room, leaving the video recording. A woman's voice could be heard faintly in the background.

"Naree?" Jae whispered, recognizing the voice.

"You are mistaken," Jungkong said off-camera. *"There's nothing here."*

"You're lying. Or did you forget I have all mage powers?" Naree suddenly appeared on the video but didn't seem to notice she was being filmed. She began opening drawers in Jungkong's room, searching for something.

"Empress, please," Jungkong said. *"I'm trying to protect you. To protect the universe."*

She ignored him, bending down and pushing the rug aside. Jungkong's eyes widened. Naree dug her fingers into the grooves in the wooden floor and loosened a floorboard. Jungkong pounced, attempting to stop her. Naree raised her hand. Crimson particles shot out at him, knocking him back against the frame of his bed.

She then reached between the floorboards and pulled out a black box decorated in a shiny red-and-gold pattern. Jungkong got to his feet just as Naree opened the box and slipped out a large silver dagger.

This time when Jungkong jumped toward her, trying to grab the dagger, Naree turned it in his direction and thrust it toward him. Jungkong fell on it, his eyes widening and his mouth falling open. Blood surged from where he was stabbed, and he stumbled backward. Naree pulled the dagger out of him and stared at the blade. For a moment, she looked scared. Her breaths came out in gasps and her hands shook.

Then a strange glow appeared in her eyes. It went away almost as fast as it had come. Her expression went stoic, and she wiped the dagger on the rug, ridding it of Jungkong's blood.

She stood, as if in a trance, and left the room with the dagger in hand.

The rest of the footage showed nothing. Jae forwarded through the recording until it got to the part where he and Mayhara entered the room.

He clicked it off, then took a step back from the computer, his hand cupping his mouth and chin as his brow furrowed.

"That's… That's…" Mayhara couldn't even finish her sentence. She was so in shock from what she'd just seen. From the look on Jae's face, he was as well.

"We need to erase this," he said, his fingers flying to the keyboard. "If the authorities get ahold of this, Naree will be locked away forever."

Mayhara stayed silent as Jae erased the footage, her emotions in battle over whether it was right or wrong to tamper with evidence. There would clearly be a police investigation into Jungkong's murder, and Jae was deleting the proof the police would need. But she understood why he was doing it. Not only because Naree was his sister, but because Jae knew she wasn't in complete control of her actions. She was being used as a pawn for Kashmeru's gain.

A buzzing from Jae's pocket sounded. When Jae pulled out the Linq, Mayhara realized it was Bruno's. She read the message displayed on the screen, which came from someone named Ghazaar.

Bruno, where are you? First dagger acquired. Headed to the meeting point in Sariska. Better hurry. Bhutano is pissed. See you at Phong's.

Mayhara and Jae exchanged confused glances.

"Bhutano is pissed?" Jae shook his head. "But I thought Bruno was possessed by Bhutano. That means—"

"Bhutano is possessing someone else" Mayhara pressed her hands to her cheeks as she put the pieces together. "Bruno was just one of the Pishacha, probably assigned to protect Naree."

"And Bhutano is still out there."

They were quiet for a moment, pondering what this meant. Then Mayhara put a hand on Jae's arm.

"They don't know what happened to Bruno," Mayhara said. "Or that you have his Linq."

"On a positive note, it means Bruno hasn't resurfaced anywhere yet. If he does at all." Jae stood. "Guess we're going to Sariska." He took a handkerchief out of his jacket pocket and wiped down the keyboard.

Mayhara nodded, mentally preparing herself for the four-hour journey. As they left the apartment, her mind raced to make sure neither of them had touched anything else. She was already a fugitive, but if the police found her fingerprints at the scene of a crime, it could make her a target for a 'shoot-on-sight' situation.

They hurried down the stairwell, neither of them saying much. When they reached the lobby, it was even more busy than it had been when they'd arrived. Jae put his hand on Mayhara's back to make sure they stuck together as they squirmed their way through the throng of people.

Bright sunshine warmed Mayhara's face as they got outside the building. To everyone around them, it was a lovely day, business as usual. But Mayhara couldn't help but think there was a dead man in an apartment upstairs who would never feel sunshine again.

They rounded the corner, headed for where Jae had parked his bike. Mayhara collided into Jae's arm as he came to a sudden stop. Looking past him, she saw the police officer inspecting Jae's motorcycle. The officer had his tablet out, no doubt typing in the license plate number.

As the officer spoke into his radio, Jae turned to Mayhara.

"We're going to need to take the sub-train." He kept his voice down and peered over his shoulder as he directed Mayhara away from the street.

"The sub-train might get us there quicker anyway," Mayhara said. "But your bike—"

"Don't worry. I'll get it back later."

Jae checked his Linq and found the nearest sub-train station, which luckily was not too far away.

The day began to heat up, and Mayhara longed to remove the head scarf from her head but kept it on to be safe. She found herself ducking her head down and eying the ground any time they crossed paths with anyone in any kind of uniform. She was thankful that Jae was so confident and determined; it helped her stay focused on their mission, whereas otherwise, she would fall apart from being overwhelmed.

The sub-train station was packed, and they were lucky to get a standing place on the train, smooshed up against a dozen other passengers. When Jae looked down at his arm, Mayhara realized she'd been clinging to it. Instead of letting go, she looked up at him and offered him a small smile. The corner of his mouth turned upward, and Mayhara relaxed a little. She leaned a little closer, both because she was terrified of being recognized, but also because him being near comforted her.

After a couple of stops, Jae pulled Bruno's Linq out of his pocket. He worried his lip as he read the screen.

"What is it?" Mayhara asked quietly.

"Ghazaar. Looks like he's getting nervous about Bruno not answering him."

Mayhara smirked. "Well, maybe 'Bruno' should answer him then."

Jae gave her a sideways look, matching her smirk. "All right. 'Bruno' will let him know he's on the way."

He typed in the message quickly and tucked the Linq away. When his eyes met Mayhara's, they both let out a small laugh.

About an hour outside Kuchaman City, the sub-train had emptied enough for Jae and Mayhara to sit. Though part of her had gotten comfortable to be holding on to Jae for physical and emotional support, she was glad to finally be able to get off her feet.

The rocking movement of the sub-train lulled her into a tranquil, almost-numb state, and before she knew it, she was waking up, having fallen asleep on Jae's shoulder. She looked around, confused and self-conscious, trying to focus on how long she'd been asleep.

"Where are we?" she whispered to Jae. "I must have passed out."

"We're about an hour outside of Sariska. And don't worry about it. You needed the rest."

She adjusted her head scarf. "Have you been awake the whole time?"

"Yeah. I'm not tired. Just anxious."

She felt the urge to reach out and squeeze his hand, but she resisted. Instead, she took a look around, noting the passengers who were busy checking their Linqs or reading books. Her eyes came across a man at the far end of the train. He was dressed in black and a black mouth mask hung at his chin. Though she knew the Pishacha wore the masks, it wasn't uncommon apparel in New United Asia, so she couldn't be sure he was one of the shadow army or simply an innocent citizen. He looked away when their gazes met, but she could have sworn he was watching her. She pulled the scarf a little lower over her brow and crossed her arms over her chest, hugging herself.

Probably just my paranoia, she thought.

She looked toward the window, but they were still underground. Nothing to see but blackness. When she turned her head, her eyes met the mysterious man's again. Her muscles tensed, and she grabbed Jae's wrist.

"What?" he asked, his voice low.

She leaned closer to him and whispered, "I think that man is watching us."

She gestured with her eyes without turning her head.

Jae made sure not to look too quickly. Instead, he kept his eyes on her and reached for her cheek. Mayhara's breath caught, not knowing what he was about to do. He leaned in closer to her, his mouth nearing her ear, and when his breath touched her skin, a thrilling shiver traveled up her spine. With his face close to hers, he turned his head slightly, as if he were about to whisper in her ear, but his eyes went to where the mysterious man sat.

She let out a breath, understanding Jae's strategy, but still she couldn't shake the fact that she'd enjoyed his touch.

"Yeah," Jae whispered. "He's watching us."

"What should we do?"

"It might be nothing. Or he might recognize you from your picture on the news."

"Or he could be Pishacha." She swallowed back her nervousness. "Should we get off the train?"

She took a chance and glanced at the man. He squared his jaw and stood, sending Mayhara's heart into a panic. The man walked toward them, purpose in his gait, and reached into the pocket of his jacket. Mayhara instinctively opened her hands, ready to defend herself. Jae did the same. They stood.

With a quick movement, the man pulled something shiny out of his pocket and threw it down the aisle. He then pulled up the mouth mask, covering his nose and mouth as he continued toward Mayhara. As white smoke filled the sub-train, the passengers began to panic, getting up from their seats and heading for the opposite side of the train. But the passengers closest to the smoke were too late, their eyes rolling to the backs of their heads as they collapsed.

"It's some kind of chemical," Jae said, the white smoke pluming toward them.

Mayhara held out her palms and shot out a cloud of crimson energy as she and Jae backed away from the man. Her crimson cloud pushed the white smoke away from them, and Jae fired off sapphire shots at the man. One hit him in the chest, knocking him back. Mayhara continued to beat back the smoke with her particles.

Jae took her arm. "Come on."

He pulled her toward a nearby door and pulled the emergency handle. The sub-train shuddered and skidded to a stop, the cabins filling with a blaring alarm. Jae pried the door open with his hands, just enough for Mayhara and him to squeeze through. He blasted one more shot of sapphire at the man, who'd gotten to his feet. This time the energy hit him in the head.

Mayhara climbed out of the train, dropping to the side of the tracks in the underground tunnels. Jae dropped down beside her and pointed in the direction they needed to run. Mayhara didn't dare turn back, for fear it would slow her down.

They dashed through the darkness of the sub-train tunnels, headed for the next station. They darted past puddles and rats as they got farther away from the compromised sub-train. Jae pulled Mayhara back to the center of the tunnel between the tracks as another sub-train charged toward them. He held on tightly to her as the wind kicked up dust and dirt and debris around them. Mayhara closed her eyes, leaning into Jae until the sub-train passed.

"All clear," he finally said, and they darted down the tunnel again.

There was a light up ahead, and Mayhara felt relief fill her chest as they neared the station. When they reached it, Jae gave her a boost, and they both climbed to the platform.

It was only then that Mayhara dared to look back. She didn't see anyone coming, but she wasn't about to underestimate the man's determination to chase them down.

"We've got to get out of here," she said.

"This way up," Jae said, putting a hand on her back and urging her toward the escalator.

They ran up it, finding themselves on a quiet street. It appeared as if it was someplace just outside of the nearby city. There were only a few people around: a woman pushing a baby carriage on the sidewalk across the street, and a group of school kids in uniforms bantering and laughing as they headed home. Mayhara spotted the faint smudge of the comet above the town, reminding her of their urgency.

"Maybe there's a bus stop or something nearby?" she asked. "Or a taxi?"

"I don't want to risk a taxi driver recognizing you." Jae checked his Linq. "We're not that far from Sariska. There's a bus station about ten kilometers from here. We're going to have to walk."

Mayhara looked over her shoulder at the sub-train station entrance. "How about we walk quickly?"

Jae let out a small laugh. "All right. Sounds good."

TWENTY

*Y*ou've done well, my love.

Naree woke in the back of the jeep to Kashmeru's voice.

We're one step closer.

She'd done it for him. All her reincarnations had led to this one. This fated one where they would finally be united.

It was always the way.

She pressed her hands to her heart. She could almost feel him there. Her heart thrummed with the knowledge they would soon be together.

Her Kashmeru.

Her love.

There's one more thing I need to you do before we can continue, my love.

"Anything," she whispered. She could barely stand another second without him. "Just tell me what to do."

I knew I could count on you, my love.

TWENTY-ONE

When they arrived in the Alwar district of Sariska, Mayhara wasn't sure what to expect. She had heard that the administration had plans to shut down the national park, but it didn't appear as if the town near the tourist attraction had been abandoned yet. The streets were still littered with patrons visiting the restaurants, cafés, and gift shops, as well as buying tickets to the tiger reserve.

Jae inspected the map feature on his Linq. "Phong's is a café a bit east of here." He pocketed his device and glanced at Mayhara. "Ready?"

"Yeah, let's go."

The town was surrounded by forests, grasslands, and rocky hills, with the road their bus had come in on snaking through the center of the tourist hotspots. Mayhara was actually grateful for the head scarf, which kept the hot sun off her scalp.

They approached the café, and Mayhara's mouth watered at the sight of the tall glasses of liquid set at the tourists' tables.

"Think we could get a drink?" she asked.

"Yeah, we probably should hydrate. Come on."

Mayhara first went to the restaurant's entrance, scoping out the tables inside. With no trace of Naree, they decided to grab a small table near the edge of the café's front terrace. They each ordered the 'delicious homemade lemonade' the café advertised, and when the drinks came, Mayhara couldn't indulge in hers quick enough.

With her thirst quenched, Mayhara felt more awake, more aware. She scanned the restaurant, wondering if they had missed Naree and Ghazaar. Perhaps they had tired of waiting for Bruno and left. But Jae hadn't gotten any more messages on Bruno's Linq, and he didn't want to initiate a message from 'Bruno,' just in case something he typed clued in Ghazaar that the messages were fake. They'd have to wait it out until they got another lead.

Jae called the waitress over and ordered two plates of *Masala Poha,* much to Mayhara's delight.

She raised a brow at him.

"We'll collapse if we don't eat anything," he said to her when the waitress walked away. "Might as well have some sustenance while we wait for them to show up."

The food came quickly, and Mayhara found herself devouring it. She had been so nervous about confronting the Pishacha, evading the police, and rescuing Naree, that she hadn't realized how hungry she was.

They polished off their meals while continuing to keep watch. Jae checked Bruno's Linq every few minutes, making sure it was actually on and the battery hadn't suddenly died.

After the waitress cleared their plates, Jae paid for the meal.

"I'm going to the ladies' room," Mayhara told him. "Be right back."

She almost felt dizzy leaving the table, but she figured it was her body catching up with everything she'd been through in the last couple of days. Her system was probably in a happy sort of shock from the food and drinks. A bit dazed in the ladies' room, Mayhara went through the motions while her mind wandered. When she stepped out of the bathroom stall, she grimaced at her reflection in the mirror. She desperately needed a shower. She pulled the head scarf down and almost laughed at her hair. She needed a brush. Or scissors.

She washed her hands and rubbed her wet fingers under her eyes and along her neck. Behind her, the door opened, and a woman walked in.

Not just any woman; it was Naree.

Naree must not have recognized her at first, because she continued to the sink beside Mayhara, rifling through her large purse in search of something.

And then it dawned on her. She froze, just as Mayhara was getting her wits about her to make a move. But in one split second, Naree threw out her palms. Her palms glowed green and before Mayhara could react, a sudden force of wind blew Mayhara back against the tile wall. Her head hit the hard surface, the ache making her squeeze her eyes shut for a second. When she opened them, Naree was gone.

Shouting a curse, Mayhara charged for the door. She looked around and caught sight of Naree hurrying through the kitchen entrance.

"Jae!" she shouted, not caring if the waiters or patrons were bothered by her outburst. She could barely make out his face out on the terrace. "She's getting away!"

Jae jumped up, and Mayhara turned on her heel. She dashed for the kitchen and spotted Naree escaping out the back door. The cooks and wait-staff yelled and hollered as she tore through the kitchen running after her. By the time Mayhara broke through the back door, Naree had slipped into the woods that bordered the restaurant's property.

Mayhara took off after her at top speed. She was barely aware that Jae was behind her, catching up. Her pulse hammered in her ears as she breached the line of trees. Jae was quickly beside her as they wound and weaved through the Kadaya, bamboo, and Dhok trees.

Naree looked over her shoulder, her brows drawn, and disappeared behind some large shrubs.

Suddenly, everything in Mayhara's vision went purple. She was blinded. She skidded to a stop.

"What's happening?" she asked, reaching out in hopes of finding Jae.

"She's using her powers to stop us."

Amethyst mage powers, Mayhara realized. Sight was one of them. And back in the ladies' room, Naree had used the emerald mage power of air to knock her back.

"It won't last," Jae said. "Trouble is, the magic diminishes the farther away she gets."

He cursed, obviously feeling defeated.

Mayhara reached out farther and found him. She took his hand. "We can catch up. Can you hear her?"

Instead of answering, he squeezed her hand. Through the purple haze, tendrils of blue energy snaked from what Mayhara could only assume was Jae's free hand.

"Okay," he said. "Watch your step."

Jae tugged on her hand, and she had no choice but to move one foot in front of the other to keep up with him. She kept a hand out to be sure she wouldn't collide with a tree, but she wasn't too sure her foot wouldn't catch on a twig or slip into a hole in the ground.

After a minute of seeing nothing but purple, the air started to clear. It was as if Jae had magically appeared out of nowhere, even though he had been guiding her the entire time. She trusted he was still listening for his sister since he seemed to be confident of which direction to go.

Up ahead, between breaks of the camouflage of trees, glowing eyes locked with hers. Something shiny gleamed from Naree's hand.

The dagger, Mayhara thought.

Naree quickly turned away from them as she slipped into a darker part of the forest. As they neared the spot where she'd disappeared, Mayhara realized it was the entrance to a cave situated in a rocky hill.

"Naree!" Jae called out, stepping forward through rocks and shrubs.

Mayhara surveilled the entrance. It appeared as though the rocky ground descended to lower depths under the hill. Even using her crimson mage powers of feeling the earth, there was no telling how deep this cave went. And there was no telling what awaited them inside.

But there was no question as to whether or not they would go after Naree. She was Jae's sister and the Lotus empress. They had no choice.

Inside, there were a few spots of light, where the sun shone through breaks in the rock above them. There were tunnels ahead, and a howling wind pushed through every now and then.

Jae listened and pointed to the tunnel on the right. "This way."

Instinctively, Mayhara opened her hands. Her palms glowed red. Jae placed a hand on her arm.

"Wait. We don't want to hurt her." He swallowed hard. "She's my sister. She might not be in the right mind to remember that, but it's still Naree inside."

"Of course," Mayhara said. "I don't want to hurt her, either."

He nodded and they moved toward the tunnel.

Mayhara tried to keep her breathing quiet so Jae could listen for his sister. As she looked around, the rocky walls reminded her of a tomb.

"Do you think this is where Kashmeru's body is buried? It would explain why they came to Sariska and why Naree brought the dagger here."

"I don't know. It's possible. I know there are a lot of temples around here. Seems fitting for the tomb of a deity. There's even a ghost town not far from here—as in occupied by actual ghosts."

Shivers crawled up Mayhara's arms. She hadn't really thought about it, but now that he'd said it, there was a chance they would be dealing with the spirit of Kashmeru. She wasn't sure if she was an elite enough mage to confront him.

The tunnel opened up, revealing a small cavern with an elevated level in front of them that led to another tunnel. In front of that tunnel stood Naree. In one hand, she held the dagger. Her other hand was raised and glowed red.

"No. Naree!" Jae put his hands up, but not to use his powers. "It's me—Jae! Don't—"

There was a blank stare in Naree's eyes, and Mayhara knew she wasn't in control. She wouldn't respond to her brother's words.

Crimson energy spilled out from Naree's palm, and the ground rumbled beneath them.

Mayhara and Jae struggled to keep their balance as the earth quaked. Mayhara fell to the side, scraping her arm as she hit the ground. Jae tripped to the opposite wall. The ground between them cracked and crumbled, the rumble growing louder.

On the upper level, Naree turned and ran into the tunnel.

Jae and Mayhara got to their feet on unsteady legs as the earth continued to shake, and the crack between them grew until it became a huge gap. Mayhara looked over the edge, but all she saw was a bottomless hole that separated her from Jae. She put her hand up, ready to use her mage powers to create a crimson-particle bridge to get to him, but the second she called upon her magic, an eruption of golden fire burst from the crevice. She shielded her face from the heat of the flames.

She looked back the way from which they'd come, but the earth had fallen into the crevice there. She couldn't turn back. She could go forward, though. There was a place where she could form a bridge to the upper level so she could go after Naree. But it was impossible to get to Jae, at least with the fire dancing its great heights between them. She doubted her crimson particles could withstand the Lotus's golden fire magic. It appeared he was trapped.

"Jae!" Mayhara shouted. "Can you move anywhere? Back toward the entrance, maybe?"

For a second, he didn't answer, and Mayhara feared he might be hurt or unconscious.

"Yes," he finally said. "I can go back. I'll try to take the other tunnel near the entrance and see if I can catch up."

"I'm going after Naree," she said through the flames. "Hopefully, one of us will be able to find her."

"Be careful!"

"You too!"

Mayhara stayed close to the stone wall, as far away from the flames as she could. She threw out her powers and formed a crimson bridge to take her to the upper level, and then raced forward to the tunnel Naree had run through.

She was plunged into darkness. She held her hands in front of her, using the glow of her palms as a source of light. It wasn't much, but at least she wasn't completely blind. She moved through the tunnel as quickly as she could, but it seemed to go on forever.

The terrain was uneven, and she had to stop now and then to catch her breath. Sweat covered her temples and back, and she wasn't sure her powers would hold out long enough for her to keep the glow of her palms going. Depleted and exhausted, she gasped when she spotted light up ahead.

Her pace picked up, and a sense of hope overcame her as she reached the end of the tunnel. It opened up into a chamber. The floor of the chamber shimmered, and there was a break in the ceiling of the cave, casting a pool of light onto the center, which refracted the light into the large space. It was as if millions of sparkles danced in the air.

She moved forward slowly, glancing around in search of Naree, squinting from the brightness of the sparkles. Footsteps to her left made her turn, and she instinctively held her palms up but didn't call upon her powers. Her tense shoulders dropped in relief when she spotted Jae running toward her.

"You made it," she said, resisting the urge to throw her arms around him.

"It was a challenge," he said as he panted. "Where's Naree?"

"I'm here," came his sister's voice from across the chamber. "I've been waiting for you."

Jae and Mayhara exchanged a look.

"Waiting?" Jae asked. "But you've been running from us."

"I only wanted to lead you here," she replied. She lifted the dagger as if inspecting it, and then she tucked it into her belt. "I thought you might wonder if this is where Kashmeru's spirit dwelled."

Mayhara took in the shimmering chamber. She doubted a deity so evil would be buried in a place so beautiful. Beside her, Jae furrowed his brow. He clearly didn't believe it, either.

"It is not," Naree said. "He's not so naïve as to let you find him so easily. But he asked me to get you out of the way. He knows you're trying to stop him. And he won't have it."

If this was not where the body was actually buried, then Mayhara deduced that Naree had only led them there to trick them, to trap them here so she could continue to heed Kashmeru's call.

"Naree, don't do this," Jae said. "Please. It doesn't have to be this way."

Naree shook her head. "I'm sorry. But it does. This is what he wants."

"But it's not what you want." Jae's hands were clenched into fists. "The Lotus always rejects Kashmeru in the end."

"That may be the case," she replied. "And if the same fate is upon him, he will destroy the universe so that every soul can share his pain."

"Naree," Mayhara said, her voice pleading. But Naree didn't look at her. "Lakshmi," she said instead, calling the Lotus by her deity name. "You know not to let this happen. You are the pure one. You must fight back."

Naree only regarded her for a moment, and then she stepped closer, closing the distance between them. "You cannot begin to understand the bond between us. Our souls are from another plane. We were created for each other."

"But you can't let the universe be destroyed," Jae said. "It's up to you to save it."

Naree's palms grew purple. Sadness clouded her face, and she stared intensely at Mayhara. "Mayhara, my crimson mage. You must help me. I'm in peril."

Mayhara stared back at her, her mind buzzing. It was shocking to hear the Lotus empress say her name. She hadn't realized the empress knew it. The empress's palms glowed a bright white, and the emotion Mayhara felt seeping into her pores was unavoidable. She had to protect her. She blinked, trying to keep her thoughts straight, but she found herself losing that battle. Something inside of her needed to listen to the empress.

"Save me, Mayhara!" the Lotus said. "It's your duty to protect me." The Lotus pointed to Jae, fear in her eyes. "The enemy is threatening me."

Across from Mayhara, Jae's face began to change. He looked back and forth between the Lotus and Mayhara. "No! I'm not the enemy. It's your brother—Jae!"

Mayhara held her hands out, replaying his words in her head. *I'm the enemy. I'm going to kill the Lotus empress.*

Yes, that was what he had said. She was sure of it. Who was this man threatening the empress?

Mayhara turned to him, stepping between him and the empress. She couldn't let her be harmed.

"No, you will not touch her," she shouted, glowing crimson particles emanating from her palms. Scowling, she thrust her energy out. Torrents of granite-like, crimson particles tore through the air toward him.

"No," he yelled. "Don't!"

He tried to defend himself with his sapphire energy, but the crimson rock found its way through, grabbing on to him and adhering to him, forming a stone trap. He shifted, grunting as he attempted to free himself, but it wouldn't budge.

His eyes went to the Lotus, desperation apparent in his voice. "Naree, stop! Stop manipulating her. Please! Don't make her do this."

Naree ignored him. "Protect me, Mayhara. It's your duty!"

Mayhara swung her arm, pitching a glowing crimson sphere toward him. It zoomed through the air and caught him in the chest, knocking him to the ground. More particles attached themselves to him, making the stone trap thicker and heavier.

He clenched his teeth as he raised his palms. Vivid blue energy crystals formed into a sphere. "Mayhara, I don't want to hurt you. Please stop. It's me. Please."

"Don't let him get to me, Mayhara," Naree shouted. "You're my crimson mage! You need to protect me. You need to destroy him!"

Mayhara's eyes widened. "Yes, Empress! As you command." The garnet on her wristband glowed, and she could feel her power intensify. She put one foot forward and hurled crimson energy at the threat. Red, glowing particles rained on the enemy, pinning him down ever more.

He coughed, trying to block the crimson dust with his sapphire energy, but not able to block it all.

"Mayhara, don't do this!" he pleaded. "She's manipulating you!"

Mayhara blinked, his words circling around her, but again she felt the distress of the empress needing her. His words were clearer in her head: *I will kill the Lotus. She will die at my hands.*

Mayhara squared her jaw and thrust her hands out farther, increasing the amount of crimson particles to form around him. It weighed down on him, trapping him, restricting his movement. She had to save her empress. She couldn't let this enemy kill her.

He winced, bringing his hands forward, worming them through the crimson rock. A bright blue glow slowly formed at his palms. He clenched his teeth as he thrust his hands out toward Mayhara.

Tendrils of blue snaked through the air until they finally reached her, swirling around her until they formed a shield of transparent blue fog.

"I'm not your enemy, Mayhara," he said. "It's me. Jae-hyun. Your friend."

This time Mayhara heard it correctly. She gasped and retracted her hands, closing her fingers into her palms and stumbling backward. She blinked, realizing what she had been doing and feeling an acidic sickness in her stomach. She'd almost killed him.

"Oh my God, Jae!" Mayhara's hands flew to her mouth. "I'm... I'm sorry. I thought—"

"No!" Naree yelled. "What are you doing? I told you to destroy him."

Jae pushed at the crimson rock with all his might, but it wouldn't budge. Mayhara reached out and pulled at the air in front of her. The crimson particles fell apart, crumbling to dust at his feet.

Naree raised her hands, palms out, ready to attack again, but Jae threw out his sapphire energy at her. It reached her before she could fight it off.

"Naree, you don't want to hurt us," Jae said. "You shouldn't let Kashmeru control you. You are the pure one. He wants to kill you."

Naree tried to wave off his particles, but they swirled around her, making their way to her ears.

"You love me, Naree. And I love you." Jae stepped closer to her.

She tried to back away, but Mayhara quickly threw out crimson particles and trapped Naree's feet. Naree raised her brows in surprise, looking first at her feet and then back at Jae.

"We're family," Jae said to Naree. "We need to stick together. Please hear me, sister. Please. We need to keep the universe safe."

Naree blinked. She lowered her hands slowly and her expression changed. "Family," she said softly.

"Yes," Jae said, his voice breaking. "Family."

Naree's hands flew to the sides of her head. She pressed in on her temples, looking as if she were waking from a bad dream. Her attention flew to Mayhara.

"Oh no, what have I done?" Naree buckled to her knees, tears streaming down her cheeks. "I… I killed people. I almost killed you both. What has he done to me?"

Mayhara and Jae hurried to her side as she sobbed. Jae wrapped his arms around her, shushing her.

"It'll be all right," he said. "We'll get you somewhere safe and put an end to this."

Naree looked up and him, and with a hiccup, she wrapped her arms around his neck and apologized through her tears.

Jae closed his eyes and squeezed her tightly. When he opened them again, he looked up at Mayhara and reached for her hand. Without making a sound, he mouthed, "Thank you."

Mayhara nodded. With a small smile, she squeezed his hand in return.

TWENTY-TWO

Under Naree's illusion power, the three of them had been able to get back to Jae's place safely. They had all exhausted themselves to the point where all they could do once they had gotten inside the apartment was collapse. Jae sent an encrypted message to Darshana to let her know everything that had happened, but she hadn't responded yet. Mayhara suspected she was in a compromised position and couldn't get back to them right away. Again, they would have to wait.

Jae had insisted Naree take his room. Mayhara had had no objections; after all, this was the Lotus empress they were dealing with. Mayhara had been born to serve her, and as far as Mayhara was concerned, Naree could have any bed in the entire district she wanted.

Mayhara curled up on the couch in a blanket Jae had brought her. She held the dagger in her hand, inspecting its fine grooves and intricate design. It was magical; she could feel it. There was practically a buzzing emanating from within it. It was almost as if it were trying to move, being drawn to someone or someplace where it was destined to be used. It had a purpose.

Jae appeared in front of her and handed her a mug. "Thought we could use something to relax our nerves," he said.

"Thanks."

"She's asleep," he said. "Of course, I keep checking to make sure. It's like part of me doesn't trust that she's really here."

"I know what you mean. And after being under her illusion spell in the caves, it's not that easy to trust anything is real."

Jae took a sip of his tea and then nodded.

They sat quietly for a while, and Mayhara couldn't help but wonder if Jae's mage power of sound included assuring the absence of noise. She would be envious of him if it did. She'd love to be able to shut off the world sometimes, even if just for a few minutes.

"I'm still bummed Bruno's phone got crushed in the crimson," Jae said, leaning back on the couch and scrubbing a hand over his face.

"Sorry about that. My fault."

One corner of his mouth crept upward.

"We still have his computer files," he said. "But the Pishacha could easily change their plans now, and we would be none the wiser."

Mayhara set her tea down on the coffee table and turned to face Jae. "I know this isn't over, and I don't know if anything is ever going to be okay. You've got to be feeling the same restlessness I am. Tell me I'm not wrong."

He pursed his lips for a moment. "You're not wrong. I'm completely on edge, but I can't let it get to me. There's too much riding on this not getting messed up."

"Oh, just the universe," she joked.

Jae smiled at her. "Just that old thing."

They each laughed, and Mayhara felt a small bit of tension fall away. She knew she couldn't go back to her old life. And she didn't want to see the collapse of the universe. As hard as it was for her to accept the fact that she had a hand to play in preventing that collapse, she knew it was the right path to take.

"We're headed in the right direction, right?" she asked. Her stomach fluttered, and there was an expanded feeling in her chest. "I hope that what we've done, getting your sister back, is enough for now."

He took her hand and squeezed it, a softness falling around his eyes. "Even if it's not, we're a team now. Whatever comes our way, we can deal with it together."

⟡

The morning sun filtered in through the living room windows, warming Mayhara's face. She yawned and stretched, pushing herself to a sitting position on the couch. The inviting smell of coffee wafted through the air, bringing a smile to her face.

When she got to her feet, meaning to head to the kitchen, the sight of Jae standing motionless in the corridor caught her eye. He held a small piece of paper in his hand. Her brow furrowed as she approached him.

"What are you doing?"

He looked at her, his mouth pulled into a frown. "Naree is gone. So is the dagger."

It took a moment for Mayhara to wrap her head around what he'd said. "What? When? How?"

He shook his head. "She must have left sometime in the middle of the night. When I got up, the bed was empty."

Mayhara wanted to reach out to Jae, but she reconsidered, figuring he might need his own space to process. They'd been through so much to find her, to get her back safe and out of the hands of the Pishacha, only for her to disappear fewer than twenty-four hours later.

"What's that?" Mayhara asked, pointing to the paper in his hand.

"A letter," he said. "*My beloved Jae-hyun,*" he read, "*I'm sorry to abandon you again, but I cannot escape my destiny. He calls me, so I must go. Though it pains me to leave you,* oppa, *I must follow my path.*"

His hand dropped, and his eyes slowly rose to gaze at Mayhara. She didn't know what to say; she was still trying to wrap her head around the fact that it had happened so quickly.

A knock at the door took them out of their introspection. Mayhara put a hand to her throat, holding back saying out loud that it could be Naree. She didn't want to give Jae any false hope.

Jae hurried to the door. When he opened it, his face remained stoic. He stood back, allowing Darshana to enter the apartment.

"She's gone." His tone proved he couldn't believe it himself.

Darshana clicked her tongue, her expression sad as she placed her hands upon his upper arms. "I'm so sorry. I was afraid the fight might not be over so quickly."

"You knew this would happen?" Mayhara asked.

Darshana walked toward her and stroked her cheek. "No, dear. I'm not a psychic. But I had a feeling either the Pishacha would come hunt her down or Kashmeru would reach her mind somehow. He won't stop calling to her, you know. Not until she either frees him… or kills him."

Mayhara swallowed hard. "So this is just the beginning?"

"We have more information now. We know what we're looking for."

"The daggers," Jae said. "I'm gathering there are seven."

"That would correlate with the legend. The Council of the Seven, the seven mages, the seven chakras, the seven deadly sins…the seven circles of hell."

Mayhara shivered. She and Jae exchanged a look.

"So we need to track down the other six Keys and get the daggers before the Pishacha do," Mayhara said. "But how do we even know where to start?"

Darshana regarded both of them, and Mayhara felt fear wash over her. Her stomach soured and her blood felt as if it were running cold. She was afraid Darshana might not have an answer for them. She was afraid they were lost.

Darshana let out a deep sigh. "I did some meditating while I was laying low. And on my transcendental journey, an image came into my mind. It took me a while to focus on it and figure out what it was. But finally, I did."

Mayhara pressed her palms together and brought her fingers to her lips, waiting for Darshana to continue.

"What was it?" Jae asked, looking as if he were about to jump out of his skin.

Darshana raised a brow. "A scroll. The answer to our problems, once and for all."

Copper Mage

Book Two

ONE

Mayhara cringed as she pulled the computer tower from the rubble, her fingers aching from the bite of the jagged pieces of stone. She couldn't use her powers on the stone; the academy building had been enchanted to withstand mage powers so the students wouldn't accidentally destroy it. Even the bricks that made up the building were unable to be penetrated by the magic. But the enchantment had done nothing against the bullets and battering rams the New Asian Administration had used to destroy the school during the Eradication.

With one final yank, she loosened the machine from where it was wedged, but dread overcame her as she took in the damage the casing had endured. She could only hope the hard drive was still intact. They were relying on the information it contained. She was quick to unscrew the casing and disconnect the hard drive. It was crushed in one corner, but she had to think positive—it would work; it would be fine.

With the hard drive in hand, Mayhara stood. Sirens in the distance caused her to freeze in place. She shouldn't be here. She shouldn't be anywhere, actually, except in a prison camp with her family—which was exactly where she'd end up if she was caught sneaking around the demolished mage academy. Instinctively, she backed up against the wall, her long dark hair falling across her face as she ducked her head.

She waited until the sirens faded, her breaths slowing in relief once they'd passed. Wincing, she realized she'd been crushing the hard drive into her chest. Her grip had been too tight, and a drop of blood bloomed against her deep brown complexion. She adjusted the hardware and steeled her feelings. The fear of getting caught was not only an issue of getting thrown into a prison camp; if she was captured now, her mission would be jeopardized. And if that happened, it could mean the end of the world.

Holding the hard drive securely, she scanned the room. She wasn't sure there would be anything else of use to her in the administration office of the school. She held what she hoped were the complete files of every student who'd ever attended the academy, but she wasn't confident it was all they would need to track down the other elite mages. At least, the ones who had survived.

She shuddered at the thought of the government's war on mages—and worse, the Pishacha's plan to terminate the elites as a direct order from the vengeful deity, Kashmeru. It was bad enough the Lotus empress had slipped from their grasp, unavoidably heeding Kashmeru's call, but Mayhara also had to deal with the fact that an ancient shadow army was out to kill her.

Deciding the hard drive would be enough, she made her way through the fallen bricks and concrete dust and into the hallway. The setting sun barely offered enough light for her to check if her path was clear. She considered using her mage powers to shine some crimson light but thought better of it. She'd just have to travel carefully.

She made it to the end of the hall and approached the stairway leading down to the main floor. Only a third of the stairs was intact, and she had to use some skillful maneuvering to make her way down. Luckily, her tight jacket and fitted, black jeans made tackling the obstacle a little easier. Once she reached the main floor, her eyes immediately went to the damaged hanging tapestry embroidered with the faces of the past Lotus empresses. Centuries of reincarnations of the deity Lakshmi were displayed along the high walls of the great hall, now partially burnt and torn, destroyed in the crossfire during the Eradication.

The only face missing was Naree's.

That was because her family had kept her hidden for years. No one knew she was the reincarnated Lotus empress aside from her family and Darshana, the empire's finest guru. The New Asian Administration didn't know—or at least they hadn't known. For all Mayhara knew, the administration could have found out. And if Mayhara's suspicions were correct and the administration was under the control of the Pishacha, then the fate of the universe was looking rather bleak.

She walked past the rubble that littered the floor and headed for the library. One of the large, wooden double doors hung partially off its hinges. Inside, desks and bookshelves were strewn about on the mosaic-tiled floor. A gaping hole in the wall let in what little was left of the sunlight, the golden beams shining upon the demolished shelves and shredded books. At the far end of the room, Jae crouched over a metal box on the floor.

"Find anything?" she asked him.

Jae turned his head toward her and dropped whatever was in his hands. "Nothing that helps."

He stood and stretched, rolling out his shoulder. For a moment, Mayhara was transfixed by his lean, muscular form, his confident stance, and the heavy set of his brows as he contemplated the situation. He raked a hand through his dark hair and sighed. When his eyes found her again, she cleared her throat and looked down at the hard drive in her hands. It wasn't the first time she'd found herself staring at him. Spending every day with him over the last few weeks, Mayhara had experienced many moments of a quickened heartbeat if he happened to brush her skin, a tingle in her body when they would share a laugh, and the desire to move closer to him while they worked. But she'd always shaken off the feeling as loneliness, as wanting to be close to someone since her family was imprisoned, or simply being in a situation together that not many others would understand. Besides, she couldn't know how he felt, and as brave as she was fighting off Pishacha, she didn't have the nerve to ask him.

Not that there was any time for that, anyway.

They were on a mission to save Jae's sister, to free the spirit of Lakshmi from the evil grasp of Kashmeru, and to ensure the safety of the universe. She had a family she needed to get out of a prison camp, so she shouldn't have wasted a moment wondering if this guy—this former classmate from the Empire of the Lotus Mage Academy—liked her back. It was trivial.

"I found the hard drive," she said, holding it out. "It looks like it took a blow, but maybe we can salvage what's on it."

He strode toward her and held his hands out. She gave him the hardware and then rested her hands on her hips, focusing on their mission once again.

"No way of telling until we get back to the temple," he said. "But the damage appears minor." He flashed her a smile. "I'm hopeful. Good job."

Mayhara ignored the compliment. "No sign of any scrolls?"

"None like the one Darshana described."

"She said it wouldn't be here. She would have recognized it from her vision if it was a scroll that had been kept at the school."

Jae tapped the hard drive against the palm of his hand. "I know. I figured I'd look anyway, just in—" He stopped, lifting his chin.

He'd heard the crumbling before she had. His sapphire powers at work.

With a gasp, Mayhara threw her hands up into the air past Jae's head. A section of the ceiling fell apart, taking with it a metal light fixture that made a direct drop toward where they stood. Quick to use her mage powers, Mayhara released streams of crimson energy, the particles rushing between Jae and the falling debris. The crimson shield solidified, forming a slanted wall that deflected the debris. Her garnet wristband glowed brightly. She pushed out her power until the wall connected sturdily with the floor. As soon as her palms were clear from the crimson dust, Mayhara pulled Jae toward her.

Dust flew around their heads, both from the destroyed ceiling and Mayhara's crimson wall. Jae gaped at how close he had been to getting hit, and then he turned back to Mayhara. They were mere inches apart.

"Are you all right?" she asked.

It took him a moment to respond. He swallowed visibly. "Yes. Thanks."

She averted her eyes. "Yeah, of course."

Her hands were still on his arms. She let them drop, then pushed her hair out of her face, taking a step back. Jae's eyes narrowed slightly, but as he opened his mouth to speak, a buzzing interrupted him.

He pulled his Linq out of his pocket but didn't look long at the screen. "It's Darshana."

"Has she found something out?"

"She didn't say. She just wants us to get back as soon as we can."

Mayhara nodded once. "Then let's go."

Two

Shiro raced after Qiang, his head kept low and his footsteps light. The heat and the stench made the air thick and difficult to move through. But that was the least of Shiro's concerns. With Qiang leading the way, Shiro and the rest of their gang were determined to make it to the eastern guard station unnoticed. It was only a matter of time before the Imperial Police discovered that the guards patrolling Shiro's camp were missing—and surely soon after they would find them tied up and stuffed in the outhouses, having been knocked out by a couple of Qiang's men. Ten minutes had passed since then, and every second flooded Shiro's heart with panic.

Shiro glanced over his shoulder at the rows and rows of bunkers at the edge of the camp. High above the camp, in the midnight-blue sky, the hazy streak of the Akutake comet marked its place as it made its approach. Seeing the encampment from this distance hit him hard. Long gone were the grassy areas surrounding the bunkers, now trodden down by the heavy boots of the Imperial Police, beaten into mud by the unforgiving monsoons. The cabins themselves appeared as if they were dying, the cracking stone greyed with time, infested with withered vines, the doors and windows falling off their hinges. The outhouses were long forgotten by the Imperial Police, who did nothing to keep them usable. Food rations seemed to get smaller by the week. Shiro had already given up believing the administration intended to keep them alive. This was a death camp. If they wanted to survive, there was no other choice but to escape.

"Keep low," Qiang called out. He signaled for a few of the men to rush ahead. Shiro closed the space between them, huddling close to Qiang's back to await further instructions.

The two men Qiang had sent ahead—Peng and Bao—were lean and light on their feet. They traveled fast, but Shiro suspected it was because they were emerald mages and used air energy to their advantage. If it weren't for Peng's reddish hair and hooked nose, he and Bao could be mistaken for brothers, all long legs and arms. Qiang nodded to Mitty, the burly golden mage whose hair was pulled back in a bun, then twisted to look over his shoulder at Shiro. Their eyes locked, and for a split second, Shiro couldn't breathe. Qiang's black hair hung loose on his forehead, and the stubble on his chin drew emphasis to how square his jaw was.

"Ready?" Qiang asked.

Shiro wasn't sure. He couldn't even keep straight in his head what they were doing. But Qiang had said he'd overheard guards talking about an oncoming attack, and they had apparently mentioned Shiro's name specifically. Qiang and the others were doing this for him. He nodded.

They stood but kept their heads low, approaching the patrol route. A short but loud grunt sounded, and the next thing Shiro knew, Mitty rushed forward, pounding a golden glowing fist into the guard whom Peng and Bao had jumped and pinned to the ground. The guard curled into a ball with a moan. Peng and Bao must have thought that was the end of the fight because they released the guard. They only realized it was a mistake when the guard jumped to his feet with a cyber baton in his grasp.

Shiro mumbled a curse. The weapon served as an advantage over mages, able to block and deflect their powers. It evened the playing field.

The guard snarled as he swung the baton in front of him. He didn't stand at his full height, obviously still affected by Mitty's fiery punch. Peng tried his luck and pounced the guard but was caught in the stomach with the baton. An electric sizzling sounded. Peng yelped in pain and fell to the ground.

Qiang sprang to his feet and rushed toward the scuffle. Mitty flexed his muscles, his fists clenched, circling the guard and assessing his possible strategies of attack. The guard swung his baton in Qiang's direction, which erupted an explosion of fear in Shiro. It would kill him to see Qiang hurt. His palms glowing orange, Shiro whipped his hands through the air. He ignored the excruciating pain that tore through him from using his mage powers and concentrated on the ground the guard stood on. A flash of ice suddenly appeared at the guard's feet. In his shock, he attempted to move back, but he slipped on the ice and landed hard on his backside. Qiang took advantage of the guard's weakened position and used his crimson power to move the earth, crimson particles forming around the guard's arms to hold him down. But the guard was quick to swing his cyber baton, the glowing stick shattering the crimson earth around his left arm.

Before the guard could get a good hit in, Qiang jumped on top of him, grabbed him by his head, and slammed it into the ground. Shiro rushed forward but skidded to a stop when Qiang suddenly slipped a serrated hunting knife out of his boot. Shiro remembered it being smuggled in, but he hadn't seen it since then. Until now. He was barely able to protest whatever Qiang had in mind before Qiang grabbed the guard's face, forced his mouth open, and sliced off his tongue.

Shiro turned away, bile rising in his throat. Tears spilled over his lashes. He hadn't wanted it to come to this. Killing repulsed him. He held his throat, begging himself not to vomit.

He turned back to face Qiang, his heart pounding in his ears. He tried to avoid looking at the guard, but his eyes deceived him. The guard gurgled as he struggled not to choke on his blood.

"Qiang, what have you done?" Shiro's voice shook.

"What? I didn't kill him." Qiang wiped his knife off on the guard's shirt, then stuck it back in his boot. "This way he can't rat us out to anyone. Let's go. We've got to reach the guard station before they find out."

Shiro could only stare after Qiang as he reminded the team of the plan. Inside his chest, Shiro's heart felt as if it had been pulverized, as if the beating had stopped from the horror of what he'd just seen. He knew they would have to go to some extreme measures in order to get out past the guards, but this just seemed unnecessarily cruel. Or had the guards deserved such treatment for all the years the mages had been forced to suffer under their watch?

Peng and Bao ran ahead, while Mitty dragged the whimpering guard into the bushes to hide him. Shiro heard a sizzle, which he imagined was from Mitty using his fire-control powers to cauterize the guard's tongue stump. At least, he hoped that was what it was.

Shiro was astounded at how Mitty never showed that he was experiencing any pain from using his powers. When they'd been captured during the Eradication, the New Asian Administration had implanted power blockers into the necks of all mages. But the devices served more like shock collars, transmitting currents of painful electricity into the mage's body upon use of their powers, rather than blocking them. Shiro hadn't been able to move for days after trying to use his water-control powers for the first time after the implant. Water and electricity were a bad mix.

A few months after imprisonment, they'd banded together and had all been practicing, training with Qiang's guidance to block out the pain. Shiro could never entirely block it out. And he suspected Peng and Bao couldn't, either, judging by the clenching of their jaws and twitching of their shoulders when they used their powers. But for Shiro, it was worse. When he used too much mage power, he would be punished with tremors of agony accompanied by a stinging nosebleed. It had always felt as if the blood was literally draining from his brain. But he was determined to endure it in order to escape.

And it was then, in those moments stolen away to train the pain away, that Shiro had grown closer to Qiang. It was then that he'd found a reason to get up every morning, a reason to fight to survive, and a reason to get out of the prison camps and be free—together with Qiang.

He'd imagined what their life together could be like, daydreamed about getting a place together, somewhere off the grid where no one could find them. Nothing big or fancy. Just some place they could call their own.

But first, they would need to escape, and that meant using his mage powers. He only needed to use enough power to get them out of the camp. He just hoped it would be as easy as Qiang had said it would be. And he begged to the gods that no one would have to die in the process.

THREE

Naree stirred, stretching with a pout as she woke from her dream. But it wasn't only a dream; it was a memory from a past life. As Lakshmi, she had sneaked out of the palace in the middle of the night to meet her love, Kashmeru. He had stood beneath a willow tree, hidden from view by the low, swaying branches. Hearing her approach, he had turned to face her, and his smile had mesmerized her.

He had held out a hand. "Lakshmi."

"I'm sorry I'm late," she had replied.

"For you, I would wait an eternity."

Her heart filled with warmth from his words, his gaze, and the intense love she could feel emanating from his core. She had taken his hand and let herself be enveloped by him. He lowered his head, his nose pressed into her hair as his hands gently caressed her back.

"Where shall I take you, my love?" he'd asked.

"Anywhere. As long as you're with me."

Naree smiled at the memory, running her hands along the soft fabric of the bed, wishing it was Kashmeru's arms instead. She wanted to lie there all day, reveling in the feeling, reliving the moments of pure, genuine love.

Lakshmi, we have some things to take care of, my love.

She let out a sigh and pushed her feet to the side of the bed. As she swung into a sitting position, her long, straight, black hair fell like silk over her shoulders. Though reluctant to do anything but lounge all day, she couldn't resist Kashmeru's call.

A knock came at the door before it opened. Bhutano stepped in, stopping just inside the room. He wore his uniform, which always confused Naree. He was a shadow spirit, possessing a human body and pretending to be the human as he carried out Kashmeru's plan. Looking at him, no one would suspect that this man would be playing a part in the demise of the universe.

She'd only met him after Bruno disappeared. Before that, Bhutano was the invisible commander, instructing Bruno to protect Naree, to bring her where she needed to be in order to carry out her part of the prophecy. Now that Bruno was gone, Bhutano stepped in to do the job of protector himself.

"Your Highness," he said with a bow.

"Yes, I know," she responded. She stood, grabbing her robe. "I'll get ready."

FOUR

Mayhara held tightly to Jae's waist as the motorcycle took a swift curve off the main road and onto a hidden path that led uphill. She wasn't sure if it was the unevenness of the road or her close proximity to Jae that was making her heart jump. As soon as they veered onto the path, the loud roar of the engine cut out. Peering over Jae's shoulder, Mayhara could see a blue glow peeking out from beneath his driving gloves. His sapphire mage powers silenced the engine so they could reach Darshana's hidden temple undetected. The heavy canopy of trees along the path helped as well.

They'd both moved into the temple with the guru shortly after Naree's sudden disappearance following their rescue mission. Darshana had insisted that Naree's knowledge of Jae's apartment was too risky. She could easily divulge his location to the Pishacha, brother or not. Then he'd be a sitting duck. It had taken some convincing, but Jae had finally agreed.

Besides, Bhutano was still out there.

They knew that Bhutano had possessed a human, and they'd assumed it had been Bruno. But after Bruno had lost the fight they had and disappeared into a cloud of black smoke, Jae had intercepted a message that Bhutano was angry that Bruno hadn't shown up at a meeting point. That was when Mayhara and Jae knew Bhutano had been possessing someone else. The problem was they didn't know who.

The temple Darshana had somehow acquired use of—details she mysteriously kept secret—sat quietly, high on the hill, invisible to the road below. Though modest in size for a temple, its pink sandstone columns and white marble tile floors gave it a welcoming, aesthetic beauty. Stone elephants as tall as Jae stood, tusks up, at the entrance, and both inside the temple and out in the gardens, statues of deities could be found—not only Kashmeru and Lakshmi, but also the gods and goddesses of the sun, moon, and sea. Jasmine trees brushed by the hilltop winds blew a calming fragrance through the space. The back of the temple opened up to a floral garden flanked by the hilltop forest. A small, stone, manmade waterfall fed into a clear pond that reflected the stars and the approaching comet at night. Lotus fountains supplied a tranquil sound of gentle, flowing water.

But more importantly, the temple felt safe.

There were more than enough bedrooms for the three of them, and Jae had set up his equipment in the ground-floor office. The laptop that held the files he'd stolen from Bruno was kept open on the office desk, being used daily in an attempt to track down the Pishacha and Naree.

Jae parked his motorcycle in the carport, and Mayhara reluctantly slipped her hands from his waist. Removing her helmet, she shook out her long, dark hair and wiped the beads of sweat from her temples. Jae flashed her a smile as he propped both helmets on the bike. He gave the bike a pat, obviously glad to have it back. After it had been found by the Imperial Police a month ago, Jae had had to abandon it, waiting for the right opportunity to get it back. Mayhara wasn't sure how he had done it, nor had she bothered to ask. She only remembered him leaving the temple one night and returning with it a couple hours later.

Now it looked like it belonged there in the carport, parked between the two used cars that belonged to Darshana. They weren't flashy cars; Darshana had purposely bought boring, ordinary ones they could use to get around without being noticed.

"I wonder what's got Darshana in a huff," Jae said, removing his gloves.

"Could be anything. But she wouldn't have called us back if it weren't something that might help."

He tapped the carrier bag at his side. "Speaking of something that might help, I'm anxious to check if these files are intact."

"Think positive," Mayhara said as they strode toward the entrance. "On both accounts."

Jae glanced at her and halted, gently grabbing her wrist. "Hey."

She blew out a shuddered breath as she stopped alongside him. "What?"

"First of all, unclench your hands."

Mayhara looked down at her white-knuckled fists, only now realizing she was clenching them. She forced herself to relax her hands and then looked up at Jae.

"It won't do us any good if you're wound up so tight." Jae loosely shook her arm, the corner of his mouth inching upward. "Let's just take this one step at a time. It's the most we can do."

"Yeah. Okay. You're right."

He gave her a wink, releasing her arm, then motioned for her to continue with him into the temple.

Out of habit, Mayhara ran her hand along the smooth surface of one of the stone elephants' tusks as they stepped inside.

They didn't have to search for her. They found Darshana in the meditation room, as they'd expected, sitting with her legs crossed, her wrists resting on her knees, and her eyes closed. Her breathing was almost indiscernible. Her long, white hair was pulled into a neat braid that hung down her back. The skilled guru's posture was impeccable; it was almost as if she were a statue. Peace seemed to surround her, like a soft glow that danced upon her being. That, along with her almost wrinkle-free skin, made her look much younger than she actually was.

Jae propped his shoulder against the doorframe and gave Mayhara a sideways smirk. They knew better than to interrupt Darshana when she was meditating. Mayhara caught Jae's expression and bit back a laugh. She knew he must have been thinking about the time they'd been waiting for Darshana to break from her trance, lurking on the sidelines, only for Mayhara to have involuntarily let out a violent sneeze, shocking the guru into losing her balance and falling backward with her legs still crossed in the lotus position in the air.

Jae smiled and shook his head, obviously infected by Mayhara's shaking shoulders as she kept her laughter locked inside.

"That's not helpful," Darshana said flatly, her eyes still closed.

"Sorry, Darshana," Jae and Mayhara replied at the same time.

Darshana placed her palms together and gracefully bowed forward. She then shook out her wrists and opened her eyes. As she got to her feet, she eyed Jae's messenger bag. "Find it?"

"Mayhara did. There's some damage to the casing, but it's probably salvageable." Jae pushed off the door frame. "What did you need us to come back for?"

The old woman moved with poise through the room, blowing out candles. "The vision of the scroll came to me again."

"That's great," Mayhara said.

"I saw more details this time. I thought we should add them to Jae's computer thingy."

"3D simulator," Jae said. "Yeah, let's do it. If this scroll is the key to saving the universe, then we need to figure out what and where it is."

"That's why I called you back," Darshana said. "I thought it best to do it while it's still fresh in my mind. I went back into meditation after I called to see if any other details would appear, but nothing else has come up."

"Okay, well, let's put in what you did see. Who knows? Maybe when you see it on the screen, something else will come to you." Jae stepped aside as Darshana walked past him and toward the office.

Jumbles of wires snaked between Jae's laptop, a couple of external hard drives, and some other equipment Mayhara couldn't remember the names of. When Jae tapped the laptop's screen, it emanated a blue glow that cast a muted light on the office walls.

"Just pulling up the program," Jae said, his face bathed in blue.

A grid popped up on the monitor, a 3D graphic of a scroll cylinder displayed in the center. Jae placed two fingers on the screen and pulled them in different directions. The scroll rotated.

"The cylinder has a curved design on both ends." Darshana pointed at the screen.

"Okay, let me zoom in," Jae said.

"Curved like the tips of flower petals, linked in a row."

"Like this?"

"No. Pointier."

Mayhara stayed in the doorway to give them room to work as Jae listened to Darshana's description of the scroll and sculpted the details into the graphic in his 3D program. She pulled out her Linq—the new one Jae had gotten for her since her old one was still in the evidence room of the police station—and scanned the news sites for any word of homicides. She knew there was a chance the government could be covering it up, but if any of the media sites let the report of a mage homicide or any other death slip through the cracks of the controlled internet, it could be a lead.

Not only were the elite mages being found murdered all over New United Asia, but seemingly innocent citizens were turning up dead as well.

Mayhara had learned that these seemingly innocent victims were actually Sacred Keys, special recruits of the empire, assigned with keeping special daggers safe from the Pishacha. These daggers were connected to the legend they'd all heard as children, one that Mayhara had found out was real.

According to the legend, the ancient deity Kashmeru had known only one true love—the Lotus empress Lakshmi. Lakshmi had been created in pure beauty and grace, a goddess of good. Though Kashmeru's spirit had been filled with evil and corruption, there had remained a connection between them that had withstood centuries. Their hearts had called to one another, time and time again. The hold was so strong, neither one could deny the bond, but Lakshmi denied Kashmeru her love every reincarnation.

She had vowed that she would never give him her heart, and he had vowed to destroy the universe because of this.

To put an end to his constant chase, the Empire of the Lotus had created the mage army, training mages to protect the empress in every reincarnation. They'd defeated Kashmeru and his shadow army of Pishacha and sealed the deity in a tomb. The legend prophesized that he would remain trapped in the tomb unless the Council of the Seven could secure the blood of the Lotus empress to set him free.

Jae's sister, Naree, was the newly reincarnated Lotus empress. And the daggers were the key to get her blood.

Mayhara fought not to hold her breath as she scrolled through the news feed. If she did that, she'd suffocate. She kept an electronic notebook full of names of the deceased mentioned on the sites, placing stars next to the names she recognized. People she'd gone to the academy with—the elite mages.

Now that they had the hard drive, she was anxious to crosscheck the names. As she made it to the end of her memorized list of news sites, she let out a sigh of relief. A day without a reported death was a small but welcome respite from her daily anxiety.

But it hadn't been the only thing she'd been searching for. With the extremist uprising in the prison camps, Mayhara feared for her parents and her sisters. She was sure her family, peaceful as they were, wouldn't get involved in extremist groups, but there was a constant dread that they'd get caught in the crossfire. Her fear that something might happen to her family had exemplified when she'd been marked as a fugitive. She was paranoid that the government would use her family as bait to get her to turn herself in. By some miracle, Darshana had used her connections to keep them safe—even if it was within the prison camp walls. Darshana hadn't been specific, but she apparently had undercover mages working as guards, and they had promised Darshana Mayhara's family would be kept out of harm's way.

She didn't know if she could count on that promise, but she had no choice but to accept it.

Again, she was relieved that her Linq search revealed no reported deaths. But that didn't mean the government wasn't hiding such news from the public. She did find a report of some of an extremist group's members being locked up in solitary confinement, but it wasn't from the camp her family were in. Mayhara shuddered to think what things must have been like in those camps. Her heart cinched at the thought of her family enduring any cruel treatment, but she had to count on Darshana's word that they'd be kept safe.

But she couldn't go on like this. Not knowing. She had to get them out of there. Somehow, there had to be a way.

"Yes," Darshana suddenly said. "That looks right."

Mayhara looked up from her Linq and stepped forward to glance at the monitor. Her eyes narrowed. "I've seen that before."

Darshana and Jae turned to face her.

"You have?" Jae asked. "Where?"

"CenSinq." Mayhara touched two fingers to her bottom lip as she stared at the scroll. "Where I used to work. It's in the director's office."

FIVE

“Wait.”

“Shiro, there’s no time.”

Shiro searched Qiang’s face, not sure what he was looking for. Perhaps a sign that Qiang was not as brutal as he appeared to be.

“I’m just… I think we should think this through.”

Qiang took Shiro’s hands. His grip was strong. “I can sense your anxiousness, but we’ve talked about this at length. Shiro, this is our chance to get out of here. We won’t get another one. We need to rebel. Now. We need to find the mages on the outside and come back and free our people.”

Shiro swallowed hard, his throat like sandpaper. “I know. It’s just… I don’t see how violence is the answer.”

“They’re not giving us a lot of choices.”

Shiro’s eyes bore into Qiang’s. “There’s always a choice.”

Qiang was locked into Shiro’s gaze, as if his words were sinking in. He nodded. “I know. This here is a choice. What we’re doing. We’re choosing to free our people. This is a necessary evil for the greater good.”

“I know, but—”

“And don’t forget, Shiro: They were coming after you. If we hadn’t left tonight, you might have been dead tomorrow.”

But we aren’t out yet, Shiro thought. There was no guarantee this escape attempt would even work. Reluctance kept Shiro from speaking, but as Peng and Bao called to them in whispers, he finally nodded once in agreement.

Qiang signaled for Shiro to follow him. They stuck to the side of the dirt path, close to the tall grass. The orange glow that had burnt through the sky when they’d left their bunker had now faded completely to black. The twinkling stars above reminded Shiro of freedom, of home. Of lying beside the koi pond at the academy with the first boy he’d ever kissed.

A boy who’d been killed during the Eradication.

Shiro shook the thought from his head. That had been three years ago. And this was no time to get emotional; he had to concentrate on the task at hand.

The guard outpost came into view. The guard booth was a metal box pushed up against a thirty-foot-high titanium fence. Inside the booth were two uniformed men, and standing sentry in front of the gate was a uniformed woman. Two more guards were checking the engine of one of their jeeps parked about ten feet away from the booth.

Qiang gathered the gang into a huddle, the five of them crouched down in the grass and reeds. Qiang held a finger to his lips, and in that moment of silence, Shiro could hear the rushing water of the nearby river. The proximity of the water filled him with a sense of purpose. He could do this. They were going to escape. Tonight.

"Five guards are more than I anticipated," Qiang said, stroking his chin in thought. "We're going to need a distraction."

"I can cause a fire just outside the gate," Mitty suggested.

"Not a terrible idea." Qiang narrowed his eyes. "I'm just worried they'll linq headquarters, and then we'll have a whole mess of guards to deal with."

"What about a storm?" Shiro asked. "I can bring hard rain, and the emeralds can whip up the wind."

Peng and Bao smirked.

Qiang nodded. "That could work. No need to call it in; it's just a storm. Then we could get close enough to take them out and open the gate."

They all nodded in agreement.

"Don't forget," Qiang said, placing a hand on Shiro's arm, "this is just the inner barricade. Once we get past this, we'll need to book it to the outer one over the bridge before anyone finds out."

"Ready to make it rain, Shiro?" Peng asked, a sly smile playing on his lips as his palms began to glow a bright green.

"Let's do it." Shiro rubbed his hands together, his gaze drifting toward the sky.

It started with small tufts of clouds appearing out of nowhere. The swirling gray grew thicker and expanded, stretching to block out the stars in a matter of seconds. It took every ounce of resilience for Shiro to withstand the piercing pain that sliced through his body. He squeezed his eyes shut, concentrating on pushing out his water energy and calling the element to do his bidding. His hair whipped to and fro haphazardly upon his head, the wind picking up thanks to Peng and Bao. The first drops fell lightly upon Shiro's face. And then it began to pour.

The rain was torrential, pelting his skin like small pebbles. Shiro could feel strands of his black and copper hair sticking to his forehead. He opened his eyes, but he could barely make out anything aside from Qiang through the curtains of rain. Leaves and debris zoomed through the air, twisting and turning and flying out of sight. The guards could be heard calling to each other to get out of the downpour, which kept violently switching directions due to the hard winds.

Shiro noticed Qiang say something into Mitty's ear, and Mitty nodded.

At Qiang's signal, they sprinted toward the guard booth. The heavy rain concealed their footfalls. As they got closer, Shiro noticed the guards stiffen. He pushed out his energy to bring even harder rainfall, immediately feeling the sting of blood in his nose. Before he could calculate what the guards' next moves would be, a blazing fireball tore through the rain. It hit the guards' station with a blast, throwing fire in every direction.

Two of the guards were flailing, dropping to the ground and rolling to get the flames off them. The other two reached for their Comm devices. Shiro sent out a blast of ice to one of them, freezing his hand in place so he couldn't contact headquarters. Bao shot air energy toward the other, knocking him back hard against the wall of the guard booth.

Shiro felt the biting shock of electricity as he was suddenly struck from behind. He fell forward, the buzz of a guard's cyber baton thrumming in his ears. He looked up to see the guard hovering over him, drenched from the pouring rain, baring his teeth as he wielded the cyber baton. Before the guard could strike again, he was tackled from the side and taken down into a puddle.

The puddle seemed to deepen, practically burying the guard, as Qiang jumped off him and to his feet, his palms glowing red. He grabbed the guard's cyber baton and hurled it toward Peng. As soon as Peng caught it, he whipped the end horizontally, catching the female guard's throat. She clutched at her neck as she dropped to the ground.

Shiro looked around. Only one guard seemed to still be alive, but he was still on fire from Mitty's fireball. Shiro directed the rain onto the guard in hard torrents, putting out the flames.

Shiro locked eyes with Qiang as the guard moaned in pain. The guard's skin was blackened, his clothes burned away, and his cries of agony continued as he tried to claw at the ground and crawl away from the mages.

"He's suffering," Qiang said. "We need to put him out of his misery."

At first Shiro could only stare at Qiang, frustrated that it had come to this. His breaths were heavy, and his heart felt as if it had been shattered. Then he nodded and looked away.

The rain stopped, and there was a *thud*. Shiro didn't look to see what had been done or who had done it.

Shiro shook, his nerves on edge. Everything felt as if it had spiraled out of control. He almost flinched when Qiang's hand stroked his cheek.

Qiang's voice was gentle. "We need to keep moving."

"No more deaths," Shiro said.

Qiang offered him a small smile. "I'll do my best. I promise."

Mitty, Peng, and Bao approached, and Qiang dropped his hand from Shiro's cheek.

"We've got about ten minutes to get to the next outpost," Qiang said. "Less if anyone saw that fire blast."

Qiang marched forward to the gate, his palms glowing red. His hands stretched out in the direction of the titanium posts holding the gate. The ground beneath the posts rumbled, the earth loosening into dust. The posts wavered, the thirty-foot gate leaning away from them. Peng and Bao threw out their air energy to push the gate farther, and Mitty charged toward the opening with his mighty strength, his arm like a battering ram, glowing with golden light.

With their combined efforts, the gate fell with a metallic *bang*. Dust flew about them in clouds.

The muscles in Shiro's neck and shoulders tightened as Qiang motioned for them to follow him.

They ran over the fallen gate together, following wherever Qiang would lead. With the clouds of dust obstructing his view, Shiro relied on the sound of the river to help him get his bearings. He knew the bridge was downriver, and he could feel more than see which way they needed to go.

Just as they emerged from the clouds of dust, blinding white light beat down on them, stopping them in their tracks. Shiro's heart was in his throat, his hand pushing out and clutching for Qiang's arm. Someone shouted over a digital amplifier for them to stop at the same time that Qiang hollered for them to split up and get to the bridge. Before Shiro could protest, Qiang slipped out of his grasp and disappeared into the glaring light.

"Qiang!" Shiro yelled, suddenly feeling more alone than he'd ever felt in his life.

It took the sound of gunshots to knock Shiro out of his shock, his body crouching as low as he could manage as he darted toward the river. If he could get as close to the banks as possible and follow it down, he might make it to the bridge and meet up with Qiang. As his feet raced, so did his mind. He had no idea what he would do if he got separated from Qiang's crew. His breaths caught in his chest, and he could feel the adrenaline in his body pushing him faster.

Finally escaping the light, he caught sight of the river. The lights of the bridge were far off in the distance, but he wouldn't stop until he got there. He ignored the dryness in his throat from his rushed breathing and the sting of his racing heartbeat. He simply needed to get to the bridge.

Without warning, his shoulder flinched back. He stumbled, only understanding what had happened when the slick, warm sensation of blood oozed down his arm. At first, there was no pain. And then a tight pressure took over. He pressed a hand to his shoulder, gasping as the throb of the bullet wound worsened. He tried to get to his feet. His vision blurred. He could hear the guards approaching, the man on the digital amplifier instructing him not to move. And he could hear the river.

He couldn't let them get to him. The punishment for attempted escape was death. Not to mention, they already wanted him dead.

No, we wouldn't let them.

The pain in his chest and shoulder worsened. It made him wish he would just pass out so he wouldn't have to feel it anymore. But that wasn't an option. Not yet. Though he was losing blood fast—and consciousness along with it—he pushed out his copper energy and called to the river. He wasn't sure if the raging water was getting louder or if it was just the footfalls of the guards, but as he squinted, he could see the water surging.

He had to believe he had enough power in him to bend the water to his will. He had to trust that the water would take him away and somewhere safe. It would not harm him.

He rolled closer to the bank, despite the shrill command of the man over the amplifier. His head spun, and his body was soaked in blood, but still he rolled, the copper glow still strong enough to control the water.

There was a split second of freefalling, and then the muffled din in his ears as water enveloped him, nearly crushing him, and stole his breath. But in the next second he was traveling upon the surface, the rushing waves carrying him away from the gun shots.

He could barely see where he was. The lights of the bridge grew closer as his vision became clouded. The pain of using his powers combined with the gunshot wound intensified, feeling like ice in his veins, and Shiro cringed as he fought to keep in control. But it was too much, and he let go, praying the water would not betray him.

SIX

Jae made sure to follow closely. Although he'd pulled up the blueprints of the building back at the temple, Mayhara knew this building. There was no reason she shouldn't take the lead. They stood quietly across from the back entrance, waiting for the moment Mayhara had promised would come. Sure enough, just as Mayhara had predicted, the support staff entrance at the back of the building opened. A short woman in a cleaning smock exited the building but propped a broom in the doorway to keep it open before she made her way to the dumpsters in the rear parking lot. Mayhara had said the woman would do this, as she had every night for the past two years. She had either forgotten the lock pad code or lost her employee keycard or was simply too lazy to reenter the code whenever she took the trash out. It didn't matter to Jae what the reason was; he was just glad they had a way in.

Once the woman was out of sight, Mayhara gave Jae a nod. "Let's go."

It was as if Mayhara were gliding over the ground; her moves were smooth and stealthy. Jae kept close behind, emitting a bit of sapphire magic to keep their journey quiet. When they reached the door, they slipped inside. Just as Jae pulled his leg in through the doorway, his toe caught the broom. It swung downward, and he held his breath as he reached out and caught the handle. Mayhara looked back at him with wide eyes. He swallowed hard, hoping she could see the apology in his eyes. But the way she clenched her jaw seemed to be from fear of being caught rather than anger that he'd almost botched their break-in.

"This way," Mayhara whispered.

They followed the corridor, which was dimly lit by small yellow lights spread out along the hall. Before they reached the turn in the corridor, Mayhara stopped and held out a hand. Jae closed the distance between them, and she tiptoed to get her mouth near his ear.

"The first security camera is around the corner."

He nodded and stretched his neck, looking past her. After slipping his scrambler out of his pouch, he aimed the device in the direction of the camera. He turned a knob on the device until the small screen on the scrambler showed a dotted red line.

"Is it working?" Mayhara asked.

"Just retrieving the signal."

The red dots on the scrambler screen merged into a straight line. Jae pushed a lever, and the line distorted into peaks and valleys. Jae nodded his head. They both rushed around the corner and down the hall until Mayhara held up her hand again. Jae scrambled two more cameras before they reached the service elevator.

Adjusting his hoodie, he let out the smallest of breaths as Mayhara pushed the elevator call button. It opened right away, and they slipped inside. Mayhara pushed a button, and then she pushed back the strands of hair that had loosened from her bun. At first, they were both silent. Jae could almost hear his heartbeat. Mayhara looked up at him, and he searched her face.

"I was afraid for a moment the elevator's recognition software would identify me, but I guess they only have that software on the employee elevator." She shifted from one foot to the other. "Then again, I've probably been erased from the system."

"Unless they haven't done it yet, and you've set off a silent alarm. We can't be sure the system hasn't alerted someone that you're in the building."

"In which case the authorities would be notified, so we better hurry."

There was a small *ding* as the elevator doors opened.

"There's a camera directly outside these doors," Mayhara told him.

Cracking one of the doors open, Mayhara leaned away while Jae scrambled the camera's signal.

In the clear, Mayhara led Jae through the double doors, which opened up to a fancy corridor. The marble floors were polished, shining in the glow of the LED lights lining the baseboards. Mayhara sped down the hall and ducked into one of the offices, the door of which had been left open.

Jae nearly collided with her when she came to a sudden full stop. Her eyes were wide as she looked around, and she wiped at her jeans as if clearing them from sweat.

"What's the matter?" he asked.

"My stuff is gone. Not that it matters—it just threw me, that's all. I should have expected it."

She only cast him a momentary glance before she circled the desk and pressed a button on the computer. The screen came to life, and Jae waited patiently as Mayhara typed something on the keyboard.

Her face changed as she let out a sigh, and her shoulders dropped. "I'm in. They haven't changed the password."

He nodded, though she didn't see it. She was too busy typing away at the keyboard. After pulling out the portable drive Jae had given from her satchel, she swiftly connected the cable to the computer.

She swiped the back of her hand across her forehead. "It's transferring. It'll take a minute."

They locked eyes, with nothing to do but wait. The glow of the computer screen softened her features, the light thrown on her lashes creating impossible shadows.

She dropped her gaze, and he realized he'd been staring at her too intensely. He hadn't meant to make her uncomfortable. The situation was nerve-wracking enough without him gaping at her in fascination.

Clearing his throat, he turned toward the enormous window that looked out over the city. The lights from the buildings were like bright stars, and the colorful neon signs from the pubs and restaurants below added flavor to the darkness. He'd never seen any city from this height before, and he had a brief shortness of breath at the overwhelming beauty of it. As he placed his palm against the glass and scanned the city streets, he thought about how, looking at this view, one wouldn't be able to tell that the Eradication had even happened. No wonder these snobby office officials were oblivious, unable to see the impact of hundreds of families being arrested—even killed—because of the corrupt government and the Pishacha.

Before he could dwell on it further, Mayhara's voice stirred him from his thoughts.

"It's done." She quickly disconnected the cable and slipped the portable drive back into her satchel.

"Where to now?" he asked.

She pulled up the zipper of her jacket. "Top floor."

After switching off her monitor, she hurried out of the room toward the service elevator. With half their mission complete, Jae felt optimistic. They only needed to get the scroll and leave the building unnoticed. He held on to the vision of them succeeding, letting it drive him to finish the job. In the elevator, Mayhara pushed the button for the top floor. It didn't go unnoticed when she ran her hand over her satchel, feeling for the hard drive. It was as if she hadn't believed she had actually acquired what they needed. When she looked up at Jae, he gave her a nod, a silent reassurance that it was true.

The door dinged open, and they repeated their routine, scrambling the camera's signal before rushing through the double doors. This floor was even fancier than the last one, with elegant vases and expensive-looking artwork lining the hall. Jae followed Mayhara past a glass-walled conference room that was able to seat at least fifty people.

"There's another camera around the corner, and then the office is just down the hall."

With the camera signal successfully scrambled, they finally reached the secretary's station outside the director's office. Jae glanced at the gold nameplate on the door, which read: DIRECTOR SHEI.

Mayhara reached under the surface of the secretary's desk, searching for something. The corner of her mouth inched up, and Jae heard a click.

"Helps to be observant," she whispered before turning toward the director's door.

Mayhara went directly for the enormous mahogany desk. In her haste, she knocked over a framed picture that sat upon the desk's surface. As she straightened it, Jae noticed a beautiful woman in the picture, her chin up and her clothes impeccable. The director, he assumed. Beside her was a girl, probably a couple years younger than he was. Jae assumed it was the director's daughter, though the young girl didn't seem pleased to have her picture taken.

Mayhara crouched and reached for the handle of one of the drawers. Her face fell when it didn't open.

Ignoring Mayhara's muttered curse word, Jae crouched down to inspect the drawer. It didn't have a keyhole or lock pad, but as he ran his hand across the front, he found a small round sensor on the handle.

"It's fingerprint-activated," he said.

"Shit." Mayhara raked her fingers over her hair.

Jae scanned the desk. "Let me try something."

He reached into his pouch and pulled out a small leather container. Taking a small transparent sheet and a tissue from the container, he glanced at Mayhara to see her staring intensely at what he was doing.

"A little trick I learned a few years back," he said.

He carefully placed the transparent sheet on the side of the director's mouse and gently pushed with the tissue. Using the light of his Linq, he inspected the sheet. The lines of a thumbprint could be seen on the sheet. Jae then placed the sheet with the thumbprint on the sensor. A miniature green light on the drawer flashed as the drawer clicked open.

Mayhara's smile was wide.

He hesitated a split second, taking in the beauty of her curved lips, but then snapped back to attention and focused on the drawer as she pulled it open.

Mayhara pulled out the scroll tube, rotated the end, and then slid out the scroll.

Jae's eyes were first transfixed on the scroll tube. Though the room was dark and his Linq light too bright, it looked exactly like the 3D image he'd created on his laptop from Darshana's descriptions. His attention then went to the scroll Mayhara had unrolled. He noticed small dots of light illuminated on a map. Mayhara rolled it back up.

"That's it," he said.

"Yeah." Mayhara slipped the scroll back into the tube and slid it in her satchel. "Let's go."

Jae bent to close the drawer, but as he began to slide it closed, he heard something move in the drawer. "Wait a second."

He reached in and pulled out another scroll tube. It looked identical to the one they'd already taken.

Mayhara's brow furrowed. "What is it?"

"I don't know, but let's take it anyway. Just in case."

Mayhara took it from him and placed it in her satchel.

His heart was hammering through his chest as they made their way out of the office and down the corridor. They only had to escape the building undetected, and their job would be successful.

As they called for the service elevator, Jae could feel the sweat intensify on his brow. Every second it took to reach them felt like an eternity. At last, the elevator dinged. The doors opened, and Jae's jaw clenched. It wasn't empty.

A security guard flinched at the sight of them but was quick to draw his weapon. "Hold it right there!"

Simultaneously, Jae and Mayhara raised their palms. The hall lit up in blue and red. Mayhara threw out crimson energy, forming a crimson particle seal over the guard's hand and gun before he could pull the trigger. It hardened instantaneously. Eyes wide with shock, the guard struggled to loosen his hand from the crimson. Before the guard could use his free hand to use his radio to call for help, Jae bent at the knees and sent a kick into the guard's stomach. The guard was knocked backward and dropped to the ground. Jae reached forward and forcefully pulled the guard out of the elevator.

The guard somehow got to his feet and swiftly turned, swinging his arm and clobbering Jae's shoulder with the crimson-covered weapon. Jae howled in pain but immediately emitted sapphire energy to cause a high-pitched ringing in the guard's ears. The guard tried to cover his ears, but his one hand was still glued to his gun. Mayhara's garnet on her wristband glowed brightly, and then she expelled a blast of crimson energy to knock the guard off-balance. He stumbled backward, falling and hitting his head hard against the crimson stone around his gun, knocking him out.

"Come on!" Jae called, holding the elevator door open for her.

She ran to him, and he pulled her against him. He only let himself hiss through his teeth after the doors closed and the elevator descended.

Aside from their heavy breaths, they were silent for a moment.

"Are you all right?" she asked, her eyes on his shoulder.

He looked down to see his jacket had ripped. He ignored the throb in his shoulder. "Yeah, I think it's just a bruise. He didn't break the skin."

She nodded as she felt at the satchel, making sure everything was there.

Jae held his breath as the elevator doors opened at the service-level floor, but no one was there.

They raced for the door, and as they got to the entrance, Mayhara let out another curse. The broom was gone, and the door was closed.

Mayhara reached for the lock pad. After quickly punching in a code, the lock pad flashed red. She typed the code in again, but again the light flashed red.

"It must be a different code than I have," she said.

"Or they changed it when you got arrested. Here."

He swiped at his Linq and pushed on the screen a few times. As he held the camera of his Linq to the lock pad, a series of numbers ran across his screen. It stopped on a four-digit code, and the lock pad's light turned green.

The door had barely clicked open before they raced out through the darkness and bolted for his bike.

SEVEN

Naree concentrated on keeping her hand steady as she fit the key in the lock. It felt like forever since she'd been to Jae's apartment, and a part of her hoped he might be home. Two Pishacha soldiers stood behind her, waiting to accompany her inside.

When she pushed the door open, she was not only greeted by a deafening silence and darkness, but memories of the time she spent in the apartment with her brother.

She'd come here for sanctuary after years of enduring her parents' insistence that she remain hidden. She'd grown up with no friends, no contact with anyone but her immediate family. She'd even been kept from meeting her grandparents, aunts, and uncles, just in case her secret would be revealed.

It was like prison, in a way. She'd spent her adolescence under the watchful eye of her parents, as they whispered and worried and cried about her safety. And when her brother had left for the mage academy, she was jealous. It was an entire school of mages dedicated to honoring her—her very own empire—yet she wasn't allowed to let anyone know she existed.

Finally, at sixteen, she couldn't take it anymore, and she ran away to find Jae.

She remembered Jae's intense discussion with their parents over his Linq as he tried to reassure them that he'd keep her safe, that she needed a little breathing room or else she might lose her mind. It took some heavy convincing, but he'd won in the end, and she was grateful.

One night when she was particularly sad, pondering her fate, Jae came to her and handed her a tiny, carved, jade dragonfly. He'd made it for her, explaining that dragonflies represented adaptability and self-realization. He'd told her that everything would work out, and she just needed to believe in herself, that he'd always be there for her.

Now, standing in his dark apartment, she longed to find the jade dragonfly. She needed a sense of meaning as well as the feeling that she could believe in herself.

"No one's here," one of the Pishacha soldiers said.

"The guard at CenSinq told the director the break-in occurred a couple hours ago," the other Pishacha said. "We need to search the place to see if they hid the scroll."

As the Pishacha began rummaging the apartment, Naree headed for the bedroom. Bending down and settling on her knees, she reached under the mattress, feeling for the place she'd hidden the dragonfly. The smooth feel of it made her smile. Quickly, before the shadow soldiers could see, she stuffed the memento into her trouser pocket.

Hiding her joy from having the gift in her possession again, she steeled herself and opened drawers and the closet doors. She doubted the scroll was here. Jae was smart enough not to stay at his apartment when Naree knew its location. He'd be somewhere she didn't know about. Somewhere secluded and concealed.

My love, I long to see you.

Kashmeru's words spread through her like warm silk. She wrapped her arms around her middle and closed her eyes. "I long to see you too," she replied.

We're getting closer, but the necessary pieces are still missing.

"I know. I'm doing what I can."

We'll be together very soon, and then nothing else will matter.

She nodded and opened her eyes.

The scroll wasn't here. What they really needed to do was get the other daggers. They were the more important elements.

She walked into the hall and called out to the Pishacha soldiers. "It's not here. We need to go."

The Pishacha stopped searching and marched toward her. With nods, they left through the door.

Naree cast one last glance at Jae's apartment before she turned to follow the Pishacha, the jade dragonfly cool in her pocket.

EIGHT

Shiro felt the soft touch of Qiang's fingers interlacing with his. He stared at their joined hands for a moment before looking up into Qiang's shining eyes.

Qiang gave him a smile that sent a ripple of shivers up Shiro's spine, almost making him giggle. Qiang stretched his neck and looked toward the night sky.

"Look," Qiang said. "There's the comet."

Shiro didn't want to break away from his gaze. He could stare at Qiang's handsome face for ages. Reluctantly, he did as Qiang urged and turned his focus to the sky.

One could miss it if they didn't look closely enough, but Shiro spotted it. The hazy streak of white looked impossibly far away, yet somehow Shiro felt its energy. He remembered learning about it when he was at the mage academy. It didn't seem to be of importance, since the Lotus had not yet been reincarnated, but they were meant to study it anyway. It was supposed to mark the return of Kashmeru and the deity's hunt for his one true love, Lakshmi.

Love.

Shiro focused again on Qiang. He opened his mouth to speak, but all he could feel was pain. Qiang seemed to disappear as everything in Shiro's vision went black. Fingers slipped away, and an agonizing ache throbbed in his chest. He felt as if he were falling.

No. Not falling. Floating.

But he couldn't see where he was.

Shiro felt as if lead weights were pasted to his eyelids. He tried again to open them, confused by his blurry vision, and confused by where he was. The lumpy bed he lay upon was unfamiliar, and whatever room he was in smelled of moss and rotting wood.

He wasn't back in the prison camp with Qiang. That had been a memory. Something that had happened almost half a year ago. They'd run away. What had happened?

He lifted his hands to rub at his eyes but froze in place as his right shoulder seized in pain.

Agony.

I was shot, he remembered. *But not dead.*

The river must have carried him to a bank downstream, where he'd washed ashore. The only explanation for finding himself in his current location was that someone must have found him and brought him here— wherever *here* was.

He was thankful it hadn't been the Imperial Police. If it had been, he'd have been back in the prison camp. Or worse.

Qiang.

Though he could barely move, panic filled him. What had happened to Qiang and the others? Were they alive? Did they think him dead?

For a torturous moment, Shiro recalled the feeling of Qiang letting go of him. Perhaps he had had no choice. Perhaps Qiang had been injured or shot and unwillingly let go of Shiro. They weren't supposed to be separated. They were supposed to escape together. Run off together. Start a new life, together.

Shiro attempted to move again. The spot where the bullet had hit him felt as if it were on fire, searing his flesh and ripping apart his nerves. He recalled a day in the academy when he walked too close to the golden mage practice area. A rogue fire ball had zipped out of control and smacked him in the gut, knocking him down. That burning ache had been the same. He'd eventually healed and gotten over the pain. He just had to believe he would survive this too.

Steadying his breathing, he listened. He heard water pouring. A rush of adrenaline coursed through him as he realized he was not alone. Using his uninjured left arm, he wiped his fingers over his lids and forced his eyes open. The blurriness slowly faded. Narrow streams of sunlight danced around the silhouette of a young woman. He found her to be the source of the water he heard, as she filled a clay cup on a cluttered table near the foot of the bed. She turned and left the room before he could get a good look at her.

He could only lift his head a fraction without pain shooting from his neck to his shoulder, so he glanced around the best he could from his position on the bed. He ran his fingertips along the rough sheets, and from what he could gather, it wasn't a real bed, but bound straw covered in blankets. This made him more aware of the room, which was constructed of thin planks of wood and bamboo, more straw and leaves fashioning the roof above him.

To his right was a small wooden table covered with flasks, glass vials, and a bunch of plants and herbs he didn't recognize. There was also a dingy mirror, cracked in a corner and covered with dust. He could see half of his face in it from his position. He almost gasped at the black, puffy eye staring back at him. The injury must have happened when he fell. His copper-streaked black hair stuck to his forehead from sweat, and his lips were cracked from being dry.

He glanced in the other direction. The doorway the young woman had left through led outside, and from what Shiro could see, the makeshift hut sat deep in a gloomy, overgrown forest. He could sense a murky water source nearby. A swamp, he believed.

The thought of water triggered a scratch in his throat. He needed to drink something. Eyeing the cup the young woman had filled, his fingers twitched. It hurt too much to move, but maybe using his powers would hurt less.

Bracing himself for the pain, Shiro raised his hand and stretched his fingers, his palm glowing orange as he concentrated on the cup of water. It began with a few drops hovering out of the cup, but those drops were soon followed by a steady stream of water that arched through the air toward him. Shiro opened his mouth and guided the water into it, instantly refreshed by the cool liquid. It wasn't until he took the last swallow of water that he realized the use of his powers hadn't caused any pain at all.

Instinctively, he reached for his neck. Instead of feeling the bulge of the power blocker beneath his skin, all he found were stitches.

"I removed it," came a crackly voice. "It will take some time to heal, but I can quicken the process."

Shiro half-expected to find the young woman from before. But in her place, there stood a boxy, elderly woman with scraggly, salt-and-pepper hair and sunken-in eyes. Layers of worn, beige material hung off her form in what Shiro supposed was a self-made dress.

Shiro's muscles tensed, not knowing what to expect of the woman. He looked her up and down, scrutinizing her, but she simply stood there staring at him.

"Who are you?" Shiro asked, his voice a bit raspy.

The old woman came closer with the help of a bamboo cane. "I'm the one who pulled you out of the river before you washed away."

"You pulled me out?" He hadn't meant for it to sound offensive, but he just couldn't picture a woman of her stature being able to drag someone from the river, even if he had been fully washed up on the banks.

"Maybe you're not aware," she said, "but mages aren't the only ones who possess magic."

Shiro looked her over, wishing he could sit up to inspect her more closely. "You're a witch."

"A swamp witch. Yes." She reached for a cloth that hung on a pole near the bed and proceeded to dab at the sweat on his forehead. "Though if I must be honest, my granddaughter did help me carry you here."

Her granddaughter. Shiro surmised it was the young woman who had poured his water. He looked past the doorway to see her sorting something into baskets outside. The girl looked to be his age, with clear, smooth skin, pale from what Shiro assumed was lack of sun. Her hair was a bit unkempt, the dark waves falling in a million different directions over her shoulders. In contrast to her grandmother's plain clothes, the girl wore a flowered skirt and a plain grey peasant top, so Shiro gathered that she must travel out into civilization now and then.

Civilization.

Shiro wondered how far away they were.

"What's your name?" he asked the swamp witch.

She gave him a slight bow. "Amalia. And that's my granddaughter, Karina."

"Not that I'm not grateful, Amalia, but why did you save me?"

Amalia pressed her lips together, her eyes narrowing. "It was an essential part of the prophecy."

Shiro almost scoffed. "Prophecy?"

"I realize you're not aware, copper mage, but the Lotus is in dire danger and needs your help."

This time he did scoff. "The Lotus? I think you've been hiding out in the swamp too long. There is no Lotus."

"On the contrary. She has been reborn. It's a well-kept secret—her reincarnation—but now the Pishacha have her, which means the empire must reunite and carry out its duty."

Shiro stared at her, unable to wrap his head around her words. "I… I don't believe you. What you're saying can't be true."

"Well, you best come to terms with it soon. Because it's the truth. If you search your soul, the mage in you should feel it in your bones. The prophesized comet is coming. The time has come, and the elite mages must assemble and fight, or it will be the end of us all."

NINE

$\mathcal{T}$he sun had barely let go of the horizon when Mayhara opened her eyes. As her muscles awakened, she felt the residual ache of the night before. It wasn't from a fight or extreme physical exertion; most of their mission had consisted of sneaking and, at most, running. But she had been on edge so much, her muscles taut with tension and her body filled with anxiety, that the aftereffects left her sore and exhausted.

When they had arrived back at the temple, Darshana had been deep in meditation. Mayhara could barely keep her eyes open, so she had gone straight to bed, knowing they would deal with the scrolls and the external hard drive in the morning. Now that morning had come, Mayhara was filled with impatience, needing to know if they had all the pieces of the puzzle they needed to move on with their plans against the Pishacha.

She quickly dressed and headed down the spiral staircase. The morning sun cast a golden glow on the marble floors, and a cool breeze blew in from the veranda. Mayhara wrapped her shawl around her, breathing in the fresh scent of mountain air. She could use a coffee, but first she headed for the office.

She wasn't surprised to find Jae leaning back in the chair, scrolling with the computer mouse as he stared at the monitor. There were bags under his eyes, and his hair was disheveled.

"Have you been up all night?" she asked.

He straightened at the sight of her, rubbing at his lids as he spoke. "I got a couple hours of sleep. But I wanted to check on this."

She found herself staring at his biceps as he raised his arms over his head to stretch. Feeling a blush spread over her face, she averted her gaze.

The external hard drive was still connected to the computer, but the light on the device was off.

"Did the program work?" she asked.

"Finished collating at two in the morning." He crossed his arms as he yawned.

"Why didn't you wake me?"

"One of us had to get a decent night's rest." He gave her a half-smile. "In any case, I haven't looked through them yet. I thought you might be better at understanding it all."

"Let me see." As she made her way over to his side of the desk, she spotted a program running in the corner of the screen. She'd seen it many times before, so she wasn't surprised that it was there. Jae had found a way to hack into the city's facial recognition program the government used to keep watch for criminal activity. But Jae had been using it to track down his sister. "Anything on Naree yet?" she asked.

He stretched his arms again and linked his hands behind his head, letting out a sigh. "Nothing solid. I'm sure she's being clever about not being spotted—or she's using mage powers to keep the cameras from capturing her face."

"Or the Pishacha are keeping her out of sight."

"Though I'm pretty sure they're using her to get the daggers, and I can't seem to figure out which of the locations on Bruno's list of addresses is the next target."

"If only we'd still had Bruno's Linq, then we could cross-reference, or track down Naree by messages or email." She bit her lip, remembering that she'd accidentally crushed the Linq of the Pishacha soldier who Naree had been traveling with. Jae had the Linq on him when Mayhara had almost buried him in crimson rock, temporarily convinced by Naree that he was the enemy.

"Hey, stop blaming yourself for that." Jae leaned toward her and placed a hand on hers. "You saved my life."

The warmth of his hand was comforting, but she suddenly felt hot from his touch. She pulled her hand away and pointed at the scrolls on the desk. "Any luck with those?"

"The moving lights on the first scroll seem to match up with the uprising in the prison camps. I've been cross-referencing with some news reports I've found, so the director of CenSinq wasn't lying about those."

"And the black triangles?"

Seven dark grey triangular dots moved about on the map. At times, one or two of them would disappear from one location and reappear somewhere else. When Mayhara had first seen them, back when she'd worked for Director Shei, she'd asked her what they were, but the director had blown her off.

"I'm not sure yet. Could be the Imperial Police, undercover agents, or—"

"The Pishacha," Mayhara guessed.

Jae rubbed at his chin. "Can't rule that out, but I don't see why Director Shei would have access to their location. What purpose would it serve? Plus, I was under the assumption that there are more than just seven Pishacha soldiers—though I could be wrong. I don't think I've seen more than three in one place at a time so far. Our best course of action would be to check it out. Unfortunately, we don't have the manpower to cover all the spots they show up. And they keep disappearing."

"I don't think it's the elite mages. Otherwise, one of those dots would be sitting where the temple should be on the map. Could it be the location of the Sacred Keys?"

He shrugged. "I don't think so. There are still seven dark dots and we know for a fact one of the Keys is dead. I'd think either the dot would stop moving or wouldn't show up anymore."

Mayhara nodded, puzzled. "What about the other scroll?"

"That one has no lights or electronic signals of any kind." He took the scroll and unrolled it. "No tech. Old school. Another map, but I can't match it up to any land. It's not any of the major cities. I need to inspect it more."

"Has Darshana looked at them yet?"

"No. I've been planning on showing her once she comes out of her morning meditation. Come look at the collated report."

Jae slid his chair over, and Mayhara pulled up another chair from the corner of the room.

She looked over the window that popped up, examining the columns of information Jae's program had generated. It extrapolated the information from the academy's database and cross-referenced the census information, listing any known locations of mages residing in New United Asia.

Jae left the room for a bit as she looked over the files. When he came back, he had two mugs of coffee. He handed one to her and sat back down.

The aroma surrounded her, filling her with a sense of calm. She knew it was just a temporary feeling; they had a lot ahead of them. But at least she wasn't doing it all alone. She took a sip of the hot liquid and let it warm her inside.

"How's it look?" he asked.

"Looks like some of the files from the academy were corrupt." She shook her head as her eyes scanned names. "There's no way of telling how many of the elite mages were imprisoned and which ones made a deal with the government. But I see two that match up. The next golden and sapphire elite mages have addresses in the census database. They must have been recruited to work for the government like I was."

He sipped his coffee as he continued to gaze at the monitor. "They might be unaware that they are the elite if they haven't heard of the murders."

Mayhara nodded. "You're right. I'll get ready and see if I can track them down. The golden mage, Huojin Cho, seems to have the closest address. It's at least a start."

"And once you get her here, that will help with manpower too."

A voice from the doorway made them lift their heads. "That's assuming she comes back with you."

Darshana stood there, a frown on her face.

"Darshana," Mayhara said. "What's wrong?"

"I have some bad news." She stepped into the room and heaved a sigh. "The Pishacha have another dagger."

"What? How?"

"I don't know." Darshana rubbed one of her temples. "I just sensed a disturbance, and I know that's what it was."

Mayhara felt as if her breath had left her for a minute. Jae pulled out his Linq and began swiping and pressing on the screen.

"A death was reported in Gangapur City this morning." He reached for the scroll, unrolling it to inspect it. "There was a mark near there. It's moved now, but I remember seeing it because my family used to visit the Shastri Park gardens for my mother's birthday every year when we were kids."

Darshana pressed her hands together and placed them against her lips.

"Does that mean it's the dagger or the Pishacha?" Mayhara asked.

"I don't think it's the dagger." Jae shook his head. "That would be too easy, and if some of them are still locked up, it doesn't explain some of the dots moving around. But let me see if the location of the closest one is anywhere near an address on Bruno's list. I can go there and see what I can find out."

"Speaking of maps—" Mayhara picked up the other scroll and handed it to Darshana.

The guru looked it over, and her eyes narrowed.

"Do you recognize it?" Jae asked.

"No, this doesn't look familiar. I can't imagine what this place is."

"Do you think it's the scroll from your vision?" Mayhara asked.

Darshana ran her hand over the material. "It's important for sure. But I don't think it's the one I saw."

"But the container looked like these?" Jae asked.

"Yes. To the detail."

"That means it was made by the same scroll maker, right?" Mayhara looked them over, examining them for any differences between the two. "Here. The markings are numbers just along this line, almost impossible to see."

Darshana inspected the markings. "Yes, you're right."

"The scroll's design is unique, though," Mayhara said. "Obviously one that's been passed down through centuries within the company. I'd be willing to bet manufacturing scrolls was kept as a family business. Jae, think you can track down the scroll maker? I don't see a company name on it anywhere."

"I know someone who can help us figure it out," Jae said. "In the meantime, if you can get the vision of the scroll back into that brilliant head of yours, Darshana, and search for the marker number, I can use that. The company must have records of the scrolls it's made, and we might have a lead as to who has the scroll you envisioned or where it might be."

"All right. I'll do my best." Darshana adjusted the deep green scarf at her neck. "But first I need to go."

Mayhara blanched. "What? Where are you going?"

Darshana tucked loose white hair behind her ears. "I need to answer a call."

"A call? Who called you this early in the morning?" Mayhara asked.

"Not a call via Linq, silly girl."

"Oh." Mayhara fought back a blush. "Sure. Of course."

"I hope to return soon." Darshana's eyes darted between them. "Be careful."

She left without another word. Mayhara and Jae exchanged a glance, and then Mayhara stood.

"I'll start with the golden mage." She typed the address into her Linq. She'd have to take one of the cars in order to get there, but she was familiar with the route. "Wish me luck."

"Wait." Jae placed a gentle hand on her shoulder before she could get past him.

She faltered, almost turning into him just to feel him against her. She cleared her throat. "What's wrong?"

His eyes searched her face. "I'm just worried. There's been another murder. For all we know, there's been more."

She offered him a small smile, placing her hand on top of his. "I'll be careful. I promise."

"Keep your head covered and your face down. Lie low if you spot the police or anyone who might be Pishacha—"

"Jae, I know," she said, cutting him off. His concern warmed her heart, but she forced herself to remain practical.

"And only use your powers if absolutely necessary."

She reassured him with a nod. "Understood. You be careful too."

TEN

Shiro scooped the last bit of hot soup Amalia had given him into his mouth, relishing the taste. She may have been a swamp witch, but she did make a rather tasty soup. He wasn't about to ruin his experience by asking her what was in it, however. He was just thankful he had one good arm he could use to feed himself. Being fed like an infant would have been humiliating.

Karina, Amalia's granddaughter, took the bowl from him. "Do you need anything else?"

"No. Thank you. You and your grandmother have been more than generous."

She offered him a smile and bowed before leaving the room.

Shiro desperately wanted to shift his position, but it hurt too much. Instead, he closed his eyes and listened to the sound of herons and warblers calling to each other in the surrounding woods. If he stayed perfectly still, he actually felt at peace.

But his heart ached, as if there was something missing.

Qiang.

It occurred to him that this was the first time in years he'd been away from Qiang for this long. He'd been so used to seeing him on a daily basis, spending time with him, training with him, indulging in a few quiet moments alone with him.

Was it so easy for Qiang to let him go?

Shiro played the moment Qiang's hand released his over and over in his head. Was it intentional, or a means for survival? He told himself he was being paranoid, but the thought crossed his mind that Qiang might not have had Shiro's best interest at heart when he'd planned the prison camp escape. Did he even care about Shiro at all?

The sound of footfalls shuffling along the wooden planks of the makeshift floor roused him. For a moment, he tensed, wondering if he'd fallen into a trap. Maybe Amalia had contacted the authorities. Lied to him about wanting to help the Lotus. She'd be sure to get a hefty reward for turning him in, enough to get her out of the swamp and living decently. But then again, she'd removed his blocker, so that theory wouldn't have made sense.

He had to blink in disbelief when he saw his former guru from the academy approaching the bed.

"What? Darshana?" He attempted to sit up but hissed through his teeth when his shoulder throbbed, the pain pulsing around the bullet wound in his chest.

"Lie back, boy," Darshana said. "You nearly died."

Amalia, who had walked in behind Darshana, came closer to inspect his bandage. "This needs changing. I'll get more gauze and healing ointment."

Amalia stepped away, leaving Darshana and Shiro alone.

"She says ointment, but she means mud," Shiro said. "It smells of rotten eggs, but it does make my shoulder feel better."

"You should trust her," Darshana said, looking him over. "She knows what she's doing."

Shiro gazed at Darshana in wonder. "I wasn't sure you'd still be around."

"You shouldn't doubt me, boy."

"How did you find me?"

"Amalia."

He didn't question it, admitting to himself that he knew nothing about witch magic or their connection with mages.

"What are you doing here?" he asked. "It doesn't make any sense."

"Once you've had a chance to heal a bit more, you'll need to come with me. The mages are gathering. We have a lot of work to do."

He searched her face. "Amalia said the Lotus needs our help. I… I have to be honest. I have my doubts as to whether or not any of this is true."

"It is true," she said. "The empress has been reborn. Her name is Naree and she's been kept hidden away by her family, who have feared for her life since the day they found out she was the reincarnated Lotus. This is the hundredth reincarnation, which, according to the prophecy, determines the fate of the world."

"The hundredth time Lakshmi would deny Kashmeru her heart."

Darshana nodded. "Bringing about the destruction of the universe."

"But the empire sealed him in a tomb. The legend says he would unleash his Pishacha in an attempt to use the blood of the Lotus to set him free."

"The Pishacha are out there, Shiro. They have Naree—the reincarnation of Lakshmi—which means they're getting closer to freeing him from his tomb so he can carry out his destruction and the end of the world. The only chance we have to stop them is the union of the elite mages."

He was quiet for a while. He rubbed under his lip with his good hand, battling the sinking feeling in his stomach. A restlessness came over him, a need to know more. When he looked up at her, his expression was serious. "So this is it? This will determine the fate of the world?"

"Yes. And it is your duty to the empire of the lotus to stop Kashmeru from destroying it."

Amalia returned and placed a bowl of smelly mud on the side table beside the bed. When she removed his bandage, Shiro held his breath. His eyes went to Darshana, who kept her expression neutral. It was only when Amalia slathered the salve on Shiro's shoulder and over his wound that Darshana wrinkled her nose. Shiro stifled a laugh, thankful for the comic relief.

Amalia cast a glance at Darshana, whose expression sobered.

Amalia gathered the old bandage and the tub of salve, ready to walk away, but Darshana's brow wrinkled. She grabbed Amalia's wrist, narrowing her eyes.

"What is it?" Darshana asked. "There's something you're not telling me."

Amalia took her time before she answered, her gaze moving between the other two. "You all know the prophecy. But there is a detail that has been lost throughout the centuries, one that is important to the one hundredth reincarnation."

Darshana raised her chin. Shiro wasn't sure if it was because she was insulted or simply curious.

"There are parts of the prophecy that remain in the ancient books."

Amalia locked eyes with Darshana. "Parts that have been forgotten throughout the generations but are of utmost importance."

"Like the daggers," Darshana said.

"Yes. The daggers. But also the Council of the Seven."

Darshana narrowed her eyes. "I assumed that meant the Pishacha. It makes sense that the shadow army would be made up of his seven greatest warriors."

"I believe the translations may have been misinterpreted. I think there are pieces missing from the puzzle, and we might be mistaken about the Council of the Seven."

Shiro winced as he sat up a bit. "But none of that matters if we rescue the Lotus, right? If there's no Lotus blood, Kashmeru can't be set free."

"But do you think all it takes is the blood of the Lotus to open that tomb?" Amalia asked. "It's been sealed with witch's magic."

"So a witch is needed to undo the spell." Darshana wrung her hands. "One that is skilled enough to carry out undoing a powerful spell."

"Do the Pishacha have a witch working for them?" Shiro asked.

Amalia shook her head. "I do not know if they have one yet, but I doubt they will stop until they acquire one. However, when they do, the witch would have to know *which* spell the original witch used in order to undo it. The spell was cast centuries ago."

"How would a witch know which spell it was?" he asked.

"A grimoire," Darshana whispered.

Shiro furrowed his brow. "Grimoire? What's that?"

"Every spell that's been cast has been journaled in a grimoire." Amalia paced, her gaze far away. "For something so important as sealing an evil god in a tomb, that spell most definitely would have been noted in a grimoire and kept in a sacred, hidden place."

"Do you know where it is?" Shiro asked.

Amalia dropped her gaze. "No. I don't. I'm afraid I can't help with that part of the prophecy, but I will try to find out. I've been shunned by many a coven, but perhaps I can find a kind soul who can forgive me for the wrongs I've committed."

Shiro almost asked her what she was talking about but thought better of it.

Darshana reached out and took her hands. "Thank you, Amalia. We'll need to find the grimoire before the Pishacha figure out they need it—if they haven't already."

They were quiet for a moment, contemplating their situation.

"So this is really happening?" Shiro asked, sitting up higher despite the pain.

Darshana released Amalia's hands and turned to him. "It is. But your help is needed." She stepped closer and sat on the bed beside him. "What is your answer, Shiro? Do you agree to fulfill your promise to the Lotus empire? Will you help us?"

He swallowed hard. It terrified him, but he knew there was only one answer. "Yes, Darshana, of course. I'll help."

Jae parked his bike off the street across from the gated house, making sure it was out of the view of anyone who would drive by. The house was a mansion, and Jae had to double-check the address to make sure he was at the right place. He still didn't know what he might have been walking into, but deep down in his gut he knew it had to be where one of the Keys lived. He just hadn't been expecting a mansion.

He jogged across the street, glad there was no one else in sight. If the black spots were Pishacha, he knew there was one not too far from here. He just hoped he had gotten to the house in time.

Glancing up at one of the gate columns, Jae spotted a camera overlooking the front entrance. The red light on the camera was on, and the lens was pointed right at him. He tightened his shoulders, his hands splaying and retracting. Fighting off his nervousness, he pushed the buzzer on the gate.

Moving his collar away from his neck, he ignored the churn of his stomach and waited. Though it must have only been mere seconds, it felt as if he'd already been standing there forever. He wondered if anyone was home—or if he was truly too late and the Pishacha had already found the place before he had.

The sound of a car engine reached his ears, and he glanced over his shoulder to see an approaching police car. He used his sapphire powers to listen to the inside of the police car. If the officer was calling in his presence, he'd have to abort his mission until it was clear. Jae ducked his head and pulled up the collar of his jacket, turning away from the street. He briefly wondered if the black spots on the map represented the Imperial Police working for the Pishacha. No sound came from the police vehicle, aside from the officer's breathing and the engine motor.

The police car passed without incident. Jae clenched his jaw and grit his teeth. He was in the clear for the moment, but he knew he still had a mission in front of him. Jae pushed the buzzer again.

"State your business," came a voice from the speaker box.

Jae knew he had to get right to the point. "I'm here in the name of the empire of the Lotus."

The silence that followed pushed in on his gut, harder every second. Still, he stood his ground, knowing the Sacred Keys' loyalty to the empress had to be strong. Otherwise, they wouldn't have been trusted with the daggers.

Unless he was wrong, and this address had nothing to do with one of the Keys. In which case, the owner could be calling the Imperial Police at that very moment.

Just as his doubts started to win over, the gate buzzed open.

The front walk was laid out in a curve, constructed in a mosaic of grey, white, and black stones, lined with perfectly manicured grass, vibrant flower beds, and water features. Jae cautiously made his way up the marble steps to the double-story, double-glass doors.

They opened automatically when he reached the veranda. Jae stepped inside, his eyes going immediately to the polished, white, baby grand piano that sat majestically in the center of the enormous foyer. A crystal chandelier hanging above it twinkled as it caught rays of sunlight. The house seemed more like a museum, everything modern and beautifully furnished. The Japanese, *ukiyo-e* print wallpaper featured gold birds and flowers, contrasting with the predominantly dark colors of the interior trim and detailing. The tall windows on either side of the main doors were paneled with colored glass panes of amber, green, and dark pink in a geometric design that represented leaves and cherry blossoms.

A burly man in a blazer entered from the right hall. Jae's muscles tightened at the sight of him. The man looked him up and down as he straightened the lapels of his dark blazer.

"Mr. Satoshi Kitaro is waiting for you in the formal dining room," the man said. "Please follow me."

Jae gave him a slight bow. The man turned, strutting back down the hallway. Jae flexed his fingers before following him, hoping he wasn't walking into trouble. They walked through a small sitting room, where a fireplace was situated on the interior wall facing a floor-to-ceiling window. The tall mantel of birch wood flanked a rectangular mirror with gold-and-white-jeweled trim.

They continued through a center arch of decorative painted columns and molding with ornamental keystone designs, commencing into the formal dining room. At the oversized, dark wood dining table, in front of yet another fireplace, sat a man in an expensive suit, finishing his breakfast.

Jae studied Mr. Kitaro, still unsure if he'd just entered the house of a Sacred Key. The man's salt-and-pepper hair was slicked back, but a few stray strands had escaped the hair gel and hung to one side of his ear. His moustache and beard were trimmed neatly, and the ring on the man's left hand had to be worth more than Jae's motorcycle.

With no time to waste on being subtle, Jae emitted sapphire energy.

"Mr. Kitaro," Jae began. "Are you a Sacred Key?"

A soft blue glow radiated in the air: Jae's truth power.

"I am," Mr. Kitaro answered.

Jae's shoulders relaxed shortly. He wasn't in any immediate danger, but it was just a matter of time before the Pishacha found them both.

"Would you like to join me, Mr.—?" Mr. Kitaro motioned toward the table, his eyes full of skepticism.

"My name is Jae. And no, thank you. I'm here on important business."

"Yes. You mentioned that, Jae." Mr. Kitaro studied Jae's face and stance. He then turned to the man who'd led Jae to him. "It's all right, Aiguo. We're just going to have a little chat."

Aiguo nodded, but he didn't leave the room. Instead, he stepped back and folded his hands together in front of himself.

"The Pishacha are tracking you down," Jae said, disregarding Aiguo's presence. "The Lotus has been compromised, under the spell of Kashmeru, and the dagger needs to be moved before she finds it."

Mr. Kitaro regarded Jae, taking a sip of his juice out of a crystal glass.

Jae's hands itched from frustration. Why wasn't this man taking him seriously?

"I understand your concern," Mr. Kitaro said. "I am aware that the Lotus has been reincarnated."

"Then you know that you're in danger. That the dagger needs to be relocated to a safer location. You should come with me. I can get you to a safe location."

"Safer than here? This house is a fortress. The dagger is in a safe. My bodyguard, Aiguo, has the strength of ten men. Why should I worry?"

"None of that matters." Jae leaned forward, his palms on the table. "The Lotus is under Kashmeru's spell, which means he can make her use her powers to get the dagger, and he can make her hurt you. You have a better chance coming with me, where the mages are gathering. They can protect you and the dagger."

Mr. Kitaro shifted in his chair. "How do you know I have no powers?"

"I'm guessing that since you're walking free and not in a prison camp, you serve no threat, meaning you have no powers. The Lotus and the Pishacha have already killed two Keys to get the daggers, and no one has caught them."

Jae waited a moment for Mr. Kitaro to process this information. The subtle clenching of his jaw told Jae that he hadn't been aware a second Key had been killed.

Jae pushed himself off the table. "There's a database filled with addresses we believe they're using to find the Keys. That's how I found you, which means every minute you stay here, you're in danger."

"How did you get this information?"

"I have my ways. And I know you may not feel the threat yet, but we've obtained a digital scroll that might be tracking some of the Pishacha. They're closing in."

"What do you propose I do, Jae?" Kitaro asked. "That I simply abandon my home, my life, and live in fear as I anticipate the shadow army's appearance?"

The alarm suddenly went off in the house. It wasn't blaring, but loud enough to alert anyone in the house.

Jae recoiled and looked around, his body more tense than before. A video screen came to life near the doorway. Aiguo hurried to check the screen. Jae was right behind him. The monitor showed Naree standing by the front gate as two Pishacha used cyber batons to cut through the locks. They pushed the door open with force.

For a split second, Jae felt conflicted. Seeing his sister, he wanted to go to her, to rescue her from Kashmeru's hold and bring her to safety. To say he forgave her and promise her she'd be safe with him. But there was too much at risk. And there wasn't any time.

"Looks like you don't have a choice, Mr. Kitaro." Jae marched to the man's side. "We need to go. Where's the dagger?"

Jae could see the uncertainty in Mr. Kitaro's expression. The man stood, nearly knocking his juice over. He rubbed at the back of his neck and frowned. He clearly hadn't thought it would come to this so soon.

"I'll… I'll take you to the safe."

Aiguo followed them as they dashed down the hall to a locked office. Mr. Kitaro fumbled as he retrieved a set of keys from his pocket. It took him three tries to get the right key in the lock. Aiguo stood behind them, looking left and right down the hall, his hands balled into fists, ready to fight off anyone who might breach the safety of the house. When Mr. Kitaro finally got the door open, he raced to a painting on the wall. Swinging it away from the wall on its hinges, he typed in the code to the safe.

Glass broke somewhere in the house, and Jae's hands glowed blue, knowing the Pishacha had shattered the front doors.

"You have a back way out of here?" he asked.

Mr. Kitaro turned with the dagger case in his hands. "Yes. Follow me."

Mr. Kitaro grabbed a small briefcase out of the safe before closing it. As Jae raced behind, Mr. Kitaro led them to the far end of the hall to a descending stairway. They reached the bottom, and a chill seeped into Jae's bones.

All sound around him faded, a low whistle filling his ears. And then, his sister's voice.

Jae, bring me the dagger.

Jae shook his head, despite knowing Naree couldn't see him. She was using her sapphire sound powers to get inside his head.

They entered a room in the basement, filled with boxes and tools. Mr. Kitaro pushed aside a trick tool shelf on one wall, revealing a hidden corridor.

I need the dagger, Jae.

"No, Naree," he whispered.

You can't stop destiny. This is meant to be. I will get the dagger one way or another. Don't cause me to hurt anyone just to make that happen.

Aiguo urged them through the dark corridor.

"This leads to the back of my property," Mr. Kitaro said. "It comes out at the far end of the greenhouse. Aiguo can get us to the car and we can take off. Can you get us to your safehouse without them tailing us?"

"I'll do everything I can," Jae said.

Jae could just make out a door on the other end. When they reached it, Mr. Kitaro punched in a code, and the door clicked unlocked. He opened it and ascended the stone steps on the other side. He tripped as he reached the top and almost dropped the dagger case.

Jae caught it in his hands. "Let me take that."

Mr. Kitaro hesitated, locking eyes with Jae.

"Trust me. In the name of the empire."

Mr. Kitaro bit the inside of his cheek before finally nodding and releasing the case.

Aiguo made his way to the corner of the greenhouse and glanced around. "I think we're clear. Let's go."

Jae grit his teeth as he kept close to Aiguo and Mr. Kitaro, hoping beyond hope that Naree and Pishacha were still in the house searching for them. They rounded the corner, and Jae spotted the garage near the front of the house.

Suddenly, Aiguo was attacked from the side and smashed into the ground. One of the Pishacha had been searching the grounds, and it had paid off. Jae's palms glowed blue, and he emitted an energy wave. The wave blasted the Pishacha off Aiguo, but not without hitting the bodyguard as well. Aiguo rolled to the side with a moan but quickly jumped to his feet.

The Pishacha rose to his knee and stomped a foot down, extending his cyber baton so that the end glowed a greenish yellow. He got to his feet and swung at Aiguo. Jae created a vibrating blue sound shield and knocked the Pishacha back. The Pishacha swung the cyber baton, which cut through Jae's shield and caught him on the forearm. Jae hissed through his teeth, and his shield collapsed. He instead created a sapphire energy sphere and whipped it at the Pishacha. The Pishacha swung at the sphere with his baton but missed. Before he could counterattack, Aiguo jumped him from behind, his thick arm wrapped around the Pishacha's neck.

The Pishacha struggled, then dropped to his knees, still attempting to pry Aiguo's arm from his neck. His face began to turn blue, his eyes bulging from their sockets.

And then the space he was in burst into black smoke. Aiguo shuffled back a few steps, his jaw hanging open. The Pishacha had disappeared. Jae had seen it before, when he'd fought Bruno. Bruno had never resurfaced, as far as he knew, so Jae had to assume that meant the shadow soldier had been defeated, sent back to the depths of whatever evil place from whence he'd come.

Jae rushed over and helped Aiguo up, only momentarily regarding Mr. Kitaro's stunned stare.

"He's gone," Jae said. "But the others are near. We need to move."

I can hear you. I'm coming for the dagger.

"They know where we are," Jae said. "We've got to move now!"

Aiguo brushed himself off. "There's no way we can get to the car before they spot us. I have an idea."

Jae flinched at the sound of more glass crashing.

"I'll divert them," Aiguo said to Jae. "Make them think we're all in the car. Can you get him out of here?"

"Yes. I've got my motorcycle. He can message you when we're safe."

"We've got code words," Mr. Kitaro said. "I'll know if he's secure or in trouble."

"Good." Jae clapped Aiguo on the back. "Good luck."

Aiguo gave him a nod, then offered Mr. Kitaro a quick bow before bolting toward the garage.

Jae crouched down behind a bush near the greenhouse, pulling Mr. Kitaro close. They ducked their heads and waited as they heard the car engine start. The car peeled out of the garage, its tinted windows hiding who was inside, and left the property just as Naree and the other Pishacha raced outside.

"Let's go," Naree yelled, running off the property.

Jae kept still, praying that Naree wouldn't be able to hear him with her powers. The sapphire on his wristband glowed a bright blue, but he knew that even his extra boost of power might not be a match for what the Lotus could do. Another car's engine roared to life and took off. Jae kept a hand on Mr. Kitaro's arm until they were long gone. Only then did he dare emerge from their hiding spot to head to his bike.

TWELVE

Naree took slow breaths in and out, using her sapphire energy to drown out the sound of the Pishacha searching the Sacred Key's house. In her mind, a battle was taking place.

Hearing Jae's voice had done something to her heart. She missed him. He had always been there for her, yet now she was on the other side of the war lines. She reached into her pocket and ran her fingers along the jade dragonfly, holding back a whimper of frustration. What was she doing? If only she could speak with him, maybe she could clear her mind.

My love, we need to stick to the course.

Kashmeru's velvety voice caressed her, and her mind whirled. It was as if her heart did a complete turnaround. Kashmeru had an effect on her she could not control. She loved him. There was no denying what she felt. And when he called, she had no choice but to listen.

Do you not want to be with me, Lakshmi?

"Yes, of course."

Why do I feel resistance?

She didn't answer.

Do you know what it feels like when I am without you? Let me show you.

In the next moment, her heart felt as though it had been rammed into by a truck. Her breath left her, and her muscles tensed in agony. She doubled over, reaching out to grab something so she wouldn't fall to the ground. She gasped for air, clutching at her throat. As tears began to trail down her cheeks, she shook her head. She didn't want to feel like this. And it broke her heart that this was how Kashmeru felt without her.

At long last, the pain left her, and she was able to breathe again.

It hurts me every second I am away from you, my love. I need you.

"I don't want to cause you pain," she whispered, her voice rasp.

Please hurry, my love. Find the daggers. The comet nears. Its energy will help us complete the ritual, but we need all the necessary elements to make it happen.

She straightened, pushing her back against the wall as she wiped away her tears. "I'll do my best, Kashmeru. I promise."

Thirteen

Mayhara adjusted her head scarf and pretended to be talking on her Linq, turning her face away from the Imperial Police car patrolling the neighborhood. She quickened her pace slightly, reaching the food festival that was taking place. It was safer here, crowded with patrons, and all cars were blocked from entering the festival area.

Glancing at her Linq, she checked her course and continued toward the address she'd noted. There was an image in her head of Huojin from her academy days, but she wasn't sure she was remembering her correctly. The girl in her mind was petite but strong, with impossibly straight, black hair and an almost non-existent nose. She wasn't the elite back then, but she'd had that fiery spirit that could carry her there. The boy who had been the elite golden mage back then had been reported murdered a couple months ago, and this girl was the next golden mage on the list who hadn't yet been assassinated.

Making her way past a *takoyaki* stand, Mayhara ignored the rumble of her tummy. She probably should have eaten something before she'd left, but she'd been so determined to find Huojin that she'd left as soon as she could. Still, one whiff of the golden balls of fried batter filled with octopus, *tenkasu*, and pickled ginger almost had her doubling back to grab an order.

On a sign post she came to a hung WANTED poster with her picture on it. Murder, it read. A lump formed in her throat. New United Asia considered her a criminal. But she hadn't killed her friend. She'd been framed. Not that anyone would believe her. She pulled at the edges of her purple head scarf and kept going.

She had to push her way through a crowd clapping along to a Bollywood dance performance, getting annoyed when some spectators refused to move out of her way. When she finally escaped the throng of that crowd, she hurried past a few more food stands and an instructional yoga presentation for children.

A helicopter hovered past the fair, and instinct made Mayhara hunch her shoulders and duck her head. She peered up to check if it was an Imperial Police helicopter and then blew out a breath of relief when she saw that it was not. Her eyes already drawn upward, she caught a glimpse of the comet, it's hazy white streak a mere smudge in the sky. Its presence reminded her of her mission. She needed to find the golden mage and do it without getting caught.

When she reached a vendor selling *aonori* and *katsuobushi*, she paused to look over her shoulder. Someone caught her attention, someone whose stare was so intense, there could be no mistaking that she was watching her. Mayhara felt her heart pound harder as she turned toward the assortment of products at the vendor stand. Maybe she was being paranoid. Maybe the woman wasn't even looking at her. Mayhara waved off the vendor who was trying to get her to purchase his goods. She had to keep moving. Instead of looking back to see if the woman was still watching her, she squared her shoulders and marched farther down the lineup of food stands.

Steam from a *jalebi* cart surrounded her. She squinted as she made her way through, taking in the tantalizing scent of the sweet, deep-fried, sugary glazed dough. Again, she ignored the growl of her stomach, pushing through until she reached a parasol vendor. She stopped and subtly turned, finding that the woman was not far behind, and she was definitely watching her. Was she Pishacha? Or maybe undercover police? She was dressed in drab, grey clothes, a long, loose jacket hanging partially off her shoulders. Somehow Mayhara couldn't picture her being Pishacha or a member of the Imperial Police. So why was she following her?

Mayhara's senses became heightened, and her heart was racing. With tightened fists, she turned away from the street, cutting through the nearest alleyway, even though it would put her off course. She needed to lose the watchful woman first, and then she could double back once she was in the clear.

After slipping through the alleyway, she blended in with shoulder-to-shoulder pedestrians. In a particularly crowded part of the street, she pulled her head scarf off her head and turned it inside out. The color was different on the other side, and it had a pattern, so she placed it back around her head with the light blue, flowered side showing in hopes to throw off anyone who might have been following her.

Making her way completely around the block, she found herself back at the *jalebi* stand. She waited there for a moment, checking all directions for the woman. She heaved a sigh and pressed her hands together to stop them from trembling, relieved that the woman was nowhere around. Pulling out her Linq, she checked the map again and continued toward Huojin's apartment.

The music from the festival faded as she got farther away from the festivities. Her Linq led her to an apartment building that looked to be going through renovations. Luckily, the workers had propped the door open to make their job easier. She walked past a man carrying cans of paint and headed straight for the stairway. The apartment number on the address she took note of told her Huojin lived on the third floor. She passed some people in costumes on the stairs, feeling a bit paranoid that she was the one being stared at.

Finally, she reached the door. She blew out a quick breath before knocking, then shifted from her heels to the balls of her feet as she waited. The door opened a couple inches, and dark eyes looked out at her. The eyes were bigger than Mayhara remembered. The young woman's hair fell in a curtain of silky black just shy of hitting her shoulders.

"Yeah?" the young woman asked, looking Mayhara up and down.

Mayhara cleared the dryness from her throat. "Huojin?"

The door opened a bit more, and Huojin narrowed her eyes, studying Mayhara's face. She could see the recognition dawning on her.

"You're from the academy," Huojin said.

"Yeah. Mayhara."

"Crimson house."

"That's right." Mayhara pushed the head scarf off her hair. "I need to speak to you."

"Why? What's going on?"

From inside the apartment, someone called out. "Huojin, who is it?"

As Huojin looked over her shoulder, the door opened more. Mayhara spotted a young woman with beautiful, dark skin and curly hair. Her heart jumped, realizing who it was. Meeting her gaze, the girl smiled, obviously recognizing Mayhara too.

Her smile widened as she got closer. "Mayhara?"

"Salina! Oh m—I thought you went back to Eritrea."

Salina ran up, immediately throwing her arms around her. She squeezed tightly and then took a step back to look at Mayhara. "I did. Back when my mom passed. I stayed to help my dad out for a few years. But, uh, Huojin needed my help, and my dad is settled now, so I came back. You should come in."

"Salina," Huojin mumbled.

"Stop worrying," Salina said, pulling Mayhara into the apartment. "We were close friends back in the day, remember?"

"You two were close friends. And you and I were close friends. But we"—Huojin gestured between herself and Mayhara—"never ran in the same circles."

"None of that matters now," Mayhara said. "The time has come for us to all band together."

"Why?" Salina asked. "What's going on?"

Mayhara looked between the two young women. "You might want to sit down."

Huojin gestured at the couch and chair in the small apartment. They sat, and Mayhara felt a churn in her stomach. This time it wasn't because of hunger, but because of what she needed to tell them.

Subtly, she glanced at their wrists. Each of them wore their golden mage wristbands, their citrine stones intact. It was a relief to see they both still wore them. Perhaps it was a sign that, somewhere deep inside, they were ready for what was coming.

She placed her hands together and stuck them between her knees. "I'm sure you've been watching the media about the Akutake comet."

"Yeah," Huojin narrowed her eyes. "What about it?"

"It's part of the prophecy. And I know this may come as a shock, but it's all coming true. The Lotus empress needs our help."

Huojin scoffed. "Lotus empress? Since when—?"

"They've kept her a secret for almost two decades. She's the hundredth reincarnation, which means Kashmeru has sent his shadow army after her. And they've got her. She's under his spell, and we not only have to try to break his spell and get her back, we need to stop the Pishacha from trying to carry out the ritual to wake Kashmeru from his tomb."

Huojin narrowed her eyes. "I don't know what street drug you're on, but—"

"I'm telling the truth." Mayhara fought to keep her voice calm. "You can ask Darshana."

"You know where Darshana is?" Salina asked.

"*She* found *me*, actually." Mayhara straightened in her seat and held her hand out toward Huojin. "And now I've been sent out to find you."

Huojin and Salina exchanged a glance.

"But doesn't she need the elite mages?" Huojin asked. "Excuse my crassness, but you weren't at the top of the class. It was Fei Ling."

Mayhara frowned. "She's been murdered."

"What?" Huojin's eyes were wide.

"No," Salina said softly, shaking her head.

"That makes me the elite." Mayhara waited as the information sunk in.

Huojin stared at her, her face falling more. "And if you're here to recruit me, that means that Kris… was killed too."

"I'm afraid so."

Huojin's lip quivered. Her head fell forward, and she began to sniffle.

Salina scooted closer and put an arm around her. "Oh my god."

Huojin wiped away her tears, lifting her chin a bit. "I used to like him. He was a great guy. He didn't deserve this."

"No one does," Mayhara said. "That's why we have to stop the Pishacha. They'll be coming after you next."

A wrinkle formed in Huojin's forehead. She blinked, then stood up. "No. No, they won't. I made a deal with the administration. They said I'm safe. I'll… I'll go to the Imperial Police and demand protection."

"They won't help you, Huojin." Mayhara looked up at her with pleading eyes. "They're in on it. The Pishacha are working with the government."

"No. I won't believe that." A sound escaped from Huojin's lips that was half-laugh and half-scoff. "They gave me this place. A job. They promised me my family's safety. I just need to work a few more years and then I can get them out. I let them put this damned blocker in my neck and vowed my allegiance to them."

"They won't follow through on their promises, Huojin. Believe me."

Mayhara stood. "I was in the same position, and they came after me. They killed the wrong girl, and when they realized what they'd done, they tried to pin the murder on me. I'm surprised you haven't seen my face on the news."

Huojin crossed her arms over her chest. "I don't read the news. It's too depressing."

Mayhara folded her hands together and held them at her chest. "You have to come with me. Both of you. Darshana has a temple hidden somewhere they won't find. We're gathering the other mages and we're hunting down the Sacred Keys—the keepers of the daggers."

"Sacred Keys? Daggers?" Huojin shook her head. "What are you talking about?"

"I can explain everything when we get to the temple," Mayhara said.

Salina stood up, wiping her hands on her skirt. She appeared ready to go with her.

"No," Huojin said, her voice calm.

"What?" Mayhara could only stare at her.

"I'm not going." Huojin held her chin high.

"What do you mean you're not going?" Salina asked. "It's the empress. We owe her our fealty."

"I can't." What might have been stubbornness in Huojin's expression changed to desperation. "They'll kill my family."

"They'll kill *you*," Mayhara said. "But if you come with me, we can beat the Pishacha, and we can set our families free."

Huojin's eyes filled with tears. "You can't guarantee that. You can't guarantee anything."

"I can only guarantee that if you stay here, they'll come after you." Mayhara slowly shook her head. "It wasn't that hard for me to find you, and I'm sure they're as resourceful as I am."

"Please," Salina said to her. "I came all this way to help my best friend. Don't let that be for nothing."

Huojin looked between them. "I... I don't know."

"Trust me," Mayhara said. "I was unsure too. But if the Pishacha succeeds, the universe will end. We can't let that happen. And the only way we can stop them is if we stick together."

Houjin's brows drew closer, and she fiddled with her wristband. Salina reached over and took her hands. Her eyes were on her, but she didn't say anything. It was almost as if they were communicating with their minds.

Huojin nodded, her shoulders dropping. "Okay. Okay, I'll come."

Mayhara felt as if she'd been holding her breath the entire time and was now able to breathe. "All right. But before we go, there's one thing we need to do."

"What's that?" Huojin asked.

Mayhara grimaced as she slipped a scalpel out of her satchel. "This is going to hurt a bit."

FOURTEEN

Shiro slowly stretched his neck left and right, wincing at the slight pain as the movement pulled at his sore shoulder muscles. For the hundredth time, he thanked the gods that the bullet had missed his heart. He breathed in the faint smell of Amalia's mud salve, which was thankfully masked by the bandage taped to the wound on his chest.

He'd anticipated worse pain when he'd gotten dressed, but it was tolerable. Whatever Amalia had put in the soup she'd given him was working its magic. He wished he didn't have to put on his prison clothes again, but he had no other choice. Amalia had nothing he could wear. At least the uniform was a plain color, nothing that would draw attention to himself out in public.

He froze in place, his fingers still on his shirt buttons. Out in public. It hit him hard that this would be the first time he'd see the city streets of New India in years.

Karina walked into the room, stirring him from his thoughts. "My grandmother packed some things for you."

"Some of that soup?" he asked.

"Yes, and more salve."

"Great." He held back a grimace. "Thanks."

Taking the sack she held out to him, Shiro bowed in gratitude and then headed for the doorway.

The humid air slapped him from every direction when he got outside. The hut sat in a dry, elevated clearing in the wetlands. Trees were all around, their roots buried in mud. At the nearest set of bamboo stalks, Darshana could be seen speaking in hushed tones to Amalia. Their expressions were grave. Darshana cast him a glance over her shoulder, and Amalia's brow furrowed with worry. Darshana set a hand on Amalia's shoulder and nodded once before turning to approach Shiro.

Darshana took a deep breath in and adjusted the strap of her rucksack. "Are you ready to begin our journey?" she asked him.

He clutched the sack of supplies to his chest. "Yes, I'm ready."

They moved forward, off Amalia's land—if that was what it could be called—and into a mud-covered area littered with murky puddles, thin, bendy trees, and bamboo. Shiro scanned the landscape before them. The mud was held in place by old, dead leaves and stems of the plants that had probably died the winter before.

"Good thing I wasn't shot in the leg," he said.

Darshana regarded him with a simple "hmm" and continued walking.

Every step they took disturbed the mud, turning it dark and blackish as they tread, causing the scent of rotten eggs to waft up and invade their nostrils. Shiro could hardly keep track of their progress because of all the mosquitoes and other flying insects invading the space around his head and arms.

Farther into the wetland, the tall reeds began to tower over their heads, with the fuzzy brown seed heads shedding their seeds into the wind. The humidity had Shiro's shirt soaked in sweat. To stop thinking about how much he wanted to change his clothes, he instead drew his attention to the jewel-bright, blue-and-red damselflies perching on the plants and the acrobatic tactics of the dragonflies hunting in the air.

"Darshana?" Shiro asked, cutting through the silence.

"What is on your mind, Shiro? I sense a lot of thoughts zipping around in that head of yours."

"What were you and Amalia whispering about when I came out of the hut?"

Darshana cast him a glance. "Please try not to step on the snails. We are the ones invading their territory, after all."

"Are you avoiding the question?"

"No."

Shiro swatted at a spider's web that hung suspended between two low-hanging branches. "I just… I just thought I should know. I'm about to do everything you ask of me, including sacrificing myself in the name of the empire, so if there's something I need to know, maybe you should tell me."

"We were discussing some points of the prophecy. It's been translated from the ancient language from centuries ago, and"—Darshana paused as she sidestepped a grass snake slithering near her feet—"we believe some of the points may have been misinterpreted—or left out altogether.

"Like the grimoire."

"Yes. And other things, perhaps."

"Such as?"

"We believe there is another factor included in the legend that has more or less been hidden from us. And I'm just now starting to put the pieces together. Of course, I can't be sure. It would be best to meditate on it. The gods will reveal the answers to me."

He didn't question her. He hadn't meditated since his academy days, and even then, he hadn't been very good at it.

After what felt like hours of trudging through the wetlands, Shiro noticed the trees beginning to spread out more. He felt a weight lift off his shoulders as they cleared the trees and were finally able to step on solid ground again. A sense of stability came over him, and for the first time in years, he didn't feel hopeless.

"You know, I used to think frogs were cute, but if I never see another one again, I'll be good with that. At least I still have my shoes. I almost lost them a couple times back there."

Darshana looked down at their feet, her brow raised. "You know, you could remove the water from the equation here."

Shiro gave her a sideways glance, and then his lips curled into a smirk. He could do what she said. It wouldn't hurt him to use his powers, he remembered. In fact, it would be rather thrilling. With his palms glowing orange, Shiro pulled the water out of the mud. Rivulets of water seeped away, leaving the hard dirt and grime to turn to dust and powder that crumbled off as they continued to walk.

"Much better," Darshana said as they reached an abandoned dirt road. "I'm parked just up here."

"Thank the gods. Don't get me wrong; it's a blessing to be able to roam freely without the threat of a guard's lashing, but that mud walk was a workout. I'll be happy to sit down for a bit."

"Speaking of being free, I have something for you."

When they reached the small blue car sitting halfway in the grass, Darshana unlocked it and opened the trunk. Curiosity peaked, he stepped up beside her to see what she had for him. He almost laughed when she handed him a black windbreaker and dark grey baseball cap.

"A baseball cap?" he asked. "Really?"

She shrugged. "I passed a novelty shop on my way here. It'll do. Take it or leave it. But I'd take it if I were you. Word is bound to have gotten out that you've escaped. The authorities will be keeping an eye out for you."

He ran his fingers along the brim of the cap. She was right, and he knew it. He popped the cap onto his head and slipped into the windbreaker, making his way to the passenger side of the car. A strange feeling came over him as he buckled his seatbelt. It had been years since he'd had to do it. Though it was a trivial thing, it deepened his feeling of freedom.

"I also have this for you," Darshana said.

He looked at her hand to see she was holding out a wristband.

"Is that—that's not mine, is it?" he asked.

"It is now. Unfortunately your original one is stuck somewhere behind the prison camp walls. But I took it upon myself to have this one made for you. It might even be more powerful than your old one."

Shiro took the wristband and ran a finger along the surface of the carnelian stone. It was smooth and shiny, and the touch of it filled him with a sense of purpose.

"Thank you," he said.

"Well, you're going to need it. This is going to be a lot more than just a training exercise."

Without another word, Darshana started the car and drove them along the dirt road, flanked by trees on either side of them. Shiro thought the dirt road would eventually lead to a paved road or a rural street. Instead, it winded through a small village. The houses were small and in need of repairs, and Shiro even spotted a well where the residents of the village were fetching water. Though the people looked poor—their clothes worn with holes and their bare feet dirty—he felt their lifestyle was still a step up from his last few years at the prison. For one, they were free. And for another thing, they weren't being hunted by the Pishacha.

Shiro's chest felt tight. He realized that as long as he was a mark, he wasn't truly free. And if Kashmeru was successful in carrying out the end of the universe, freedom meant death.

"I guess I always wondered what I was going to do if I ever got out," he said, "but it looks like the only plan on the horizon is to fight the Pishacha."

"You learned this at the academy, Shiro. The mages have a duty to serve the empire, to do everything necessary to ensure the Lotus reigns and the world does not fall into the hands of evil. An elite's responsibility is even more important, as the head of their house, the role model and example to all mages, bestowed with supreme control of their power."

Shiro reflected on this for a moment, gazing out the window as they departed the small village. "But you're not just seeking out the elite, right? We should be gathering all the mages we can."

"I agree." Darshana nodded as she took a turn onto a more developed street. "And I do, in fact, have a mage who is not an elite under my charge. Strength in numbers rings true. Unfortunately, most of the mages are in prison camps, and my priority is to have the elite ready."

"How many do you have so far?"

Darshana worried her lip. "We have the crimson mage… and you."

Shiro's jaw dropped. "Two?"

"Mayhara is currently tracking down the golden mage. I have no doubt she will succeed in her mission. And we have intel on the possible location of the sapphire mage. That would mean we're nearly halfway there."

"That doesn't sound as impressive as you think it does."

Darshana glanced in the rearview mirror. "The prophecy states that the elite will be key to keeping Kashmeru at bay. I believe I am doing my part as quickly and efficiently as possible."

"All I'm saying is a little backup never hurt."

Darshana spared him a quick glance. "Is there someone in particular you have in mind?"

He thought about Qiang but shook his head. He didn't want to incriminate his friend if it wasn't necessary, especially after the brutal things Qiang had had to do. And the truth was, he was still hurting. Qiang had let go of him, had let them get separated. He had broken his promise to be by his side through it all. Part of him gave Qiang the benefit of the doubt that the blast of gunfire and desperation to stay alive had torn them apart, but another part of him wondered if it had all been a lie, if Qiang had just been using him as manpower to help him escape, with no intention of being involved with him afterward.

Shiro felt the presence of water nearby. Sure enough, scanning the road ahead, he spotted a sign for the New Jaipur bridge. A sense of nostalgia came over him when he thought about the last time he had been in New Jaipur. He wondered how much it had changed.

The car shook, and Shiro wondered if they'd hit a pothole. He heard a horn honk loud and long, and the car shook again. Someone's tires squealed.

Darshana clenched her jaw as she held fast to the steering wheel.

"Is it an earthquake?" Shiro asked, his hand gripping the side of the car.

There were only two other cars visible on the bridge. The oncoming car swerved as the bridge trembled, crashing into the side railing. The car behind them stopped, switched on its hazard lights, and made a hasty U-turn.

Darshana stopped the car.

"What is it?" Shiro asked.

In the middle of the bridge, strutting toward them, was a young man in a long, black trench coat. Behind him were three men who looked like ninjas.

"Are those Pishacha?" Shiro's voice was a whisper.

"I believe the three in the back are. Yes."

Darshana squinted. "I have a theory, but I thought it was just a myth."

"What's your theory?"

Before she could answer, the car wobbled. The man at the front of the group held his arms up, palms facing Darshana's car. Shiro let out a shout as the bridge rocked and the car was violently upheaved, flipping onto the driver's side. Darshana moaned in pain, her temple bleeding against the shattered glass from the driver's side window. Shiro quickly unbuckled his seatbelt, practically falling onto her. He got her free from her seat and mustered every bit of strength he had to lift her, despite the throbbing ache in his shoulder.

The Pishacha were fast approaching. Shiro used the dashboard and seats as footholds and hoisted the half-unconscious Darshana from the car. Her head was bent, and she moaned with every move. They both nearly fell as he maneuvered her over the side and got her onto the street. He then quickly carried her to the side of the bridge, breath labored and muscles screaming, his hands covered in her blood.

The mysterious young man at the front of the group raised his hands again. Shiro jumped to his feet and copied his stance, his palms glowing orange. Pulling energy from the river below him, Shiro shot out spheres of water, blasting hard into his adversaries. The Pishacha flinched back as they were hit, and then they ducked and moved, their bodies appearing as impossibly fast smoke and shadow.

The young man at the front stomped on the bridge, and it began to crack.

Shiro lost his balance, his shoulder aching as he caught himself from falling. He got to his feet and threw his water energy at the man, blasting it in an unrelenting stream. If he could keep the man from breathing air, he might get the advantage over him.

The Pishacha closed in, wielding cyber batons. Shiro backed up, ducking and dodging their swings, his adrenaline kicking up as he realized this could be the end. He hadn't come all this way to be killed on this bridge. Practically growling with frustration and panic, Shiro called upon his powers, pushing harder than he ever had before.

The bridge cracked some more, shaking and jerking, but below them, the water began to crash and rise. The usual gentle river became raging rapids, spraying up and pushing the bridge. Shiro focused and moved the water, pushing the waves toward his attackers. The water reached up like arms, the liquid fingers grabbing the Pishacha and flinging them downriver. They burst into black smoke before they could be submerged, disappearing into the wind.

One Pishacha remained. The mysterious man sneered at Shiro, his hands outstretched like claws as he came closer. Shiro thrust his palms forward. This time, he controlled the water in the man's body, lifting him from the ground. The man's eyes widened, his arms and legs flailing. Shiro clenched his teeth and flung the man back, hard, against the road. There was a crack as the man's head hit the ground.

He said something, something Shiro didn't understand, and in the next moment the last remaining Pishacha glided toward the man, lifting him into his arms, and the two of them disappeared into a cloud of black smoke.

Panting, Shiro stared in confusion. For a moment, he held steady, anticipating their reappearance. But after a minute without their return, he let his shoulders drop. The water below him dropped back to its normal level, the rushing slowing to its usual pace.

So this was what they were up against. He'd never imagined powers like what he'd just seen. They had learned nothing about Pishacha having the ability to evaporate into smoke. And the mysterious man—who was he? And what did he have to do with the prophecy? As he tried to wrap his head around it all, he heard Darshana moan.

Getting his wits about him, he darted for the guru. Dropping to his knees, he put his hands on her shoulders, looking her over.

"Are you all right?"

She lifted a hand to her head, retracting it immediately upon contact with her bleeding wound. "I can't tell. Dizzy."

He gently let go of her and looked toward their car. They couldn't stay on the bridge. The car's engine didn't appear to be affected by the flip, but there was no way to tell without testing it. Clenching and releasing his fists, Shiro walked over to the top of the car and used all his remaining energy to push. After a few tries, the car fell back onto its tires. The driver's side door was busted and wouldn't open, so he went through the passenger's side and got into the driver's seat. He held his breath as he turned the key. Miraculously, it sputtered back to life, and Shiro released his breath. It worked now, but he didn't know if it would last long enough to get them somewhere safe.

Crawling out of the car, he rushed back over to Darshana. She hissed when he got her to her feet.

"You're losing a lot of blood," he said. "We need to get you help."

"We can't go to a hospital." Darshana grabbed him by the shirt. "They'll find us and end us both."

"How far away is the temple?"

"Still far. I don't know if the car will make it, especially up the hill we need to drive."

Shiro shook his head. "What do we do?"

She leaned against him, her lids heavy and her shoulders sagging. "I know of an abandoned supply warehouse near here. We'll go there and try to send for help."

FIFTEEN

The top of the temple came into view as the car took the hidden path and rounded the final curve. Out of the corner of her eye, Mayhara caught Huojin's raised brows and widened eyes. Salina leaned forward from the back seat to get a better view.

"Whose place is this?" Huojin asked.

"Darshana hasn't exactly told us," Mayhara said as they pulled into the carport.

She put the car in park and paused for a second, noticing the other car wasn't there. Jae's motorcycle was parked in its spot, however, so relief washed over her at knowing he was back. Hopefully, his venture was as successful as hers had been.

She reached for the key to turn off the engine but stopped when the announcer on the radio mentioned the approaching comet.

"…The New United Asia's National Space Association has sent a probe to gather pictures of the Akutake comet as it nears. It's still too far for civilians to pick up with ordinary telescopes, but NUANSA promises to upload any images they capture on their website. Scientists predict that the comet's intense energy waves may disrupt electrical equipment and devices when it gets closer…"

Mayhara suspected it would do more than that. It was mentioned in the prophecy that the comet's appearance would be the pinnacle of events surrounding Kashmeru's reemergence. Its approach was like a time bomb, the closer it got, the less time the mages had to stop Kashmeru from destroying the world.

Mayhara grabbed her satchel and opened the trunk for the two golden mages. They had thrown some things together to bring with them, not knowing if or when they'd be able to return to their old lives. They couldn't take much, for risk they'd draw too much attention to anyone who might have seen them leave, so they'd had to restrict themselves to two duffle bags.

As Mayhara led them toward the entrance, a strange feeling came over her. She and Jae had only been working together for a few weeks, but she felt as if a bond had built between them during their time together. They were a team and they relied upon each other alone—aside from Darshana, whom she saw more as their leader. And even though she knew they needed all the elite mages in order to carry out their mission, the shift in dynamic made her inexplicably uneasy.

Once they were inside, Mayhara set her things down.

"You guys live here?" Huojin asked.

"It's temporary," Mayhara said. "I mean, I don't know what's going to happen after, you know, everything. But for now, it's where we hang our hats, I guess."

"It's so fancy," Salina whispered. "Like a museum."

"The main thing is it's safe." Mayhara led them into the main room, which stood in the center of the temple.

Peering out the doorway of the office, Jae looked their way.

"Damn, who's the hottie?" Huojin's voice was a whisper, only loud enough for Salina and Mayhara to hear, but Mayhara had to wonder if Jae might have been able to hear her with his sapphire powers. She couldn't judge by his expression, which remained serious.

They approached each other, and Jae studied Mayhara, as if checking if everything were okay. She did the same, glad to see he didn't appear injured.

"Hey." Jae reached for her when they were close enough, but he then retracted his hand and shoved it in his pocket. "I see you've made some progress."

"You could say that."

"Did you have any problems?"

"No. I did think I was being followed. A woman seemed to be watching me as I travelled through the city's festival. Maybe I was being paranoid, but her eyes made me uneasy. I managed to lose her, though."

"Did she look familiar to you?" he asked.

She shook her head. "No. I don't think I've seen her before. And we were careful heading back to the car, so I don't think we were followed."

"Good," Jae said.

Mayhara gestured at the golden mages. "Jae, this is Huojin and Salina. Do you remember them from the academy?"

"Sure, hard to miss golden mages with your skills." Jae gave them a small bow, which they reciprocated. "Welcome to the temple. Sorry it's under such dire circumstances."

Huojin tilted her head. "I remember you now. You kept to yourself a lot." Mayhara tried not to notice how Huojin's eyes traveled up and down his body. "But I seem to recall you had some decent skills yourself. Are you the elite now?"

"No. No, we're still tracking down the rest of the elites, *including* the sapphire elite. I believe you're the golden elite now, Huojin."

Her expression changed, her flirtatious smile disappearing. "Yeah. It's still sinking in. The whole thing."

"Salina was staying with Huojin when I found her," Mayhara said.

"I've been away for a while," Salina explained. "I don't know if anyone remembers, but I left the academy when my mom passed away—this was months before the Eradication happened. Moved back home to Eritrea. But Huojin reached out to me recently, and I promised to come help her out. My father isn't in danger since Eritrea is out of New United Asia's jurisdiction, but Huojin's parents are in a prison camp, and the plan was I would pitch in whatever credits I could earn so she could afford to get them out once she was able to petition for their release. But I guess things have changed now."

"We'll get them out," Mayhara said, placing a comforting hand on Huojin's arm. "We'll get them all out."

Jae looked between them, eyeing their bags. "Why don't I show you the free rooms so you can put your stuff away? Darshana is out at the moment, but I know she'll be happy to see you."

"Sure." Huojin reached for the bandage at her neck, the remnants of where Mayhara had removed her blocker. She winced for a second, then turned to Salina. "You're so lucky you didn't have to endure getting a blocker or having it removed."

A man in a button-up shirt entered the room from the kitchen. He had a cup of coffee in his hand. Mayhara's brow furrowed and her eyes went questioningly to Jae.

"It's okay," Jae said. "This is Mr. Kitaro. He's a Sacred Key."

Mayhara's jaw dropped. "A Key? Does that mean you have one of the daggers?"

Mr. Kitaro extended a hand to Mayhara. "You must be Mayhara. Jae's told me about you."

A small smile found its way to her lips as she shook his hand. "I'm sorry. How rude of me. Yes, I'm Mayhara." When she released his hand, she offered him a bow. "I was just surprised at the expedience of Jae's success. Seems he tracked you down rather quickly."

"Well, it wasn't without its difficulties," Jae said. "I only got to him moments before Naree and a couple Pishacha did. Thanks to Mr. Kitaro's bodyguard, Aiguo, we managed to escape safely with the dagger."

Mayhara stared at Jae, worry washing through her as she checked him over, making sure he wasn't injured in any way. And seeing Naree had to have been difficult for him. She knew he wanted to rescue her. It was detrimental to their cause. But she wasn't here; he would have told her if she was. The frown on his face was enough to tell her that wasn't what had happened. She longed to comfort him. He caught her gaze, and her expression sobered. Internally, she told herself she was being overprotective and obsessive.

"Yes. Aiguo is a good man," Mr. Kitaro said. "I'm still waiting to hear from him to see if he got away."

"Pishacha," Salina remarked, shaking her head in disbelief. "That's crazy."

"I'm sorry." Mayhara pressed her fingers against her cheek, embarrassed by another rude blunder. "Mr. Kitaro, these are Huojin and Salina. Huojin is the golden elite."

They all exchanged bows.

"You are all rather young to have such an important task on your plates," he said, studying them.

"We were trained by the best," Jae said in defense.

"Yes, but your training was incomplete." Mr. Kitaro took a sip of his coffee. "You'll be up against entities that are centuries old. And a god with unparalleled powers."

"It can't mean nothing, though," Salina said. "Why would mages even exist if not to protect the Lotus, to ensure that the empire doesn't perish? We may be young, but I believe we've got destiny on our sides."

Mr. Kitaro appeared as if he were biting back a smile. "You make a good point. And for all our sakes, I hope you're right."

"Mr. Kitaro, I don't recall anything about Keys from the legend," Huojin said.

Mr. Kitaro took another sip of coffee and made his way to one of the couches. He took a seat, and Huojin and Salina sat on the couch across from him. Mayhara stood beside Jae behind them.

"Long ago, after the first reincarnation, the elders of the empire were concerned about Kashmeru's threats to destroy the universe. When the elders asked the prophet who'd announced the prophecy if there was any hope, he told them to look to the mages. Kashmeru had his army; the Lotus had to have hers as well."

"But where do the Sacred Keys come into play?" Mayhara asked.

"There is an order of the elders. They are the ones protecting the tradition, passing down the prophecy, doing what they can to ensure the empire doesn't fall. They were unable to stop the Eradication, but I think they knew it was coming to this, because they entrusted the Keys with the daggers."

"It was inevitable," Jae mumbled. "Unstoppable."

"But not without hope," Mr. Kitaro said. "The daggers were a hidden part of the prophecy. When the elders learned of them, they took necessary precautions to disperse them and hide them, knowing they were the keys to bringing Kashmeru back to life. The Sacred Keys were given the duty of protecting the daggers."

"How are Sacred Keys chosen?" Mayhara asked. "Is it some kind of connection to the empire?"

"We have direct blood ties to the Lotus." Mr. Kitaro straightened his back as he said it, as if showing his pride. "Not the reincarnated one of today, but of reincarnations passed."

Huojin shook her head. "And what are these daggers for?"

"They are bound with a magic that connects to Lakshmi's soul, through her blood."

"Meaning… her spilled blood." Mayhara's voice almost broke when she said it.

"Yes." Mr. Kitaro stretched out his legs. "The seven daggers are needed in order to begin the ritual to bring Kashmeru back to life."

Jae rubbed at the back of his neck. Mayhara put a hand on his arm, wanting to calm him. No one felt easy thinking about the empress being stabbed, least of all her brother.

"Can I see it?" Huojin asked.

"The dagger?" The Key studied her. "It is hidden somewhere safe. And it's probably better if you don't know the location."

"The problem is we only currently have one." Jae cracked his knuckles. "The Pishacha have two of them. Not only do we have to recover them, we have to find the other four."

"*Seven* daggers?" Salina asked.

Mr. Kitaro nodded. "Seven mage houses. Seven chakras."

"Seven deadly sins," Huojin added.

"They are all connected," Mr. Kitaro said, lifting his coffee for another sip.

"Why didn't anyone tell us about the Lotus being reborn when we were at the academy?" Salina asked.

"Only a handful of people knew. My parents feared for my sister's life because of the prophecy."

Huojin tilted her head. "I didn't even know you had a sister."

Jae shoved his hands in his pockets. "My family kept her a secret. And I had to pretend I was an only child. Darshana knew. Apparently, she had a vision and came to see my parents when Naree was born. I don't remember it because I was just a toddler at the time."

"Maybe they should have told us," Salina said. "Maybe we could have done something to stop the Eradication if we knew the one hundredth reincarnation had come to pass. We might have been prepared for some kind of attack."

"It doesn't matter now," Mr. Kitaro said. "We couldn't stop the Eradication, and now Lakshmi—Naree, now—is under the control of Kashmeru."

"What is he doing to her?" Huojin asked. "Besides tricking her into setting him free?"

"He's making her collect the daggers," Mayhara said. "Even if she has to kill to get them."

Jae compressed his lips and dropped his head. Mayhara felt terrible for saying it, but it was the truth. And the other mages had to know how far Kashmeru would go to make the prophecy come true.

"Do we have a lead on the other mages?" Salina asked.

"Yes," Mayhara said. "That's actually how I found you."

Jae's Linq let out a tone, and a wrinkle formed between his brow. He studied the screen and gnashed his teeth. "It's Darshana."

Mayhara came closer, trying to catch a glimpse of his screen. "Something wrong?"

"I… I don't know. She sent a location Ping, but it disappeared."

"Because it would be dangerous if someone else were to see it," Mayhara guessed.

Mr. Kitaro stood. "She must be in trouble."

"We need to find her." Mayhara's blood grew hot, and she got a churning feeling in the pit of her stomach.

"Let's go then," Jae said, addressing the mages.

"Do we leave him here?" Salina asked, referring to Mr. Kitaro. "Should I stay?"

"The temple is safe," Jae said. "I don't know what kind of trouble Darshana is in, but we could use the manpower if it's the Pishacha."

Mr. Kitaro looked up from his Linq. "My bodyguard is on the way. I won't give him the exact location until he's sure he wasn't followed to the nearby gas station."

"Are you sure he hasn't been compromised?" Jae asked.

"We used our code word." Mr. Kitaro nodded. "It's safe."

Mayhara clenched her hands into fists. "Let's hope you're right.

SIXTEEN

Naree felt exhaustion wash over her. Bhutano insisted they travel to the next address on the list in an attempt to find another dagger, but their speculations were wrong. The house did not belong to a Sacred Key.

Naree had felt her energy drain as the Pishacha soldiers killed the family in the house, despite their innocence.

She wasn't sure she could do this anymore. The darkness in Kashmeru's core was destroying her. She was pure light, a goddess existing in goodness, yet Kashmeru's hold on her was too strong to resist. Whatever magic he had used to put her under his spell was tearing at the very fabric of her being. She could feel herself getting more lost every moment she spent under his hold.

Time is running out, my love. This is no time to back down.

"I'm just tired."

Soon we will be together, and you can relax in my arms. We can spend a thousand moons doing nothing but holding each other, you enraptured in the blissful cocoon of my love.

An energy came over her, as if Kashmeru himself was holding her. She almost moaned from the feeling of sheer exhilaration.

Come to me, my love.

"Yes."

Find the daggers. We need them all.

"I'll do as you say, Kashmeru. I promise. But the mages have one of them."

Get it back for me.

"I will."

Do whatever is necessary to retrieve it from them. It's the only way.

"I don't know where they are."

Find them.

She was about to protest that she didn't know how to do that when her

Linq buzzed. She glanced at the screen and concentrated on the Ping location that flashed on. She quickly double tapped it to zoom in, memorizing the location on the map before it disappeared.

"I think I know where they are."

Excellent. Get the dagger. Our fate depends on it.

SEVENTEEN

Shiro paced the concrete floor of the dark warehouse. It had been at least an hour since Darshana had used her phone to contact the mages she was working with. Since then, she'd been slipping in and out of consciousness. He'd put together some old boxes he'd found in the warehouse and covered them with a picnic blanket from Darshana's car. He didn't believe it was comfortable for her, but it was the best he could do.

The blanket was already soaked with blood. The warehouse's outdated first aid kit had provided him with a solitary strip of gauze and some medical tape, which he'd fastened to her wound as best he could. He checked constantly to make sure she was breathing. Other than that, all he could do was wait.

He wasn't sure whom to expect, but he hoped he'd recognize them when they arrived. She'd told him Mayhara's name, and he thought he had a pretty good picture of her in his head from memory, but that was from back during the academy days. She could look completely different now.

Darshana stirred, and Shiro ran to her side. Her eyes fluttered open halfway, and she opened her mouth as if to speak, but no sound came out. Her lips appeared dry, so Shiro held a hand over her face and formed a few drops of water, pulling from the humidity in the warehouse air. She licked her lips and swallowed, and then her eyes drifted closed again.

He watched her for another twenty minutes, afraid to look away. He'd wrung his hands so tightly, he could have sworn he broke a finger or two. His chest felt as if it were being compressed with a wire that was getting tighter every silent minute that passed.

What was he going to do if she didn't make it? What would happen to him if the other mages didn't find him? He had no idea where to go or how to find them. He'd be lost. A fugitive with nowhere to go. With no sanctuary.

A loud *clang* sounded from somewhere in the warehouse. Shiro jumped to his feet. Though he knew Darshana had sent for the other mages, the fact was that there were still Pishacha after them. His first instinct was to protect himself and Darshana. He readied his stance, palms up but not yet aglow. The sound of approaching footfalls grew louder. Shiro's nerves were on fire from the anticipation.

"Darshana?" someone called. The voice was female. Friendly.

Shiro dropped his arms and stood up straight. He took a chance. "Mayhara?"

First there was a pause, and then four figures came into the room.

At first, Mayhara's appearance threw him off, but as she came closer, he could see she was the same girl he'd remembered from the academy. Only more grown-up. Behind her were other mages from the academy he couldn't recall the names of.

"Who are you?" Mayhara asked him. "And how do you know my name?"

"I'm Shiro. I'm the copper elite." He glanced back at Darshana, who was still unconscious. "Darshana found me and was bringing me to the temple, but we were ambushed. She's hurt."

Mayhara and the male mage rushed to Darshana's side.

"She's been in and out," Shiro said. "She's lost a lot of blood. I thought about slowing the bleeding by controlling the water in her blood, but it would be too risky. I could stop her heart if she's too weak."

"No, it's a good thing you didn't," the guy said. He stood and turned to Shiro as Mayhara held Darshana's hand. "I'm Jae. This is Huojin and Salina."

Shiro nodded, recalling their names now that Jae had said them.

"What happened?" Mayhara asked. "Was it the Pishacha?"

"Yes. And someone else."

"Was it the Lotus?" Jae asked.

"No. It was some man. Some creepy guy dressed in black with dark eyes. He was in front of the Pishacha, and he used powers to destroy the bridge we were on and flip our car."

Mayhara and Jae exchanged a confused glance.

"Who was it?" Mayhara asked.

"I don't know. But Darshana said she had a theory. Then they attacked us, and Darshana was injured. She never had the chance to explain her theory to me. I used my mage powers to defend us, and they disappeared."

"Let me guess," Jae said. "Into clouds of black smoke."

"Yes, exactly."

"You're in prison clothes," Huojin said. "Did Darshana get you out?"

Shiro shoved his hands in his pockets. "No. I escaped. Well, barely. Got shot and fell into the river. Luckily, I'm a copper and was able to make the water help me. Until I passed out, that is."

"How did you survive?" Mayhara asked.

"It's a long story."

Darshana let out a small moan, but her eyes were still shut.

"We've got to get her back to the temple," Jae said. "We've got medical supplies there. I can stitch her wound."

"It's dark now," Salina said. "Will she be okay if she's moved?"

"I think so." Jae was already lifting her, cradling her like a baby. "Let's get to the car."

They headed back the way they'd come in, their footsteps echoing throughout the warehouse.

"I hope you weren't followed," Shiro said, adrenaline rushing through him now that they were finally moving from their hiding place.

"So do I," Mayhara replied.

"We can't take her car," Shiro said. "It's barely running. I hope you've got room in yours."

Jae opened the door to the outside. A small car sat on the curb. "It'll be a tight squeeze, but we'll have to manage."

Salina opened one of the back doors, and Jae placed Darshana inside in a seating position. "Okay, just be careful. Sit on either side of her to keep her steady."

Shiro scanned their surroundings before he got in the car. Huojin squeezed in beside him, but she was petite, so it wasn't impossible. Salina moved Darshana's head onto her shoulder, not bothered by the blood. Darshana moaned, and her eyes fluttered open and closed.

"It's okay," Shiro whispered to her. "We're with the other mages now."

Jae started the car, and Mayhara glanced back at them from the passenger side. "You'll be okay, Darshana. We've got you."

They took off in the darkness, and Shiro didn't know what to expect.

"Do you guys have a plan for all of this?" he asked.

"We're still putting the pieces together," Jae explained. "We've acquired one of the daggers. In fact, we've got a Sacred Key at the temple."

"A Sacred Key?" Shiro tried to remember everything Darshana and Amalia had spoken about regarding the prophecy. He had to admit it wasn't all clear to him. "Is he alone?"

"He has a bodyguard." Jae glanced at him via the rearview mirror. "Though I'm not sure if he arrived safely."

Shiro was about to question him, but the car began to shake. The car jumped, and there was a commotion of alarm between them. Darshana fell from Salina's shoulder, almost collapsing onto Shiro's lap. He caught her and pulled her back.

Not this again, he thought, his arms shooting out to brace himself.

Jae skidded to a stop. Before them, the road was torn apart, pieces of earth jutting from the paved ground. Dust kicked up, hovering around them.

"Oh no," Mayhara said.

Shiro bent forward in the seat. Through the windshield, he spotted a beautiful young woman standing in front of them, glaring as her palms glowed a brilliant crimson.

Eighteen

"It's Naree," Jae said, locking eyes with his sister. At the same time that he feared the look in her eyes, a sense of relief came over him that she was still alive, that no harm had come to her. Yet.

"How did she find us?" Mayhara asked.

"It might have been from when Darshana sent me her pinged location."

"What do we do?" Huojin asked.

"We get out of the car." Jae threw his door open.

"Leave Darshana here," Mayhara said to Shiro. "We shouldn't move her any more than needed."

Jae kept his eyes on his sister. As she came closer into view, he saw that Naree was flanked by four Pishacha and two other people dressed in black. They were partially hidden in shadow, but there was no mistaking the contempt in their expressions. The ones without mouth masks had matching tattoos on their necks, though Jae couldn't quite place the design. He didn't know who they were or why they were with his sister, but there were many pieces of this puzzle of a prophecy he hadn't quite grown to understand.

"That's the guy," Shiro said, coming up beside him. "The one from the bridge."

"And that's the woman I saw at the street fair." Mayhara grabbed Jae's arm. He could feel the panic in her touch. "She's one of them."

The one Shiro said was from the bridge glared at Jae, sneering as he lifted his chin. Goosebumps broke out all over Jae's skin, his brow slicking with sweat. He didn't know this enemy. He wasn't sure what to be prepared for.

"What are they?" Huojin asked.

"Some kind of dark soldiers," Shiro said.

The earth shook again, the ground around them cracking and rumbling. Naree's hands were completely covered in red glow; it was so intense, it reflected in her eyes.

The ground rose around them. Not just the mages, but around Naree, the Pishacha, and the dark soldiers. It was as if they had created some kind of arena, a cave-like place for them to battle. At first, Naree and the Pishacha and the others sunk into the depths of the darkness, but Naree's palms glowed red from using crimson powers, illuminating their location.

The mages huddled closer together.

"She's the Lotus?" Huojin asked.

"Yes," Jae said. "But, like I said, she's under a trance."

They watched from the cave entrance as Naree stood in the center of the space, glaring at them all. When her eyes went over Jae, he swallowed hard, wondering if the trance had disconnected her from him. Did she no longer see him as her brother? Had Kashmeru broken her emotions to the extent that she was willing to kill her own family?

Her gaze went past him and onto Shiro.

Jae's eyes narrowed. Naree's red glow morphed to white. The dark soldiers seemed to be laughing silently.

"Shiro," Naree said, her voice echoing in the raised earth around her.

"Why is she calling you by name?" Jae whispered.

Shiro shook his head. "I… I don't know."

"Shiro, I need you to bring me the dagger."

Jae looked over at Shiro. His face seemed pale, his jaw trembling.

"I don't have it," Shiro said, his voice unsure.

"But you can get it for me." Naree's feet barely seemed to touch the ground as she slowly walked forward, as if she were gliding instead. "I'm willing to make a trade for it."

Shiro visibly swallowed. "Trade?"

"Qiang for the dagger." She smiled at him. "What do you say?"

"Who's Qiang?" Huojin whispered.

"Must be someone you care about," Jae guessed. "Don't believe her. Look at her hands. She's using diamond mage powers to read your emotions. She's lying."

Shiro blinked, searching Jae's face. "Are you sure?"

Jae clenched his jaw. He pulled from his sapphire powers, trying to reach out with his truth powers to see if Naree was telling the truth, but she was blocking him. He couldn't read her; her power was too strong. Reluctantly, he shook his head.

"It's a simple trade, Shiro. Qiang for the dagger. And if you don't agree, then I have no use for him."

"We need to go in there," Shiro said. "We can't let her hurt him."

The mages exchanged looks, and then Mayhara nodded.

They followed Shiro in, Mayhara tight at Jae's side. Jae gestured for them to move carefully. There was no telling if the ground would give way. The cave walls concealed them on all sides, shutting out most of the light. The farther into the cave's darkness they got, the colder the chill that snaked over Jae's body.

Shiro glanced around. "Where is he?"

"He's not here, silly boy." Naree raised a brow. "But neither is the dagger I need."

Jae concealed himself partially behind Shiro so that Naree couldn't see his glowing blue palms.

"How do I know you won't hurt him after I get you the dagger?" Shiro asked.

"I give you my word," she said, smiling her brilliant smile.

It was only for a second, but Jae's truth power broke through.

Naree's smile fell away. "If I did have him, he'd be dead."

She gasped, and then a sneer took over her face.

"She doesn't have him." Jae grunted as she pushed back on his energy, almost burning his hands.

The ground rumbled again. Naree's hands glowed red again. Jae could see Mayhara's hands also glowing red. She was trying to stabilize the earth.

"Where is the dagger?" Naree demanded to know.

Her hands switched to blue. She was trying to use truth to get them to confess. Jae mustered up enough sapphire energy to silence the mages. Even if they were to speak, Naree wouldn't be able to hear them.

"Fine," Naree screamed. "Have it your way. I'll get the truth out of one of you, even if I have to kill the others in the process."

She turned to the Pishacha and said something Jae didn't understand.

On her command, the Pishacha advanced, their bodies seemingly emitting black tufts of smoke as they marched. Jae's hands were already awash in a blue glow as the four Pishacha shot forward to attack them.

Jae and Mayhara took a defensive stance. The others followed suit, wristbands aglow. The golden mages thrust out their hands, and golden fire shot out at two of the Pishacha, knocking them back. A path of ice quickly snaked over the cave floor, knocking one of the Pishacha's legs out from under him. The other Pishacha stopped dead in his tracks, an earthy formation trapping his feet. He looked down and growled, then disappeared.

Naree's hands glowed emerald, her jaw clenched as she glared at them. A vicious wind ripped through the cave, throwing half of them to the ground. Mayhara grit her teeth, using crimson energy to keep her balance. She reached down and yanked Jae to his feet.

The Pishacha all popped out of vision, leaving black smoke, then reappeared in different locations, charging toward the mages. This time, the dark soldiers, who had been standing protectively beside Naree, crouched forward and held out their palms. No light glowed from them, but dark tendrils of black particles streamed through the air.

The sounds of crimson, copper, sapphire, and golden energy forces buzzed between them, colliding with the dark energy the mysterious soldiers on Naree's side were casting at them. The Pishacha pushed in, whipping out cyber batons and swinging them at the mages. Jae lost track of the others, focusing on the Pishacha in front of him. He barely had enough strength in his sound wave sphere to block the impact of the cyber baton.

Suddenly beside him, Mayhara jumped with a guttural roar and landed hard on the ground in a crouch, her hands aglow in red. The red glow traveled from her hands, over the cracks in the ground, and into the nearest two Pishacha. The one attacking Jae stumbled back but disappeared into a cloud of smoke before he fell. Jae was sure he would reappear again soon, though he didn't know when. The Pishacha only disappeared for good with a critical hit. If they wanted to be rid of them, they'd have to up their game. The other Pishacha clambered to his feet but got struck with a fireball that sent him spinning.

The Pishacha who had attacked Jae reappeared behind him, but the sound reached Jae before the Pishacha could execute his attack. Jae blasted the shadow demon with a resonating sapphire energy sphere, sending the Pishacha flying back hard into the cave wall. The Pishacha morphed into smoke. Jae's breaths were heavy as he glanced around. He hoped the hit was critical enough to have banished the Pishacha for good.

The dark soldiers were still on them, but the mages held their ground.

"They have powers. Are they mages?" Salina asked.

"I've never seen mages like those," Mayhara said. "They don't fall into any classification of the empire houses."

"Watch out!" Shiro yelled.

They dodged a blast of dark energy, breathing hard as they jumped back into a defensive stance. A mixture of crimson earth and golden fire energy merged together into a gush of lava, the burning embers forcing the dark soldiers back.

Naree let out a growl and held her hands in the air. Copper light glowed in her palms. Rain began to fall, putting out the lava fire. The dark soldiers smirked as they advanced.

Mayhara threw out her crimson energy and formed a barrier between them.

Shiro's palms grew orange. The rain that fell seemed to be pooling together in midair. It grew until it was as big as a wave, which then was propelled into the Pishacha and dark soldiers.

They sputtered as they tried to get air to breathe. The female soldier raised her palms and pushed the water away, crouching low to the ground as she advanced. She headed straight for Jae.

Jae sent a sapphire sphere once, twice, each time sending the female soldier back a few steps. On the third strike, he yelled as he pushed his energy out, adding an earsplitting ring to the sphere and making the soldier close her eyes and cover her ears, her head obviously full of the noise. Jae took advantage of the soldier's weakened state and pushed a final sapphire sphere at her, knocking her off her feet and back against the cave wall. Her head connected with a jagged piece of hard rock, causing her to fall to the ground, unconscious. A Pishacha appeared, wrapped his arms around her, and they both disappeared.

Naree's palms grew golden. A massive flood of golden fire scorched in a circle around them. The mages huddled together, flinching from the flames. Mayhara threw out crimson energy, causing the earth barrier to rise around them like a shield, while Shiro called upon his water powers to send a wave over the flames.

Naree sent fireballs into Mayhara's shield, knocking it down, piece by piece.

Huojin was exposed first.

"Don't even think about it, bitch!" Huojin yelled, heaving a fireball at Naree.

"Don't!" Jae yelled. "We can't kill her!"

Before the fireball reached her, Naree held her hands up, glowing green. Huojin's fireball ricocheted, zipping back toward Huojin. It hit her with an explosion, fire crackling over her body.

"Huojin!" Salina screamed, running to her side. "No! No, please!"

Huojin fell to her knees as the gold fire energy coursed over her body. Her limbs dropped to her sides, and her eyes glazed over.

Shiro shifted his focus and quickly expelled water energy, putting the fire out. Huojin let out a deafening scream as some of her scorched skin peeled away. Steam rose from her body as she threw her head back in agony.

Salina yelled in a rage, spinning fast toward Naree and raising a glowing, gold palm.

"No!" Jae yelled, pulling Salina's arms back. "She's the Lotus."

Salina screamed in frustration, the golden energy flying from her hands. But Jae had thrown off her aim. Salina's fireball hit the remaining dark soldier. He screamed in anguish, flailing until the flames went out. One of the last Pishacha swooped in behind him. He wrapped his arms around the dark soldier, enveloping him in his dark cloak before they disappeared into a cloud of black smoke.

Naree's face was red with rage. She breathed heavily, looking around as if to surveil her position. She was alone with one Pishacha. Surely, she would see that she was outnumbered.

"This isn't over," she said, her eyes boring into Jae.

The last remaining Pishacha drew near her. Purple energy wafted through the air, emanating from Naree's glowing palms.

The purple energy grew thicker, filling the cave in a dense fog. Jae couldn't see anything, blinded by the amethyst power. The fog seeped into his lungs. He began to cough, and he heard the others coughing too. They were choking on the fumes.

"Mayhara!" Jae called when he could catch his breath.

The fog began to thin.

"Jae!" she answered.

"Mayhara." He waved at the air in front of him, catching a glimpse of her. "Are you okay?"

"I'm right here."

He reached out, and she found his hand with hers. He pulled her into him, wrapping his arms around her.

The purple fog thinned more, dissipating into nothing.

Jae looked around. Naree and the remaining Pishacha were gone.

Shiro and Salina were crouching next to Huojin, who was moaning in pain.

"She's hurt bad," Salina said, a sob in her throat. "These have got to be third-degree burns."

"We need to get her to a hospital," Shiro said.

"We can't." Jae clenched his jaw. "They'll find her and kill her. We need to get her and Darshana back to the temple. Darshana left me the number of an emergency contact in case we needed medical attention. It's the best we can do."

Salina helped Huojin to her feet and nodded. "Okay, but let's hurry."

Shiro wrapped his hands around his neck and threw his head back. "Those dark soldiers. They were mages, weren't they?"

"They weren't Pishacha," Mayhara said. "They were like us. Except… filled with bad energy."

Jae looked her over. There was a cut on her temple. He placed a gentle finger on her cheek to examine it. "Are you okay?

"I think so." Her eyes were still darting around, as if paranoid the Pishacha would show up again. "You?"

He let out a deep breath and shook his head. "This is far from over. She won't stop until she gets the dagger."

"We need to find the others before she does—and somehow get the two she already acquired."

Jae rubbed a hand over his sweat-covered brow. His chest was tight, and his muscles felt like they were on fire. "Let's get back to the temple and recoup, figure out our next plan of action. We need to make sure the Sacred Key, the scroll, and the dagger are safe. First, we have to make sure Darshana survives."

"Yes," Mayhara said, her body aching from exhaustion. "We need her more than ever."

Jae studied her face, but Mayhara could tell his thoughts were on the mission.

"I have a feeling there's more to the prophecy than what she's told us," he said. "Let's hope we can put all the pieces together before it's too late."

GOLDEN MAGE

BOOK THREE

ONE

Salina pushed aside the gauze curtain and gazed out at the koi pond. The clouds had parted enough to allow some beams of sun to dance upon the water. She took a deep breath in through her nose and released it through rounded lips, attempting to clear her mind and ease her tensed muscles. She'd hardly slept, keeping vigil over Huojin as she lay wounded and suffering in her bed at the temple.

The newscaster on the televiewer caught her attention when he mentioned the Akutake comet. Turning away from the window, Salina tucked a golden-brown curl behind her ear and grabbed the controller, turning up the volume a bit. A petite woman with short, brunette hair tilted her head slightly at the camera. In the corner of the screen, a still image of the oncoming comet was displayed.

"This is Akutake's second cycle through our solar system, the last one—182 years ago—bringing it roughly twelve million kilometers away from Earth. Astrophysicists at the New United Asian Space Agency predict the comet will come exceptionally closer this year, approximating the proximity to be a mere seven million kilometers from Earth. Its closest range will align with the air space above the city of New Delhi in India's district of New United Asia in less than a month.

"Though NUASA reassures us the comet does not impose a risk, a movement of the devout population across New India, between New Jaipur and New India, has encouraged citizens to offer greetings to Akutake in the form of prayers, meditation, and festivals honoring the comet. Because of this, the governor of New Jaipur has arranged a number of festivals to welcome the comet in its various phases of approach, beginning with the Navratri Festival, taking place next week."

A rustling of sheets made Salina turn. With a furrowed brow and a hiss through her teeth, Huojin stirred. Her dark hair was damp and clung to her temples. She wasn't able to move too much, with half her body covered in severe burns. Though Huojin would have been best treated at a hospital's burn center, it was too risky. Mages were outlawed, and walking into a medical facility, which would no doubt be occupied by Imperial Police, would mean certain imprisonment. Or worse.

Jae had acquired the help of a doctor who was willing to keep his mouth shut for compensation. The doctor had provided burn creams and ointments, dressing Huojin's wounds to the best of his ability with what little resources he could provide. Left with pain pills and instructions on how to change her bandages, the mages were on their own to help Huojin to heal. Only time would tell if it would be enough.

Luckily, Huojin's fire powers drew most of the heat from the burns, converting the element into vapers that were released into the air. The result was a very humid room.

Salina hurried to Huojin's side. Huojin's eyes opened a fraction of an inch, her gaze resting upon Salina.

"Sal—" Huojin's raspy voice was cut short by harsh coughing. She winced as the coughing fit jolted her body.

"Take it easy." Salina's voice was gentle as she reached for a washcloth on the side table. She dunked the washcloth in the small basin of water before gently dabbing at the sweat beaded on Huojin's forehead. It was one of the only places not burned by Naree's fire magic.

"Where... Where is everyone?" Huojin asked, her face still contorted from the pain. "What happened with Darshana? Is she okay?"

"Don't worry about that right now. You need to heal before you can deal with anything else."

"But is she alive?"

"Yes. But she hasn't woken up yet."

It had been a series of harried events since the battle with Naree and the Pishacha. Huojin's injuries had been the worst of them all, but Darshana had been hurt even before the battle had begun, and she had yet to awaken.

"I need some water," Huojin said, shifting slightly to sit up.

Salina poured her a glass from the pitcher on the side table. "Here."

"I can't remember everything," Huojin said as she took the glass. She winced as she sipped, and then she handed the glass back to Salina. "I remember the fire. I remember Naree and the Pishacha disappearing. And you bringing me to the car. But I must have passed out from the pain."

Salina released a shuddered breath, feeling the panic as if it were happening all over again. She pushed through the feeling and focused on the events that had followed. "We brought you here. Jae got a doctor to bandage you up."

"I think I remember that. It felt like a dream. A really… agonizing dream."

"He gave you a shot of morphine and left us some pills. But Shiro said he knows of a witch who could heal you better than any doctor could."

Huojin scoffed. "A witch?"

"Yeah." Salina gave her a half-shrug. "Unfortunately, he can't remember how to find her, and Mayhara thought it was too risky for him to wander off searching for her. He said we'd have to wait for Darshana to come to. If she ever does."

"Didn't the doctor help her?"

Salina stood and began pacing. "Yes, of course. He tended to her injury but couldn't do anything more. He couldn't be certain if she would remain unconscious or not without a scan. But since we can't take her to a hospital…"

"We can't do anything but wait." Huojin shifted again, drawing in a breath through her teeth.

"What do you need?" Salina rushed back to Huojin's side. "What can I do?"

"Maybe those pain meds?"

Salina didn't waste any time. She quickly uncapped the bottle of pills and slipped two capsules into Huojin's bandaged hand. Huojin slid them into her mouth and took the glass Salina offered her.

As Huojin leaned back against her pillow again, Salina felt a heavy weight on her heart. She hated seeing her best friend like this. Huojin had been her saving grace when Salina had arrived at the mage academy, taking her under her wing. She'd been there for her whenever she had needed someone, which Salina had often needed, being so far away from her own country. And she'd been her personal mentor during golden mage training, especially when Darshana had been too busy to advise her. She was her home away from home, the one who'd comforted her when her mother had died and had paid for her ticket home, and Salina would do anything for her.

To see her suffering like this was killing Salina.

"Are the pills helping any?"

Huojin squirmed, her face twisted in pain. "Not yet. I think I need a distraction. Talk to me about something."

"What should I talk about?" Salina steadied her breath, fighting off tears.

"Anything pleasant. Tell me about your home."

"Massawa was originally a small, seaside village. It extended over the same area as the Kingdom of Axum, which used to be called the Kingdom of Zuma. It has the oldest mosque in Africa—the Mosque of the Companions—which is believed to be the first mosque on the African continent."

"So it's old," Huojin said with the hint of a smirk on her lips.

Salina smiled, relishing in the fact that her friend still had her sense of humor. "Very old."

Huojin licked her lips and swallowed hard, her eyes drifting halfway closed. "Tell me more."

"It is very hot in Massawa. There's not a lot of rain. Like, ever. It's famous for having very high summer humidity despite being a desert city. The desert heat and the high humidity together make it seem unbearably hot. But the sky is gorgeous. It's always clear and bright throughout the year."

"What about the food?" Huojin asked. "I bet the food is divine."

"I think it is." Salina laughed. "But my absolute favorite is anything with *hilbet*. It's like a paste made from lentils and fava beans. I remember coming home after grade school and my mother would already be preparing dinner. She'd make a stew called *tsebhi* and flatbread and *hilbet*. And I would always eat the most *hilbet*, which made my brother mad."

"Yeah, that sounds like you." Huojin smiled at her. "It sounds lovely. I wish I could visit there."

"You can one day. I promise. I'll take you there myself."

Huojin's smile widened. Her thin wisps of black lashes almost entirely blocked the view of her chestnut brown eyes. "Tell me more."

"Well, even though it's called the Red Sea, it is the bluest of blues you'd ever see." She let her head fall back as she recalled her youth. "I remember going to the shore with my family when no one had to work or go to school. Those were the best days. They were precious to us. We didn't have a lot of money, but we felt rich because of the love our family had for each other."

When Salina looked back at Huojin, her eyes were closed, and a small smile rested on her lips. Her slow, steady breathing told Salina she'd fallen asleep.

Salina stood, her heart feeling compressed with worry. It wasn't so long ago that she had lost her mother. She wouldn't be able to bear it if she lost her best friend too.

TWO

Mayhara adjusted her eyes to the darkness of the old shop. It wasn't that it didn't have any lighting inside; it was more as if the shop owners were relying on the bright sunlight coming in through the windows to illuminate the shop. The only problem was it was a partly cloudy day, and the sconces in the shop were merely faint yellow glimmers on the walls. The place smelled like metal and paper, and Mayhara distinctly heard the ripping sound of a buzz saw buzzing coming from behind the far wall.

Jae, who had ventured deeper into the store than she had, studied a few of the scrolls on the dusty shelves before nodding at her. They were in the right place. Now they just had to speak to the right people.

Jae spread his gaze around the shop, running a hand through his dark hair and then over the hint of stubble at his jaw. Mayhara noticed his eyes flit to the upper corners of the space.

He's checking for cameras.

Adjusting the dark blue scarf that covered her long, silky, black hair, Mayhara followed Jae across the red-tiled floor. He headed toward the mahogany counter, where a woman in a flowered, green *cheongsam* dress and a man in a black *tangzhuang* jacket stood. They appeared to be ordinary workers, probably a decade older than Mayhara and Jae, neatly groomed with a graceful manner in the way they moved. Mayhara worried that they might not have any information about the scrolls she and Jae had stolen.

Jae approached and bowed to them. The young woman looked him up and down, her brows drawn down. Jae glanced back at Mayhara for a moment.

"May I help you?" the man behind the counter asked. His smile seemed genuine.

"I've passed by this shop a few times but never came in here. It's charming." Jae gave him a nod.

"Thank you," the man answered. The woman remained quiet, her face hard to read.

Mayhara sidled up beside Jae.

"How long have you been working here?" Jae asked.

"For as long as I can remember," the man answered.

"Ten years," the woman said, her hand planted on her hip.

"But we practically grew up in the shop," the man said. "I learned to walk right over there. Nearly destroyed a shelf of vases."

Jae let out a small laugh along with the man's throaty chuckle. The woman remained stoic.

"So, you're part of the family who owns the shop?" Jae asked.

The woman crossed her arms, her lips in a straight line. When Jae met her gaze, her eyes went to the counter as she adjusted her *fa-zan* hairpin.

The male tilted his head slightly and studied Jae for a quick moment. His eyes then flit over to Mayhara. "Is there something in particular you're curious about?"

"I'm sorry." Jae pressed his palms together and bowed. "I don't mean to be rude. My name is Jae, and this is my friend May—" Mayhara and Jae exchanged glances momentarily. They couldn't be sure the shop workers would recognize Mayhara from police bulletins stating she was wanted for murder. Better not to give them her real name. "Maya."

"Nice to meet you," Mayhara said.

After a short pause, the man gave them a slight bow. "I'm Nian, and this is my sister, Zhen."

Zhen made a quick movement Mayhara didn't quite catch, and Nian responded by letting out a muffled *oomph* and reaching for his lower leg. Mayhara bit back her urge to laugh, knowing Zhen must have kicked him. Perhaps she didn't want people knowing her name.

"Your family's scrolls are beautiful," Jae said.

Nian cleared his throat. "Thank you."

"Have you learned the art of scroll making, or are your duties strictly to manage the shop?"

Nian glanced at Zhen, as if unsure to continue speaking freely.

"It is a family business," Zhen said. "And as such, we must learn every aspect."

Jae nodded.

"Would you be able to tell your scrolls from others?" Mayhara asked.

"Of course." Zhen lifted her chin. "It would be a dishonor not to be at least somewhat of an expert on the subject of the family business."

"The reason we ask is because we're looking for some information on a couple scrolls. They appear to be from your company." Mayhara swung her canvas bag forward and retrieved the scroll tubes, laying them on the counter.

Zhen rested her hand on her chest, just below her throat, and stepped closer to her brother. Nian's gaze went between Mayhara and Jae before gently placing his fingers upon the end of one tube. With narrowed eyes, he slipped the scroll from the first tube and turned it over in his hand. He held it at an arm's distance as he unrolled it. As he studied it, Zhen looked up at Mayhara, her mouth in a straight line.

"This one looks familiar." Nian spoke slowly. Deliberately. "But the digitalization tells me it was made in connection with an outsourcing company that installs the software for this type."

"You wouldn't be able to tell us what or who those lights are assigned to?" Mayhara asked.

"Not without getting the coding documents from the digitalizing company." Nian rolled up the scroll and stuck it in its tube.

"Can you take a look at the other scroll?" Jae asked.

Nian breathed in deeply through his nose. He didn't seem irritated, and Mayhara wondered if he had something to be afraid of. Paranoia scraped at her skin as she wondered if Nian and Zhen might have in fact recognized her after all. She watched their hands, making sure they weren't tripping some emergency call button that might alert the Imperial Police. Had they already called for them? Were Nian and Zhen just biding their time until the authorities arrived?

Mayhara instinctively looked toward the window, fidgeting with her head scarf as Nian opened the other scroll. His brow wrinkled, and he blinked a couple times as he scanned the scroll.

Zhen pursed her lips and backed away. "We don't recognize this one."

Nian swiveled his head her way and began whispering in harsh tones in Mandarin. Zhen argued back.

Mayhara didn't understand their words, but she recognized the sound of it. She turned to Jae, wondering if he knew the language.

"They're arguing about whether or not they should help us," Jae said, loud enough for the two siblings to hear him. "She's telling him she doesn't trust us."

"Trust has to be earned," Zhen suddenly interjected. Her hands were balled into fists. "There are wars taking place no one knows about, no one could even dream about, and you don't get to decide if we are pulled into them or not."

Nian placed a gentle hand on her arm and said something to her in calming tones. Zhen crossed her arms and backed away from him but didn't argue further.

Squaring his shoulders, Nian tilted his head slightly. "Could you, perhaps, state your motivation for wanting to find the meaning of this scroll?"

Jae leaned closer over the counter and lowered his voice. "We know of these wars. Believe me. We are a part of them. We are mages, the loyal warriors of the Empire of the Lotus."

Zhen and Nian stared at them for a moment. The only sound that could be heard was their breathing.

"Mages are outlawed," Zhen said. "It is illegal for us to help you."

Nian turned quickly to his sister. "Where do your loyalties lie, sister? We have always served the empire. The Lotus has always been our sovereign goddess."

Zhen jutted out her chin. "My loyalties would lie with the empress, of course. But there has been no news of her rebirth."

"It's been kept secret," Jae told her. "It's the one hundredth reincarnation, and according to the prophecy, the Lotus is in danger. Her reincarnation has been kept secret to protect her from the Pishacha."

Nian and Zhen exchanged glances, and then Nian dropped his gaze. Jae raised his hand, and his palm began to glow a bright blue. Zhen's eyes widened and her bottom lip trembled.

"I have a feeling this doesn't surprise you," Jae said to Nian. The blue glow grew, illuminating Nian's face.

"We have heard about her reemergence, yes. But only recently."

Zhen swallowed hard.

Mayhara pushed back her head scarf. "And you understand this is the one-hundredth reincarnation?"

Nian nodded.

"If you honor the Lotus, we need your help," Jae said. "Kashmeru has his shadow army out, and they already have the Lotus in their grasp. She's under his spell."

Zhen's jaw dropped. "We are doomed, then. We've already lost."

"No." Mayhara laid her hands flat on the counter. "That's what the mages are for. We're going to rescue her. We have the power to fight the Pishacha. But we need all the help we can get. Our guru says this scroll is one of the keys that will turn things in our favor."

Zhen turned to Nian and spurted out something in Mandarin again. She shook her head at her brother, but he calmly reached out to stop her from flailing her arms as he spoke to her. Mayhara didn't have to understand the language to know Nian wanted to help them, despite his sister's protests.

Zhen let out a huff and took a step back, placing a hand on her hip and almost pouting at Mayhara and Jae.

"Will you take another look?" Mayhara asked, this time directly to Nian. "Maybe something on it looks familiar to you?"

"We think it's a map," Jae said. "But we can't tell what location it might be."

Nian pulled the scroll closer and took a better look, running his hand along the material.

"It's very old," Nian said. "The paper is different from the modern kind we use today. There are some smudges in the ink, almost as if someone made this in a hurry."

Mayhara and Jae waited patiently as Nian followed a few of the ink markings with his fingers. After what seemed like a long while, Nian looked up at them.

"I'm sorry," he said. "That's all I can tell you at this point. I can speak with some older family members. Perhaps they can be of better assistance."

Zhen began yelling in Mandarin, but Nian shouted back, silencing her.

"Can we keep the scroll here so that I may show one of them?" Nian asked.

"I don't think that's a good idea." Jae rolled up the scroll and put it back in its tube. "I can leave you a number to call when you've found someone who might be able to help. We can come back."

"It's also for your safety," Mayhara said. "If the Pishacha come looking for this, you could be in danger."

"That's the first sensible thing you've said," Zhen mumbled under her breath.

Mayhara ignored Zhen's comment and nodded to Nian. "Thank you for your help."

A buzzing from Jae's pocket forced him to turn away. He and Mayhara stepped away from the counter as he checked the screen of his Linq.

With a quick glance at Mayhara, Jae held his Linq to his ear. "Shiro?"

Mayhara waited for a second.

"Okay, we're on our way." Jae swiftly tucked the Linq away.

Mayhara searched his face. "What is it?"

"It's Darshana. She's awake."

THREE

Naree stood on her balcony, overlooking the gardens. The villa was quiet, and all she wanted to do was breathe in the tranquility and sip her tea. The last few weeks had been a struggle. There were times when she was unsure of what she was doing, like she was living a dream. And there were times when she felt as if her mind was separated from her body, when she could see what actions she'd been carrying out but had no control over them.

Because of him.

She took a deep breath and looked upward. Birds danced in the air, circling each other as they soared across the sky. She breathed in, the scent of her rooibos tea mixing with the smell of fresh spring flowers in the gardens. She allowed herself to close her eyes. A memory from another life began to play out in her mind.

She stirred her tea, a soft breeze playing with the hem of her skirt as she sat at an outdoor table at her favorite cafe. He approached the table. His thick, black hair was a bit longer now, the ends extending enough to tuck behind his ears. His dark brows gave a strong contrast to the tiny flecks of silver in his anthracite gray eyes. His smile lit up his face, and when he took her hand to place a kiss upon it, she blushed.

"My love," he said as he slid into the seat across from her. "This is the highlight of my day. You are an absolute vision of beauty."

"As are you," she replied with a sheepish smile.

He laughed. "You find me beautiful?"

"Yes, I do." She leaned forward and filled the cup in front of him with tea.

He continued to smile at her as he sipped, watching her face.

She narrowed her eyes. "What is it?"

"I'm sorry. I don't know what you mean." Still, his grin did not fade.

"Something is up. I can tell."

He tilted his head. "I should have known better than to try to hide something from you."

"What are you hiding?"

He set down his teacup. "I was going to wait until this evening, after our stroll through the park."

"Now you must tell me," she insisted.

"I suppose I have no choice."

She giggled. "You don't."

"Very well, then." He reached into his trousers pocket and pulled out a rectangular, black, velvet box.

Her eyes widened as he set it on the table and slid it closer to her.

"For me?"

"My love, everything I have and everything I am is for you."

She practically swooned at his words.

"Open it," he said. His smile was child-like.

She almost danced in her seat from excitement. The box was soft under her touch. When she opened it, her breath caught in her throat. Inside was a shiny gold chain-link necklace, a tiny charm of a dove in flight sitting in its center.

"It's lovely," she exclaimed. "But why? What occasion could it be that I deserve such a gift?"

"The occasion—" he stood and took the necklace from the box. "—that I am utterly and completely in love with you."

A flutter in her stomach caused her to fiddle with her blouse. With a feather-light touch, he swept her dark brown hair off her neck, draping it over her shoulder. He placed the necklace around her neck, his fingers softly brushing against her bare skin as he closed the clasp. She gasped as the cold metal of the charm touched her chest.

His hands rested on her shoulders. "Do you love it?

She ran her fingers over the gold as she stood and turned to face him. "I do."

He placed his hands on her waist and urged her closer. "Do you love me?"

Their gazes locked. She reached up and traced a finger along his cheek and down to his jaw. He leaned down and gently pressed his lips against hers, his hands slipping behind her to pull her even closer. She deepened the kiss, letting him take what he desired, letting his passion fill her with want.

It felt so right, yet…

She gasped and pulled away. Her hands flew to her lips.

"My love?" He searched her face. "What's wrong?"

Fear filled her. His eyes now appeared black as coal. There was a presence within him, something sinister that loomed like a dark cloud, a shadow that chased away the light.

Evil.

Deep inside, Kashmeru lurked. His evil is what she felt radiating off him. But she couldn't say it.

She took two more steps back. His brow furrowed.

"No." A scowl began to form on his face. "Do not cast me away."

She shook her head and backed away even more. "I... We... We can't. This. This is wrong."

Before he had a chance to object, she turned and ran.

"Your Highness."

Naree turned to find Bhutano standing by the sliding doors of the balcony, his hands clasped behind his back and his uniform crisp and wrinkle-free.

"Yes?" She stirred her tea, which she knew had to have gone cold by now.

"The dark mages are ready to accompany you. We need to find the next dagger." He gestured toward the door, indicating she should follow. "Time is closing in on us."

She sighed, leaving her cold tea behind on the balcony railing. "All right. Let's go."

FOUR

Mayhara's heart pounded the whole way back to the temple. Though she was relieved to hear Darshana had awoken from her coma-like sleep, she needed more information. Was Darshana coherent? Was she in pain? Impatience tore at her so much, she nearly yelled at Jae to ignore the speed restrictions and drive his motorcycle faster. Instead, she forced herself to practice the breathing techniques Darshana had taught her to keep her calm.

Wind whipped at her face, but the sound of the motorcycle's motor was cloaked under Jae's sound magic. Under the stifling press of her helmet, she felt hot, the anxiety of needing to see Darshana causing her to sweat.

Once they reached the carport of the temple, Mayhara hastily tore off her helmet and dismounted Jae's bike. She could hear Jae struggling to keep up with her.

Jae called out to her to slow down, but she hardly acknowledged his words. She needed to know Darshana was okay. Somehow, she felt as if it would be a bad omen for their mission if Darshana wasn't all right.

Mayhara rounded corners and skidded down halls until she reached Darshana's room. The door was open, and both Shiro and Salina turned to her as she entered. On the bed, propped up with pillows, lay Darshana. Her eyes were closed, fine lines settled above her cheeks and lips, and her long, white hair fanned out over her pillows.

Mayhara's heart sank. "I thought she was awake."

"I *am* awake." Darshana opened her eyes a fraction of an inch. "Can't an old woman rest her eyes without the world thinking she's dead and gone?"

Despite herself, Mayhara laughed. This brought smiles to both Shiro's and Salina's faces.

Mayhara hurried to Darshana's side. "We're so relieved you're awake. We thought—"

"Never mind what you thought. I taught you not to dwell on the negative, didn't I?"

Mayhara bowed her head, her gaze staying on the guru. "Yes, of course."

"Do you need anything?" Salina asked, stepping forward and attempting to adjust Darshana's pillows.

Darshana waved away her efforts. "First of all, stop fussing over me. Second, I need you to tell me exactly what happened with Naree and the Pishacha."

Jae suddenly appeared in the doorway. "Darshana."

Darshana let out a deep breath. "Yes, yes. I'm fine. My dears, time is of the essence. What happened in the battle with Naree?"

Everyone began speaking at once, and Darshana's expression showed she was having trouble keeping track of who was saying what.

"They somehow found us when we left the warehouse."

"Naree created a cave in the middle of the road."

"She said she wanted the dagger."

"We fought inside the cave."

"Not only the Pishacha there, but others."

"Mages."

"Dark mages. Like the one we saw on the bridge."

"They fought alongside her."

"But we matched them in might, and they disappeared."

"But not before Naree unleashed a firestorm on Huojin."

"She's badly burned."

This last part made Darshana sit up. Everyone was quiet for a moment.

Salina looked around at everyone, then put a hand on Darshana's arm. "The doctor who tended to you treated her as well. He did everything he could."

Darshana swiped strands of hair away from her face. "Where is she?"

When Darshana threw back her covers, Mayhara protested.

"No. Don't get up," she said.

"She's resting," Salina told her. "She's healing, though."

Darshana shook her head. "I want to see her. I need to put my hands on her to see what's going on inside."

Mayhara and Jae exchanged glances.

Shiro sighed and took a step back, nodding. He pushed his copper-streaked, dark hair off his forehead, averting his gaze.

"All right," Jae said. "Just… take it easy."

They gathered around her as if she were the most fragile thing in the world until she scowled and waved them away, mumbling about minding people's personal space. Huojin's room wasn't far down the hall, but Darshana was still breathing heavily once they got there.

It had been a couple days since Mayhara had seen Huojin. She knew the elite golden mage needed rest and time to heal, and Mayhara had been busy helping Jae track down the scroll maker's shop. Looking at her now, Mayhara's heart hurt. Some of Huojin's burns seemed to have healed, but blackened, blistering skin still covered a good portion of Huojin's body.

Darshana pursed her lips as she approached the bed where Huojin lay sleeping. Closing her eyes, the guru reached out toward Huojin. Her hands came so close to the golden mage, one would think she was actually touching her. Darshana moved her hands over the space above Huojin's skin, now and then wincing as if feeling Huojin's pain. Everyone remained quiet, waiting for her to finish her analysis.

At long last, Darshana pulled her hands back and opened her eyes. She turned to the group, her mouth in a straight line. "She's healing, but not as fast as I'd like."

"Is there something we can do to help her?" Salina's brow was creased with worry.

Before Darshana could answer, Shiro spoke up. "I was thinking maybe the swamp witch could help her. The same way she helped me. I'm sure she must have something that could heal Huojin's burns."

Darshana nodded. "Yes. I think she might. Amalia's understanding of mage powers would be beneficial in providing the perfect tincture or salve needed to help the healing process along."

"Can we trust this Amalia?" The deep voice from the doorway made them all turn.

Mayhara had almost forgotten that the Sacred Key had been staying with them at the temple. Darshana narrowed her eyes at the man with slicked-back, salt-and-pepper hair, taking in his white, button-down shirt and dress pants. She hadn't been aware of his presence. They'd never had the chance to tell her about him before she'd been injured and fallen into her coma-like sleep.

The Sacred Key bowed. "I'm sorry to interrupt."

"It's okay," Jae said to Darshana. "This is Mr. Kitaro. He's the Sacred Key I located using the scroll."

"It is a pleasure to meet you, Guru Darshana. I've heard great things about you."

She bowed in return but still did not smile. "Sacred Keys are connected to Lotus empresses of the past. I must assume you are related to the late Anjana Patel."

"Yes." Mr. Kitaro's eyes soften. "She was my great-aunt. Older sister to my grandmother."

The hint of a smile materialized in Darshana's expression. "Yes, I had the pleasure of meeting her—and working with her when she lived at the palace. Seems like ages ago."

"It's been over twenty years since she passed."

A shadow fell over Darshana's face, and her gaze seemed far away.

"We have the dagger he's been guarding," Jae told her.

This seemed to bring Darshana out of her daze. She clasped her hands together and faced the Sacred Key. "Mr. Kitaro, what do you know of the dark mages?"

"I've heard some theories, but I can't be sure if any of them are correct. The detailed existence of dark mages seems to have been kept from the Sacred Keys. Or at least attempted to be kept from them."

She kept her eyes on him, scrutinizing his face as if trying to determine if he was covering up something.

"You don't believe me," he said. When she smirked in response, he let out a small chuckle. "Okay. Why don't you tell us *your* theory, and I'll let you know if any of it matches with the rumors I've heard."

Darshana looked around the room. "Perhaps we should move to the living room and give young Huojin some peace and quiet."

FIVE

Salina and Mayhara sat on the living room couch. Shiro stood at the back of the room, one arm wrapped around himself and the other propped up as he stroked his chin. Jae settled on the arm of the couch, his hands pressed into his legs right above his knees. Darshana paced the room as she spoke, while Mr. Kitaro stood and listened with his hands clasped in front of him.

"Kashmeru has sent his shadow army to capture the Lotus. We know this to be true. We've all witnessed this manifestation firsthand. The legend says the Council of the Seven needs Lakshmi's blood to unlock Kashmeru's tomb. The Council of the Seven has always been described as dark mages, but the elders and gurus of the empire have always counted on the notion that the Seven were elite Pishacha soldiers—spirits as ancient as Kashmeru who have been at his side through the centuries. But seeing the dark mage who attacked us on the bridge, I'm leaning toward the theory that they are not Pishacha. That they are people born as mages, just like you." Darshana gestured to the mages and then folded her hands together as she continued to pace.

"The ones we saw in the cave looked around our age," Salina said. "But they weren't from the academy."

"I'm not sure of their background," Darshana said. "Or why their existence has been kept secret."

"Probably for the same reason the reincarnation of the Lotus has been kept secret," Mr. Kitaro said. "To have an upper hand in this war."

"So they've been training to fight for Kashmeru?" Shiro asked. "Training with whom? And where?"

Darshana shook her head. "More mysteries I don't have the answers to."

"Kashmeru must have created them," Jae said.

"It makes sense that they're working with the government." Mayhara raked her fingers through her hair. "Mages are illegal. Yet these mages walk free."

Darshana eyed the Sacred Key. "How does my theory stand against what you've heard, Mr. Kitaro?"

Mr. Kitaro's gaze roamed about the room. He took his time before he spoke, as if measuring his words. "Most of the rumors circling the elders of the empire have been of the existence of mage children who were not brought forward. It didn't make sense at first because we do not force anyone to swear themselves to the Lotus if it is not their will. Most mages, of course, feel honored to be a part of such an important society, to be invited to the mage academy—when it existed—to train. And those families who declined the invitation were few but documented in the Sacred books. We respected their wishes. Therefore, it had become curious that rumors surfaced of hidden mages, families who hid their children from existence."

"These families must have been seduced by Kashmeru." Darshana wrung her hands. "Kashmeru could have sensed the presence of dark mage powers and… I don't know. Promised them something great for their loyalty, perhaps."

Mr. Kitaro nodded. "Most likely an agreement to spare them from the downfall of the universe. A place in his kingdom when the rest of humanity would be erased."

"And now they've come out of hiding and are leading the fight." Salina's voice was barely audible.

"The Council of the Seven." Mayhara looked at Jae. "There are seven of them."

"And there are seven elite to match their power," Jae said. "We just need to find them."

"But they won't be able to fulfill the prophecy without the daggers, right?" Shiro asked. "They play a part."

Salina stood. "Then we need to get the rest of the daggers. Before they do."

SIX

Jae found Mr. Kitaro standing alone in the middle of the downstairs hall, staring at one of the stone statues. The older man held a coffee mug in his hands, his expression grim.

"Mr. Kitaro?"

He seemed to snap out of his trance and turned toward Jae. "Oh, I'm sorry. Did you need me for something?"

"Um, no." Jae stepped closer. "Is everything all right?"

Mr. Kitaro let out a long sigh. "To be honest, I was thinking about Aiguo."

"Your bodyguard." Jae furrowed his brow "Did you hear from him?"

"Not since he diverted the Pishacha from following us, no. And if I'm telling the truth, I'm not too optimistic about ever seeing or hearing from him again."

"You… You think they killed him."

"I hate to admit it. I don't want to simply give up hope, but it's not looking good." Mr. Kitaro gazed down at his coffee. "He saved our lives. He was a good man. He was loyal, did his job, and he has brought honor onto himself."

"I'm sorry for your loss," Jae said quietly. He drew closer to the Sacred Key and placed a hand on his shoulder. "We will beat the Pishacha, Mr. Kitaro. Whatever it takes. We won't let Aiguo's sacrifice be in vain.

The air was stifling. Salina swiped a hand over her throat and walked toward the rear sliding doors that led to the patio. She needed some air. As soon as she slid the door open, a cool wind caressed her skin. The mountain air was slightly damp, but Salina didn't mind. It refreshed her. It nourished her need to escape for a moment.

Sitting on the ground by the koi pond was Shiro. He stared at his fingers as he braided two blades of grass together. Taking slow strides, Salina concentrated on easy, deliberate breaths as she headed for the white, wooden bench Shiro was sitting in front of.

For a moment, they simply sat there. Together but separate.

Shiro tossed his braided-grass creation into the pond. A copper glow emanated from his palm as he waved his hand to the side. The water in the pond responded to his powers by rippling toward the floating grass braid, pushing it along the surface of the water.

One of the koi in the path of the ripple changed direction and quickly swam away from the charging braid. Shiro twisted his wrist, and the braid chased after the fish.

After a minute of watching his shenanigans, Salina couldn't help but let out a laugh. Shiro glanced over his shoulder at her. The corners of his mouth inched upward.

"I'm glad to see you actually have a smile." Shiro shifted to face her. "I was beginning to think one didn't exist in your culture."

Salina raised a brow. "I could say the same about you."

He ducked his head and chuckled.

Salina raised her chin as her gaze went to the sky. The faint, streaky haze of the Akutake comet stared back at her, as if encouraging her to stay strong for their mission. She breathed in a shuddered breath, hoping Huojin would heal and be able to fight their fight.

"That about sums it up," Shiro said. "That sigh. It's made of a million words and a billion emotions."

She nodded, but her eyes were still fixed on the comet. "It's been hard. I don't know if you remember, but back at the academy, I was notorious for being a positive person. I was always able to find the good in any situation. But after my mom passed… and now, not knowing Huojin's fate… I don't know if I even have it in me to stay positive."

When she turned toward him, she found he'd been studying her face.

"You really care about her," he said.

"Yes, of course."

He continued to stare at her, and she found the intensity unnerving.

A light coming to life inside the temple caught Salina's attention. She spotted Jae through the glass doors aiming a remote control at the televiewer. The news popped up on the screen, and Jae and Mayhara watched with concentration as they sat together on the couch. Salina couldn't hear the televiewer, but the newscaster on the screen reminded Salina of all the times Huojin would watch the news for word on the prison camps. It suddenly hit her that Huojin had spent years worried about the wellbeing of her parents, and now it was Huojin who was in critical condition, and her parents had no idea.

She turned to face Shiro. He wasn't staring at her anymore.

"What was it like in the prison camps?" she asked.

Shiro's eyes widened for a second, obviously surprised by her question.

"I see what you mean about always focusing on the positive," he joked.

"I'm sorry. I was just… wondering about Huojin's family."

"Ah. Okay." He ripped another two blades of grass from the ground and began folding them together. "It was awful, if I can be honest. It was like being stripped of your humanity and not knowing what terrors the next day might bring."

"I'm sorry you had to go through that."

"It got a little easier when Qiang took me under his wing. He not only gave me tips on how to survive, he gave me a reason to survive."

"Yeah." She gave him a half-smile. "Huojin did the same with me."

"It made all the difference in the world. I grew to love him, to the point that I knew I could only exist if Qiang was in my life. That without his love, I could perish." He finished folding his blades of grass and looked up at her. "Is that how you feel about Huojin?"

Her smile was soft. "No. I mean, I love her, but not like that. She's my best friend. Not that I think there's anything wrong with your love for Qiang."

He averted his eyes.

"Did I say something wrong?" She placed a hand on her heart. "I'm sorry if I offended you."

"No. It's not that." He threw the blades of grass to the side and pushed himself to his feet. Shoving his hands in his pockets, he shrugged. "I've come to realize that I don't know if Qiang feels the same way for me. There was a split-second moment during our escape where we got separated. And it seemed all too easy for him to let me go."

"But you can't really judge his feelings from a moment of panic."

Shiro shrugged again, kicking at the dirt. "I've been looking online, searching for any prisoner deaths, just in case. But I can't find any news. So if he's dead, they're keeping it a secret. And if he's alive, why hasn't he tried to contact me?"

"Shiro, it's not exactly easy to find us here."

Shiro shook his head. "He would find a way. His ingenuity is one thing I admired about him."

Salina pursed her lips. Her attention was drawn back to the televiewer. On the screen was an image of a building ablaze with fire. Curious, she stood and headed inside. Shiro followed.

Video footage on the screen showed fire fighters battling a burning building.

"—the police station is a mere one hundred kilometers from New Jaipur. Damages are extensive. The fire claimed the lives of six Imperial Police officers and left another four with critical burns. Authorities have not yet had a chance to investigate the source of the explosion, but word is an extremist group is suspect in the attack."

"An explosion?" Salina asked, crossing her arms.

"Do you think it was really an extremist group?" Mayhara asked. "Or could it be the Pishacha? Or the dark mages?"

Shiro worried at his chin, shaking his head.

"They're working together," Jae said. "Why would they attack the ones working with them?"

"Maybe they messed up." Salina shrugged. "Did something they weren't supposed to do."

The image on the screen changed first to a close-up shot of the Akutake comet and then changed to a number of people dressed in suits and a handful of uniformed Imperial Police entering the town hall.

"—to discuss the events welcoming the Akutake comet. Due to the alleged extremists' attack on the Alwar police station, the chief of New Jaipur's Imperial Police is scheduled to accompany the governor, along with an advisory committee. Governor Laghari will lead the opening ceremony of the Navratri

Festival, giving what is sure to be a spiritual speech for the citizens of, not only New Jaipur, but all of New United Asia. The nine nights of the Navratri Festival will be filled with music and performances, with traditional—"

Mayhara stood from the couch. "That woman who was standing beside the chief of police. That was my boss back at the census bureau."

"And the officer next to him," Jae added. "He's the guy from a picture Mayhara and I saw at Bruno's club.

"He was at the office, too." Mayhara tapped her chin with a finger. "He had a meeting with my boss. They're all connected with the Pishacha."

"Your boss is the one who had the scrolls, right?" Salina asked.

"Yes." Mayhara began to pace.

"Are you thinking what I'm thinking?" Jae asked her.

"We should go to the festival?" Mayhara bit her lip.

"What?" Shiro scoffed. "We can't just show up, an escapee nod a wanted murderer, to a place crawling with Imperial Police."

"They must have information on the whereabouts of the first dagger," Jae said. "We could follow them or listen in on their conversations. It could be a long shot, but we've got to do what we can to get that dagger."

"It's risky," Salina said.

Jae got up from the couch and stood beside Mayhara. "So is doing nothing."

"We'll need to keep out of sight." Shiro rubbed at his chin. "But you're right. One of them could lead us to the dagger."

"Long shots are still shots." The voice was Darshana's.

They turned to see her standing in the doorway. She had a thick shawl wrapped around her shoulders.

"Darshana, where are you going?" Jae asked. "Shouldn't you be resting?"

"I've rested long enough." She shuffled a set of keys between her hands. "I'm going back to the swamp to see if Amalia can help Huojin."

"Alone?" Mayhara asked.

"Mr. Kitaro has agreed to watch over Huojin, and the rest of you have work to do. The rest of the daggers are out there, as well as Sacred Keys whose lives are at stake. And we're still shy a few elite mages." She nodded once to them before she turned on her heel and left the room.

"She's right," Jae said. "Let's get moving."

"I'll get the scroll. We can start there." Mayhara turned to Shiro. "And I'm close to getting an exact location on one of the elite. I'll narrow down an address so you can follow that lead."

Shiro nodded. "Let's do it."

SEVEN

Naree gazed out the car window as the dark mage put the vehicle in PARK. She'd been twisting the same strands of hair between her fingers during the long drive, fighting off the feeling of being on edge. Anytime she felt the panic inside her coming to the surface, she could hear Kashmeru's voice telling her everything was evolving as it was supposed to. That they'd be together soon.

One of the dark mages who had accompanied her opened her car door and stepped aside. Naree climbed out, still staring at the view before them.

"It's been a long time since I've seen the shore," she said, her voice calm.

"Yes, Your Highness." The mage motioned for her to walk in front of him. "We can enjoy the view later. First we must get this dagger."

With a sigh, she turned away from the sea and led the way.

EIGHT

ayhara checked the scroll again, the wind blowing over the nearby sea causing her hair to whip around her head. She could feel Jae's body heat as he drew near. His breath was warm on her neck, but she knew his eyes were on the map.

"This must be it," she said, more to convince herself than anyone else.

There was nothing around for miles except a tall, red-and-white lighthouse. They'd traveled over fifteen hours to Jamnagar, following suspicious activity on the scroll, only to come to a lonely and seemingly abandoned but functioning lighthouse on the coast. Jae and Mayhara had decided to chase the lead, while Salina and Shiro traveled to New Delhi to track down the amethyst mage.

Waves crashed upon the shore, and a brutal wind bit into Mayhara's skin. She wasn't used to the chill in the air, and she felt the need to close the distance between herself and Jae, seeking out his warmth for comfort.

"The two black triangles that were flashing on the map have disappeared." Mayhara looked up at the top of the lighthouse. "It's got to be the dark mages. Do you think they disappear if they're inside a building?"

"I wouldn't rule it out. Let's go in and find out."

He nodded to her, a silent message for her to be prepared. If a dark mage—or two—was inside the building, they were going to be ready for a fight.

Seagulls squawked through the foggy air. Mayhara's fingers twitched as she and Jae stomped over rocks and wet sand. They had one dagger, and the Pishacha had one. If one of the daggers was still here, she would feel like they might be okay. Like they stood a chance in this fight. But if there was no dagger here, if the Pishacha had gotten to it first...

The pathway in front of the lighthouse was cracked and broken, demolished beyond repair, the earth beneath it uneven and full of sunken-in gaps. Mayhara opened her fingers, her palms still aimed at the ground. The red glow of her garnet wristband matched the red in her palms. She pushed out her power, reaching for the earth below them. The ground shook as the dirt below the broken path evened out, the gaps disappearing. She and Jae picked up their pace to get to the lighthouse door.

Taking a chance, she turned the knob. The door was unlocked. She gave Jae a nod before pushing it open and stepping inside.

They paused in the entryway in front of the spiral stairway that led up the tower. Jae held a finger up, his neck stretching upward. His palms glowed a bright blue.

"It's quiet," he said. "I don't think anyone is here."

"Who'd hide a dagger in a lighthouse?" she whispered.

"Who'd think to *look* for one in a lighthouse? Let's go up and see if we can find anything."

Their footfalls sounded on the metal steps. Jae quickly used his powers to silence them. Mayhara felt as if every nerve in her body was on high alert as they climbed. It felt as if they'd never reach the top, but at long last, the bright blaze of the turning beacon came into view.

Mayhara held tightly to the railing at the top of the stairs. The windows around them were enormous, the view stunning. But the lighthouse was empty.

"Did we make a mistake?" Mayhara asked. "Was the map wrong?"

"Maybe they took the dagger *and* the Sacred Key."

"There are no signs of a struggle." Mayhara shook her head. "I don't know. Something's not right."

"Maybe a Key hid the dagger here but didn't stick around to guard it."

"Doesn't sound like something a Sacred Key would do."

"I know. Let's head down and see if we can find any clues."

When they reached the bottom of the stairs, Mayhara put a hand on the wall, following it around.

"There's a door back here," she said.

"I think that's the control room." Jae pressed an ear to the door. "I can hear the motor for the beacon, but nothing else."

Mayhara turned the door handle and slowly pushed the door open. When she switched on the light inside the room, she and Jae gasped.

In the middle of the room was a wooden chair. A man was tied to the chair, his head slacking to the side and his eyes rolled back. A trickle of dried blood stained his face from the corner of his mouth to his chin.

"You think he was a Key?" Mayhara asked.

"Why else would he have been killed?"

Mayhara forced herself to look away from the corpse and focus on the other objects in the room. A desk was overturned, its drawers ripped from their places and tossed on the floor. A short bookshelf sat empty. Folders, papers, and books were strewn about, and a cabinet stood with its doors wide open, its contents obviously rifled through. A nail stuck out of one wall, the picture frame that must have been hanging there broken on the floor. "If there was a dagger hidden here, chances are they found it. All the shelves and drawers appear to have been searched already."

Jae scrubbed a hand down his face and nodded. "Okay. But maybe they didn't find it. We need to be sure. Let's feel around. Maybe there's a loose brick in the wall or something, a hidden spot they might not have found."

After searching for a few minutes, Mayhara backed away from the wall, almost tripping on the small rug that sat underneath the wooden chair. An idea hit her when she looked down at it. Crouching down, she placed her hands on the floor and reached out with her mage powers. She could feel a lack of earth below her, a place not occupied by the ground.

"There's something under the floor. A room, I think." She looked up at Jae, her mouth set in a straight line. "We have to move the body to get underneath."

Jae took a deep breath and nodded. "Okay. We'll set him on the floor off to the side. Let's untie him."

"Be gentle." Mayhara knew it was a useless request. The man was already dead. Still, she couldn't help but feel they needed to treat the Sacred Key with respect.

After they undid the ropes, Jae and Mayhara lifted the man's slumped form out of the chair. He was heavy, but Mayhara did her best not to drop him. Still, the man's bald head thumped on the floor once they set him down. Mayhara grimaced and whispered an apology to the dead man.

Jae picked up the chair and moved it aside. Mayhara rolled back the rug. She didn't see any difference in the floorboards, but she felt around to be sure. On one end of a board, there was a tiny notch just big enough for a finger to fit.

"A trapdoor," she said.

She stuck her finger in the notch and pulled. There was a creaky groan as she lifted the door. Using his Linq, Jae lit up the area to look into the hole in the floor.

"Another staircase," he said. "I'll go down first."

Jae disappeared down the stairs. As Mayhara began to climb in after him, she heard a click, and the space lit up fully. They found themselves in an underground room. There were cabinets and a desk. A small military-style bed was pushed up against the wall. It was like an underground bunker.

Mayhara wrinkled her brow. "Nothing looks out of place. I don't think whoever killed the man knew this room was here."

"Then we might be in luck."

The two of them wasted no time searching the room. They opened all the drawers, felt for false bottoms, and reached behind the furniture for where a box might have been securely taped. Reaching for an oversized book on the bookshelf, Mayhara pulled, only the hardback cover slipped away, revealing a black box standing on its side.

"Jae."

He came over as she took the box off the shelf. It was decorated in a shiny red-and-gold pattern. Mayhara held her breath as she turned it right-side-up and opened it.

Inside, lying neatly in a velvet mold, was a silver dagger. It had the same intricate design and grooves as the one they'd taken from Naree.

"They never found it," she said. "The Sacred Key did his job. He protected it."

She and Jae exchanged glances.

"We've got to get it back to the temple. The Pishacha might come back."

Securing the black box in his canvas bag, Jae led the way back up the stairs. Mayhara replaced the rug, and Jae set the chair on top of it.

"What about him?" she asked, her eyes on the Sacred Key.

Jae let out a shuddered breath. "I'm afraid we can't do anything. I can call in an anonymous tip to the Imperial Police, though they might already know about this if they're working with the Pishacha."

"Won't they trace the call?"

"No, I have a program that hides that information. Don't worry."

Mayhara bent down to close the Key's eyes. "No. Don't call them. They won't treat him with any respect. I have a better idea. Will you help me carry him outside?"

He did as she requested, the two of them lugging the honorable man outside of the lighthouse.

"Over here." Mayhara gestured with her chin.

After they set him down on the ground, Mayhara closed her eyes. She recited a prayer in her head, thanking the gods for the Sacred Key, giving thanks for his help. Then she held her hands out, focusing on the ground around him. As her palms glowed a bright red, the earth shook, the dirt and sand around the man falling away. It was as if the earth was enveloping the Sacred Key in its arms, pulling him in and forming a shelter around him. As his form disappeared into the earth, Mayhara waved her arms over the ground, and the earth evened out. No one would be able to tell anyone was buried there.

"May he have peace," she said.

Jae put a gentle hand on her shoulder. "That was nice of you."

"He didn't deserve to be left there for the flies."

Jae nodded, not saying a word.

Together, they turned away from the makeshift grave and headed for Jae's bike.

NINE

Mayhara sat across from Director Shei, her hands folded in her lap. Glancing over at one of the large windows in her office, she caught a glimpse at her reflection. She swiped a strand of hair behind her ear. There was something different about the way she looked. This was not how she looked now. This look was from her past. From when she was younger.

"I have to admit I'm impressed with what I've read." Director Shei's voice caused Mayhara to turn away from her reflection.

She swallowed hard and forced a small smile. "Thank you."

"Your records show you excel at administrative work. I think you'll be a great asset to the team." Director Shei's brown eyes flit over Mayhara's face. "Do you understand the responsibilities we're about to place in your hands?"

"Yes, of course."

Director Shei set her elbows on the desk and pressed her smooth hands together, her beautifully polished nails clicking together as she did so. "Your family will be kept safe. We promise you that, in exchange for your services to the firm. I know how important family is."

Mayhara followed Shei's gaze to the picture frame standing on the corner of her desk. In the photograph, Director Shei stood beside a girl about Mayhara's age. She had straight, black hair and thick streaks of eyeliner. The young girl was not smiling and looked as if she were about to turn away from the camera.

"Is that your daughter?" Mayhara asked.

"Yes. That's my Ruolan. I call her 'Ru.'"

Mayhara reached for the picture frame, but her hands were unsteady. The frame fell, and when Mayhara reached for it, Jae's hand suddenly appeared to pick it up.

"We need to hurry," Jae said.

Mayhara looked around to find herself in the dark. Jae placed a piece of sheer, plastic material on Director Shei's mouse and pressed it against one of the drawers of her desk. The drawer opened.

It was the night they'd broken into her old office building.

Mayhara gasped, sitting upright in bed. Two memories had converged in her dream, and each of them was connected to an important piece of the puzzle.

She threw her sheets off and grabbed her robe, barely fitting her feet into her slippers before she charged out of her room and down the stairs. She ran past the office, but no one was in there. The lit-up monitor told her Jae must have been awake, so she quickly changed direction and darted for the kitchen.

"Jae," she called.

When she skidded into the kitchen, Jae stood with a cup of coffee. Darshana was in front of him. They both turned to her, concern on their faces.

"Darshana, Jae." She put a hand on her chest, begging her heart to stop trying to slam through her chest.

"Slow down, child," Darshana told her.

"What's wrong?" Jae asked. "Did something happen?"

"The girl. The female dark mage from the cave, the one who followed me through the street fair—"

"Yeah?" He narrowed his eyes, waiting for her to continue.

"She's director Shei's daughter."

Jae blinked, shaking his head. Darshana closed her eyes and placed her fingertips together, resting them on her chin.

"How do you know this?" Jae asked.

"I know it sounds crazy, but it came to me in a dream. Something my mind remembered from the director's office."

Jae put his coffee cup down. "What was it?"

"There was a picture on her desk. Do you remember when we broke in? I knocked it down."

"I... vaguely remember?"

"There was a girl in the picture with the director. That girl is the same one I saw at the food fair when I went to get Huojin. She's the dark mage we fought in Naree's cave. And in my dream, I remembered when I was first being interviewed for the company. Director Shei told me it was her daughter. I'd just forgotten about it."

"That explains why she's connected," Jae said. "She plays a bigger part in this than we thought."

"We'll have to tell the others," Darshana said. "It makes me wonder about the other dark mages. Perhaps there are more people in power because of their dark mage offspring. Jae, would you mind having everyone gather in the meditation room?"

"Yes. Right away." Jae bowed and left the kitchen.

"It's probably not the breakthrough we were looking for," Mayhara said to Darshana, "but it's something. Especially after Shiro and Salina came to a dead end searching for the other elites."

"It could very well help."

Mayhara had some hope in her heart. Her information on the last known residences of the other elites had turned out to be nothing but abandoned apartments. The only documented elite mage in a prison camp was the emerald mage. Mayhara doubted any of the mages knew they were now elite. And one of them was currently in a prison camp.

When they were all gathered in the meditation room, Mayhara was surprised to see Huojin. Salina had to help her walk, but her healing process seemed to have accelerated. The salve Darshana had fetched from the swamp witch was working wonders.

Salina helped Huojin sit on a yoga pillow and then took a seat herself.

"I thought this would be a good opportunity to catch up on where we are." Darshana sat cross-legged facing them. "The comet is getting closer, and the festival will begin in a couple days. Huojin is healing, and Mayhara has just informed me that one of the dark mages is the daughter of the census bureau's director. We have two daggers, and the Pishacha—as far as we know—have one. Jae has told me that the scroll makers have not yet gotten back to him with information on the cryptic scroll we have."

"I'll pay them another visit," Jae said. "They may be avoiding me because of the Pishacha."

Darshana nodded. "Then be careful. They might be watching the shop."

"I've been tracking the black triangles on the other scroll. But so far,

I've come up empty," Shiro said. "I'm beginning to believe the Pishacha aren't able to locate the other daggers, either."

"All this aside," Darshana said, "I want you to remember that we will inevitably be fighting the big fight. You will have to call upon your training from the academy as well as learn some lessons you never had a chance to learn because the school closed down."

Mayhara took a deep breath.

"What if we can't learn in time?" Huojin looked down at her bandages.

Darshana kept her chin up. "The elite mages are destined to go into battle no matter what you have learned and what you haven't."

"We don't have all the elite mages yet," Salina said. "And some of us are not in the best shape."

Darshana waved a hand in the air. "Mind over matter. Do not dwell on the problem. Focus your mind on the solution. You have to believe the universe will deliver the answers. The other elite mages will be found, and your powers will excel as they should to protect the world from Kashmeru's destruction."

Huojin ducked her head. Salina grabbed her hand and squeezed it.

"But first," Darshana said, "we must meditate."

The following days were a whirlwind of activity. Jae returned to the scroll shop to put pressure on the scroll maker family, but he still had no answers. The other elite mages were nowhere to be found. The locations of the remaining daggers also remained a mystery. When the mages weren't running around trying to get a leg up in the war, Darshana made them train.

While Mayhara literally made mountains out of molehills, Jae irritated Shiro by practicing his truth power on him. Huojin started back slowly, but in a matter of days, she was able to practice with the rest of them. She was still weak, but Salina encouraged her, telling her she was getting stronger every day.

Darshana now told her it was time to push herself, so they all went into the field behind the temple for a mock battle of ice and fire. Shiro against

Huojin.

Huojin looked to Salina, who gave her a confident nod.

Taking their stances across from each other, Shiro and Huojin held their hands up.

"Remember, Huojin," Darshana called out, "control your breathing. Inhale through the nose and exhale through the mouth."

Shiro, who seemed to be waiting for Huojin to stop breathing so heavily, flipped his wrist and shot out a blast of ice. Huojin grunted as she threw a fireball to deflect it. The fireball nicked the ice but didn't quite repel it. It zoomed close to Huojin, who had to dive to the side to avoid it.

"Your flame needs to be more contained to give it strength," Darshana said.

Huojin huffed out an agitated breath and took her stance again. This time she shot fire at Shiro first. With a wave of his hand, a shield of ice formed, virtually swallowing Huojin's fireball.

"The heat needs to flow through you effortlessly," Darshana instructed. "Like the breath of a dragon."

Huojin squared her jaw and shook out her hands.

"You can do it, Huojin!" Salina called out.

Huojin assumed the position, her breaths deliberate.

Shiro nodded to her, as if giving her a heads-up. He crouched low and threw his hands out. Ice bullets shot from his palms.

Huojin shouted as she placed both hands in front of her and created a wall of fire. The fire wall deflected most of the ice, but one ice bullet got through and hit her in the arm. Huojin spun as she was knocked backward, falling to her knees as she grabbed the spot that had been struck.

"Your emotions are fueling your fire, but you do not have them under control." Darshana linked her hands in front of her. "You need to harness your anger and your frustrations without letting them burn the power out of your flames."

"I'm trying," Huojin said, her voice cracking. "I can't do it."

"This isn't up for debate. You *must* do it."

"Darshana," Salina began, but the guru cut her off.

"I'm sorry, but there is no room for being lenient. Every elite has to do their part. The universe is counting on you. And you owe it to the Lotus to fight this battle."

Tears flowed down Huojin's face. She shook her head and stormed off, heading inside the temple. Salina ran after her.

Mayhara exchanged looks with Jae, not sure what to do. She'd never seen Darshana like this.

"Darshana." Mayhara's voice was gentle as she approached her. "Are you okay?"

Darshana closed her eyes and rubbed at her temples. When she opened her eyes again, she let out a long breath. "Please forgive me. I lost control and forgot my mindfulness. I believe I need to take a silent walk and reflect on my actions."

"Yes, of course."

The guru bowed to the remaining mages and walked past the koi pond and into the trees.

Jae, Mayhara, and Shiro stood in silence, not knowing what to say. The stress was getting to them. To all of them. Mayhara raked a hand through her hair, wondering if they had what it took to win this battle or if everything was going to fall apart.

Naree approached the young man and smiled. He looked up from his desk and tilted his head.

"May I help you?" he asked.

She studied his face for a moment, and then her palms glowed blue. "You're the sapphire elite," she said.

"Yes." He narrowed his eyes at first, noticing her palms.

Naree smiled. He could not lie; she'd used truth powers on him. He had a blocker chip in his neck, so he couldn't stop her without causing himself pain.

Then, the Pishacha and dark mages entered the office behind Naree, and the young man's eyes widened. He tripped as he shot up from his chair, his hands held out to regain his balance.

"W-What's going on here?" He visibly swallowed. "How'd you get in here?"

"Shhhhh." Naree playfully held a finger to her lips. "You're not going to scream, are you?"

His gaze whipped quickly between the men behind her. His jaw quivered as he shook his head. "N-No."

"Hmm. Cross your heart?" Naree stepped even closer, her palms raised to face him. "Hope to die?"

Eleven

Huojin turned away from the mirror. It wasn't just that her burns looked awful, but she couldn't seem to face her reflection at all. There was no fire behind her eyes anymore. She felt lost. Disappointment from the last three days of training weighed heavily on her heart to the point of proving unbearable.

Darshana's outburst during the first training at the temple still echoed in her head. Since then, Darshana's words had been strictly helpful criticism, absent of the harsh tone she'd used with Huojin that day. Apparently, the guru had done some mindfulness meditation and cleared the cruelty from her instructions. But Huojin still felt Darshana's dissatisfaction with every word.

There was a knock on her door, which had been left slightly ajar. When Huojin spotted Salina peeking into her room, she smiled at her and waved her in.

"You coming to dinner?" Salina stepped into the room wearing a simple yellow dress, but the way it looked on her was like runway fashion on a supermodel.

"Yeah." Huojin felt as if Salina could tell her smile was fake. "Let's go."

Salina didn't question her façade. Instead, she hooked her arm through Huojin's and walked beside her as they headed toward the dining room.

As they descended the marble staircase, Huojin's stomach began to churn, and not from hunger. Though she had faced Darshana every day, it never got easier. In fact, she could swear that the stress of not believing she could fulfill her destiny was eating a hole in her heart.

The dining room was more like a banquet hall. The gray and white ceramic table was big enough to seat twenty. The tabletop reflected the warm lights of the lotus-shaped chandelier above it. Darshana, Jae, and Mayhara were already seated and looked up at Huojin and Salina as they entered. Huojin's gaze immediately dropped to the floor when she and Darshana caught each other's eyes. She followed Salina's lead as they slipped into their chairs.

"Smells delicious," Salina said.

Shiro emerged from the adjoined kitchen carrying a large serving bowl of steaming rice, which he set upon the table between a plate of yakitori chicken and *goma-ae*. A waft of herbs and spices filled the air.

"The chicken is a little spicy," Shiro said. "I hope everyone is okay with that."

"The spicier the better," Salina said.

"I think I can handle it." Jae grabbed his cloth napkin and spread it out on his lap.

"Looks divine," Darshana told Shiro as he sat down to join them.

Mr. Kitaro appeared at the entrance in a nice button-up shirt. "I hope I'm not too late."

"Not at all, Mr. Kitaro," Shiro said, gesturing for him to take one of the empty seats.

"This was a lovely idea, Shiro." Darshana nodded at him. "Thank you for going through all the trouble."

"My pleasure," Shiro replied. "I felt like everyone's been working so hard, we deserve a small reward. Something to keep the spirit alive and full of thanks."

Huojin simply stared as the rest of the group began placing food on their plates. She had no appetite. The feeling of failure filled every inch of her, not leaving room for anything else. She looked around, studying the faces of her fellow mages, her guru, and the Sacred Key. This dinner was for them. Not her. She hadn't done anything to deserve it.

As the conversation gradually transitioned from how delicious the food was into their theories on the Pishacha's strategies, Huojin could do nothing but set her hands in her lap and force back the lump in her throat. Except for being shunned as a mage, she'd never felt like an outsider before. But during the past few days, she'd felt more and more like she didn't belong. Like some higher power had made a mistake in including her with the mage community. Like she was an imposter.

Salina leaned closer to her. "You okay?" she whispered.

Huojin looked up at her, wanting to reveal everything she was feeling, but she couldn't do it here in front of everyone.

Salina's eyes suddenly widened. "Oh, you're bleeding."

Everyone stopped talking and focused on Huojin. She followed Salina's gaze to her leg, where a blossom of blood had begun to spread through the leg of her trousers. She hadn't realized she had been digging her fingers into her thigh, breaking open one of her wounds.

"Let's change your bandage before the blood dries." Salina stood. "Hopefully the bandage hasn't slipped like last time. We don't want cloth stuck to your skin."

When Salina held out a hand to her, Huojin took it and stood, not even acknowledging the pain of her open wound. She nodded to the rest of the group.

"I'm so sorry. Please continue your meal without me."

"It's no problem at all, Huojin." Mayhara set down her fork. "Do you need any help?"

"It's okay," Salina said. "We've got this. But thanks."

Huojin walked ahead of Salina, her arms wrapped around her midsection. She was so nauseous, she couldn't even look behind her to see if Salina was still there. It wasn't until she reached her room that she knew Salina was still with her.

"Sit down." Salina motioned toward the bed. "I'll get the bandages."

Huojin wiped at her cheek, catching a tear. She grinded her teeth, frustrated that she felt trapped in a place where nobody wanted her.

"Actually," Salina said as she studied her, "you're going to have to get out of those pants."

Huojin sniffed back more tears as she nodded, standing and unbuttoning her pants. She slipped them off and tossed them toward the wastebasket near her door. "They're ruined anyway."

Salina looked as if she wanted to say something to that, but the tightening of her lips told Huojin that Salina had changed her mind. Perhaps it was one of Salina's family recipes on how to get blood out of clothes. Normally, she would have been glad to hear Salina's advice. Normally, they would conquer such a project together, no doubt falling into a fit of hysterics over their clumsiness.

But not tonight. Tonight, more than anything, Huojin wanted to escape.

She sat far enough over the edge of the bed that Salina could unwrap her bloodied bandages. She winced at the burn of the cloth being torn from her wound but bit her tongue to keep from making any remarks.

"Sorry," Salina said. "I'll be quick. Looks like you punctured it. Probably with your nails. Why were you squeezing your leg so hard?"

Huojin looked into Salina's eyes, unwilling to tell her the truth about how she was feeling. "It was itching. I didn't realize I'd scratched at it so hard."

"It's okay." Salina gave her a half-shrug as she unrolled a fresh spool of gauze. "It happens. Do you remember when I scraped up my hand when I first started training at the academy? I couldn't stop scratching at it. Had to wear a glove to class just to keep me from messing with it."

Huojin offered her the smallest of smiles, but there wasn't enough feeling behind it. It was as if the disappointment she felt in herself kept her from enjoying anything, even the smallest of things.

"Okay." Salina stood and looked at her own hands, which were spotted with blood. "You can get dressed. I'm going to wash up."

"You should go back to dinner," Huojin told her. "Shiro went through all the trouble to cook."

"What about you?"

"I'm not actually feeling so well." She rubbed a hand across her belly. "I don't want to make it worse by introducing hot spices to the mix. But please tell Shiro I'm sorry."

"He'll understand. Don't worry." Salina picked up a stray piece of gauze from the floor and tossed it in the trash. "You going to rest, then?"

"Yeah, I'm going to lie down for a bit."

"I'll come back later. Do you need anything?"

"No need to come back. I'm probably going to sleep." Again, Huojin forced a small smile. "Enjoy your evening. I'll see you in the morning."

Salina came forward, holding her blood-stained hands out to her side, and hugged Huojin with her forearms. "I need to go wash up. Goodnight."

After Salina left, Huojin closed her door. Pressing her head against the wood, she swallowed the lump in her throat and sniffed back the tears that began to flow. She was suffering, both physically and mentally. She wasn't sure how she was going to get through this.

TWELVE

Huojin could hear the mumble of conversation and trickles of laughter from downstairs. She turned in her bed, her eyes catching the illuminated digits of the clock on her nightstand. The group had to be done with their dinner by now, but it appeared the evening of camaraderie wasn't over. Huojin thought her dose of pain medication would have helped her to fall into a deep sleep; however, it seemed to have the opposite effect tonight. Though she longed to drift away, it simply wasn't happening.

Throwing her covers off her body, Huojin slipped her legs over the side of the bed and sat up, staring at her balcony doors. Maybe some fresh air would do the trick. Darshana always said that the surroundings of nature helped, and there was no better view of the mountaintop woods than from the second floor of the temple.

A soft wind swirled around her as she opened the balcony doors and stepped outside. The tender chirp of crickets welcomed her, and the stars twinkled above her. Her eyes went to the white streak of the comet only momentarily before she tore her gaze away from it and looked down at the koi pond in the rear gardens. She didn't need another reminder of how she was failing to fulfill her duty.

The distant sound of a car horn caught her attention. If she leaned out enough and turned to the right, she could just make out the road that traversed the mountain. She watched a few cars drive by, imagining the people below going about their everyday lives, free to go wherever they wanted without the responsibility she had on her shoulders. Why were they so lucky to be free? Why did this major accountability have to be her destiny?

Her hope was gone. There was no way she could do this. Someone or something out there had made a mistake in picking her to carry out this task. It would be better if she left.

Tears ran down her cheeks. She never thought she could be this disloyal to the Lotus empress. She'd devoted her whole life to her, yet now, she didn't believe she had anything left in her to offer the empress. Nothing but failure.

Turning swiftly on her heel, she charged back into her room and grabbed her duffle bag from the closet. She couldn't stay here anymore. She had nothing to contribute to the cause. She would only be a burden to the group, and she'd lost the skills to be able to fight the Pishacha anyway. She had to leave.

She threw her things into the duffle bag and slipped on dark pants and her forest green sweatshirt. She quickly grabbed some supplies to change her bandages and a bottle of water and stuffed them in the duffle bag as well. Tying her hair back in an elastic band, she went to her door. She pressed her ear against the wood, listening. She could hear the others speaking in calm tones. They sounded as if they were in the living room. She wouldn't be able to make it past them without being spotted. She'd have to find another way out.

She remembered that there was a towering rose trellis next to Mayhara's window. She knew the wood must have been strong for an object so tall; it had to be strong enough to hold her. Throwing on her jacket, she grabbed the duffle bag and headed for the door. Luckily, the doors in the temple didn't squeak or squeal, so she was able to open it without sound. She listened again to be sure no one was coming up the stairs, and then, with stealthy footsteps, she glided toward Mayhara's room.

Though Mayhara's door was closed, Huojin was relieved to find it wasn't locked. She didn't turn on the light, thankful the moon shone brightly enough through the window for her to maneuver through the room. Mayhara kept her room impeccably clean, her bed made so neatly one would think it had never been slept in. The few items Mayhara did bring with her to the temple were organized methodically on her dresser. To Huojin, these were signs of someone who was well put together. Someone who was secure in who they were and what they were doing. Confident in what they could contribute to a worthy cause.

Biting her lip, Huojin ignored the feeling of unworthiness rising inside her and raced to the window. After sliding it open, she peered outside to check the trellis. It was secured to the wall of the temple with steel clamps.

Huojin's eyes went downward to estimate the height. If she fell, she'd surely be paralyzed. Luckily, her duffle bag had mostly clothes in it and nothing breakable. She hoisted it through the window and let it drop to the ground. Holding her breath, she listened for the impact, and then let out a sigh of relief after the *thump*. It hadn't been too loud; no one should have noticed.

Ducking her head, she shifted her body to climb through the window, reaching out her hand to grab a wooden beam of the trellis. When she felt it safe enough, she wriggled the rest of the way out and positioned herself fully on the trellis. She held back a yelp when a thorn from the rose vines pricked her arm, concentrating instead on making her way down as quickly and quietly as she could manage. Fear that Salina would go against her request and check in on her kept her moving. After a few more thorn pricks, Huojin finally made it to the ground. Without hesitation, she grabbed her duffle bag and darted for the cover of the woods.

She decided to follow the road down the mountain but kept out of sight under the cloak of the nearby trees. By the time she was halfway down, she was covered in sweat and out of breath. She paused by a tree stump and unzipped her duffle bag to retrieve her water, grateful that it hadn't been damaged when she'd dropped the bag from Mayhara's window.

After a few gulps of water and steadier breaths, Huojin continued her trek down the mountain. She wondered if anyone might have noticed she was gone. A deep, dark part of her wondered if Darshana would be glad she'd left.

Pushing away her discouraging thoughts, she picked up her pace and made it down to the main road. She knew there was a small town nearby. If she could somehow make it to a sub-train station, she'd be able to get far enough away that the other mages couldn't stop her and force her to come back.

It was a forty- minute walk to the town. The streets were relatively empty, since it was so late at night. Most of the small houses in the small town had dark windows, the people apparently turned in for the night. She followed the distant sound of a sub-train, knowing it would take her far away. She only hoped her heartache wouldn't follow her.

About twenty minutes later, she was relieved to find a sub-train station. She had no idea of where to go, but something inside her was driving her to go to the abandoned academy. No one would be there. And it used to be home to her. And maybe—just maybe—she'd find some peace.

There was no one at the station at first, just the moonlight gleaming off the tracks to hold her attention. A shadow moved, and she spotted a figure approaching the far end of the station. Her senses were on high alert, and she forced herself to steady her breathing. She checked the digital display to see it was a two-minute wait until the sub-train would arrive. The man didn't approach her. Instead, he remained at the far end, taking a seat on a bench. She told herself she was acting paranoid. No one knew she was here, and no one would think to find her in this small town. She stared at the digital display, counting down the time until the sub-train arrived.

When the sub-train pulled in, Huojin inconspicuously watched the man at the far end of the station. He stood and boarded the train without looking her way. Breathing a sigh of relief, she stepped onto the train and slumped down into one of the seats, resting her weary bones on her duffelbag.

The property appeared to have been left untouched for years. Past the cast-iron fence, the remnants of the massive academy building stood in the moonlight. The Eradication had demolished most of the building, but what was left of it stood tall and proud, like the last remaining hope in a devastating war, a soldier that refused to give up.

Huojin shuddered. She didn't feel like such a soldier. Perhaps if she went in and felt the soul of the place, it might give her a last spark of hope.

The grounds, which had once been meticulously manicured and blossoming with life, were now scattered with rubble and weeds. A hare stood on its hind legs to watch her approach the main entrance before it scurried off into the darkness of a nearby field.

Her breaths were steady as she got closer to the school that had once been her home. She used to be proud, walking the halls of the palace, strutting onto the battlefield, receiving honors as one of the top golden mages in her house. But she felt none of that now. She pushed open the dilapidated doors of the front entrance and took a step inside.

"Lakshmi," she prayed with a whisper, "I'm lost."

She took deliberate steps, one foot in front of the other, hoping inspiration and faith would come to her. The tiles at her feet were destroyed and covered in dust, much resembling the feeling in her heart. Tears hung on her lashes as her heart ached.

"Lakshmi. Please."

She stopped in the middle of the foyer, closing her eyes and waiting. Perhaps her goddess would send her a sign, an answer. Huojin pressed her lips tightly together as her tears flowed freely over her cheeks. She could barely hold back the shudder of her shoulders as sobs threatened to crumple her to the ground.

A metallic *clink* sounded from somewhere behind her.

Her eyes shot wide open, and she stopped breathing so she could listen. Turning slowly and squinting against the darkness, she scanned the area, searching for the source of the sound. Had the hare from the field followed her inside? Perhaps it had knocked over a bit of tile in its travels?

She wanted to speak out, to ask who might be there. But what purpose would that serve? Unless it was one of the mages or Darshana, whoever might be there, whoever might have tracked her to this spot, could only serve as a danger.

Her heart pounded in her chest. A dark figure moved into a beam of moonlight. The figure moved slowly, carefully.

Huojin dropped her duffle bag and closed her hands into fists. She could barely feel the surge of golden energy in her palms. It was weak, but it was there.

"Ah," the figure said, moving closer into view. "So you're the golden elite."

Huojin gasped and looked down at her hands. The faint golden glow could be seen through her clenched fingers.

"Who are you?" she asked. "What do you want?"

"I see I have you at a disadvantage, me knowing who you are, but you not knowing who I am." The young man took three more steps until moonlight surrounded him. "We met before. But I can understand if you don't remember me. There was a lot going on at the time."

Huojin studied his face, her heart racing. He looked familiar, but she couldn't place him. When he shifted to adjust his fingerless, black leather gloves, she realized where she'd seen him.

"You're one of the dark mages."

Though tall and built of lean muscle, his face was almost boyish, with thick lips and a narrow chin. His eyes were half-concealed by this mane of dark brown hair, which stuck out from his head in one direction, as if it had been blown by a strong wind and frozen in place. He wore a black jacket with fur lining the collar, and the ends of his sleeves were a bright red that covered the wrists of his gloves.

Huojin held her chin up. "You shouldn't be here."

"You underestimate me. But that's because you don't know me. So let me introduce myself. My name is Avi. Avi Laghari. Perhaps you've heard of my father, Governor Laghari?"

Huojin's jaw dropped slightly. "You're the governor's son? And a dark mage?"

"It's typical, don't you think? With great power, blah blah blah."

Avi took another step toward her. She immediately fell into a defensive stance.

"Stay where you are." The faint glow remained in her palms as she held them up.

He let out a chuckle. "Or what? I can see you're injured. Your glow is weak. And you've been crying."

"You can go to hell. I'll fight you if I need to."

"You don't understand." Avi shifted his stance, as if ready to attack. "There's no hope for you. Kashmeru is bringing those faithful to him to the promised land. The rest of you are doomed. So you might as well give up now."

"Over my dead body."

He smirked. "Thanks for the invitation."

She felt the heat before anything else. But it wasn't fire that came at her. Not flames like she could produce. It was as if a wave of hot electricity coursed through the air at her. She could see the plumes of energy distorting the air, and then the pain hit her. She let out a cry as her body was pushed backward. Her palms glowed golden, and she found her bearings.

With a guttural shout, she pushed out her fire energy at him. Streams of golden flames shot toward him, the most she'd been able to generate since suffering her injuries.

The scowl on his face was illuminated by her fire. Avi shifted his arms dramatically, extending one above his head and the other out at his side. He then brought his hands together hard in a loud clap. The energy in the air shifted again, the waves catching Huojin's fire and ricocheting the flames back toward her.

With a gasp, she jumped to the side and tucked into a roll that brought her into a crouch.

"It doesn't have to be this way," Avi said, lowering his arms. "Join us and live forever. Pledge your fealty to Kashmeru and be saved."

"Never!"

Avi tilted his head and chuckled again. "Wrong answer, sweetie."

His arms shot out and whirled in a circular motion. Huojin jumped to her feet and pushed out her arms, palms facing him. But the glow in her hands faded as an explosion of distorted energy rippled through the air, buzzing around her until finally the ripple hit her, crushing her bones and ripping the life out of her.

THIRTEEN

Salina's heart was in her throat as she ran from Huojin's empty room to the office where Jae and Mayhara were working. For a second, she was afraid to speak. Afraid of what it might mean.

"Salina?" Jae asked when he looked up from the computer.

"Have you guys seen Huojin?" Salina wrung her hands.

Jae shook his head. "I haven't seen her all morning."

A wrinkle formed on Mayhara's forehead. "She's not in her room?"

"No. And her duffle bag is gone."

"She ran away?" Mayhara stood so fast, her chair skidded away behind her. "Why? Why would she abandon us?"

Salina raked a hand through her curls, her brows drawn together. "I think she was feeling the pressure. I think it was getting to her. We've got to find her!"

Shiro suddenly appeared behind Salina. The color had been drawn from his face.

"Wait, guys," he said. "I know where she is. Come see."

They all followed as he led them to the living room, where the news program had been paused on the televiewer. Darshana and Mr. Kitaro were on the couch, waiting for them. Shiro clicked a button on the remote, and the news program rewound by thirty seconds.

"—last night, where fans of the traditional festival performance were astonished at what appeared on stage. Warning: the images we're about to show you could be too graphic for sensitive viewers."

On the screen, a video clip was shown of a small, outdoor stage at the Navratri festival. As the curtains opened, a form crumpled on the floor, center stage, was revealed. The crowd gasped and began to murmur, some of them fleeing the area in a panic. As the footage continued, the newscaster went on.

"… because the victim suffered multiple broken bones all over her body, officials believe that foul play was the cause of death. Authorities have since removed the body and taken it to the city's coroner's office for examination. Initial fingerprints have revealed that the victim to be Huojin Adachi, who has recently been reported missing by her employer at Fukuhara Systems, Incorporated. One of Miss Adachi's co-workers, who happened to be attending the festival and was close to the victim, stepped forward to speak to the Imperial Police and has speculated the victim's death to be linked to a jealous boyfriend…"

The corner of the screen displayed Huojin's picture. Salina's hands flew to her mouth, her eyes wide and filling with tears.

"No," Mayhara said, her voice barely audible. "No, it can't be."

"This wasn't some jealous boyfriend," Jae said. "It was the Pishacha."

Shiro rubbed at his jaw. "They left her body in a public place to send a message."

"Sick, pathetic animals," Mr. Kitaro said with clenched teeth.

"No." Salina shook her head, tears flowing down her cheeks. "No. I… I don't believe it. How could she be—? No. How did this happen?"

Mayhara went to her and enveloped her in her arms, stroking Salina's hair as she sobbed. "I'm so sorry."

Salina backed away from her, her eyes wide. "We've got to go get her."

Mayhara blanched. "What?"

"Her… body. Her corpse." Salina bit her lip. "We can't just leave her for the government to do who-knows-what to. We've got to take it from the coroner's office."

"That's a bad idea," Darshana said, not meeting anyone's gaze.

"What?" Salina scoffed.

Darshana raised her chin, her lips in a frown. "They'll be expecting that."

"She's right." Jae crossed his arms and squeezed at his chin. "That's why they left her in a public place. They knew it would make the media channels and we'd find out. They're betting on us wanting to get to her body. It's a trap."

"Jae." Salina's voice cracked. "We have to."

"It's a trap, Salina," Darshana reiterated.

"I don't care. We owe it to her." Salina straightened her shoulders. "We need to find a way. We can't leave her body in their hands." She turned to Shiro, locking gazes with him. "Please. She was my best friend."

Shiro clenched his jaw, studying Salina's face. His eyes then went to Jae, who searched the faces of the rest of the group. Darshana let out a sigh and dropped her head.

"All right." Jae placed a hand on Salina's shoulder. "Of course. We'll do whatever we can."

Salina nodded, wiping her tears away. "Thank you."

Jae and Shiro sprinted ahead through the confetti-covered streets, well ahead of Salina and Mayhara. Darshana followed somewhere behind. Mayhara had to trust that the guru would keep up. The coroner's office was located two blocks away from the main street where the festival was taking place. It was still early in the day, and the streets weren't full yet. But between the handful of patrons, stand workers, and performers practicing for their shows, there was enough of a cover to keep the focus off the mages' mission.

Jae almost stumbled as he threw his back against the wall of a building. He signaled for the others to keep out of sight. As Mayhara caught up, she spotted the two Imperial Police officers making their rounds near the building housing the coroner's office.

Pushing a sweet-bun cart, an elderly man strolled along, most likely hoping for some early sales. His bright orange umbrella was big enough to create some cover, so the group headed toward him.

"Easy now," Shiro whispered. "Don't draw attention."

The elderly man stopped as they approached, displaying a friendly smile, despite the fact that he was missing some teeth. "Fancy some sweet buns?" he asked. "Buy two, get one free!"

"Sure." Jae pulled out his Linq and showed the screen to the vendor. "We'll take three."

The vendor used his scanning device to receive Jae's payment, all the while oblivious to the fact that Shiro and Salina were scanning the street for more police. Darshana's eyes darted back and forth as she accepted the bag of sweet buns.

"It looks clear," Salina said. "We should go in now."

A loud bang sounded in the air, causing everyone to turn their attention toward the main street. When a pink puff of smoke billowed up from a group of partygoers, Mayhara's shoulders relaxed.

"Just some kids goofing around," Shiro said.

"Okay, let's—" Salina froze, her words gone.

Mayhara turned to see three Pishacha standing in front of the coroner's office. Their eyes were like black coals above their mouth masks, glaring at the mages.

"Shit," Jae mumbled. "We've got to get out of here."

"No." Salina shook Mayhara's hand off her arm. "We can fight them. We need to get in there and get Huojin."

"We'll draw the attention of the police," Darshana said. "And there are far too many officials here. We'll all be arrested on the spot."

"Darshana's right." Jae put his hands together, pleading with her. "Even if we got through the Pishacha and the first pair of police, there'll just be more following. This place is crawling with them."

The three Pishacha began marching their way.

"Come on." Mayhara put her arm around Salina. "We've got to go."

"We can't leave her!" Salina cried.

"We have no choice," Darshana said. "I'm sorry."

"No. This isn't right."

The Pishacha picked up their pace.

Shiro grabbed Salina's arm. "Let's go!"

As they began to run, Mayhara's palms and bracelet glowed a crimson red. She only glanced behind her for a second, pushing her palm in the direction of the Pishacha. The pavement beneath the Pishacha shifted with such force, a huge block of earth rammed through the street, blocking their path.

"Go!" Jae yelled.

The five of them charged back toward the alley they'd used to get to the street. Jae checked over his shoulder to make sure they'd all kept up. Mayhara grabbed the guru's arm and pulled her along so she wouldn't get left behind. When they reached the main street, they swerved around an enormous fountain that decorated the town square. As the Pishacha emerged from the alley, Shiro threw out copper energy, not halting his stride as he did so. The fountain burst, hard streams of water shooting out in every direction and knocking the Pishacha down.

"Go, go, go," Mayhara urged, knowing their car was just a street away.

They slipped through another alley, and this time Mayhara used her power to rattle the earth behind them. The buildings lining the alley shifted, bricks and stones getting knocked out of place, crumbling down into the alley into a huge mountain of debris.

Jae was the first to reach the car. The five of them were heaving breaths and quick limbs as they clambered into the car and took off.

No one spoke for a good fifteen minutes. They were already on the main highway when Salina began to cry.

"Salina." Mayhara put a hand on her arm.

"I've failed her," Salina said.

No one said anything. As they continued to drive toward the temple, Mayhara felt as if they had all failed Huojin. They'd failed her the moment she'd decided to leave the temple in the first place. If only she had noticed how desperate Huojin had been, if only she could have spoken with her and reassured her that they were on her side, maybe she wouldn't have felt the need to run away.

By the time they got back to the temple, everyone's spirits were low. Salina had stopped crying, but everything about her stance and expression told Mayhara there was a storm brewing underneath. When they got inside, Mayhara caught up with her, squeezing her shoulder.

"Salina, Huojin would never blame you."

Salina shook her head. "I don't know what to think anymore."

Darshana, who appeared behind her, folded her hands together. "It's best to not dwell on it, as nothing can change what's happened. What we need now is to get you ready."

Salina blinked, her brow creased. "Get me ready for what?"

"You are now the elite golden mage," Darshana said.

Salina turned to Mayhara.

"She's right," Mayhara said. "You're next in line."

Salina's mouth opened as if to speak, but she could only shake her head.

"We are all mourning the loss of Huojin," Darshana said gently. "But we cannot lose sight of the fact we have a universe to save. This is our life's mission, and we must adhere to our cause."

Salina stared at Darshana for a moment, and then she turned and grabbed at her own chest. Bent over slightly, she dragged in ragged breaths.

Mayhara rushed to her. "Are you all right?"

"No." Salina shook her head and rubbed at her throat. "My heart hurts. I can't breathe. It's as if the temple is falling in on me."

"Try to relax your thoughts," Darshana urged.

"*Relax my thoughts?*" Salina stood up straight and pointed a finger at her. "This is all your fault, you know. You pushed her too hard. You wouldn't let her stop forgetting that she wasn't living up to your expectations."

"They are not my expectations," Darshana said sternly. "It was her responsibility as part of the empire."

"But we're still people with feelings." Salina's fists tightened. "I think you've mistaken us for robots."

Darshana bowed her head and pressed her lips together. "Perhaps you're right. Perhaps I did push her too hard. All of you. I, too, am feeling the pressure of this great responsibility. I didn't mean for this to happen."

"Well, it's too late to be thinking about how your words and actions can affect someone now." Salina's voice cracked. "She's gone."

The room echoed with her voice. Salina picked up a nearby vase and threw it across the room, where it shattered into a hundred pieces. With a frustrated grunt, Salina turned on her heel and stomped out of the room.

Mayhara glanced at Darshana, who was still staring at the ground. "Don't worry. It's grief that's driving her right now. I'll talk to her, but she's going to need some time."

"I want to say I understand," Darshana said. "But time is one thing we don't have a lot of."

FOURTEEN

aree blinked. She couldn't remember how she got to where she was standing. The water in the sink splashed as it flowed from the faucet, and her hands were covered in blood.

Another death.

Lakshmi, the pure goddess of light whose soul was her own, was crying out inside of her.

What have I done? This is wrong.

Naree glanced at the mirror. Tears stained her cheeks. Every death was adding up and weighing her down. It was as if she could feel each of the victim's souls pass through her as they died. She felt their pain, their agony. Inside her, Lakshmi was weeping as well.

My love, Kashmeru spoke. *Do not give up on me. We're so close.*

Her breath shuddered as she washed the blood off her hands. She nodded as she held back a whimper.

Are you still with me, my love?

She pressed her lips together and then forced a small smile. She nodded again, her head spinning. "Yes. Yes, I'm with you."

FIFTEEN

Jae stared at the screen of his Linq, a wrinkle etched in his brow. It took him a second to realize who was calling him. He walked to his window and glanced up at the night sky as he held the Linq to his ear.

"Yes?"

"Hello. This is Nian from the scroll shop. You asked me to contact you about the content of a scroll."

"Nian, yes, of course."

The line was quiet for a moment, and Jae wondered if they'd been disconnected.

"We heard about the body left in the city square," Nian said. "I assume it was a… friend of yours. An elite mage."

Jae stiffened. "That's none of your concern."

"We think it is. It tells us what could happen to those in your circle. And by us helping you, we might be considered part of that circle."

The mark in the sky noting the comet's position caught Jae's eye. "Did you call to tell me that you no longer wish to help?"

"No. We have some information on what the other scroll is. We have contacted our great-aunt. She says she might know of the map that's on it."

"We can't be sure it's a map. We've studied it and can't match a location."

"Think on a smaller scale," Nian said. "We think this is a more specific map. Of a place somewhere hidden. Perhaps underground."

"How can we be sure?"

"Bring the scroll in. Next week, Wednesday. Our great-aunt will be in town then and can take a look at it."

Jae rubbed at his chin. "I don't know if we have that much time."

"That's all I can offer you."

"Fine. We'll be there."

Jae marked the date of the meeting in his Linq and slipped the device back into his pocket. He thought about waiting until the morning to tell

Mayhara, but part of him was glad he had a reason to see her again before he turned in for the night.

Running a hand through his hair, he headed out of his room and down the hall. He straightened his shirt before knocking on her door.

✿

Mayhara opened her door, surprised to see Jae standing there. She might have been imagining it, but she could have sworn there was a reddish tint to his cheeks.

"Hey," he said. "Did I interrupt you?"

She followed his glance to the Linq in her hand. "Oh. No, sorry. I was checking for more news."

"Find anything?"

"No. Just the usual." She walked over to her dresser and placed her Linq on it. "What's up?"

"I just got a call from Nian about the scroll. He said they have a great-aunt who might be able to tell us what it is."

"That's great."

"He wants me to come by next week so she can take a look at it. I thought you'd like to come."

"Yeah, Count me in."

"Great." He tapped his fingertips against the doorframe as he studied her face. "Hey, are you all right?"

"Yeah. I think I'm still processing it all. This whole thing with Huojin got me thinking about my family."

"Darshana said she got them transferred under a different name. They won't connect them with you. They should be safe."

"For now."

"We'll get them out."

"You can't promise me that." She shook her head and sighed. "I wouldn't ask it of you."

He took two steps into her room and held out his hand. "Come here," he said softly.

Though she was taken aback by his request, she reached out and took his hand. He pulled her closer and wrapped his arms around her. She didn't question his intentions, but instead let herself take comfort in his warm embrace.

"We'll be okay," he whispered. "We're in this together, remember?"

She pressed her head against his chest. "Yes. I remember."

He kissed the top of her head. Goosebumps sprung to life all over her body.

"Goodnight, Mayha," he said, using the shortened version of her name she'd only ever heard from her parents.

"Goodnight."

He backed away slowly, his eyes still on her as he gently released her. She smiled, but her vulnerability caused her to wrap her arms around herself. With a nod, Jae turned and disappeared out her door.

As his footfalls dissipated, Mayhara closed her bedroom door and pressed her back against it. Without thinking, she touched the spot on the top of her head where Jae had kissed her. The hint of a smile formed on her lips as she brought her fingers to her mouth. She suddenly felt hot, as if someone had turned up the heat in her room to full blast. She blew out a breath and headed for her window. Maybe she just needed some air.

When she slid her window open, she spotted movement in the trees nearby.

Salina?

Mayhara leaned out to get a better look, but Salina—if that was who it was—sprinted too quickly through the trees. Without hesitation, Mayhara grabbed her Linq, darted out of her room, and hurried down the stairs, thankful she hadn't yet taken off her shoes. Everyone must have been in their rooms, because she didn't spot anyone downstairs. Her heart began to race as she ran outside and in the direction she'd seen Salina go. She wasn't sure what she was up to, but she guessed it had something to do with Huojin. Would she really be venturing out to retrieve her body? What was her plan, exactly? Even if she took the train, how would she bring Huojin's body back to the temple? Besides, it was too dangerous for one mage to go wandering off alone in the middle of the night. And with Salina's fragile emotional state, Mayhara had even more reason to worry.

Mayhara used her mage powers of stability to keep her balance as she maneuvered through the trees and underbrush, chasing Salina. She could feel Salina's footsteps through her connection with the earth, making it easier for her to catch up.

"Salina!" she called when she caught sight of her.

Salina's shoulders tensed as she skidded to a stop. Her golden-highlighted curls swung around her head as she turned to face Mayhara. There was a wild look in her eyes that gave Mayhara pause.

"Where are you going?" Mayhara asked between bated breaths.

Salina stared at Mayhara, inhaling and exhaling so hard it moved her entire body. "If Darshana's not going to take responsibility for Huojin's body, I'm not going to sit back and do nothing."

"Salina, it's too dangerous. Huojin wouldn't have wanted you to put yourself in danger."

"You didn't know her like I did. Nobody did. She wouldn't have wanted to be abandoned like this. I can't just leave her there and forget about it."

"No one's asking you to forget." Mayhara stepped closer. "We just can't risk any more lives."

"Don't you get it? She's worth the risk. Nothing you say will change my mind. I owe this to her."

Mayhara held her hands up, signaling that she wasn't going to argue with her. "Okay. Okay. Then… at least let me go with you. Let me help you get her body. I can't let you do this alone."

Salina took a long, deep breath in through her nose and blew it out her mouth, her eyes studying Mayhara.

"Fine. But I'm not waiting. I've got to hurry to the next sub-train station. We need to move now before they dispose of her body disrespectfully."

"Okay. But how about we drive? Or did you have another plan on how we're going to bring Huojin back here?"

Forty-five minutes later, Mayhara parked the car near the city center. She didn't think it was the best idea to be out near the festival again, but she didn't know any other way to make sure Salina didn't suffer the same fate as Huojin.

The square was much more crowded now than it had been when they'd been there earlier. People attending the festival were dressed in traditional garb, the red, yellow, green, black, and blue of their *Ghagra choli* and *kurta* clothes reflected in the street decoration. Loud music played as festival performers showcased traditional dances. Judging by the jovial looks on everyone's faces, one would never suspect the end the world might be nearing.

Salina rushed from the car and began zigzagging through the crowd.

"Salina, wait!" Mayhara had to push through patrons to catch up with her.

She wasn't sure Salina had even heard her, for Salina didn't stop, didn't hesitate. She carried on as if she were drawn to the coroner's office by a powerful magnet. There were too many people getting in Mayhara's way. She knew better not to use her powers where there were so many witnesses, but she had to stop Salina before something bad happened. Discreetly pulling up her powers, she quickly aimed energy at Salina to throw her off-balance. Because it was tight quarters, a handful of patrons near Salina also lost their footing. To anyone else, it would have appeared as if the lot of them had accidentally bumped into each other and stumbled. But Salina knew the cause of the disturbance. As she found her bearings, she glanced back at Mayhara with a squared jaw. Mayhara quickly closed the distance between them and put a hand on her elbow.

"I said we'd do this together," Mayhara said. "Please trust me."

Salina raised a brow. "You didn't have to trip me."

"Apparently, I did."

Salina bit her cheek. "Okay, fine. Let's go."

"What is your plan, exactly?" Mayhara walked beside Salina, trying to keep up with her pace. "How are we going to get in?"

"I'm going to set off the fire alarm. Someone's bound to open the door once that goes off."

"And draw attention from the police and fire brigade? I don't think that's going to work."

Salina pursed her lips. "Fine. Plan B. I'll short-circuit the lock pad. My brother showed me how to do it once."

"Once? Have you ever done it yourself?"

Salina gave her a sideways glance. "There's a first time for everything."

Mayhara looked around, scanning the crowd for Imperial Police or

Pishacha. Festivalgoers danced through the square, the choreography extremely enthusiastic and energetic. Everyone was caught up in the fun. No one paid Mayhara or Salina any attention.

There was still no sign of Imperial Police or the Pishacha when they reached the door of the coroner's office. From what Mayhara could see through the narrow windows flanking the door, the lights were off inside the building. She was relieved by the thought that the office was closed for the day, but she wasn't about to release the breath she was holding quite yet. There were still too many eyes around, and some of them could have been watching them from the shadows.

Salina set her hand on the lock pad. Her palm emitted a golden glow.

"What are you doing?" Mayhara shifted her position to block the view of the lock pad from passersby.

"I'm overheating the circuits." Salina's glow grew brighter. "This will cause the system to crash and shut down temporarily. It will take three seconds for the emergency power generator to reboot the system, so that means—"

The red light of the lock pad went out as a beep sounded. Salina grabbed Mayhara's arm with one hand and pushed the door open with the other.

"Three. Two."

The door closing behind them took the place of Salina's count of *one*.

"Where, exactly, did your brother learn that?" Mayhara whispered.

"Let's just concentrate on one crime at a time, okay?"

As Mayhara's eyes widened, Salina let out a small laugh. Though Mayhara was still curious about Salina's hotwiring, she was somewhat comforted to see her smile again.

"I'm kidding." Salina urged Mayhara forward, behind the main desk, and toward the door marked *Examiner*. "He's studying electronics at university."

They both stopped in front of the beveled-glass window of the door, and Salina's mouth turned down into a frown.

"Do you think…" Salina let out a trembling breath. "She's in there?"

"We've come all this way." Mayhara placed a hand on Salina's shoulder and gave her a gentle squeeze. "Let's find out."

hey used the glow of their palms to light the way. The door creaked as they opened it. Mayhara was hit with the smell of formaldehyde, causing her to flinch and blink rapidly.

Salina extended her arms, holding them high to illuminate a greater area of the room. Two bare, metal examination tables stood four feet apart from each other in the center of the room. One wall of the room was lined, floor to ceiling, with dull, metal cabinets, each displaying a row of labeled square doors.

Salina went to the cabinets and leaned closer, reading the labels. Mayhara stood beside her, searching for Huojin's name.

"There," Mayhara said. Stunned to actually see Huojin's name on the door, she couldn't find the strength to point.

Salina followed her gaze, her breath hitching when she spotted her friend's name. Her shaking hand reached for the electronic button next to the label. Her finger hovered there for what seemed like an eternity. With a visible swallow, she pushed the button.

A beep sounded, and the drawer slid out. White, frosty mist escaped from within the drawer, dancing above a pristine white sheet covering a form below it.

Salina chewed at her cheek, hesitating before reaching for a corner of the sheet. A freezing chill traveled along Mayhara's skin as Salina slowly peeled the cover back to reveal Huojin's blueish face. Salina's knees gave out, and she grabbed on to Mayhara for support. Mayhara had to close her eyes and muster her strength to keep from falling herself.

She was really dead. It wasn't a trick. Though Huojin's skin was blue and her features seemed to have sunken in a bit, Mayhara knew it was her corpse, kept frozen in a mortuary cabinet until her autopsy could be completed.

"Do you think they've done anything with her yet?" Salina asked, her voice a soft whisper. "She doesn't look cut into or anything."

Mayhara shook her head. "I don't know."

"If the Pishacha are involved, maybe they haven't planned on examining her at all. They already know what killed her."

"Probably. They might be keeping her here just to cover—"

A click sounded from outside the room. A muffled voice could be heard on a radio transmitter.

"The police!" Mayhara quickly pushed the button on the drawer door. As Huojin's body slid back into the cabinet, Mayhara grabbed Salina's hand. "We've got to go."

"But—"

"We're going to end up in the drawers next to her if we don't get out of here. Come on!"

They raced to the back of the room to another door. Mayhara hoped it led to a way out instead of just a closet or storage area. They needed to find a way out of the building without getting caught.

The door opened to darkness, but when Mayhara pushed out crimson energy into her palm, the red glow revealed a hallway in front of them.

"We must have triggered a silent alarm." Mayhara pulled Salina along, hoping the hall led to an exit.

Salina threw a spark out that traveled down the hall. Before it fizzled out, Mayhara spotted a couple of places where the corridor branched out. She had no idea of the layout of the building, but she would have to take a chance that they'd pick the right hall.

As they raced down the corridor, a loud bang sounded behind them. A thin, red beam of light shone over Salina's shoulder.

"Stop right there!"

Mayhara gathered her powers and aimed a shot at their pursuers, knocking them off-balance. The red beam shifted upward and disappeared from their sight. Mayhara picked up her pace, but her grasp on Salina slipped as they reached the first turnoff in the corridor. Mayhara practically dived to the right, grateful when she spotted the exit sign at the end of the corridor.

But when she glanced beside her, Salina wasn't there. Mayhara skidded to a stop and swirled around, frantically searching for her friend. A glowing blast of fire caused her to shield her eyes. As she backed up, trying to adjust to the change of light, she caught sight of an Imperial Police officer swinging a baton across the back of Salina's head. She crumpled to the ground. Mayhara slapped a hand over her mouth to keep from screaming and backed up against the wall behind a stack of boxes.

The beam from a tactical streamlight shown down the hall. Mayhara backed up even more and held her breath. Her heart was beating so hard, she thought the police would hear it for sure. When the light disappeared, she listened.

"Is someone else there?" one of the officers asked. "I thought there were two."

"Are you sure, Rico? I only saw one."

"Could have been her shadow," Rico said. "Okay, let's get her upstairs and contact Bhutano. Find out what he wants done with her."

Mayhara heard more footsteps and muffled voices. Backup had arrived, which meant the police had been informed. She wasn't sure she could take on all of them, and chances were that more officers would arrive. She couldn't make a move. Not yet.

She pressed herself hard against the wall until the voices and shuffling of feet disappeared. Her heartbeat pounding in her throat made it hard for her to breathe properly. When it was finally quiet, she whipped out her Linq and pressed Jae's contact button.

"Mayhara?"

She was relieved to hear his voice. "Jae. They have Salina."

"Wha—Where are you?"

"At the coroner's office."

"What? Why? Didn't we just agree how dangerous that is?"

"Jae, there's no time to argue. The police took her. But they said they're bringing her upstairs and contacting Bhutano. They're not arresting her. If I can find her before—"

"No! No, don't move. Are you hidden?"

"Not for long." Mayhara peered down the dark hallway. "I'm sure this place will be flooded with police and Pishacha soon."

"Get out and find a place to hide. Shiro and I are on the way. Wait for us. You can't take them on alone."

Mayhara didn't answer. Could she really wait for Jae and Shiro? What if Bhutano showed up before they got there? If there was a chance to somehow save Salina, get her out of wherever they were holding her, she didn't think she could wait.

"Mayhara!"

"Right," she said, not wanting him to argue with him. "Hurry."

She pressed the END CALL button and tucked her Linq away, sinking to the floor as she tried to control her heavy breaths.

The silence of the hall pressed in on her. She turned her head toward the exit sign. She could easily break out of the building and find a place to hide and wait for Jae and Shiro. But was that the right thing to do?

Mayhara stood and clenched her fists. Time was not on their side. It would take Jae and Shiro at least half an hour to get to them, even on his impeccably fast motorcycle. By then, who knew what might have happened to Salina. They'd already lost one friend. They couldn't bear to lose another.

Mayhara stretched out her neck and shoulders, preparing herself. She'd do what she could to avoid being spotted, but she had to be ready, just in case.

She hadn't spotted any stairs on her way into the building, but maybe there was an elevator entrance she'd passed without noticing. Retracing her steps, she continued down the corridor toward the coroner's office. The rooms she passed seemed to be laboratories and other offices. Between two of the doors, a fire extinguisher was mounted on the wall, and beside it, a fire escape plan. According to the plan, she wasn't too far away from the elevators. But being trapped in one and cornered by the police or the Pishacha was not going to be beneficial when it came to finding Salina. Instead, Mayhara opted for the stairs.

The first two upper floors led to more labs and offices and one giant computer room. When she arrived at the fourth floor, the hallway was lit up. Mayhara backed up from the stairwell door and listened for movement or voices. The doors on this floor were closed, and the hall appeared empty.

"Here goes nothing," she whispered to herself as she eased out into the hall.

Stealthily moving from room to room, she found a filing room among some offices. As she continued down the hall, she came upon a wall of windows. A giant oval-shaped conference table took up the majority of the floor space. She was about to breeze past the room until she spotted a 3D image of the Akutake comet up on a viewing screen. She glanced around at the rest of the freeze frame, noting the star-filled sky at the top of the image. At the bottom of the screen was an illustration of what appeared to be a tunnel leading down into a cavern. The entire image mesmerized her. She immediately pushed open the door and entered the conference room, searching for the projector that shone the image onto the screen. Up near the ceiling, the beamer was mounted on a shelf, but the wires connected to it went behind the wall. She didn't see a computer anywhere, but there was a remote at one end of the table.

Checking over her shoulder to make sure no one was in the hall, she rushed over to the remote and pushed the *play* button. The video began to play, but there was no sound. She concluded that someone had turned the speakers off when they'd left the room but hadn't bothered to turn off the computer or the beamer. She couldn't understand what she was watching, so she hit the *rewind* button and played the clip from the beginning.

There were no words on the screen explaining anything, so she had to pay attention to try to figure out what the clip was about. The 3D animation showed the comet coursing through the sky over what appeared to be the horizon of the Earth. At one point, the horizon highlighted the tunnel that led to some kind of cavern. The video image then displayed lines that must have represented vibrations from the comet growing and reaching the cavern.

Mayhara stopped the video and played it again. She couldn't figure out where this cavern might have been or what the significance of the vibrations reaching it meant. Her head spun with confusion, and she knew she had to continue searching for Salina, so she took out her Linq and played the video again, this time capturing the whole thing with her camera.

She slipped out of the room and looked up and down the hall again. There was still no sign of any police or Pishacha, but she knew the clock was ticking. After checking a few more rooms and finding nothing, she began to lose hope. She was about to give up when she came upon a locked door. All the other doors had been unlocked, which made Mayhara suspect this one had something to hide. Hopefully, it would be Salina.

She pressed her ear against the door but didn't hear anything or anyone inside. Pulling on her mage powers, she felt through the floor, her connection to the gravel in the concrete allowing her to sense if anyone might be behind the door. She could sense the weight of something or someone in the corner of the room, but she couldn't be sure if it was even a person, let alone Salina.

She desperately wanted to knock and call out to her friend, but if it wasn't her, if it was someone else, or if what she felt was an object, like a couch that weighed as much as a person, and someone heard her, she'd be caught for sure.

Her Linq vibrated. She slipped it out to check the screen, but just as she caught a glimpse of Jae's message to sit tight, the elevator down the hall dinged. Mayhara swiftly put her phone away and took a defensive stance. She tried to ignore the weak feeling in her legs and the sensation of suffocation. She couldn't afford to be afraid.

The three police officers who emerged from the elevator charged at her, one of them pulling a gun. Mayhara ignored their protests and shouting, shooting crimson energy balls at them. One guard was knocked back by the energy ball, his head cracking as it impacted with the wall. The guard with the gun shot at Mayhara, but she quickly formed a crimson shield that blocked the bullet, propelling it off to the side. Mayhara used her stability powers to throw off the remaining guards' balance, but one of them was charging at her so fast that even with the shift of balance, he managed to careen into her, knocking her back onto the floor. By the time she got her wits about her, the other guard had approached and drawn his cyber baton. Its head buzzed as the guard held it near her ear.

"Move and I tear this through your face," he said.

Mayhara's heavy breathing and the buzz of the cyber baton was all that could be heard for a good minute. The guard who'd shot at her grabbed her by the arm and pulled her to her feet.

"Throw her in with the other one," he said. "Looks like Bhutano gets two instead of one."

Her arm was pinched in the guard's grasp. The other kept the cyber baton dangerously near her head. She had no choice; she had to do as they said. The only silver lining was that they would take her directly to Salina.

They dragged her to a room at the end of the hall. Mayhara kept an eye on the lock pad as the guard punched the code in, dropping her gaze when he checked her face.

"Secure her like the other," he said once they'd gotten into the room. "We don't want her escaping."

Pain erupted in her wrist bones as electro-cuffs were secured around her wrists behind her back. The other guard pushed her into a chair and tied a black rope he'd unhooked from his belt loop around Mayhara's midsection. He sneered at her as they backed away and out of the room.

As soon as the door closed, Mayhara scanned the room. It appeared to be some kind of informal meeting room, with two short couches facing each other and the chair Mayhara was tied to next to a small table. Just past one of the couches, Mayhara spotted feet.

"Salina!"

Salina's body sagged against the floor. She was tied with the same rope as Mayhara, but to the leg of a small end table. Mayhara bounced in the chair, moving it enough to get a better look at her. Salina's head was bent at a strange angle against the end table. Mayhara could only hope she was still alive.

"Salina! Salina! Wake up!" Mayhara reached out with her powers and made the floor below Salina quake.

A moan escaped Salina's lips as she slowly sat up. Mayhara released a quick breath of relief. She was alive. Her wrists were also locked in electro-cuffs. She looked up at Mayhara, and then her eyes widened.

Thank the gods!

Salina shifted, trying to look behind her. "What happened?"

"They hit you from behind. They're working with the Pishacha. Bhutano is on his way. We've got to get out of here."

Salina looked down at the black rope around her chest. Narrowing her eyes, she glared at the rope. A thin trail of fire energy emerged, traveling from behind her where her hands were trapped. Salina guided the fire trail to the rope. Gold cinders burned through the rope and smoke wafted up into Salina's face. Salina guided the fire trail to the rope. Gold cinders burned through the rope and smoke wafted up into Salina's face. As soon as the ropes fell away, she stretched, wriggling to her feet with her wrists still cuffed behind her. She hurried to Mayhara's side.

"I'm going to burn your rope. It's better if I'm touching them, which means I have to turn around and do it behind my back. Let me know if I get too close. I don't want to burn you."

"Okay." Mayhara moved her head back just in case.

Salina's fingers felt the rope, and her palm emitted a golden glow.

"Jae and Shiro are on the way," Mayhara said as the rope began to burn. She tried not to think about how close Salina's fire was coming to her body. "And I know the keycode. But we're both stuck in these electro-cuffs."

Salina looked toward the door as Mayhara's ropes fell away. "Even if we managed to get the door open, we'd be at a disadvantage out there in these cuffs."

Mayhara shrugged, her shoulders slumping. "I'm sorry."

Salina backed onto the arm of the couch. "It should be me apologizing. I'm the one who got us into this. And I couldn't even save Huojin's body."

They were quiet for a moment, reflecting on their situation.

"If only I had known how she was feeling," Mayhara began. "I didn't realize she felt like running away."

"I think it was more than that. I knew she was feeling the pressure," Salina said. "But I didn't know how much she was suffering."

"She would forgive you, you know?"

"I guess I need to step up now," Salina said with a nod. "I'm the golden elite. Going forward and playing my part to win this war is what I have to concentrate on now."

Footfalls sounded in the hall. Salina and Mayhara jumped to their feet. Though their hands were still trapped behind their backs, they took defensive stances. It would be a tricky fight, but they weren't about to give up yet.

The hall echoed with a couple of thumps and what sounded like people falling to the floor. Mayhara and Salina exchanged glances, shifting their balances in case the door opened.

"Check those rooms. I'll check these." It was Jae's voice.

Mayhara gasped and ran to the door, Salina in tow. "Jae! Shiro! We're in here!"

Mayhara kicked the door a few times to get their attention.

"We're here!" Salina added.

"Mayhara? Salina?" came Jae's voice from the other side of the door.

"Yes!" Mayhara pressed her forehead on the door. "The lock pad. The code is 468225."

She and Salina stepped back as they heard Jae punching the numbers in. With a final beep, the door clicked open. Mayhara couldn't help the smile that appeared on her face when she saw Jae standing there.

He placed his hands on Mayhara's shoulders. "Are you all right?" His eyes went from her to Salina, but his hands remained on Mayhara.

"Yeah, but we're cuffed," she said.

Behind him in the hall, Shiro bent down over a body sprawled on the floor. With a smirk, Shiro stood, producing a set of keys.

"I found something," Mayhara said as Shiro unlocked her cuffs. "Something to do with the comet and some cavern. I took a video with my Linq."

Salina shook out her hands after Shiro unlocked her.

"Okay," Jae said. "We'll have to wait until we're out of here to look at it. There's a hoard of Imperial Police downstairs. Shiro and I managed to evade them until we got up here and ran into this one." He pointed to the officer on the floor. "But we can't risk taking the elevator or the stairs down."

"Though they are a little busy with a flooding problem at the moment." Shiro gave everyone a wink. "But what about the fire escape?"

"Exactly what I was thinking," Salina said.

SEVENTEEN

Jae couldn't stop checking the rearview mirror of his motorcycle. They'd made their escape seemingly unnoticed. The cacophony and throng of the celebration had offered enough cover for them to make it down the fire escape, through the mass of partygoers, and to the safety of their vehicles unscathed and unnoticed.

Jae was glad when Shiro had offered to drive Salina in the car. She had been too distraught about Huojin to drive, and Jae needed Mayhara near him. He hadn't said so out loud, but if Shiro hadn't taken the initiative and proposed to drive Salina, Jae would have insisted. He would have found a way to keep Mayhara with him.

Jae had panicked when Mayhara had called him for help, as if the walls had been crashing in on him and his heart would thrash through his chest. Now that he'd found her, he didn't want to let her out of his sight. They were elbows-deep in the middle of a war, but as long as Mayhara's arms were wrapped around him and they weren't being followed, everything would be all right.

When they got back to the temple, Jae didn't want her to let go. As he set his kickstand down, her hands slipped off his waist, and he held back a frown. He couldn't help but stare at her as she pulled off her helmet and handed it to him.

"Thanks," she said when he took it.

"You okay?" He set both helmets on the bike.

She nodded but wrapped her arms around herself. "Shaken up. I hope Salina's all right."

"Me too." He knew he was staring, but he couldn't tear his eyes away. It was taking every ounce of willpower he had not to pull her into his arms. "Mayhara…"

She watched his face, her brows drawn together. "What is it?"

The lights of the car Shiro drove lit up the carport as it approached.

"Jae, what's wrong?" Mayhara asked.

Taking a step closer, he reached out to her. He opened his mouth but couldn't put his feelings into words. Not now. Not here. "You, uh, you've got some dirt on your face."

His eyes still locked with hers, he gently brushed her cheek with his thumb.

Her lips parted.

"Hey," Shiro called, walking over from the car with Salina. "Everyone all right?"

Mayhara cleared her throat and turned to him. "Yeah. Salina, how are you?"

Salina's gaze was trained on the ground. She gave a shrug. "I don't know. I know we had to get out of there, but it feels so disrespectful to just… leave her there."

"We tried, Salina." Mayhara held her hands. "There was nothing else we could have done."

Tears began to flow down Salina's cheeks. Mayhara let out a sympathetic whimper and pulled Salina in for hug.

"Let's go inside," Shiro said. "I can make us some tea if you'd like."

Salina nodded, backing out of Mayhara's arms and wiping her cheeks. "That sounds nice. Thanks. Maybe it will help with this headache."

"You were hit pretty hard," Mayhara said. "You probably should ice it."

"Oh, that I can definitely help with." Shiro held his palm out to Salina, and the copper glow was soon covered with a small block of ice.

For the first time that day, Salina smiled.

They'd fallen asleep in the living room, their half-drunken tea now cold on the coffee table. Darshana cleared her throat, and Mayhara opened her eyes. Her head was resting on Jae's chest. She didn't remember falling asleep in that position, but she wasn't complaining.

"What time is it?" Mayhara sat up and squinted at the sun coming in through the windows.

"Nearly noon," Darshana answered. "When did you get back?"

Jae stretched, blinking as he woke. "In the middle of the night. I guess we fell asleep."

Salina shifted, pressing her hands against her temples, and Shiro yawned loudly.

Mr. Kitaro appeared behind Darshana, sipping a coffee. "Good morning. You all look better than I expected. I can't tell you how tempted I was to call the police about a possible kidnapping. Luckily, Darshana helped me see the error of my ways."

"Now that you're awake, I have to tell you what I saw." Mayhara pushed her dark hair out of her face. "It was some kind of graphics simulation in one of the conference rooms I stumbled upon last night."

Darshana took a seat in the chair across from her and folded her hands in her lap. "Go on."

"It was an animation of the comet." She grabbed her Linq from the coffee table and walked over to Darshana. She'd already played the video she'd recorded for Jae and the others while they'd drunk their tea, but if anyone might have more of a clue as to what the details of the video meant, it was Darshana.

Mayhara started the video and showed Darshana the screen. When the image of the comet hovered over the tunnel that led to a cavern, and the lines that must have represented some kind of vibration appeared on the screen, Darshana let out a *hmm*.

"Jae thinks it has something to do with Kashmeru's tomb," Mayhara said.

"I would guess the same." Darshana played the video again. She pointed to the bottom of the screen. "I don't seem to recognize any of the markings here. But if we can figure them out, we might have a better idea of where this is."

"Wait." Salina sat upright. "You mean you don't know where the tomb is?"

"It's been kept secret," Mr. Kitaro explained, stepping closer and tapping his fingers on his coffee cup. "Only the mages who sealed him in the tomb were aware of its location. The empire thought it best not to have the information public. Can you imagine the chaos it would create if it were common knowledge?"

"But this means the Pishacha—and the government—know where it is."

"It's probably heavily guarded." Shiro rubbed at his chin. "Crawling with Pishacha, I'm sure."

"So when the comet is in the right position, they'll bring Naree there." Jae raked a hand through his hair.

"They're not going to be able to do anything if they don't have all seven daggers." Salina looked between Darshana and Mr. Kitaro. "Right?"

"That's the theory," Mr. Kitaro said.

They were quiet for a moment, but the silence was interrupted by a buzzing sound.

Jae pulled out his Linq, a wrinkle forming above his brows.

"What is it?" Mayhara asked.

"A message," he answered.

"From whom?" Darshana asked.

"Blocked ID," was all he said. And then he showed them his screen.

You'll find what you're looking for at the Danta Ramgarh Observatory

The car sped down the highway. Naree chewed on a nail while a battle raged in her head.

My love, please remember: they will try to deceive you. They will tell you our love isn't real. But it's the most real thing in the world. It has existed from the beginning of time and it will live on forever.

Naree closed her eyes and took a deep breath, trying to exhale her doubt.

They will try to make you believe I am using you. But only you know how I really feel. Only you understand how much I am devoted to you. Everything I have and everything I am is for you. Never forget that my love.

She put a hand on her heart. It swelled with memories from past lives, each of them filled with the existence of Kashmeru's love for her. Her body felt as if it were floating. Her skin tingled. Her mind cleared.

Never forget, my love.

"Never."

NINETEEN

Salina parked the car and looked through the windshield at the observatory on the hill. The building was a standing silhouette in the twilight. The four mages stepped out of the car, none of them sure about what awaited them. Salina stretched out her legs, her nerves partially numb from long drive. She had asked to be the one to drive to keep her mind occupied with something other than the loss of her best friend. Heavy traffic had turned the two-hour journey into three hours of frustration.

"This mysterious message you got," Shiro said to Jae. "You think it was from the scroll makers?"

"That's what I thought at first." Jae adjusted the collar of his leather jacket. "Now I'm not so sure."

"Who else could it have been from?" Salina asked. "What was the message again?"

"Just that we'd find what we were looking for here."

"I don't know." Mayhara pulled the zipper of her jacket higher. "I've got a funny feeling about the whole thing."

As they continued toward the entrance of the observatory, Mayhara caught up with Salina. It wasn't the first time Mayhara had approached Salina like this in the past two days, checking to make sure she was all right. Though Salina hadn't come to terms with Huojin's death yet, she knew in her heart that she had to carry on with the mission, even doing so in Huojin's name.

"Hey." Mayhara bumped elbows with her. "You sure you're up for this?"

"Yes. I need to. Anything is better than obsessing over why Huojin was killed. It's time to put a stop to this before anyone else dies."

The observatory's lights were on, but no one could be seen inside. The glass doors at the entrance were locked, so Shiro pushed the call button. After what seemed like forever, a tall, thin woman with glasses and her reddish-brown hair in a bun came to the glass doors, studying them. She pressed the key code into the lock pad and gave them a polite smile.

"May I help you?"

Jae glanced at his friends. He couldn't very well say *we received a message to come here*, especially if this woman had no idea who they were or what they were looking for.

"Are you closed?" Salina asked.

The woman let out a small laugh. "This is a research observatory for scientists, not a public venue."

The mages exchanged glances. The message must not have come from this woman. But then, who was it from?

"Oh." Salina slapped a hand on Shiro's back, causing him to take a step forward. "Well, as luck would have it, Shiro here is a man of science. Isn't that right, Shiro?"

"We're part of his research team," Mayhara added. "Doing a paper on the Akutake comet."

"Uh, yes." Shiro fidgeted but then raised his chin, giving off an air of confidence. "It's all very... scientific."

"Be that as it may, our protocol is for scientists to make an appointment beforehand." The woman flashed a fake smile, but she was clearly irritated. "Showing up out of the blue like this, especially at such a late hour, is highly unusual. Please call or use the website to make an appointment and I'd be happy to assist you."

She began to close the door.

"Please." Salina put her hand on the door. "You can make an exception, can't you?"

"I'm really sorry, but I can't. Goodbye now."

"Wait!" Mayhara said.

The woman ignored her and pushed the door harder to close it. Mayhara's palm glowed crimson, and suddenly a chunk of the floor in the doorway burst upward, creating a makeshift doorstop.

The woman's eyes grew wide, first fixated on the protrusion and then darting between the mages. She backed away. "No. No. I know who you are. Dark mages."

"No, we're not," Mayhara insisted.

"Of course you are. I've heard about you. Which one of you is the governor's son? Ha! Like I'd stick around to find out."

She turned to run.

Jae reached out with his sapphire magic as he called to her. "No, wait. You're mistaken. We are mages, but not dark ones. We're soldiers from the Empire of the Lotus."

His truth energy floated around her like blue sparkles as she stopped and turned to face him.

"You can trust us," Jae said, stepping into the building.

Salina, Shiro, and Mayhara followed close behind.

"I… I do," the woman said. "I don't know why I do, but, somehow, I know you're telling the truth."

"What's your name?" Jae asked.

"Asano."

"Asano, I'm guessing since you know about dark mages, you're also familiar with the Sacred Keys."

Shiro stepped closer. "She's one of them, isn't she?"

Asano looked to the blue glow of Jae's hands. "I am. I'm the keeper of one of the sacred daggers."

Salina and Mayhara exchanged glances, and then Mayhara drew closer.

"We need you to give it to us, Asano." Mayhara's voice was gentle but even. "You're right to fear the dark mages. They're coming, and so are the Pishacha. It's just a matter of time before they find you and the dagger."

"But we can offer you protection," Jae added. "A hidden sanctuary and a safe place to hide the daggers."

"We'll have to move fast, though." Salina looked over her shoulder at the door, which was still propped open by Mayhara's floor bump. "Can you take us to the dagger?"

Asano wrung her hands and nodded. "Yes, of course. Follow me."

She led them from the lobby, up the metal stairs, and to the main observing floor. This floor, which was constructed of planks of metal grates, curved around the inside of the round building. The group passed a control room, which was filled with computers and other equipment, as well as a wall of monitors. One screen seemed to be devoted to monitoring solar flare activity, while another was focused on the Akutake comet. In the center of this building's level, the observatory's massive telescope stood like a colossal metal giant.

Asano brought the mages into a room that was lined with panels of dull gray, rectangular metal. Every panel looked the same, but Asano didn't even waver as she confidently approached one and pressed two pressure points. The panel slid out of the wall electronically like a small drawer, revealing a shelf holding a box.

Salina recognized the black-and-red object. She'd seen one just like it at the temple. It was the box that held a sacred dagger.

Asano used delicate movements as she retrieved the box. She blew out a shaky breath, presenting the box to Jae. Salina, Shiro, and Mayhara drew closer as Jae lifted the lid. They had to be sure the dagger was really inside.

Jae lifted the dagger and held it up to the light.

"We'll take that. Thanks." The voice came from behind them.

Salina turned, stunned to see a dark mage, flanked by two Pishacha in black mouth masks. The dark mage wore a long, dark gray cloak, and a loose, white, button-up shirt that exposed most of his chest. His hair was buzzed short on the sides, the remaining dark hair pulled back into a ponytail. One of his eyebrows had slashes in it, as if the hairs had been cut with a razor.

"No!" Salina immediately crouched and shot off a blast of fire at the intruders. The dark mage covered his face from the flame. As soon as the wave of heat died off, he extended his arms. All the metal in the room warped, including the floor. Asano and the mages stumbled. Stunned by the unexpected move, Mayhara had to take a second before she could reach out and stabilize the mages' balance.

In that instant, Asano grabbed the dagger from Jae and spun away. Her movements were so calculated, they were almost too fast to catch as she darted for a section of the wall indistinguishable from any other section. But this one had a secret doorway she slipped through, and in an instant, she was gone, and the door was shut.

"Mayhara! Shiro!" Jae shouted. "Go after her. Salina and I will handle these guys."

"Yeah, come *handle* us," the dark mage taunted. "Give us a chance to get rid of another one of you."

Everything seemed to happen at once.

Mayhara and Shiro ran to the wall, pressing random spots in the damaged metal in hopes of finding the secret pressure point to release the hidden door.

Salina filled with rage at the dark mage's words and threw her arms forward, blasting the enemy with a horizontal cyclone of fire. The dark mage and Pishacha backed into the hall to shield themselves.

Salina and Jae then charged into the hall. The enemy had spread out, moving steadily, as if they were predators stalking their prey. Their heavy, black boots scraped across the metal floor as they advanced.

Jae lifted his chin and shifted closer to Salina. "Cover your ears," he said to her.

She did as he'd commanded. Jae raised his glowing palms and slapped them together hard, creating a huge blast of sound. The waves tore through the air and forced the Pishacha and the dark mage back. The dark mage crashed into the side of the telescope. The Pishacha disappeared into clouds of black smoke before they collided with the metal equipment situated around the floor.

Taking advantage of their enemies' struggles, Jae and Salina ran for the stairs.

"Mayhara and Shiro are gone," Jae said as they raced for the door.

"They must have figured out how to get through that secret passage," Salina said. "It has to lead outside somehow. That's the only thing that makes sense."

Just as they reached the entrance to the building, the Pishacha reappeared in front of them. One of them unfolded his black cloak to reveal the dark mage, who stepped out with a sneer. They must have grabbed him with their magic and brought him with them.

With a cry of rage, Salina threw her hand out. A long whip of golden fire extended from her palm. She flailed it out, the end of it whipping at their enemies. Smoke appeared as the Pishacha disappeared again. The dark mage hissed as he recoiled from the whip.

"I hear them." Jae lunged forward and out the door. "They're across the cliff."

Salina sprinted behind him, trusting his power of sound to track Asano and their friends. She heaved each breath as her feet pounded the ground.

Overhead, the sky had darkened to night. Only the moon lit their way over the uneven surface of the cliff.

At last they spotted Mayhara and Shiro running not far from the edge of the cliff. Asano was a small distance in front of them, and Mayhara was shouting for her to stop.

"You tricked me!" Asano screamed. "You used some kind of magic on me to make me believe you're on the side of the Lotus."

"No, that's not true." Mayhara was fast, closing the distance between them. "We *are* on the side of the Lotus."

Jae's palms glowed blue, but Salina could see the others were too far away for his truth powers to work.

"Please, stop!" Shiro yelled.

Mayhara grunted, her palms glowing red. She aimed for the ground by Asano's feet. In the next second, Asano stumbled and fell forward. The dagger flew from her fingers, skidding across the dirt and landing inches away from the cliff's edge.

"No!" Asano scrambled to her feet and jumped for the dagger. She stood, shaking, with the dagger in her hand.

"Asano." Jae held his hands up in a peaceful gesture, his palms still glowing blue. "We are with the empire. We are telling you the truth. We don't want to hurt you."

Asano breathed heavily, but her features softened. The wind whipped her hair around her head as she kept her eyes on Jae. After what seemed like forever, she nodded.

"Okay. I believe you." Asano took a step forward, but the earth fell away at her feet. Her eyes widened and her mouth went agape as she dropped.

A scream as loud as thunder erupted from Mayhara as she raced forward, crimson energy tearing through the air toward Asano.

The mages rushed to the edge of the cliff. When they got there, they could see a small section of rock jutting out from the cliffside. The dagger had landed on it, but Asano was clinging to it by her fingertips. Debris fell from the rock where her fingers held on.

"Save the Lotus," Asano said, her voice quavering.

Jae dropped to his chest to reach down for her, but her fingers slipped away then, and she plummeted down. The mages could only stare, their hearts hammering in their chests, as the Sacred Key disappeared into the darkness below.

TWENTY

Jae closed his eyes and dropped his head to the ground, his heart aching for the woman who'd just fallen to her death. There was nothing they could have done to save her. Mayhara had tried, but her efforts had been in vain. Jae stayed on the ground for a moment, coming to terms with what had just happened. He could hear the other mages get to their feet behind him, but for the moment, he couldn't move.

"Jae," Mayhara said. There was something in her voice that set off alarms in his head.

He lifted his chin and pushed out his hearing powers. There were footsteps. It sounded like a lot of people approaching.

His eyes landed on the dagger, but he didn't pick it up. Perhaps it was best to leave it there for now. He turned and got to his feet, following the gazes of the other mages. They were approaching—the Pishacha, the dark mages… and Naree.

His eyes locked with hers as she stomped up the hill, flanked by two dark mages. In front of her were the two Pishacha from the observatory, their coal-black eyes boring into each of the mages, one after the other. Jae searched Naree's face, trying to see some remaining clue of the sister he'd grown up with, the sister he'd do anything for. But she simply sneered back at him with a hatred in her eyes that shook him to the core.

"Naree. We're not here to fight you," Jae said. "Not again. We want you to come with us. We are *your* army."

The dark mage beside her— the one from the observatory—laughed, casting a glance at his fellow dark mages. "We are her army now. She has Kashmeru. She has no need for you any longer."

"Naree," Jae said, ignoring the dark mage. His palms glowed blue, reaching out to her with his truth powers. "Please, listen to your soul. Even as Lakshmi, you must know this isn't right. We can help you, get you back on track to doing what's right."

There was a blue glow in her palms as well. Her expression didn't change. It was as if she hadn't heard him at all. Naree stretched out her shoulders. "What is it you hope to achieve? I'm not here to be saved. Kashmeru has promised me peace, an eternity with him, a life beyond the destruction of the universe. You can't stop destiny. Kashmeru and I were made for each other, to be the ultimate gods, together. Forever."

"Naree," Jae pleaded. "Kashmeru is lying to you. You were meant to rule, but in pure love and peace, not in the dredges of his evil ways."

Naree shook her head. "Kashmeru told me you would try to manipulate me, to feed me lies. I won't fall for it. You are nothing to me."

The words stung, but Jae knew deep down that it wasn't his sister saying these things. Her mind was poisoned by an evil god. There had to be a way to win her back.

"Fine." Naree crossed her arms and raised a brow. "You don't want to fight? Give me the daggers."

Jae slowly shook his head. "You know I can't do that."

She let out a laugh he wasn't familiar with—another indication that his sister wasn't herself. "And *you* know I'll get them one way or another. You have one right now, don't you? Where is it?"

The glow in her palms turned from blue to purple. She was pushing out her power of insight, trying to get the location of the dagger. Jae wasn't sure his power over lies would hide it from her.

"We don't have it," Shiro said, stepping in beside Jae. "And even if we did, we'd do anything to prevent you and your crew of lackies from getting it."

"You think you intimidate me. How cute." Naree looked from Shiro to Salina to Mayhara to Jae. "You honestly believe it will be a problem for me to defeat all four of you at once?"

"What about eight?"

The voice seemed to come out of nowhere. It made Naree, the Pishacha, and the three dark mages turn around searching for its source.

Stepping out of the shadow of night and into the moonlight were four mages. Jae only recognized two of them, but he knew they all must have been on their side. The purple, green, blue, and white glow of their palms gave him hope.

Mayhara shifted closer to Jae. "Elites?" she whispered.

Jae's eyes drifted to her for only a moment as he nodded.

The mage who'd spoken up held her hands open at her sides, her palms alit with purple.

The amethyst mage.

She had thick black hair that hung in loose waves. Even from as far away as she was standing, Jae could see the flecks of purple in her eyes. She wasn't one of the ones he recognized, but she appeared to be the leader. The ones he did remember from the academy were Loni, the emerald mage, and Kamal, the sapphire mage. Loni looked the same as when he'd last seen her, except perhaps thinner, as if she hadn't been eating properly. And her straight, dark hair had grown to way below her shoulders. Kamal appeared taller than when Jae had last seen him, but he still sported stringy black hair that hung in his face. The auburn-haired girl whose palms glowed white was not a familiar face, but because she looked so young, he assumed this diamond mage hadn't been at the academy long before the Eradication.

Could these be the elites? What were the chances that they'd all found each other and shown up exactly when Jae and his friends needed them?

Naree looked between them, her breaths heavy as she considered what to do.

The amethyst mage stepped around Naree and her group, the other mages following her until they were next to Jae and the others. The Pishacha and the dark mages kept their eyes on them, their jaws squared and their fists clenched, ready to do as Naree commanded.

"You may have us outnumbered," Naree said, "but that doesn't mean you can overpower us."

Naree nodded to the three dark mages. The one from the observatory held out his palms. The air around them seemed to vibrate. Shiro gasped as his feet slid forward, as if he were being pulled by an invisible force. Mayhara rushed forward, stepping in front of Shiro to stop his movement, and held her palms up at the dark mage. Crimson energy flew from her palms, and the earth beneath the dark mage trembled. He crouched down and slapped his hands on the ground to keep his balance.

Naree sneered. "Destroy them!"

Chaos erupted as particles of energy flew back and forth between the two sides. Air whipped through the enemy, knocking them back a few feet, but they soon recovered and sent shockwaves of pain at the elite mages and Jae, causing them to cry out. It was as if their bones were being crushed.

The diamond mage grunted through the pain and stepped forward, throwing out her hands. Blinding white light emitted from her palms and formed a shimmering, curved shield over the elites and Jae. The shockwaves stopped, the energy bouncing off the diamond mage's shield.

One of the Pishacha disappeared from beside Naree and reappeared on the elite's side of the shield. He jumped into the air in a flying kick and planted the heel of his left boot into Jae's chest. The momentum knocked Jae hard on his back. As Jae rolled to the side to get back on his feet, Salina grabbed the shadow soldier by his cloak and pushed him over the edge of the cliff. He disappeared into a cloud of black smoke before he had a chance to fall.

The other Pishacha sneered as he tried his turn, disappearing and then reappearing on the mages' side of the shield. But Shiro manifested blocks of ice around the Pishacha's legs, sealing him in place as Mayhara slammed into him with two hammering fists. The blows knocked him backward. As he collided with the hard ground, he made his smoky exit.

Naree's eyes glowed as she raised her hands. A white light to match the elite diamond mage's poured from her palms and shot toward the diamond shield. The shimmering diamond energy from both sides rammed into each other, emitting a high-pitched screeching sound like metal scraping metal. Naree kept pushing, trying to penetrate the shield, but it was too strong.

"Kamal," the amethyst mage called. "Mute us!"

Kamal's blue glow expanded until it stretched farther than the diamond mage's bubble. He nodded to the amethyst mage.

"Do you have the dagger?" she asked Jae.

"It's near," he answered.

"You're going to have to grab it on my signal, and then we need to hurry down the hill. You have a sanctuary?"

"Yes. You can follow us there."

"We won't have much time. I can only hold them off for so long."

Jae nodded, then cast a glance at Shiro, Mayhara, and Salina. They each nodded in agreement.

"Now!" the amethyst mage yelled.

The diamond mage dropped her shield. The amethyst mage held her arms out in front of her and aimed her palms at the Pishacha and dark mages. Purple crystals pushed out into the air toward them. Loni, the emerald mage, blasted out air to hold them back while the purple cloud of energy reached them.

With a wild scream, Naree dropped to her knees, covering her eyes. The dark mages flailed and thrashed, eventually dropping to the ground as well.

Sight. The amethyst mage had temporarily blinded them.

Jae didn't hesitate. He bent down, reached past the cliff's edge, and seized the dagger, thankful it was still there. "Let's go!"

Naree threw out air, fire, earth, ice, and blaring sound, attempting to stop the elites, but she could not find them. The elites and Jae raced down the hill, keeping their balance thanks to Mayhara's energy. The steep slope aided their progress, and soon they were at their car.

"You have a car?" Jae asked the amethyst mage.

"It's hidden around the corner. Meet us there and we'll follow you. The blindness will wear off soon, so we need to hurry."

"What's your name?" Jae asked her.

"It's Apinya. But everyone calls me Penny." Penny pointed to the other mages. "You know Kamal and Loni. This is Yuki."

Jae nodded his greeting to them. Jae and Loni only looked at each other for a moment before averting their gazes.

"I'm Mayhara," Mayhara said before pointing to rest. "Salina and Shiro."

"I don't mean to be rude," Salina said, "but we don't have time to be social right now. We've got to go."

"She's right," Kamal said. "Time for chitchat later. They're going to be coming for us, and they're already beyond pissed."

"We'll follow you," Penny said.

"Wait." Jae put a hand on Penny's arm. "Were you the one who sent the message with this location?"

"Yes," Penny said. "I knew the dagger was here."

"How?" Jae asked.

"I know where all the daggers are. I'll tell you more when we reach your sanctuary."

Jae could only stare for a moment, watching as she hurried to her vehicle. She knew where the daggers were. The odds might have just changed to be in their favor. He was still wrapping his head around it as he turned to get into the car, but the purple haze at the top of the hill caught his eye.

Naree.

She was up there. Part of him wanted to rush back up and grab her, force her to come with them. But it was too risky. And she would fight him. Clenching his jaw, Jae hit a fist against the top of the car, then swung the door open to climb inside, hoping he'd still get a chance to save his little sister.

Emerald Mage

Book Four

ONE

Loni Saengkaew stared at the emerald stone on her wristband as the car climbed a hidden road headed uphill. The stone caught the light of the moon, reminding her of the many nights she'd spent fearing the fulfillment of the prophecy. Things had been a mess since the destruction of the academy, but the last few months, in particular, had turned her life upside down. She sucked in a sharp breath through her nose and crossed her arms, clenching her hands into fists and tucking them in at her sides

In the driver's seat, Penny spared her a glance, the flecks of purple in her eyes sparkling from the streetlights. Out of the four mages in the car, she and Penny had been together the longest, venturing as a team through the post-Eradication chaos to get to where they were now.

Loni had been squatting in an abandoned Linq factory for almost three months when Penny had found her. It was just one of the many places she had camped out while on the run. Penny had simply shown up, in her dark purple leather jacket and knee-high, black boots, telling Loni she needed to come with her. Thankfully, Loni had remembered Penny from the academy, but they hadn't been in touch in years, so it had been a surprise to see her. As the elite Amethyst mage, Penny had used her power of insight to find her, but because Loni had moved around so much, she hadn't been easy to track down.

The trees flanking the small road they were driving on began to decrease in number. Up ahead, at the top of the hill, the surroundings cleared to reveal a beautiful temple. Loni leaned forward and took in a deep breath, as if inhaling the sacredness of the temple, hoping for comfort. The truth was she was a wreck inside. Physically, mentally, and, most of all, emotionally. The only thing keeping her going was justice. She'd promised herself she would see this through. She would destroy Kashmeru herself, if she could.

The car in front of them—the one they'd been following—pulled into a carport. Another car was already parked there, along with a motorcycle that she recognized.

When they parked, Loni looked over at Yuki—the diamond mage—who removed a hairband from her wrist and swept up her shoulder-length, auburn hair into a messy bun. Yuki yawned, and Loni almost made a joke about it being past her bedtime but refrained. Yuki had heard it all before. At seventeen, she was probably the youngest elite mage to have ever existed.

The four mages emerged from the car simultaneously. Kamal—the elite sapphire mage—stretched his arms above his head and slightly arched his back. As he kicked out his long legs, he looked around at his driving companions, his ever-present, cocky grin twisting his lips to one side.

The four passengers from the other car were already waiting for them. Jae—whom Loni knew well—signaled for them to follow and headed toward a door seemingly guarded by a white, stone elephant. He looked almost the same as she'd remembered, with his short, dark, hero hair and his square shoulders. He did seem a little more worn for the wear, but the rugged look suited him.

For being so close to the busy road at the bottom of the hill, the temple was quieter than Loni had expected. She had to admit, though, that the pink sandstone columns and white marble floors were a far more pleasing aesthetic than the murky, soiled, and rotten-egg-scented places she'd been used to camping out in during the past couple of years.

Up ahead of her, the crimson mage—Mayhara, she remembered—ran her hand along one of the stone elephants' tusks before she entered the temple door. There was no denying she was beautiful. Her flawless creamed-caramel skin contrasted nicely with her thick, dark hair. Jae placed a hand on the small of Mayhara's back as he followed her inside. Loni wondered, with an itch of jealousy, how long they'd been a couple.

"Come on inside." Shiro—the copper mage—held up the dagger, which he'd wrapped in a red cloth. "I'm going to store this somewhere safe and catch up with you."

Inside, the temple's ceilings were at least ten feet high, and the marble floors were polished. It didn't feel like a temple. The feeling Loni got was more like it was an extravagant home, filled with comfortable furniture. Though, she wasn't too familiar with many homes decorated with elegant stone statues of various deities. A gentle breeze floated in behind the mages as they entered the building, carrying with it the pleasant scent of jasmine.

An archway to the right of the main entrance hallway led them to a spacious kitchen. In the breakfast nook, sitting at a small black ceramic table, were two older people. Loni recognized the woman as Darshana, her guru from the academy. The man, however, she'd never seen before.

Darshana eyed the group coming in and jumped to her feet. Her hands flew to her mouth, trembling slightly. Her white hair was pulled back into the long braid Loni was familiar with, and she still had stunning skin for someone her age.

"I can't believe it." Darshana walked over to the four new mages and took each of them by their hands, one after the other. One by one, they bowed to her in greeting.

The salt-and-pepper-haired man at the table stood. Loni had expected him to be taller than he was, probably due to the sense of importance he seemed to convey. He certainly dressed like someone important. He bowed as he approached them. "Judging by the amount of jovial energy flooding the room, I assume these are the other elites we have been looking for. It's a pleasure to meet you. I am Mr. Kitaro."

"He's a Sacred Key," Jae explained. "A keeper of one of the magic daggers."

"Cool," Kamal said, flipping the bangs of his stringy black hair with a jerk of his head.

Jae raised a brow at his comment, causing Loni to bite the inside of her cheek to keep from laughing.

"I'm Apinya. But everyone calls me 'Penny.'" Penny bowed to Mr. Kitaro.

"Ah. *Apinya*." Mr. Kitaro nodded. "It means 'magical powers.' How fitting. You have wonderful specks of purple in your irises, matching your amethyst mage powers. How perfect."

Penny's forehead creased for a fraction of a second. "Thank you?"

Next to her, Kamal bowed again while sticking his hands in his pockets, typically combining an air of respect and apathy in one move. "I'm Kamal, and I guess I'm the new elite sapphire mage. Penny just found me a week ago to let me know, so I'm still trying to wrap my head around it."

"Nice to meet you, Kamal," Mr. Kitaro said.

Since she stood beside Kamal, Loni decided to go next. She raised her hand and then stuck it behind her back. "I'm Loni. Emerald elite."

"One of my best friends from childhood was an emerald mage." While Mr. Kitaro smiled, it didn't reach his eyes.

Loni refrained from questioning whether or not that friend was still alive.

Everyone's gaze then went to Yuki. She looked around with her wide eyes as if unsure of what to do. Relief seemed to wash over her when Penny spoke up for her.

"Yuki is the diamond elite."

"I should probably be shocked by such a young elite," Mr. Kitaro said. "But diamond mages are so rare that I imagine the former elites who were... *eliminated* by the Pishacha were few in number."

Yuki's only response was to drop her gaze as she nodded, tendrils of her long, auburn hair slipping from her hairband and falling in front of her pale, narrow face.

"You all look famished," Mr. Kitaro said.

"I'll make more tea," Darshana said, heading for the stove and grabbing the kettle to fill.

Kamal raked a hand through his hair. "I mean, I could use a shower and a beer if we're offering things."

"Why don't I whip up something to eat?" Jae's gaze fell upon Loni before he headed for the cupboards.

"I'll help," Mayhara said. Her smile told Loni she hadn't caught the look Jae had just given her.

Though Loni couldn't be sure what meaning might have been behind that look in the first place. Because the last look he'd ever given her had been one of disappointment.

They'd moved into the dining room so everyone could sit comfortably around the table and eat. Penny moved her food around her plate but hadn't taken a bite. Though *bibim gooksu* Jae and Mayhara had whipped up smelled delicious, with the scent of spices and vinegar filling the air, Penny simply had too much to divulge to the group and was in no rush to eat.

"So you saw my Linq number in your head?" Jae asked, reaching for the water carafe to fill his glass. "I didn't know amethyst mages could do that."

"Normally, we can't," Penny said.

"It's a highly unusual skill," Darshana added.

"Good thing, too." Kamal snorted. "Otherwise, amethysts everywhere would be stealing credit account numbers and winning lotteries on the fly."

Yuki gave him a disapproving look.

"It took a lot of meditation," Penny said, ignoring Kamal's remark. "And when I finally pinned it down, I contacted you right away."

"Via a mysterious message." Salina pointed her chopsticks at Darshana. "Which actually led us to one of the daggers."

Penny shrugged. "I figured it would be diligent to kill two birds with one stone. Plus, I didn't want to identify myself in the message, just in case it was intercepted."

"Which it might have been," Mayhara said. "Would explain why the Pishacha showed up."

"So you know where the other daggers are, then." Shiro narrowed his eyes as if he were trying to calculate some major mathematical equation.

"Yes." Penny set down her chopsticks. "The Pishacha have three of them."

Shiro almost choked, sputtering as he tried to clear his throat. "Three? I thought they only had two."

"Yeah, we counted two," Salina added.

"One was acquired recently." Penny dropped her gaze, as if disappointed in herself. "They got to it before we could."

Darshana put a hand on her chest, taking a deep breath. "Yes. Yes, you are right. I'd felt a disturbance, but I believed it to be Huojin's downfall."

Salina frowned. Penny could feel Salina's sorrow over her friend's demise as if it were her own loss.

Mr. Kitaro bowed his head and closed his eyes. "Another Sacred Key has fallen."

It was quiet for a moment. And then Mayhara spoke up. "They have three, and we have three. There's one left. You know where it is?"

Penny nodded. "I do."

A tingling sensation traveled in a repeating wave through Penny's head. Her senses were on high alert. Someone was approaching the temple.

"We should probably—" Jae stopped mid-sentence when Penny abruptly turned her head and stood from the table.

As she proceeded from the dining room toward the front door, she could hear the others following her.

"Penny," Loni called. "Should we be afraid?"

Penny didn't stop walking, her boots clunking along on the marble floor in a consistent rhythm. "I'm not sure. Something is wrong, but I can't tell."

Searching her mind, she found something blocking her insight powers. It had to be magic; that was the only thing that made sense. But what was it? She could just make out the faint glow of the various-colored light behind her as the other mages prepared themselves for a possible fight. But Penny couldn't sense that they were in any danger. Unless her senses were betraying her.

She opened the door.

There, not ten feet from where she was standing, was a young woman with smooth, pale skin and dark, unkempt hair hobbling toward the door. On one arm, she propped up an older woman with scraggly white hair.

"Amalia?" Darshana said from behind Penny. Her eyes were on the older woman.

"Help," the young woman said. "She's dying."

TWO

Shiro ran forward to the other side of Amalia and wrapped her arm over his shoulder. He immediately felt the dead weight of the old woman leaning on him. Amalia whimpered with every step she tried to take. Karina—Amalia's granddaughter—squared her jaw and grunted as they worked together to get Amalia through the front door.

"What happened?" Shiro asked.

"It was a dark mage." Amalia's voice was hoarse and weak. "He did something to me. It feels like poison is running through my veins."

The rest of Amalia's words were lost beneath a barrage of coughs. Karina and Shiro carried Amalia to the living room couch and gently set her down. Amalia gasped in pain as they released her.

Darshana, Mr. Kitaro, and all the mages gathered around, baffled at this new development.

"How did this happen?" Darshana asked, sitting herself down on the coffee table in front of the couch so that she was eye level with her friend.

"I was out collecting herbs." Amalia scrubbed a trembling hand over her face. "They cornered me."

"The Pishacha," Karina added.

"Oh my God," Loni exclaimed.

"Why did they corner you?" Shiro asked.

"They wanted me to help them."

"With what?" Shiro shook his head. "Why you?"

Amalia shifted on the couch, wincing. "Kashmeru was sealed in a tomb by the empire, but they used a witch to bind him there magically. In order to keep a being as powerful as a god locked in a tomb, they had to use a powerful spell performed by an even more powerful witch."

"That's a lot of *powerfuls*," Salina whispered.

"And because it was sealed by a witch," Amalia said, "it can only be opened by a witch."

Kamal scratched the back of his head. "So what's that have to do with you?"

Loni smacked him on the arm. "She's a witch, dumbass."

Kamal cleared his throat. "Y-Yeah, okay. I just, uh, figured that out."

"Not just any witch." Karina looked around at the group. "She's probably the most powerful one in the world."

Shiro nodded slowly, putting the pieces of the puzzle together. "So that's why they cornered you. They wanted you to do the unbinding spell."

Mayhara crossed her arms. "And the dark mage attacked you because you refused."

Amalia opened her mouth to respond but fell into a fit of coughs. She could barely nod to answer Mayhara.

Karina rubbed her grandmother's back but looked up at the mages. "Of course she refused. And in return they tried to kill her."

"No. No. They didn't try to kill me." Amalia waved a feeble arm in the air, catching her breath. "The dark mage who attacked me—he was rail thin and had green, spiky hair—he used a power on me I didn't know a mage could have. It was as if needles were penetrating my skin and injecting me with a burning, itchy acid. I could barely breathe, and I lost control of my body and fell in the mud. He pushed me down with his boot and told me I had seventy-two hours to change my mind or else his magic would kill me. Then he and his Pishacha bodyguards disappeared. They left me writhing in the mud."

Karina's brows drew together, her mouth set in a frown. "She'd been gone longer than usual, so I went looking for her. When I found her, she told me to bring her here. The dark mage's magic has been in her system for about eight hours now."

"Amalia, we're going to do everything we can to help you." Shiro took her hand in his. "You saved my life. I'm going to do whatever it takes to save yours."

Yuki began to pace, her eyes far away. "I don't understand the Pishacha's plan. If you still refuse, and they let you die, they're out a witch anyway."

Amalia put a hand on Karina's knee. "That's another reason I wanted Karina to bring me here. You need to keep her safe."

"We're not giving up on you," Darshana said. "But of course, we'll keep Karina safe."

"Thank you, Darshana." Amalia bowed her head to her.

"So, theoretically," Jae said, sitting in the chair next to the couch, "they could find another powerful witch to do the unbinding spell."

"Hope there're not too many of them around." Kamal held up his hands. "No offense."

"It's not as simple as that." Amalia grunted as she shifted, leaning her elbow on the arm of the couch. "There are a couple of other things required in order for the witch to harness enough power for the spell to be in full effect. The same elements required when they sealed Kashmeru in the tomb, but… reversed, in a sense."

"What things?" Yuki moved to the floor, sitting next to the coffee table and tucking her legs beneath her.

"When the tomb was sealed, there was a celestial event—a full solar eclipse. The powers of the seven elite mages at that time were combined and channeled through the Lotus. And a powerful witch performed the binding spell. To open the tomb, the Pishacha need a celestial event—"

"The comet," Mayhara said, sitting on the arm of Jae's chair.

"The council of the seven would draw the power from the Lotus through her blood using the seven daggers, and a powerful witch is needed to undo the binding spell." Amalia held up a finger. "But not every witch has knowledge of the spell."

"But you do, right?" Kamal asked.

"No," Amalia answered.

"What?" Kamal scoffed. "Then I have to ask again, what does all this have to do with you?"

"Shut up, Kamal," Loni whispered.

"The spell is in a grimoire," Penny said. She had been quiet during the entire exchange, standing at the back of the room, listening.

"What's a grimoire?" Salina asked.

Penny let out a sigh. "It's a book of spells, usually very ancient. Not something you'd like an enemy to get ahold of."

"So we just have to keep the grimoire away from the Pishacha." Salina looked around, hopeful.

"Where is this grimoire?" Darshana asked.

Both Amalia and Karina shook their heads.

Amalia wrung her hands. "It is in a place called The Archives. A hidden place made by witches where important books and items are kept safe. I was there once when I was very young. But to protect me, my mother performed a charm that made me forget its location. I have no idea where it is."

Mayhara stood and turned to Penny. "Please tell me you know where it is."

Penny shook her head. "Not exactly. It's protected by magic, like Amalia said."

"Okay," Loni said. "But if we don't know where it is, it's highly unlikely that the Pishacha will be able to find it, either. So it's moot. We've just got to make sure to get all the daggers so they can't perform the ritual."

Kamal shrugged. "That does seem like the most logical plan."

"All right, then it's settled." Jae nodded once. "Let's get those daggers."

THREE

It was three in the morning when they finally decided to turn in. The men had generously offered to clean up the dinner dishes, and Darshana brought Karina and Amalia to a guestroom on the ground floor to stay in. Amalia could barely walk, but Karina proved herself to be pretty strong. She had to have been, since she'd rescued her grandmother from the swamp to bring her to the temple.

"There are a few more rooms upstairs," Mayhara said. "Plenty enough for everyone. Salina, will you help me get the ladies settled while the boys finish up?"

Salina fought the small churn in her stomach. "Sure."

Mayhara led the way upstairs, bringing the young women to the first empty room down the hall. Salina followed behind them. She couldn't be sure, but she felt as if Loni had been avoiding making eye contact with her. After all these years, could she really still be angry with her?

"Here's the first room." Mayhara opened the door and took a step back so the others could look inside. "They're all pretty much the same."

"I'll take it, if no one minds." Yuki covered her mouth as she yawned. The dark circles under her eyes were a dead giveaway to how exhausted she was.

"Good night, Yuki," Penny said, placing a hand on Yuki's arm. "Sweet dreams."

"Night, everyone." Yuki gave them all a tired smile, her eyes half-closed as she wandered into the bedroom and closed the door.

A few steps down the hallway, Penny turned to Mayhara. "She's been through a lot. Two diamond elites were killed by the Pishacha before she became the new elite. She knew she was next. When the Imperial Police asked her to come in to answer some questions, she knew it was a setup. She could feel their emotions and knew they were hiding something. She made them think she was cooperating, gave them the slip, and escaped. It was only a matter of hours before her parents were slaughtered in the prison camps."

"That's awful," Salina whispered, a hand on her heart.

Mayhara frowned in silence. Salina wondered if it was because her parents were still trapped in the prison camps.

"She's tougher than she looks," Penny said. "But she's still young, and I can't help but feel responsible for her."

Mayhara stopped in front of the door to another empty room. "You seem to have adopted a sort of mother role to the others."

Penny shrugged and let out a sigh. "I had to find them, and I knew their lives would never be the same. As the cornerstone of that pivotal turn, I just feel—"

"She's been amazing," Loni said. "Like, really there for us. At least, she has been for me."

"I think it's something that I've always felt I needed to be able to do." Penny pushed her hair behind her ears. "My parents were killed in a car crash when I was young, so I had to take care of myself for a long time. I think I relayed that into an almost maternal instinct for those in need."

"You're awesome at it," Loni said softly.

Penny gave Loni a small smile and reached out to squeeze her hand. "I'm about to drop right here in the hall, so I better get to sleep."

Loni pointed to the door across the hall. "If that one's available, I'll take it."

Salina couldn't help but notice that Loni had directed the statement to Mayhara. She hadn't imagined it; Loni was avoiding looking at her, much less talking to her.

"Yeah, sure," Mayhara said. "Sleep tight."

Salina rubbed at her shoulders, not sure how she felt about Loni's clear dismissal of her. They walked halfway down the hall before she realized Mayhara had been speaking with her.

"I'm sorry. What?" Salina bit her lip. "I was spacing out and didn't hear what you were saying."

"It's okay. We're all really tired. I was just saying we might have a shot, now that Penny is here. If she can track down the rest of the daggers, the Pishacha won't be able to fulfill the prophecy."

"Right. Yeah. I think we might actually have the ball in our court for once."

Mayhara studied her face. "Are you all right?"

"Yeah. Sorry." Salina shook her head. "I just got a little flummoxed around Loni. I wasn't expecting that kind of reaction from her."

"What do you mean?"

"You didn't notice the tension between Loni and me?"

"Sorry. Maybe I'm still on edge because of everything that's happened tonight. The battle on the cliff, the appearance of the other elites, and Amalia showing up poisoned on our doorstep—my brain hadn't even taken it all in yet." Mayhara looked over her shoulder before continuing. "What happened? Why is there tension between you?"

Salina opened her mouth to answer but couldn't bring herself to dive into the story. Not at three in the morning, anyway.

She crossed her arms. "It's a long story. Probably shouldn't get into it in the middle of the night. I think I'm just going to turn in. Darshana's probably going to have us training before the sun comes up, and my battery is on empty."

"Same here. But I'm here if you need to talk."

"Thanks. Good night, Mayhara."

Mayhara gave her a nod. "Good night."

FOUR

aree splashed cold water on her face, the droplets trailing down to her forearms as she stared at her reflection. She couldn't quite remember how they'd gotten back to the mansion. But she'd grown accustomed to the lost time and blackouts in her memory. Kashmeru had always been there—at least audibly—to let her know everything was all right.

Only this time, he hadn't spoken to her yet. Deep down, she could feel his rage. It was so strong, it shook her bones. And she understood his anger.

She had failed him.

She raked her thick, long, dark hair away from her face and tried to stop her bottom lip from trembling.

A softer voice inside of her—Lakshmi's loving voice, which was her own—told her to be strong. As the reincarnation of the Lotus empress, Naree was very powerful. She was, to her core, a strong leader, the sovereign of the Empire of the Lotus. Revered. Respected.

Yet Kashmeru was her undoing. The feared god was the darkness to her light, and he had control over her.

He'd asked her to acquire the arcane daggers needed to set him free from the tomb where he lay imprisoned. And she had failed.

There were seven daggers. She had three. The most recent face off with the elite mages was not successful. She'd been so close. She could have taken the dagger she'd been after away from the elites. Instead, she and the shadow army were ambushed. They'd been outnumbered, outwitted, and ultimately lost the dagger to the elites. The elites now had the upper hand, and Kashmeru knew it.

She took a deep breath and waited for his words. He loved her. She knew this. It was pure fact, centuries old. But to suffer his silence when she knew he was furious with her was something she couldn't endure.

As frustration tore at her, she pushed herself away from the bathroom sink and headed into her bedroom. Finding nothing but silence, she made her way downstairs.

The mansion's lounge area was a lavish room with a sixteen-foot ceiling, tall windows, and an enormous fireplace. The large, oak, double doors we accented with colored glass panes of amber and violet. Between the ivory statues and plush furniture, Naree should have felt like pampered royalty. Instead, she felt like a child about to be punished.

The murmur of voices caused her to turn toward the terrace sliding doors. She took in the sight of Bhutano waltzing in, speaking in low tones with three of the dark mages. She perked up, anxious to hear what they might be discussing, especially since Bhutano was the only other person Kashmeru spoke to besides her. He was Kashmeru's messenger, after all. His right-hand man, so to speak.

When their eyes met, Bhutano stopped speaking, holding a hand up to signal to the dark mages to halt the conversation. The dark mages pressed their lips together and eyed Naree as they continued to follow Bhutano through the lounge and through the oak doors to the mansion's conference room.

Bhutano cast her one last glance before closing the doors and leaving her in the room alone.

Naree crossed her arms and swallowed back the lump in her throat. She felt as if her stomach was turning inside out. She knew Kashmeru was mad, but she could only imagine what he had expressed to Bhutano for him to have given her that look of disapproval. She could barely hold back the tears as her insides soured, as if they were filling with acid. She plopped down on the couch and rubbed at her arms, biting her lip as she pondered what she could do to make things right.

FIVE

Loni opened her bedroom door to find Penny standing in the hall, waiting for her.

Loni held back a curse. "You'd think I'd be used to that."

"Good morning, sunshine. Darshana has requested our presence in the courtyard."

"This place has a courtyard?" Loni stepped into the hall with a scoff and closed the door behind her. "Not that I'm ungrateful. It was beyond wonderful to sleep in a bed that big and that comfortable after all the hellholes I've spent nights in."

"It's a nice change." Penny looked away from her as they walked.

"What is it?" Loni asked.

"Sorry?"

"I know that look, Penny. There's something you're not telling me."

They descended the stairs in silence. Loni waited patiently, hoping that giving Penny space would allow her to open up.

"I can't see it." Penny stopped at the bottom of the stairs. She turned to face Loni but still didn't look her in the eyes. "The day Kashmeru is released from his tomb. The vision won't come to me."

"But that's good, right? That means it's not going to happen."

"Not necessarily. I don't see anything past when the comet reaches the tomb. That could mean anything. It might be that our fates haven't been decided yet. It might also mean nothing exists beyond that point."

Loni's eyes widened. "Wow. Penny, you really know how to lighten the mood. Are you going to tell the others?"

Penny wrung her hands. "Not yet. I want to see if the vision comes to me... eventually. I'll meditate some more, and we'll see if it does."

"And if it doesn't?"

"Then we'll need all the luck we can get."

Shiro wiped the sweat from his hairline with a towel, catching his breath after the morning's training session. Though Darshana had been generous enough to give the mages an extra hour of sleep than usual, she'd pushed them extra hard today as well.

He had to admit, though, that it had been thrilling to observe the new mages using their powers. It had been years since he'd participated in a proper combat training with all the houses of mages, and he'd forgotten how magical it was. At one point during the training, he had aimed ice pellets at Loni. She had masterfully used her air power to whip them away from her. They'd zipped through the air in Salina's direction, and if Salina hadn't been so quick to use her heat shield to block them, she would surely have been hit.

"Hey, nice work out there." Kamal took a swig of his water bottle and gave Shiro a wink.

"Thanks. You too. I think my ears are still ringing from that sound blast you created."

"Cool, right?" Kamal crossed his arms and leaned against the archway of the meditation room. "You know I can control the pitch? I could make an entire song if I wanted."

Shiro eyed Kamal, who was smiling to himself as if pleased with the praise he lavished on himself. Didn't he know there was a war going on? Not that Shiro wanted to be a downer, but he felt as if Kamal was only interested in being in the spotlight.

"I'm going to go take a shower," Shiro said, making his way toward the hall.

"Can't you just water blast yourself or something? Save some time?"

"I'm pretty sure this clean-up requires some soap."

Kamal laughed as if Shiro had told him the funniest joke he'd ever heard. "All right. Catch you later, then."

Shiro held back from rolling his eyes and ventured into the hall and toward the stairs. As he walked by Amalia's room, he heard a continuous mumbling. Curiosity got the better of him, and he slowly pushed open the door, which stood slightly ajar.

Amalia was in her bed on top of the covers, lying still with her eyes closed. If it weren't for the rise and fall of her chest, he would have worried.

Kneeling on the floor beside Amalia's bed was Karina, the source of the mumbling. When he took a step closer, he realized it wasn't mumbling, exactly. Karina was chanting in another language. His best guess was Latin, but he wasn't exactly sure.

He stood silently for a moment, listening. But then she stopped.

"You're very good at being quiet," Karina said, opening her eyes, "but I smelled you ever since you walked down the hall."

Shiro bit back a laugh. "This coming from someone who bathes in an actual swamp."

"We don't bathe in the swamp," Amalia said, grunting as she sat up. "We're no water mages, but we know how to boil water."

"Though magic does help it look less murky," Karina added.

"What are you doing?" He gestured at the floor. "With the chanting, I mean."

Karina stood and stretched, exchanging a look with her grandmother. "Trying to do a magical detox. I don't know if whatever the dark mage did is a reversible kind of magic, but it's worth a try."

"Is it working?" Shiro asked.

Amalia tightened her jaw and grabbed the bedsheets, clenching them until her fingers turned red.

Shiro shifted from one foot to the other. "I'll take that as a no."

"I'm not giving up." Karina walked over to Amalia and rubbed her back. "I'll try some other herbs and… maybe a different spell. There's a full moon coming; I could try to harness the power of—"

"Karina, stop." Amalia covered her mouth to cough. "There's no use. That dark mage knew what he was doing. He wouldn't have done something to a witch that a spell would undo. That would be foolish."

"Maybe a spell isn't what is needed." Shiro scrubbed at his jaw.

Karina narrowed her eyes. "What do you have in mind?"

"The plasma in human blood is ninety-two percent water. I'm assuming it's the same with swamp witches?"

"Yes." Karina smirked. "Except it's dirtier with possible tadpoles and dead mosquitos thrown in the mix."

Shiro felt his cheeks grow hot. "Sorry."

"What are you suggesting?" Amalia asked, cringing as she shifted on the bed.

"Well, it was your idea to do a detox." Shiro gave a half-shrug. "I'm just thinking of going a different route."

Karina stared at him a moment and then quickly turned toward her grandmother. "Manipulating the water in your blood? You think it would work?"

"It couldn't hurt," Amalia said.

"Actually… it might." Shiro cringed and came closer to the bed. "If I successfully extract poison from your body, it's going to have to come out somehow."

"Like…" Karina appeared as if she were holding back a wince. "She might throw it up?"

"That, or it could be pushed out through her pores. In any case, the poison is probably going to take a toll on whatever it comes into contact with."

Amalia took a deep breath and let it out slowly. With a nod, she leaned back until her head rested on her pillow. "Okay. Let's do it."

"Grandma, are you sure?"

"It's worth a try." Amalia closed her eyes. "I'm ready."

Karina swallowed hard, backing away from the bed.

Shiro wanted to tell her he would be careful, that he wouldn't let anything bad happen to her. But he couldn't promise that, and he didn't want to lie.

Amalia stretched out her fingers and blew out a breath. Her eyes were still closed, but she nodded once, giving Shiro the green light.

Shiro placed his palms together. He needed to take his time and do this right; otherwise, he could harm her heart or shatter her veins. For a moment, he had reservations about having mentioned his idea. If it didn't work, if he ended up killing Amalia, Karina would never forgive him. And he would never forgive himself.

He stretched out his arms, reaching toward Amalia until his fingers were mere inches away from her skin. The carnelian stone on his wristband caught the light. He felt outward with his power, tuning in to her blood.

The current of her blood flow tingled in his fingertips.

He flinched, pulling his hands back for a second. Something hurt him. It was like splinters cutting through his skin. The farther he reached in, the sharper the pain. Sword tips. Razor blades. Hot, burning needles. Whatever magic the dark mage had used on her, it was killing her harshly.

Ever so gently, he pulled with his powers. Amalia let out a hiss, arching her back. Karina stepped forward quickly, worrying her hands, but she didn't approach the bed. Shiro carefully shifted his hand to the side. He could feel the poison crawl through her veins as he did so. Amalia clenched her teeth, but her moan of pain still escaped.

"Maybe we should stop," Karina said, her eyes darting between Shiro and her grandmother.

"No!" Amalia shook her head frantically. "Keep trying."

Shiro moved his hands horizontally, trying to separate the poison from Amalia's blood. He closed one hand into a fist and pulled it upward. Amalia let out a wail, grabbing at the sheets by her sides. Shiro pulled his power farther upward, his hands shaking.

"Shiro?" Karina scrubbed her hands down the sides of her face.

"Just a little more," he said, his voice strained. He could feel the muscles in his neck tightening. He squeezed his fist tighter and yanked his arm upward.

Amalia gagged, rolled to her side, and vomited violently.

Shiro let go, his gaze flying to Karina as she ran to her grandmother's side. It wasn't until Amalia's second heave that Karina got the wastebasket under her head in time to catch her grandmother's sick.

A mixture of blood, yellow slime, and black particles landed in the wastebasket. It bubbled and sizzled, and it took all the control Shiro had not to throw up himself.

"Oh, Grandma," Karina cried, stoking her head.

Shiro wiped sweat from his brow and took a step back.

"Was that all of it?" Karina asked, her eyes brimming with tears.

"No." He took a deep breath and exhaled, shaking his head. "There's more. Lots more. But she's in a lot of pain. I think she should rest."

"No," Amalia said, her voice raspy. "Let's keep going."

"Amalia, the poison is strong. If I do too much at once, it'll rip your insides apart."

Karina's eyes grew wide. "He's right, Grandma. Let's take a break. Replenish your strength. We'll try again once you've rested."

Reluctance was etched on her face, but Amalia nodded. She rolled back onto the bed, trying to catch her breath. "All right. Just a little rest."

"I'll give you some space." Shiro turned to head out of the room, feeling as if his nerves were about to dissolve. Before he closed the door, he took one more glance at Amalia. She was breathing more steadily, but her face was pale, her eyes pinched closed.

Karina held her hand and looked up at Shiro. Her expression of sorrow and fear tore a hole in his soul.

SIX

Penny inhaled, counting in her head. She tried to concentrate solely on her breathing, but she could literally feel Shiro's frustration. He sat in the lotus position, his eyes closed, attempting to meditate, but his frustration was palpable. She knew what he was trying to do, and she knew it was taking a toll on him.

She exhaled and then breathed in again. This time it was Yuki who distracted her. Her yoga moves were too fast, not at all graceful and fluid. She was more like a cheerleader practicing her jumping techniques.

"Why do we need to learn all this yoga anyway?" Kamal asked as he tried to copy her reverse warrior pose. "Seems silly."

She scowled at him. "So we can do things like this."

She was so fast, Penny almost couldn't track her movements. Yuki had swung her arms down to the mat and extended her right leg out in front of her. She swept it swiftly to the side, catching Kamal's leg and knocking him flat on his back.

Yuki smiled at Kamal's groan of pain. "Still seem silly to you?"

Penny pushed their conversation away and closed her eyes. For a while, a whirlwind of thoughts went through her mind. She ignored them, blocking them from her train of thought as she tried to draw a blank slate. After a while, her thoughts were clear, and she slowed her breathing.

A picture popped into her mind. The interior of some house, but seen through tunnel vision. Everything at the edges of the scene was blurred out. A fireplace. A pastel painting hanging above it. Someone walked by it, but she couldn't see who it was. In her vision, she followed them. They went down the nearby hall and entered a dark room. They took a key out of their pocket and unlocked a door inside the room. The door led to what looked like a storage area, a large walk-in closet with shelves. And on the shelves were three red-and-black boxes. The daggers.

"All I'm saying is if I knew you were going to attack me, I would have been ready," Kamal said to Yuki.

Penny grunted in frustration. Even Shiro sighed with impatience.

"Can you two keep it down?" Penny asked.

Yuki and Kamal sheepishly apologized, and Penny closed her eyes again.

Come on, daggers. Show me where you are.

She cleared her mind once more. She searched for the vision, wanting to call it back so she could figure out where this place in her vision was.

Darkness. Shadows. Water.

Water?

She followed the thought. It was as if she were swimming through the water in her mind.

Bubbles. Fish. People looking through glass and pointing.

Penny's eyes flew open as she gasped.

"I found it," she said, jumping to her feet. "I know where the last dagger is."

There were still a few patrons at the aquarium. They had about fifteen minutes left before closing time, and the workers had already begun to rope off sections. Kamal used his sapphire-based charm to walk up to the straggling patrons, whispering to them. Loni watched them listen to him. Each person he approached seemed to nod in agreement with whatever he said and proceeded to leave. None of them noticed the blue glow of his palms, which he kept hidden behind his back.

Once the leftover patrons had gone, Kamal proceeded to get the workers to go. One of them removed their keys from their belt loop and handed them to him. Loni almost laughed at the extremes Kamal had gone to for this mission.

Once they were in the clear, Penny called them over. "Follow me."

They made their way down a tunnel that went through the water. Fish swam above them and to their sides. At the end of the tunnel, the room opened up facing a gigantic wall of glass. Behind it loomed a wall of coral littered with sea anemones and flower-like clusters of pink polyps. Crown-of-thorns sea stars rounded the bases of the coral walls, and small mandarinfish swam around, searching for food. But what made Loni drop her jaw was the sand tiger sharks that loomed nearby.

"There are sharks in there," Loni whispered, as if they could hear her.

"There's also a dagger in there. An important one." Penny took her hands. "Shiro will help try to steer them away."

Loni looked up at Shiro.

"Yeah," he said. "I've, uh, only done it with smaller fish, but how different could it be?"

Loni fought off a shiver that crept up her back. "You're filling me with confidence, you know that?"

"Do you see that section of coral there?" Penny pointed, her finger on the glass. "Next to that blue starfish."

Loni drew closer to the glass and peered at the spot Penny spoke of. "Yeah."

"That seaweed should break away. The box is behind it."

Loni took a deep breath. "Okay. I can get it."

"You know what you're going to do?" Penny asked.

"I'll dive in and create an air bubble around my head so I can get low enough without having to come back up for air. But Shiro *has* to keep those sharks away."

"Guys," Kamal called. He waved them over to a door he'd unlocked. It read, "Staff Only."

They followed him through the door and made their way up a set of metal stairs. The stairs brought them to a platform that was suspended above all the tanks. The sound of the filters whirred in the air, and Loni could feel the vibration shaking her bones. Or maybe that was just her nerves.

They rounded the shark tank and Loni squatted down.

"Are you ready to do this?" Penny asked.

"As ready as I'll ever be," she answered.

Loni took off her shoes and swung her legs over the water. She winced as she dropped her feet inside. "Cold," was all she said.

Her palms glowed green, and she held them near her ears. Instinct had her hold her breath as she jumped, but there was no need to do so. As soon as she was in the water, a bubble of air surrounded her head. She took a chance and breathed, hoping the bubble wouldn't pop. The green of her palms grew brighter, as she was determined not to lose her air bubble.

She looked up at Penny and the others, but they were blurry and wavering in her vision. It looked as though Kamal was giving her a thumbs-up. She turned her attention downward. The spot Penny told her about seemed so far away. She looked left and right, searching for where the sharks might be. She caught sight of one, but it was moving away from her.

It's now or never, she thought.

Loni shifted her position and kicked her feet, diving deeper into the water. Her eyes focused on the blue starfish. Panic threatened to do her in, but she forced it out of her mind. She had to get the dagger. This was their chance to get ahead of the Pishacha. Just a little bit farther.

A school of clownfish swam past her bubble as she reached for the seaweed Penny had told her to pull away from the coral. She muttered a curse directed at Shiro. He couldn't even keep the little fish away. But when she looked over her shoulder, she saw why. A tiger shark was twisting in the water, making its way toward her.

Loni gasped. Her feet kicked to back away from the shark, and her foot caught a sharp bit of coral. Holding back a yelp, she tried to keep from flailing. A small cloud of blood trailed away from the back of her foot.

No, no, no!

She stared wide-eyed at the approaching shark, afraid to move. The shark went left and right, jerking his head as if fighting off something causing resistance. Loni's breaths began to cloud the bubble. She fought back her panic and told herself to steady her breathing. The shark snapped its teeth in the water, aggravated by the unseen force that was keeping it from getting near Loni.

Thank you, Shiro, she thought.

Quickly, she turned and made her way back to the blue starfish and the seaweed. There was no telling how long Shiro could keep the shark away from her, and Loni knew there was at least one more in the tank. Her odds wouldn't improve if that one decided to join his friend.

The seaweed was slippery, but she managed to pull it away from the coral. Sure enough, there was a small section carved into the coral where the red-and-black box sat. It was wrapped in clear, tight plastic and tape.

She pried the box out of the hole and held it against her chest.

Checking once more for the whereabouts of the sharks, she focused on the surface of the water and kicked her legs as hard as she could. Using a little more air power, she boosted herself to the surface. Her bubble popped as soon as she broke through.

Shiro and Penny pulled her out and set her on the platform. Kamal took the box. Even though she'd had air the entire time, she gasped as though she were breathing for the first time.

"You did great, Loni," Penny said.

"If I never see another shark for the rest of my life, it'll be too soon." Loni stood and wrung water out of her clothes. She grimaced at the murky grime that clung to her skin. "Let's get out of here. I need a shower."

SEVEN

Mayhara slipped her hands off Jae's waist and dismounted his bike. As she removed her helmet, she scanned their surroundings for Imperial Police and Pishacha. It was risky returning to the scroll shop, but they had the chance to find out more about the mysterious scroll they were in possession of. Even Penny wasn't able to give them insight on what the scroll was or why it was important.

The bell above the door chimed as they stepped into the cluttered shop. The siblings Mayhara and Jae had met during their last visit to the shop looked up as they entered. Nian, the more cooperative and cordial of the siblings, packaged a purchase by a short, plump customer and wished her a nice day before nodding his greeting to Jae and Mayhara. Nian's sister, Zhen, simply raised a brow at them as she continued to dust a shelf of vases.

They were dressed similarly, Nian in a blue-and-black *tangzhuang* jacket and Zhen in a blue-and-black *cheongsam* dress. Nian's black hair was slicked back, while Zhen's thick, dark mane was pulled up and held in place with a matching blue *fa-zan* hairpin shaped in the form of a peacock.

Jae and Mayhara waited until the customer Nian had tended to was finished with her purchase. Mayhara pretended to inspect a carving of a dragon as the customer passed by her. For a second, the woman stopped. Mayhara's heart began to hammer in her throat. She calmly adjusted her turquoise headscarf and turned away from the woman. Forcing herself to breathe normally, Mayhara told herself the woman might just have been browsing the shelves once more before leaving. Finally, the woman continued walking. When the bell above the door signaled her departure, Mayhara let out a sigh of relief.

Nian walked around the counter and bowed to Jae. As Mayhara made her way over to them, Zhen scoffed and rolled her eyes. Mayhara shot her a questioning look, but Zhen ignored her and disappeared behind a curtain into what Mayhara assumed was the stockroom.

"Good to see you again." Nian bowed to Mayhara as she joined them. "You too," she answered.

"Zhen is getting our great-aunt. I'll lock the door and close the shop temporarily so we can talk in private."

Jae nodded and glanced at Mayhara. She pushed back her headscarf and rocked onto her heels, fighting off a flutter in her stomach. Could this great-aunt of theirs really be able to solve the mystery of the cryptic scroll?

The curtain was pushed aside, and Zhen appeared, followed by a short, round-bodied, older woman with straw-like white hair and thick glasses. She hobbled behind Zhen as they approached the counter.

"This is our great-aunt Baozhai," Nian said.

"She can probably help you," Zhen said. "She's very old."

Nian scowled at Zhen and elbowed her hard.

"She's not wrong." Baozhai smirked. "She's also not in my will."

Zhen frowned and mumbled something in Mandarin.

"Thank you for offering to help." Jae bowed to her. "I realized there's a risk to working with mages, so we do appreciate it."

"Hmm. Don't thank me yet." She held out her hand. "Let's have a look first."

Jae and Mayhara exchanged a glance. Zhen and Nian watched them expectantly. Baozhai's hand was still out as she waited. Clearing his throat, Jae opened his messenger bag and withdrew the tube that held the scroll.

Baozhai took it, running her hand over the surface as if checking to see if it was authentic. She turned as she slipped the scroll out and then unrolled the delicate fabric on the counter. She used her fingers to smooth out the material. Adjusting her glasses, she leaned closer and studied the illustration.

Mayhara bit back her impatience. She desperately wanted to ask the woman what she saw but knew it was better not to interrupt her.

"First the bad news," Baozhai finally said. "I haven't seen this scroll before. It's from before my time. You can tell from the fabric that was used and the almost blueish tone of the ink."

Mayhara and Jae leaned closer to inspect the things she'd described.

"Since I haven't seen the scroll before," Baozhai continued, "I can't say with certainty I know what it is."

"Okay," Jae said. "I'm hoping there's some good news to counter that fact."

Baozhai squinted as she smiled at him. "There is. You see this symbol?" She pointed to a small square near the bottom of the scroll. The square had diagonal lines connecting the corners, forming an 'X' and a vertical line running through the middle of the square. "That's the symbol for *witch*. And this symbol next to it is an old language style of writing *book*."

"Witch book," Mayhara said to herself. "A grimoire?"

She and Jae exchanged a look. Amalia had mentioned a grimoire. Perhaps this was connected.

"And you think this is a map?" Jae asked Baozhai. "Nian mentioned the possibility."

"These twisting and turning lines"—Baozhai traced the lines with her wrinkly finger—"to the common eye, they might appear to be the borders of land, but they could also represent the walls of a tunnel."

Mayhara put her hand on the corner of the scroll and adjusted her perspective. "Okay. But where is this?"

"I can't be sure." Baozhai shook her head. "But these symbols on the sides might be clues. Someone would have to decipher them."

"So basically, this scroll is a treasure map to a grimoire." Jae crossed his arms and pressed a thumb to his lips. Mayhara could almost see the wheels in his brain spinning.

"That's what it looks like." Baozhai rolled up the scroll and slipped it back in its tube. "I'm sorry I can't help you more. Most of those symbols are foreign to me, so unless you know where to find a witch—"

A hard banging on the door made them jump.

"Who is that?" Mayhara whispered.

"Imperial Police! Open up!"

Mayhara's hand shot out and grabbed Jae's arm. "Oh no. That woman who was in the shop. She must have recognized me and called the police."

Jae's head whipped around to face Nian. "Is there a back way out of here?"

"Yes, follow me."

Mayhara's head swam as she and Jae rushed through the curtains into the back room. The police had found her. This could all go bad very fast. The room was jampacked with inventory, making it difficult to maneuver.

There was a large door at the back of the room labeled WORKSHOP, but that wasn't where Nian led them.

Kicking a large box to the side, Nian grabbed a wall-high set of shelves and pried it away from the wall. Behind it was a hidden door.

"This way," he said, throwing the door open. "Keep going to the end of the hall. It comes out on the opposite side of the block into an alleyway. From there, you're on your own."

Mayhara nodded. She could hear Zhen telling the police the lock was stuck, asking for their patience.

"Thank you," Jae told Nian.

"Good luck," he replied.

He shut the door behind them, and they raced down the hall. Mayhara's jaw was set, and she flexed her hands, preparing herself to use her powers if necessary.

At the end of the hall, Jae yanked the door open. Mayhara squinted against the sun, adjusting her eyes to the change of light so she could better assess their escape route.

"Through here," Jae called, already at the gate of a chain-link fence dividing the alleyway.

Mayhara almost tripped over a crate blocking her way but managed to slip through the gate unscathed. They dashed to the end of the alleyway and pressed their backs against the wall of one building. Mayhara could hear the deafening sound of buzz saws through the workshop windows. Jae peered around the corner.

"Okay, let's go." Jae nodded to her once.

They only made it twenty feet before a loud voice boomed through the air.

"Imperial Police! Stop where you are!"

Mayhara made the mistake of looking over her shoulder at the officer who had shouted at them. In that instant, Jae had veered off to dive behind a dumpster, yelling for Mayhara to come with him. But that moment cost her a precious second of judgement. Another officer appeared in front of her, his gun drawn.

Mayhara's vision hazed over for a second. She could hear one of the officers say "back up" and "fugitive" into his radio while the other commanded that she not move.

No. She had to concentrate.

A crimson glow came to life in each of her palms. The officer with the gun shouted at her to lower her hands. Instead, she forced out crimson energy on each side of her. The earth exploded between her and the Imperial Police, a barrage of debris kicking up and striking the officers, throwing them back. The officer with the gun trained on her fired his weapon, but the explosion had knocked him off balance, and the bullet missed.

Setting off another explosion, Mayhara crouched down and doubled back. She leaped to the spot Jae had gone and grabbed his arm. "Let's go!"

"This way," he said. "I can hear their backup coming from the other direction."

She didn't question him; she just ran. They didn't stop until they were two blocks down and had rounded the corner. As they paused to catch their breaths, Jae checked behind them.

"We've got a head start, but we can't stop."

She gaped at the blood on his jaw. "Oh my God, did I do that?"

"No, don't worry. I clipped it on the dumpster." He peered around the corner. "We can make it back to my bike if we cut through those buildings. You ready?"

She steeled herself and nodded. "Yeah, let's go."

EIGHT

It was peaceful in the garden. Naree watched a hummingbird flit around from flower to flower collecting nectar. It seemed tranquil, happy as it completed its task. Naree could almost forget the anguish she'd been in over the last few days at not completing her task.

Almost.

She stretched on the lounge chair and glanced through the sliding glass door. Seeing Bhutano come toward her, she sat upright and swung her legs off the leg rest to place her feet on the floor.

His short, dark hair was slicked back, his shoulders broad and squared. His heavy brows were drawn over his intense black eyes. His expression was pure business, yet the clenching of his jaw told Naree he had some bad news.

"Bhutano?" She had to clear her throat when his name hadn't come out right.

"Your majesty."

The fact that he called her this was already a good sign, in her mind. "Has something happened?"

"I've called a meeting with the council of the seven. They'll be arriving shortly, and you should attend."

"Of course," she said. "What's this about?"

"One of the elites had a run-in with the Imperial Police near a scroll shop in the city."

"A run-in?"

He nodded once. "They almost had her, but she managed to escape. Your… Your brother was with her."

Naree flinched. She wasn't sure what to think or how to feel. She'd been trained not to think of Jae as family. Naree was a reincarnation of Lakshmi, and Lakshmi had no brother.

Bhutano searched her face.

Maybe this is a test, Naree thought. *To make sure I'm still on Kashmeru's side.*

She cleared her throat, keeping her expression neutral. "A scroll shop? Does this have anything to do with the scrolls that were stolen from Censinq?"

"We believe so," Bhutano replied. "We're sending a team in to interrogate the shop staff."

Naree breathed in deeply and exhaled slowly. "And if they can't give us any answers?"

"Then our dark mages will have to step in and *make* them cooperate."

NINE

Mayhara and Jae split up as soon as they got to the temple. They'd agreed to divide their tasks. As Jae went to find Darshana and fill her in on the information they'd found out about the scroll, Mayhara headed off to find Amalia. She hadn't expected to find Karina in the hall, with her back pressed against her door. And she hadn't expected to find her crying.

"Karina! What—"

The sound of Amalia's strained moan from behind the door gave Mayhara pause.

Karina winced, wiping the tears from her cheeks.

"What's happening in there?" Mayhara whispered, placing a hand on Karina's shoulder.

"Shiro's trying to pull out the poison."

Mayhara's jaw hung open as she tried to process that. "He can do that?"

Karina shrugged. "It hurts her, though. I don't know what's worse: her suffering from the poison or from the extraction."

"Well, if it's working—"

"That's just it. He can only do it in short sessions without tearing apart her insides. Then, by the time she's rested enough for him to do more, he checks to see how much poison he can feel in her body, and it's multiplied. It's growing faster than he can remove it. He can't keep up with it, but neither one of them wants to give up."

Another moan of pain sounded from behind the door. Amalia's cry made Mayhara's heart tense up.

Karina drew her lips in, suppressing a sob. "I… I can't bear to watch or listen anymore."

Mayhara drew closer and put her arm around Karina. She could practically feel Karina's worry seeping out of her pores. "Maybe you should take a walk, get some air."

Karina sniffled, nodding her head.

Mayhara took a step back and studied her face. "And if you're up for a distraction, I could really use your help with something."

"Sure." Karina fell into step with Mayhara as they made their way down the hall. "What is it?"

"We acquired a scroll that has something to do with the prophecy. Apparently, the symbols on it might be able to be interpreted by a witch. I was hoping you'd be able to take a look and see if you can translate any of it."

"Of course." Karina took her hand and squeezed it. "If it helps putting an end to Kashmeru's tyranny, count me in."

Jae leaned on the back of the couch, watching Darshana pace as she took in the information about the scroll. Mr. Kitaro and Penny, seated in the living room area, kept their eyes on her as well. Kamal, Loni, and Salina waited for her to speak, undoubtedly processing the news themselves.

"And Mayhara's asking Amalia to translate the symbols?" Darshana asked.

"Yes," Jae answered.

"Actually," Penny said, interrupting, "she asked Karina. They're out by the pond, looking over the scroll right now."

"How do you know that? You've been sitting here all…" Kamal scoffed. "Not going to lie. It's scary when you do that."

"Okay, so there's a chance we could figure out where the grimoire is." Salina raked her hands through the curls at her temples. "I mean, I know we said we were going to concentrate on getting the other daggers, but we've totally got to follow up on that, right?"

"Cover our bases." Mr. Kitaro nodded, coddling his coffee cup. "Yes, it's a strategic move."

"Should we really be deciding that yet?" Loni's tone was full of skepticism. "We don't even know if Karina can decipher the scroll, let alone figure out where The Archives are. We could be wasting our resources if we split up, especially if this turns out to be a wild goose chase."

"Have a bit more faith, Loni," Darshana said, finally standing still after pacing the entire room. "These things fall into our laps for reasons, especially when it comes to the prophecy. I don't think it's a coincidence that Amalia and Karina found their way to us in a time when needing a witch proves useful."

"Spooky," Kamal mumbled.

"We'll use our cognitive lessons from back at the academy," Salina said. "Make a plan."

"Yeah, between the group of us, we can come up with something that will work."

The back sliding door slid open. They all turned to see Mayhara and Karina stepping inside. Mayhara tapped the scroll tube against her palm.

"We've got something," Mayhara said.

Jae felt goosebumps spring up all over his skin.

"There are symbols at the bottom right of the scroll. Mayhara said she and Jae thought they might be Wiccan. But they're not Wiccan numbers. They're Bhahmi numerals."

"Numbers?" Jae asked. "Referencing what?"

"The way they're lined up," Mayhara began, "we think they're coordinates."

TEN

A flash of color soared through the air toward Loni, and with it came an earsplitting, high-pitched tone that almost made her lose focus. Her palms glowed emerald green, and when she pushed out her mage powers, creating a blast of wind, the sound became muffled and distorted, and then disappeared. At the opposite end of the training field, Kamal smirked at her.

"Jerk," she mumbled.

The trill of laughter caught her ear. Loni followed the sound and spotted Mayhara on the far end of the field. Jae handed Mayhara a towel but playfully whipped it away before she could take it. Mayhara giggled and smacked Jae's bicep, her hand lingering there a second or two longer than Loni was comfortable with. Jae lifted the towel and hung it over Mayhara's shoulders.

Loni's insides grew hot, her breath like steam escaping from her nostrils. A part of her wanted to send a blast of emerald energy their way and knock Mayhara off her feet.

In that moment, Loni was pummeled into and slammed to the ground with force. It took her a minute before she realized it was Salina who'd collided with her.

Loni clenched her jaw and pushed Salina off her. "Watch it!" She rolled to the side and jumped to her feet.

Salina furrowed her brow as she regained her footing. "Sorry."

"My fault," Shiro called, running up to them. "That last ice blast was more powerful than I meant it to be."

"I didn't mean to crash into you," Salina said. "It's just that Darshana is pushing me extra hard now that I'm the golden elite, and keeping focus is—"

"I don't want to hear your excuses." Loni used her air powers to blow stray grass and leaves off her clothes. "It's always excuses with you. Maybe you should start taking responsibility for your actions for a change."

Salina scoffed. "What the hell is your problem?"

Loni was about to retort, but the other mages were approaching. Out of the corner of her eye, she spotted Darshana, watching them intently from the temple's terrace.

"Everything okay?" Jae asked.

"It's fine," Loni answered irately.

"A pity." Kamal rested his hands on his hips. "Thought we might get to see a catfight."

He began to meow, but Penny smacked him on the arm.

"Pig," Yuki mumbled.

A *ping* sounded, and Shiro took out his Linq. "Oh no."

"What is it?" Mayhara asked.

"There's been an attack on town hall," he answered.

The mages gathered closer, huddling over Shiro's shoulders to watch video footage a citizen had caught and uploaded to social media. The shaky video showed an explosion erupting through a section of windows on New Jaipur's town hall building. Passersby screamed as they fled.

The man holding the camera shouted, "I think a bomb just went off in the town hall! Smoke is filling the air. People are running away in case another bomb explodes. Who would do this?"

"Extremists?" Salina asked.

Kamal shrugged. "Who else could it be?"

Loni noticed Shiro's jaw tense as he put his Linq away.

"It was uploaded about half an hour ago," Yuki said as she pulled the elastic band out of her hair. "Let's go inside and see if any of it has made the news yet."

Loni took her time, trailing behind as the rest of the group headed inside to the living room televiewer. Her eyes followed Jae and Mayhara as they walked side by side. They weren't holding hands, nor did Jae have his arm draped around her shoulder. But there was a vibe between them that felt like a knife in Loni's gut. She knew she had no reason to feel territorial about him. She hadn't seen him in years.

They made it inside, followed by a curious Darshana and Mr. Kitaro. Loni's thoughts were interrupted by the televiewer coming to life. Similar video footage to the one they'd seen on Shiro's Linq displayed on the screen.

"—that the involvement of extremists in the attack is just speculation at this point. However, the perpetrators seemed to have left a calling card of sorts, a symbol that denotes responsibility for the act. A small, black, plastic card with a gold skull and crossbones illustration was found at both the scene of the attack today as well as the incident at the Alwar police station last week."

The image on the screen changed from the burning town hall to a shot of the governor and his family being escorted into a limousine.

"Governor Laghari and his family were not physically harmed in the explosion, as they were in a different section of the building at the time for a press-related photoshoot, but they are scheduled to meet with a security specialist due to the upcoming costume gala in New Jaipur."

"Avi." Yuki's hands flew to her mouth.

"What?" Salina asked.

"The governor's son." Yuki visibly swallowed. "Avi. He's a dark mage."

"Are you sure?" Shiro asked.

"Yes," she said, dropping her gaze.

"Wait." Jae turned to the other mages. "That makes sense. The Sacred Key from the observatory—when she accused us of being dark mages, she asked which one of us was the governor's son."

"So it's true," Mayhara said.

"But how did you know?" Shiro asked Yuki.

Yuki pursed her lips.

"They used to be a couple," Kamal said.

"Not a couple." Yuki smacked his shoulder and crossed her arms. "We went on, like, two dates. But this was before I found out he was a dark mage. As soon as I found out, I cut ties with him—which he wasn't too happy about. So I used my emotion powers to convince him he was fine with the break."

"Wait. Dates?" Salina asked. "Aren't you fourteen?"

Yuki narrowed her eyes at her. "I'm seventeen."

"Penny?" Mayhara asked.

Everyone turned to see Penny holding the controller, which was pointed at the televiewer. The screen was frozen on the interior of a building. Loni realized it was the building the gala would take place in. The shot zeroed in on a fireplace. Two tall cast-iron candle holders stood on either side. Above it was a painting of a girl smelling a lotus.

"Penny, what is it?" Loni asked.

"I've seen this before. This fireplace, the painting. I've seen them in my visions." Penny turned to the others. "I think I know where the Pishacha are hiding the daggers."

Everyone's eyes went to the screen.

"At the governor's mansion?" Jae asked.

"We've got to go get them." Kamal stood, puffing out his chest as if ready to go.

"Don't be so hasty." Darshana, who had been quietly watching them for some time, stepped closer. "They will have armed guards at all times of the day and night. Especially now, with the recent attacks. No one will be able to get close to that place."

"But they will on the night of the gala," Yuki said.

"Only prominent people." Loni swiped her hair out of her face. "I believe it's invitation-only."

"So we get invited," Jae said.

"What?" Mayhara shook her head. "How's that supposed to happen?"

"It shouldn't be hard for a sapphire mage to convince whoever is at the door that they belong there." Jae looked pointedly at Kamal. "It's a costume ball. Everyone will be wearing masks."

"It could work," Mr. Kitaro said, also stepping forward from the back of the room. "If we got someone in, they might be able to get to the daggers."

"Sure," Kamal said. "I can do that."

"You shouldn't go alone," Penny said. "This isn't a solo job. Plus, you'd have a better chance at not raising suspicions if you had a date. Not me, though. I need to go into vision-mode to figure out where the daggers are, and people might notice."

"I'll do it," Loni said. "I love masks."

"I can get some devices so Penny can communicate with you over an earpiece," Jae added. "A couple of us can be near but out of sight to make sure we've got a clean escape route."

"Okay, it's settled," Darshana said. "And while we await the gala, we can try to figure out how to find the grimoire."

A warm, comforting feeling filled Jae's heart when Mayhara opened her door and smiled at him. He'd been rehearsing in his head what he wanted to say to her, but now, gazing into her deep brown eyes, he was at a loss for words.

"Jae?"

"I wanted to… Is it okay if I come in and talk to you?"

"Of course." She opened the door wider and stepped aside.

Her bedsheets were slightly pulled back. Jae wondered if she had been lying down, and for a moment he felt bad for disturbing her. But he'd been driven here by a force he couldn't ignore, so instead of apologizing, he decided to open up.

"Mayha, maybe this is going to sound ridiculous, but I can't get it out of my head. I tried to play it off all day, as if it hadn't affected me, but I just can't shake it."

"What is it?"

He cleared his throat. "Yesterday, when you almost got caught… I… I thought my heart was going to stop."

"It's not ridiculous." She offered him a small smile. "I'm pretty sure mine did. At least, for a few seconds."

"I don't know what I would have done if they'd taken you away." He let out the smallest of laughs. "I mean, I do. I would have done anything in my power to get you away from them. But one of them took a shot at you. The panic that brewed up inside me… I could feel it in my throat."

She reached up and ran a finger along the laceration on his jaw. "Looks like you actually got the worst of it."

He trapped her hand with his, holding it to his cheek. "It's just a scratch. Especially compared to how my fear for your life tore a gaping hole in my heart."

She searched his face, her lips parting. Her thumb caressed her cheekbone, and she took a step closer.

Jae let his face hover nearer to hers, his eyes taking in every tiny movement of this moment, the way her lids grew heavy, the soft brush of her breath against his skin. Slowly, he closed the distance between them. There was no second-guessing now. The moment he'd been dreaming of had come to fruition.

Her lips were soft and warm, and as she drew in a breath—the kiss along with it—she pressed her chest against him. Jae cupped his hands around the back of her head, like he was afraid the kiss would end too soon.

Before his heart could explode, he moved his lips to her cheek, her temple, her forehead, and then he pulled her into a crushing embrace. Her hands traveled up and down his back as he stroked the back of her head. He wasn't sure if the hammering in his chest was coming from her heart or his.

"I was afraid," she whispered, "to let myself believe you could feel this way about me."

"You never have to be afraid with me. We're in this together, remember? You're stuck with me for a while."

"For a while?" She chuckled.

"Forever," he said. "Or until the end of the world. Whichever comes last."

She laughed softly as she drew back. He took her hands and gazed at her a moment longer.

"I should let you get some sleep." He let go of her hands and raked his fingers through his hair. "To be honest, today has left me exhausted."

"Me too." She gave him a warm smile. "I'll see you in the morning."

He reached out and trailed his thumb down her cheek. "Good night."

He left the room with the feeling he was floating. His heart thrummed with exhilaration and his breaths came easy. It was as if he'd just removed a layer of armor. He had to stop himself from skipping to his room like a kid. If anyone were to see him, they'd think he'd already singlehandedly won the war.

But someone did see him.

At the end of the hall, standing with her hand on her doorknob, was Loni.

Jae's smile faded as he walked past her. His stomach felt heavy when their eyes met for a split second. The look she gave him was filled with mixed emotions he couldn't quite interpret. He didn't even want to guess what she was thinking.

He forced himself to look away, continuing to his room. He didn't have time to deal with Loni right now. He was too exhausted. And he wasn't about to let her rain on his parade.

ELEVEN

Mayhara turned over in her bed for the hundredth time. But this time it wasn't dark mages and approaching comets keeping her up. Though she felt a little guilty for dwelling on it under such dire circumstances, she couldn't get the kiss with Jae out of her head. It wasn't that she hadn't wanted it to happen, and it wasn't that she regretted it. But she couldn't shake the twinge of guilt lurking in her bones for finding a hint of happiness while others were imprisoned and getting killed.

She punched her pillow with a grunt and then threw her covers off her body. Sighing, she sat up and swung her legs off the bed. Maybe a tea would help settle her nerves.

When she got to the kitchen, she found Kamal sitting in the breakfast nook, scarfing down leftovers.

"Don't mind me," he said between bites. "I'm always hungry."

"I noticed." She opened a cabinet and took out a tea cup.

"Can't sleep?" he asked.

She filled a kettle and set it on the stove. "Can't shut off my brain."

"Maybe a plate of *chana aloo* would help."

"I'm fine with green tea. Thanks."

She could feel him watching her as she prepared her hot drink. She wanted to ignore him, but it finally got to her.

"What?" There was no malice in her voice. Just exhaustion. She walked over with her tea and sat across from him at the table.

"Is it your family?"

"Is what my family?"

"The reason you can't sleep."

She tried to hide the blush that blossomed in her cheeks by taking a sip of her tea. If she wanted to share her feelings about Jae with someone, Kamal wasn't exactly the first person she'd seek out. "One of the reasons," she said. "What about you?"

"Oh, I don't have a family. Not a real one anyway."

"What does that mean?"

Kamal set his fork down and wiped his mouth with a cloth napkin. "It means my mom abandoned me when I was a baby. No idea who my dad is. Spent my youth bouncing from one foster home to another. The closest I'd come to calling someone family was Sunan."

"The sapphire elite at the time of the Eradication," she noted.

"Yeah. And obviously, he's not around anymore—nor are the other sapphire elites ahead of me. Otherwise, I wouldn't be here."

Mayhara toyed with the handle of her cup. "I'm sorry. I didn't know your history. It sounds rough."

"Kind of falls into the shadows. You know, with the possible end of the world coming about. But yeah."

A noise in the corridor cut into their conversation. Kamal raised his brows, his eyes locked with Mayhara's. Her brows, however, went in the opposite direction. She tried to ask him what the source of the sound might be without speaking, but he only shrugged. He didn't seem interested, but Mayhara was too curious. Besides, they had enemies out there. She had to make sure no one had broken in with the purpose of murdering them all.

Keeping light on her feet, Mayhara slipped out of the breakfast nook and headed toward the corridor, her hands stretched and ready, just in case. Peering into the darkness, she spotted Loni slipping on a leather jacket.

"Loni?" Mayhara whispered.

Loni froze for a second but averted her gaze when she realized it was Mayhara who'd called her name.

"Where are you going?" Mayhara asked.

Loni set her jaw, her mouth in a straight line. She narrowed her eyes at Mayhara. "Out."

Without another word, Loni whipped around and charged out the door. For a moment, Mayhara stood there, dumbfounded. When she sobered and went back into the kitchen, Kamal was still eating, seemingly disinterested in what had taken place in the hall.

"That was Loni," Mayhara said, still puzzled by the encounter. "She just… left. Said she was going 'out.'"

Kamal nodded as he finished chewing. "Yeah. She does that."

Mayhara blinked. "What do you mean?"

"Granted, I've only been pulled into this group recently. But I've noticed it enough. She disappears when she's upset about something."

"I mean, we're all upset. But running out in the middle of the night is reckless."

"I don't think she's upset about the same thing you are." Kamal pointed his fork at her.

"What makes you say that?"

"Because I know something I'm guessing you don't."

Mayhara scoffed. "What are we, eight? Just tell me." She lifted her tea, slowly sipping.

Kamal licked his fork and placed it on his empty plate. "Fine. I think Loni's having a hard time seeing you and Jae together because they used to be a thing."

Mayhara choked on her tea, coughing and spurting as she tried to catch her breath. "Wait. What?"

Kamal smirked. "See. You didn't know."

"First of all, what makes you think Jae and I are together?"

"Oh, okay." He raised a brow. "That's how you want to play it."

Mayhara was about to object, but she knew if she did, Kamal might not tell her about Jae's past relationship with Loni. And she really needed to know.

"Fine." Mayhara checked the doorway, listening to make sure no one was coming. "We might have… a connection. But it's not like we've had a chance to define it or even talk about old flings."

She waited, but Kamal just shrugged and brought his plate to the sink.

"So, they were a thing?" she finally asked. "Back at the academy?" She tried to remember seeing them together, but it wasn't something that stuck out in her mind.

"No. After the Eradication."

"After?" Her face felt hot, and her heart began to speed up. "How?"

"From what she told me, Jae rescued her. They escaped together when the government tore up the school."

Mayhara felt a heaviness in her stomach. She placed a hand on her throat, finding it a little hard to breathe. "What happened? I mean, why aren't they together anymore?"

"I don't know." Kamal stuck his hands in his pockets. "You should ask Jae."

She felt as if she'd been separated from her body, looking down on herself, unable to move. Kamal watched her for a second, his eyes flitting around her face.

"Yeah," she finally said. "I probably will. But, um, do me a favor? Don't say anything to him. Or to Loni. About this conversation, I mean. I just need to wrap my head around it a bit more before I bring it up with him."

"Sure thing." He gave her a wink and headed out of the kitchen. "Good luck."

TWELVE

Rain made the streets glisten under the light of the moon. The streetlamps were reflected in the puddles Loni passed as she navigated through downtown New Jaipur. She knew this area was far from safe. She knew because she'd been here before on more than one occasion. And her reasons for being here hadn't exactly been honorable.

Ignoring the sweat beading along her hairline, she concentrated on keeping alert as she passed a group of homeless people. They were gathered around a trash can, a blazing fire inside it warming their hands. One of them—a man with a dirty beard—watched her closely. She pretended not to notice. When he took a step toward her, she used her emerald powers to feed the fire with a burst of air. The fire roared as the flames shot upward, bright embers kicking up into the air. The group, including the man who had been watching her, flinched from the sudden change. Loni kept her head down and continued down the street.

Checking the street signs, she noted she was two blocks away from her destination. She knew she shouldn't have been going there, and she knew this course of action was one of self-destruction, but she couldn't stop herself. She needed a fix. And she needed it now.

When she reached the alleyway, she looked down and adjusted her jacket. Her body was shaking, but she couldn't tell if it was because of the cold wind the rain had brought or because of the anxiety that had crept into her veins.

A sense of relief overcame her when she spotted the familiar face, but it was short-lived when she remembered he'd denied her his services the last time she'd gone to him.

Li Jun sat on the back steps to a long-abandoned restaurant kitchen, the place that was now what he liked to call his laboratory. His head was shaved, allowing the large tattoo over his left ear to be visible, and there was an intentional cut in one of his eyebrows. His army-green trench coat clung to his muscles as he ran his knife along a sharpening stone. The sound grated Loni's nerves.

She inhaled deeply and let out a long breath when his eyes met hers. Rubbing the back of her damp neck, she approached him. His second-in-command—Nadia, Loni remembered—stepped between them and glared at her with her light gray eyes. A tiny blue jewel piercing jutted out over the right side of her mouth.

"How dare you show your face here again." Nadia clenched her teeth.

"Nadia, let her approach."

"But, Li Jun, last time—"

"I have a feeling Loni wants to apologize for last time. Isn't that right, Loni?" Li Jun raised a brow as he waited for her to answer.

Nadia swept her short, pink bob behind her ears and stepped aside so Loni could approach.

"Well?" Li Jun kept his eyes on Loni as his blade slid against the stone. "What's it going to be?"

Loni desperately wanted to cross her arms to stop herself from shaking, but she didn't want to seem weak. Weakness in this part of town could mean death.

"Look, Li Jun. I'm sorry about trying to scam you last time. I was… I wasn't thinking clearly. It was the *Moxy* controlling me."

"If I were to forgive you, what's to stop you from trying to pull that crap off again?"

She averted her gaze. "The scar Nadia left on my body is a solid reminder not to repeat my mistakes."

Nadia rested her hands on her hips and smirked.

"So I assume you didn't come here just to apologize." Li Jun smiled, but it didn't reach his eyes.

"No. I need a hookup." Loni's voice was small.

"It's been a while," Li Jun said. "I thought maybe you decided to get clean."

"I wanted to." Loni's head filled with visions of her sister screaming for help. She ran a hand over her face to stop the memory. "Look, are you going to sell to me or not?"

"You've got credits?" Li Jun asked.

Loni pulled out her Linq. "I've got eighty-two."

He sucked at his teeth. "That'll get you a hundred milligrams."

Loni's brow wrinkled. "That's it?"

"What can I say?" Li Jun shrugged. "Inflation."

"That's like two pills. That's not going to last very long."

"Well, you got something else to bargain with?" Li Jun inspected his knife.

"She's got a shiny jewel on that bracelet of hers," Nadia said.

Loni put a hand over her emerald. Part of her wanted to rip if off and hand it over, trade the stone for double the Moxy. But deep down, she knew she'd need its power to keep her alive when the time came to fight the Pishacha.

"No." She stuffed her hands in her pockets. "I can't trade it."

Nadia stepped forward. "Now I'm even more interested in it."

"I said it's not an option. I'll just take the hundred for now."

"Come on, Loni." Li Jun tilted his head. "Throw in the wristband and I'll make it three hundred milligrams."

She stiffened, gritting her teeth. Her mind volleyed her choices, and her stomach clenched with unease. She couldn't risk it, no matter how much she needed the Moxy. She was the elite emerald mage. She needed to keep her wristband.

"Not this time," she said, trying to throw them off.

"Fine." Li Jun tucked his knife away. "Transfer the credits."

Loni pulled out her Linq and tapped a few buttons on the screen. She then extended the end of the Linq toward Nadia. Once Nadia touched her Linq to Loni's, a *bleep* sounded, notifying them that the transfer was complete. Li Jun dangled a tiny, sealed plastic bag between two fingers. Loni swallowed hard as she reached out and took the bag.

"Pleasure doing business with you, Loni," Li Jun said, his tone sarcastic.

"See you soon." Nadia chuckled.

Loni kept her pace steady as she turned away from them and left the alleyway. She cursed her body for continually shaking. All she could think about were the pills in her pocket.

As she reached the street, a siren blared. Red and blue flashing lights illuminated the surroundings as the Imperial Police car raced in her direction. Loni held her breath, turning away from the car and ducking her head. She breathed in deeply through her nose and exhaled slowly, attempting to calm her thrashing heart. Closing her eyes, she listened as the siren grew closer. Then, in a dizzying moment, the tone of the siren changed. The car passed, continuing its race down the street.

As the blare of the siren faded, Loni pushed down the nausea that threatened to bring up her dinner. Her fingers closed around the bag of pills in her pocket. The Moxy called to her, promising to dull her grief and give her an escape from her sorrow.

She couldn't wait until she got back to the temple. She needed her fix now. It was only two pills, enough for one hit. But maybe this could be the last time she'd need a fix. She'd quit after this. One last fix of Moxy, and then she'd be done.

Checking over her shoulders, she ducked into an abandoned shop whose door stood slightly ajar. The streetlights lit up the windows. The shop was mostly empty except for a counter and shelves covered in blankets of dust.

Loni pressed her back against the wall near the door and pulled the bag of pills out of her pocket. Fingers shaking uncontrollably, she grasped the small, round, white pills. Her breaths came fast and heavy as she stared at them. This was wrong, she knew it. This was not behavior becoming of an elite mage. But it was the only way to stop the ache in her heart. And she was going to quit anyway, wasn't she?

She shoved the pills in her mouth and closed her eyes, letting the plastic bag drop away. Her eyes still shut, she slid down the wall until she was sitting on the floor.

Images of her sister, Kanya, filled her mind. Tears spilled down her cheeks as she thought about her sister's smile, her laugh, her embrace.

Kanya was dead, and Loni hadn't even tried to save her.

Guilt pressed in on her chest, threatening to suffocate her. Sobbing, she pulled her knees closer. Her grasp on her legs was so tight, she thought she might tear holes in her jeans.

The memory of the last time she saw Kanya played out in her head.

It sounded like fireworks were exploding around them. Smoke filled the air, and the ground shook. Loni ran to the window, looking down at the courtyard, and spotted her sister scrambling for cover with the rest of the students outside.

"Kanya!" Loni banged on the glass, but Kanya didn't hear her.

Loni's breath hitched. She ran from the dorm room to the stairwell. Screams echoed all around her. Loni didn't know what was making the building shake, but it was causing her head to throb as she bounded down the stairs.

Using her air power, she skipped the last few steps, landing on the main floor with a thud. When she reached the door to the courtyard, a blast of fire and debris threw her back. Her head caught the marble column in the hall. Everything went black. She couldn't move. Sounds faded in and out.

Someone grabbed her from under her arms and dragged her. She wanted to shout to the person to leave her alone. She didn't want these intruders to take her away. She needed to get to her sister. But even opening her mouth to speak sent shockwaves of pain shooting into her brain. The ache was too much. She felt herself slipping in and out of consciousness.

Another explosion went off somewhere in the school.

She opened her eyes to find that the person who'd dragged her from the hall was a boy she only slightly remembered seeing around the academy.

"What's happening?" she asked him, barely able to pronounce the words.

"It's the Imperial Police. The government has approved the Eradication proposal. They're abolishing the academy."

"Oh my God!" She sat up, her head spinning. "Kanya!"

She ignored the boy's protests as she charged for the hole in the wall where the door used to be. Smoke and flying debris blocked her vision. She threw out her emerald powers to clear the way so she could find her sister.

At the far end of the courtyard, Kanya was being forced into electro-cuffs by Imperial Police.

"Kanya!"

"What are you doing?" The boy grabbed her, sounding scared.

"That's my sister." She shook off his hand. "Kanya!"

Kanya whipped her head around and found Loni. Her eyes were wide with fear and tears stained her cheeks. Her temple was bruised and bleeding, and the sleeve of her blouse was torn.

"Loni!" Kanya flailed away from the police officer who was cuffing her, attempting to run to her sister. But she was suddenly struck with a long glowing baton that crackled with electricity as it made contact with her neck. Kanya fell *to the ground, her fingers reaching toward Loni.*

Loni screamed. She tensed her muscles, ready to run toward her sister, but the boy grabbed her arms and pulled her back just as another explosion went off close by.

"No. Don't go out there. You'll be killed." He was stronger than she'd guessed. "Come with me. I know a place to hide."

Loni almost gagged as the Imperial Police struck Kanya again. This time, Kanya didn't move.

"I need to save my sister," Loni yelled at the boy, her voice cracking with her sobs.

His hold on her was firm as he peered through the chaos. "She's already dead. I'm sorry. We can make it out alive, but you need to follow me."

Her breaths were drowned by her sobbing as she let him pull her along. Her mind swirled with fear, sorrow, anger, and confusion. What was happening? How had it come to this?

And Kanya... Kanya was dead.

The next thing she knew, the boy was leading her down stone steps. The went through a long corridor that eventually led to a double door made of withering wood. The boy pulled her inside.

Loni looked around, her vision clouded by her tears. "Is this a cave?"

"I guess you could call it that," he answered.

They were surrounded by stone, but the center of the room had a dropped bottom, and a large column of lights stood, reaching from the cavern floor far below up to the rock ceiling above them. It was a spiral edifice split into seven sections. Each section was divided by glowing particles of different colored elements: red at the bottom, swirling upward through orange, yellow, green, blue, and purple, then ending at the top with a brilliant white.

Loni wiped the tears from her face, but her body still shook. "What is this place?"

"We're under the school. I think this has something to do with the Lotus." He looked back at the door. "But I don't think anyone knows about this place. They shouldn't be able to find us here. We can wait until the attack is over. Until they leave. When it's clear, we can escape. I know a place we can lie low."

Loni sniffled. "Why are you helping me?"

"I'd help more if I could, but the attack was so fast, and you were the only

one nearby.”

She was quiet for a moment, staring at the column of magical lights. “Thank you,” she finally said. “My name is Loni, by the way.”

“Nice to meet you, Loni. I’m Jae.”

The sound of glass breaking stirred Loni from the memory. Her head spun as she jumped to her feet. Though her face and fingers and skin felt numb from the Moxy, her brain was scrambling to be on high alert.

It might have just been a rat that had made the noise. But she couldn’t be sure.

She steadied her balance and scanned the store. Adjusting her eyes to the dark, she spotted two figures moving toward her from a back room.

Gasping, she raised her hands between herself and the strangers. The room seemed to tip to the side as her vision doubled. Were there really four strangers now? She squeezed her eyes shut and shook her head, quickly opening them again.

No. Only two.

But she was intoxicated, and her reflexes were off. She had to get out of there. Whether they were Pishacha or ordinary street thugs, she didn’t have the time or the opportunity to figure it out.

Steeling herself, she bolted for the door.

“Get her!” one of them said as they raced after her.

The cold, damp air helped to partially clear her mind. But still, she was unsure she could fight off her pursuers. Her shoes splashed through puddles as she ran. She knew she was heading in the wrong direction, what with the sub-train station east instead of west, but she couldn’t stop now. The strangers weren’t far behind. She’d have to try to lose them and double back.

With a quick glance over her shoulder, she made a move. Her palms glowed green as she cast out her power. The manhole in the street was blasted upward by air, hitting one of her pursuers hard in the face. Loni only looked back long enough to see he was knocked out—or possibly dead.

One down.

She turned the corner, nearly losing her balance. She could barely catch her breath, but she couldn’t afford to slow down. Her crucial mistake was veering into an alleyway that stopped in a dead end.

Muttering a curse, she raised her chin and looked upward. With her powers at full capacity, she might have been able to generate enough air to lift her to one of the rooftops. But the buildings swayed in her vision. The numbness taking over her skin had reached deeper inside her, making her muscles limp. There was no way she'd make the jump. Not like this.

She'd picked a fine time to indulge her addiction. If she had just waited until she'd gotten back to the temple—

The other man appeared in the alleyway, blocking her only exit. Loni's breaths were frantic as panic began to set in.

"What do you want?" she yelled.

The tall, lanky man came closer, ignoring her question. She could just make out the sneer on his face.

"Stay away from me!" She squared her shoulders, despite her urge to shrink into herself and disappear.

Still, he neared.

She couldn't stop the whimper that escaped her mouth. Her instincts took over, and she raised her palms in his direction. One second, he was smirking, clearly reveling in his victory of having trapped his victim. The next second, the man froze, his eyes practically popping out of his head and his jaw hanging open. He grabbed his neck, his face drained of color as choking sounds erupted from his throat.

Loni's breaths were gasps as she kept her powers trained on him and gave him a wide berth, moving past him. He shot one hand out to reach for her, but she backed away, concentrating on keeping the air out of his lungs. And when he dropped to his knees, Loni turned and ran as fast as she could.

THIRTEEN

The cup of coffee warmed Mayhara's hand. She held it close as she entered the office where Jae was working. It was almost symbolic. Like she was keeping something familiar and comforting between her and Jae. She was trying to get her nerve up to ask him about his alleged past relationship with Loni, but she was going to need a lot more than coffee to give her courage.

On the other hand, she couldn't even be sure Kamal had been telling the truth about the relationship. It was one of the sapphire powers, after all: Making people believe lies.

"Good morning." She slipped into the chair across from Jae, despite her temptation to lean into him and give him a kiss.

He stopped typing and looked up at her. His smile seemed to cover his entire face. "Morning. How did you sleep?"

"Great." She hoped he wasn't using his powers to detect her fib. She needed to shift the focus off of her. "What about you? It looks like you've been up for a while."

"Karina translated the coordinates from the scroll, so I plugged them in. They point to the Bhaja Caves in Pune."

"Pune? That's like twenty hours from here."

"If there's no traffic, yeah. So I'm trying to get as much intel as I can before we plan a trip out there."

"We?" A blush crept up her face.

He grinned. "Are you up for it?"

"Sure." She squeezed her coffee cup, fighting off the butterflies in her stomach.

"We need to wait for Karina to finish interpreting the rest of the symbols on the scroll first. But if we want to get our hands on the grimoire before the Pishacha do, we need to be sure we know where to look."

She nodded. It wasn't that she wasn't paying attention to him, but she couldn't stop staring at his lips.

Noticing her gaze, Jae leaned forward on the desk. "You okay?" he whispered. His grin wasn't as wide as before, but it was still there.

The question she'd been dying to ask him all morning danced in her mind.

I should just ask him.

She opened her mouth to speak, still not sure exactly what she was going to say, but Shiro walked into the room. She lifted her coffee and took a sip.

Jae and Mayhara both sat back in their seats, widening the distance between them.

"How's it going, Shiro?" Mayhara asked. "Any progress with Amalia?"

Shiro scrubbed his hands down his face, the dark circles under his eyes a stark contrast to his color-drained face. "You want the sugar-coated version, or do you want the truth?"

Mayhara grimaced. "That bad?"

"I thought the syphoning was working," Jae said.

"Yes and no." Shiro raised his arms above his head to stretch. When he lowered them, he released a sigh filled with exhaustion. "I can only get so much poison out without ripping her apart. And then the problem is that any poison left inside her multiplies until it fills her again."

Mayhara had no response. She realized that deep inside her, she had believed Shiro's plan would work. She had held on to the hope that together they could accomplish anything. Now, suddenly, a seed of doubt was planted, and she feared it might sprout and spread and destroy any optimism she had that they could win this war.

"Way to bring down the room, right?" Shiro leaned forward and picked up a paper from the desk. "What's this?"

"That," Jae said, pointing to the paper with a pen, "is the blueprint to the governor's mansion. Penny took a look at it and said she couldn't see any room that matched what she saw in her vision, so we're going on location."

"How are we getting in?" Shiro asked.

"They've started preparations for the gala." Jae shrugged. "Kamal and I can use our powers to convince them we're part of the staff."

"As long as there's no Pishacha around," Mayhara added.

"If there are, we'll lie low," Jae said. "But at the very least, we can get a lay of the land, figure out escape routes and weak spots."

"Yeah." Shiro nodded. "Sounds good. Count me in."

"Are you sure?" Mayhara shook her head. "No offense, but you look like crap. Don't you want to get some sleep?"

"I don't think I could if I wanted to," Shiro replied. "My mind would just be running circles around this puzzle with Amalia. Might do me some good to get out and concentrate on something else for a bit."

"All right." Jae gave him a curt nod. "It's a plan."

"What's that one?" Shiro pointed to another set of blueprints.

Jae pushed the paper closer to Shiro. "This one is a blueprint of the Bhaja Caves. It's where the coordinates encrypted in the scroll point to, so we're betting the grimoire is hidden somewhere inside. Between that and the website's virtual tour videos, I can't seem to find anything that might lead to a space that matches the illustration on the scroll."

"Karina's still interpreting the other symbols on the scroll," Mayhara said. "So hopefully it'll give us more insight."

Shiro studied the blueprint. "The Bhaja Caves."

"Have you ever been to them?" Mayhara asked.

"When I was a kid." Shiro gave them a half-shrug. "The memory is kind of a blur."

Jae shifted in his chair. "So you wouldn't remember if there was some blocked-off section, maybe restricted access or construction or something?"

"No." Shiro raised a brow. "But I bet we'll find it if we know where to look."

The day had grown hot. Or maybe it was just Shiro's exhaustion catching up with him. He pulled at the collar of his T-shirt, attempting to get some air to cool off his sweat-covered skin. He desperately wanted to remove the cap from his head, but he couldn't take the risk. The cap and sunglasses weren't the best of disguises but were necessary to keep from being recognized.

Kama's voice came to him over the earpiece. "Heading to the south entrance."

Shiro resisted touching the device in his ear. It would look too suspicious. "Watch out for the gazebo. There's a handful of Imperial Police headed that way.

"Copy that," Kamal answered.

"I'm going to try to slip in with the decorating staff," Jae announced.

"I'm keeping an eye on the north entrance." Yuki's voice was small and reflective of her age.

"Just make sure you're keeping your distance," Jae said. "We don't want that ex-boyfriend of yours spotting you."

"He's not my ex-boyfriend," Yuki said. "We only saw each other a couple times."

"Still, keep out of sight." The earpiece clicked as Jae signed off.

Yuki wasn't supposed to be scoping out the location with them. Since Loni would be attending the gala with Kamal, it made sense for her to become as familiar with the governor's mansion as possible. But apparently Loni had told Darshana she wasn't feeling well and stayed in bed. Penny was back at the temple meditating with Darshana about the dagger location, Salina was keeping an eye on Amalia, and Mayhara was taking notes with Karina as they tried to break the code in the scroll.

Yuki wore sunglasses, and a dark blue headscarf covered her auburn hair. As long as she kept herself inconspicuous, there shouldn't be a problem.

Shiro pretended to be a tourist photographing the city as he snapped pictures of the windows, the staff entrances, and the stations of security personnel. There was no doubt security would be at least doubled for the gala, but the mages would have a basis to build on.

The lavish two-story mansion stood regally behind an eight-foot cast-iron fence. Terracotta columns lined the building on three sides. The circular driveway at the front was adorned with ancient banya trees. Trucks were parked along the service entrance side, with hired help setting up tents and carrying in rented tables and festive decorations for the upcoming gala.

"Uh, guys," Kamal said. "We've got a problem."

"I hear it." Jae muttered a curse.

Shiro lowered the camera and glanced around. He couldn't hear anything, but he didn't have the advantage of having sapphire powers.

"This doesn't feel good," Yuki said. It sounded as if she were running. "There's a lot of anger and hostility coming this way."

"Pishacha?" Shiro asked.

"I don't know," Yuki answered. "But it's big."

The hairs on Shiro's neck stood at end. Part of Yuki's diamond mage powers was emotion, Shiro noted. And if she was panicking about a force of anger and hostility heading toward them, then he was going to follow her lead.

He turned and hurried in her direction but froze in place suddenly when gunfire ripped through the air. Screams erupted around him. Women grabbed their children and ducked low to the ground. Others darted behind shops and stands to take cover.

He heard the shouts and chants of protest then.

Extremists.

More gunshots sounded.

A little girl, standing alone by a fountain, released the balloon she'd been holding and began to cry. Her mother, who hid behind a bench holding a baby, called out to her. It was apparent she didn't want to expose the baby but desperately wanted her child to come to her.

Shiro ran to the child and swooped her up in one quick movement. In a matter of seconds, he placed the girl at her mother's side. The woman blubbered her thanks.

A crew of Imperial Police marched through the square, guns at the ready. The angry mob of extremists plowed into the open, setting off red-colored smoke bombs and shooting fire bullets through the windows of the governor's mansion. Bursts of ice blasted through the square, connecting with the drawn guns of the police and encasing the barrels. Chaos ensued as the swarm of extremists whipped Molotov cocktail bombs at the horde of police and released a wave of fire bullets onto them.

In the center of the army of extremists, he emerged.

Qiang.

Shiro's heart stopped for a moment. Qiang was alive. All the nights Shiro had spent crying over the possibility of the love of his life being dead were suddenly for naught. Here Qiang was, his muscles lean, his black hair hanging a bit longer than Shiro remembered, and scruff covered his square jaw. His thick brows were drawn. He was clearly present and determined. And he was alive.

Shiro's heart sped up again. It hammered in his chest and threatened to crack him into pieces. Qiang was leading the extremists into a dance with danger. He was making fatal moves with grave consequences.

"We've got to get these people out of here," Jae said through the earpiece.

"I've just cleared out the south quarter," Kamal announced. "Headed your way."

"I've calmed the people by the bridge," Yuki said. She had the advantage of her diamond mage powers to help control the emotions of the crowd near her. "The last of them are safely out of range."

Qiang marched closer, shouting orders and instructing his troops. With his crimson powers, he shook the ground and brought the oncoming police to their knees. Peng and Bao, the long-legged emerald mages who took part in their prison escape, used their powers to choke the first row of police officers. Mitty, the burly golden mage, tossed firebombs from his glowing palms over the cast-iron fence onto the lawn of the governor's mansion.

Shiro longed to call out to Qiang, but he feared getting caught in the crossfire. Besides, he needed to get the people in the square to safety. Taking a deep breath, he summoned his powers. He wasn't sure what good it would do, but he was willing to try anything at this point. Clouds moved in and rain began to trickle down. The drops spotted Yuki's headscarf as she rushed toward Shiro.

"Everything's going to be okay," she said to the frightened people around Shiro, gesturing with her palms, which were aglow in bright white, for the stragglers to depart the area.

Shiro helped the young mother by guiding the little girl to follow her.

The rain came down faster, making it hard for the extremists to clearly see the barrage of Imperial Police charging in from out of nowhere.

Shiro couldn't help himself. He followed Qiang's movements as he fought off the police. Shiro made his move once the opportunity arose and darted toward Qiang. In his vigilance to stand his ground, Qiang raised his palms toward Shiro, ready to fight. But the second he realized it was Shiro coming toward him, his mouth hung open and he dropped his hands.

Shiro grabbed Qiang and hurriedly pushed him back and out of harm's way. They ducked behind a large statue of the sun god Surya.

Qiang placed his hands on the sides of Shiro's face. "How can this be?"

"You're alive."

Qiang let out a laugh. "That's what I was going to say. I thought you were shot."

"I *was* shot."

"But you live." Qiang pulled him closer and wrapped his arms around him.

Shiro squeezed him tightly and closed his eyes. Gunshots rang in his ears.

"Qiang." Shiro pulled back and searched his face. "What are you doing?"

"What do you mean?"

"This." Shiro gestured at the mansion. "These attacks."

"We can't let them get away with what they're doing, Shiro. Our families are still imprisoned. They have the grounds to deem mages illegal. We need to fight for our rights."

"But this way? It's dangerous. There were families out here. Children. You're not considering the innocent lives you might be destroying."

Qiang searched his eyes, his expression grim. "Shiro, we're in a war. War has casualties."

"But if we can prevent innocent people from being killed—"

"Survival and freedom come at a price."

Shiro's brows dropped. "Is that why you gave up on me? Why it was so easy for you to accept that I was dead? Because lives are expendable during war?"

Qiang put his hands on Shiro's shoulders. "Shiro, no."

Shiro shrugged him off, his jaw tightening. A crackle in his earpiece interrupted his next sentence.

"Shiro! Yuki!" Jae sounded out of breath. "We've got to go. Kamal's been shot!"

FOURTEEN

It wasn't the mumbled voices in the temple that woke Loni; it was Kamal's grunts and moans. She covered her head with her pillow, begging the noise to stop. Every sound was like a giant needle being driven into her skull. Eventually, Kamal grew quiet, but the mumbling persisted.

Loni felt a wave of nausea as she forced herself out of bed. Her head pounded with every cruel beat of her heart. Curiosity drove her to find out what all the noise was about, but more than that, she needed water. An ocean's worth of water, judging by the sandpaper feel of her throat.

She reached the bottom of the stairs just as Darshana was closing the door behind someone.

"Who was that?" Even speaking made Loni's head throb.

Darshana placed her hands together in front of her, palms touching. "The doctor."

"What… What happened? Is it Amalia?"

"No. It's Kamal. He's been shot."

The shock of the news partially cleared Loni's mind, letting her push aside her own pain for a moment. "Is he all right?"

"Come see for yourself." Darshana headed for the living room.

Loni was relieved to see Kamal conscious on the couch. His pants had been cut over his thigh, exposing a thick bandage taped to his leg.

"Kamal." Loni hurried to the couch and kneeled beside him. "What happened?"

She glanced around. The only mage missing was Penny. Mr. Kitaro stood near Darshana—which seemed to be the norm as of late—with his hands stuffed in his pockets and a frown on his face. The others were gathered around, looking beat. Kamal, on the other hand, seemed rather pleased to be doted on, Loni thought to herself.

"Extremists," Jae answered. "Kamal got caught in the crossfire."

"They were using some kind of mage-made bullets," Shiro said, "made of stone and fire."

"Seared right through me." Kamal sucked in a breath through his teeth. "You should have seen the look on the doctor's face when he pulled it out."

"He's actually lucky it didn't rupture his femoral artery," Mr. Kitaro added.

Loni looked him up and down. "But you're okay?"

"Not exactly." Kamal hung his arm over the back of the couch. "No one's even offered me a snack yet. I mean, what's a guy got to do around here to get a bag of chips?"

Yuki let out a small laugh. "I'll get you some. Just stop whining like a baby."

Mayhara bit back a smile. "He's on pain killers."

Loni turned to Shiro. "What happened with the extremists?"

Shiro ran a hand through his hair. "They attacked right outside the governor's mansion. We managed to get the civilians out of there, but Kamal got hit."

"I've been monitoring the media channels," Mayhara said. "There aren't a lot of details in the news. Not yet, anyway. But apparently the rebels were cleared out."

"Does that mean they were arrested or killed?" Loni asked.

Salina sat down in the chair across from the couch. "I'm sure the media has been persuaded to bury the real story. Probably because they don't want anything ruining their gala."

Loni furrowed her brow, which sent a small wave of dizziness through her head. "Wait. They're still going through with it?"

Mayhara shrugged. "Apparently."

Shiro let out a defeated sigh. "Which makes me wonder if there's an underlying reason for the event."

"Either way," Jay said as he rested on the arm of the couch, "if the other daggers are stashed somewhere in the mansion, they might be planning to move them because of today's attack."

"Well, I hate to tell you this." Kamal fiddled with the cut hem of his ruined pants. "This bullet wound might cause a slight setback as far as my dance moves are concerned."

Yuki, coming back into the room, tossed the bag of chips in his lap.

"You can't even hobble to the kitchen for a snack. There's no way you're going to that gala."

"No." Mr. Kitaro let out a chuckle. "A limp like that would certainly act as a hindrance."

"Jae will have to go instead," Darshana said. "We need a sapphire mage to get in the door."

Jae and Mayhara exchanged a quick glance.

"Yeah." Jae cleared his throat. "All right."

Loni's temperature seemed to rise. Her head swam, threatening to throw her off-kilter. It was a good thing she was kneeling on the floor. If Jae was taking Kamal's place, that meant she and Jae would be posing as a couple at the gala. She ignored the heat that scorched her cheeks.

"That's not the only alteration to the plan."

Everyone turned to look as Penny entered the room, Karina in tow.

Darshana narrowed her eyes. "What did you see?"

"A possibility," Penny said as she and Karina sat on the floor around the coffee table. "It's going to be tricky getting the daggers *and* leaving with them."

"You have a plan?" Mayhara asked, joining them on the floor.

"Karina does." Penny nodded at her.

"Penny kept envisioning different scenarios where the Pishacha and the dark mages catch you retrieving the daggers. The visions were different each time, but we're certain the Pishacha and dark mages will be at the gala."

"I don't like the feel of this," Yuki remarked.

"Neither do I," Karina said. "Which is why I came up with something that I hope will help. At least temporarily."

"Go on." Mr. Kitaro stepped closer.

Karina looked around at everyone. "I can do a boundary spell to trap them."

"What's a boundary spell?" Kamal asked.

"It's a spell that can seal someone—or in this case, a group of people— in a space for a certain amount of time. The mansion itself is too big to do the spell on without a powerful talisman or a celestial event."

"What about the comet?" Yuki asked.

"It's not close enough yet," Penny explained.

"But if the Pishacha and company can be led into one place—say, the room where the daggers are hidden—I can trap them there so you can escape without them being able to follow you."

"But what about their black-smoke disappearing trick?" Salina asked.

"They wouldn't be able to leave the boundaries of the room in any form, so if they did disappear, they'd only be able to reappear within the room."

"So cool," Kamal said.

"But there's a catch," Karina added.

"Figures," Shiro muttered.

"The spell I'm using pulls its magic from a special anointed candle. The boundary spell will only last as long as the candle burns."

Jae rubbed at his jaw. "How long is that?"

"It depends on how strong I need the spell to be. And I'm guessing, with the force of the entities in that room, it'll need to be a pretty strong spell."

Loni shifted, pulling her legs out from under her and gathering her knees closer to her body. "So we pretty much have to get out of there as fast as possible, just in case."

Karina nodded. "Pretty much."

"How are we going to make sure the Pishacha find Jae and Loni?" Shiro asked. "That is, without drawing the attention of the governor and the Imperial Police and all?"

"Maybe I can help with that," Yuki said. She straightened her shoulders. "Avi is sure to be there. I'll make sure he sees me and lead him to the room. I'm sure the others will follow."

"We don't know for sure they'd follow." Salina rubbed her hands together. "But it could work. We'd have to time it just right, though."

"I'll talk them all through it with the earpieces Jae made," Penny said. "That way I can keep you apprised of how fast Karina's candle is burning."

They were all silent for a while, deep in thought. Loni felt a hard knot in her chest, and her fingers trembled slightly. This was a huge mission, and she was one of the key players. A mild sweat began to form on her brow. As her stomach began to churn, she tried to push away the craving for more Moxy to ease her nerves. But her addiction was putting up a fight.

At long last, Darshana spoke. "It's risky, yes, but I think it could work. The others can stand by outside of the mansion gate in case something goes awry."

"We have two days," Penny said. "If anyone thinks of anything we missed, you better bring it up before the plan goes into action."

As the rest of them agreed, Loni bit her lip. Her skin began to itch, and her heart felt heavy. She wasn't sure she could hold herself together enough to pull this off. She knew she had to, but it was going to be a challenge. And she couldn't shake the feeling that desperate times were calling for desperate measures.

FIFTEEN

Kashmeru's thumb traced small, delicate circles in Lakshmi's palm. She watched the strokes as her skin began to tingle and the tiny hairs sprung to life along her arms. When she looked up at him, his eyes were soft yet intense. And the small upturn of the corner of his mouth made her blush.

"When I'm with you," he said, "everything else fades away."

She smiled and averted her eyes, overwhelmed by the feeling of joy inside of her.

"See how good it is when we are together?" he asked, moving closer.

"Yes," she replied, following his lead and closing the distance between them.

She could feel his breath on her lips, but at the last second, he pulled away. She blinked at him in surprise.

His smile disappeared. "Perhaps next time, you won't fail."

"What?"

Naree sat upright, stirred back to the present. Kashmeru had finally spoken to her after a silence that seemed like forever. But his message was clear. He was disappointed in her failure to secure all the daggers, but he was giving her another chance. "Kashmeru," she called from the sofa where she had fallen asleep earlier. "I'm sorry."

I know, my love.

Her heart practically burst with gratitude that he had answered her.

I believe you have learned your lesson and will do as I wish.

"Of course. Anything for you."

We will be together soon. You just need to get the daggers so we can begin the ritual. The reward will be worth it, I promise you.

Tears spilled over her lashes, but her smile reflected her delight. She wanted to be with him again. To feel his thumb trace circles in her palm. To be near him again and not have him pull away from their kiss.

The door to the lounge opened, and Bhutano marched in.

"Your highness." He gave her a slight bow.

This time, she was not afraid of what he would say. Kashmeru was with her again, and this was her chance to prove to him that she would succeed. To prove her love to him.

She stood, holding her chin high. "Yes?"

"There's been an attack on the governor's mansion. Extremists."

She hadn't been prepared for this news. She furrowed her brow, trying to wrap her head around it. "Did they get inside?"

"No."

"Was anyone hurt? Avi?"

"Avi is unharmed. But we lost a couple Imperial Police in the chaos. The area is secured now, and measures are being taken to ensure the mansion can't be infiltrated."

She had to be certain the daggers hidden in the mansion weren't taken. If they were, she'd lose any footing they had in this battle.

"We need to stop them from further endangering our plan," she said.

"I agree. I've sent a team of Pishacha on a manhunt. We will find them and eradicate the situation. We're also discussing the destruction of the prison camps. With the mage families trapped behind the walls."

She flinched. "How will you carry that out?"

"We're devising a plan. It might take a bit of time to coordinate in a way so as not to turn the public against the government. We want to pin the blame on the extremists."

"Do you think the public will believe the extremists would destroy their own people?"

"We hope to make it appear as if the deaths of the mage families are collateral damage. That the extremists meant to attack the camp guards but destroyed everything and everyone in their path instead."

She inhaled deeply, considering the plan. "It could work. But I'm also concerned about the daggers."

"I'll discuss moving them to a more secure location with the governor. I'm certain we can come up with a solution."

She nodded, her mind whirring.

"As for the remaining daggers," he said, studying her face. "I have an idea in which you play a vital role."

SIXTEEN

Crickets chirped, filling the night air with their song. Jae watched Mayhara's face as she gazed at the comet. Moonlight shimmered on her features, like tiny sparkles he wanted to chase with his lips. She'd been quiet all day, and he wondered if she might have regretted their kiss.

They'd spent the day training, honing their skills for the possible showdown at the gala the next day. Though she'd smiled at him whenever he looked her way, he couldn't help but think the smile didn't quite reach her eyes. Of course, he could just be paranoid. After all, this plan of theirs was risky. Mayhara's distance could simply be the way she dealt with worry.

"What are you thinking about?" Jae kept his voice low and soft.

Mayhara tucked a strand of hair behind her ear. "When I was little, my father and I would sit outside when it got dark and watch for shooting stars. Then, as I began to come into my powers, I saw one, and I wished that I would become the best crimson mage there ever was."

He smiled at her. "And now you are."

She nodded. "Now I am. And I didn't expect to feel so overwhelmed."

Taking her hand, Jae stroked her skin with his thumb. "Have you already forgotten what we said? We're in this together. You're not fighting this fight alone."

She smiled back at him and squeezed his hand.

The buzz of Jae's Linq interrupted them. Jae's brows pulled together when he saw Loni's number appear on the screen. He spared Mayhara a glance before he answered.

"Yeah?"

"Jae, I need help." Loni breathed hard into the Linq.

"Where are you?"

"Downtown New Jaipur."

"What? I didn't even know you left the temple."

"Jae. Please. I think I'm being followed."

"Okay. Ping me your location. I'll come get you." He hung up, a stiffness in his neck and jaw.

"Who was that?" Mayhara asked.

He let out a hard sigh. "It was Loni. She's in New Jaipur."

"What? Why?"

He was reluctant to answer. A slow anger bubbled up inside of him. If his suspicions were correct, Loni had fallen into her old habits again. Or perhaps she'd never given them up at all.

He shook his head. "I need to go get her."

"I'll come with you."

"It'll be faster on my bike. She thinks someone might be following her. If so, I can evade them easier on my bike."

Mayhara blinked and crossed her hands over her chest. "Oh. Okay. Be careful."

"I will. "

He leaned closer to her, hesitantly. When she didn't pull away, he kissed her gently on the lips. It was just a peck, but it was somehow reassuring. He nodded his goodbye and headed for the carport.

Dashing to his bike, he clenched his teeth. It was typical of Loni to get into trouble. As long as he'd known her, she had never been able to avoid it. And this wasn't the first time he'd had to pull her out of it.

He was still searing with anger by the time he found her almost an hour later. She stood near an old, out-of-service vending machine at an abandoned gas station, keeping to the shadows with a sweatshirt hood pulled low over her face. She looked over her shoulder as she shuffled to his bike.

She stumbled when she reached him. Jae stuck out his arm and caught her before she could fall.

As she straightened out, he pulled off his helmet and studied her. "Are you okay?"

She shivered. "I don't know."

"Look at me."

When she didn't listen to him, he grabbed her by her shoulders. She gasped and gaped at him. Her eyes were wide and bloodshot. She pressed her lips together and began tipping to the side, her lids drooping closed.

He knew it. She was high.

"Loni!" he shouted through his teeth. "How could you do this?"

There was a *crash* nearby, like a metal trash can had been knocked over. They both turned their heads, scanning the dark for movement. Though he was still fuming, he knew they shouldn't stick around.

"Come on." He handed her the spare helmet. "Let's go."

As soon as she was securely on the bike, her hands holding his side, he revved his engine and took off. The streets downtown were in bad shape, so he swerved around potholes and braced himself as they maneuvered over gravel-covered cement.

He heard another engine approaching. A glance in his side mirror led him to let out a curse and speed up. The headlights of the car behind him were getting closer.

"Hold on." He wasn't sure if Loni had heard him, but her grip stayed true.

Up ahead, the lampposts on either side of the street began to bend into the road.

Dark mages!

Jae flew toward the next intersection. He sped up and veered right, hopping up on the sidewalk. Cutting the corner, he heard the squealing tires of the pursuing car. They weren't happy with his stunt, and their own magic got in the way of their chase.

Jae hunkered down as his speed increased, and Loni's hold on him became tighter.

The car wasn't far behind. He had to lose them. There was no returning to the temple with dark mages on his tail.

He skidded sideways and zoomed into an alleyway, cutting between buildings. The car screeched to a stop, but the crates, barrels, and dumpsters in the alley began moving into the center of Jae's path. He had to zigzag to dodge them, barely scraping by. Loni let out a whimper. All this movement had to be brutal on her, especially in her state of mind. He was just glad she hadn't let go.

After they broke free from the alley, Jae skidded into another turn and raced to the next intersection. He was sure the dark mages following him would be clever enough to go around the block to catch up with them, so there was no slowing down now.

When he turned the next corner, he spotted a construction site ahead of them. He used his sapphire powers to quiet the motor.

"Loni, I'm going to need your help."

She stiffened. "Okay."

"See that work site up the street?" He felt her shift behind him.

"Yeah."

"Big mountain of dirt?"

He felt her let go with one hand. "Got it."

He hoped she understood what we wanted her to do, because a glance in his side mirror told him their pursuers were not far behind them. As they neared the construction site, an emerald glow appeared behind him. Dirt kicked up and floated into the air. At the same time, the scaffolding surrounding the building began to shake, metal poles detaching from the structure and flying toward the road. Jae knew this move had been caused by the dark mages.

"Loni!"

"I'm trying!"

The wind picked up. The particles from the mountain of dirt began to swirl as they rose, forming what looked like a tornado. Loni grunted, and the tornado moved toward the road, behind the bike and in front of the car. Small bits of debris struck Jae's helmet, but they'd cleared the whirlwind. Jae watch in his side mirror as the car flipped on its side from the swirling storm of dirt and debris.

Not wanting to take any chances, he shifted into top gear and raced out of the city before anyone else could catch them.

SEVENTEEN

Jae barged into the temple, gritting his teeth. He told himself to calm down. Loni was a wreck, and chances were she wouldn't even remember half of what had happened tonight. He went into the kitchen to get some water. Loni followed. As he sipped his water, she simply stood there, not saying a word. She rubbed at the skin under her eyes, which were still bloodshot.

"What happened, Loni?" He didn't yell. He didn't want to wake the whole house.

She crossed her arms. "I don't know."

"How could you risk this? Especially after what happened to Kamal. We can't afford to lose any more manpower. We can't afford to lose an elite."

"You never got it, did you?" She raised her arms and dropped them at her sides. "The pressure is crippling."

"Of course I get it. But you don't see the rest of us giving in to our demons to deal with the pressure."

"Well, maybe I'm not cut from the same cloth as the rest of you. Maybe I'm not as put-together as everyone else."

His hands were clenched into fists, but he kept them at his sides. "How did you even pay for it?"

She averted her gaze.

"Loni."

"I traded for it." Her voice was so quiet, he almost hadn't heard it.

"Traded what?" When she didn't answer, Jae scrubbed a hand down his face. He'd lived this before. She'd stolen from strangers—and from friends, no less—to pay for drugs. She'd always felt horrible afterward, but it had definitely made Jae lose his trust in her. "Did you take something from one of us?"

"No."

He narrowed his eyes at her.

"Not from one of you." She sighed. "I took one of the small golden trinkets from the dining room."

"So you thought: house full of fancy things, easy way to get something worth trading for drugs?"

"You don't understand. I have no control over it. I can't stop it. Believe me, I'm trying. But my sister… I can't get her out of my head. It's like there's something evil inside me and it's clawing at my old wounds and ripping them open again."

"That's no excuse, Loni. We're in a war."

"Exactly. There's so much pressure."

They both turned as Mayhara walked into the kitchen. Her eyes darted between them. "What's going on?"

Loni wiped her tears from her face and looked away from her.

Jae rubbed the back of his neck. "It's… Don't worry about it."

Mayhara's brow wrinkled. "I don't understand. Loni, what were you doing in New Jaipur? Does this have anything to do with why you left the temple a few nights ago?"

Jae set his jaw. "You've done this more than once since you've been here? Loni, this is an addiction. Can't you see?"

"Addiction?" Mayhara studied Loni, who wouldn't look at her. "Are you…? Is this about drugs?"

Loni rolled her eyes. "Listen, Miss Perfect. You know nothing about me."

Mayhara scoffed. "Is that why you were out there? To get a fix? Drugs are so important to you that you would put us all in danger?"

"It's my own business," Loni said through gritted teeth.

"No." Mayhara pressed on her temples. "It could affect us all. You not realizing that is selfish. And selfishness is not a luxury any of us can afford."

Jae stepped between them. "Okay, that's enough."

Mayhara narrowed her eyes. "What? Jae, you're defending her?"

He let out a sigh. "You don't know the whole story."

"I don't feel I have to. This could endanger our whole—"

"Mayhara, drop it. Please."

His voice was stern, and Mayhara flinched. Loni raked her hair away from her face.

Mayhara looked between them and lifted her chin. "Fine."

She turned and marched out of the kitchen.

"Mayhara," Jae called, but she didn't look back. He planted his hands on his waist and glared at Loni.

"Don't give me that look," Loni said. "I don't need your judgement, and I don't need you to defend me."

She knocked a bamboo bowl off the counter before she stomped away.

Kamal suddenly appeared, hobbling in on crutches. He grabbed a cookie from the cookie jar and then leaned back against the counter. "Chicks. Am I right?"

"Shut up, Kamal."

Jae hurried out of the room. He needed to catch up with Mayhara. Darting up the stairs, he hoped she'd give him a chance to explain. He sucked in a breath as he tapped lightly on her door, praying to the gods she wouldn't ignore him.

His shoulders dropped in relief when she opened the door. But the look she gave him made his stomach churn.

"Mayhara, I'm sorry. Can we talk?"

She pressed her lips together, simply looking at him for a moment. Fear rose in his veins that she'd turn him away. But then, by some miracle, she nodded.

"Yeah, sure." She opened the door wider and turned away, walking toward her window.

He walked halfway into the room. The last time he'd been in here, they'd shared a kiss. "I should explain why I stopped you from berating Loni."

"Berating?" She scoffed. "Jae, she could have ended this all for us. You said she thought she was being followed, and the only thing I can think of is that the Pishacha or dark mages found her."

He stuffed his hands in his pockets. "Yeah. She was being followed by dark mages. But we lost them."

"But the fact that she went out there in the first place—for drugs, no less—was a bad move."

"I know. Believe me, I told her that."

"So it's just that you didn't think *I* should tell her that? You think we should have an elite who's hooked on drugs?"

He took a step toward her, but she took a step back. He pushed a hand through his hair and dropped his gaze. "I just… I thought it would just make it worse if we ganged up on her. I was already giving her the shame speech."

"So, because you have some history with her, you thought it should be you."

He flinched at her words. He'd never mentioned having a history with Loni to Mayhara. "Did she say something to you?"

Mayhara averted her gaze and shook her head. "No. But it's true, right? You have a history?"

He nodded slowly.

She crossed her arms. "Maybe you should tell me about it."

"The day of the Eradication, we escaped together."

She took a deep breath and let it out. "Okay."

"We stayed hidden until the Imperial Police left, and then we ran away. But something else happened that day. Loni's sister, Kanya, was killed. Right in front of her eyes. And there was nothing either of us could do to stop it. And she carried that with her when we escaped. We sheltered in a few obscure places as we made our way to her family, and we got close. We grew to depend on each other and became comfortable with each other's company. But she would cry at night and have nightmares about Kanya being killed, and then one day, she began disappearing for hours at a time in the middle of the night."

"She was going out to get drugs."

He nodded. "When I found out, we fought. I told her this wasn't the way to deal with her grief. And at first it worked. I thought she was clean when we got to her parents' place. But she had to tell them about Kanya, and she had to tell them they needed to find a place to hide from the government. They'd started arresting the families of mages and placing them in prison camps."

Mayhara rubbed at her arms, slightly hunched over as she thought about her own parents, still trapped behind the walls of their prison camp.

"We helped them pack up," Jae continued. "And I was supposed to bring her to join them in a hidden cottage in the mountains before I headed back to Korea. But having to see the looks on their faces when they learned they'd lost a daughter… For Loni to have to explain to them that she'd watched her sister die… Well, it wasn't long before she turned to something that would numb the pain again. I tried to stick by her and break her of the habit, but she's an addict. She went behind my back. Finally, I couldn't deal with it anymore, and I told her she had to choose. She didn't choose me. And after that, I never saw her again. That is, until she showed up with the other elites at the observatory."

Mayhara watched him a bit longer. After a while, she uncrossed her arms. "It's a sad story," she said softly. "I'm sorry for her loss."

"I didn't know she was still doing it."

Mayhara pursed her lips. "Maybe I should go with you to the gala."

"No, that's too dangerous. If they recognize you, you'll be arrested. Or worse."

Her brows sunk down, heat rising in her throat. "Is that the real reason? Or is it you'd rather go with Loni?"

He tried to close the distance between them. "Mayhara—"

She backed away. "You know, I knew you two had a past. But I had to find out from Kamal. *Kamal*, Jae. Do you have any idea what that felt like?"

"I didn't think it was important. That was in the past."

"Was it?" She shook her head. "It looked like you were more than happy to defend her just now."

He took another step toward her.

She held up her hands. "No. I need some space. This is…" She scoffed. "This is not right. We should be concentrating on getting the daggers. Not on a silly fling."

"Mayhara."

"I said *no*. This"—she gestured between them—"is not why we're here. Not why I'm here. We need to beat Kashmeru. We need to ensure the safety of our families. Of the world. So that's the only thing I'm going to be putting my efforts into."

She marched to her door and held it, waiting for him to leave. She wouldn't look at him as he walked past her, and he could feel his heart crack into an infinite number of pieces as she closed the door behind him.

Eighteen

ayhara refused to cry any more. It had been an hour, and she was out of tissues. She didn't want to wonder anymore if Jae still had feelings for Loni. She didn't want to concentrate on the fact that Loni was the one who'd ended it. She didn't choose Jae. It had probably broken his heart. It didn't matter. There were more important things at hand. Yet she couldn't ignore the tightness in her chest. There was no denying she had feelings for him, and their relationship fizzling out before it even had a chance to begin made her heart sink. But she had to find the will to tuck away those feelings, just for now, just for the moment.

A knock on her door made her jump. Though she didn't want to fight with Jae anymore, she couldn't stop herself from answering. Deep down, she wanted to see him.

She blinked in surprise when she opened the door to find Salina.

"Oh," Mayhara said. "Hi. It's the middle of the night."

"I know." Salina grimaced. "Sorry. But I wanted to see if you were okay."

Mayhara grimaced. "Did you hear us fighting? I'm so embarrassed."

"Don't be embarrassed. Tensions are high around here."

Mayhara let out the smallest of laughs. "You could say that."

"Did you break up?"

Mayhara bit her lip. "Come in."

Salina stepped into her room and sat on the corner of the bed. "I thought you might want to talk."

Mayhara wrapped her arms around herself. "What's there to talk about, really? We weren't even really together, were we? It was just one kiss. Well, two. But the second one was just—you know what? It's not important."

"That doesn't mean it doesn't hurt," Salina said. "I see the way he looks at you."

"It doesn't matter." Mayhara rubbed at her eyes. "I can't think about that right now. I'm the root mage; I need to stay grounded. What the hell am I doing, putting matters of the heart in front of the fate of the world?"

They were quiet for a moment, and then Salina sighed.

"We used to be friends, you know? Loni and I."

Mayhara sat next to her on the bed. "Used to be? What happened?"

Salina opened her mouth to speak, but instead of words, a sob escaped her lips. She covered her face with her hands as tears began to fall.

Mayhara leaned closer to her. "Salina, what happened?"

Salina took her hand and shook her head. "I'm sorry. I'm sorry. This wasn't supposed to be about me."

"No, it's okay. Don't worry."

"It's just... It's Huojin."

"Salina, it's okay. It hasn't been that long. We're all still torn up about it, but you were her best friend. It makes sense that you—out of everyone—must still be the most devastated over her death."

"I thought I was holding myself together so well."

"But you don't have to. You're allowed to grieve." Mayhara pulled her in for a hug.

For a moment, Mayhara forgot about her fight with Jae. She let Salina cry on her shoulder, shedding tears herself for their fallen friend.

When she released her, Salina gave her a small smile.

"Did you still want to tell me about you and Loni?" Mayhara asked.

Salina nodded, sniffling back the last of her tears. "We actually became friends through Huojin."

"Really?"

"Huojin and Loni's sister, Kanya, were a couple. But Kanya was very temperamental, and Huojin was very stubborn, so it didn't last. They had a bad breakup. Two strong personalities like that... It got hostile."

"I don't think I ever noticed."

Salina swiped at her cheeks. "They mostly fought in the golden mage dorms. They didn't want Darshana to find out. Anyway, the breakup ended up pitting Loni and me against each other."

"How awful."

"The comments and criticisms between the four of us got out of control and became aggressive, and one day Loni got in Huojin's face, and I wanted her to back off. My temper got the best of me and I… I accidentally burned her arm."

Mayhara's eyes widened. "You *burned* Loni?"

"I hadn't meant to. I apologized, but she didn't want to hear it."

"After all this time, she may have put it behind her."

"I don't know." Salina shrugged. "She doesn't exactly have friendly conversations with me now. I don't think we're in a good place yet."

Mayhara shook her head. "Loni's just not in a good place, period."

Salina grimaced. "I heard."

"You did? From whom?"

"Kamal."

Mayhara raised a brow. "Of course."

"I guess Jae wasn't enough comfort for her to deal with her grief. So she turned to drugs."

Mayhara let out a sigh. "I can understand she's fighting an addiction, and I guess I should have some sympathy regarding that. I just hope she doesn't let that get in the way of our mission." Mayhara shook her head. "Otherwise, we're never going to win the battle, let alone the war.

Nineteen

ireworks filled the night sky. They would be set off all night, as was tradition at the governor's mansion on gala night during the Navratri festival. But this time, the celebration was bigger, as a symbol of welcoming the Akutake comet.

The governor and his staff had certainly pulled strings to get the broken windows replaced and the damage to the property covered up in time for the party.

Everywhere Loni looked, people were dressed in extravagant ballgowns, dashing tuxedos, and, most importantly, gorgeous and elaborate masks to hide their faces. Some attendees even wore top hats or fascinators to complete their look. She was surrounded by glitter, feathers, and flowing champagne.

"Are you all right?" Jae asked her.

Her arm was hooked through his as they entered the mansion. She fought to ignore the churn in her stomach. "Yeah. Sure."

"You're supposed to be enjoying yourselves," Yuki said from behind them. "Maybe smile or something?"

Loni's earpiece crackled. "Let us know your progress," Penny said. "Karina's got everything prepared for the spell here. Yuki, remember: You've got to place the talisman in the room we want to trap them in."

"Yep," Yuki answered softly. "Got it."

They'd made it to the front porch without incident, but they were approaching the door, where every guest was being checked off a list.

"Looks like you're up," Loni said to Jae, faking a smile.

"Don't worry. I'll help," Yuki said.

Loni glanced over her shoulder to see that Yuki was smiling. And something told her it wasn't fake.

"Name, please." The woman at the door wore a black-and-yellow ballgown and held a clipboard. Her mask was one that had to be held up with a stick, but she simply kept it in her hand with the clipboard, probably tired of lifting it between talking to every guest.

Jae put his hands behind his back. Loni moved closer to Jae to block the view as he called upon his sapphire powers.

"You don't need our names," Jae whispered to the woman. "The three of us are welcome to join the party."

Yuki leaned forward. "And you're very happy to see us."

Loni resisted the urge to roll her eyes.

The woman blinked at Jae and then grinned. "Welcome to the party! I'm so glad you could join us."

Jae's smile was genuine this time. He bowed graciously to the woman and then proceeded inside with Loni and Yuki in tow.

"Why do I feel like I'm part of a vampire gang?" Loni asked.

"Good thing she invited us in, right?" Jae joked.

The foyer was lit by an elegant chandelier. Loni was willing to bet it was normally the center of attraction when entering the mansion, but tonight it had to compete with the barrage of paper lanterns, dragon steamers, and bamboo-paper hanging fans that decorated everywhere one looked. Ikebana flower arrangements were displayed on marble pedestals.

Travelling farther into the house, Loni realized most of the décor was based on New Jaipur's flag colors: red, yellow, white, green, and blue. Beads with these colors were strung around the staircase handrails, laid out on tablecloths, and hung from the ceiling. The decorating team had also lain out LED strips along the baseboards to create a mystical ambiance.

"Mayhara? Shiro?" Penny's voice came over their earpieces. "You're in position?"

"All clear here," Shiro answered. He and Mayhara were waiting by the cars, ready to take off as soon as the daggers were acquired.

"Your attention, please."

The voice came from the ballroom. Loni, Jae, and Yuki worked their way into the grand room to find a woman standing near the large, glass, double patio doors in a deep red ballgown with a plume of feathers in her hair.

"That's Shei," Jae whispered to Loni and Yuki. "Mayhara's old boss at the census company. She's involved with the Pishacha. Her daughter is a dark mage."

"I have the honor of welcoming you all to this year's Navratri Festival Gala," Shei said. "Governor Laghari and his family and staff have been organizing this gala for six months now, and despite attempts to thwart our efforts, the gala has commenced with success."

The crowd applauded. As Shei introduced the governor to address the partygoers, Loni studied the people surrounding him. Shei said something to the young woman beside her. She was willing to bet the girl in the silver dress was her daughter, Ru. She recognized the young man whispering in Ru's ear as Harish Patel, the son of the wealthiest man in New Jaipur. He had a narrow face and a prominent nose, and there was almost a wildness in his eyes as he glanced around the room. Loni made a note to keep an eye on him. There was something about him that gave Loni the feeling he was also a dark mage. The way these groups were intertwined, it wouldn't surprise her. Slightly behind the governor stood his wife and his son, Avi. Loni recognized him from the news. He had a boyish face, with thick lips and a narrow chin, but his body was pure lean muscle. His mane of dark brown hair spiked out from his head in one direction She could see why Yuki had been interested in him.

Once Loni and Jae found the room the daggers were in, Yuki would have to lead these three—and any Pishacha who might be around—into the room so that Karina's spell could trap them. Loni wondered if the other four dark mages were at the party.

"As soon as you see the fireplace, let me know," Penny said into their ears. "I'll describe what I saw in my vision and lead you to the room."

The crowd applauded again as the governor ended his speech. "Thank you, everyone. Please, enjoy the party."

Music began to play. Yuki moved closer to Loni and Jae. "Okay, you two try to look inconspicuous while I search for that fireplace."

"Good luck," Loni told her.

Jae lifted his chin, staring into space for a moment.

"Jae?"

He shifted his attention back to her. "Come on. Let's dance."

She was surprised when he took her hand and led her to the dancefloor. He seemed to be bringing her to a specific spot. She glanced around and realized they weren't far from where Governor Laghari, Director Shei, and the chief of police were sipping champagne and conversing.

Jae swung around to face Loni and assumed a dancing stance, his hands on her waist. It was a familiar feeling, having his hands on her. She'd almost forgotten how right it felt. Though she wished he would, he wasn't looking into her eyes. She knew he was eavesdropping on the conversation being held with the governor.

"The chief of police is asking Shei if she's secured a place to move the daggers." Jae spoke in a low voice so only Loni—and the other mages listening in—could hear.

As they turned in their dance, Loni glanced over to the chief of police. The governor's brows were drawn as he spoke.

"Governor Laghari is reluctant to move them until the festivities are over," Jae said. "Too many eyes."

"Okay," Loni said. "But at least we know they're still here."

Jae stiffened. "Oh my God."

"What?" Loni asked.

Her earpiece clicked. "What's wrong, Jae?"

Jae swallowed hard. "The governor just called the chief of police 'Bhutano.'"

Loni's jaw almost dropped. "Bhutano? As in Kashmeru's spirit messenger?"

"Yeah." Jae spared the man a glance. He stood tall, his shoulders broad, his hair extremely short, and he kept his lips in a straight line. "We thought he'd been possessing a man named Bruno, whom Naree was seeing before she fell under Kashmeru's spell—or because of his spell, I can't be sure. But we beat Bruno in a fight, and he disappeared like the Pishacha do, and Bhutano was apparently still around. Looks like we were wrong about his identity."

"I guess it makes sense," Loni said, "with the way the police and the government are mixed up in this."

"Bhutano says he's sent out some of his dark mages to get rid of the extremist. The ones who were not expected to be at the gala."

"So that means they're not here. Hopefully, they're not near enough to interfere with our plan."

Jae bit the inside of his cheek.

"What now?" Loni asked.

"They're talking about taking care of the prison camps, but I don't know what they mean. Something they've been planning to do. I'm afraid they want to destroy them—and everyone inside of them."

Loni froze in place, nearly stumbling mid-dance. "They can't do that."

"What's stopping them?" Jae urged her to continue dancing.

Loni dropped her gaze. Destroying the prison camps would mean the deaths of millions of mage families. "What do you think will happen to the government if we beat Kashmeru?"

Jae took a deep breath and let it out. "If we can get the empress where she belongs—on the throne and in charge—order should be restored. Naree will deem mages legal again, the prison camps will fall, families will be released, and if there's any justice in the world, those who were involved with the Pishacha will be removed from their positions."

Loni looked around at all the masked women in the room. "Do you think Naree is here?"

"I don't know. If she is, it would be hard to recognize her."

Loni's hands trembled, and she felt a dull ache in her head. Her addiction was calling to her. It was her body's response to dealing with the stress. But she had to push the craving away. She had to concentrate on the task at hand. Glancing at Jae, she decided to change the subject to keep her mind off the threat of nausea.

She adjusted her mask. "It's funny. All that time we spent together and you never mentioned that your sister was the Lotus."

"I had to keep it a secret."

"Even from me?"

Jae averted his gaze. "You weren't exactly trustworthy, sneaking off in the middle of the night, getting yourself into trouble."

Her shoulders hunched and her cheeks burned. "I'm sorry, you know?"

"Loni." Jae shook his head, letting out a humorless laugh. "Now's not the time."

"I know. I just… I just need you to know that. I was stupid. When you told me to choose between my vices and you? Choosing my vices… That was the stupidest decision I ever made in my life."

Jae gazed at her for a moment. She wished she could see his whole face. She wished she could tell what he was thinking. After a moment, he broke eye contact and looked over her shoulder.

"Are you… feeling better?"

She sighed. "I don't even know what that means anymore. The word 'normal' is lost on me."

"Guys." It was Yuki's voice on the earpiece. "I found the fireplace."

Jae stopped dancing and slowly led Loni out of the ballroom.

"You sure it's the right one?" Penny asked.

"Two tall cast-iron candle holders stood on either side," Yuki said. "A painting of a girl smelling a lotus."

"Yep, that's it," Penny said.

"We're on our way, Yuki." Jae took his time getting through the crowd. They didn't want to draw too much attention by rushing. They feigned smiles and acted polite as they wormed through silk and beads and feathers to get to where Yuki was.

"Okay," Jae said. "Let's find the room and make sure the daggers are in there before we lure the dark mages in."

"It's a hall to the right," Penny told them. "Second door on the left."

As they made their way toward the door, they discovered two security guards standing sentry in the hall, along with a handful of gossiping partygoers.

"My turn," Loni said. "Try not to breathe too deeply for a sec."

She felt the power in her palms as she diminished the air in the hall. The people who were congregating there began to clear their throats. The men pulled at their collars, and the women patted at their throats. One by one, they departed the hall.

The guards, though visibly uncomfortable, stood their ground.

Jae approached them, his palms glowing blue. "Looks like you two need to go out and get some air."

Loni released her hold on the air pressure as the guards left their stations.

"What's the code, Penny?" Loni asked.

After getting the door open, she, Jae, and Yuki entered the room.

Jae gestured at a door at the far end of the room. "That must be it."

Penny gave them the code for this door as well. Loni's heart pounded as the door clicked open and they slipped inside. It was a walk-in closet with shelves. On one of the shelves were three black-and-red boxes. Jae opened one of them to confirm.

"We've found them," he said.

Yuki walked up to the shelves and took a small charm out of her clutch purse. It was a round, wooden charm with the image of a flame engraved into it. Karina had charged the figure with a magical force to connect it to the candle she was about to burn.

"The talisman's in place," Yuki said.

"Karina has started the spell," Penny told them.

"I'll go get Avi's attention." Yuki tilted her head and left the room.

"Let's take these, then." Jae removed the first dagger from the box and slipped it into the inside pocket of his tuxedo jacket.

Loni took the next dagger and placed it in a secret pocket in the skirt of her dress as Jae secured the final dagger.

"I can't believe we've got them all," Loni whispered.

"Let's not get too confident yet." He adjusted his lapels. "We've got to get out of here first."

"Okay, he sees me," Yuki said. "Headed your way. The other two are with him."

Black smoke burst in the room, and Jae and Loni flinched when two Pishacha appeared.

"I guess word travels fast," Loni said.

As the Pishacha approached, Loni mustered all her strength and threw out a wave of her power. The two Pishacha froze, grabbing their chests. They both disappeared, black smoke swirling.

"What was that?" Jae asked.

"I sucked the air out of their hearts. I don't like doing that; it's draining."

Yuki ran into the room, spinning around to face the door just as Avi, Ru, and Harish stomped in behind her. Avi squared his jaw and raised his palms.

"Watch out!" Yuki shouted, stepping in front of Jae and Loni and throwing her diamond shield between them and the dark mages. "Avi's a bone crusher. Stay behind the shield."

"Penny," Jae said. "How's it looking?"

"Karina's almost done. She needs another minute."

Loni held her palms up. Avi's eyes widened. He threw his hands around his neck and gasped. As he dropped to his knees, the two Pishacha who had disappeared reappeared at Avi's side. Ru held her palm up, and framed pictures that hung on the wall tore away and zipped through the air. One hit Yuki on the side of the head. Her diamond shield dropped.

The Pishacha advanced.

Jae threw out a blast of sound. Everyone in the room covered their ears, including Loni and Yuki. He hadn't had time to warn them. Harish held his palms up, and all the lights in the room burst. Electricity flashed in the air.

"Penny!" Jae yelled.

"Okay, go," Penny said. "But the candle is burning faster than we anticipated. You need to book it."

Loni raised her palms again and then closed her hands into tight fists. The three dark mages and the two Pishacha gasped as they clutched at their hearts, backing away.

"Go!" she screamed, grabbing Yuki's hand and pulling her out of the room.

Jae was close behind. As they made it into the hallway, they looked over their shoulders just long enough to see the Pishacha disappearing and reappearing in the room, filling it with smoke as they tried to escape. The three dark mages were in shock, because they couldn't get past the doorway.

"Come on," Jae said. "Don't run. It'll look suspicious."

He raised his palm once more and aimed it at the doorway. The yells and hollers from within the room were suddenly silenced.

"The candle is almost out," Penny said.

"We're headed out the front door as we speak," Jae said.

TWENTY

enny let out a long breath and took the earpiece out of her ear. "They made it. They're on their way."

Karina nodded, staring at the wick of the candle that was no longer aflame. "That was close."

Penny glanced at the others, not yet able to relax. Inside of her, the anxiety of the situation still bubbled. She'd have to find a chance to meditate to clear the unwelcome feeling from her body.

"They got the daggers?" Darshana asked.

"Yeah, they got them," Penny answered.

"Brilliant," Mr. Kitaro said, straightening his blazer.

"I can't believe the chief of police is Bhutano," Salina said, sitting on the couch with her hands pressed between her knees. "No wonder the police are against us."

"All this excitement has made me hungry," Kamal said. "Penny, would you mind getting me a little something?"

"Not now, Kamal."

"Please?"

"I'm going to help Karina clear this stuff away first." Penny gestured at the candle and the herbs spread out over the dining room table.

"Fine." Kamal turned to Salina. He gave her a sly smile."

"Not a chance," Salina said. "You need to get back on your feet eventually."

"I think I'll go check on Amalia," Darshana said. "Make sure she's comfortable."

"I'll go with you." Mr. Kitaro smiled as he joined her.

"What's up with those two?" Kamal asked once they were out of earshot.

Penny shook her head. "I'm sure it's none of your business."

Karina placed the candle and herbs in a small box and stood. "I'll go put these away. I'm glad the spell worked."

"It was perfect, Karina." Penny gave her a nod. "Thanks for your help."

"I'm almost done with the translation of the scroll, too." Karina sighed. "It's just taking a little longer than I thought. But if my grandmother is feeling better tomorrow, maybe she can help too."

"That would be great." Penny nodded.

Karina left the room, and Penny raked her hands through her hair.

Kamal smiled and nodded. "We've got all the daggers."

"Yeah. Hard to believe." Penny said.

"I don't think I'll believe it until I see it with my own eyes," Salina added.

"Now we just need to—" The sound of glass breaking stopped him. He grabbed his crutches and stood from the dining room table. "What was that?"

A vision hit Penny. She let out a curse. It had somehow been blocked from her mind until now.

"The other four dark mages," she said. "They're here."

Kamal shifted, his grip tightening on his crutches. Salina jumped to her feet.

"And the Lotus," Penny whispered, her chest tightening with fear. "Naree is here."

She signaled for Kamal to keep quiet and then ran to the hall. Salina raced beside her. Throwing open Amalia's door, Penny stared wide-eyed at Darshana, Mr. Kitaro, Karina, and a sleeping Amalia.

"Don't make a noise," Penny said. "And don't open the door, whatever happens."

"Penny, what is it?" Darshana asked.

"I'll explain later."

"I'll stay with them," Salina said, closing the door.

Penny heard it lock. She raised her palms, aiming them at the door. A purple glow surrounded the door, and in the next second, it disappeared from sight. Invisible to whomever might come along.

As she ran back to the dining room, a thump and a scream stopped her in her tracks.

Again, she called upon her magic. This time she cloaked herself. She couldn't hold this magic very long, but she just needed to get to Kamal so she could hide him. And then she'd have to fight off the four dark mages—and, if it came to it, the Lotus—on her own.

When she reached the dining room, Kamal's crutches were sprawled out on the floor, and beside him—

"Kamal!" She let go of her magic.

There was a lot of blood. Kamal wasn't moving. Blood gushed from his chest. He'd been stabbed.

"No, no, no. Kamal."

He wasn't breathing. Penny began to hyperventilate.

Something clicked behind her, like shoes on the marble floor.

Before she could turn around to face the intruders, a cloth sack was shoved over her head. She screamed, but in the next second, something strong and hard struck her above her ear and the world faded to black.

Sapphire Mage

Book Five

ONE

Park Jae-hyun let out a sigh of relief when the cars finally reached the temple. Jae had spent the entire drive checking the side mirror while Mayhara had driven. He couldn't believe their luck; they hadn't been followed. Both cars had safely raced away from the celebrations at the governor's mansion before anyone could discover that the Pishacha and dark mages had been trapped in one of the rooms. Of course, the spell that had trapped them there had to have been broken by now. It had only lasted as long as Karina's enchanted candle burned. Which was why Jae's eyes had been trained on the road behind both getaway cars.

Mayhara shut off the engine once they were parked and glanced at Jae. Her long, dark hair fell softly over her cheeks. Things were still tense between them, and Jae felt a vise tightening around his heart. She had been hurt because he hadn't disclosed the truth about his past relationship with Loni. She'd basically ended whatever had been growing between them before it could really even begin. He desperately wanted to find a time to sit down with her and explain himself. To tell her how he truly felt about her. But she continually brushed him off, stating that she needed to concentrate on their mission. Their relationship was purely professional now. Just two members of the band of mages who vowed to protect the legacy of the Empire of the Lotus and prevent the dark god Kashmeru from destroying the world. No big deal.

Shiro, who had been driving the other car, nodded to Jae once, pushing back the strands of his black and copper hair as he sighed. The expression on his face was one of concern. Jae figured Shiro must have felt the same as he did about their escape from the party: uncertain and skeptical about their victory. They'd been successful in acquiring the daggers, but that didn't mean they'd won the battle. They still had to find and rescue Naree—Jae's sister, who was the reincarnation of the Lotus empress—and break the spell she was under. The dark god Kashmeru was controlling her every move, using the lure of their centuries-long, complicated, love-hate relationship to manipulate her to do his bidding. He needed her to break the spell that kept him locked in a cursed tomb. But he couldn't be released without the arcane daggers.

And the mages now had all seven.

Mayhara averted her gaze when Jae caught her looking at him. The hair on the nape of his neck stiffened as she turned and headed for the temple entrance without a word. Jae, Shiro, Yuki, and Loni followed Mayhara toward the door. The skirts of the ball gowns Yuki and Loni wore swished as they walked.

But then, Yuki suddenly stopped.

Jae and Shiro turned to her when they noticed her standing frozen, her face pale against her auburn hair. The other mages stopped to study her as well. She wrapped her arms around her middle and shivered.

"What is it?" Jae asked. "What's wrong?"

"Fear." Yuki bit her lip. "I feel fear, coming from inside the temple. And… something else. I think it's… death."

Jae and the others widened their eyes, their bodies tensing.

"Amalia," Mayhara said with panic in her voice. She turned on her heel and bolted into the temple.

Jae was close behind, the others in tow. He silently prayed to the gods that Amalia—the swamp witch who'd saved Shiro's life—was all right. Her blood had been poisoned by a dark mage, and despite Shiro's attempts at using his powers to syphon out the poison, Amalia was getting worse.

If she was dead…

The mages burst into the temple and began to search for the others who had stayed behind. But their search stopped short when Loni screamed in the living room. The rest of the mages hurried to find her.

Loni, looking pale as she stood, trembled, with her dark waves falling from her hair clip, her hands covering her mouth, and tears flowing down her cheeks.

Jae gasped at what was on the floor in front of her.

"Kamal!" Mayhara rushed to the body sprawled out on the cold marble floor surrounded by a pool of blood.

Jae bent down beside the long form of Kamal's body and immediately used his sapphire powers to listen for breathing or a heartbeat. Neither one could be found.

"He's dead," Yuki whispered. "His spirit has left him."

As the diamond mage, Yuki would have been able to sense his spirit. If Jae had doubted himself about not hearing a pulse, he would have to believe Yuki's words. Their sapphire elite was dead.

"What… What happened here?" Shiro looked around.

The place was in a shambles, furniture knocked over, drawers ripped from cabinets, and the sofa torn to shreds. Even paintings had been stripped from the walls.

"They were here," Jae said. "They found the temple, and they were looking for the daggers."

"And they killed Kamal in the process." Loni's voice broke on their fellow mage's name.

"Where are the others?" Mayhara stood with her hands clutched to her chest and ran to the hall.

They all followed her to Amalia's room, but when they arrived at where her door should have been, they discovered it gone. The mages looked around at each other in confusion.

"What happened to her door?" Loni asked. "This doesn't make sense."

"Sight," Mayhara said, feeling the wall where the door used to be. "Penny must have cloaked the door with her amethyst powers."

Jae watched as Mayhara's hand clamped around a space of air.

"I found the knob." Mayhara jostled at it and then shook her head. "It's locked."

Yuki placed her hands on the invisible door, her palms glowing white. "They are in there. They're afraid. That's the fear I felt."

Jae lifted his palms, the blue glow reflecting off the wall where the door was hidden. He didn't know if Penny's cloaking spell had blocked the sound out, but he had to let the others inside Amalia's room know they were there.

"Hello, can you hear me? It's Jae." He pushed his sound powers through the wall. "Darshana? Penny? Salina? Are you in there?"

Still using his powers, he heard Karina—Amalia's granddaughter— swallow hard. The sound of a chair screeching against the floor followed.

"Jae! Yes!" Karina answered. "We're here."

"Can you unlock the door?" Jae asked. "Or is it spelled shut?"

In a few seconds, the lock clicked, and a wide-eyed Karina opened the door, which magically materialized before their eyes. Karina gasped in surprise, pushing her dark, unkempt hair away from her face.

The mages rushed inside. Mayhara first embraced a trembling Darshana and then Salina, Shiro crouched down next to the bed to feel the sleeping Amalia's forehead, and Loni asked Mr. Kitaro—the Sacred Key, keeper of one of the magic daggers—what had happened.

"We're not sure what happened," Mr. Kitaro said. "Penny told us to keep quiet and lock the door. We heard a lot of ruckus, but we followed her instructions."

Jae, Shiro, and Mayhara exchanged glances.

"They found the temple," Loni explained. "The Pishacha. Or the dark mages. Or both. And they… they killed Kamal."

Karina slapped a hand over her mouth and backed up against the wall. Darshana closed her eyes and bowed her head, her mouth drawn into a frown. Mr. Kitaro ran a hand down his face. Salina's jaw hung open in shock.

"They must have been searching for the daggers," Jae added.

"Wait." Mayhara's head whipped around. "Where's Penny?"

TWO

There was a buzzing in Penny's head. Like wires transferring electricity, each pulse a dull ache in her temples. Her eyes slowly drifted open, and she found a pair of dark eyes staring back at her. The face was unfamiliar, the young man's mouth kept in a straight line. Her eyes drifted momentarily to the scar running from one eyebrow to his cheekbone.

"She's awake," he said, looking over his shoulder as he stood upright. "Ru, get Bhutano."

The girl he spoke to looked up from filing her jet-black nails and wrinkled her lip in response. She tucked away the nail file and headed for the metallic door. With a wave of her hand, which emitted tendrils of black smoke, the door opened for her, closing as soon as she stepped outside the room.

Penny took in a deep breath, remembering what had happened. The dark mages and Naree had infiltrated the temple… and killed Kamal. She swallowed hard, remembering the blood. Her head spun, and the spot on her head where she'd been struck throbbed.

Something sharp and metallic pierced the skin at her wrists when she tried to move. She figured they were electro-cuffs that bound her wrists together behind her back, securing her to the chair she'd woken up in. She bit back the panic that rose in her throat. It wouldn't improve her situation to lose her calm. Plus, she needed to minimize her movements. She didn't want to feel the shock of the cuffs if she were to try to get free.

She glanced around the room, taking in the six remaining figures spread out in the cold, dimly lit, windowless space. Was she in a basement? She couldn't tell.

Penny recognized the only female of the seven—the one who had left the room—as the daughter of Director Shei, head of the census division of the government. Mayhara had been the one to put the pieces of that puzzle together. From what Penny could gather, Ru had telekinetic abilities, able to move things with her dark mage powers. With her straight, black hair hanging in her face and her ever-present frown, Ru was the gloomiest looking one out of the seven.

Penny's focus shifted over to two of the dark mages who stood together on one side of the room. They whispered something to each other that Penny couldn't hear. She recognized these two from the news. Avi was the governor's son. With his wild hair, boyish face, and thick lips, Avi was easily the best-looking of the group, and Penny could understand why Yuki had fallen for him. Beside Avi was Harish, the son of the richest family in New Jaipur. The wildness in his eyes overshadowed his prominent nose and thick brows.

The one with the scar on his cheek moved into her line of vision. He gave her a cynical sneer as he leaned closer to her. "Where are your friends to help you out now, mage?"

"Daiki," Avi called. "Get out of her face. Bhutano said to back off until he talks to her."

Daiki twisted his mouth sideways and ran a hand roughly over his mop of messy hair. "Yeah, whatever."

She wasn't familiar with Daiki, and a glance at the others told her how uneducated she was on the dark mages. She made a note to try to read them with her powers when they lowered their guard.

The door to the room opened again, and Ru stomped in. She plopped down on a chair and lifted her feet, her heavy boots coming down hard to rest on a small table. Entering the room behind her were the chief of police—whom the mages recently learned was being possessed by Kashmeru's evil spirit messenger, Bhutano—followed by Naree—the reincarnation of the Lotus Empress Lakshmi.

The chief of police was impressive, with his pristine uniform, impeccable coifed hair, and perfect posture, but it was Naree whom Penny was mesmerized by. Penny could tell from Naree's eyes and cheekbones that she was Jae's sister. The family resemblance was unmistakable. But Naree also had an allure about her, like she was made up of pure magic. Her wavy, brunette hair fell loosely over her temples, and there was a magical draw to her chestnut brown eyes. Penny had seen her before, of course, but never this closely.

Harish stepped forward and placed a chair opposite Penny, which Naree sat in, her eyes locked with Penny's. Harish then strode back to join the other dark mages as they witnessed whatever it was Bhutano had planned to do.

"Hello, Penny," Bhutano said, pacing beside her with his hands clasped behind his back. "You might be wondering why we didn't simply kill you along with your fellow mage back at the temple."

Penny shifted her gaze from Bhutano back to Naree.

"It might have crossed my mind," Penny answered.

"Yes," he continued, "well, we went to the temple with the intention of collecting what belongs to us. But you surprised us by being clever enough to hide them where even the most powerful being could not see."

They didn't find the daggers?

Penny dropped her gaze. She knew she had to be very careful around Naree. Naree had all the powers every class of mage had. That included amethyst mage powers—vision, insight, illusions, and secrets. If she used her powers, she could see what Penny was thinking. She could find out their secrets. She had to clear her mind as much as possible so Naree wouldn't see.

"I could feel the magic of the daggers," Naree said. "But their exact location was fuzzy in my mind. It was as if a witch had cast a cloaking spell on them."

Again, Penny pushed all thoughts from her head. She didn't want the enemy to find out about Karina. They'd already poisoned Karina's grandmother. She had to keep Karina safe from their destructive ways.

"We searched the temple, so perhaps they were in another location." Naree held out her hands. Her palms glowed with bright blue light.

Truth, Penny realized.

"Where are the daggers, Penny?" Naree asked.

Penny felt the pull of Naree's power. Though she tried not to speak at all, there was no fighting the force of the sapphire powers Naree used on her.

"I don't know." Penny's eyes widened at her own words. She didn't know. Penny realized what she'd said was actually the truth. The daggers had been moved. They weren't where she remembered them to be.

Logically, it made sense. There was no doubt that when the other elites discovered Kamal's body, they would have realized the temple was no longer safe and decided to move to a different location, bringing the daggers with them. And since she had no idea where the mages would have gone, she was clueless as to where the daggers were.

She paused, the thought of Kamal filling her thoughts. Her heart tightened up, like it was being crushed beneath a heavy weight. Kamal was dead. They'd killed him.

And now they were holding her prisoner, sparing her life only if she could give them some answers.

"What do you mean, you don't know?" Bhutano asked, his jaw tight with anger.

"At this point, I don't know where the daggers are." Penny lifted her chin. "They've been moved. I don't know the new location."

"But you can use your insight to find out," Naree said, her voice calm.

Penny tilted her head. "You know as well as I do that the daggers are cloaked in magic."

Naree pursed her lips. "But you were able to track them down before."

Penny didn't offer an answer. The blue glow returned to Naree's palms.

"Meditation." Penny let out a sigh, finding it too hard to fight the sapphire mage power of truth. "It takes time."

As Naree studied Penny's face, something occurred to Penny. Naree hadn't been to the academy. She hadn't learned the ins and outs of mage powers like the mages who had attended the academy had. Although Naree held all the power of each class of mage, she wasn't trained in using them. She didn't know the rules.

"It's possible for me to track them down," Penny said. "But I'm not exactly in the ideal mindset or physical comfort to do that." She gestured at her arms, still bound behind her back.

Naree glanced at Bhutano. He stopped pacing and gave Naree a single nod.

"Perhaps we can arrange something," Naree said. "But understand this. I will be able to see your visions. Any information you try to conceal in that pretty little head of yours will be found out. So there's no use trying to hide it."

Penny took a deep breath, holding Naree's gaze. There was more at stake than just the daggers she needed to keep hidden from the Pishacha. She forced herself not to think about the grimoire. If the Lotus used her amethyst powers to see Penny's thoughts, she might find out about their plans to get the grimoire, and she needed to stop the enemy from gaining any more advantages.

THREE

The somber mood in the air was almost tangible. Jae followed Mr. Kitaro along with the rest of the group. They carried with them what they could from the temple, the weight of their belongings nothing compared to the weight of losing Kamal.

With the Pishacha having discovered the location of the temple, the group would have been sitting ducks if they'd remained. And just because the dark mages hadn't been able to find the daggers on their first ambush of the place, that didn't mean they wouldn't return and do everything in their power to find them on a subsequent visit.

They were at a loss as to where to go, and so Mr. Kitaro had suggested a safehouse he had tucked away in a remote area just outside the city. Jae glanced back at Shiro, who was helping Karina get Amalia down the concealed path that led to the safehouse. The cars and Jae's bike were hidden behind a cluster of trees and bushes not far from the house, but the short walk, which progressed through rocky and uneven terrain, felt like miles to Jae.

None of them had had any sleep since before the festival. And the adrenalin rush after finding Kamal dead and Penny missing was quickly fading.

Up ahead, walking beside Darshana, Mayhara cast a quick glance over her shoulder at him. Their eyes only met for a second, but in that small moment, Jae felt his heart being crushed. She'd barely spoken to him since their fight. And of course, with everything that had happened since she'd told him she couldn't be with him, there were more urgent things to deal with. But still, he longed to have a heart-to-heart with her and let her know how he felt about her.

Salina reached the door to the cabin right after Mr. Kitaro. She looked back at the crew and let out a sigh. Though her posture showed she was as exhausted as the rest of the group, there was a fire in her eyes that told Jae she was prepared to fight for their cause. To go to any lengths to get Penny back. She'd lost enough. They all had.

"It's modest," Mr. Kitaro said as they all caught up and gathered on the front porch. "But it's off the grid, and, as you could probably tell from the trek here, virtually impossible to find."

Jae was going to mention how well the temple had been hidden as well before it had been found, but he bit back his words. He needed to think more positive if he was going to get through this.

As if she could sense his struggle, Darshana cast him a glance.

Mr. Kitaro flipped open a control panel beside the door and punched a code into the lock pad. The light on the lock pad changed from red to green, and Mr. Kitaro opened the door.

"I just need to turn on the main generator to get the power up," Mr. Kitaro said.

There were a few clicks of metal Jae couldn't see. In the next second the lights inside automatically came on as Mr. Kitaro stepped into the house.

"As I mentioned, it's not as grand as the temple. Rooms will have to be shared."

"I'm sure we'll manage," Mayhara said, offering him a thankful smile.

Mr. Kitaro placed a hand on Karina's shoulder. "I think the first room down the hall on the right would suit Amalia and you. We should get her settled."

"Thank you," Karina said.

Amalia, whose eyes were droopy, gave him a slight nod. Her jaw was tense and her grip on her granddaughter was tight.

"I'll help them settle in," Shiro told him.

Loni and Yuki squeezed past Jae, and when Yuki caught Jae's eyes, he wondered if she was using her diamond mage powers to read his emotions. Salina had paired up with Mayhara and disappeared down the hall.

Jae set down the motorcycle helmets and glanced around the quaint space, stretching out his back muscles. "This place is actually nice."

"It's safe." Mr. Kitaro pointed to the windows in the living room. "Bulletproof glass." He moved over to a monitor near the kitchen and swiped the screen. The monitor came to life, showing four different views of their surroundings. "Hidden cameras set up around the perimeter with silent alarms that will alert us if anyone trespasses."

"Great setup."

"I take the position of Sacred Key seriously. Though I haven't had the opportunity to use this place as a sanctuary until now."

"Yeah, speaking of which…" Jae ran a hand over the stubble on his chin. "Do you think this place is safe enough to hide the daggers?"

Mr. Kitaro placed his hands on his sides. "I spoke with Darshana about it. Neither of us are one hundred percent certain it's a good idea. If the Pishacha do manage to track us down, the chances of them finding the daggers could sway in their favor. Darshana decided to meditate on it as soon as she gets settled. We'll have a meeting once everyone is rested and decide what to do. Together."

Jae nodded. "Sounds good. I guess I'll go see if any beds are left and settle in."

With a sigh, he made his way down the hall where the rooms were located. Karina, Amalia, and Darshana were in the first room. The door was open, and Jae spotted Karina propping the pillows in the bed Amalia lay in. Darshana pulled the comforter over Amalia's legs, her brows low in worry.

Farther down the hall, Yuki and Loni were unpacking in the room they'd claimed. Jae noticed there was a third bed in their room and suspected they were being optimistic about finding Penny. He hoped they were right.

Yuki turned to face Jae, though he hadn't made a sound. Loni didn't seem to notice when Yuki headed toward the door to approach Jae. He took a step back as she continued into the hall and closed the door behind her.

"She's hanging on by a thread," Yuki whispered. She held up her hand and opened it to reveal the white glow in her palm. "I'm doing what I can to keep her grounded, but it's exhausting. I think it's best if you give her some space. Her emotions really go out of whack when you're around, and I just don't have it in me to stop that rollercoaster."

Jae nodded solemnly. "Understood. Thank you for watching out for her."

She gave a half-shrug. "Just doing my part." She studied his face. "You're a cluster of turmoil and anxiety yourself. Let me know if you need some time with me, just to calm your nerves."

"Thanks." He offered her a small smile. "I'll be okay."

She nodded before returning to her room, and Jae continued down the hall. He almost collided with Mayhara as she exited the room she was sharing with Salina. She took a step back, breathing in deeply and stuffing her hands in her pockets as she averted her eyes. He wanted so much to embrace her and tell her how much he missed her company, but he refrained.

"Hey," he said.

"Hey." Her voice was soft. She glanced up at him, her thick lashes hiding the full view of her eyes.

"You all right?"

She shrugged as she nodded. "As best as I can be, under the circumstances. Torn up over Kamal and hoping Penny is okay."

"Yeah. Me too." He glanced down the hall. "Mr. Kitaro said we're going to meet later to talk about where to keep the daggers."

"That's a good idea. It's crucial we keep them out of reach of the Pishacha. And the fact that we have them all means those targets on our backs just got a lot bigger."

"Normally, I'd take a shot at brainstorming and making a list of possibilities, but I'm just too—"

"Exhausted." Mayhara let out a sigh. "Yeah, me too."

For a moment, they stood in silence, their locked eyes speaking volumes. The second Jae worked up the courage to breach the topic of their feelings, Mayhara took a step back.

"I'm going to…" She pointed over her shoulder. "I'd like to get a shower in before we all meet with Darshana."

"Oh." He rubbed the back of his neck. "Okay."

She turned and disappeared into her room, closing the door behind her. Jae had to clear his throat in order to swallow back his disappointment.

Everything seemed to be pressing in on him. He hoped the buzzing in his head was just a side effect from exhaustion mixed with his emotions being pushed to extremes. The alternative would be that his powers were on the fritz.

At the end of the hall, Jae found a room to the right and one to the left.

"That one's Mr. Kitaro's," Shiro said, poking his head through the doorway on the right. "You can room with me if you want."

"Perfect. Just point me in the direction of my bed. If I could just close my eyes for twenty minutes, I might be able to keep them from popping out of my head."

"Yeah, good idea." Shiro's mouth formed a slight smirk. "Not even you could pull off that look."

FOUR

Darshana sat at the dining room table, her hands splayed, palms down, on the tabletop. Her eyes were open, but Jae could tell her focus was elsewhere. Experience told him she was trying to hold on to the visions she must have seen when she'd meditated.

Yuki and Loni were already seated near Darshana. The warning look Yuki flashed Jae caused him to pick a seat far from Loni. Mayhara and Karina were next to join them. To his surprise, Mayhara sat across from Jae. Karina hovered near the kitchen island behind the dining room table. Mr. Kitaro strode in, looking dignified as always, and took the seat next to Darshana.

Shiro gave everyone a nod as he entered the room and went immediately to Karina's side. "How's Amalia?"

Karina shook her head and crossed her arms over her chest. "She seems worse. She's resting now, but even in her sleep, she looks like she's suffering."

Shiro placed a hand on her arm. "I'll come see her after this and try to help her a little."

She mouthed a *thank you* that didn't quite hit the air.

As soon as he sat down, Salina rushed into the room. Her eyes were wide and frantic. "Your pictures just hit the news sites."

Jae held his hands up, as if to slow her down. "Wait. What's going on? Whose pictures?"

She slid into a chair. "Yours. And Yuki's and Loni's. They've pegged you for an attempted terrorist attack on the governor's mansion."

Almost all of them whipped out their Linqs to check the web. Jae's jaw dropped when an image of his face appeared with the label "Fugitive" in one of the news reports. Next to him were images of Loni and Yuki.

"How did they know it was us?" he asked. "We had masks on at the ball."

"Because the Imperial Police are working with the Pishacha," Mayhara said. "And Naree knows it was you."

"It probably didn't take much to figure out who the others were," Mr. Kitaro added. "Especially if they obtained information from the academy. Or if they used Naree's amethyst powers."

"Great," Loni mumbled.

"It doesn't matter," Yuki said. "We already knew we'd have to go into hiding. This doesn't change anything."

"Except that we can't show our faces in public anymore." Loni tucked her Linq away. "It's going to make things a lot harder."

Darshana waited for them to settle down, keeping her chin high and her expression blank. They all seemed to notice she wanted to speak, so they stilled their voices and sat attentively. It was like being back at the academy again.

Darshana placed her hands together, her eyes meeting each elite mage, one by one. "I'll start with the good news. Penny is alive."

"You found her?" Loni asked, leaning forward in her chair.

"Not exactly." Darshana ran a finger from her temple down to her jaw, her gaze elsewhere. "I felt her presence. She's afraid, which tells me the Pishacha have her. But she's still alive, which tells me they need her for something."

"The daggers," Mayhara said. "They want her to tell them where they are."

"But we've taken them with us," Salina said. "She doesn't know where they are."

"She's an amethyst mage," Jae put in. "She can find them with her mind. She's done it before."

"Which means she's got every right to be afraid," Mayhara added. "The dark mages will likely do whatever it takes to get that information from her."

"She won't tell," Loni insisted. "Even if it costs her her life."

"On the other hand…" Shiro glanced at Karina for a split second. "It's reasonable to assume they won't kill her. As long as she withholds any information from them."

"Unless their methods of torture break her down." Karina's gaze was trained on the floor. "Cause her pain until she can't withhold from them anymore."

Jae knew Karina was thinking about what the dark mages had done to her grandmother. They'd poisoned her, threatening to leave her for dead if they didn't give them the information they'd wanted. Of course, Amalia had refused, which was why she was lying in her bed suffering. Even Shiro's blood syphoning wasn't working to get rid of the poison. It just kept reproducing and growing inside her.

If the dark mages poisoned Penny to get her to talk, she might not be able to keep the location of the daggers a secret.

"Which is why," Darshana said, "I've come up with an idea of what to do with the daggers."

Everyone waited with anticipation for Darshana to continue. Jae would have held his breath if his heart hadn't been hammering so hard.

"The Sacred Keys separated the daggers for a reason." Darshana gave Mr. Kitaro a nod. "If the daggers are not all in one place, it will make it harder for the enemy to find. I propose that we follow the Keys' logic and do as they did."

"Meaning?" asked Shiro.

"Meaning the six of you should each take a dagger and find an undisclosed location for it without telling the others where it's hidden—just as the Sacred Keys did."

"This makes sense, especially now," Mr. Kitaro added, "because of the possibility of the Pishacha getting Penny to use her powers to track down the daggers."

Darshana gave a nod. "She won't be able to see them all at once or try to get into any one person's head to find them."

"That's true," Yuki said, leaning forward in her chair. "It took her a while to track down each dagger before we found them. And even then, we were too late for some of them."

Darshana let out a slow breath. "Does everyone agree?"

Everyone nodded, looking around at each other. Jae's mind scrambled to think of a place to hide the dagger he'd be given. It would have to be somewhere clever, somewhere the Pishacha wouldn't think to look.

"I'd like them hidden as soon as possible," Darshana said. "You don't have to stick to Mr. Kitaro's property, but please do take care when traveling elsewhere to keep out of sight, and make sure you are not followed." Darshana let out a breath. "Mr. Kitaro will find a place for the seventh dagger in Penny's absence."

Everyone seemed deep in thought for a moment, no doubt trying to figure out where to hide the daggers.

After a moment, Darshana spoke up again. "We have another problem: the grimoire. What we need to do now is find the grimoire before the Pishacha find out about it from Penny."

Jae raised his hand. "I'll go. I've been to Pune before, and I think getting there on my bike will be easier than in a car."

"I'll go with him," Mayhara said.

Jae studied her face, but she kept her eyes on Darshana. He caught Loni's eyes shifting between them, but he quickly averted his gaze.

Jae cleared his throat. "Okay, good. We can leave in the morning. Get a fresh start. It's a long drive."

Darshana placed her hands together. "Very well. I'm going to try reaching out to Penny again."

"If you can locate her," Salina said, "we'll be ready to go in for a rescue."

"Yeah." Loni raked her hands through her dark hair. "Count me in. I'll do anything to get her back."

Jae glanced around at everyone. There was one more pressing issue on his mind. "I wanted to bring up what I heard the chief of police and Director Shei discussing at the ball."

"You mean about the prison camps?" Yuki asked.

"Yeah." Jae rubbed at his chin. "Anyone have any ideas of what we can do about it?"

Shiro lifted his hand. "Maybe I can reach out, try to find Qiang. He could have some intel on what's happening at the prison camps—or could at least find out. If we know the government's strategy, we might be able to figure out how to stop them."

"Good idea." Darshana breathed in deeply and let out a slow breath. "There's one more thing. Something that came to me while I was searching for a sign of Penny."

Mayhara furrowed her brow. "What was it?"

"It's about the comet." Darshana's expression was troubled. "The vision of it appeared to me, and with it, a strange, pulsing, static energy. It was like waves of power disrupting everything it touched. I focused on it further and understood that its energy conflicted with the energy of mages. Like polar opposites ricocheting off each other."

Yuki tilted her head. "What does that mean?"

"I believe," Darshana said, "as the comet gets closer, it will interfere with your powers."

"You think it will leave us powerless?" Jae asked.

Darshana shook her head. "I don't know. I don't think it's a permanent effect, but rather something that will occur as the comet is in close proximity."

Mayhara shifted in her chair. "Is that why the prophecy mentions Kashmeru being reborn upon the comet's arrival? Because our powers will be weak?"

Shiro scratched at an eyebrow. "Giving Kashmeru and the Pishacha power over us."

Darshana and Mr. Kitaro exchanged looks.

"Yes," Mr. Kitaro answered. "I believe it is so."

"Well, that sucks." Loni threw her hands in the air. "How are we supposed to fight them if we're stripped of our powers?

"I hope it doesn't come to that," Darshana said, "But if it does, then by any means necessary that will keep things balanced in our favor. The time has come to tie up any loose ends. Get the grimoire. Hide the daggers. And figure out a way to get the Lotus out of Kashmeru's grip."

FIVE

The morning sun filtered through the gauzy curtains as a slight breeze brought fresh air to play with Naree's hair. She sat at her vanity, holding a hairbrush and studying her face. Her skin was flawless, her hair thick and lustrous. She wore a silk robe and her bedroom floor was heated. She'd slept comfortably and had a delicious-smelling breakfast waiting for her downstairs.

This was the life Kashmeru was offering her. He promised to always take care of her, and he was keeping that promise.

My love.

"Kashmeru."

I can feel the time nearing when we can be together.

"Yes. I've made some progress."

You have all the daggers?

She bit her lip and set down the hairbrush. "Almost"

There was a pause, and Naree's nerves tightened. For all the love she felt, why did Kashmeru frighten her? She stood from the vanity and began to pace, worrying her hands.

You need to hurry, my love. The comet is approaching.

"I'm doing my best."

Please do. It won't be long before we'll be together and I can hold you in my arms again.

"I know. I long for that as well. I promise, I'm doing my best."

Six

The hot shower did wonders for Jae's exhaustion, but it hadn't made a dent in the anxiety that clung to every inch of him. He pulled on a clean T-shirt and raked his fingers through his thick, dark hair. As he took his hand away, he focused on his fingers. Darshana's words about the comet's influence on their powers replayed in his mind. He didn't feel any different, magic-wise. He wondered how close the comet had to be in order to feel the effect.

Stepping out into the main room, he found Darshana standing by the window, sipping tea. Nearby, in the open kitchen, Loni was pouring herself a cup. She only spared him a glance.

"Heading out?" Darshana asked when she turned to face him.

"It's a long drive." He grabbed his leather jacket, which hung over a dining room chair. "As it is, we won't get there until tomorrow. The sooner we leave, the better. I'm just waiting for Mayhara."

Loni turned toward him and leaned back against the counter, staring into her tea.

"Jae." Darshana took a breath and let it out calmly. "We haven't really spoken about your newly inherited station."

Jae rubbed his chin as he nodded. "Elite sapphire mage. Yeah. I've, uh, been trying to wrap my head around it."

"Yes, I know." Darshana stepped closer to him. "I can feel your struggle."

Jae and Loni exchanged a glance. Loni raised a brow and sipped her tea.

"You feel it?" Jae slipped the jacket on and adjusted the collar. "Sounds a little diamond-mage-ish."

"She's an empath," Loni put in. "Why do you think she's making me drink this disgusting tea?"

Jae furrowed his brow. "I don't understand."

Darshana walked over and put a hand on Loni's shoulder. "I believe

Kamal's death and Penny's disappearance have hit Loni hard. Along with Yuki, they were all Loni knew for a while. The four of them were like family. And the loss of family is a major trigger to her emotions."

Loni held up her cup, raising a sarcastic brow. "Nothing a little tea won't fix, of course."

Jae studied her. There was no mistaking the deep sadness in her eyes. Her leg was bouncing a bit, and a small film of sweat blanketed her hairline. Her drug addiction was calling her. The pain of losing Kamal and possibility of losing Penny was causing her to crave a fix.

"And the tea helps?" he asked.

"It has a calming effect," Darshana answered. "It will help with her nerves."

Jae stretched out his shoulders. "Maybe I should drink some."

Darshana held a hand up. "No. You're going to be driving, and the tea will make you sleepy. With the police and the Pishacha out there, you're going to want to be alert and focused."

Jae gave her a nod. "Right."

"I know this is taking its toll on you." Darshana set her teacup on the table. "Your position as the elite means you're a target, and that means there's a chance your own sister may try to attack you."

Jae's gaze dropped to the floor. "She's tried to kill me before. I mean, not directly. She sort of hypnotized Mayhara into believing I was the enemy and had her attack me. I was nearly crushed to death under crimson rock."

Darshana placed the tips of her fingers together. "But you got through to her to stop her. To stop both of them."

"Mayhara tried to kill you?" Loni asked. "And you still—?" Loni snapped her mouth shut and turned away from Jae, burying her face in the steam of her tea.

"My point is," Darshana continued, "you found a way to get through to Naree. She heard you. And I believe that is going to be the key to getting her back. I'm relying on the strength of that connection."

Jae pressed his lips together and nodded. "So am I."

Darshana put a hand on his arm. "Jae, the gods would not have bestowed this task upon you if you weren't worthy enough to handle it. You must believe it is within you to follow through with our part in this war. I believe in you. You should too."

He breathed in deeply, his eyes locked with hers, as if staring at her long enough would convince him of her words.

She patted his arm, as if to stop him from staring, and then returned to drinking her tea.

"All right." He took out keys from his pocket. "I'm going to check my bike and make sure it's in order for the trip."

Darshana nodded and headed for the counter. Jae figured she needed a tea refill. He grabbed the helmets, casting Loni a second's glance before he exited the house. His concern for her was like a pull in his chest. Like muscle memory from their days on the run. He hoped she could keep grounded and resist any cravings for a fix.

It had only been five seconds since he'd closed the door behind him when it opened again. He turned to find Loni stepping out onto the porch. Her mouth was set in a straight line.

"Loni?" He knew he had to tread lightly around her. Resisting approaching her, Jae tightened his grip on the helmets. "Are you—? What are you doing out here?"

"I needed to see you before you go. Just in case." Her voice cracked on the last word.

"Try not to be pessimistic, Loni."

"How can I not be?" She lowered her gaze. "I'm sorry. I don't mean to be so glum. I'm just… I'm worried about you. I lost the closest person to me, and it devastated me. And maybe you don't feel for me anymore what I thought you felt, but I still hold you as one of the most important people in my life. The thought of possibly losing you…"

Tears spilled over and trailed down her cheeks. Her lips trembled and her hands were clenched at her sides.

Jae set the helmets down on the porch and pulled Loni into his arms, unable to stop himself. "Believe me, Loni, I will do everything in my power to keep that from happening."

He felt her nod against his chest, and he kept his arms around her as she wept. He believed she needed this, though he could hear Yuki's warning playing over and over in his mind.

Loni squeezed him tightly, her sniffles disappearing into his jacket.

Just give her another minute, he said to himself.

Right as he was about to let go of her, the door opened once more. His eyes widened when Mayhara stepped out. He knew that when he took a step back from Loni, it must have appeared as though it was because of Mayhara's presence. He didn't want either of them to think that.

Loni looked between Jae and Mayhara as she swiped at her cheeks and cleared her throat.

"Um. Good luck, then," was all she said before heading back into the house.

Mayhara zipped up her leather jacket and tightened the scarf at her neck as she walked past Jae.

A dozen things to say flew though his mind, but he knew every single one of them was wrong. Maybe they'd get a chance to talk during their trip. They'd be on the road for a while, so he'd have plenty of time to think of the proper things to say to her. But for now, all he could think of was, "Ready to go?"

Mayhara adjusted the straps of the backpack she carried. "Yeah. I've got the scroll and Karina's interpretations of the symbols. Plus drinks and food for the road."

"I've got some provisions too. Hopefully, we won't have to stop too often for gas."

He bent down and grabbed the helmets then handed her one. As she took it, he watched her face. He wanted so much to clear the air before they got on his bike, but he knew she would tell him that it wasn't the time. He'd have to find the proper time to do it, if the gods allowed.

They were making good time up until they were four hours into their journey. Jae spotted a roadblock up ahead on the highway. He muttered a curse to himself, remembering that his face was plastered all over the news sites. Both he and Mayhara were wanted by the police. He moved into the slow lane and used his powers so Mayhara could hear him through their helmets and over the sound of the bike and other vehicles.

"Imperial Police up ahead. Can't go back, and there are no exits before the roadblock. I'm going to use my powers to convince them to let us though."

He felt her nod against his back. He figured she wasn't sure if he could hear her or not. Her hands were resting at his sides, and the closer they got to the police who were checking vehicles, the more her hold would tighten.

The car ahead of them advanced, and Jae forced himself to remain calm. His riding gloves hid his glowing palms, and he focused on the police officer's face as he was waved forward.

The Imperial Police officer studied his face through the helmet's visor. "Where are you headed today?"

Jae pushed out his sapphire energy as he spoke. "To the festival in Vadodara. I promised my girl I'd get her there so we can get a better view of the comet."

It might have been his imagination, but it felt as if Mayhara's hold on his waist had tightened even more when he'd said, 'My girl.'

The officer shifted his gaze back and forth between Jae and Mayhara. Jae continued to push out his power to convince the officer he was telling the truth.

"Can I see some identification, please?"

It hadn't sounded like a question. Jae moved his hand closer to the officer. Startled by his movement, the cop reached for his taser pistol but didn't pull it out. Jae had to act fast to keep him from recognizing them.

"We're not the fugitives you're looking for. You're going to wave us through and wish us a pleasant day."

For a moment, Jae began to panic. The officer hadn't reacted right away. Was the comet blocking his power already? Jae swallowed hard and waited, internally counting the seconds.

The officer took his hand away from his weapon and waved them through. "Have a pleasant day."

Jae gripped the handlebars and nodded his thanks.

It wasn't until they were miles away that he felt Mayhara's hands relax on his waist.

SEVEN

Shiro wandered the grounds around the house, contemplating a place to hide his dagger. He wasn't sure if the other elites were sticking to the property or venturing outside of the area. And he wasn't supposed to ask.

Movement near the house caught his attention. As Karina lifted her arms, chanting with her eyes closed, Shiro tucked the dagger into the back hem of his jeans and began walking toward her. He made a point of keeping quiet, but his trek was through high grass and dead leaves.

Karina lowered her hands and stopped changing. When she opened her eyes, she focused on Shiro.

"Sorry," he said. "I didn't mean to interrupt."

"No, it's fine." Karina offered him a small smile. "I was finished anyway."

"What were you doing? If you don't mind me asking."

"Darshana asked me to put a protection spell on the house."

"You can do that?"

She let out a small laugh. "I can't attest to the level of my skills, but it's worth a try. I guess I can't be sure if the spell works or not. I did one on our place in the swamp, but my grandmother was attacked outside of our territory, so… it's likely."

"How is she doing?"

Karina bit her lip and shook her head. "It doesn't look good. And when I try to focus on thinking positive, my heart hurts, like it knows it's a lie."

"I've been meaning to see her. I could try another syphoning therapy."

She gave a half-shrug. "I don't know if they're helping. But let's go see if she's awake and ask her. I'm willing to give it another try if she is."

"Yes, let's do that." He held out his arm, gesturing toward the house.

With a nod, she turned toward the house and led the way.

The house was quiet, and Shiro wondered if the other mages were trying to figure out where to hide their daggers. Jae and Mayhara had left earlier that day, but he hadn't really seen much of Yuki, Loni, or Salina.

His thoughts were cut short when Karina opened the door to her room and the sound of Amalia's ragged breathing reached his ears. He felt his heart plummet to his gut, sending a wave of acid surging into his stomach.

Amalia was so pale, her skin appeared gray. Her hair was dry and brittle. Shiro was sure it would crack and break off if it were to be touched. She had lost almost all color in her eyes, leaving them looking like glass. Every small movement she made was done with uncontrollable shaking. And she'd lost a lot of weight, her bones prominent in her arms and fingers.

Shiro came closer, his sympathy riddled with fear. Karina, who sat by her grandmother's side, glanced up at him as she sopped up the sweat from Amalia's forehead with a cloth. He gave Karina a nod, wanting her to be the one to bring up the syphoning therapy.

Karina faced her grandmother and tilted her head. "Do you need anything, Grandmother?"

Amalia's trembling hand clasped on to Karina's. "Just your company, dear."

Karina squeezed her hand. "Shiro is here because we wondered if you need him to get more of the poison out."

Amalia gave her a strained smile, tears pooling in her eyes. "No. It won't do any good."

Shiro took another step forward. "But your pain—"

"I've been speaking with my ancestors," Amalia said. "I am not worried about my pain."

"Grandmother?" Karina's voice was a whisper.

"What does that mean?" Shiro asked. "Speaking with your ancestors?"

"Some witches gain this ability to speak with members of their coven who have passed on. Especially witches closer to death."

Karina's head dropped, her grasp still tight around Amalia's hand.

"It's not important anymore. My suffering." Amalia licked her dry lips. "There is a scroll."

Shiro furrowed his brows. "You mean the one with the cryptic map?"

"No. Another. It is hidden in the spine of the grimoire. I believe this is the scroll Darshana has been having visions of."

The gears in Shiro's brain began turning. "What does the scroll contain?"

"It's a spell the Pishacha never want you to find." Amalia gave Shiro one solid nod. "A spell that can destroy Kashmeru for good."

Shiro held her gaze, his breath catching in his throat. There was a spell to kill Kashmeru. This was the key. The way to end the war. To win the war. To save the world. "It's in the grimoire? The same grimoire that contains the spell to release Kashmeru from his tomb?"

Amalia nodded. "The same. It's a failsafe."

"Why wasn't it used on him before?"

Karina lifted her head, her brows drawn down. "Because they're connected."

Shiro blanched. "You mean… the Lotus."

Amalia glanced between Karina and Shiro. "Yes. They are linked. It is very likely that killing Kashmeru would also mean the demise of Lakshmi."

A million thoughts tore through Shiro's mind. Jae and Mayhara were on their way to find the grimoire. He needed to text them to let them know about the second, hidden scroll. Though part of him was afraid to tell him the part about the possibility that the spell could kill Jae's sister.

His thoughts were cut short when Yuki suddenly entered the room.

"Yuki?" he asked. "What's wrong?"

Yuki put her hands together. "I'm sorry to interrupt, but there's been a development."

Shiro's heart stopped for a moment, and he feared that something had happened to Jae or Mayhara. Or both.

"It's the extremists." Yuki grabbed her hair and quickly pulled it into a ponytail. "There was a news bulletin about an attack on the New Jaipur City Development Authority Office. I checked the location against the director's scroll that tracks the rebellious activity. They're on the move, but if we hurry, we might be able to catch them."

It took a second for Shiro to wrap his head around this information. This was his chance to talk to Qiang and ask him about the prison camps. He turned toward Karina and Amalia. Karina gave him an understanding smile.

"Yeah." Shiro turned back to face Yuki, his heart thumping in his chest. "Yeah. Let's go find them."

EIGHT

Penny had waited alone in the basement for Naree and Bhutano to return. Hours must have passed, and she was sure it was the next morning. A part of her held on to the hope that the other elites would be doing what they could to find her. But they had no clue where to start looking. Penny didn't even know where she was.

She'd been left with Daiki—the dark mage with the cheek scar—and another mage whom Daiki called "Rikuto." While Daiki sat across from Penny, giving her nonstop menacing sneers, Rikuto seemed bored, occupying himself by continuously bending and unbending the blade of a double-edged *tantō*. She knew one of the dark mages was able to manipulate metal, and Rikuto proved to be him. His hair was buzzed short on the sides, with the rest pulled into a ponytail. He wore a long, dark gray cloak over a loose, white, button-down shirt. And there was a prominent tattoo on his neck, a symbol Penny didn't recognize.

She wondered if so much bending and unbending was damaging the *tantō* at all. She couldn't imagine the blade upholding its sturdiness and being useful after so much manipulating.

"Hey, Penny," Daiki called. The smirk on his face made her cringe.

"What?"

"Are you afraid of scorpions?"

She shot him a questioning look, noticing his gaze falling to her knee. She flinched when she found a scorpion there, crawling up her leg into her lap. She held back a scream, but small sounds of panic emerged from her throat as the scorpion crept along.

Suddenly, the door opened. Naree and Bhutano strode in, their faces stoic.

Penny glanced back down at her leg, her forehead wrinkling when she found the scorpion gone. Had it crawled under the chair? Had it managed to get inside her clothing? She tried not to squirm so as not to anger it if it was near her skin.

"I hope this time we've given you has provided a moment for you to think," Bhutano said, checking his watch. "You simply have to cooperate with us, and no harm will come to you."

Naree seemed to glide through the room. She looked rested, as if she'd gotten some sleep. Her hair was like silk, and her skin was glowing. She didn't seem like a prisoner, like she was being controlled by an evil god. She looked as though she was being pampered and cared for. But Penny knew it was all a ruse. Kashmeru was controlling her, making her believe that her life was better with him, convincing her that this was where she was supposed to be by showing her how good life was in his world. But the truth was she was being held in a golden cage, trapped in deceitful beauty, with no freedom of her own.

"Like I said before," Penny said to him, "I don't know where the daggers are. And they're not easy to track down."

"But this time, it will be different," Naree said, settling into the chair across from her. "We can search for them together. With the influence of my powers and your connection to the other elites, it should be easier than when you had to do it before."

The wheels in Penny's head were spinning as she desperately tried to find a way to keep Naree from seeing the daggers. If she could even find them with her mind. "Fine. I can't do it like this, though."

"What do you mean?" Naree asked.

"I need my hands free."

Daiki moved forward, his fists resting on his waist. "Aren't they?"

Penny almost scoffed. "They're bound in these electro-cuffs."

Daiki smirked. "What electro-cuffs?"

Penny furrowed a brow and moved her hands. They didn't meet any resistance, and she stared in wonder at her wrists as she brought her hands in front of her face.

"How did—?"

From the back of the room, Penny heard a low chuckle. Bhutano pushed himself off the wall where he was leaning and straightened the cuffs of his Imperial Police uniform. "I see you've got things under control, Your Highness. I'll leave you to it. I've got something else Kashmeru wants me to take care of for now, but I'll be back to check on your progress."

Bhutano locked eyes with Penny as he left the room, his gait full of self-confidence.

Penny's gaze went back to Daiki, who was still smirking at her.

Naree shifted in her chair. "Daiki has the power to manipulate your thoughts. You only believed you were cuffed because he made you think it was so."

Penny scratched her tongue with her teeth as she took in this information. That explained the scorpion. He'd only made her believe there was one, but it had been an illusion. These mages had powers she hadn't known existed. Not knowing what you were up against made things much scarier to deal with. She really needed to watch her step.

She glanced around at the other dark mages, and Naree followed her gaze.

"I suppose you're curious about the other soldiers," Naree said, "and what they might be able to do."

Penny kept her mouth in a straight line, not wanting to answer but curious still.

Naree crossed her legs and leaned back in the chair. She pointed to Rikuto, the one who'd been bending and unbending the *tantō*. "That's Rikuto. An orphan, like you. He has the power to manipulate metal."

Rikuto stuffed his hands in the pockets of his dark gray cloak and stretched out his neck. Penny got a glimpse of his neck tattoo, noting that it matched the one on Director Shei's daughter.

"The bald one in the corner is Kun," Naree said, gesturing in his direction with her chin. "He's got a very special power. Able to sicken his victims, even to the point of infecting them with poison."

Kun had a thin face, almost skeletal. His eyes were as black as coal, and dark circles lurked beneath them. He too had a tattoo on his neck. Penny wondered if they all had the tattoo and she'd just never noticed it.

"Then, of course, we have Harish." Naree nodded to him. "Son of the wealthiest family in New Jaipur, and a syphoner. He can drain energy of any kind, whether it be electrical, mechanical, human, or magical. And our little lady by the table is Ruolan Shei, daughter of the government's census director. I'd love to tell you she has a beautiful smile, but I'm afraid I've never seen it. Ru can move things by pulling and pushing energy. A telekinetic, if you will."

"The quiet one over there," Naree said, pointing to the dark-skinned young man with short brown hair, "that's Jin-woo, and he's got a special talent. He can manipulate the slithery things of this world. Insects, snakes, weeds, vines… things of that nature."

Jin-woo had a beautiful face, almost feminine. Perhaps that was why he'd shaved lines into his eyebrows, to give him a more edgy look. Jin-woo held up a hand, which emanated black tendrils of smoke that made their way toward Penny. The tendrils turned into creeping vines, sliding along the floor as if they were snakes and finding Penny's legs. The vines circled her legs and wrapped themselves around them until she was bound.

Daiki let out a laugh. "Now you really are tied up."

Naree looked over her other shoulder. "And of course, there's Avi: the bone crusher. I believe some of your colleagues are familiar with him."

Penny looked away from him, not wanting him to see her fear.

Naree leaned forward, her arm draped over her knee. "Together, they make up the Council of the Seven. Kashmeru has gifted these special talents to them, chosen them to be the powerful assets in his shadow army. You see what you are up against, and that doesn't even put a dent in what I can do to you." Naree studied her. "Are you ready to cooperate now?"

Penny chewed at her lip as she weighed her options. "It might not work, you know?"

"It's totally worth a try, though. Isn't it?" Naree flashed her a wicked smile.

Penny's heart thrummed in her chest. She knew there was no way out of this situation, but that didn't mean she had to play entirely by the enemy's rules. After all, meditation was a way for her to reach out with her mind. Who was to say that she wouldn't *accidentally* reach out to Darshana?

Penny nodded. "Fine."

"Good," Naree said. "Let's begin."

Penny took a deep breath, concentrating on breathing slowly. She cleared her mind, erasing thoughts of electro-cuffs and scorpions and bendable *tantōs*. She listened to her breaths and relaxed her shoulders, her arms, her hands.

"Good," Naree said in a gentle voice. "Now picture the daggers. Picture the blade, the hilt, the design. Pull that picture of it up in your mind. Search for it."

Penny thought of Darshana. Her kind smile. Her wise words. The motherly way about her.

Her eyes came into focus in her mind.

"What are you doing?" Naree asked, seeing what Penny saw.

"I'm looking for the daggers."

"But that's your guru in your head."

"Maybe she's near them." Penny hoped Naree would buy her excuse.

Darshana. Can you hear me?

Instead of an answer, Penny's mind zoomed out to see Darshana handing Mr. Kitaro a box.

"What was that?" Naree's voice was sharp.

Penny opened her eyes to find Naree glaring at her. "I don't know."

"Don't lie to me."

Naree raised one of her hands. Avi stepped forward with a sneer on his face. Black tendrils of smoke swirled through the air. A shooting pain erupted in Penny's pinky finger. She bent forward and cried out in pain, feeling the slicing burn of her bone being crushed.

Penny gasped. "I'm not lying. I swear. I don't know what that was." As tears came to her eyes, she tried to breathe through the pain.

"Don't you see that that was totally unnecessary?" Naree asked. She clicked her tongue a few times. "If you'd just stay the course, we could have avoided that."

Penny bit back a whimper. Her eyes flit over Naree's face, confused at how she could have turned out this way.

"Why are you letting him control you?" Penny asked.

Naree blanched, not having expected the question.

"Can't you see he's poisoning you?" Penny placed her hand in her lap and tried not to think about her pain. "The longer you stay under the spell, the more you lose yourself."

"You wouldn't understand. Our love, our fate, the pull between us…These are things that have existed for centuries, so I wouldn't expect a mere mortal to truly wrap their simple mind around it." Naree took a deep breath and let it out. "He loves me."

"Kashmeru has a twisted idea of love, Your Highness."

Naree's lips pressed into a slash. She clenched her jaw and stretched out her neck. "You know, I don't believe you've ever been in love. You wouldn't know the lengths one would go to for you, or you for them. You wouldn't understand sacrifices and compromises. And you certainly wouldn't understand the feeling when someone you're meant to be with holds you and promises you the world."

"Naree." Penny tried a different approach. "Lakshmi. You're pure good. You represent all that's right in the world. You know Kashmeru is evil. You have to break free from his hold on you."

Avi stepped forward again. "I think that's enough out of you. Unless you want another little taste of my special medicine."

Penny could feel her finger throbbing. She dropped her gaze, unwilling to face more pain.

"Here." Naree reached into her trouser pocket and pulled out a tiny, carved, jade dragonfly. She admired it for a moment, turning it between her fingers. "Maybe this will help you get a better connection. Jae gave this to me."

"And you still have it," Penny remarked. "It must mean something to you."

Hope bloomed in her chest at the realization that Naree was still holding Jae near to her heart. She was sure she saw something there in Naree's eyes when she was gazing at it. Maybe there was still a chance to get through to her.

Naree looked up at her and scowled. "It serves only as a connection to him so that I can reach him and convince him to give up his fight. Perhaps it will serve as a connection for you to find him and the location of the daggers." Naree placed it in Penny's hand. "Try again."

Penny frowned. She didn't know how to get through to Naree and free her from Kashmeru. And now she herself was being forced to work for their side. Her stomach roiled and her chest felt as if it were caving in on itself.

Penny cleared her mind again. She felt the cool surface of the jade dragonfly between her fingers. It began to warm in her hand, and her mind was drawn to it. Suddenly, Jae's eyes appeared before her in her mind. It was as if a camera were zoomed in on his face, the focus smudged around the edges. Her mind's eye zoomed out slowly, and she could see Jae speaking to Mayhara. They were near his motorcycle. She couldn't make out the words. Jae was filling the bike with gas, and Mayhara was checking her backpack. She pulled out a scroll.

Penny snapped her mind shut, not wanting Naree to see. The jade dragonfly slipped from her fingers and fell to the floor. When she opened her eyes, she could tell it was too late. Naree had seen what she'd seen. She hadn't meant to show her the image, but her mind had gone right to Jae when she'd held the dragonfly.

Naree smiled. "Now we're getting somewhere."

NINE

By the time Shiro and Yuki got to the New Jaipur City Development Authority Office, the only traces of the extremist group to be found were the scattered rubble and the smoke still wafting in the air from the explosion they'd set off in the building. Shiro looked around at the damage Qiang and his gang had done in their attempt to strike back at the government for making mages illegal. He shook his head, still in disbelief of the lengths Qiang would go to. This was the same man who'd taken care of him in the prison camps. The same man who'd cried in his arms when the life of one of their own had been brutally taken by prison guards. Shiro never would have imagined that the kind, gentle man he'd fallen in love with would be able to cause so much death and destruction.

Shiro scanned the area. There was a cleanup crew tending to the area, but it seemed like most of the police had cleared out along with the fire department and the medics.

"Any idea of where they went?" Shiro asked.

"The scroll will only show where the extremists attacked. The lights eventually fade after the event ends." Yuki checked her Linq. "I don't see any more reports on the news sites, but I'm going to check the Spottit app. They have a sub-thread for people who've witnessed riots or protests and stuff. Maybe someone saw something after the extremists took off, and we can get a lead."

As Yuki scrolled through the app, Shiro checked to make sure the four Imperial Police officers patrolling the area didn't recognize them. Especially Yuki, since her picture had just been up on the recent new bulletins. He hoped the officers were too preoccupied with the aftermath of the attack.

"Okay, got it." Yuki's eyes widened. "Someone spotted them entering an abandoned building on South Gaoling Street."

"That's this way." Shiro gestured as he briskly walked toward the street in question.

It took some maneuvering to avoid the police, but eventually, they reached South Gaoling Street. A few old shops were scattered along the street, with very few patrons. The place looked like it had been hit hard by recession. Trash spilled out from receptacles along the sidewalks, and mud caked the gutters. It seemed a likely place for the extremist group to lie low. It was just a matter of finding the abandoned building they were in.

Shiro glanced in windows as they made their way down the street. Yuki's hands were closed into fists, but Shiro could just make out the faint white glow she was trying to conceal.

Yuki hissed through her teeth. "Feeling some strange hostility up ahead."

"Okay. It's probably that theater. I think it's been closed for a couple of years now, and it looks big enough to hold a group like Qiang's."

They picked up their pace, not wanting to miss their opportunity to catch Qiang. Shiro checked over his shoulder as they made their way to the entrance. For a moment, he became paranoid that someone might post about them on the Spottit app.

The sound of Yuki jiggling the door handle snapped Shiro from his thoughts.

"It's locked," she said. "Maybe if we go arou—"

Suddenly, he felt as if the world were turning upside-down. It wasn't until he landed on his arm—and Yuki landed on her back next to him— that he realized someone had used crimson powers on them.

Shiro and Yuki called upon their powers, their palms glowing as they shifted to stand.

"I wouldn't do that if I were you." The woman who spoke hovered above them, glaring. Her glowing red palms were aimed in their direction. Her hair was short and spiky, and her sleeveless top exposed her lean muscles.

A large, dark-skinned man appeared at her side. "What are we going to do with these two, Kyoko?"

"Let's get them inside before someone sees." Kyoko lowered her hands.

The big man bent down and grabbed Shiro and Yuki by their shirts, lifting them to their feet.

"Wait." Shiro held up his hands in surrender. "We're here to see Qiang."

"Keep it down," Kyoko snapped. She eyed her partner. "We can put them in the back, Rajim."

"You think they really know Qiang?" Rajim asked.

Kyoko scoffed as she led the way to a side door. "Doubt it."

Shiro flinched as Rajim shoved him through the door. "I do know Qiang. We're close, personal friends."

"Funny." Kyoko looked him up and down. "I've never seen you around."

Shiro glanced at Yuki.

"It's okay," she said in a soft voice. "Stay calm. We'll get this sorted."

He wasn't sure if she was using her powers, but he noticed his heartbeat slowing and his breathing coming easier.

"Listen," Shiro said to Kyoko. "We don't want any trouble. But I need to speak with Qiang."

Kyoko pursed her lips. "Well, Qiang's not here right now. And I can't very well let you go without knowing your objective, so Rajim and I are just going to have to keep you locked up in the back until he gets back."

Rajim grabbed Yuki's and Shiro's arms and forced them through the theater. Members of Qiang's extremist group gathered in the large room, some sprawled out on the seats, and some grouped together near the stage, checking their weapons. All eyes were on Shiro and Yuki as they were led across the room and through a door.

Rajim pushed them toward a couple of chairs. "Have a seat."

Shiro and Yuki did as they were told.

Kyoko held out glowing red palms and pushed out crimson energy at their feet. Crimson earth sealed their feet to the floor. "Just so you don't get any clever ideas," she said, smirking.

"When will Qiang be back?" Shiro asked.

Kyoko let out a laugh. "I guess we'll just have to wait and see, won't we?"

She hit Rajim's arm with the back of her hand, and the two of them exited the room, locking the door behind them.

TEN

Jae mumbled a curse when the CLOSED ROAD sign appeared ahead. A wide wooden barricade blocked the street, and just beyond it, he could see the tents, lights, and rides of the Vadodara festival. They had just gassed up the motorcycle, and he'd thought they could cut down their travel time by driving through the night. But this threw a wrench in their plans.

He pulled over as the road ended and cut the engine. Along the sides of the road, dozens of vehicles were parked, some of them in the grass, filling a makeshift parking lot for the festivalgoers.

Mayhara pulled off her helmet. "Looks like the road is closed because of the festival. It's like your lie became a truth."

"We'll need to double back and find an alternate road to Pune. We might have to find a back road, which could unfortunately take longer."

"Mind if I stretch my legs for a minute?" Mayhara asked. "I'm starting to cramp up."

"No, go ahead." Jae dismounted after she did and hooked their helmets to the bike. "I could use some stretching myself."

They paced the side of the road a few yards. Jae noticed that Mayhara seemed to be creating more distance between them, as if she needed to be farther away from him after having held on to him for hours. He let out a sigh and let her wander. He knew she needed time and space; he just wished he were more patient in giving them to her.

Fireworks began going off over their heads. The sounds of music and chatter from the festival reached his ears between the bursts of light. Jae admired the fireworks display for a minute, caught up in the feeling of sharing the moment with Mayhara—even if she stood more than twenty feet away. He longed to stand beside her and take her hand, but he knew she might pull away and break his heart all over again.

"Jae."

He tore his eyes away from the sky to find Mayhara plodding his way, staring wide-eyed over his shoulder. Following her gaze, he noticed three Imperial Police on foot, patrolling the grounds of the festival and headed their way.

Jae was about to bolt back to his motorcycle when he spotted a patrol car slowly advancing toward them.

At that moment, a van full of teenagers unloaded, the rowdy youngsters whooping and laughing, pointing at the fireworks as they made their way past Jae and Mayhara, heading to the festival.

"Come on," Jae said once Mayhara was near enough. "Blend in."

He took her hand and led her toward the barrier. They caught up with the group of teenagers and walked in close enough proximity that it could appear they were part of the entourage. Mayhara glanced over her shoulder at the Imperial Police as she lifted her scarf to cover her hair.

"We're going to have to wait until they're gone before we can risk going back to the bike." Jae gave her a reassuring nod.

She nodded back, visibly swallowing.

As they reached the throng of festivalgoers, Jae spotted a hat that had fallen onto the ground near a novelty stand. Without stopping, he stooped down to pick it up and placed it on his head, sparing a glance behind him.

"There are police everywhere," he whispered close to Mayhara's ear. "I feel like we just waltzed into the lion's den."

Mayhara scanned the crowd, confirming his words. "How are we going to get out of here?"

"I'm not sure." Jae looked around, examining the surrounding buildings on the outskirts of the festival. "Let's find a place to lie low until we can figure out how to evade them."

She gave him a nod. Jae still had her hand in his as he led her through the crowd. He kept his head ducked to avoid getting noticed by the police or anyone else who might recognize him from the news bulletin.

As he glanced at an officer standing near a sweet bun stand, panic shot through him. The officer had noticed him and was following his movements. Jae wasn't sure if he'd recognized him or if he was just curious. Trying not to seem too obvious, Jae picked up his pace. As they got closer to one building, he noticed a worker in uniform exit the basement entrance of a shop. The worker carried a large box that mostly obstructed his view.

With his arms full, the worker attempted to close the door behind himself by kicking it. He continued up the stairs and on his way, and Jae noticed the ground shift at the doorway. Crimson earth had formed a doorstop, keeping the door from fully closing.

Jae turned to Mayhara, whose hand was raised, the faint glow of red fading from her palm.

"Good catch," he said.

"Thanks. Let's go."

He checked once more to make sure they weren't being watched. The officer who had spotted him before was no longer at his station. Jae wasn't sure if he'd followed them, so he picked up speed. Jae and Mayhara descended the stairs together quickly and slipped into the basement door. Mayhara waved her hand, and the crimson doorstop disintegrated.

It was dark inside the basement room, but festival lights shone through a narrow window that had a view of the street, giving them enough illumination to see where they were walking. Jae checked out the window, seeing mostly the bottom halves of festivalgoers' legs.

"I don't think anyone followed us, but I can't be sure." He turned back to Mayhara, who was lowering her scarf from her head. "I want to give that officer a little time to forget he saw us."

Mayhara let out a sigh. "Yeah. Sounds good. Otherwise, we'll have to stay here until the festival is over."

"These things tend to go until dawn. I don't think we want to wait that long."

Jae watched her as she came to stand beside him at the window. His eyes traveled over the curve of her cheek, the plumpness of her lips. Her nearness stirred up the urge inside him to talk to her.

"Mayhara, I know this probably isn't the right time—"

"No. It isn't."

Jae let out a slow breath. "I've got the feeling we're going to be short of right times, given the situation."

She crossed her arms over her chest and took a step back, but she didn't turn away from him. "What is it?"

His heart thrummed in his chest. His mind scrambled for the words as he internally reminded himself that he was a sapphire mage, the very mage who ruled the throat chakra, and he should be a master of communication.

"I don't want there to be any bad feelings between us. I hate that you can't even look at me without hate in your eyes. I'm sorry for not telling you about Loni, and I wasn't taking her side over yours. I was just trying to stop the fighting and keep things from escalating."

Mayhara searched his face. "I don't hate you, Jae. I could never."

Partial relief bloomed in his heart. "My feelings for you haven't changed. You've got to know that."

She narrowed her eyes. "Really? Because you seemed awfully chummy with Loni on the front porch this morning."

"No. No, that was nothing. She's in a bad place and I was offering comfort. As a *friend*."

She bit her cheek, her brows drawn down. "I don't think she sees it that way."

"I… I know. But I can't be responsible for how she feels. I can only be responsible for how I feel."

She seemed confused as she blinked, rubbing her arms. They were both quiet for a long moment, and Jae felt his hope plummet.

"I understand that you feel we can't be as close as we were before, but I would be devastated if our friendship was unsalvageable."

She tucked a strand of hair behind her ear. "It's not… unsalvageable."

"It's not?"

"Of course not." Her voice was a whisper.

He kept his gaze on her a moment longer. A noise outside the window caught their attention. Four pair of legs in Imperial Police uniforms marched by the window. Jae and Mayhara backed up, ducking out of sight.

"We need a distraction," Jae said.

Mayhara's palm lit up, and she held the red light closer to some boxes on a shelf. "This could work."

Jae came closer and read the labels on the boxes. "Fireworks?"

"Fire*crackers*. The kind that go off on the ground and make a lot of noise. If we set one off in the alley where no one is, it could distract the police, and we could make a break for it."

He nodded. "Okay. Yeah, that could work."

Jae grabbed a box off the shelf while Mayhara checked the window.

"Okay, no sign of the police." Mayhara went toward the door. "Get ready."

With Mayhara leading the way, they climbed the stairs and headed for the alley. It was a long corridor and—as luck would have it—totally vacant.

"There," Mayhara said. "Behind the dumpster."

As they raced down the alley toward the dumpster, Mayhara pulled her scarf over her hair. She and Jae crouched near the side of the dumpster, and Jae set the box down.

"This is a big box," Jae said. "It's going to cause quite a racket."

"Just what we need."

As Mayhara created a small glow to give them some light, Jae pushed the button on the electro-lighter and held it to the corner of the box. As soon as the flame caught, Jae dropped the lighter and pulled Mayhara to stand.

"Let's go."

Their hands were still joined as they hurried out of the alley and pushed their way through the crowd. Jae checked left and right as they zigzagged through the throng of people. A couple of Imperial Police noticed them, giving curious looks, but the moment one of them began to move their way, the loud, tumultuous popping and clattering of firecrackers echoed throughout the air. The noises made everyone flinch. The police wasted no time rushing to find the source. Many people in the crowd screamed, mistaking the noise for gunfire. Some panicked and fled away from the offensive racket.

Jae welcomed the surge of people running from the festival, using the opportunity to mix with the crowd and get to his bike. If anything, any suspicious police would find the swarm of panicked citizens an obstacle. He just had to make sure not to let go of Mayhara's hand.

The crowd spread out as they reached the barricade on the road that separated the festival from the street. Jae and Mayhara checked behind them as they sprinted to Jae's bike. Jae unhooked Mayhara's helmet and handed it to her.

But the second he picked up his helmet, a voice materialized in his head.

Jae.

He froze at the sound of Naree's voice. Shock pushed through him, and he had to turn around and scan the crowd to make sure she wasn't actually there.

"What is it?" Mayhara asked.

He was about to answer when he heard his sister's voice again.

I see you. You shouldn't run. It's of no use. I will find you.

Jae wasn't sure if he should answer. His heart wanted to reason with her, to tell her to come to him so he could rescue her from the evil god controlling her. Instead, he turned to Mayhara. They needed to get to the grimoire before the Pishacha did. He just hoped Naree didn't know that that was where they were headed.

"We've got to go," he said to Mayhara. "She's going to catch on to our plan."

A wrinkle formed on Mayhara's forehead. "Who?"

"Naree. She's talking to me in my head. She's trying to stop us. We don't have any time to lose."

"Yeah. Okay." Mayhara seemed to fight off a shiver. She shoved the helmet on and nodded. "Let's go."

Jae mounted the bike, still glancing around to convince himself Naree wasn't there, that there wouldn't suddenly be an army of Pishacha ready to jump them. He started the motorcycle, and as soon as Mayhara's hands were around his waist, he drove off.

Eleven

Karina took the teacup from Amalia's trembling hands. They didn't have access to the special herbs Amalia usually used in her teas, but Darshana had made her a brew that was supposed to keep her more comfortable.

"Any better, Grandmother?"

"I'm pretty sure it has valerian root, which means I'll get tired rather quickly."

Karina stroked her arm. "That's okay. You need to rest."

"But we still need to talk, dear."

"Grandmother, we can talk later."

Amalia reached for her hand. "No. We might not get a chance, and I have a lot to tell you. We should speak now."

A shiver traveled up and down Karina's spine, but she resisted shaking it off.

"What did you want to talk about?" Karina feared she knew the answer, but she wasn't sure she was ready for it.

Amalia shifted, and Karina immediately helped her by fixing her pillows to prop her up.

"Your mother passed away when you were a baby, so you wouldn't remember what happens at a witch's funeral, what needs to be done."

Karina wrung her hands. "I… Do we have to talk about funerals?"

"I think we do. And it's important for you to know. And it's relevant for what could be your part in the prophecy."

"My part?" She inched closer.

"A very powerful witch is need for the spells involved with the prophecy. The Pishacha need a powerful witch to release Kashmeru from his tomb, and the Empire needs one to destroy him."

"You think the Pishacha have a powerful witch?"

Amalia shook her head slowly. "I don't know."

"And you think the Empire will need me to destroy Kashmeru?"

"You are already at their disposal. But beyond that, I believe fate has handed you to them."

Karina bit her lip. "I don't know if I'm that powerful. I wasn't even sure I cast the protection spell on the house properly."

Amalia patted her hand. "You come from a long line of powerful witches. It's in your blood. But what I'm about to tell you in regards to my death—and my funeral—will ensure that you are powerful enough when the time comes."

Karina furrowed her brow, bracing herself. "Okay. What is it?"

"When a witch dies, it's important she is returned to the earth. Witches are devoted to nature, and we are put back to the place from whence we came. Given our situation, I will have to be buried on Mr. Kitaro's property. So it's important that you consecrate the ground in which you'll lay my body."

Karina squirmed in her chair as she nodded. She wasn't ready to face the fact that her grandmother would die soon, but she knew these details were important.

"Now here's the vital part," Amalia continued. "My powers will be buried with me and flow into the earth, but you can perform a ritual to transfer that power to you."

Karina's head was spinning. "What does the ritual involve?"

"I will teach you the incantation you need to recite. But to increase its effectiveness, you'll need help from the mages. Even one mage can help with the potency of the spell, but all seven would push its power to the fullest. I truly hope Penny is found and rescued when the time comes, but if not, the other six will do."

"What do the mages have to do?"

"Each mage must generate energy particles from their powers, and these particles must be strewn over my grave while you recite the incantation. The particles will then dissolve into my grave, drawing out my power. This power will then flow to you and become yours, making you one of the most—if not *the* most—powerful witch in New United Asia."

Karina looked at her hands. There was a tenseness in the pit of her stomach that caused her to bite the inside of her cheek. "I understand."

"I'm not saying your destiny is to unlock Kashmeru's tomb. Perhaps the Pishacha have a witch to carry out that part. But should you have the chance to destroy Kashmeru, if it comes to that, you will have the power within you to carry through with it."

Karina locked eyes with her grandmother for what seemed like forever. Amalia breathed in a ragged breath and began letting out a barrage of coughs. Karina scooted closer and rubbed her back, her face contorted in worry.

As Amalia's coughs faded, she waved off Karina. "It's important for you to understand that, because of this power, the Pishacha will be after you. They will know you can open the tomb, and they will do anything they can to get their hands on you."

Karina took her hand and held it to her chest. "I'll be careful. I promise."

Amalia stroked her cheek. "I love you, Karina."

"I love you, too, grandmother."

Amalia smiled, and for a moment, Karina didn't see any pain in her face.

"Now, dear," Amalia said as she patted Karina's hand, "that valerian root is kicking in. So if you don't mind—"

"Oh! Yes, of course." Karina adjusted the pillows. "Get some rest. I'll check on you later."

"I'll teach you the incantation after my nap."

"All right."

As Karina fixed the bedsheets, Amalia closed her eyes. By the time Karina left the room, Amalia had fallen asleep.

When Karina made it to the main room, she found Darshana, Loni, and Salina sitting cross-legged on the rug. Darshana's eyes were closed, but Loni and Salina had their eyes open. Karina's brows sunk down, and she aimed a questioning look at them. Loni held a finger to her lips to signal to her to keep quiet. Salina gestured to Darshana with her head and then placed her fingers on her temples. Karina understood the message and sat quietly on the couch to wait for Darshana to finish meditating.

"You're not as quiet as you think you are," Darshana said, her eyes still closed.

Loni and Salina whispered their apologies.

Darshana opened her eyes and let out a sigh as she uncrossed her legs and stood. "It's no use."

"You can't find her?" Salina asked.

"I see glimpses of her. I know she's trying to figure out how to get out of the Pishacha's grasp. But I don't know where she is. It's as if the signal is blocked, or as if there is a thick glass standing in the way between us. Something is interrupting the telepathic bond."

Loni looked between Darshana and Salina. "So what do we do?"

Karina inched forward on the couch. "Maybe I can help."

Loni raised her brows. "How?"

"I don't know what magic the Pishacha are using to keep her location concealed, but I could try to do a locator spell."

Salina sat up straighter. "It's worth a try, right?"

"Yeah." Loni nodded. "Let's do it."

"What do you need?" Darshana asked.

"I need something of Penny's. Something personal with meaning. The more meaning, the better. I also need a paper map. A map of New United Asia is probably best, since we're not sure how far the Pishacha may have taken her. And I need a knife."

Loni and Salina stood.

"I think I know what personal object might work," Loni said. "I'll go get it from our room."

"I will ask Mr. Kitaro for a map," Darshana said. "I have a feeling he will have one."

"And I guess I'll get the knife," Salina said. "What are we talking? Steak knife? Butter knife?"

Karina smiled at her. "I need it to slice my palm, so it's going to have to be sharper than a butter knife."

Salina grimaced. "Gotcha."

Salina was the first to return, seeing as the kitchen wasn't far from the main room.

A few moments later, Loni showed up holding a necklace. "This was her mother's. Her parents passed away after a car accident. Of all the things Penny kept after their death, this is the only thing she still has. The rest was lost or destroyed during the Eradication."

Karina held her hand out to take it. "That'll work."

Darshana entered the room. Not only did she have a map with her, but she was also accompanied by Mr. Kitaro. "One map of New United Asia. Though, from the looks of it, it was before some of the border changes."

"It should still work," Karina said as she took the map and lay it on the floor.

Kneeling so that the map was in front of her, Karina held the knife in her left hand and swiped the blade across the palm of her right hand. She then placed her palm on the map, in their current location, and began moving her hand in a circular motion. Blood smeared along the map as she continued to move her hand, the circles she formed growing bigger until she'd covered the map in her blood. As she recited the chant she had learned when she'd been younger, she held Penny's necklace in her bloody hand and closed her eyes. She imagined Penny's face as she repeated the chant.

"Whoa," she heard Loni say.

Karina opened her eyes. On the map, the city of Agra stood out, cleared of Karina's blood.

"That's where she is?" Salina asked.

"Looks that way." Karina set Penny's necklace down. "Though it's a lot of ground to cover."

Loni began pacing. "Okay, I say Salina and I head to Agra. I think it's a four-hour drive. In the meantime, maybe you guys can get a hold of a detailed map of that city. Karina, will the locator spell work if you did it again on that map?"

"Yes, it should."

"And then we'll have the location narrowed down some more." Loni looked expectantly at Karina, hope in her eyes.

"Yeah. We can linq you the location once we've figured it out."

Salina rubbed her hands together. "Perfect. I'll get my jacket."

"Me too." Loni pointed at Mr. Kitaro. "Can you get the map of Agra?"

Mr. Kitaro nodded. "Yes. No problem."

Loni and Salina swept out of the room to prepare for their trip. Karina went to the kitchen to wash the blood off her hands and the necklace. She took a deep breath and let it out slowly, hoping she had helped. Her mind moved to her grandmother's words about gaining more power, and a chill rushed through her at the thought of being able to carry out magic more powerful than a simple locator spell. It was exciting but terrifying, especially when it came to the fate of the world.

She turned to Darshana, who was folding up Mr. Kitaro's map. She could see the worry in her expression and hoped that Loni and Salina would find Penny before it was too late.

TWELVE

Naree stepped into the kitchen just as one of the staff had finished making her tea. She needed a short break from using her powers on Penny. She hadn't imagined it would be so difficult to break her so they could find the daggers. Sipping her tea, she told herself not to give up. Progress was slow, but it was still progress.

As she leaned her hip against the counter, something in the pocket of her slacks pressed hard against her. She set down the teacup and reached into her pocket, pulling out the jade dragonfly. Running her thumb over the smooth, cool surface, she couldn't help but think of Jae and when he'd given it to her.

"Jae, I don't want to go back. Mom and Dad are suffocating me." Naree plopped down on the couch in Jae's tiny apartment and crossed her arms over her chest.

Jae sat next to her on the couch and bumped her with his elbow. "I know. You can stay here for a while. I talked to them, and they finally agreed."

Naree gave him a small smile and rested her head on his shoulder. "Thank you."

"You don't sound so overjoyed."

"Because I know I'll eventually have to go back." Naree sighed. "I know deep down that they are right. That there is something sinister our there just biding its time before it can get to me. And I know they want to protect me from that. But I feel like a prisoner. I haven't even met anyone outside our immediate family, and I don't have any friends."

Jae put his arm around her and squeezed her. "I'm sorry you're going through this."

"I mean, imagine an entire school of mages dedicated to honoring me, and I can't even attend it. I can't even let any of them know I exist. Do you know how frustrating that is? I have my very own empire, and I'm not even allowed to let anyone know I'm the Lotus."

"Well, I know you are." Jae shifted to face her. "I have a feeling it won't always be like this. Maybe one day, something will change, and you will be able to take your place on the throne and witness your empire with your very own eyes."

The smallest of smiles tugged on her lips. "That would be lovely."

"In the meantime, I can't offer you a throne, but I can give you this as a reminder of adaptability and self-realization."

He pulled a small object out of his jacket pocket and handed it to her.

She gazed upon the small, jade carving of a dragonfly. It represented change.

"This is gorgeous," she said. "Thank you."

"I made it just for you."

"You made this? Wow, that's incredible." She threw her arms around him, pulling him in for a hug. "I know I don't know a lot of people, but I have to say you are the best brother ever."

He laughed and hugged her in return.

One of the kitchen staff entered the kitchen and spotted her teacup. "Did you need more tea, ma'am?"

Naree slipped the jade dragonfly back into her pocket and tucked a strand of hair behind her ear. "No thank you."

The staff member nodded and headed for the pantry, probably to prepare the next meal.

Lakshmi, my love.

A pang in Naree's chest caused her to hunch over slightly. "Yes?"

The comet is approaching. Do not let me down.

"I won't." She cleared her throat and squared her shoulders. "I promise."

With her chin lifted, she exited the kitchen to head back to the room Penny was being held in. She had a mission, and she was going to keep her promise and see it through.

THIRTEEN

Penny was exhausted. Though Naree pushed her to concentrate on the daggers, Penny was doing everything she could not to. When Naree would call her out, Penny would lie and tell her the meditation wasn't working. But the truth was she did have a strong connection to the elite mages and her powers, partnered with Naree's, would probably be enough to track them down.

But she couldn't let that happen.

The door to the room opened, and Bhutano walked in. He only spared Penny a glance before directing his focus on Naree.

"Your Highness, are we making any progress?"

She cleared her throat. "Small steps."

"What does that mean?" His eyes darted to Penny for a second before addressing Naree again. "Have you found the daggers or not?"

Naree tightened her jaw.

Bhutano straightened the cuffs of his uniform. "I see. Perhaps she needs a bit more motivation."

Naree averted her gaze and nodded. "Yes, of course."

"I'm certain you can handle this with five of the seven?" he asked. "I have a special assignment for Harish and Daiki."

Naree gave him a slight nod. "I understand."

Penny turned her gaze away from Bhutano.

Naree scooted closer to her. "Do not disappoint me, amethyst mage. Do not forget whom I have at my disposal. Even five of the seven would be too much for you to handle. Now close your eyes and concentrate."

Penny took a deep breath. She didn't want to anger Naree, especially with Bhutano in the room. But she also wanted to hear what special assignment Bhutano had for two of his dark mages. She closed her eyes, pretending to get into the meditative state, but her ears were tuned in to Bhutano's conversation.

"We're ready to move forward with our plan regarding the prison camps." Although he kept his voice to hushed tones, Penny could still make out his words. "I've got Pishacha soldiers setting up detonation devices throughout all the prison camps. Daiki, I need you to change the views of any witnesses so that they believe these devices were set up by the extremists. Harish, you are to find any uprising in the camps and drain the powers of the rebels. Syphon their powers and dispose of them."

Penny swallowed hard. Bhutano meant that he should kill them.

"Take some of the Pishacha soldiers with you," Bhutano continued. "I have to meet with the governor to organize details behind the scenes and finalize our story to the press."

Penny's eyes were still closed, but she could picture Bhutano checking his watch before heading out of the room. Hearing the door close confirmed that he had left.

This wasn't good. They were getting ready to destroy the prison camps. It was genocide, and they were going to blame the extremists for the terrorist attack.

She had to alert Darshana. She cleared her mind and attempted to reach out to her. She knew Penny might see, but if she could get a message to Darshana and the elites could somehow intervene and obstruct the enemy's grand scheme, it would be worth it.

Darshana, please hear me.

The sound of a chair scraping against the floor caused Penny to open her eyes.

Naree stood before her, her nostrils flaring and her fists clenched at her sides. "You deceitful hag!"

A sudden pain in her hand exploded as her ring finger snapped. Avi stood behind Naree, black tendrils of smoke wafting from his hand. Penny cried out as the pain in her ring finger triggered the pain in her pinky finger. She felt as if half her hand had been run over by a tank.

Naree shook her head, teeth gritted together. "Will you never learn?"

Sweat drenched Penny's temples as she bared her teeth. "You are working with monsters! How could you sit idly by while Kashmeru destroys human life? Why would you let thousands of innocent people die?"

Rikuto curled his lips as she marched forward with the *tantō* knife.

Penny gasped for breath. Before Rikuto could reach her, Kun put a hand up to stop him.

"Wait," Kun said, smirking. He cracked his knuckles and stretched out his neck. "I have a better idea."

Kun—the poisoner—extended his arms out toward her and twisted his wrists. Penny shuddered as acid filled her stomach. She felt as if her blood were curdling, and she doubled over in pain. It was as if she were being stabbed from the inside, her stomach being ripped to shreds. Bile rose in her throat as the acid threatened to bubble over and out of her. She fell onto all fours on the floor, heaving as her muscles felt like they were on fire.

"All right," Naree said. "That's enough."

Slowly, the stabbing pain stopped, but the acid was still lingering inside her.

"Though she doesn't deserve it, let's give her a moment to recover. She's proven to be a slow learner, but I'm sure she'll cooperate from now on."

Salina pulled Loni back behind a parked truck to duck out of sight as an Imperial Police car drove by. They were both quiet and standing still until the car was out of sight. As soon as it was gone, Loni yanked herself from Salina's grip and stomped off down the sidewalk.

"Hey," Salina called. "How about a *thank you*?"

Loni stopped and turned around. "Excuse me if I don't like being grabbed. Or do you not remember the last time you did that? I can show you a scar if you need a reminder."

Salina let out a slow breath, regretting that she had accidentally burned Loni back when they'd been in the academy. "Loni, I told you I didn't mean that. Tension was high. We were all hostile toward each other back then."

"But I never physically hurt *you*."

"I… I know."

Loni crossed her arms, waiting for her to continue.

Salina let out a grunt of frustration. "You know, why did you even volunteer to come with me if you can't stand being around me?"

"Let me be clear." Loni pointed a finger at her. "I didn't do this for you. I did this for Penny. At least *she* knows how to treat people. *She* knows what it's like to be a true friend."

They had been walking for what seemed like forever, trying to track down Penny's location, but every building, every house, had been a dead end. Darshana had linqed them to let them know Karina needed more time. They still hadn't covered the whole town yet, so Salina wasn't about to give up hope. But spending this much time with Loni alone was proving to be a tricky dance of not letting their past get in the way of their mission and focusing on what needed to be done before time ran out.

"Loni." Salina came closer to her, wanting to put a comforting hand on her shoulder but refraining. "I wish I could take it back. I'm sorry things became so unpleasant between us."

Loni pursed her lips. "I thought we were friends. The four of us. And then when Huo-jin and Kanya broke up, it was as if I didn't matter to you anymore. Like we were suddenly enemies on opposite sides."

"We're not the same people we were back then, Loni. We've both been through a lot since then, and we've grown as people. And we know, now, what it's like to suffer loss. You're not the only one who's had to let go of someone who meant the world to them."

"Believe me, I know."

Salina dipped her head, knowing Loni was speaking about her sister who'd died in the government's attack on the academy. "We've both lost a lot."

Loni sighed. She studied Salina's face for a moment, as if she was searching for the right thing to say. "It might take some time to get over it. But I'll try."

It was quiet for a moment as they regarded each other. Salina wondered if they were finally at a point where they could bury the hatchet and move forward.

The chirping of her Linq stirred her from her thoughts. She checked the screen.

"It's Darshana." Salina scanned the area around her before she turned on her speakerphone. "Hey, Darshana, have you found the location?"

"We have the map, and Karina's done the spell. But it isn't narrowing it down enough. They must have some kind of magic blocking their exact location."

"How far has it narrowed down?" Salina asked. "Anything's better than nothing."

"I'll send you a picture of the area," Darshana told them. "Karina said she'll keep trying, but until she can get a precise location, you'll have to search on your own."

A chirp sounded. Salina held her Linq at arm's length so she and Loni could study the picture. It was zeroed in on a neighborhood. Salina checked the street names to try to figure out where they needed to go.

"Okay, got it," Salina said. She exchanged a look with Loni and gave her a nod. "We're headed there now."

"Good luck."

FOURTEEN

The copper glow in Shiro's palm fluttered and went out. Water pooled at his fingertips. He was trying to make an ice pick to try to free himself and Yuki from Kyoko's crimson foot trap, but his powers didn't seem to be working right. He blinked in confusion and shook out his hand.

"What's wrong?" Yuki asked.

"I don't know. I tried to push out my powers and they fizzled."

"You think it's the comet?"

Shiro forced himself not to panic. "Could be. I'll try again."

This time, the glow held. In a matter of seconds, a shiny, solid ice pick formed in his hand. He breathed a sigh of relief and exchanged a look with Yuki.

Before he could even use the pick, the door to the small room opened. Rajim charged in, eyes wide, and placed his golden, glowing hands on the ice pick. It melted as Rajim pried it out of Shiro's hands.

"I guess I should have bound your hands as well," Kyoko said.

"Come on." Shiro swallowed hard. "You can't blame me for trying. You never said when you'd be back."

"I don't think you're in any position to make demands or excuses." Kyoko glanced over her shoulder. "Or did you not notice the roomful of mages we have on *our* side?"

Just then, a figure in the room caught Shiro's eye.

"Mitty!"

Both Kyoko and Rajim looked over their shoulders. In the room, Mitty—one of the mages who'd escaped with him and Qiang—squinted at Shiro.

"Oh, hey, Shiro," Mitty said. "What are you doing in there?"

Mitty, who was even bigger than Rajim, stomped closer. His hair was pulled back in a bun, and he was missing a tooth. Shiro suspected the tooth had been lost during their escape. Though, with the number of attacks the extremist group had been involved in, it could have been lost at any point in time.

"You know this guy?" Kyoko asked Mitty.

"Yeah. We were in the camps together. Got out together too. Well… sort of." Mitty shook his head at Shiro. "Where'd you go, man? We lost you back there."

"I got shot," Shiro explained. "Fell in the river."

"No way! And you survived?" Mitty whistled. "Dude, you must have nine lives."

"Maybe. Hey, Mitty, can you tell these two I know Qiang? We came here to talk to him."

Mitty approached Kyoko, raising a brow. "Enjoying your power trip, Kyoko?"

"Hey, I don't know these guys." Kyoko glared at Shiro. "They could be undercover."

"You can see they're mages."

"They could be double agents sent here by the government to usurp us."

Mitty scoffed. "I know paranoia drives you, but trust me. They're on our side."

Kyoko pursed her lips and held a hand out at Shiro's and Yuki's feet. The crimson stone disintegrated to powder. Her glare was still intense as Shiro and Yuki stood.

"Thank you," Shiro said. "Is Qiang here?"

Mitty waved for him to follow. "I'll take you to him."

As they walked through the auditorium, Mitty cast a look over his shoulder at Yuki. Shiro realized he didn't know who she was.

"This is Yuki, by the way."

Mitty smiled at her. "Nice to meet you, Yuki. What class of mage are you?"

"Diamond," she answered.

Mitty's eyes widened. "Really? I don't think I've met too many diamonds. They're rare."

"Yeah." Yuki cleared her throat. "I hear that a lot."

"I don't think we even have a diamond mage in the rebellion." Mitty rubbed at his chin. "If you're thinking of joining, I could put in a good word for you."

Shiro flashed him a look. "Don't get any funny ideas, Mitty."

Yuki let out a small laugh. "It's okay, Shiro. He's just being nice. Trust me; I can tell."

Shiro gave her a nod. "If you say so."

"It's this way," Mitty said to them both as he gestured toward a staircase.

As they climbed the stairs, Shiro glanced at the crowd of mages who made up the extremist group. They were all following Qiang, all devoted to his purpose. He marveled at what Qiang had created, even if he didn't agree with his tactics.

When they reached the top of the stairs, Mitty opened the door to an office. Sitting in a chair by an electronic whiteboard was Peng, one of the two emerald mages who'd escaped the prison camps with him. The other emerald mage, Bao, was sitting at a desk typing on a computer. The two thin, long-legged men were not brothers, but—aside from Peng's red hair and hooked nose—they looked identical.

Leaning against the back wall, Qiang first narrowed his eyes, and then widened them, his thick brows raising in surprise. It might have simply been because Shiro hadn't seen him in a while, but Qiang appeared more handsome than ever, his body tall and lean, his shirt sleeves hugging the muscles in his arms, and there seemed to be a glow about his high cheekbones.

Qiang shook the hair out of his eyes. "Shiro?"

Shiro's heart pounded. The sound of Qiang's voice sent goosebumps over his skin, and Shiro's breath was caught in his throat.

"Man, Shiro," Peng said. "I knew you weren't dead."

Bao stood from the computer and walked over to pat Shiro on the arm. He then sidled up to Peng and pulled his Linq out. Peng did the same, and there was a beep when the two Linqs' heads touched. Shiro was about to accuse them of placing bets on his life, but he refrained. He was there to see Qiang.

Qiang took a few steps forward before his eyes went to Yuki. "Who have you brought me, Shiro?"

"This is Yuki. She's the diamond elite."

"Is that so?" Qiang asked. "Seems pretty young to be both a diamond mage *and* an elite."

"Definitely pretty, though," Mitty added.

Out of the corner of his eye, Shiro spotted the white glow in Yuki's palms. The next second, Qiang, Peng, and Bao burst into giddy laughter. Peng bent over, holding his stomach. Bao wiped tears of laughter from his eyes. And Qiang—well, Shiro had never seen him laugh like that before. It made him smile. Mitty scratched his head, totally perplexed at what he was witnessing.

Yuki dropped her hands, and the white glow faded away. The three men sobered, clearing their throats as the laughing stopped.

Qiang blinked, running a hand over the stubble at his chin. "Okay. She's the diamond elite. Not sure making people laugh counts as a weapon, though."

"I needed to do something harmless," Yuki explained. "Instead of, oh, I don't know, something like this."

She raised her hand so fast, Shiro almost didn't catch the movement. Diamond bullets flew through the air with a zipping sound. Qiang stared in shock as the wall behind him was marked with gouges from where they'd made impact.

"*Damn*, girl," Mitty mumbled.

"If you can pry those out," Yuki said, "you can consider them my contribution to your cause."

Qiang gave her a sideways smirk, shaking his finger at her. "I like this one, Shiro."

Shiro gave him a nod. "With all due respect, that's not the reason I'm here."

"Okay." Qiang came nearer, closing the distance between them, sending a warm shiver up and down Shiro's spine. "What is it?"

"We overheard something at the governor's mansion," Shiro began.

"What were you doing there?" Qiang asked.

"He wasn't." Yuki raised her hand for a second. "I was. With a couple of other elites. We were in disguise—on a mission—when we overheard the chief of police and the director of the national census discussing something."

Shiro noticed she didn't mention the daggers and thought it was best if he didn't, either.

Qiang looked between them. "What were they discussing?"

Yuki let out a sigh. "They said they were going to destroy the prison camps and blame it on the extremists. You."

Qiang studied her face. His gaze then went to Shiro. "I haven't heard this from any of my sources. But I'll look into it and find out what I can."

"Thank you, Qiang." Shiro gave him a slight bow.

"I'll deal with it because it's the right thing to do. But, Shiro, you might not agree on how I intend to stop them."

"I wish it wouldn't come down to violence." Shiro gave a small nod. "But I also understand you'll do what you have to do to save our people."

There was a small hint of a smile on Qiang's face. He took Shiro's hands, rubbing his thumbs against his knuckles. Shiro let out a shuddered breath, a fluttery feeling filling his stomach.

"Can Shiro and I have a moment alone?" Qiang asked the room.

Yuki gave Shiro a questioning look, to which Shiro responded with a nod to let her know it was all right.

Everyone cleared out and left them alone to speak privately. The moment the door closed behind them, Qiang pulled Shiro into his arms.

"I want you to know, I mourned you. I thought you were dead."

Shiro buried his head in Qiang's shoulder, breathing in the scent of sandalwood and musk. "I thought you gave up on me."

"I wouldn't have, had I known you survived." Qiang stepped back and locked gazes with Shiro. "I promise, when this is all over and both of us manage to stay alive, I'll find you."

Qiang placed a slow kiss upon Shiro's lips. Shiro felt lightheaded, fully aware of the beating of his heart. When the kiss ended, they embraced once more, and Qiang caressed the back of Shiro's head.

Though Shiro wanted the embrace to last forever, he knew he couldn't stay. They exchanged Linq numbers to keep in touch and update each other on their progress, and in a blur of longing and heartbreak, they parted.

Shiro's mind replayed the kiss and Qiang's promise as he and Yuki left the theater. They'd done what they'd come to do, and they stepped into the night with a small sense of relief.

Halfway down the street, Yuki turned to him, placing a hand on his back. "He truly cares about you, you know?"

He was about to question her but closed his mouth, knowing she had used her powers to read Qiang's emotions. Allowing himself a small moment to take in that fact, Shiro smiled.

FIFTEEN

Four hundred feet above the village of Bhaja, in the city of Pune, a group of twenty-two rock-cut caves comprised of prayer halls called *stupas* made up the famous Bhaja Caves. Jae stared up at the structure, feeling exhausted. His legs were weak, and his slack of sleep was causing waves of hot and cold to wash over him. He wasn't sure if the ringing in his ears was because of the messed-up magic from the approaching comet or because he and Mayhara had driven the entire night non-stop.

"I feel mentally numb," Mayhara said as she stretched out her back. "I was so afraid I'd fall asleep and fall off the bike."

Jae raked a hand through his hair. "Same here. I think we better eat something and hope the rise of insulin wakes us up."

Mayhara opened her backpack. "Protein bar?"

"And an energy drink, I think."

The smallest hint of a smile flashed across her face as she handed him the provisions.

"So, what's the plan?" she asked between bites.

Jae took out a pamphlet of the Caves. "I was looking at Karina's notes, and I think one of the translations she wrote down matches with cave number eight in the structure."

Mayhara looked at the graphic of the spot Jae pointed at. "Why do you think that?"

"Out of all the caves, it's the only one that is partially destroyed. One of Karina's translations was the word 'broken.' I think that fits."

"Only one way to find out." Mayhara chugged her drink. "You ready?"

Jae pulled out his Linq. "One second. Apparently, Shiro sent me a text. He says there's a scroll hidden in the spine of the grimoire. An important one." Jae tucked the Linq away. "I guess we should make sure it's intact when we find it."

"Did he say what was important about it?"

"No. But we can sort all that out after we actually get our hands on it."

"True."

Tours of the Caves took place daily. Jae and Mayhara posed as tourists as they bought their tickets. Along with Mayhara's head scarf, she also wore a pair of sunglasses to hide her eyes. Jae, who still had the baseball cap he'd stolen from the festival, donned sunglasses as well.

The Caves were beautiful and rich with cultural and religious history, but Jae knew he had to concentrate on their mission. When they got to the eighth cave, Jae and Mayhara hung back from the crowds, pretending to inspect the sign that explained the history of the cave.

Jae ran his hands along the texture of the stone walls, waiting until there was a gap in the crowds of tourists. When no one was around to witness, he put his hand on the small of Mayhara's back and led her through the entrance of the cave.

At first there wasn't much to see, short of some wooden beams and a section that looked like it had collapsed, but as they made their way to the rear wall of the cave, Jae noticed a symbol on the wall. It was almost invisible to the eye, but the bumps and grooves were definitely there.

"I need the scroll," he said, keeping his voice to a whisper.

"Did you find something?" Mayhara pulled out the scroll from the backpack, checking over her shoulder that no one else was coming into the cave.

"I think so."

Mayhara kept watch as Jae checked the scroll.

"It doesn't look like it lines up with any of the lines," Jae said. "Is this symbol in Karina's translations?"

"Let me check."

Jae ran his fingers over the symbol and inspected the cracks in the wall as Mayhara checked Karina's list.

"Pull," she said.

Jae wrinkled his brow. "You sure it's not 'push'?"

"It says 'pull.'"

Jae felt around for something to grasp on to—a lever or a latch or even a groove deep enough for his fingers—but found nothing. "I'm not sure how anyone is supposed to pull on this wall. There's nothing to pull."

Mayhara studied the wall for a moment. "Because it's not supposed to be pulled open by just anyone. It's supposed to be a witch. Pulling it open with magic."

Jae felt his throat close up and his hope fizzle. When he mumbled a curse, Mayhara let out a small laugh.

"What so funny?" Jae asked.

"Oh, I don't know. Can you think of another way we can move a big hunk of rock?"

She raised a brow, and Jae had to smirk.

He playfully bowed and held his hand out toward the wall. "Of course. Be my guest."

Jae stepped back as Mayhara raised her hands, palms aimed at the wall and glowing red. The floor shook as the wall began to rumble. Sand and debris fell as the part of the wall Mayhara used her powers on pivoted like a big, thick door. Beyond it was an abyss of darkness and the stale scent of dust.

When the opening was wide enough for them to fit through, Mayhara lowered her hands. Jae glanced at the entrance of the cave to make sure no one was watching.

Mayhara adjusted the strap of her backpack. "Ladies first?"

"Only if you're sure."

"I can use my powers to feel the ground and walls and make sure we're not suddenly stepping into a pitfall."

"Good idea." He threw a look over his shoulder one last time. "And we better hurry and close this behind us before someone notices. Or follows us in."

They slipped inside, and Jae used his Linq light to illuminate the area they'd stepped into. The red glow of Mayhara's crimson power shone as she closed the secret door. The scraping sound of rock and sand echoed in the chamber as the external light was shut out.

Mayhara's palms glowed as she held her hands out in front of her. "Okay, this way."

It was difficult to see because Jae's Linq light was bright against the old, dusty walls, but he could discern that they were in a narrow passageway riddled with spiderwebs and moss that had grown between stones. Mayhara was quiet as she led them down the passageway, the sound of her breathing steady. After a minute, the narrow corridor opened up to a larger, circular cavern. In the middle of the cavern was a pile of rocks covered with a large slab of stone.

Mayhara put her hands on the slab. "There's something under here. A large space."

"You think it's a trapdoor or something?"

"I'm not sure. But I can move this off so we can see."

Jae stepped back as Mayhara used her powers to move the stone slab. It noisily scraped against the pile of rocks until it cleared them. Once it was removed, they could see that it wasn't just a pile of rocks, but a circular structure resembling a well.

They moved forward and tried to look into the well, Jae's light shining on a deep shaft surrounded by slick, brick-like stones. His light would only travel so far.

"I hear water," he said. "A waterfall, I think."

"There are waterfalls at some of the Caves, right?"

"Yeah. Maybe this leads to one. Or is fed by one."

"I wonder how far down it goes." She created glowing particles and dropped them into the well. The tiny lights traveled down so far that they were impossible to see, disappearing into the abyss.

"You think we need to go down there?" Jae asked.

She ran her hand along the top of the stones. "I think there's a symbol carved into these rocks. Let's check it against Karina's translations."

Jae pulled out the translations and compared the symbol to Karina's list. "Downward."

Mayhara sighed. "I guess we go down. But maybe I can make it a little easier for us. Can you light it up again?"

Jae held his Linq in the well, lighting up the rocks. Mayhara lowered her hand into the well, the glow of red filling the shaft. One by one, stones began to protrude from the well wall, every foot or so, forming footholds and handholds.

Jae smirked. "That'll make it a lot easier."

"It's still slippery, so move with caution." Mayhara waited as Jae packed away Karina's translations. "You ready?"

"Yeah." He let out a hard breath. "Let's go."

Mayhara sat on the edge of the well wall and swung her legs over into the hole. As she found her footing, Jae readied himself, tucking away his Linq.

Jae, please.

He hesitated, getting a chill from his sister's voice in his head. Especially now, in the dark.

Jae, you must help me. Kashmeru demands the daggers. If I don't hand them over to the Pishacha, he'll have me killed.

Though Jae's instinct was to listen to his sister's pleas, he tried to ignore her, knowing it was a trick. He forced himself to take steady breaths as he sat on the edge of the well wall, ready to follow Mayhara down.

They'll kill me, Jae. Do you want that to happen?

He felt a cinch in his heart. "Of course I don't."

"What?" Mayhara called from inside the well.

"N-Nothing." He shook his head, even though Mayhara couldn't see him from where she was. "It's Naree again."

"She's trying to distract you. Come on."

He knew she was right. Kashmeru was using her to manipulate the elites. Jae squared his jaw, forcing himself to concentrate on the task at hand, and lowered himself into the well.

The climb down was slippery and grueling. It seemed to take forever, foothold after foothold, with only their glowing palms reflecting against the stones lighting the way. At long last, he heard Mayhara grunt along with the sound of a splash.

"I've reached the bottom," she called up at him. "I'm ankle-deep in water."

Jae looked down as he descended the final few feet. He could see the light from Mayhara's Linq illuminating the water below. He jumped when the walls of the well came to an end and landed in a small stream of water that swallowed his feet.

Mayhara already had the scroll out and was checking the map as she glanced around. "There's a tunnel here. I think this is where the map on the scroll begins."

After about twenty feet, they came to a fork in the path.

"This way," Mayhara said after studying the map.

Another twenty feet, and the ground rose above the water. The tunnel curved to the right, getting tighter. Jae wondered if they had picked the right way, but Mayhara was following the map on the scroll, so he gave her the benefit of the doubt. When the tunnel widened again, he was glad he hadn't questioned her.

After they walked a bit more, they came to a section where the tunnel forked off in multiple directions. Mayhara stopped, tilting her head as she brought the map closer to her face.

"What is it?" Jae asked.

"This section isn't shown on the map."

He came closer to take a look for himself. Their heads were right next to each other, and he could hear her breaths. The faint smell of vanilla and jasmine wafted around him. He had to force himself to not think about how close she was to him, but instead to figure out their path.

"What about this symbol here?" he asked, pointing to a mark on the map that stood alone along a line.

"There are no forks in the road there, but maybe that's part of the puzzle." She lifted her head, glancing around. "Look to see if this symbol is marked on any of the tunnel entrances."

Using their Linq lights, they searched the walls of the tunnels, feeling for carvings or grooves and bumps. Jae hadn't found anything yet, and he tried desperately to fight off the feeling of defeat.

"Wait," Mayhara called.

Jae felt a weight lift off his heart. He hurried to her side, to where she was crouching on the ground. Her fingers ran over some cracks in the floor of the tunnel.

She checked the symbol on the map once more. "This is it."

It was barely recognizable, but she was right. They stood and continued down the tunnel.

"It's like a maze," Mayhara said.

"More like a labyrinth."

"What's the difference?"

"There's only one way out of a labyrinth. It's a good thing we have this map. Witches can be very clever in hiding things. And with something as important as the grimoire at stake, I'm willing to bet the other corridors don't lead to just dead ends. There could be traps that could kill someone."

Mayhara shuddered, shaking out her shoulders.

"Who do you think carved out these tunnels?" Jae asked.

"It's a hefty job. I'm guessing the witches were working with some crimson mages. I can imagine a team of them would be able to carry out the construction of these tunnels.

After another hundred feet or so, the tunnel opened up to a large cavern. Jae's eyes widened as he took in the sight before them. It was like a giant, underground storage room. The space was filled with a cornucopia of items. Jae figured some, if not all of them, were magical. Old, withered books were piled on what looked like an altar. There was a pile of materials, and when Jae got closer to inspect, he lifted one to find it was a cloak of some kind. A silver telescope stood amongst a stack of other objects he couldn't begin to identify. There were shelves of jars containing various liquids and items. A chill ran up and down his spine at the thought of what vile things might be inside.

"What is all this stuff?" Mayhara's voice was a whisper, as if she were afraid to wake something that might be sleeping in the cavern.

"I don't know, exactly." He picked up a gold hourglass to inspect it. A glittery liquid swirled inside. "But I'm willing to bet some of it's worth a fortune."

Mayhara nodded. "Hidden here by the witches. Probably for good reason. We just need to find where the grimoire is hidden." She checked the map. "There are a series of symbols here. Four of them in a row. Maybe the grimoire is labeled with them?"

He took a look at the symbols. "Maybe. Let's start looking."

They began searching through the things, going first through the pile of books. Something standing beneath a stack of canisters caught Jae's eye. At first, he thought it was a low table, but when he crouched down to inspect it, he realized it was a chest.

He removed the items that were stacked on top of the chest and ran a hand along the surface. It was made of a dark wood and adorned with intricate carvings. When his eyes went along the edge of the lid, he spotted a number of symbols that were similar to the ones on the map.

"Mayhara, take a look at this."

"What did you find?"

"The symbols on the edge of this lid. Some of them look like they match the ones on the map."

She crouched down next to him and ran her fingers along the symbols. "Yeah, you're right. But there are a lot more than the four in the scroll. There must be twenty different symbols here."

Jae placed his hands on the lid and tried to pry the chest open. It wouldn't budge. Mayhara joined him as he tried again.

"Let me try my powers," she said when it didn't work.

Her palms lit up in glowing red, her gaze intense as she pushed out her powers. But still, the lid wouldn't budge.

"Sealed with magic," Jae mumbled.

"Then why the symbols on the map?" She looked at the map again, her eyes flitting to the lid every few seconds. "Wait. It's a combination."

Hope sprung in Jae's heart. He watched with a quiver in his stomach as Mayhara pressed the symbol on the chest's lid that matched the first symbol on the scroll. The wood shifted inward, as if it were a button she had pressed. Her eyes widened, the small hint of a smile on her lips. She searched for the second symbol and pressed it, then the third and fourth.

The popping sound of a metal latch opening filled the cavern. Jae and Mayhara glanced at each other with anticipation and then inched forward, placing their hands on the lid. Together, they pried the lid of the chest open. There was a thunderous *crash* as it hit the back wall, exposing the open chest.

Mayhara swallowed visibly. Jae held his breath as Mayhara reached in and pulled out a dusty book. She and Jae exchanged a look, and Jae was almost frightened to believe their luck.

They'd found the grimoire.

SIXTEEN

Penny felt as if her mind were being pulled in a million different directions. She had a clear picture of the daggers in her mind, but her visions were jumbled, scattered, and blending into each other.

"Are you sure she's the elite?" It was Ru who'd spoken.

Penny opened her eyes to see her carving into the table with the *tantō*.

"I think she's bluffing," Jin-woo said.

Penny squared her jaw. "The daggers are not easy to find. If they were, anyone would be able to find them."

Naree held a hand up, gesturing for everyone to stop quarreling. "No one asked for commentary. Penny just needs to get out of her own way and concentrate harder."

Penny jumped when the door opened. Bhutano entered the room, and Penny's mind brought up the words he had spoken before. He'd said he was meeting with the governor to discuss the prison camps. A sick twisting wormed its way through Penny's stomach as she considered what they might have decided to do. She felt helpless to stop the enemy from carrying out their plan. She hoped that Jae had remembered Bhutano's conversation at the ball and somehow devised a plan to thwart their efforts. Only time would tell.

"Tell me," Bhutano said, "have we found out the location of the daggers yet?"

"Not yet," Naree answered.

He straightened the lapels of his uniform jacket. "Kashmeru is growing impatient. The comet gets closer every minute and we don't have the daggers *or* the grimoire."

"We'll get the information out of her," Naree insisted.

"Well, perhaps we're thinking too small. No more messing with little fingers. I think we should aim for something bigger. Like her legs."

Penny held back a gasp. Her hand was in enough pain as it was. She couldn't fathom what it would be like to have her legs crushed to the point of not being able to walk anymore. And Avi wouldn't hesitate to do it, either. They didn't need her to walk. They only needed her to talk. Penny bit the inside of her cheek, knowing she had to oblige.

"I'll do it," she said. "I'll find them."

Naree shifted in her chair, smiling. "That's more like it."

"No more games, amethyst mage." Bhutano crossed his arms over his chest. "You best deliver or be ready to deal with my wrath."

Penny swallowed hard and nodded. Closing her eyes, she pushed all thoughts from her mind. This time, she forced herself to really concentrate on the daggers, to bring to mind what they looked like and what they felt like. She remembered holding one in her hand and inspecting it. The shiny blade, the intricate design of the hilt, the elegant box it was stored in.

The image of a dagger solidified in her mind, but as she zoomed out, the location was unclear.

"Do you see them?" Bhutano's voice was harsh and impatient.

"No." Penny kept her eyes closed as she shook her head. "Not them. Just one."

"What do you mean?" he asked.

She furrowed her brow. "I don't see the others. I... I don't think the daggers are together."

Hearing a loud crash and Bhutano's roar of anger, Penny jumped in her seat, but she kept her eyes closed so as not to further infuriate the man.

She felt soft hands on her arms and felt Naree come even further into her mind.

"She's right," Naree said. "It's just one dagger. Buried, near a stream. But it's unclear. I don't recognize the area."

"Search harder," Bhutano ordered. "Kashmeru demands it."

Penny pushed her powers out and reached for one of the mages. If she could see one of them, maybe she would have a better idea of what had happened to the daggers. Flashes of light and fragments of images passed through her mind in a dizzying display until finally, it landed on Jae.

Penny believed it was Naree's connection to him that made him pop into her mind so easily.

She zoomed out her focus on him and found him in a strange cave, crouching beside Mayhara. Mayhara ran her hand over the leather cover of an old book covered with dust.

Naree gasped. "What's this?"

Penny realized what they were looking at. They'd found the grimoire that contained the spell that would unlock Kashmeru from his tomb. But now Naree saw it as well. Penny scrambled to clear her mind. "Nothing. I don't know what that was."

"Liar."

The harshness of Naree's voice made Penny's eyes shoot open.

Naree whipped her head around to face Bhutano. "It's the grimoire. They now have it."

Bhutano lifted his chin, the corner of his mouth inching upward. "Very good, young mage. You've unwittingly disclosed the last piece of the puzzle we need to complete Kashmeru's awakening and saved us the trouble of fetching it."

Penny bit back a curse. Now Jae and Mayhara would be even bigger targets than they had been before. There was nothing she could do to stop the Pishacha from going after the grimoire, and it was just a matter of time before they found out where all the daggers were hidden.

"We have had a witch trying to track down that old book, since we couldn't get the information from the swamp witch." Bhutano checked his watch. "But now that it is within our reach, we can have the witch concentrate on learning the spell to break the bond that locks Kashmeru's tomb."

"And then I can be reunited with my true love," Naree added, her eyes softening.

"Do you have the location?" Bhutano asked.

Penny tensed all her muscles, trying to block the information from Naree's sight. But it was a futile attempt.

"I know where it is. Yes." Naree stood from the chair and faced Bhutano. "The Bhaja Caves. They're underground. In some secret tunnel."

Bhutano snapped his fingers. "Ru. Jin-woo. Get to the Caves and do whatever you deem necessary to retrieve the grimoire."

Penny swallowed hard as the two dark mages disappeared, leaving clouds of black smoke behind them.

Salina and Loni approached the massive iron gate of an exquisite villa. Behind the gate, the front lawn sported a lush garden of manicured bushes and thick, green grass. The stone pathway that led up to the house was impeccably clean, flanked by purple Aubrieta flowers on either side. On the wide stone porch, an Imperial Police officer stood guard.

Salina narrowed her eyes as a man dressed in black with a mouth mask came out of the house and spoke to the guard. The guard nodded and went around the back of the house, and the masked man went back inside.

"Was that a Pishacha soldier speaking to the officer?" Loni asked.

"Yeah," Salina answered. "I guess we got the right house."

"Did you see that?" Loni pointed to the front door.

"No. What?"

"He didn't put a code in the lock pad. I think it's unlocked."

Salina put her hands on the bars of the gate. "But this gate isn't. Tell me if you see someone coming."

Loni scanned the area as Salina put her hand on the gate's lock pad. The golden glow of her palm lit up the device until it emitted a low beep, and the red light on the device went out.

"What did you do?" Loni asked.

"I overheated the circuits. It crashed the system, but we need to hurry before it restarts."

They pushed the gate open and slipped through, closing the gate before the lock pad rebooted. Using the landscape to help them approach, Salina and Loni managed to get to the front door undetected.

Salina wasn't sure where the officer had gone, but she didn't want to stick around to find out. Luckily, the entry to the house was laden with windows. She peeked inside to make sure the coast was clear and then pushed on the latch of the door. It opened without incident.

"You were right," Salina whispered. "Let's go."

The interior of the house was like nothing Salina had ever seen. The temple had been gorgeous, but this villa had a unique modern look to it.

Telling herself she needed to focus on the task at hand instead of the villa's decorative style, Salina scanned the area and listened for movement.

As the two of them got to the main room, a figure moved at their side. *Pishacha.*

Salina clenched her jaw and pulled up her golden powers. At her side, Loni did the same with her emerald powers. Together, they launched a torrential gust of fire at the Pishacha, who flailed as his cloak caught the flames. Just as Salina and Loni were about to throw another offensive strike, the Pishacha disappeared.

The sound of fast footfalls echoed down a side hall.

"This way," Salina exclaimed.

She and Loni took off down the corridor. They made it to the end in time to see a dark mage about to descend a staircase.

The dark mage shot black particles at them before darting down the stairs. Loni held up her hands, and a glowing wave of green knocked the particles to the wayside before the black light could make impact with them. The two of them took off after the dark mage and found a door at the bottom of the stairs.

The dark mage had had no time to stop their advancement, and Loni and Salina crashed into the basement room. There, sitting in a chair, her legs bound with what looked like vines, was Penny.

"Loni! Salina!" Penny tried to stand, but her bound legs made it difficult.

Taking a defensive stance were three dark mages, two Pishacha, the chief of police, and Naree.

Though they were outnumbered, Salina figured they had the element of surprise on their side.

Salina thrust out her hands, and golden fire raced out at two of the Pishacha, knocking them back. A rush of wind was sent out by Loni, which raced over the floor and knocked one of the dark mage's legs out from under him.

Another dark mage lifted his hands, black tendrils of smoke swirling through the air at Salina. She summoned a fire whip and slashed it through the air, whipping his energy away. She snapped it once more, and the whip caught around his waist. He cried out in pain as the fire burned him. Salina cracked the whip to the side and sent the dark mage crashing into the wall. One of the Pishacha grabbed him and they disappeared together.

Penny lifted her hands, the purple glow set in her palms. The room began to cloud up in purple smog, but suddenly, she dropped her hands and cried out in pain. Salina's jaw dropped, and she had to blink, unsure of what had happened.

The chief of police—or Bhutano, as they had learned he truly was—advanced on Salina. A sneer grew on his face, and he pulled out his taser-pistol from his holster. Behind him, Naree grabbed Penny and held her by the neck.

Salina raised her hands toward Bhutano, who was fast upon her. She aimed her fire whip, but before she could strike, a blade flew through the air and hit him, slicing into his heart. Salina gasped. She looked over to see that it had been Loni who'd used her air powers to send the knife—a *tantō*—at him. He stopped in his tracks, staring down at his chest, which was gushing blood.

"No," Naree called out, her brows drawn together. Her grip tightened on Penny.

Bhutano stumbled backward but kept on his feet. He quickly turned toward Naree and teetered to her, grabbing on to Penny's arms and staring into her face.

Salina readied herself, unsure of what Bhutano was going to do.

With his hands clamped on to Penny, he muttered something Salina couldn't hear. Naree's eyes widened. Dark dust and smoke surround all three of them before the police chief crumpled to the ground. Penny's head fell back, and her eyes fluttered shut.

The remaining Pishacha and the two dark mages hurried to Naree, who was propping up the now-unconscious Penny. Sneers covered their faces as the black cloaks of the Pishacha wrapped around them all, and in an instant, they disappeared in a swirling cloud of black smoke, leaving Loni and Salina gaping in shock. Left behind, the police chief lay dead on the ground, his blank eyes staring up at them.

SEVENTEEN

Darshana wiped the sweat from Amalia's brow as Amalia recited the last lines of the power transfer incantation to Karina. She tried not to wince at the raspy sound of Amalia's breathing, choosing instead to concentrate on the dampness of the cotton cloth. Karina carefully wrote down the lines, repeating them back to her grandmother to make sure she'd gotten them right. They'd been sitting with Amalia for over an hour, making sure they got all the information about the ritual written down, as she insisted.

"Are you sure you got it, dear?" Amalia's voice was hoarse and gruff.

"Yes," Karina answered. "I checked every word."

"You were always a clever young woman." Amalia gave her a small nod. "Best student I ever had."

Karina's mouth turned into a slight smirk. "I thought I was your only student."

Amalia took her hand. "It was my greatest achievement, teaching you. I know you'll be able to do this. I totally believe in you."

The last word was cut off by dry coughs followed by wheezes. Amalia pressed a hand to her chest, her face twisted in pain.

"Grandmother?" Karina stood, setting the notebook and pen down on the nightstand.

Darshana reached for Amalia's shoulders, trying to help her sit up. Karina grabbed a glass of water and tried to offer it to her, but Amalia waved her off, shaking her head. Amalia cleared her throat, her eyes watering. When Karina set the glass of water down, Amalia took her hand.

"Karina, you have… an important role… in all of this. Don't… forget. Make me proud… and save the world."

Karina nodded as she bit her lip. "I will, Grandmother."

Amalia slowly turned her head to Darshana. "Take care… of her, Darshana.

Darshana set a gentle hand on her arm. "I promise. I will."

Amalia nodded slowly and turned to Karina again. Her hand trembled as she raised it to stroke Karina's cheek. "I… love you… Karina." Her last word came out as air.

Karina's tears were flowing, and Amalia's eyes fluttered closed. Her ragged breathing slowed, and then her mouth dropped open as the last breath left her body.

Darshana wiped the flowing tears from her cheeks. It felt as if her heart were folding in on itself, each beat sending a heavy, biting ache through her body. She could only imagine what Karina was going through, losing the woman who was practically her mother, the woman who'd raised her and taught her everything she knew, cared for her from when she'd been an infant until she'd blossomed into a young woman. The woman who had been her everything.

Karina dropped her head to her grandmother's arm, her hold still tight on her hand. Her body shook as she sobbed uncontrollably.

Even if she weren't an empath, it would have been unbearable. But as it was, Darshana had to leave the room. She thought it was respectful, in any case, to give Karina time and space to mourn.

As she closed the door and stood in the hall, she felt lightheaded and had to balance herself by holding the wall. Her sobs shook her, and she let them come. She, too, needed to mourn.

A noise from the main room snapped her from her grief, and she forced herself to regain her composure. When she reached the main room and spotted Shiro and Yuki, she almost burst into tears again. Their sad faces reflected her own.

"I have some bad news," she said to them.

Yuki nodded, wringing her hands. "We know. Amalia is no longer with us. I felt it."

Darshana stepped forward, and Yuki and Shiro closed the distance to embrace her as she cried.

"We were friends for a long time," Darshana said as the tears dissipated. She took a step back and wiped her cheeks. "We studied together when we were young. But even as life took us in separate directions, we remained friends. We only saw each other once a year, perhaps, but we always picked up where we'd left off. No matter the time in between."

Yuki squeezed her hand. "I'm sorry for your loss."

"I'm sorry I couldn't help her." Shiro shook his head.

Darshana patted his arm. "Do not blame yourself. This was not your fault, but the fault of the enemy. They did this to her, and we must not let her death be in vain."

Yuki nodded, her gaze trained on the floor.

The sound of Shiro's Linq chirping disrupted the moment.

Shiro checked the screen. "It's Salina."

Darshana nodded, and Shiro pressed the button for the speakerphone.

"Salina," he said, "did you find Penny?"

"We… did." Salina sounded hesitant. "But there was trouble. A battle. Loni killed Bhutano."

Shiro's eyes widened. The three of them exchanged looks.

"Do you have Penny?" Yuki asked.

There was a pause.

"No," Salina said. "They took her and disappeared. Penny is gone."

Eighteen

They were almost out of the well. Jae climbed after Mayhara, forcing himself not to curse every time his foot slipped on the footholds. He wasn't going to let the difficult climb get him down. They'd found the grimoire. They had all the daggers. Things were looking up for them.

Mayhara let out a grunt as she reached the top of the well. Jae could just make out the glow of her palms as she grasped on to the edge to lift herself up.

Just then, a low howl sounded in the well. Jae glanced down to see black smoke swirling below him.

Jae whipped his head back toward Mayhara. "Hurry! Get out of the well."

Mayhara gasped, looking down to see what Jae saw.

The Pishacha were there.

Black tendrils of dark magic swirled around him like a rope, tightening around his body. A look down revealed a dark mage sneering at him, directly below his feet. A hand clamped around Jae's foot. He kicked, nearly losing his hold on the brick Mayhara had turned into a handhold.

Above him, Mayhara stood above the well, having cleared herself from it. She had her hands extended, and red crimson energy shot downward. Jae's foot was released, and he looked down to see the dark mages and Pishacha slipping rapidly down the well shaft. Mayhara had gotten rid of the other footholds, giving them nothing to hold on to.

"Hurry!" she called out, extending a hand to him.

Jae forced his legs to go faster. Below him, clouds of black smoke revealed that the Pishacha had disappeared with the dark mages.

Mayhara yanked on Jae's arm and pulled him out of the well. She was just lifting the stone slab of the well, intending on sealing it, when she was hit with a downpour of rocks from behind. The rocks pushed her to the ground, and Jae had to hurry to pull her free from the weight of them.

In the cavern, opposite them, stood two dark mages and two Pishacha. One of the dark mages Jae recognized as Ru, the daughter of Director Shei. She was the one who had attacked Mayhara with the rocks. The other dark mage was the one who'd tried to pull Jae down in the well. He had short hair and dark skin, with shaved lines cut into his brows. Other than his menacing sneer, he had a mysteriously beautiful face.

Jae and Mayhara moved away from the well and adopted defensive stances, their hands raised, palms facing their enemies.

The dark-skinned mage aimed his hands outward. Black tendrils swirled around the cavern, some of them sinking into the well. In the next instant, massive, reaching vines slithered up and out of the well, along with a barrage of creeping insects, chirping and droning as they crawled out of the well and wriggled toward them. There were so many of them that Jae couldn't see the cavern floor anymore.

Mayhara shuddered and closed her eyes for a moment, most likely trying to block the image from her mind. She held up her hands, the blinding flash of red light pulsing in her palms as the earth moved. Gaps and holes were created, swallowing the insects into its depths bit by bit.

Jae's head snapped back as a sphere of black energy struck him in the head, sending him tumbling back. He retaliated by throwing both hands forward. Glowing particles of sapphire energy flared as he hurled them at the dark mage who'd attacked him. The dark mage grunted as he was knocked back and crashed against the stone wall.

Ru stomped one foot forward as she pushed out her powers, tossing a large boulder at Mayhara. With eyes wide in shock, Mayhara was quick to dive toward Jae, pushing him out of the way and getting them both a safe distance from the boulder. A massive crash sounded as the boulder hit the well, destroying both at impact.

As Jae lifted his head, he realized the contents of Mayhara's backpack had spilled all over the cavern floor. He gasped as he spotted the grimoire lying a couple of feet away.

He reached for it, but he was lifted from the ground by black smoke and hurled across the room. His head slammed into the wall, causing everything to momentarily go black.

Mayhara scrambled to the grimoire and held it to her chest. She turned, held her palm up, and let her powers go. Crimson particles wrapped around her like a shield, blocking her from everyone's view.

Ru growled and her power pulsed in the air. The crimson shield cracked and then fractured, and a deafening eruption filled the room as the shield was obliviated, sending rock and sand and earth sailing in all directions. Jae just caught sight of Mayhara darting from the explosion before he was grabbed by one of the Pishacha and thrown toward the dark-skinned mage. Jae's body was flipped around by the dark mage, and in the next second, Jae was punched in the jaw. He mustered all his energy to retaliate, striking the dark mage in the stomach.

Blow for blow, the punches struck over and over, like pounding drums in a volatile dance.

There was a roar in the cavern, and Jae turned in time to see a pulse of energy erupt from Ru's hands. Jae and the dark mage were thrown in opposite directions. When Jae turned his head, he spotted Ru's arm wrapped around Mayhara's neck as she ripped the book from her hands.

The dark-skinned mage smirked at Jae right before he was enveloped in the black cape of the Pishacha soldier at his side. Ru quickly backed up into the other Pishacha soldier, her glare still set on Mayhara. In an instant, they were gone, and black smoke filled the room.

Jae felt his stomach drop. He rushed to Mayhara, both of them coughing from the smoke.

Mayhara took his hand and led them to the room's secret door. A red glow appeared as the smoke began to dwindle, and the sound of the stone door scraping against sand and dirt reverberated in their ears.

They stumbled out into the cave, which was fortunately vacant. Mayhara doubled over, coughing. Jae put his hands on her arms and helped her to stand.

"Are you all right?" Jae pushed her hair back and checked her face.

She placed a hand on his arm, gasping for breath. "Yeah, I'm okay. What about you?"

"Just some cuts and bruises." He glanced back at the opening to the secret passage, spots flashing in his vision. "They got the grimoire."

She let out a breath. "I'm sorry. I couldn't stop them from taking it."

She reached behind her and pulled something out from beneath her jacket. "But they didn't get this."

Jae's eyes widened as Mayhara held her hand up. His throat closed up as he gasped for breath, unable to believe what he was seeing. Clasped in the safety of her fingers was a tiny scroll.

"Is that—?"

"Yes. I took it out of the grimoire's spine without them seeing." She shook her head. "We're not lost yet."

AMETHYST MAGE

BOOK SIX

ONE

The breeze that blew over the meadow was unusually warm. It made Karina think of the swamp—their home—and she knew her grandmother would have been pleased.

Karina swept her dark hair out of her face as she continued to consecrate the meadow—a piece of land on Mr. Kitaro's property—with her mixture of sandalwood, patchouli, and jasmine oils. She repeated the blessing as she paced the ground surrounding her grandmother's grave. Once the blessing was complete, Jae and Shiro lowered the satin cocoon that was wrapped around Amalia's body, placing the deceased swamp witch in her grave.

Karina was the first to toss a handful of earth onto her grandmother's body. She did so with a tightened jaw and a heavy heart. Steadying her breaths, she forced herself not to break down. Not now. She had a ritual she needed to complete before she could allow herself to let the grief crawl in.

Darshana, the wise guru who led the mages, followed suit, gently throwing dirt upon the silk cocoon. She stood back, gazing upon the corpse of her lost friend, and closed her eyes as wind played with her long, white braid.

The others soon fell in line. Once they'd all had their turn, Jae and Shiro filled the grave. Watching her grandmother slowly disappearing beneath the soil, Karina took deep, heavy breaths and prepared herself for the incantation.

It was as if any sense of happiness or joy was being buried along with her grandmother. Her heart felt like a stone in her chest. It was a struggle just to stand. But she'd made a promise, and she intended to keep it.

Once the grave was filled, Mr. Kitaro—the Sacred Key who had accompanied the mages for much of their journey—handed each of the elite mages a candle. The mages spread out, equidistant from each other, surrounding the grave. Darshana moved away to stand beside Mr. Kitaro, and Karina, with a trembling breath, gave them a nod.

Closing her eyes, Karina recited the words of the incantation her grandmother had taught her. When she got through all the verses once, she opened her eyes and spread out her arms.

Each of the six mages held their candles secure in their left hands as they held out their right, palms facing Amalia's grave.

Karina began the incantation again. She would have to repeat it until the transfer of power was complete. Her grandmother's witch powers would first return to the earth, which was bonded with her magic. The incantation would pull those powers from the consecrated earth and guide them to Karina, who would then absorb her grandmother's magic and combine it with her own. The mages served as a power booster, the pull of their elements guiding as much magic as possible to its new home base.

Amalia had said even one mage involved in the spell would supply enough power to amplify the transfer. Penny—the elite amethyst mage— was still missing, but Karina's spell was still empowered immensely by the remaining six elites.

It was the red glow of Mayhara's power—the power of the elite crimson mage—which reached the soil of Amalia's grave first. Mayhara's long, dark waves danced around her lovely oval face, the wind causing the ends of her hair to play with her full lips.

The crimson particles were next joined by the copper glow of Shiro's power—the power of the elite copper mage. The glow mirrored the copper tips of his slightly disheveled black hair. Though Shiro stood with squared shoulders and a solid stance, there was a softness in his eyes—a sadness— that Karina couldn't miss.

The red and orange flow of magic now swirled with the golden glow of Salina's particles. The elite golden mage had her eyes narrowed as the wind tousled her golden-highlighted curls against the dark skin of her high cheekbones.

Loni—the elite emerald mage—pushed out her powers, the glowing green particles floating in to join the red, orange, and gold. Sweat glistened at her temples, dampening the black hair framing her face. Karina wasn't sure what demons Loni was struggling with, but she suspected Loni was doing her best to conquer them.

The bright blue glow of Jae's sapphire particles swept in and spiraled around the wave of the other magical molecules, joining the surge as the massive collection of magic entered the ground. Jae was the newest elite, having inherited the station when their friend Kamal had been killed. But Jae had another connection to the prophecy that linked the two ancient deities responsible for the war that could end the world. Jae's sister, Naree, was also the reincarnation of the divine goddess Lakshmi. Of all the mages, Jae must have had the most intense personal struggle with this war.

The last mage to infuse her powers into the strain was Yuki. She was the youngest elite mage, and as a diamond mage, also one of the rarest. Yuki looked so small, her auburn hair coming loose from her hairband, and wind made her black blouse and skirt thrash around her petite form.

Karina recited the lines of the incantation once more, raising her hands higher and opening her mind to receive the flow of magic.

It started slowly, a mild weakness in her legs. She forced herself to stand straight and hold her stance, fearing that she'd crumple to the ground if she gave in. Her body felt as if it were being hit with flashes of extreme hot and cold, and she found it difficult to breathe as lightheadedness set in.

Tunnel vision caused her to focus on the bright light surfacing from her grandmother's grave. The glittering white light hovered over the grave for a moment and then seemed to be sucked into Karina's skin. Tiny pinpricks covered her body. She heard a ringing in her ears, and the wind picked up violently, the blast of it causing her eyes to water.

And somewhere in her head, she could swear she heard her grandmother's voice, but she couldn't make out the words.

The flames of the candles each of the mages carried went out all at once, and Karina felt every muscle in her body tense.

The wind suddenly died, and Karina could feel a warm glow in her chest—a glow that seemed to slowly grow and expand until it filled every inch of her being.

Is this it? she wondered. *Is the transfer complete?*

A gasp from Loni snapped her out of her shock. Karina turned to see Loni gaping at a figure just out of her line of vision.

"Penny?" Salina said, shaking her head, her eyes wide.

Karina turned to see if it was, indeed, their long-lost amethyst mage, but the movement and the shift of balance overwhelmed her, and she felt herself falling to the ground.

Two

For a moment, Mayhara was frozen. She couldn't get her mind to wrap around the fact that Penny stood there, not fifty meters away from her. She was sure it was her. She had the same black, wavy hair, the same intense gaze, as if she could see things no one else could. She wore what Mayhara remembered her wearing when she last saw her, except a bit more disheveled. Unless Penny had a twin, it had to be her. Mayhara's eyes narrowed as doubt circled her. Could Penny really be in the meadow with them?

She flinched as Loni ran past her, shocking her out of her stupor. The second Loni pulled Penny into an embrace, Mayhara knew it couldn't be an illusion.

"Penny," Mayhara called. Her legs carried her forward before she could even catch her breath.

In her peripheral vision, she could see Shiro rushing to check on Karina, who'd crumpled to the ground after the transferal spell. If Mayhara could split herself in two, she would make her other self join Shiro to make sure Karina was all right. But her first instinct was to find out how Penny had escaped from the Pishacha's grasp.

Loni had just released Penny when Mayhara reached them. Mayhara threw her arms around Penny and squeezed her. Penny seemed stiff, not returning the embrace. Mayhara realized Penny hadn't returned Loni's embrace, either.

She's either in shock or is frozen with trauma from what happened to her, Mayhara thought.

She took a step back and looked Penny over. Aside from a bandage wrapped around one of her hands, she seemed to be okay. "It's really you."

Jae, Yuki, and Salina were soon beside her, their expressions of confusion reflecting her own.

Glancing over her shoulder, she spotted Shiro, Darshana, and Mr.

Kitaro attempting to prop up the still-unconscious Karina.

"What happened?" Yuki asked Penny, placing a hand on her arm. "How did you escape?"

Penny's eyes were wide and unblinking as she glanced around at the mages surrounding her.

"You're trembling." Jae removed his jacket and wrapped it around Penny's shoulders. He nodded at the rest of the group. "Let's get her inside. Yuki, maybe you can make her a tea. I think she's in shock. We can sort everything out in the house."

Mayhara instinctively stepped to the other side of Penny so she and Yuki could lead her to the house. In a whirlwind of activity, the group made its journey. Jae helped carry Karina, seeing as she hadn't yet woken up. Penny's eyes scanned the area as they walked, obviously unfamiliar with the territory.

It seemed a grueling effort, but once they were inside, Mayhara let out a breath of relief. Jae and Shiro placed Karina on the couch in the main room, and Yuki swiftly had water boiling for tea. Loni led Penny to one of the comfortable chairs in the main room, and Salina fetched a blanket to cover her trembling legs. The rest of the mages either stood around her or sat on the carpet near her feet.

"I'm so glad you're all right," Loni said, her eyes red as tears threatened to spill.

"How did you find us?" Mayhara asked, curling her feet underneath her on the carpet.

Penny opened her mouth as if to speak but simply looked around at everyone with a confused expression.

"Give her some time." Darshana wrung her hands as she watched Penny. "She's undoubtedly suffered a lot of stress and needs a minute to breathe."

Mayhara glanced at Karina, who was still passed out on the couch. Shiro had set a wet cloth on her forehead. Mayhara wasn't sure when he'd had the time to fetch it, but in that moment, everything seemed surreal.

Yuki came into the room holding a steaming cup. She tentatively approached Penny, her eyes searching her face. "Penny?"

Penny slowly turned her head and looked up at Yuki. At first, she only frowned. Yuki's brows were raised with anticipation. And then, Penny blinked quickly, as if waking from her trance, and reached up to take the teacup.

"Thank you," Penny said.

Mayhara felt a collective sigh of relief release from the group.

They gave Penny a moment as she sipped her tea. Mayhara felt as if goosebumps were exploding all over her body. She had so many questions but knew she'd need to wait until Penny was ready to answer them.

"Let us know if you need anything," Salina said, her voice a gentle whisper.

Penny swallowed and set the teacup on the blanket covering her legs. "To be honest, I'm not a hundred percent sure how I got here. It was like I was drawn here. Like a magnet. I reached out with my mind to Darshana, knowing she'd have the strongest connection because of meditation. And then I just followed the pull."

"I'm glad your powers didn't give you any trouble," Mayhara said.

Penny stopped mid-sip and lowered her cup. "What do you mean?"

"Oh." Mayhara sat up straighter. "You don't know about the comet's effect."

"Yes." Darshana ran her fingers down her long braid. "It's something that came to me as I was meditating. Trying to find you, actually. Apparently, the closer the comet gets, the more it interferes with mage powers. Shiro has experienced it. And so has Jae. Salina's had trouble getting her fire to hold as well."

"My feel of the ground doesn't seem as strong as it normally does," Mayhara added.

Penny visibly swallowed. "Oh. That's... troubling."

"To say the least." Loni clicked her tongue.

Yuki crossed her arms. "Not good news when we need all the power we can harness to keep Kashmeru at bay."

Penny dropped her gaze to her lap. She seemed to be calculating something in her head. "No. I suppose not."

"Like I said," Mayhara put in as she relaxed her shoulders, "I'm glad your powers didn't give you any trouble."

"But how did you escape?" Salina asked. "The last we saw, Naree had you captive, and you disappeared with the Pishacha."

"Leaving the chief of police dead on the floor," Loni added.

Penny nodded as she raised the teacup again. She took a long, slow sip, her gaze far away. Mayhara figured Penny was reliving the scene in her head.

"I passed out," Penny continued. "When I awoke, we were somewhere I didn't recognize. To make a long story short, I waited for the right opportunity and managed to escape. I made sure I wasn't followed, but every time I close my eyes, I see them. The dark mages. Their powers are unlike any I've ever seen."

Yuki placed a hand on Penny's shoulder, but Penny flinched. Yuki frowned and pulled her hand back, wanting to give Penny more space.

Yuki cleared her throat. "You're safe now. We're here."

"And we won't let you out of our sight." There was a slight quiver in Loni's voice.

"What happened to your hand?" Jae asked. "We haven't had a doctor out here yet, but if you need medical attention—"

"No. I took care of it." Penny shook her head. "I mean, it hurts, but it will heal. What about you?" Penny asked. "What did I miss while I was… away? Are the daggers safe?"

"Yes," Darshana answered. "We've taken a page out of the Sacred Keys' book and decided to hide them individually."

"Oh?" Penny's brows squished together.

"Instead of them all being in one place for the Pishacha to find," Mr. Kitaro began, "we spread them out. Each one hidden by an elite mage, and each location kept a secret."

Penny handed her empty teacup to Yuki. "So, none of you knows where the others have hidden theirs?"

"No." Salina let out a breath. "And hopefully the Pishacha won't come close to discovering any of the locations."

"Wait." Penny furrowed her brow. "You said the elites hid them, but there were only six of you until I showed up. What about the seventh dagger?"

"I took it upon myself to hide that one," Mr. Kitaro said. "It felt in keeping with my original duty to protect the dagger."

Penny nodded slowly, taking in the news. "And what about the grimoire?"

Mayhara and Jae exchanged looks.

"Well, we found the grimoire and lost it in the same day." Jae raked a hand through his hair as he scoffed. "Practically in the same hour. We had to battle with a couple of those dark mages. But the good news is—"

"She's waking up!"

They all turned at the sound of Shiro's voice. He hovered over Karina, who let out a small moan as she shifted on the couch. Karina's small form shifted slightly, the pallor of her skin paler than usual. Her dark, unkempt hair fanned out on the sides of her face. It wasn't until Karina opened her eyes and sat up that Mayhara could release the breath she'd been holding. She sent a silent thankful prayer up to the gods that everyone in their group seemed to be all right. At least for the moment.

THREE

Bhutano closed the bathroom door and locked it. Now that he was alone, he could finally let down his guard. He turned to the mirror and slowly ran a hand down the face of the body he was inhabiting. The girl's skin was smooth and soft, her eyes intense with small specks of purple.

They'd bought it. They believed he was Penny, the elite amethyst mage.

He'd reached her in time, the night of the attack. He'd felt his spirit leaving the police chief's body, and he'd only had a matter of seconds before his hold on the police chief's essence would unravel and Bhutano's spirit would be sucked into the parallel realm. But he'd successfully transcended from the chief of police's dying body into full-of-life Penny. And the plan was to go to the other elites to find out where the daggers were—without the elites being tipped off about who he really was.

So far, so good.

Possessing the body of an elite mage was an entirely new feeling to him—even as an ancient spirit who was the right hand to the greatest deity in the universe.

Penny's magic coursed through her veins, and Bhutano felt every flutter, every vibration, the warm core of it pulsing inside. Her powers of insight allowed him to understand her journey, how she'd acquired the daggers in the first place, and how close she'd become to the other elites. He knew her story, how she was an orphan, and how she now considered the elite mages her family.

He knew all this, and most importantly, he knew he could use Penny's magic when he needed to.

Bhutano took the Linq out of his hidden pocket and pressed the button to call Naree. Leaning closer to the door, he listened to make sure no one was in the hall to hear him. Though he would still sound like Penny, he didn't want the elite mages to hear what he was discussing. Talking to anyone on the phone would be suspicious enough.

"Hello?" Naree sounded hesitant.

"It's me," Bhutano said. "I'm in."

For a moment, Naree didn't respond. Bhutano figured she was still unsure that it was truly him.

"They believe you're her?" Naree asked.

"Yes. There's no reason for them to doubt it."

It was the same as when he'd possessed the body of the Imperial Police chief. No one had suspected he'd really been the spirit messenger—except, of course, those who'd been in on the entire operation, those who were followers of Kashmeru and his cause.

"Did you find the daggers?" Naree asked.

"It's more complicated than we believed," Bhutano explained. "The elite mages have hidden the daggers separately and have kept the locations of each a secret from each other."

Again, Naree was quiet, no doubt contemplating this new problem. "Should we come in with the dark mages? Force them to disclose the hiding places?"

"With the daggers spread out as they are, it would be difficult to do. I can't see that plan being a hundred percent successful. But I have another idea."

"What is it?"

"They believe I'm their friend. I can get them to open up to me."

"But if they're keeping the locations a secret from each other—"

"I'm not going to ask them where the daggers are. I suspect they won't tell me." Bhutano grinned to himself. "I'm going to lower their defenses, and then I'm going to use our dear amethyst mage's powers of insight to search their minds and show me where the daggers are. Without them even knowing it."

"Do you think you can manage it?" Naree asked. "You don't exactly have much experience using her powers."

"It worked enough to find this dismal place they're holed up in. I have confidence I can figure it out." Bhutano took another look in the mirror, moving Penny's dark waves away from her cheeks. "I learned something else."

Naree sighed into the Linq. "Something good or bad?"

"That depends. The guru says the approach of the comet is affecting the mages' powers."

"Affecting them how?"

"Apparently, it's causing some kind of disruption. Their powers aren't working to full capacity. Have the dark mages reported anything of that nature?"

"Not that I know of, but I'll talk with them and let you know for certain."

"Good. How are things going with the grimoire?"

"Tien Thi is studying it. She says some of the language is ancient, words witches nowadays don't tend to use anymore. But she believes she understands enough to find the correct spell to unlock Kashmeru from his tomb."

"Good." Bhutano just hoped their witch was powerful enough to do the spell once she found it. "If not, I may have another plan. There's a witch here they seem to hold in high regards. I'll do some digging and find out if her level of power exceeds that of Tien Thi. If that's the case, then we can use her instead. But we'll have to wait to grab her until after we've acquired all the daggers."

"It seems to all be falling into place."

Bhutano smiled. "Yes. It does. I need to go before they get suspicious. But I'll report back with what I can find out. We can send dark mages in bit by bit when I discover a location. That way, we can steal the daggers back one by one, right from under their noses."

Penny was screaming. But no one could hear her. She wondered if Bhutano had somehow muted her voice in the space he occupied in her head. She could see everything he saw, hear everything he said, and witness everything he did. But she was powerless to stop him. She heard his plan to trick the other mages into revealing where they'd hidden the daggers, but she could do nothing to warn them.

There was no way to control Bhutano's movements as he moved her body into the dining room to join the others.

"Are you sure you don't need to lie down for a while?" Salina asked.

Salina, it's not me. It's Bhutano. Please. He's lying to you.

"I can lie down later," Bhutano said with Penny's voice. "I'm actually starving."

Salina smiled and pulled out Penny's chair for her.

"How's Karina?" Jae asked Shiro as he placed a large serving plate of stir-fried noodles on the table.

Jae, please! Bhutano's got you fooled!

"She's getting some rest," Shiro replied. "She apologized for not joining us. I think she's trying to get used to the power transfer."

"Power transfer?" Bhutano asked in Penny's body.

Everyone looked at Penny.

"We won't know if it worked for sure until she tests it," Darshana said, taking a seat at the head of the table. "But I think we should give her time to mourn. It can't be easy to concentrate when you've just buried your grandmother."

Bhutano shifted in the chair. "I'd like to offer my condolences to her later. When she's up for it. I still can't believe Amalia's gone."

Penny wanted to grit her teeth and pound her fist against the table, but she couldn't do either. Bhutano hadn't even known Amalia, and he was pretending to grieve her passing, all as a ruse to find out if Karina was powerful enough to unlock Kashmeru's tomb.

"It's a bittersweet day," Mr. Kitaro said with a nod. "We've said our goodbyes to Amalia, but we are also grateful to have Penny back."

The elite mages followed Mr. Kitaro's lead and raised their glasses.

"Welcome back," Darshana said.

Penny could not stop Bhutano from raising his glass in return. If she could, she would have thrown the glass and shouted to them all that they were being duped.

Help me, Darshana. Hear me!

FOUR

Karina ran her fingers along the length of the small scroll, feeling the tiny bumps in the golden clasp on the side. Was it a code? Or simply imperfections? She couldn't be sure. All she knew was they'd had the scroll for over a week now and still had no idea how to open it. It was about half the diameter of the other scrolls they'd been dealing with, and three-quarters the length. It appeared to be sealed by the golden clasp, but none of them could pry it open. They had tried for days when Jae and Mayhara had brought it back from the Bhaja Caves, but then they'd had to organize Amalia's funeral, and thoughts of the scroll had had to wait.

With a sigh, she went to the window. The sky was cloaked in a pinkish orange hue by the horizon. She was struck with a memory from her childhood, when she'd been at the swamp with her grandmother. Amalia had been teaching her about which herbs to use in a certain potion, and the sun had begun to set. Amalia had stopped, mid-speech, and smiled at the sky.

"What is it, Grandmother?" Karina had asked.

Amalia had gazed down at her, giving her a sideways grin. "Did you know that when you were very small, you had lighter hair?"

Karina had giggled. "Strawberry blonde, right?"

"It was an odd thing," Amalia had remarked. "But a few of our ancestors have been blessed with the feature when they were small as well. They'd all grown out of it, of course. But they were all—each of them— also blessed with being very special witches with extraordinary purposes."

"You think I'm special too?"

Amalia had stroked her cheek. "Indeed."

Karina had screwed up her face and looked at the sky. "But why are you smiling at the sky, Grandmother?"

"Because, truly, your hair was more the color of the sky right now at the horizon than a strawberry blonde."

Karina blinked away the memory, focusing again on the tinged horizon. Was she a special witch with an extraordinary purpose? She knew her grandmother had to be right. And taking in her current situation, helping the elite mages in their attempt to save the world, she believed it must be her fate.

So what was missing? Why couldn't she open the scroll? It had crossed her mind, more than once, that the answer might lie in the grimoire that had been stolen away at the most inopportune moment.

She let out a grunt and held the scroll to her forehead.

"Come on," she said to herself.

She had to try again. Grimoire or not. Her brain scrambled for a spell she hadn't tried yet. For what seemed like forever, she paced her room, searching the recesses of her mind for a spell that would work.

Setting down the scroll, she gathered a few of her grandmother's candles and placed them on the floor. After she lit them, she sat cross-legged in front of the flickering flames and placed the scroll on her leg. It was so small, that, if not for the length of it, she could hide it in a closed fist. The golden clasp reflected the flames, and Karina felt hypnotized by the changing lights.

She closed her eyes and waited for the spell to come to her. Sounds became louder in her ears. She let them in and listened for a message. Between the sound of the wind outside, the call of birds, the buzzing of insects, and the muffled movements of the others in the house, a low whisper reached her ears.

At first, Karina felt a jolt, like a tremor of fear exploding in her head. She forced herself to stay her ground and keep listening. The murmur grew louder. Was it her grandmother's voice? Her heart pounded, and she listened harder.

"*…deceiving you!*"

Karina's mouth hung open. She started shaking. But she didn't want to break the connection. "Grandmother?"

She listened more closely, trying to tell if it was her grandmother's voice or not. It was still too staticky to tell for sure. The murmur echoed, as if it were being spoken through a tunnel. "*…deceiving…*"

A ringing began in her ears. She tried to keep listening to the voice, but the ringing grew louder. An ache blossomed in her neck. Her shoulders scrunched up, and she gritted her teeth. The ringing became unbearable, until she had no choice but to cover her ears and scream for it to stop.

The candles went out all at once, and Karina's breaths were heavy. But the ringing had stopped.

The door to her room was thrown open, and Karina looked up to see Salina standing there.

"Are you all right?" Salina scanned the room. "I heard a scream."

Karina scrubbed her hands down her face. "Sorry. It's okay. I'm fine."

Salina took a few steps into the room. "What happened?"

Karina sighed. "I was trying to figure out how to open the scroll, and then…"

"And then what?"

Karina bit her lip. "It's going to sound crazy."

"With everything we've been through in the past month, *crazy* might actually be normal."

"Okay." Karina grimaced. "While I was trying to listen to the voice in my head to figure out the right spell to use on the scroll, I thought I heard my grandmother's voice."

Salina offered her a small smile. "That's not crazy; that's normal. When my mom passed away, I swore I heard her calling my name a hundred times in about as many days. I think it's the heart's way of holding on to the loved ones we've lost. I still hear Huojin's voice on occasion."

"You do?"

"Yeah. She hasn't been gone that long." Salina frowned.

"That's true. And you've hardly had time to grieve." Karina sighed once more. "I guess it's just something I need to get used to. For now."

"I guess. It'll get better. And if you ever need anyone to talk to, you know where to find me."

"Thanks."

Salina gave her a single nod and then turned to leave the room.

Karina picked up the scroll from the floor and ran her fingers over it again. She would keep trying. Whatever it took.

"*…deceiv—*"

Karina dropped the scroll and slapped a hand against her chest.

Swallowing hard, she recalled what Salina had said. It was just her heart's way of holding on.

She forced herself to calm down. But even after her breathing slowed to normal, she had to wonder: Why would her heart be telling her that someone was deceiving her?

FIVE

Jae ran the program for the fifth time, leaning back in the hair at the desk in Mr. Kitaro's office. He locked his fingers behind his head as he waited for the system to run through its files. His eyes were tired from staring at the monitor, and his hope of finding Naree was slowly depleting.

Part of him wondered had he been there when Loni and Salina had found Penny, if he would have been able to convince Naree to come with him. To leave Kashmeru's grasp and join the side she was meant to be on. He'd convinced her before, when he and Mayhara had chased down Naree in the caves near Sariska. Of course, his victory had only lasted one night, and his sister had been gone in the morning. Stolen away again by Kashmeru.

Now all he had to rely on was the facial recognition software. Maybe she'd slipped up when she'd fled the villa with the Pishacha. Maybe some street camera had caught a shot of her. Then he'd have a clue where to start looking.

He needed his sister back—in her true form, not this delusional, bad-boy-obsessed version of her that fought him every step of the way. And not just because he promised his parents, but because the world depended on it.

And he was running out of time.

"The news is talking about Police Chief Min's funeral." Darshana stood in the doorway of the office. "I hope I'm not interrupting."

"Not at all." Jae leaned forward in his chair. "Are they still claiming it was a heart attack?"

"That's their coverup story, yes."

Jae tapped a button on the keyboard. A window appeared on the screen displaying a muted news reel. Sure enough, the Imperial Police chief's photo was featured in the report.

Another figure appeared at the office door, and Jae straightened in his chair. "Karina. How are you feeling?"

Karina stepped inside the office and sat in the chair opposite Jae. She had her hair pulled back in a low ponytail, and the dark circles were gone from under her eyes. "I feel… different. I guess my body is still adjusting. I can't tell if I need to go for a run or if I'm too exhausted to move. My brain feels numb and full of a million thoughts all at once. And everything… tingles."

Darshana stepped forward and rested a hand on Karina's shoulder. "I'm afraid I can't guide you through this. Mage powers, I can help with. But witch powers are out of my skillset."

"Then I guess you won't know how I'm supposed to crack this puzzle." Karina held up the small scroll Mayhara had luckily slipped past the dark mages and the Pishacha when the grimoire had been stolen from them.

According to Karina, the scroll was said to contain a spell that could destroy Kashmeru for good. No one in the empire had known about it, and Jae suspected the Pishacha were also clueless about its existence. The only hint that the scroll existed was the vision Darshana had had of it. The scroll was small enough that Jae hadn't noticed Karina holding it when she'd first come into the room.

"It still won't open?" Jae asked.

Karina shook her head and sighed. "I'm not sure if it needs a spell to unlock it, or a secret word, or… a hammer."

Darshana let out a laugh. "I'm sure it will come to you. A witch locked it, and it will take a witch to open it."

"I just thought, with my grandmother's powers…" Karina grew silent.

Jae and Darshana exchanged a glance.

"Perhaps it can only be opened when it's needed," Darshana suggested. "Some kind of guarantee the witches who created it thought up so it wouldn't be destroyed."

"Maybe." Karina didn't seem convinced.

Jae's eyes wandered to the monitor. The image of Director Shei appeared in the newsreel window. Leaning forward, Jae clicked the button to make the window full screen and turned on the volume.

"Shei, who is in charge of the comet's arrival celebration at the Bahá'í

Lotus Temple in New Delhi, has stated that plans are moving forward despite the unexpected death of Police Chief Min. She's quoted as saying that he would have wanted the celebration to continue, knowing how important welcoming the Akutake comet is to the citizens of New United Asia. The celebration coincides with the temple's grand reopening, after almost five years of extensive renovations. Astronomers say the comet's closest proximity to Earth will take place at the end of next week when it will be exactly above the temple's apex."

"That's it," Darshana said.

"What?" Jae watched as Darshana's eyes narrowed in thought.

"That's where Kashmeru must be buried."

Karina shifted in her chair to get a better look at the guru. "What makes you think that?"

"The temple has been under construction for the last five years. No one's been in there except authorities and construction crews, and as we all know, the government is tied in with the Pishacha. The comet will be closest when it reaches the sky directly above the temple—which has a star-shaped window at its top, called the symbol of the Greatest Name."

"A conveniently placed window," Jae said.

"Exactly. One should be able to see the comet's light through it," Darshana said.

"And feel its energy," Karina added.

"So, you think Kashmeru's tomb is somewhere in the temple?" Jae asked.

"My best guess is it's under the temple. But directly below that window."

Jae smirked. "I guess we'll find out."

Darshana gave him a nod in agreement. "I also wanted to talk to you about this meteor shower that's taking place later this week."

"What meteor shower?" Karina asked.

"It's not a big deal," Jae said. "We have them all the time, actually. But I think people are focusing on this one because it's taking place so close to the time of the comet's arrival."

"Yes, and it gave me an idea," Darshana said, placing her hands together.

"What is it?" Jae asked.

"So meteoroids are rock and debris that have burned off from comets that circle the sun, and the Earth occasionally crosses the orbit of these comets, causing us to traverse through the cloud of debris. And if this cloud, which we are approaching—or is approaching us, whichever way you want to see it—gets in the way of the Akutake comet, couldn't it be that it somehow disrupts the disruption?"

Jae picked up a pen and tapped it on the desktop. "You mean lessen the effect of the comet?"

"Precisely." Darshana raised a brow and waited for him to answer.

"Perhaps." He clicked away on the computer keyboard. "Let's put it on our schedule. We could go to the nearest hill, whichever is the highest point, and test out your theory."

Darshana gave him a wink. "Smart boy. That's what I thought you'd say."

SIX

Shiro concentrated on his fingers as he pushed out his magic. Like a leaky faucet, small drops of water pooled at the fingertips and slowly dripped, one by one, to the ground. He made a fist and looked up at the blue sky, gritting his teeth in frustration. Closing his eyes, he called upon Darshana's breathing technique.

Breathe in for four seconds. Hold for seven. Calmly exhale for eight.

He could sense the heavy weight lift from his shoulders and a warmth radiating throughout his body. Feeling calmer, he opened his eyes and took in his surroundings.

The meadow was peaceful. He could hear the babbling of the nearby stream, and the call of white-cheeked barbets echoed around him. He breathed in and out again. This time, when he extended his hand and pushed out his powers, pellets of ice shot out and zoomed into a nearby tree. The birds in that tree took off, frightened by the sudden impact.

The release of energy was exhilarating. Still, he worried his lip with his teeth. This interference of power the comet was causing was bad news. In the heat of battle against the Pishacha, there would be no time for breathing exercises. The elite mages needed to be at their best when the time came. Their powers needed to be fully loaded and ready to go.

"That's good, isn't it?"

Shiro turned to see Penny standing in a patch of flowers nearby. Her head was tilted, her hands clasped behind her back, and her smile was small.

"Yeah." He rubbed the back of his head and gestured to the tree pocked with ice. "It's not my best work, but at least I'm able to get my powers to work at all."

Penny came closer. "It's strange, this unexpected effect of the comet."

"I'm worried about how much worse it might get."

The buzz of Shiro's Linq interrupted his train of thought. When he spotted Qiang's name on the screen, his heart skipped a beat.

He glanced at Penny and held a finger up before answering the call. "Qiang?"

"Shiro, I'm in Guwahati. And it looks bad."

"What happened?" Shiro's eyes went to Penny, who gave him a questioning look.

"Every mage I've managed to come into contact with inside the camps—their powers have been stripped."

Shiro rubbed the crease in his forehead, letting out a curse. "It's the comet. It's affecting their powers."

"I'm not so sure," Qiang said. "I've seen the effect with my own team. Timing is off, force is weakened, but the powers are still there. These mages in the camps, they have nothing left. It's like their power has been drained entirely. All of them. All at the same time."

Shiro blinked in confusion as he processed Qiang's words. "Any trace of explosives? Jae said the police chief and Director Shei mentioned blowing up the camps."

"If there are any here, they're well hidden. We didn't exactly walk in the front door and ask for a tour. We had to sneak in just to speak to the prisoners. Mitty and Bao checked where they could but didn't find anything suspicious. And I don't even want to get into the diversion we had to create just to get back out of the camps again."

Though he knew Qiang couldn't see him, he nodded. "Thank you, Qiang."

"We'll head to Jabalpur next and see what we can find there." Qiang let out a breath. "I heard the chief of police died."

"He is dead," Shiro responded. "But the media and the government are covering up how he died."

"Why would they do that?"

"Because he was killed by an elite mage. And because it wasn't really him at the time."

"I'm not sure I know what you mean."

Shiro glanced at Penny once more, not sure if his words would serve as a trigger for what she'd gone through at the villa. "Min was possessed by Bhutano, Kashmeru's spirit messenger. His death occurred in a fight with two of our elites."

Qiang was quiet for a moment. "Do you think Bhutano died with him? Or do you think his spirit left Min's body?"

"I can't be sure of anything."

There was noise in the background. Shiro heard Qiang's muffled voice and waited for him to speak again.

"I need to go. There are too many Imperial Police in the vicinity. We're about to leave for Jabalpur."

"Okay. Qiang?"

"Yes?"

"Be careful."

"I will."

Shiro tucked his Linq away and let out a shuddered breath.

"What was that about?" Penny asked, coming closer.

"Qiang and his team are checking out the prison camps. He said all the mages there lost their powers."

Penny gawked at him for a moment before wrapping her arms around herself. "That's terrible."

Shiro rested his hands on his sides and dropped his head in thought. Penny put a hand on his shoulder.

"You're worried about him," she said.

"Yeah. I mean, that's Qiang. He's always thrown caution to the wind. But the thought of him getting caught—of getting hurt or killed—I don't think my heart could bear it."

"Tell me about him." Penny offered him a small smile. "How did you meet?"

The prisoners were given chores inside the camps. Shiro was assigned to the agricultural team, and the guards placed them all—probably close to a hundred mages—in one large bunker together, filled with bunk beds and thin, itchy blankets. Shiro's duties were comprised of plowing a field with a small handheld shovel, since the prisoners weren't to be trusted with tools that could double as a weapon. The fact that the shovel was dull and constructed of a light wood made Shiro's task that much harder.

The guards enjoyed hovering while the prisoners worked. The sun was especially cruel, and there were no protective hats provided for anyone other than the guards. Shiro was covered in dirt and only stopped digging for a moment to wipe the sweat from his eyes.

"No slacking, inmate!"

Something hard hit Shiro in the back, causing him to fall forward into the dirt.

Holding back a grunt, he pushed himself up to his knees. Glancing to his left, he spotted the nearest fellow prisoner. The young man looked to be his age, his black hair slicked to his forehead with sweat. His kind eyes seemed to reach out to Shiro, to tell him to hang in there.

Shiro gave him the smallest of nods and then shoved his shovel into the dirt again to continue his work.

The guard paced behind him, no doubt scanning the others to make sure they were doing their jobs. Risking a glance over his shoulder, Shiro noticed the weapon the guard carried. The one he'd used to hit him in the back. It was the same weapon the Imperial Police had used when they'd attacked the academy. Cyber batons, he'd heard one of the other mages call them. They were something new the Imperial Police were armed with to use against mages in case the blocking devices in the mages' necks didn't stop them from using their powers.

The guard whipped his head around and caught Shiro gawking. Baring his teeth, the guard marched forward and lifted his weapon. "I said, no slacking!"

In the next second, Shiro was struck across his cheek. Electric pulses vibrated through his head in a violent tempo. The next thing he felt was his head hitting the ground. Black spots danced before his eyes as he tried to clear his double vision and right himself. Footfalls met his ears mixed with a high-pitched ringing.

"I never liked bullies," came a voice from behind him.

There was a thump and a grunt, and Shiro opened his eyes wide enough to see the guard, face-down in the dirt beside him, blood streaming from his temple.

Shiro let out a gasp and backed away from him. He turned to see the black-haired young man extending a hand.

"Come on," the young man said. "You don't belong in the mud."

Shiro took his hand and let him pull him to his feet. His heart raced, but not just because this young man had fought back against a prison camp guard.

The guard let out a moan, and Shiro swallowed hard.

"He's getting up." Shiro almost stuttered his words.

His fellow prisoner gave a nod. "Looks that way. I'm Qiang, by the way."

"Shiro."

"You might want to get out of here, Shiro."

"But he could kill you."

"He'll try."

Shiro noticed the big rock Qiang gripped in his hand. The field was mostly mud and dirt. Where had Qiang gotten the rock from? Unless…

Qiang gestured toward another prisoner about fifty meters away. "That's Mitty. Go to him. He'll take care of you."

"What about you?"

Before Qiang could answer, the guard shot up into a crouching position and swung his cyber baton, cracking Qiang across his legs. Qiang let out a shout as he buckled to his knees.

"Go, Shiro!"

Shiro was ready to ignore Qiang's instructions and jump in to help, but he spotted two more guards racing toward them.

Qiang delivered a quick fist to the guard's jaw. "Shiro! Go!"

He could feel his heartbeat pounding in his throat as he backed away from the fight. A fight he hadn't been involved in. He realized then that Qiang was trying to keep Shiro innocent in the whole ordeal so he wouldn't be punished. He swallowed hard and turned to dash toward Mitty.

It was a blur after that. And it wasn't until night fell that Shiro saw Qiang again.

Shiro was lying in bed, staring at the underside of the bunk above him, when the door to their bunker was torn open and someone was tossed inside. A low grunt was let out by the person sprawled out on the floor, and the guards at the door delivered anyone who could see a menacing scowl before slamming the door shut again.

Those closest to the commotion got up to inspect the situation. Shiro shot out of his bed, knowing it must have been Qiang. He pushed his way through the dozens of inmates gathered near the door to find Qiang beaten black and blue. His bare back exposed long, swollen gashes of bloody flesh where the guards must have tortured him—probably with their cyber batons. Though Qiang's condition looked terrible, Shiro was happy he was still alive.

"Move out of the way." Mitty appeared, the large mass of him, moving through the crowd and toward Qiang. He crouched down and slung one of Qiang's arms over his muscular shoulders. "Make room!"

Shiro followed them to what must have been Qiang's bed. He hissed through his teeth when he saw that one of Qiang's eyes was swollen to the size of a softball, purple and red and practically swallowing the eyeball.

"Qiang," Shiro said hesitantly.

Qiang glanced up, his one visible eye softening when he caught sight of Shiro. He gave him a nod, letting him know it was all right to come closer.

"I'll see if anyone's got any bandages," Mitty said before stepping away.

Shiro dropped down on his legs beside Qiang's bed. "I'm so sorry. This is because of me."

Qiang winced as he turned his head to face Shiro better. "No, Shiro. Don't ever blame yourself. We are the victims here. They are the bad guys. Don't ever forget that."

Shiro blinked as he nodded. "Did you... That rock that was in your hand. Did you use your powers to make it?"

Qiang searched Shiro's face. "Yes."

"But the blocker? How were you not shocked by it?"

"I was," Qiang said. "But I've built up a tolerance. One day, I'm going to get out of this place. Nothing these jackasses do can keep me here. Blockers. Torture. No matter. I will prevail. Our people don't deserve to be in here. We did nothing wrong. And I'm going to make it right. Somehow."

Shiro sat in wonder of Qiang's determination. He felt some small spark of hope. "Will you teach me?"

Qiang's brow furrowed. "What?"

"How to tolerate the pain. I want to help you."

The smallest hint of a smile tugged on Qiang's lips. "Yes. I will. I'll teach you."

"He sounds too good to be true," Penny said, stirring Shiro from his memories.

Shiro took in a deep breath, his mind circling for a moment—from Qiang, to the extremists, to their war against the Pishacha, to the daggers, and finally to his need to make sure he had control over his powers—before he could properly register Penny's comment.

"No. Of course not." Shiro let out a laugh. "Nobody's perfect. But I can't think of anyone more perfect for me."

SEVEN

"**A**re you near?"

Naree scanned the area, her focus landing on the quaint cabin tucked away in the distance. It was a small source of light in the landscape of night. "Yes, we're near."

"Good," Bhutano said into the Linq. "The dagger is in the bank of the stream. I would have marked its exact location, but I was being watched. Look for the bend near the woods."

"We'll find it." Naree walked in the direction of the stream, signaling for the two dark mages who were with her—Ru and Avi—to follow. "They still don't suspect you of impersonating the elite?"

"No."

"And one of them simply let you see their thoughts? Just like that?"

"I had him tell me a story from his past. Made him focus on something emotional so his defenses regarding the dagger were stripped down enough for me to see into his mind."

"Fantastic."

"Find the dagger," Bhutano instructed. "I'll make sure no one leaves the house tonight. But keep out of sight, just in case."

He ended the call, and Naree slipped her Linq into her pocket.

They trudged through the untended fields, over rocky terrain and patches of mud. Once they reached the stream, it didn't take them long to find the spot Bhutano had mentioned. Naree reached out with her crimson powers to feel the earth and sand at the stream's bend, tuning in on where the dagger was hidden.

"It's in the water. Here," she said to the dark mages at her side. "Buried under some heavy rocks."

"Want me to go in?" Avi asked.

"One moment." Naree extended her hands, the orange glow of her copper powers emanating in the palm of each. As if the world were tipping on its side, water moved away from the edge of the stream, moved as if a wall were being created to keep it away, exposing the slick earth and pebbles of the bank. She kept her arms extended and gave Avi a nod. "Now."

Avi scrutinized the exposed riverbank and jumped into the area that was free from water. His shoes partly sunk into the squishy bottom. He glanced behind him as if checking that the stream was being held back by Naree's invisible, magical dam. Crouching down, Avi moved his fingers around, digging them into the mud and feeling the rocks embedded in the sides of the riverbed.

"Let me help," Ru said, reaching out with her powers. One by one, the bigger rocks lifted from the mud, breaking free with a sucking and popping sound.

"I see it." Avi reached into the muck and pried free the metal object. He stood and wiped the blade, smiling at the way the moonlight reflected off it.

"Get out of there," Ru urged, motioning for him to hurry. "We still have to leave the property before anyone sees us."

The moment he cleared the riverbed, Naree released her powers. The water rushed back in place, splashing against the bank.

"We got it," Avi said, his eyes twinkling.

Naree threw her hair back from her shoulders, but she didn't smile. There was still much more to do, and they'd only just started. Still, they were headed in the right direction.

She gave him a curt nod. "Yes. We got it."

Naree slunk down into the hot water, bubbles rising and covering her skin. She breathed in the steam and closed her eyes, resting the back of her head against the cool edge of the tub. It was a smaller tub than the one at the villa, but it did the trick just as well. Though the villa had been comfortable and luxuriously pleasing, the penthouse apartment they'd gone to after escaping was just as cozy, even if it was only a portion of the size. Plus, it had a breathtaking view of the New Sudamapur city skyline.

She had to admit, the change of location was not as jarring as the change in Bhutano's host. When the police chief had collapsed before her eyes, she hadn't been sure Bhutano's spirit had transferred at all. It wasn't until the eyes of the amethyst mage had opened and she'd spoken that Naree could accept what had happened. It was strange listening to Bhutano's messages being said in Penny's voice, but once he'd laid out his plan for her and the dark mages, she had no doubt that it was really him.

She glanced over at the sink. Next to it, on the counter, lay the dagger. After bringing it back from the river, she'd washed it off and set it on the counter to dry, and then decided her body could use a good soaking as well.

You've done well, my love.

She ran her fingertips along her soapy skin and grinned at Kashmeru's words.

You're proving your worth.

"The comet's getting closer," she said. "It's almost time."

We'll soon be together and rule over our own new realm.

"Rule… together?" She was filled with a tingling warmth that brought tears to her eyes.

Yes, my love. We are so close.

EIGHT

Salina clutched the hairpin in her hand, staring into her cup of tea as she sat alone in the kitchen. The pin's sharp edge pinched the skin of her palm, but she didn't loosen her grip. The pain reminded her of the loss she hadn't had the proper time to mourn.

"Why are you sitting alone in the dark?"

Salina looked up to find Penny approaching the table from out of the shadows.

"The kettle's still hot if you'd like to join me," Salina said.

"Sounds perfect." Penny fetched a cup from the cupboard and picked out tea leaves from a canister. "Can't you sleep?"

Salina sighed. "I guess you could say silent ghosts are keeping me up."

"Ghosts?"

Salina opened her hand and placed the hairpin on the table. "Huojin. This was her hairpin. I found it within my things as I was getting ready for bed. It was just… there."

"You don't remember bringing it with you?" Penny watched her as she sipped her tea.

"Maybe absentmindedly. But tonight… I don't know. It was like it was speaking to me. Telling me to remember Huojin. To hang in there and fight this fight for her. Like she'd want me to."

"She meant a lot to you." It was more of a statement than a question.

"She was my best friend." Salina ran her fingers over the golden grooves of the pin.

"I don't really remember her that well," Penny said. "From our academy days. Tell me about how you became friends."

Salina shifted in her chair, a small smile forming on her lips. "Well, we were both in Golden House…"

Salina lowered her hand. She'd hit the target, just as her guru had instructed, but she couldn't help but compare her skills to her classmates. Was her fire not as bright as theirs? Slower somehow? She could have sworn a couple of the other golden mages had snickered when she'd taken her stance during her turn.

Her stomach roiled, but she refused to drop her head. After all, she wouldn't have been admitted to the academy if her skills weren't up to par.

"All right, class," their guru called. "That's all for today. Make sure you practice your small flames for next week's precision exam."

As they began to clear out of the training area, three of her classmates approached her.

"You're the new girl, right?" the only male of the three asked. He had light brown hair that stuck up in all directions. Salina suspected he was trying to make it look like fire.

"Yeah," Salina answered. She forced herself to stand tall, like her mother always told her to do. "Two weeks now."

The boy held out his hand. "I'm Ken."

"Yes, I know." Salina offered a small smile as she shook his hand. "You're the golden elite."

"You've been paying attention," Ken said with a smirk.

"I'm Salina."

"This is Lin and Cora." He tilted his head to each side to gesture toward them.

Lin and Cora, whom Salina realized were twins, gave Salina a half-nod mixed with a half-bow, which Salina returned.

"A bunch of us were going to meet up at the cemetery for a party tonight." Ken looked her up and down. "You up for it?"

"Um. The cemetery?" Salina crossed her arms. "Isn't that off-campus?"

Lin shrugged "And?"

"I thought we're not allowed off-campus after curfew."

"You got a problem with breaking curfew?" Cora raised a brow.

Salina was about to pass on the invitation, but part of her was flattered that the golden elite and his friends were inviting her to a party. To include her in their group. Maybe even to call her one of their own.

"No, no problem." Salina waved a dismissive hand, deciding to give in

to temptation. "I'll see you there."

"Great." Ken flashed a smile with his perfect teeth.

They parted ways, and Salina gathered her things to head back to her dorm.

She was filled with an excitement that made her tremble. She'd been so nervous coming to New United Asia without her family. Not a minute went by in which she hadn't longed to linq home and hear her parents' voices. She didn't want to dwell on how much she felt alone, but in the two weeks since she'd been at the Empire of the Lotus Academy, every day she faced made her feel like an outsider.

But now she had the opportunity to be part of something, to shed her outsider persona and actually feel like she belonged.

She hadn't brought much with her from Eritrea, but her mother had given her a couple of nice outfits for special occasions. She opted not to wear the dress. It seemed like a cemetery-party fashion faux pas. Picking out a vibrant blouse and a snug pair of black jeans, she set out to fix her hair and apply a little makeup. Using her golden mage powers, she carefully heated the tip of her kajal eyeliner and emphasized her golden-flecked brown eyes.

Her heart beating quickly, she checked out the final result in the mirror. She had to admit she looked like she could fit in with the popular kids. All she needed to do was slip on her boots, and she'd be ready to go.

She took long, deep breaths as she stepped out into the hallway. Glancing down the hall, she caught two girls from her house watching her and whispering. She ignored their giggles, forcing herself to walk past them. Who did they think they were anyway? She'd made new friends, and they were popular—one of them was the golden elite! Soon she would be the one laughing. She'd show them.

As she turned toward the stairwell, a hand suddenly wrapped around her arm. She turned in surprise to find a girl with big, dark eyes and silky, shoulder-length, black hair with bright pink streaks. There was no smile on her face, and for a second, Salina was worried about what the girl might say to her.

"Don't do it," the girl said.

"What?"

"The cemetery. It's a setup."

Salina narrowed her eyes. "What do you mean?"

"Ken and his lackeys. They like to prank the new kids. Get them in trouble by making them break curfew. You wouldn't be the first to fall for it."

"What?" Salina shook her head. "Why would they do that?"

"I guess some kids get bored."

Salina scoffed. "Playing with fire isn't enough for them?"

The girl let out a small laugh. "Right? I'm Huojin, by the way."

"I'm Salina."

"Nice to meet you." Huojin gave her a sideways look. "So listen. It's no party in the cemetery, but do you want to come hang out with me and my sister? Our parents just sent a care package, and I swear we've got, like, a million packs of chocolate-coated biscuit sticks, if you like those."

"I love those! Sure."

Huojin smiled and hooked her arm through Salina's. "Great."

"So you became fast friends after that?" Penny asked.

Salina's mind wandered for a moment as she was stirred from the memory. Thoughts of Huojin led to a reminder of their mission, their fight with the enemy, and the daggers. She blinked as she processed Penny's question.

"She basically took me under her wing. I was far from home, far from family, and Huojin made it a lot easier to adapt."

"Whatever happened to Ken and his gang?"

"They got busted for tricking another newbie. Detention for weeks." Salina let out a laugh. "I was always grateful to Huojin for saving me. Not just from detention—though that would have been a terrible way to begin my studies, with that black mark on my academy records. But I was grateful that she took me in and showed me there are still decent people in the world."

"Yes." Penny sipped her tea before she continued. "There certainly are those who will fall on either side of the blade of decency. It's good to know on which side the people in our lives fall."

NINE

enny wasn't sure how much more of this she could take. Every fake conversation Bhutano was forcing her to make, every manipulative act he made her do, felt as if it were damaging her heart.

She sat at the dining room table, joining the others for dinner, but it wasn't her who controlled her movements. As Bhutano made her look around and greet her allies, Penny was begging for someone to realize it wasn't really her.

Please. Somebody. You have to see it's an imposter. It's not me!

"Karina, how are you?" Mayhara asked.

Bhutano followed Mayhara's line of vision and Penny watched Karina approach the table.

Karina! Please. There must be something in your witch magic that makes it possible to hear me.

"I'm doing better," Karina said. "Thank you."

"This looks delicious, Mr. Kitaro," Salina said, serving herself a bowl of Agedashi tofu in black pepper broth.

"I can't take all the credit." Mr. Kitaro gave Shiro a wink. "Shiro made the green tea rice."

"It all smells amazing." Salina gave Shiro a nod.

Salina! Your dagger is not safe. Bhutano has told Naree where it is. They're going after it as we speak!

"Save some for me," Bhutano said with Penny's voice, adding a convincing laugh as he took the serving spoon from Salina.

Please. You're all in danger. They've already got Shiro's dagger. Somebody, please hear me!

Her frustration built up inside her. She felt as if she were going to explode. She needed to take control of her body back.

In that moment, Bhutano knocked a fork off the table. Penny gasped internally. She had done that. She'd been trying to grab the reins and take control, and in some miniscule moment, she'd been able to move her own hand.

"Sorry about that," Bhutano said in her voice. "I guess I'm a little clumsy tonight."

It's possible, she said to herself. *I don't know how, but it's possible.*

But try as she might, she couldn't manage to do it again. She knew Bhutano was aware of what she was doing and was fighting against her. She had to find another moment where he was more vulnerable to her persuasion.

I won't give up. I need to keep trying.

TEN

The small church sat high on a hill, the cherry blossom trees surrounding it littered with falling petals. It was almost noon, and the place was practically empty.

Naree climbed the stone steps to the building's open double doors. Peering inside, she gave a nod, signaling for Avi and Ru to follow. She removed her sunglasses and pushed back the scarf covering her hair, scanning the rows of pews and the altar. A handful of people in prayer were spread out throughout the building. The altar was vacant, the lights above it out.

Naree moved silently through the church, both to remain unnoticed and also to not disturb the praying patrons. The dark mages followed, their footsteps undetectable to Naree's ears. They made their way past the altar and turned down a passage that led to a set of stairs.

The stairwell led downward, and only a single wall sconce lit the way. Reaching the bottom of the stairs, Naree found herself in a dark chamber. The only beacon of light in the dismal room was from a long, wooden votive candle stand upon which sat rows and rows of small red candles. Each row was elevated behind the first. Only about two dozen of what must have been over a hundred candles were lit here and there, but in the rear row, in the center, were a cluster of seven lit candles. Their flames seemed higher and brighter than the others.

"This is it," Naree said.

"How do you know?" Ru asked.

Naree reached for the candles. "It's exactly how Bhutano described it from the golden elite's mind."

As her hands got closer to move the candles, the flames grew hotter and more intense. She narrowed her eyes and withdrew her hands. "Hmm."

"What is it?" Avi asked.

"Bhutano said they have a witch working with them."

"The witch Kun poisoned?" Ru scoffed. "I'm surprised she's still alive."

"No. It's another witch," Naree replied. "Her granddaughter. I think she helped the golden elite hide this dagger. There seems to be some kind of spell to protect the hiding place with fire."

Avi studied the votive shelf. "You sure you can't just blow them out?"

"No." Naree didn't look at him as she shook her head. "That won't work. But it's fine. I'm known to have powers of my own that might help."

She raised her hands, her palms glowing a bright gold. Concentrating on pulling the fire away, she moved closer, inch by inch. The flames stretched from their wicks to her palms, flickering as her powers sucked away the heat. As the last of the flames disappeared into a tendril of smoke, Ru and Avi reached for the candles and moved them off the shelf.

"There's a latch," Avi said.

Naree bent closer and pulled on the latch, which opened a hidden compartment. The corners of her mouth tugged upward. They'd found another dagger. Her heart sped up, and there was a slight tremble in her hands as she removed it from its hiding place.

Bhutano's plan was actually working.

ELEVEN

Mayhara wandered into Mr. Kitaro's office to find Jae studying something on the screen. Jae glanced up as she continued toward the desk. Her eyes flit around the monitor, narrowing as she tried to figure out what he was working out. He could tell she'd recently showered; the smell of her jasmine shampoo wafted around him like a gentle caress. He forced himself not to think about it.

"It's the Baha'i Lotus Temple," he said before she had a chance to ask. "A blueprint of it, anyway. And an old one—before they started renovating it."

Her focus moved from the screen to Jae's face. For a moment, their eyes locked, and Jae felt his pulse quicken. His hopes for a reconciliation elevated when she didn't back off right away. He took a deep breath—a delicious whiff of jasmine scent along with it—and in his mind, he would be perfectly satisfied if the moment were to last beyond minutes, hours, or even days. When she finally took a step back, he released the breath but kept his eyes poised on her.

"What's the plan?" she asked as she settled in the chair across from him.

"I'm preparing for a worst-case scenario."

"Oh? Has it come to that?"

Before he could answer, two more figures appeared at the door. Jae shifted in his chair as Yuki and Loni entered the office. There was a split second of a warning look to Jae from Yuki when she caught sight of Mayhara sitting across from him. He read her expression loud and clear: *Be careful what you say.* She'd already warned Jae about Loni's vulnerable state. Loni had made her feelings for Jae clear, so finding him with Mayhara was sure to stir up jealousy in her. And with Loni's drug addiction looming in the background, Jae only hoped that Yuki's diamond mage powers were keeping Loni grounded.

"What's going on?" Yuki asked. "I feel like we're waiting for the other shoe to drop."

Mayhara gestured to Jae. "Jae was just about to reveal his big, worst-case scenario plan."

"Well," Loni said, leaning back against a cabinet. "Let's hear it."

Jae turned the monitor so they all could see. "Well, it's not a solid plan yet."

"We're all here to help," Mayhara put in.

"What is that?" Loni asked, narrowing her eyes at the screen.

Yuki took a step closer. "Looks like the Lotus temple in New Delhi."

Mayhara and Loni gave her a bemused look.

Yuki shrugged. "I had to do a paper on it, back at the academy. I wish I could have seen it before it closed for renovations."

"What's happening at the temple?" Loni leaned forward to get a better look. "Aside from the comet welcoming ceremony. What are they calling that again?"

"The Akutake Festival." Jae rubbed one of his brows. "Darshana believes Kashmeru is buried in the temple."

"What?" Yuki's forehead scrunched up. "Where exactly?"

"Where *exactly*, we're not sure," Jae replied.

"Well, he's said to be in a tomb." Mayhara gave her earlobe a scratch. "Are there sublevels to the building?"

"Yes." Jae clicked around on windows on the screen. "But I can't find anything that might resemble an area that could contain a tomb."

"Hidden, then." Yuki stuck her hands in her pockets. "Somewhere not apparent on the blueprints."

"So, what do you mean by 'worst-case?'" Loni asked. "I'm a little confused."

Jae stretched his neck out, uncomfortable with the theory he was about to explain. "Darshana and I were wondering if it were possible for the Pishacha to have figured out a way to release Kashmeru from his tomb without the daggers."

"No." Mayhara slowly shook her head. "It's not possible. The legend says so. The blood of the Lotus."

"But it doesn't say anything in particular regarding the daggers." Jae scoffed. "We didn't even know about them until the Sacred Keys started getting killed. The Pishacha have the grimoire with the spell to unlock the tomb. They have my si—They have the Lotus. Acquiring her blood could still be accomplished without the daggers, speaking practically."

"Practicality has nothing to do with it," Loni said. "This is legend and magic we're dealing with. Why did they go through all the trouble of hunting down the daggers if they didn't need them?"

Jae rubbed at the space between his nose and his upper lip. "I asked myself the same questions. But… But let's say they do it. Somehow. Let's say they find a way. What do we do?"

"We'll need to stop them," Yuki replied. She glanced once more at the blueprints on the screen. "So we're planning an ambush."

"The small scroll." Mayhara's voice was soft, as if she were still thinking it over. "We need to get it open so we can use the spell to destroy Kashmeru if they manage to set him free."

"No." Loni shook her head. "Why are we waiting? Why don't we attack now? Destroy the tomb with Kashmeru inside before the Pishacha get a chance to release him. Strike before the comet takes away all our powers."

"No." Mayhara didn't look at Loni. Instead, her eyes were far away, obviously playing out the scenario in her head. "I don't think that will work. We won't be able to get in. That place is going to be locked up tight until the night of the festival."

"We could figure out how to get in," Loni insisted.

Jae looked between the two of them and sat back in his chair. "No, Loni. Mayhara is right."

All three women stared at him, and he knew it was for different reasons. Mayhara's stare, with her slightly raised brow and parted lips, told him she was pleased that he'd agreed with her. After not taking her side in the last dispute between her and Loni, Jae was relieved that he could justifiably defend Mayhara's views.

Loni's look of shock was most definitely because he disagreed with her, and Yuki's was probably more a look of fear at how Loni might react.

"It's heavily guarded," Jae continued. "And if we're right, and they plan to release Kashmeru next week when the comet arrives, they'll have made it impossible to get to. And even if we were to miraculously find a way in, destroying his tomb doesn't mean we'd be destroying Kashmeru. I doubt it's as easy as that to kill a god."

Loni narrowed her eyes at him, her jaw squared.

Jae turned to Mayhara, who lifted her chin as if she were claiming a victory.

"But the night of the Akutake Festival," Jae continued, "the doors will be open."

Yuki crossed her arms. "It's invitation only, though. Government officials. All the higher-ups."

"It'll be catered." Jae waved a hand through the air. "That's our way in."

Loni worried her lip. "We pretend to be staff and sneak off to look for the tomb?"

"Yes." Jae gestured at the monitor. "Which is why I've got the blueprints pulled up. Hopefully, the renovations haven't changed the layout too much. We'll make a plan now so we know where to start looking. We've got three things working in our favor: We've got all the daggers, we've got presumably the most powerful witch in New United Asia, and we've got the small scroll with the spell to destroy Kashmeru."

"I'd say the priority would be to stop them before they release him at all," Mayhara said.

"Yes." Jae splayed his fingers out on the desk. "Especially if it means his return could kill my sister."

"But the spell…" Loni's words faded. She closed her mouth tight and her face went pale.

"What about the spell?" Jae furrowed his brow.

"The one that will destroy Kashmeru." Loni visibly swallowed. "Did no one tell you? Your sister is bonded to him. If we destroy him, and she hasn't already died from the blood sacrifice, we'll most likely kill her as well."

TWELVE

Loni was avoiding Jae. After she'd dropped the news about the spell like a bomb in his lap, she couldn't look him in the eye any longer. She hated being the one to have told him about how the spell could destroy his sister, but on the other hand, he had the right to know.

But that wasn't the only reason she needed to leave the room; every time Jae looked at Mayhara, she could practically feel his adoration for her seeping from his pores. It sickened her. It crushed her heart and created a vacuum in her chest that sucked at her very soul.

Her hands shook, and she felt she couldn't breathe. It was too hot to stay indoors. Or, at least, it felt that way. She pulled the collar of her blouse away from her skin, stretching her neck in an attempt to get more air.

Stepping onto the porch, she raked her fingers through her hair. Her body ached for a hit of Moxy. It was the only thing that could possibly ease the torment she was going through. But she was stuck in the middle of nowhere, empty-handed. Dry. She had no choice but to push through the cravings. Push through the withdrawal.

She paced, concentrating on her breathing. She told herself that each breath was taking her one step closer to getting through this episode. The acid roiling in her stomach made her cringe, but she closed her eyes and ignored the bitter taste in her mouth, as if turning off her attention to the drug's call. Shaking out her hands to rid herself of the trembling, she blew out a hard breath, begging the ache to leave her system.

"Are you all right?"

Loni opened her eyes and spun around to find Penny watching her. She cleared her throat and wrapped her arms around her middle. "Fine. I'm fine."

Penny tilted her head. "You know me better than to think I'll buy that."

Loni's head dropped. She held back the urge to sob. "I don't know if I'm going to make it through this without breaking."

"Is there anything I can do?"

"No." Loni held her palms against her cheeks. "I'm afraid it's up to me to fight my own demons."

"Did something happen?"

Loni shook her head, though it was a symbol of her frustration rather than an answer to Penny's question. "It's… Jae, mostly. I don't know why I can't get over him. What's wrong with me?"

Penny smiled. "Nothing. Magic powers or not, you're human. And your heart—I mean, when you open your heart, you open it completely. So there's no wonder you can get easily hurt."

"Yeah, it's, uh, one of those stupid emerald mage curses, the heart thing."

Penny let out a small laugh. "I know. And I can't blame you for being hung up on him. There was a time you two were inseparable."

Loni dropped her head, her gaze lost in a memory.

Her hair was soaking wet, sticking to her face, but she didn't care. Her hand was safe and warm in Jae's, and their pursuers hadn't been able to keep up. They ducked into the back of the small abandoned delivery truck they'd been staying in the past couple of days and crept onto the old, itchy throw rug Jae had salvaged from the dumpster outside a furniture store. It wasn't the perfect place to stay—or the safest, by any means—and a funny smell lived in the floor, but it was dry and kept them hidden from the Imperial Police. Temporarily, at least.

Jae set the bag of food they'd stolen between them and smiled at Loni. "Dinner is served."

"What do you think it is?" Loni asked with a big grin.

"Smells like eggrolls."

Loni wagged her brows at him as she peeked inside the bag. "Winner, winner, eggroll dinner."

She practically tore the bag open as she grabbed an eggroll. Jae let out a laugh as he took one for himself.

"Thanks for this," she said between bites.

"I didn't do it alone."

"No, I know. But I know you don't like stealing."

He lowered his gaze and nodded. "That's true. But this was a life-or-death situation. We haven't had a bite to eat in two days."

"Still, thank you." She held her half-eaten eggroll up. "To the better half of the team."

"Oh, I wouldn't say that." He tapped the end of his eggroll against hers. "You can be pretty amazing yourself."

She blushed as his eyes traveled over her face. The blush was warm enough to make her temporarily forget about the cold, wet night outside their truck bed sanctuary. She didn't care about any of that. As long as she was with Jae, she knew she could withstand much worse.

"What's the saying? That which doesn't kill us…?"

Penny came closer and placed a hand on Loni's arm. "It's true, though. Especially with you. You're one of the strongest people I know."

Loni offered her a small smile. Her mind wandered for a second, scenes flashing in her head of how far she'd come, her situation now with Jae, the struggle against Kashmeru, and the need to keep the daggers away from the enemy. "It doesn't feel that way. But thanks."

Penny's words seemed to have helped the trembling subside. Maybe Loni didn't need Moxy as much as she thought she did when she had such a caring friend to lift her up when she was down.

THIRTEEN

The moon was hidden behind looming clouds, making the area dark and difficult to navigate. Naree approached the hidden cave Bhutano had described. No, not a cave. A tunnel. A hollowed-out passage in the small mountain. It could have served as an underpass if any vehicles found themselves in the area. But it was highly unlikely any would, because the property was hidden away in the middle of nowhere.

It was part of the land owned by the Sacred Key the elite mages were staying with. Naree couldn't see the house from where she and her two dark mage companions were standing, but she felt a pull to investigate it.

After we find the dagger, she told herself.

Rikuto and Kun—the metal manipulator and the poisoner—came up beside her as she stopped at the entrance of the tunnel. In the vacuum of the tunnel, the mountain winds whistled and hummed. Naree felt as if the tunnel were singing her an eerie welcome song. A shiver ran up and down her spine as she scanned the curves inside of the space, searching for the spot the emerald elite had hidden the dagger.

She spread out her fingers and tugged at her own emerald powers. Playing with the wind, she guided the breeze over the inside surface of the tunnel. The tone of the whistle changed at one point. Naree moved the air back and forth over the bricks at the targeted spot a few times, narrowing in on the difference in sound.

"It's there," she said.

Rikuto stepped forward and blasted the surface with dark elemental powers. The black particles he released caused the clay and bricks to crumble, breaking away from the tunnel's inner arch. There was a loud *clunk* as the dagger broke free from its spot and dropped to the ground.

"Clever," Kun said.

Naree ignored him and bent to retrieve the dagger.

We're getting closer, my love.

Naree shivered at the sound of Kashmeru's voice.

It won't be long now.

A warm sensation filled her. She stood and faced the dark mages. "Let's go."

There was almost a skip in her step as they headed back the way they had come. Something guided her closer to the house, and her heartbeat grew stronger when she realized Jae was leaning on the railing of the porch. He was a good distance away, but she could tell it was him, even in the faint glow of the porch light. Without explaining what she was doing, she wandered closer to the house but kept hidden in the shadows of the trees.

And then suddenly, she couldn't get closer.

Her brows were drawn together when her body stopped. Something blocked her. She was unable to get past an invisible wall.

"What the—?" Rikuto pressed his body against the invisible barrier but was unsuccessful in his efforts to move past it.

"It's a protection spell," Naree said. "Probably cast to keep out those will ill intent." She held out her hands and threw every element of magic she had at the barrier, but she couldn't break through.

As the dark mages tried with their powers, Naree glanced at Jae, checking to see if he'd spotted them, but he was facing in the other direction.

"Don't," she said, placing her hands on each of the dark mage's shoulders. "Stop."

The dark mages flashed her curious looks as they dropped their hands.

"Bhutano wouldn't want us to mess up his plan." Naree gestured toward the road with her head. "We've got the dagger. Let's head back and wait for further instructions."

Rikuto and Kun nodded in agreement and joined her as they left the property.

Naree threw one last glance over her shoulder, a strange ache in her chest as she moved farther away from her brother.

FOURTEEN

The mages were gathered in the main room, watching the news coverage of Police Chief Min's funeral. Shiro sat beside Loni, who bit her nails as her leg bounced. Something told him her mannerism wasn't because of the funeral, but because of something else entirely. On his other side was Salina, who sat so still, he wasn't sure if she was breathing. Her hands were clasped together tightly and held between her knees. He wondered if she was thinking about Huojin and how she'd never had a funeral. Shiro shifted in his seat and looked back at the televiewer.

The newscaster droned on about the police chief's career, his accolades, and accomplishments. When she mentioned his leadership in the Eradication, Shiro wasn't the only one to squirm in his seat.

The screen showed a wide drone shot of the cemetery, slowly zooming in to the shiny coffin holding Min's body. The coffin was covered in poppies and stood above ground, ready to be mechanically lowered into the grave. It was surrounded by a large crowd of people, mostly police officers and government officials. Standing beside Min's family were Director Shei and Governor Laghari. Director Shei's silky, black hair was pulled into an impossibly perfect bun, and not a wrinkle could be seen on her form-fitting, high-collared dress. Her mouth was in the straightest of lines as she kept her eyes trained on the ground. Governor Laghari wore a suit that screamed of expensive taste. His hair was slicked back as always, and his brows were plunged downward as if in deep thought.

In the row behind them, two young faces caught Shiro's attention. Ru—the daughter of Director Shei, and Avi—the governor's son, both of whom the elite mages knew of as two of the Pishacha's secret weapons. Dark mages. Shiro almost remarked on how inappropriate it was that dark mages were attending the police chief's funeral, but then it occurred to him that everyone at the cemetery was probably on the side of the enemy. They were all in on it. All cheerleaders for the dark god.

"… that with all the preparations for the Akutake Festival, a new police chief has yet to be assigned. Governor Laghari has stated that the position will be appointed in the days following the festival."

Jae scoffed. "Because Laghari thinks Kashmeru will have risen by then, and things like the Imperial Police won't be necessary anymore."

"They'll all be part of Kashmeru's army," Shiro added. "In the new beginning. The new world."

"New worlds?" Yuki asked.

"I heard some guards talking about it when I was in the prison camp." Shiro leaned forward and set his elbows on his knees. "Kashmeru's followers believe this world we live in will end when he is released from his tomb. The Pishacha and everyone else who worships him would be delivered unto a new realm he'll have created, and everyone who is against him will perish in this world."

"Is that why this comet event at the Lotus temple is invite only?" Salina asked.

"That's precisely why." Mr. Kitaro made his way to the center of the room, his hands planted in his pockets. "This world, the universe, it will all be destroyed as punishment for his incarceration in his tomb. Plus, the centuries he had to wait for Lakshmi to give him her heart. When it is destroyed, everyone will perish. But Kashmeru, having been released from his tomb, untethered because of the blood of the Lotus, will reward his faithful followers by granting them a resurrected life in his newly created world. That includes his love, Lakshmi, who will have made the biggest sacrifice. She will be reunited with him at last, and together they will rule as sovereigns over the new era."

Mayhara shook her head. "That's… I don't even know the right words to describe it."

"Hard to swallow?" Loni put in.

"What kind of world is that supposed to be?" Yuki tucked her hair behind her ears. "Ruled by a dark god. Living under a cruel leader."

"It would be madness," Salina said, staring down at her hands.

"They're foolish to want that," Shiro added.

"And the Lotus at his side?" Salina narrowed her eyes. "What does that mean? That she would succumb to his darkness and lose her sense of right? Of light and purity?"

Jae worried his lip, undoubtedly thinking of his sister.

"It's scary to imagine," Mayhara said.

Shiro glanced around. When his gaze landed on Penny, he realized she'd been tight-lipped the whole time. Maybe she'd seen something about the future with her amethyst vision she wasn't sharing with the group. He was about to question her when Darshana gasped.

He followed her gaze to the televiewer, where chaos was breaking out. It took a second before Shiro could wrap his head around what was happening.

Near Min's coffin, a small crowd was huddled at the ground. Around them, panic ensued. Imperial Police had their weapons drawn, some of the officers running off in one direction, as if pursuing something or someone, but all of them with looks of confusion on their faces.

"I repeat, Director Shei appears to have been the target in an obvious assassination attempt. We cannot, at this time, confirm if she has been critically wounded. All we know is some sort of projectile struck Director Shei in the neck, at which point she immediately dropped to the ground and was swarmed by her concerned family, as well as by Governor Laghari and his wife. No one seems to understand how this happened. There is no word yet on the source of this attack or the motivation behind it. This was certainly a senseless and cruel assault on an already somber occasion. We are told medics have been contacted and are on the way, but judging by the lack of movement and the grim faces of those surrounding her, it may already be too late to save the director."

Shiro covered his mouth with his hand and stood to pace. He just barely made out what the others in the room were saying.

"Oh my gods!"

"It must be the extremists."

"Who would attack at a funeral?"

"Do you think she's really dead?"

Shiro's gut twisted. He knew it had to be Qiang or one of his gang members. He raked his fingers through his hair, his neck and cheeks burning hot, and turned back to face the screen. If it was Qiang, he was in danger. If he were to be found, the Imperial Police would surely shoot him on sight.

He quickly pulled out his Linq and furiously typed a message to Qiang: *Call me. Please.*

The camera zoomed in as the crowd around Director Shei's body slowly dispersed. Shiro's eyes landed on Ru—Shei's daughter—who held her mother's limp arm in her lap, blood soaking them both. Ru's eyes were red and full of rage as she screamed and sobbed. Avi's hands were on Ru's shoulders, trying to calm her down.

Shiro's attention was glued to the televiewer, his anxiety at its peak as he waited for word of the attacker's capture. He constantly checked his Linq screen, but it didn't light up with any message. After several minutes, it was announced that no suspect could be found at this time, but the Imperial Police were calling in backup to investigate further.

As medics confirmed Director Shei's death, the cameras focused in on her daughter. Shiro swallowed hard as Ru flared her nostrils. Her tears mixed with her dark eye makeup, causing black streams to flow down her cheeks. Her straight, black hair framed her tense face as she turned toward one camera. Her jaw was clenched, and her chest heaved as her breaths came hard. And her glare was filled with the promise of vengeance.

FIFTEEN

Mayhara held her arms out from her sides and pushed out her crimson energy. For a moment, nothing happened. She gritted her teeth in frustration but kept pushing. She was the elite crimson mage. This was her calling, her purpose. She had to believe that she would have control of her powers when the time came to use them. There was no way it was destiny's plan that the comet that empowered Kashmeru's rise would also strip the good guys of their powers.

She adjusted her stance and took a few calming breaths. A breeze blew her hair back from her face. She could do this. She had to.

Running her fingers over her wristband and feeling the smooth surface of the garnet stone, she reached deep down inside herself and pulled up all the confidence she could muster. With the next breath she took, she held her hands out, palms facing the ground, and told herself it would work. The red glow in her hands felt warm. Repeating to herself that she could do it, she pushed out her powers, demanding the crimson elements that flowed from her palms to work with the earth.

The ground began to tremble, tiny pebbles bouncing along the surface of the soil. A feeling of gratification filled her, and she raised her hands. A cloud of dirt and debris rose from the ground like a fog and swirled around her. Faster and faster until her smile turned into laughter.

"That's impressive," came a voice.

All at once, the swirling cloud stopped and the dirt dropped. Mayhara swung around to find Penny approaching.

"Sorry," Penny said, closing the distance between them. "I didn't mean to scare you. I see you've got your powers under control."

"Well, it's taking more effort than it's supposed to. Which makes me very uncomfortable."

"I get a feeling that's not the only thing that's been making you uncomfortable lately."

"What do you mean?"

Penny smirked. "I know we've all been focusing on the war against the Pishacha, but we'd have to be pretty oblivious not to have noticed the tension between you and Jae."

"Oh." Mayhara pursed her lips. "That."

Penny didn't push, and Mayhara relaxed a little.

"Yeah." Mayhara gave her a small shrug. "I don't know what's going on there."

"I thought the two of you were a hot item. I mean, I know he and Loni have history, but I see the way he looks at you."

Mayhara felt heat bloom in her cheeks. She also felt strange that Penny—who was apparently a close friend of Loni's—sounded like she was rooting for Jae choosing her instead of Loni. "It doesn't matter. We're not really in a position to worry about relationships at the moment. We've kind of got bigger fish to fry."

Penny tilted her head. "Yeah. But, I mean, what are we doing all this for? When you think about it, we're fighting for all the things that make life worth living. Isn't *love* one of those things?"

Mayhara swallowed. *Love?* Was that what this thing was between her and Jae? She couldn't be sure. She only knew she'd never felt the way she felt about Jae with anyone else.

She looked up to find Penny studying her. For a moment, it looked like Penny was annoyed.

"Is everything all right?" Mayhara asked her.

Penny blinked and her frown disappeared. "Yeah. Sure." She cleared her throat. "Hey, tell me about your family. They're in the prison camps, right?"

Mayhara's brows pulled together from the quick subject change. "Um, yeah. My parents and my sisters."

"You must be really worried about them."

"I am." Mayhara crossed her arms over her chest. "But Darshana somehow got them moved under fake names so they couldn't be tied to me."

"Moved out of the prison camps?"

"No. Darshana couldn't manage that. She just arranged for them to be placed in a more low-key location. I don't even know which camp they're in."

Penny gave her a nod, but her gaze seemed far away.

"Why do you ask?"

Penny seemed to snap from her thoughts. "Oh, I'm just... I wanted to catch up with everyone and, you know, get to know you better. Understand your struggles."

"Oh. Okay. That's nice."

"Were your sisters at the academy too?" Penny suddenly asked.

Mayhara felt like her head was spinning, trying to keep up with Penny's train of thought. "Um, no. They were too young at the time. But my younger sister Kakoli would have started last year if the academy had still been open. I think she would have really enjoyed it. She's a bit of a showoff. I just hope she's not drawing attention to herself in the camps. For her own safety."

"If she's as level-headed as you, I'm sure she's lying low." Penny let out what sounded like a defeated sigh. "Well, I'll let you get back to training. Keep up the good work."

"Thanks." Mayhara watched as Penny turned and walked back toward the house, puzzled by her odd behavior. She wondered if something more had happened while Penny had been abducted. Something Penny wasn't ready to share with the rest of them.

Bhutano checked to make sure no one was around as he pulled out the Linq and pushed the button to contact Naree. The reflection in the window startled him for a second when he found Penny's eyes staring back at him. He pushed her hair away from her face and turned away from the window.

"Bhutano?"

"Hello."

"What's wrong?" Naree asked. "You sound troubled."

"I'm hitting a wall with the crimson elite. I can't seem to crack into her mind to find the dagger."

"Do you think it's because of the comet's influence on the amethyst mage's powers?"

"No. I don't think so. Her defenses are strong. She's got some thick walls up. I just need more time."

"What about the others? The diamond or… sapphire?"

Bhutano's eyes narrowed when Naree had hesitated before referencing her brother. "I think I'll try the Sacred Key first. I have a feeling he'll be easier to wear down."

"All right. Um, Bhutano?"

"Yes, Your Highness?"

"When we were last on the property… There was a moment where we came near the house, and there was a point where we couldn't come any closer."

"What do you mean?"

"It was a protection spell, I think. You said they have a witch."

Though she couldn't see him, he nodded. "They do."

"She must have cast a spell to protect the house. We could only get so far before we hit a barrier."

"Strange." Bhutano rubbed at Penny's chin. "I guess I was able to get through because I'm in the amethyst's body." Bhutano stood straighter. "Wait. Why were you coming close to the house?"

Naree was quiet for a moment. "No reason. Curiosity, perhaps."

"Don't do it again. We're getting far, but we can't afford to mess up this mission."

Again, silence filled the seconds. "Yes, I understand."

"I'll contact you when I find out where the next dagger is hidden. Until then, stick to the plan."

SIXTEEN

Mr. Kitaro handed the small scroll back to Karina. He scrubbed at his face as if trying to scrub away his frown. "I don't think we can risk melting the gold without damaging the scroll itself."

Karina bit the inside of her cheek. "So you think only magic will open it."

It wasn't a question, but Mr. Kitaro nodded anyway. "I'm sure that whatever witch spelled it shut meant for it to only be opened by another witch. Hence: Magic."

"I figured you'd say that." Karina sighed. "I guess I was just hoping for a Hail Mary or something. But deep down, I knew it was going to have to be magic."

A figure appeared in the doorway of Mr. Kitaro's room. "*What's* going to have to be magic?"

Mr. Kitaro tucked his hands behind his back. "Ah, Penny. How are you feeling?"

"I'm fine." Penny offered him a small smile. "Thanks for asking. What, uh, were you two talking about? If you don't mind me asking, that is."

"The small scroll," Mr. Kitaro answered.

"We still can't figure out how to open it," Karina added.

Penny's brow furrowed. "What scroll?"

Karina and Mr. Kitaro exchanged a look.

"My dear." Mr. Kitaro shook his head. "Did no one fill you in on the scroll Jae and Mayhara took from the grimoire?"

The color seemed to drain from Penny's face. Her jaw dropped open as Karina held the scroll out for Penny to see.

"I can't believe we didn't tell you," Karina said. "You were still trapped by the Pishacha when Jae and Mayhara brought it back. With all the chaos and my grandmother's funeral, news about the scroll slipped through the cracks."

Penny's eyes were still on the scroll. "What do you mean *from* the grimoire?"

"It was hidden in the spine," Karina told her. "Mayhara managed to take it out before the dark mages stole the grimoire from the Bhaja Caves."

"What… What is it? What's it for?" Penny blinked rapidly as she pushed her hair out of her face.

Karina rolled the scroll in her hands. "Before my grandmother died, she said she got a message from our ancestors. The scroll apparently contains a spell that will destroy Kashmeru. Forever."

Penny flinched and swallowed hard. "What? I've never heard of such a thing. Are you… Are you sure?"

"Well, there's no way of telling for sure if anything's in here at all." Karina tapped the scroll against her palm. "Since we can't get it open."

"Okay." Penny nodded slowly, taking it all in. "So that's what you were talking about when you said it was going to take magic."

"Yes. But there's one more thing you probably should know." Karina pursed her lips and glanced at Mr. Kitaro.

"The spell," he said, "won't destroy only the dark god. Because the two deities are linked, it's believed the spell will destroy the Lotus as well."

Penny seemed to only be able to stare at Mr. Kitaro in disbelief. He took a step back and waited, giving her a minute to absorb the information.

"Right," Penny finally said. "Well, we don't want that."

"But if I could take a look at the spell," Karina said, "then I could make sure. Or maybe I could find a loophole."

Penny narrowed her eyes. "Good idea."

"But first, I'd need to open it." Karina turned toward the door. "Which I'm determined to figure out."

She gave them a curt wave before she left the room. Penny could only stare after her.

"We were pretty stunned when we found out as well." Mr. Kitaro gave Penny an apologetic nod. "I'm sorry it took us so long to realize you weren't briefed on the whole situation. I thought for sure one of the others had already told you."

He placed a hand on her shoulder.

Penny turned to him. Though her smile seemed forced, her eyes seemed more in the present than they had been moments before. "I understand. I'm sure the others thought the same. So, um, did you not know about any of this? I mean, wasn't that something you learned as a Sacred Key?"

"No." Mr. Kitaro straightened his shirt. "There are still many mysteries associated with the legend. I had to learn a lot before I was handed the responsibility of protecting the dagger, but I have to be honest, a lot of what's come to light in the last couple of months is brand new information."

"I see."

"I'm surprised you didn't."

"Didn't what?"

"See." Mr. Kitaro gave her a wink. "Amethyst insight powers and all."

"Oh." She let out a small laugh. "It doesn't always work like that. And who knows? Maybe the comet's blocking my *vision*."

"Perhaps."

"And what about the concept of the new world Shiro talked about?"

"Are you asking if I heard of the theory when I became a Sacred Key?"

"Yes." Penny went to a nearby chair and sat down, crossing her legs. "What did you learn about it?"

"Throughout the centuries, there have been many theories of how Kashmeru's revenge would unfold. And yes, one of them was the idea that he would create a new realm in which to exist, a new world of his creation governed by his rules."

Penny studied his face. "Do you think it could be true?"

"I truly hope never to find out. Kashmeru needs to be stopped before destruction of *this* world ensues."

"But what if they're right?"

Mr. Kitaro's brows scrunched together. He shook his head. "If the worst happens, and Kashmeru triumphs, it's not a world I would want to be part of."

Naree glanced at the screen of her Linq and stepped out onto the balcony to answer it. "Bhutano?"

"I have good news and bad news," came the reply.

It was a female voice, but Naree knew it was really Bhutano. It had taken her a while to get used to hearing him speaking with Penny's vocal cords.

"Let's have them, then," Naree said.

"I know where the next dagger is hidden."

Naree relaxed her shoulders a little. "Great."

"But the bad news is you won't be able to get to it. It's in the house. And because of the protection spell, it's off-limits to you."

"What's the plan, then?"

"There is an opportunity coming up when everyone should be out of the house. The meteor shower. The guru has a theory she wants to try out with the mages, something that has to do with the comet. Anyway, there's a hilltop on the property where we're all going to test this theory out the night of the meteor shower, and when we all head up there, I'll find an excuse to come back early and get the dagger then."

Naree nibbled on her pinky nail. "Are you sure you won't get caught? They could get suspicious if you slip away."

"I'll try to be convincing. They have no reason to suspect me of anything. I'm their very good friend Penny." Bhutano cleared his—or rather, Penny's—throat. "There's one more thing. When the grimoire was stolen, the elite mages took something that was hidden in the spine."

"Hidden?" Naree grabbed the strands of hair that were blowing in her face from the wind. "What was it?"

"It's a problem."

"Bhutano, come on."

"It's a small scroll. Miniature."

"I guess it would have to be to have been hidden in a book spine." She turned and headed back inside. "What's in the scroll?"

As he told her the scroll's purpose and how it could mean her death, her skin became prickly and her stomach twisted in the tightest knot. Her mind felt as if it were being smothered in a thick, wet, itchy blanket.

"They won't use the spell," she insisted.

"How do you know?"

She hesitated. "Jae-hyun would never do anything to harm me, much less kill me."

"I think you might be underestimating your brother."

Naree raked her fingers through her hair, unable to fathom that Jae would simply sacrifice her to win the war. "So you plan to steal the scroll as well?"

"Yes. I've spoken to Kashmeru, and we agree that it's imperative. We don't want them having any advantage over us. We must do whatever it takes."

SEVENTEEN

Shiro's breath left him for a long moment when Qian's name flashed on his Linq's screen. He couldn't push the button to accept the call fast enough.

"Qiang?"

"Shiro, I'm glad I caught you."

Shiro expelled a breath of relief. "Where are you? Are you all right?" They weren't even half the questions Shiro wanted the answers for, but he could hardly hear past his heart thumping in his ears.

"I'm all right." Qiang was quiet for a moment. "As for where I am, I probably shouldn't say, just in case someone is listening."

Though Qiang couldn't see him, Shiro nodded. "All right. As long as you're okay. You can't imagine how tense I've been wondering if you've been captured by the Imperial Police."

"I take it you saw the funeral."

Shiro opened his mouth and then shut it again. He wanted so much to ask him if he was the one who'd killed Director Shei, but he wasn't sure if he could do it. It wasn't a defensive move or something done to save someone's life. It was a full-on attack. And Shiro didn't know if he could accept Qiang point-blank murdering someone. A part of him knew it wasn't the first murder Qiang could be involved in. There were bound to be fatalities in the bombings and vicious attacks the extremists had been responsible for. But there was something more personal in targeting Director Shei. Something more direct in killing just one person in a moment of innocence.

"I did," Shiro said. "I saw it."

There was silence again, and somehow it was all Shiro needed to hear to know Qiang had done it.

"Any news on the camps?" Shiro asked instead.

"We were running into dead ends all over the place. Most of the mages who'd lost their powers couldn't tell us what had happened. But then we came upon a sapphire mage who'd used her powers to keep the truth untouched inside her head. She told us about two men coming to the camps. One of them would somehow drain the mages' powers, and the other would convince them to forget what had happened."

"She was able to resist them?"

"Yes. Somehow."

"She must be very skilled."

Shiro wondered if she might be close in line to be the next elite. The news also gave him hope that the elites might be able to fight off the powers of the one who was draining powers.

"And what about explosives?" Shiro asked.

"We found them at that camp and were able to disarm them. We would have never been able to find them if it hadn't been for that girl. We're going to check the other camps and see if they're using the same method of operation for hiding the explosives. I just don't know if we can find them all and disarm them before the government decides to use them."

Shiro raked a hand through his hair. "Okay. Be careful. Please."

It took a second before Qiang answered. "I will, Shiro. You too."

Darshana rubbed her temples. Something was off, but she couldn't be sure what it was. She knew she should meditate, but she felt as if the throbbing in her head wouldn't let her. It was almost as if someone were tapping on the back of her skull over and over, harder every minute, demanding her attention.

She went to the kitchen, hoping a peppermint tea might help alleviate the ache. As the water kettle heated up, she heard footfalls approaching. She thought, at this late hour, everyone was already asleep—or at least in bed. So it surprised her to find Penny coming toward her.

"Is there enough hot water for two?" Penny asked.

"Plenty." Darshana took another mug out of the cabinet. "Why are you still up?"

"I was just thinking about the meteor shower. It's the day after tomorrow, right?"

"Yes."

Penny let out a small, humorless laugh. "I'm just so mixed up lately. Losing track of the days."

"It's understandable. We've been hiding out here for so long. And you were kidnapped. I can just imagine what that must have done to your head."

"Yeah." Penny looked through the cannisters and selected a tea. "I was thinking we should all stick together. You know, when we go up to the top of the hill for the meteor shower. Not just you and the mages, but all of us."

"Karina and Mr. Kitaro?"

"I think it would give us a real sense of being a team. One big, united front, supporting each other."

"Yes, that would be nice." Darshana filled their mugs with the boiling water. "Is that what was keeping you up?"

"Well, not just that." Penny stirred her tea. "I guess it's nerves. Wondering if my powers will hold out when it comes down to the, uh, big moment."

Darshana sighed. "Yes, I'm afraid your teammates are feeling the same apprehension. And that worries me. I need to find a way to boost your collective confidence. A big part of winning a battle is believing that you can."

Penny sipped her tea, studying Darshana's face. "Yes. I think you're right."

Don't, Darshana. It's a trap!

Penny tried with everything she could muster to get Bhutano to somehow slip up. To stutter. To drop the tea. Anything that might tip off Darshana that she was being duped. Time was running out. Darshana and the others were falling for every trick Bhutano was pulling. And the elites had everything to lose.

EIGHTEEN

The sun had almost completely disappeared behind the horizon when the elite mages departed the house to begin their journey to the hilltop. Originally, only the elites and Darshana were going to go up to see the meteor shower, but Penny had insisted that they should all stick together, Karina and Mr. Kitaro included.

Karina had to admit, she was curious about how the meteors might affect the mages' powers. Plus, she'd only seen a meteor shower from the swamp, and the prospect of seeing one from the top of a high hill made her a bit excited.

The excitement was what kept her moving. The first half of the walk had been manageable, but once they started climbing the slope of the hill, Karina's legs began to feel the burn. She distracted herself from the ache by listening to Penny asking Jae about what it had been like growing up with the Lotus as a sister. Their conversation took up a good portion of the ascent, and Karina felt she learned a lot about Jae she hadn't known before.

By the time they'd reached their destination, the night sky was littered with millions of stars. The Akutake comet was visible, making its prophesized approach. Darshana had laid out a large picnic blanket and sat cross-legged as she watched the sky. Karina sat beside her, leaning back on her hands. Mr. Kitaro had a small notepad in his hand and a pen in the other, ready to jot down any changes that might occur in the mages' magic.

Shiro seemed to be scoping the sky for clouds, prepared to lend a hand of moving any nebulous obstacle out of the way, if his powers would allow him to. Salina pointed out something—a constellation, Karina thought she'd heard—to Mayhara. The speculation was that the three of them might be more directly affected by the comet and the meteors than the others would. The meteors were comprised of dust and rock fallout from previous comets, the comet itself was ice at its core, and they all were inflicted with fire burning away at them as they made their journey through space.

Of course, Loni had argued that they all traveled through air, meaning they were deeply connected to her as well. But Yuki had debunked her theory by reminding everyone that there was no air in space. It was a vacuum. She went further to say that sound waves could not travel through a vacuum; therefore, Jae's connection was also not as strong as the crimson, copper, and golden elites'.

"It's starting," Salina said. She stared, wide-eyed, as a pair of meteors shot across the sky. She stuck her hands in the back pockets of her jeans and smiled. "Whoa!"

"The idea was not to enjoy a show," Darshana called out. "It was to test out your powers during the shower to see if they improve."

"But how will that help us?" Loni asked. "I mean, when we're trying to fight off the Pishacha and keep Kashmeru in his tomb."

"Perhaps our crimson mage could replicate such a celestial event," Darshana said, "to give us an edge."

Everyone turned to Mayhara, whose expression suggested this was the first she'd heard of the idea.

Salina pulled her hands out of her pockets and blew out a breath. "Right. Let's do this."

Taking it upon herself to go first, Salina planted her feet in a defensive stance. She pushed out her palms in front of her, her fingers visibly taut.

Karina watched as Salina focused on her hands, seemingly pushing out her energy. It seemed like the seconds were ticking by with nothing happening. And then finally, a spark appeared, and two seconds later, a fireball shot from her hands and zoomed across the hilltop, barely missing a tree.

Karina wasn't sure if this was better or worse than what Salina had been experiencing since the comet had started interfering with her powers, but Mr. Kitaro must have had an idea, as he scribbled furiously onto his notepad.

As Shiro took his turn, Penny slid over quietly to Darshana and put a hand on her knee.

"Will you forgive me if I head back to the house?" Penny grimaced as she waited for Darshana's answer.

"Is everything all right?"

"I've been hit with a terrible migraine. And I know it was me who suggested we make a team effort out of tonight, but I think I need to lie down."

Darshana studied her face. "Do you think it's because of the meteor shower?"

"It could be." Penny glanced at the sky. "I was fine until I came up here."

Darshana offered her a small smile. "Of course, dear. Will you be all right going alone? Or should I send someone with you?"

"No, I'll be fine." Penny patted her knee. "I just need darkness and silence and my pillow."

"All right." Darshana nodded. "We'll see you later. Feel better, dear."

"Thank you. And good luck with your tests."

Karina gave Penny a nod and watched as she left. She wondered if it was the combination of the comet and the meteors affecting Penny's head, attacking the base of her powers where her visions and insight manifested.

A bright white light flashed out of the corner of her eye and drew her focus away from Penny's descent down the hill. She turned to see a sparkling dome of diamonds shielding Yuki. Yuki had a look of intense concentration on her face.

"Seems to be working," Karina said to Darshana.

Darshana pursed her lips. "It's taking more effort. More time. I thought perhaps the layer of debris between the mages and the comet might throw off the disruption, but I can see now the comet is too strong."

"What does that mean?"

"It's not good." Darshana blinked slowly. "But I'm going to have to trust that my mages can pull through when it counts."

Karina breathed in deeply, exhaling as she watched Mayhara forming crimson bullets and shooting them off the hilltop. The sound of each bullet rung in her ears. The ringing intensified, and Karina flinched as the sounds merged into one high-pitched tone.

As the ringing wavered, Karina swore she heard a whisper. She narrowed her eyes, trying to concentrate on the voice.

"*...the scroll!*"

She placed her hands over her ears, confused by the voice. She grit her teeth and listened harder.

"Don't… the scroll!"

Karina's eyes shot to Darshana, who was watching her with a curious gaze. A strange pull stung in Karina's chest. She sprang to her feet.

"What is it?" Darshana's eyes flit over her face.

"I don't know." Her breaths came quickly. "Something about the scroll."

"About how to open it?"

Karina shook her head. "I'm not sure. But something's… It doesn't feel right. Something's telling me to go to it. I need to keep it near me. To keep it secure."

Darshana sat up straighter, uncrossing her legs. "Are you hearing a voice?"

Karina nodded as she released a shuddered breath.

Darshana gestured with her head. "Then you must listen. Go on. We'll catch up later."

With a wildly thumping heart, Karina turned and hurried back to the house.

NINETEEN

Bhutano's breaths came hard as he approached the house. Tonight, he would kill three birds with one stone. He cut off the Linq call to Naree, having successfully delivered the message as to where the sapphire elite had hidden his dagger. Jae's mind had opened up to Penny so easily when asked about growing up with his sister. It was almost too easy to search his mind and find the dagger's hiding place. He thanked the fates that Jae's dagger wasn't in the house. Naree and the dark mages would only have to travel to a small musical instrument shop on the outskirts of New Jaipur, where Jae had concealed the dagger inside the casing of an amplifier. Bhutano was positive Naree would have no trouble finding it. Though he still hadn't pinned down the location of Mayhara's dagger, he did manage to see the location of the dagger the Sacred Key had hidden. He'd just have to retry his manipulation technique with the crimson elite mage later. For now it was up to him to get Mr. Kitaro's dagger and find the scroll.

The house was dark. Bhutano checked behind him to make sure no one was coming. He tried to use Penny's power of insight to his advantage, but he wasn't getting any visions. He wondered if the comet might be affecting the amethyst mage's powers after all.

He didn't have any time to waste. With a sense of urgency, he headed straight for Mr. Kitaro's office and switched on the small desk lamp. There was a screwdriver waiting for him in the desk drawer. Bhutano had placed it there earlier so it would be accessible, especially considering the time constraint.

Screwdriver in hand, he dropped to his knees and pried the tool between the two floorboards he'd seen in Mr. Kitaro's mind. The boards loosened easier than he'd guessed, and in a matter of seconds, a black box with a shiny red and gold design was staring back at him. He gently pulled the box from its hiding place. He could hear Kashmeru singing his praises in his head. It wouldn't be practical to take the whole box, so Bhutano opened it and removed the dagger. The blade glinted, even in the low light of the desk lamp.

After tucking the dagger into the inside pocket of Penny's jacket, Bhutano returned the box and moved the floorboards back into place.

Step one was complete. Next step: the scroll.

Bhutano switched off the desk lamp and quietly exited the office. He paused in the hall and listened but was met by nothing but silence. The mages were surely busy testing their powers at the top of the hill, and he believed they'd be there for another hour, at least. Still, he should hurry and get the job done.

Continuing on to Karina's room, he clicked on the light and scanned the area. "Where are you keeping it, little witch?" he whispered.

Careful not to make a mess of anything, he rifled through drawers and checked the bookshelf. A buzzing suddenly went off in his head, and he froze.

Someone was coming.

Bhutano quickly flipped off the light and backed up, squeezing into a space between a cabinet and a corner of the room. Anyone coming into the room wouldn't be able to see that someone was there.

He held his breath as the door opened and Karina walked in. She didn't seem to be aware of anything except for the reason she'd come into the room.

She grabbed a wicker bag that hung on the back of a chair. Reaching into the bag, she pulled out the scroll. Bhutano grit his—or rather, Penny's—teeth, furious that he hadn't checked the bag.

Kill her.

The sound of Kashmeru's voice made Bhutano flinch.

Kill her and take the scroll. She could destroy me with that spell. She could ruin everything.

Bhutano swallowed, realizing Kashmeru was right. He had the opportunity to stop her right there in that moment. No one else was around. He could convince the others, as Penny, that someone had broken in and attacked her. Pishacha or a dark mage, for example. He could claim they'd stolen the scroll. He could even fake an injury as proof that Penny had tried to stop them. They wouldn't have any reason to doubt Penny.

Bhutano reached inside the jacket's inside pocket and pulled out the dagger. He took a quiet step forward as Karina stuffed the scroll into a small canvas satchel. She hung the satchel over her shoulder, the strap crossing diagonally over her chest.

Bhutano raised the dagger, high over his head, ready to pounce.

The door suddenly swung open again, and Bhutano almost gasped. He promptly reverted back into the corner, pressing against the wall to keep out of sight.

Karina turned toward the door. "Shiro?"

"I was worried when I saw you leave the hilltop," he said. "Darshana told me you needed to get the scroll, so I thought I'd make sure you were okay."

She patted the satchel. "Yeah, I got it. I can't explain it; it's like I feel like it's precious cargo. I think I need to keep it on me."

"Probably a good idea."

"But you didn't have to leave the hilltop. I'm all right."

"I did, though." He offered her a small smile. "I promised Amalia I'd take care of you. I owe her that much."

"Thank you." She returned his smile. "We can head back up if you want. Is the meteor shower over yet?"

"I think Jae said we've got about another half hour or so."

"Great. Let's go." She ran her fingers down the strap as if making sure it was secure.

As they switched off the light and closed the door behind them, Bhutano let out a breath and stepped out from his hiding spot.

Get the scroll. It's imperative.

Bhutano cursed under his breath. He'd missed his opportunity and let down his god. But now he knew where the scroll would be at all times. He'd get another chance. And he wouldn't screw it up next time.

TWENTY

Yuki sat in the meadow, closing her eyes as the sun broke through the clouds. The grass touched her legs, making them a little itchy, but she tried to ignore the sensation and concentrate. They would be leaving in a few days to infiltrate the Lotus temple and usurp the enemy's plans. And she wasn't sure if she was ready. Darshana wanted them to be in the right mindset for their upcoming battle, so Yuki decided to meditate. The flowers in the meadow caused a pleasant fragrance to waft through the air. It helped to calm her mind.

Breathing deeply, she reached down into the source of her power. Theoretically, a mage whose power included controlling emotions should be able to keep everyone confident, including herself. Maybe it was the comet's interference, but she was having a hard time managing the elites' moods. And what made it worse was that she could feel her own confidence plummeting along with everyone else's. But she had to believe she could overcome it.

She had to.

Something in the air changed. A different emotion, like waves of something darker entering her vibration.

She opened her eyes.

"Don't mind me," Penny said. "I was just taking a walk to clear my mind."

"That's okay." Yuki smiled and patted the ground beside her. "That's why I'm here too."

Penny returned her smile as she crouched down and sat beside her. Yuki told herself the dark emotion she felt from Penny must have been her doubt, which was understandable. A part of her feared Penny might have seen something with her amethyst powers—something about the outcome of their situation—and she wasn't telling them. It would explain why Penny's dark emotions were much grimmer than the others'.

"I take it you're worried about this showdown too," Penny said.

Yuki twisted her lips. "I hate to admit it, but yeah."

"I was hoping you might have a better influence on our spirits. We could really use it."

"Believe me, I'm trying." Yuki shifted, tucking her legs underneath herself. "It's like there's this looming cloud, filled with heaviness and uncertainty, pressing down on us, and I'm fighting to clear it. Because I know if I do, we can come out on top."

Penny nodded. "And things have been complicated for you too."

"What do you mean?"

"I saw your expression when Avi appeared on screen during Min's funeral. And when Shei was hit, you jumped in your skin. Something made me think maybe part of you was worried Avi might have been hurt too."

Yuki furrowed her brow. She wasn't sure how she had felt about that. "No. I think I was just shocked by the unexpected attack."

"And if it had been *Avi* who'd been attacked?"

Yuki blinked in puzzlement. "I don't know. I mean, when I found out he was a follower of Kashmeru, it pretty much cut off all romantic feelings I had for him." She bit the inside of her cheek. "I mean, most of those feelings, anyway."

Penny tilted her head. "You never told me how you met."

"Didn't I?"

Yuki carried the tray of coffee, zigzagging through the people crowding the city streets. She'd been working for a kimono designer who thankfully didn't ask a lot of questions about her past. Being so young, she didn't have much as far as office skills, but the designer and her staff were adamant coffee drinkers, so Yuki found herself making coffee runs at least three times a day. She didn't mind. They paid her enough credits to rent a tiny, one-room apartment, and they often had enough leftover takeout that she didn't have to worry about feeding herself.

It had been almost two years since the Eradication. Two years since the government had abolished the academy and taken her into custody, proposing she work for them in order to keep her family safe. But her powers had told her they were lying, and so she'd fled when the opportunity had arisen. The next thing she knew, her parents had been killed.

Of course, something told her that they would have been killed anyway, at some point.

On the run and fearing for her life, she used her powers to land herself a meaningless job, changed the cut and color of her hair, and kept herself out of sight from the Imperial Police as much as she could.

So when she saw a police officer in her path on her way back to the kimono studio from the coffee shop, she quickly turned on her heel to change direction.

And smacked right into a young man, nearly dropping all the coffee.

"I'm so sorry," she blubbered, readjusting her grip on the carrier tray. If she had lost even one coffee, she'd have to go back to replace it or have to face the wrath of one of her bosses.

"No, it's my fault," the young man said. He had a boyish face and spikey hair that Yuki found interesting.

"How is it your fault?" She laughed. "I practically clobbered you with six liters of caffeine."

"Yeah, that seems like a lot for such a petite young lady."

"It's not all for——" She let out another laugh, caught off guard by his amazing eyes.

"I know." He flashed a smile that made her blush. "So who are you running away from?"

Her eyes widened. "What? No, I'm not... uh... What makes you say that?"

"I'm pretty good at reading body language."

Normally, she would have rolled her eyes at the line, but her emotion sensors weren't setting off any red flags. He was genuinely interested in her. "Okay, you got me. I'm... avoiding someone. But I've got to get this to my bosses, so I'm taking a detour."

He studied her face and bit his lip. "Well, how would you feel about company?"

"What?" She almost giggled.

"It's the least I could do for almost making you spill all that coffee. I'll

escort you safely to your destination, coffee intact, and in return I get to enjoy the pleasure of refreshing conversation."

"And he walked with you the whole way back?" Penny asked.

"He did." She sighed. "And he wasn't creepy or anything. He was actually charming and kind of funny. Which is why I went out with him a few times after that. But then, on one date, we overheard these university kids discussing deities. And when Kashmeru's name came up, Avi started acting strange. He made some off comments and mumbled about how they were idiots who didn't understand the world. I got a real bad vibe when I read his emotions. That's when I figured out whose side he was really on."

Penny shifted as if she were uncomfortable. "That's when you ended things?"

"I had to. Plus, I found out he was the governor's son. You can just imagine how complicated that could get. But bigger than that, how could I keep seeing someone with such screwed-up ideologies?"

Yuki's thoughts flashed in her head: finding out the truth about Avi, the dark mages, her need to be strong in the battle, and keeping the daggers out of the reach of the enemy.

Penny's eyes narrowed for a second. Yuki felt a chill run up and down her spine. Something wasn't right.

"You're right," Penny said. She stretched and got to her feet. "No one should have to compromise their beliefs." She glanced over her shoulder. "I'm going to head back to the house. I'll see you later."

With a wave, Penny departed. Yuki felt as if her stomach were being eaten away by acid. Penny's emotions didn't match her expression. Yuki couldn't figure out what was happening, but she knew it wasn't good.

TWENTY-ONE

Mayhara paced Karina's room while Karina attempted to make a list of every spell she knew. It was just a few days before they'd be leaving for New Delhi, and Mayhara felt dreadfully unprepared.

"Why can't I get this skepticism out of my head?" Mayhara asked, not really expecting Karina to answer. "We have all the daggers, and even if Jae's theory is correct, there's no guarantee the Pishacha's witch can even unlock Kashmeru's tomb. And even if she does, we have a spell that could destroy him for good."

"Except that I can't get the scroll with the spell open," Karina rebutted.

The door to Karina's room opened, and Mayhara turned to see Yuki walk in. There was a strange look on her face, and she was wringing her hands.

"Yuki?" Mayhara stopped pacing. "What's wrong?"

Yuki looked over her shoulder. "Not here," she whispered. "Would you two like to go for a walk with me?"

The look in Yuki's eyes told Mayhara that whatever was on her mind couldn't wait. Mayhara and Karina exchanged a look, and Karina nodded. In silence, they gathered their things. Karina already had the satchel with the scroll slung around her. None of them said a word as they made their way through the house and out the front door. Mayhara was grateful they hadn't run into anyone along the way.

Mayhara couldn't help but wonder whom Yuki was trying to prevent from hearing their conversation. She almost suggested that they get Jae so he could use his powers to soundproof them as they spoke, but then she wondered if it might be Jae's ears Yuki was trying to get away from. She hoped it wasn't.

They walked for what seemed like miles, with Yuki constantly looking over her shoulder. They were on a path that went through a thick forest of khair and sandalwood trees, hidden from view so no one would spot them.

Mayhara could hear the babble of a nearby stream. The air was colder here, and Mayhara shivered.

"There's something… wrong." Yuki stopped and turned to them. Her arms were wrapped around herself.

"What is it?" Karina asked.

Yuki tucked her hair away from her face. "It's Penny."

Mayhara flashed her a questioning look. "What about her?"

Yuki shook her head. "I can't be sure. We were talking, and something strange happened. She was being friendly, but everything I felt coming from her was anger, rage, and vengeance."

At first Mayhara simply gaped at her, but then she recalled something that had happened. "She and I had a conversation recently too, and she was acting really strange. She kept asking me questions."

"What kind of questions?" Yuki asked.

"About me and Jae. About my family and which prison camp they were in. I couldn't make heads or tails of why she was being so inquisitive. And she kept switching topics, like she was trying to get me to say something in particular."

Karina's eyes widened. *"Don't. The scroll."*

"What?" Yuki and Mayhara asked her at the same time. Karina let out a shuddered breath, her hand tightening on the strap of her satchel. "I've been hearing a voice lately. In my head. At first I thought it was my brain's way of grieving, but now I think it's actually my grandmother speaking to me from… wherever she is."

"Speaking to you about what?" Mayhara asked.

"I could only get a few words. The first few times it was 'deceiving you.' And then, then other night, on the hilltop, it was 'Don't. The scroll.' The sentences were broken up, so I had to piece things together myself." Karina patted the satchel. "That's why I left that night to get the scroll. I've been keeping it at my side ever since."

"But why would Penny be lying to us?" Mayhara's forehead was scrunched up so much, it began to ache. "Why would she want the scroll?"

"Thinking back," Yuki said as she paced back and forth in a short line next to them, "things started to get weird ever since she showed up here after being captured by the Pishacha."

"Yeah." Mayhara tapped her chin. "That in and of itself was strange. I think we were so grateful that she'd returned we simply accepted that she'd easily escaped and found us with no trouble. With no one chasing her."

"So, what are we saying?" Karina worried the satchel strap, her eyes darting between the other two young women.

"That Penny switched sides?" Mayhara asked.

"Or…" Yuki visibly swallowed. "That Penny isn't… Penny."

"What?" Karina scoffed. "What does that even mean?"

"The police chief. Min." Mayhara practically slapped a hand against her mouth as the pieces started to come together. "He was being possessed by Bhutano—Kashmeru's spirit messenger. Loni and Salina said that right before Min died, he grabbed Penny. That black smoke escaped his body just before he fell to the floor."

"You think Bhutano's spirit left Min and transferred to Penny?" Karina asked.

"It fits," Yuki said. "It explains all the strange ways she was acting."

"So it's not Penny," Mayhara said. "It's Bhutano. This whole time. But what was he doing? Biding his time? Why didn't he just kill us all when he had the chance?"

"Because he needed something from us." Yuki's eyes widened. "The daggers."

"But Penny—I mean, Bhutano," Mayhara corrected herself, "never asked me anything about the scrolls."

"An amethyst mage wouldn't have to." Karina narrowed her eyes in thought. "She'd just have to get you talking so the defenses of your mind were lowered enough that she could slip in there and find out the information for herself."

"I don't know what scares me more," Mayhara said. "That Bhutano is able to use Penny's powers or that our daggers could all be gone."

The three of them gawked at each other as the revelation sunk in.

"But what about Penny?" Yuki asked. "The real Penny, I mean."

"She's probably still in there," Karina said. "Judging from what I know about possessions."

"So how do we get her out?" Yuki shook her head. "How do we rescue her?"

"You don't," said a figure, stepping onto the path.

TWENTY-TWO

Karina and the others quickly huddled together, raising their hands to defend themselves. Karina's fist clenched around the satchel strap as she struggled to keep her knees from buckling.

Penny—whom they now knew to be Bhutano—smirked at them. In that moment, Karina could no longer see the person before her as Penny. Though it looked like her, it was the enemy, Kashmeru's henchman, they were dealing with now.

Bhutano was not alone, she came to realize. Waltzing up to stand behind him were Avi—the dark mage—and a Pishacha soldier dressed in black.

"Well, well, well," Avi said with a smirk. "Look what we've got here."

"I have to admit," Bhutano began, "that I didn't expect you lot to figure out my secret. But I guess we're all full of surprises, aren't we?"

"This isn't over," Mayhara said.

Bhutano raised a brow. "Is that what you believe? It looks like Kashmeru's side is at an advantage now. I don't see what hand you think you have to play."

"You won't win," Yuki said. "Evil never does."

Bhutano let out a laugh. "You are a delusional child. Do you know that? Just admit that we're better at this than you are."

"By tricking us all into revealing where all the daggers were hidden?" Mayhara scoffed. "That's why you kept hounding me with all those questions. To find out where I'd kept my dagger."

Bhutano smiled through Penny's face. "Actually, it didn't work on you. Until now, that is. Thank you, crimson mage, for letting me into your mind. Now I have everything I want." He pointed at Karina. "Except for that."

Karina gasped and backed up, her hands covering the satchel Bhutano pointed at.

"In fact, we'll take you as well, little witch." Bhutano looked her up and down. "You've absorbed your grandmother's powers. I can just imagine the magic you now possess. Releasing Kashmeru's tomb should be a walk in the park for you."

Karina bared her teeth. "You'll have to kill me first."

Bhutano smirked. "Ask and it shall be granted. Avi?"

Avi glared at Karina and stepped forward. He raised his hand and lowered his chin. A burst of black cloud formed in his palm. They'd called this dark mage the bone crusher, and Karina's heart felt as if it were about to leap out of her chest in fear.

"No, Avi! Don't!" Yuki screamed. She stepped in front of Karina and raised both hands. Gritting her teeth, she released a barrage of diamond bullets. Mayhara and Karina ducked down, covering their heads.

Avi jerked back, gripping his shoulder. Blood pooled at his side as well. The sneer didn't leave his face as he stumbled back and fell to the ground.

It had happened so fast, Karina had missed it, but the Pishacha soldier was gone. Only a small puff of black smoke could be seen where he had been, so Karina couldn't be sure whether he had been struck or not.

Bhutano had been knocked back into a tree. He pressed against a gushing wound on his upper arm and squared his jaw. "You'd really sacrifice your friend? Avi never mentioned how brutal you were, little girl."

The look on Yuki's face told Karina she hadn't meant to hit Penny's body with the bullet. Yuki trembled, shaking her head as she backed up. Karina wanted to go to Penny and stop the bleeding. If Penny was still in there, she didn't want her to be hurt. She knew a spell. She would just have to put her hands on her and recite it.

"Let me help." Karina's voice sounded desperate as she raised her hands. "I can close the wound."

Bhutano narrowed his eyes, panting in pain, back pressed against the tree as Karina approached. Karina kept her eyes on Bhutano's, hoping he would let her get close enough to help Penny.

Just as she reached him, she felt a hard jerk on her shoulder. With a gasp, she swung around to find Avi, who had crawled toward her and snatched the satchel from her shoulder, ripping the strap. Before she could stop herself, Karina flung herself at Avi, her hands closing in around the satchel. They both fell to the ground. Avi screamed in pain as Karina landed on his wounds.

Karina stumbled to her knees and flung the bag toward Yuki and Mayhara. As Mayhara caught the bag, Avi sprung to his feet and ran at her. Yuki's hands began to glow white.

Karina pointed her palms at Yuki and Mayhara, a spell spilling from her lips. The next moment seemed to go by in slow motion. A wave of energy pulsated outward from Karina's hands. Yuki and Mayhara were engulfed in a white light that emanated from Yuki's palms. Avi jumped and dived at Mayhara, his hands aiming for the satchel. As Karina shouted the last words of her spell, Yuki's white light intensified. Karina had to shield her eyes from the flash.

Suddenly, everything was much quieter. Karina opened her eyes. The spot where Mayhara and Yuki had been standing was empty. They were gone. With the scroll.

But so was Avi.

Karina's breaths were hard and heavy. She scanned the area, wondering what might have happened. Her spell was supposed to move them to safety, but she could only surmise that whatever magic Yuki had been generating had melded with her spell and cast them off somewhere else. But she didn't know where. And they were not alone.

She quickly turned to check if Bhutano was still there. She found him still backed up against the tree but slunk down a bit.

"What have you done?" he asked, cringing from his wound. "Where are they?"

Karina pressed her lips together, refusing to answer. Not that she could.

She jumped when a pop of smoke erupted beside Bhutano. The Pishacha soldier was back. The soldier bent to help Bhutano stand. Karina felt as if she were frozen as she watched the two of them. If she could just snap out of her shock and get her legs to move, she'd be able to run back to the house and warn the others.

"Let's get back to the Lotus," Bhutano said to the soldier. "We'll figure things out from there." He eyed Karina. "And bring the witch."

Diamond Mage

Book Seven

ONE

Darshana tensed her muscles, a rush of adrenaline coursing through her as her pulse hammered in her throat. She gritted her teeth, pacing the main room of the house, as her heightened senses set off alarms in her head.

Danger.

Her mind raced, trying to make sense of the overload of images ripping through her head. Her breaths came hard and fast as she tried to see and hear everything at once, but the visions were muddled, unclear, and she found it hard to put them in the right order.

"Darshana?"

She flinched, as if the voice knocked her from her thoughts. She turned to the man, her mind slowly coming to the realization that it was Mr. Kitaro speaking to her. He tilted his head, his salt and pepper hair, which was usually slicked back, sat unusually disheveled.

Wringing her hands, she gave an apologetic bow to Mr. Kitaro. "I'm sorry."

"What's wrong?" he asked, studying her. "Has something happened?"

"I believe so." She solemnly shook her head. Her fingers reached for her long braid which lay over her shoulder and worried the white strands. "But I can't make heads nor tails of it."

Mr. Kitaro glanced over his shoulder, seemingly unsure of what to do.

"Check on the elites." The words barely left Darshana's lips before she darted toward the bedrooms.

Mr. Kitaro followed, and they each knocked on and opened the doors down the long hallway, calling out the names of the others.

Loni wrinkled her brow as she came to the door and met the anxiousness in Darshana's eyes.

"What's wrong?" Salina's golden-flecked eyes were wide with concern as she stepped out into the hall.

Jae and Shiro soon joined her, obvious confusion on their faces.

"Did something happen?" Jae asked. "Is it Naree?"

Darshana slowly turned to them, her gaze intense as she pressed her fingertips together. "Where are the others? Mayhara, Yuki, Penny, and Karina?"

The others exchanged glances.

"They're not in the house? But it's dark outside." Salina marched toward the kitchen.

Loni furrowed her brow and darted toward the front door, leaving it open as she ran outside.

Jae whipped out his Linq. Shiro did the same. Darshana pressed her fingertips to her lips and forced herself to keep her breathing steady.

"Mayhara's Linq goes straight to voicemail," Jae said after pressing his Linq to his ear for a moment.

"Yuki's as well," Shiro added.

Salina returned from the main room, chewing on a nail. "Are they out training? Not that we're panicking for no reason?"

"This late at night?" Shiro asked.

"Maybe they wanted to test their powers again." Salina shook her head, as if she knew her theory was unlikely.

Loni stomped back into the house. "I can't see them anywhere."

Darshana's hands were clammy, the hairs lifting from the nape of her neck. "No. They're in trouble. I can feel it."

"But where are they?" Mr. Kitaro asked. "The property is big, but they can't have gotten far."

"Maybe you're forgetting," Loni said to him, "that the Pishacha can travel in clouds of smoke. They could have easily popped in for an attack and left again."

"We'll need to search the property, then," Mr. Kitaro rubbed a hand across his jaw. "If they're injured and lying out in one of the fields…"

"No." Darshana held her palms against her cheeks, her eyes narrowing. "No, they're not on the property. They're far. And I can't be sure, but I feel as if their energy is dispersed."

"Dispersed?" Jae asked.

"Like they're not together?" Shiro asked.

"You think they were kidnapped?" Salina asked.

Loni squared her jaw. "It wouldn't be the first time."

"What do we do?" Salina asked.

"Well, whatever we decide—" Mr. Kitaro's glance darted between them all. "—we can't stay here."

Salina blinked rapidly. "What?"

Darshana let out a sigh, her brows drawn together. "We have to come to terms with the fact that we've most likely been compromised. If the Pishacha have indeed kidnapped the others—or worse—then we cannot remain here as sitting targets for another attack."

Mr. Kitaro suddenly flinched, as if something troubling occurred to him. He turned on his heel and bolted into his office. Darshana exchanged looks with Jae. In a matter of seconds, Mr. Kitaro reappeared in the hall.

"It's gone," he said, color draining from his face.

"What is?" Salina asked.

"The dagger I was in charge of." He swallowed hard. "It's been stolen."

Darshana worried the knuckles of one hand. "I have a feeling it's not the only one missing."

Loni pressed her fingertips to her temples and let out a curse.

"We can check." Salina's hands clenched into fists. "Take inventory to see where we stand. But then what? What do we do? Where do we go?"

Darshana inhaled deeply, pushing down her panic. "We need to try to locate the others. To figure out how to rescue them. I can feel they need us. But in the meantime, we'll move on towards the Lotus temple. It's earlier than originally planned, I know. But it's the next logical step."

"And then what?" Shiro asked.

"And then we hope the gods have blessed us with a miracle to win this war."

.

Karina's pulse was like a jackhammer, pounding with the force of a thousand cannons and threatening to break her into pieces. She found it hard to breathe, and the only thing that kept her from completely losing it was the determination to save Penny from Bhutano's control.

Her eyes were still trying to adjust from the blast of black smoke that had filled her vision when the enemy had grabbed her and teleported with her from Mr. Kitaro's property. She must have blacked out when it had happened because she couldn't remember anything up until this moment. She replayed the scene in her head, trying to figure out what exactly might have happened to Mayhara and Yuki. She swallowed back the lump in her throat, her muscles tensing as she tried to slow her heartbeat.

There had been six of them in the woods. Karina had walked there with Mayhara and Yuki to discuss their suspicions about Penny. And Penny—whom they now knew was being possessed and controlled by Kashmeru's spirit messenger, Bhutano—had shown up with a Pishacha soldier and one of the dark mages.

Their sudden appearance had resulted in a standoff for the scroll Karina had carried. But Karina had tossed the scroll to Yuki and Mayhara, along with a spell that would transport them somewhere safe. The problem was Karina wasn't sure where that safe place might have been.

This concern was coupled with the fact that Yuki had fired diamond bullets with her mage powers in order to stop Avi—the dark mage—from crushing their bones with his magic. One of the stray bullets had hit Penny. And even through it had been Bhutano controlling Penny's body, Karina knew the real Penny inside would surely die along with Bhutano if Karina didn't use her magic to help them.

To top things off, Avi, who had also been wounded by Yuki's bullets, had somehow gotten sucked into Karina's spell and disappeared with them.

Although Karina suspected Yuki's diamond magic might have mixed with her, and she had no idea what the consequences of such a magical combination could be.

Lastly, Karina felt an urgency to get word to the other mages and Darshana. They were all in danger, and the enemy had stolen all the arcane daggers from them. With the daggers and the grimoire in their hands, they had all the ingredients they needed to release Kashmeru from his tomb, which meant the certain end of the world.

But Karina was helpless to do anything because Bhutano and Pishacha had abducted her, and she had no idea how she was going to turn the tables on the enemy.

As she blinked away the last of the smoky dust from her eyes, she glanced around and studied her location. It wasn't what she'd expected. Judging from the view out the window, she was in an extravagant apartment in some high-rise. Probably the penthouse. She wasn't sure what city they were in, though. Not far from where she sat, the most beautiful young woman she'd ever seen hovered over Penny and inspected her injury.

Naree. The empress. The reincarnated goddess they called "the Lotus."

She could tell just by looking at her that she was royalty. Her thick, long, dark hair looked as if it were spun silk. Her brown eyes practically glittered like jewels. There was an aura around her that was mesmerizing. Karina had never seen such perfect, glowing skin before.

Karina was on the floor, her back against the wall, and her legs trapped in warped metal clamped around her thighs. When she lifted her gaze, she spotted a dark mage watching her from a chair in the living room. Though he was indoors, he wore a long, dark gray cloak over a loose, white shirt. His hair was buzzed short on the sides, but the longer portion from the top was pulled back into a ponytail. She could just make out the top of a tattoo decorating his neck. He smirked when his eyes traveled down to the warped metal. The look of pride on his face told Karina that he was the one who had manipulated the contraption.

"She's awake," the dark mage called out.

Naree looked up and stood straighter.

Bhutano sat on a barstool, his jaw clenched and hands covering the bloody wound. "Thank you, Rikuto." The purple-flecked brown eyes that were really Penny's drifted from the dark mage over to Karina.

Naree waltzed over to her as if she had all the time in the world. "So you're the witch."

Karina breathed deeply through her nose, her eyes trained on the beautiful empress.

Naree lifted her chin and glanced back at Bhutano, who slowly made his way over to join her.

"She doesn't look like the most powerful witch in New United Asia," Naree said.

Karina had never been one to fuss about her appearance, but the way Naree was looking at her made her want to tame her wild hair and hide the tears in her clothes.

"But she is," Bhutano said, wincing. "I don't know what spell she used, but she made two of the elite disappear, and Avi along with them. Who knows what alternate realm she might have spelled them to?"

"Hmm." Naree placed her hands on her hips. "That does pose a problem."

A figure lurking near the door stepped into the room. The woman appeared to be in her mid-to-late thirties. A small touch of wrinkles marked the space between her dark brows. Her dark hair lay flat, almost oily in texture, with a few gray strands tucked behind her ears. The most prominent feature on her face was her nose, below which hung a round, silver piercing. "She absorbed her grandmother's powers, but she still has no control over them."

Karina narrowed her eyes at the woman. Why would she say such things? This woman didn't even know her.

The woman traipsed over to her, studying her with judgement in her eyes. The closer she got, the more Karina was filled with the need to protect herself.

"You don't need her," the woman said. "My skills as a witch are exemplary. And I'm in control of them." She reached for Karina's hair. "My powers are far more—"

The second her fingers curled around a lock of Karina's hair, the woman's eyes widened and her face went pale. She quickly retracted her hand as if she'd been stung, pulling it to her chest and covering it with her other hand, gaping at Karina.

"How did you do that?" the woman—the witch, Karina now comprehended—asked in shock.

"Her hair." Bhutano shifted closer, clutching at his wound. "The strands Tien Thi touched…"

Karina threw him a questioning look. She grabbed at her hair and pulled it forward so she could see it. The small section of hair in her hand had strands that had gone from messy, dark brown to silky, reddish gold. Her jaw dropped for a second. This was what her hair had looked like when she'd been a child. The conversation she had had with her grandmother when Karina had been young came to mind, where Amalia had told her that witches born with this color hair were special and fated for particular destinies. Karina quickly snapped her mouth shut and stared at her captors.

"I told you she was powerful," Bhutano said with a strained voice.

The bandage covering his wound was already soaked with fresh blood, and Karina worried Penny was running out of time.

Tien Thi pursed her lips and narrowed her eyes, her hand still cupped against her chest. "She had no control of it, though. Her magic is too wild."

Naree raised a hand. "That's enough, Tien Thi. I will decide if she has value or not."

Karina's mind was racing, trying to figure out how to use her status to her advantage. "I can control it." She kept her chin up and erased any evidence of doubt from her features. "And I have a proposition."

Bhutano and Rikuto exchanged a wary glance, but Naree kept her eyes on Karina.

"What is your proposal?" Naree asked.

"We both want something here," Karina began. "We both have something to negotiate with."

Tien Thi scoffed. "We're not here to negotiate with you, you imbecile."

Naree squared her jaw. "I said *that's enough*, Tien Thi. Let her speak."

Karina's gaze darted between them. "You need a powerful witch to unlock Kashmeru's tomb. I'll agree to be that witch, perform the spell for you."

Tien Thi appeared as if she were about to retort, but Naree flashed her a warning glare.

"Continue," Naree said to Karina. "What is it you want in exchange? I'll admit Tien Thi is annoying, but she has a point: You're not exactly in a position to negotiate."

"You know I can do it," Karina insisted. "You've only got one shot at getting that tomb open, and I'm your best bet. I've absorbed my grandmother's powers, and I was marked a special witch as a child." She swallowed hard. "I hate to admit it, but all signs turn to one undeniable fact: I was born to do this."

Naree scrutinized her face. "And what is it you want in return?"

"Release Penny."

At first, Naree simply gaped at her.

Karina continued. "Let me heal her wound and then set her free from Bhutano's possession."

"That's an awfully bold demand," Naree stated. "You expect me to simply release an enemy from my control?"

"It won't matter in the long run, if you think about it." Karina winced as she tried to shift within her metal trap. "The comet is just a couple of days away. You have all the daggers. There's nothing to stop us from releasing Kashmeru."

"Then why would it make a difference if we released your friend when she's doomed anyway?"

"It makes a difference to me." Karina shook her head. "I'll know I did everything I could… for her. To end her suffering. And anyway, if you deny me, I'll refuse to help you."

Naree looked her over. "I believe she means it."

"Your Highness?" Bhutano appeared skeptical.

Naree turned to him. "You have many of Kashmeru's followers available, ready to serve as a vessel for your spirit. And as for the amethyst mage, I can sweep her mind."

Karina gasped. "What? No!"

Naree's head swiveled back to face Karina. "Those are my terms. You may heal your friend, and we will release her. But her mind will be erased. Take it or leave it."

Karina could hardly breathe. She looked into Penny's eyes, hoping she could make her understand that she was doing this for her. The lump in her throat almost choked her as she swallowed it back.

Naree crossed her arms, one brow raised as she waited for Karina's answer.

"Very well," Karina finally said.

Naree smirked and uncrossed her arms. "Rikuto, you may remove her binds."

Rikuto kept a straight face as he approached Karina. He held out his palms toward her, and a dusty black mist emerged, traveling from his hands to the warped metal. Karina felt the pressure ease on her thighs as the metal loosened and eventually unraveled. When she was free enough, she hurried to her feet but kept close to the wall, just in case.

"This is absurd," Tien Thi said, her hands balled into fists. "What of me? Do you just expect me to stand by and allow this to happen?"

Naree frowned at the witch. "No. That's not exactly what I had in mind."

"Then what?" Tien Thi stared at her expectantly.

Naree eyed Rikuto. "It looks like we no longer have the need for the lesser witch."

Tien Thi gasped. Rikuto gave Naree a nod.

Faster than Karina could follow, Rikuto shifted his wrist, and a jagged sliver of the metal ripped itself from the piece that once bound her legs. It flew swiftly toward Tien Thi and sliced across her neck.

Karina slapped a hand over her mouth as blood gushed and spurted from the witch's throat and she dropped, wide-eyed, to the floor.

THREE

Yuki felt sick to her stomach. Her head spun, and her vision blurred. She wasn't even sure she was standing upright. Stretching out her hand to find her bearings, she felt someone's fingers wrap around hers.

"Mayhara?" Yuki blinked and squinted, hoping the hazy fog that obscured her vision would clear.

"I'm here," Mayhara answered. "Wherever *here* is."

Bit by bit, Mayhara's face came into view. There was fear and confusion in her big, brown eyes, and small wrinkles formed on the forehead of her heart-shaped face.

Yuki took in deep breaths, trying to calm the bubbling churn of her stomach. She glanced around, taking in their surroundings in an attempt to figure out where they might be.

"What happened?" Mayhara asked, raking the fingers of one hand through her dark brunette waves. In her other hand was Karina's small satchel. "How did we get here?"

Yuki wiped her shaking hands on her jeans and shook her head. "I'm not sure. I used my powers to divert our plane momentarily—"

"Wait? What? I… I don't know what that means."

"Okay. Sorry. It's a power diamond mages can develop. We're connected to spirituality and the spirit realm."

Mayhara's eyes widened slightly. "Are you saying we're in the spirit realm?"

Yuki glanced over her shoulders, unsure of how to answer. "I didn't mean for us to land here. I didn't even know it was possible. I was just trying to shift our place in our plane of existence so Avi couldn't get to us." She eyes the small bag Mayhara clutched to her chest. It contained the scroll that held the spell that could destroy Kashmeru. "I couldn't let him get his hands on the scroll."

Mayhara ran her hand over the satchel as she nodded. "Right. Okay. So then, how did we end up here?"

Yuki replayed the scene in her head. She remembered Karina shouting words she didn't understand. And she remembered feeling a wave of energy wash over her.

"Karina cast a spell. I can't be sure what the spell was, but I think it somehow melded with my powers and… sent us here."

"Wherever *here* is." Mayhara slowly turned her head, her eyes scanning the area. "If we landed here, I wonder what happened to Karina."

"And Penny. I mean, I know it was Bhutano controlling her, but I still believe Penny was in there somewhere. I hope they're all right."

Yuki pushed her auburn hair out of her face and surveyed their surroundings. Everything around them seemed slightly out of focus, as if some kind of filter was on that caused a slight glow. At their feet, a low fog traveled, touching upon everything as it floated along. The air was cool, almost chilly, and smelled as if there might be a bonfire nearby. The buzzing of insects seemed higher-pitched than normal. But the most unusual thing was a shimmering, multicolored haze that danced slowly around the sun. The haze changed hues as it moved, reminding Yuki of the *aurora borealis*, the northern lights that were predominantly seen in high-latitude regions. Also marking the sky was a dark streak. It was like the negative image of the comet, and Yuki wondered if the blackness of it was symbolic of impending doom.

"So now the question is," Mayhara began, worrying the strap of the satchel, "how do we get out of here?"

Yuki tried to steady her breaths. She could feel Mayhara's anxiety, and it matched her own. At least she *thought* it was Mayhara's anxiety. She briefly wondered if her own emotions were so strong, she couldn't feel past them. But she had to try to keep them both calm so they could use their heads and figure out their next move. It wouldn't do either of them any good if she gave in to her panic.

A snapping of a nearby branch made them both jump. They huddled together, both raising a hand with their palms facing outward, preparing for whoever or whatever might be approaching. This realm was unfamiliar, and Yuki didn't know what to expect.

Movement caught her eye. Yuki's breath caught in her throat when she spotted Avi—the dark mage who'd tried to kill them just moments before—stumbling out from behind a far-off tree.

"No. How did—?" Mayhara couldn't even finish her question.

"He must have got caught in the magic mashup or something." Yuki kept her voice low, but it was too late. Avi had already noticed them.

Wild brunette hair framed his boyish face, but instead of his usual pompous and arrogant expression, his features here riddled with a combination of fury and pain. He bit on his thick bottom lip as he hobbled toward them. Yuki could see blood seeping through his clothes at his waist and shoulder.

A part of her felt bad for having injured him. She had cared for him once, when they'd first become involved with each other. He had been charming and funny, and she'd never been looked at by anyone else the way Avi had looked at her.

But everything had changed when she'd found out what side he was on. She felt like the whole thing had been a lie. And now, he seemed hellbent on killing her. On killing her and Mayhara both.

Avi gritted his teeth and lifted a blood-soaked hand. Yuki grabbed Mayhara's arm and began to pull her back, away from Avi. But when he frowned and examined his hand, Yuki took a relieved breath. There had been no black tendrils, no cloud of black smoke, and more importantly, no pain. It appeared Avi's bone-crushing dark magic had failed.

"His powers," Yuki whispered. "They're not working."

"Not that I'm not grateful," Mayhara said, shaking her head, "but why?"

Avi bared his teeth and began stumbling toward them.

"I can't seem to form any particles." Yuki gestured at Mayhara's free hand. "You try. Try to form a rock or something. Anything."

Mayhara's brow furrowed, but she did what Yuki had suggested and lifted her hand, palm up, between them. Her eyes were wide and full of panic. "It's not working. Why isn't it working?"

"Maybe it has something to do with where we are." Yuki looked up at the sky again. The shimmering haze had more of a bluish tint now as it traveled around the sun. "I've only read a little about this realm, and my memory seems to be failing me at the moment."

Avi snarled as he got closer, stumbling and grunting every few steps as he clutched at the wound in his side.

"We need to get away from him, though, just in case. We don't know if this lack of magic is temporary or not." Yuki patted the satchel. "The comet is only a couple of days away. It's needed to destroy Kashmeru. We need to figure out how to get back and get the scroll to the Lotus temple before it's too late."

Mayhara gave Yuki a solid nod, glancing once at the approaching dark mage before taking her hand. They pushed forward, making their way through the puzzle of trees and bushes, unsure of which direction they should be heading. The only thing Yuki knew for sure was it had to be in the direction away from Avi.

FOUR

Loni adjusted the straps of the backpack she carried to the car. She was used to being on the run, but this was different. There was an urgency that bit at her brain and a lurking sense of doom.

They'd gathered what they could from the house and were almost done packing up the vehicles. Loni was afraid the Pishacha now knew what their cars and Jae's motorcycle looked like and could have the police keep an eye out for them, but they had no other way to get to New Delhi quickly while avoiding being seen in public.

"Then I guess Karina's protection spell didn't work," Shiro said to Mr. Kitaro as they loaded a couple more bags into the trunk of one of the cars. Shiro paused to run a hand through his copper-tipped, black hair. "Since the Pishacha were somehow able to get into the house and take your dagger."

Salina appeared beside the other car, having placed some provisions on one of the seats. She eyed the others.

"We have to remember," Mr. Kitaro answered, "that we do not fully understand what the dark mages are capable of."

"You think they have powers that could undo a witch's spell?" Loni asked.

Salina bit her lip. "That's a scary thought."

"Perhaps not all spells." Mr. Kitaro clapped invisible dust off his hands. "Otherwise, they'd have been able to break the spell sealing Kashmeru's tomb."

Shiro shrugged. "I mean, essentially that's what they're doing. With their magic and the dagger, they'll be breaking a witch's spell."

"No." Mr. Kitaro shook his head. "Not without a witch to reverse the sealing spell. Hence all the fuss about the grimoire."

Loni's attention diverted to Jae, who was tying a duffle bag to his bike with elastic rope. He didn't seem to be paying attention to the conversation.

Upon closer inspection, Loni spotted wrinkles worrying his forehead. He'd been far away in thought since they'd found out the other elites and Karina were missing. Though she knew he cared for the safety and well-being of all their missing friends, there was no doubt his heart was hurting most because of Mayhara's absence. And knowing that was tearing a hole in her soul.

Still, she wanted to be there for him. But just as she got up the nerve to speak to him, Darshana appeared and cleared her throat.

"We'll need to depart soon. I can't imagine the Pishacha will grant us any more time than they already have, whatever their plan is."

"I think their plan was to disband us," Shiro said. "And leave us to keep guessing what their next move might be."

Salina crossed her arms. "Well, I'll give them credit. Their tactics are definitely unnerving."

"In any case, I have to agree with Darshana." Mr. Kitaro checked his watch. "We should make haste."

"I could ride up ahead," Jae announced, finally giving the conversation attention. His eyes met Loni's for a mere fraction of a second. "Alone." He cleared his throat. "The bike is packed pretty full. But, uh, I can keep an eye out for what's in front of us. I'll be wearing my earpiece and monitoring traffic updates. I can signal if we need to change our route."

"I can drive one car," Shiro said. "Or at least take the first shift."

"Shifts sound good," Salina agreed. "I'll drive the other one."

"Shotgun." Loni gave her a half-smile.

"I'll accompany our copper elite, then," Mr. Kitaro said.

"I'll ride wherever I fit, I suppose." Darshana gave them all a nod. "Let's say five minutes to grab any last-minute items?"

They all agreed, and though Loni longed to speak to Jae, she instead took the opportunity to double-check her room. She had shared it with Yuki and Penny, and now both of them were missing. Leaving the room now, before anyone knew where they might be, felt strange. Like abandoning them and then jetting off somewhere where they couldn't be found.

"Ready?" Salina asked as she found her in the hallway.

"I guess, yeah."

It wasn't until they were a good half hour into their drive that the nausea and shakes began. Loni kept her eyes on Jae's motorcycle in front of them, wishing to get rid of the acidic taste in her mouth.

Her brain was screaming, *"Moxy!"* And it was taking every ounce of willpower she had to not divert Salina in the direction of her dealer. She already felt guilty for abandoning Yuki and Penny. Her helplessness in losing her sister added to her desperate emotion, and watching Jae—the man who'd broken her heart—ride up ahead of her, knowing his mind was on someone else, just made things worse.

When she let out a shuddered breath, Salina glanced her way.

"Are you all right?"

Loni bit the inside of her cheek. "Fine."

"Loni."

"What?"

"You're not fine. Look at you."

Loni wiped sweat from her brow and dug her nails into her seat. "I'm working through it."

"Okay." Salina glanced her way again, worry etched on her face. "Hey. I'm here, okay? I know we don't exactly have the best history, but we're in this together now. And despite what you might think, I do care about you."

Loni squeezed her seat more tightly as she nodded. Salina's words were like medicine for her heart, but they didn't quite help stop the acid churning in her stomach.

Salina reached out, and Loni took her hand, forcing herself not to dig her nails into Salina's skin.

Up ahead, Jae signaled for them to veer off.

"What's happening now?" Salina muttered, following his directions.

Loni released her hand so she could have better control of the wheel.

Shiro followed behind them as Jae led them into a humble highway rest stop.

Salina parked the car next to Jae's motorcycle and let out a sigh. Shiro pulled up on the other side of the car and glanced their way as he cut his engine. Everyone got out of their cars, and Jae dismounted from his bike. The group gathered around Jae as he removed his helmet.

The rest stop was comprised of a row of parking spots situated along a lonely sidewalk. A small building containing restrooms stood among weeds and unmanicured bushes. A few picnic tables sat in the grass. All but one were unoccupied.

Loni glanced at the group of three young people—probably the same age as her—sitting at the table that was occupied. They were messily dressed and didn't seem to care much about the state of their hair. One of the young women had bloodshot eyes protruding over thick, dark bags. The young man kept bouncing one leg and hunched his shoulders as he glanced around. The other young woman was constantly flicking her lighter on, her cigarette dangling from her dry lips.

Loni couldn't help but think the group was using drugs. It might not have been Moxy they were indulging in, but Loni was sure it was something that could take off the edge. Her mouth filled with saliva, and her hands started to shake. She crossed her arms in an attempt to steady them.

She tried as hard as she could to concentrate on what Jae was saying and ignore the threesome at the picnic table, but she found herself glancing over at them every few seconds.

"The Imperial Police have got road control set up about ten miles up the highway," Jae said, addressing the whole group as they gathered around him. "According to the traffic report, they're set up in intervals all the way from here to New Delhi. We're going to have to take the next exit and stay on the back roads."

"How long is that going to take?" Shiro asked.

"It depends, but definitely longer than we anticipated."

Loni's focus drifted back to the threesome at the picnic tables. They had to be using, she could tell. How easy would it be for her to go over and find out?

"All right," Shiro said. "Sounds like we have no other choice."

"We can manage," Salina put in. "We'll make it."

"Sounds like here's no time to lose, then." Darshana gave Jae a nod. "We'll be right behind you. Let's be on our way."

As they made their way back to the vehicles, Shiro seemed to take a detour to Jae's bike. Loni couldn't hear what they were saying, but there was an unmistakable sadness in Jae's features when Shiro lightly slapped his back. She tried to listen more intently, but the only clear sentence she heard was, "We'll find her."

Mayhara.

That was where Jae's mind was. She had no doubt about it. Though it tore Loni up inside, she knew Jae's feelings for Mayhara were stronger than anything he'd ever felt for her. Her brain felt numb as she came to terms with it, but there was nothing she could do. She'd lost him.

A far-off siren sounded. Shiro looked over his shoulder at the road. Whatever the source of the siren, it wasn't near. Yet.

Loni watched as the threesome at the picnic table hurriedly gathered their things and scrambled to a rusty, white compact car. She was sure the small plastic bag the young man stuck in his pocket was their drug of choice. Her heart felt as if it were caving in on itself. She told herself to fight off the urge to run up to the man and ask him to sell to her. She didn't even care what it was. She needed something, anything, to stop her suffering.

Shiro ran to his car and climbed in. Jae pulled his helmet on. Salina started the car, but Loni still stood with the passenger side door open.

The threesome closed their door and the car's lights came on.

"Wait," she let out.

Salina ducked into the car and faced her with drawn brows. "What?"

Loni's heart pounded, and her mouth watered. Her head spun from the anguish. She swallowed hard and then shook her head. She had to avoid the temptation. The fate of the world was at stake. No matter how much she wanted to ease her pain, she had to put their mission first. "Never mind. It's nothing. Let's go."

FIVE

Karina shook out her hands, blowing out shuddered breaths as Rikuto stared her down. He hadn't taken his eyes off her the entire time since they'd been left alone. Though the situation she was in was making her skin crawl, she wished Naree and Bhutano would return from wherever they had escaped to so she wouldn't be alone with Rikuto any longer than she needed to be.

She was relieved when the door to the apartment opened. But instead of Naree and Bhutano returning, another dark mage entered the room. This one had no hair, though he had the same tattoo on his neck as the other dark mages. His face was slim, and he walked with a gangly gait. He only spared Karina a second's glance before traveling over to sit beside Rikuto. In his hands were two small cylindric containers containing some kind of liquid. He handed one to Rikuto.

"Is this from Yung's?" Rikuto asked.

"No. Yung's was out of my way. It's from Sampan."

"Kun, man, Sampan is a rip-off. It's mostly watered-down broth and barely anything else."

"Just shut up and eat, Rikuto. You want Yung's, you can get it yourself."

Rikuto snarled at Kun, but he took the plastic utensil Kun handed him and opened his container, placing the lid on the coffee table.

The delicious scent of oyster sauce and bay leaves wafted through the air. Karina's stomach let out a small gurgle of hunger. She quickly placed her arm over her midsection to quiet the sound. She didn't know if the Pishacha had any intention of feeding her, but she wasn't about to ask the dark mages.

"Your hair's not growing back yet," Rikuto said between slurps. "It's because you're not getting any nutrition from Sampan's soup. You need to go to Yung's."

"It's growing back. Shut up."

"You should have left it like it was. The green suited you. Fit with your whole *poison* persona."

Karina's breath stuck in her throat. *Poison.* This was the dark mage who'd poisoned her grandmother. Who'd ultimately killed her. Karina dug her nails into her palms, forcing herself not to react. Forcing herself not to jump up from the chair and attack him.

You're outnumbered. Stay calm.

She could use a spell, but chances were that Naree would return and use mage powers to take her down. Or she'd make Rikuto slice her throat like he had with Tien Thi.

"It still smells like blood in here," Kun said. "Didn't they get it all?"

"They got most of it," Rikuto answered after another slurp of his soup. "Doesn't matter. We're leaving tomorrow."

"Well, they should have had Harish syphon the blood away with his powers."

"That's not how it works. He syphons magic."

"Witch's blood is magic, isn't it?" Kun let out a chuckle. "He and Daiki still out at the camps? I thought they'd be done setting up the explosives by now."

"Yeah, I think they're almost done." Realizing what they'd just said, Rikuto turned to look at Karina.

Karina kept her head down, pretending not to listen to their banter. When the door opened again, her chin shot up.

Naree practically glided in. She was so graceful; it was as if she were floating. Her eyes locked with Karina's as she continued into the apartment. Behind her was Bhutano in Penny's body, followed by a uniformed Imperial Police officer.

No. Not an officer. A captain. Karina could tell by his uniform. The captain's uniform was grayish blue in color, whereas the police chief's was more of a navy blue. And there were stars above the New United Asia emblem on his chest, which set him apart from the normal Imperial Police officers. It figured Bhutano would pick someone with authority to possess. Karina wondered if this captain was next in line to be the new Chief of Police. Whoever he was, he looked eager to let Bhutano possess his body.

Karina almost cringed at the lengths Kashmeru's followers would go to for him. Blindly following an evil god for what had to be an empty promise of immortality.

Bhutano moved slightly slower than the other two, cringing now and then because of the wound in his shoulder. Penny's blouse was tinged with blood, and Karina felt an urgency to heal her.

Karina wrung her hands as the three people who entered the room came over to stand in front of her. She almost forgot Rikuto and Kun were there, until Rikuto sneered at her as he backed away.

"How do you want to do this?" Naree asked Bhutano while sizing up Karina. "The healing first?"

"No." Bhutano locked eyes with Karina. "For all we know, this could be some clever trick where the witch incapacitates me. Or traps my spirit somewhere like she probably did to Avi."

Naree crossed her arms and lifted her chin. It was as if she had already decided Karina was guilty of Bhutano's accusations.

"We'll do the transfer first. Put me in a safe place." Bhutano turned to the police captain and held him by his shoulders. "Are you ready, Captain Kang?"

"It is my honor to serve my god." Kang kept his shoulders squared as he held Bhutano's gaze.

"Kashmeru will reward you in the new world." Bhutano intensified his grip on the captain's shoulders.

When the eyes that were really Penny's glazed over and turned the blackest of blacks, Karina felt her breath leave her body for a moment. She could only gape in disbelief when Penny's jaw dropped and a swarm of black particles emerged from her mouth. It was like an intense cloud of tiny flies floating out between Bhutano and Kang. Karina felt a sharp twist in her stomach watching the scene play out. Kang's mouth then widened, and the black particles moved in a snake-like motion through Kang's lips.

In the next second, Penny's eyes rolled to the back of her head, and she released Kang's shoulders to crumple to the floor. Karina gasped and ran to her, crouching down to gather Penny into her lap.

Captain Kang's eyes also rolled back, but before he could fall, Rikuto and Kun rushed forward to catch him under his arms.

"Take him to the couch," Naree told them. "It usually takes a moment for his spirit to settle in the new host."

Karina swallowed; it was hard to find her voice. "What about Penny?"

Naree shrugged. "We shall see. Perhaps she wasn't strong enough to survive Bhutano leaving her body. Perhaps his presence was the only thing keeping her alive."

Karina's jaw hung open. But Naree ignored her and moved over to observe Captain Kang. She whispered some directions to the dark mages that Karina could not hear.

Karina shifted her focus to Penny's face, pushing her hair away from her eyes, hoping she would wake up. The slow rise and fall of Penny's chest sent a wave of relief through her.

She's alive. But for how long?

Karina moved the material of Penny's shirt aside and peeled back the bloody bandage. The wound was clean; Naree had extrapolated the bits of diamond bullet from Penny's shoulder, but she was still losing a lot of blood.

I can't wait any longer. I need to do this now.

Karina placed a hand over Penny's wound and closed her eyes. Her lips began to move, the whisper of a healing spell barely loud enough for her to hear herself. Her hand began to warm, but she wasn't sure if it was the spell or Penny's blood causing the temperature change.

She repeated the spell once more, just to be sure, before she dared to open her eyes. The glare that was set upon her when she looked up made her flinch. Kun rubbed his chin and scrutinized Penny. Karina averted her eyes and moved her hand away from Penny's wound.

Just as Kun started toward them, Naree spoke up. "He's waking up."

Kun turned away from Karina to join the empress, and in that moment, Penny stirred.

Karina held back a gasp. "Penny," she whispered.

Penny tried to sit up but froze and winced.

"Don't move." Karina put a hand on her elbow. "The bleeding has stopped, but you still need time to—"

Captain Kang stood and stretched out his neck. He flexed his arms and then straightened his uniform.

Karina knew there was no time to lose. She squeezed Penny's elbow tightly and locked eyes with her. Leaning closer, she pushed out her magic and whispered, "Remember."

Penny blinked. "Wh—"

"That's all the time you get," Naree announced, coming over to stand above them. "You've done all you can do, and now I shall do what I said I would."

Karina wanted to protest, but Naree's glare stopped her. She got to her feet and helped Penny stand up. "You mean you'll release her now."

Naree sighed. "That too, I suppose. I do keep my word. But first, her mind."

Penny's breath shuddered, and she stared wide-eyed at Karina. Karina kept her lips pressed together and squeezed Penny's hand. She wasn't sure if the spell she'd just casted would work, but she had to believe it would.

Naree held out her hand to Penny. Penny visibly swallowed and stepped toward the empress.

"Is this really necessary?" Karina asked.

"We made a deal," Bhutano said through Kang.

Karina wrapped her arms around herself as Naree placed her palms near Penny's temples.

A purple glow emanated from her hands, reflecting off the sides of Penny's face. Karina felt as if the procedure went on forever. She hadn't even known wiping someone's mind was something a mage could do. Penny's eyes went from wide to droopy-lidded, and then Naree pulled her hands away.

Karina waited, watching Penny's face, but her expression remained void of awareness, empty of emotion. She half-expected her to fall to the ground, but Penny simply stood there, like a statue. "What did you do to her?"

"Don't worry." Naree gestured to Rikuto to take Penny's arm. "She's in a sedated state for now, but my dark mages will escort her somewhere safe. Somewhere where she can't cause any trouble."

"How could she cause trouble?" Karina refrained from shouting despite the anger bubbling inside her. "You've erased her memories."

"One can't be too careful," Naree replied. "Especially in times of war."

"Where exactly will they take her?"

Naree smirked. "Do you really think I'd be foolish enough to tell you?" She gestured to her dark mages again, indicating the door.

Kun and Rikuto held each of Penny's arms and led her out of the room. Penny's legs moved her along, but her stoic expression remained. Karina's heart pounded as they disappeared, worry stabbing her like a sharp axe to her chest.

"And now," Naree began, "for your part of the bargain."

Naree pulled a necklace out from the neckline of her blouse. Karina noticed a small key hanging from it. With graceful movements, Naree glided over to a cabinet and unlocked one of the drawers. From it, she pulled out a large, withered book.

The grimoire.

The faded brown leather had a few cracks in it. The spine was a softer material, probably purposely designed so it had more give. The pages were a yellowing parchment, worn at the edges. It smelled of dust and sage.

Karina wiped her sweaty palms on her pants, shifting her feet.

"You might want to get comfortable, dear." Naree tilted her head. "You've got an important spell to learn."

SIX

As they traveled farther, Yuki noticed the landscape around them. Their position seemed to be elevated, as if they were on a mountain. In the distance, in one direction, a desert stretched, its sand a soft beige color. In the other direction, there was a lush green forest and a vast, crystal blue lake.

Yuki's mind scrambled as she tried to remember what she might have learned about the spirit realm. She knew it was a parallel plane that existed with their world, sort of overlapping with it. But she couldn't recall much else. Her mind insisted, however, that if there was a way in, then there had to be a way out.

Luckily, they seemed to have lost Avi. For now. She knew he was persistent and would stop at nothing to get to them. Though she couldn't be too sure he'd survive his injuries much longer.

"How do you know where to go?"

Yuki was roused from her thoughts. She looked over her shoulder at Mayhara, who seemed to be struggling to keep up with her. "Sorry, what?"

"You seem to be leading us as if you know exactly where we're supposed to go."

The statement made Yuki stop. She turned to face Mayhara full on and blinked for a minute in confusion.

Mayhara's deep brown eyes were wide, obviously still shaken by the fact that they were trapped here. Their constant movement and the humidity in the air turned her usual silky, brunette waves into a bit of a thick, frizzy mess. But Yuki had to admit, she was still beautiful despite it all. Mayhara adjusted the strap of the satchel as she fought to keep her balance.

"I don't know," Yuki finally said. "I guess I just feel… a pull."

"A pull to where?"

"I'm not sure. But I know it's right."

The tiniest of smiles came to life on Mayhara's face. "Okay. I trust you."

Yuki reached out and gave her hand a squeeze. "I'm sorry I got us into this mess."

"What? No. You probably saved my life. Both of our lives. If you hadn't tried to get us away from Avi, we could be dead right now."

Something pink with transparent green wings fluttered by Yuki's ear. When she tried to swat it away, it flitted over to her other ear, buzzing incessantly. "I'm not entirely sure we *aren't* dead right now."

Mayhara let out a laugh as they continued to walk. "I thought you read up on this place when we attended the academy. Wasn't it on the course requirements for diamond mages?"

Yuki pushed past a bush with glowing lilac flowers. "Well, I mean, I guess it was more theoretical. Because who would be able to get information on this place without actually coming here?"

"A skilled diamond mage, maybe? Or an amethyst mage might have seen it? Or… Darshana."

Yuki huffed a laugh. "True. She probably knows all about this place. Oh, watch your step here."

Mayhara looked through the fog where Yuki had gestured. Rocks and pebbles were embedded in the soil. The uneven land was riddled with dips and holes and slants that could make even the most graceful walker stumble. Mayhara had already remarked on what terrible timing it was that she couldn't use her earth-manipulating powers to make their journey easier.

"So, what *did* you learn about this place?" Mayhara asked, her hand tight on the strap of the bag.

"Well, mainly that it was created by a rupture in the cosmic and communal coherence. You know the Yin and Yang?"

"Of course."

"So it's like that space in between. Yang is the manifested side of existence, and Yin is the side yet to be. The hidden, or the potential of life. So the spirit realm is sort of like that plane connecting the two."

"So is it like purgatory?" Mayhara asked. "The plane between Earth and heaven?"

"Would it help you if I said, 'yes and no'?"

Mayhara chuckled. "No, but I wouldn't expect a more fitting answer when it comes to this stuff."

"Right?" Yuki smiled at her.

"So, since it's the spirit realm, does that mean there are actual spirits here?"

"That's the theory. But to be honest, I don't think anyone has testified to having proof. Like, even the few people who've experienced death for a couple of minutes before they were revived, they've talked about seeing a light. Probably that." She pointed to the sun. "And maybe hearing voices of loved ones they lost. But honestly, who's to say?"

For a small moment, Yuki allowed herself to imagine discovering her parents here. They'd been killed when she'd run away from the government, and she'd never had any closure when she'd found out they were dead. She pushed down the feeling of hope, however, not wanting to eventually face disappointment.

"Well, if it's any consolation," Mayhara said, "I'm glad we're together here. Not alone."

The snapping of a branch caused them to freeze.

"Speaking of not being alone…" Yuki swallowed.

Cutting through the fog, Avi hobbled toward them. Yuki wasn't sure how he'd managed to catch up, but there was no time to deliberate.

She and Mayhara took off, trying their best not to trip and fall because of the bumpy terrain. They had to dodge a few prickly bushes that popped up in their path. The fog seemed to grow thicker, swirling around them as they ran.

Yuki heard Mayhara grunt and looked over her shoulder. "You okay?"

"Fine," she answered between breaths. "The strap of the satchel ripped on a branch or something. Keep going."

They picked up their pace, and at one point, Mayhara managed to get in front of Yuki, holding the satchel in her hand.

The fog thinned a bit, and Yuki could just make out the ground below their feet. Or, in their case, the lack thereof.

"Wait! Stop!" She reached out and grabbed Mayhara by her arm.

They skidded to a stop just in time. But in Mayhara's effort to right herself, the satchel slipped from her grasp.

Directly in front of their toes, the earth fell away. They stood at the edge of a cliff, and though they were safe at the top, the satchel containing the scroll plummeted down into the abyss.

"No!" Mayhara futilely reached for it. Yuki had to pull her back.

Yuki risked looking over the edge, tracking where the satchel had gone. As it dropped, it dispersed the fog around it. She was sure it was a hundred-meter drop at least, but she watched it land near a tree with bright red flowers.

Mayhara let out a curse. "There must be a way down. Other than this, I mean."

Yuki heard a rustle behind them. "Avi's gaining ground." She quickly glanced around and spotted something that might help. "Look!"

They backed away from the cliff and found wide, stone steps that appeared to descend in a curve around the mountain. But there was a large gap—an empty space that dropped into a low ditch—between where they stood and where the steps began.

"We'll need to jump for it," Mayhara said. She seemed to be calculating the distance. "We can make it. I doubt Avi can. Not with his injuries."

Yuki felt skeptical, but there was no time to lose. "Okay, let's do it."

Avi neared, sneering at them.

They took off running for the gap. Yuki held her breath as they pushed off into a jump. She let out an *oomph* as she landed. Her legs felt sore and she'd hit her knee against the stone, but they'd done it. They'd cleared the gap.

They stood on the stone steps, finding their bearings, and turned back to face Avi. He clutched his side, soaked in blood and surveilling the gap. He was in no condition to jump it, and he knew it. Yuki locked eyes with him as he backed away. She was sure he was searching for an alternative route to get to them.

With labored breaths, she placed a hand on Mayhara's arm. "Okay, let's go find that satchel."

SEVEN

The words on the page began to blur. Karina had been staring at them for hours. She wanted to close the book and rest her eyes, but she was being watched. Though not intently watched anymore. It was just Kun and Rikuto in the room with her, left by Naree and Bhutano, who had made it clear they had things to prepare. After the dark mages bored their gazes into her for twenty minutes, they slowly lost interest, resorting to checking their Linqs and not really paying attention to her. After all, the only thing she'd been doing was reading one solitary page of a book.

She had to admit when Naree had first put the grimoire in front of her, she'd been fascinated by it. The moment she'd touched it, her fingers had tingled from the thought of the centuries of witches who'd written in it. She'd run her hand over the words, half-afraid her fingers would make the ink smear. It was a relief when she found she was able to read the ancient language it was written in, but the thought of releasing Kashmeru from his tomb and unleashing pure evil upon the world caused her skin to crawl. The spell she was learning the words of was the spell that had locked Kashmeru in his tomb, a spell cast by a very powerful witch. Karina's job was to learn the spell so she could undo it, to basically turn the spell on its head and break the bond.

She desperately wanted to flip the pages, to see what else might be in the book, and maybe figure out how to use the small scroll that had disappeared with Mayhara and Yuki. Information that would only be useful if they would somehow return from wherever she'd accidentally sent them.

She held the corner of the page and eyed the dark mages. Would they notice if she were to flip the page? They weren't even looking her way. Her pulse thrummed faster as she got her nerve up to peel the page back. But as soon as she lifted the page, the door to the apartment opened. Karina quickly smoothed down the page and shifted in her seat. The two dark mages lounging in the living room straightened up, tucking their Linqs away.

Karina expected Naree and Bhutano to return, but instead, the female dark mage stomped into the room. She was thin and fast. Her dark hair hung to just above her shoulders, and her eyes were like black coal.

"Hey, Ru. Think fast." Rikuto threw something at her head.

Karina didn't register what the object was until Ru used her powers to stop it in midair.

Ru had her hand raised, and when she twisted her wrist, the crumpled ball of metal turned. With a flick of her hand, the metal ball shot back in Rikuto's direction. He let out a playful *ugh* as it hit him in the stomach.

"You here to relieve us of our watch?" Kun asked.

"Yeah." The annoyed frown didn't leave her face. "It was supposed to be Harish and Daiki, but they're not back from the Kadma prison camp yet."

"Gods, how many more camps do they need to boobytrap?" Rikuto asked, tossing the metal ball into the air and catching it before it hit him in the face.

"Kadma's the last one, I think. They've been busy hitting the others all day." Ru plopped down on the couch next to Kun, casting a glance at Karina.

Karina couldn't stop looking at her. The image of Ru at Police Chief Lin's funeral when her mother—Director Shei—had died in her arms held strong in her mind, along with the haunting look in Ru's eyes that had spoken of pure vengeance.

Ru scowled. "What are you looking at?"

Karina almost dropped her gaze, but a little voice inside her head told her to stay strong, to not show weakness.

Ru stood, not breaking eye contact. "What is it?" She squared her jaw and took two steps toward Karina.

Karina couldn't help but think of Qiang. She remembered the look of deep concern on Shiro's face when he'd told her that Qiang had been ultimately responsible for Director Shei's death. "Nothing."

Ru narrowed her eyes. "I don't believe you."

Karina forced herself to keep her chin up. "It's just… I recognize you. From the funeral that was on the news."

Ru searched her face. "And?"

Karina tried to hold her gaze. "That's it. Nothing else."

"Why don't I believe you?"

Karina shook her head. "It doesn't matter."

Ru raised her hand. The crumpled piece of metal Rikuto had thrown at her earlier jetted through the air and stopped a mere inch from Karina's left eye. Karina gasped but held still. A jagged point sticking out from the metal ball taunted her iris.

"Does it matter now?" Ru sneered.

Karina swallowed hard and tried not to shake.

"I know there's something you're not telling me," Ru insisted. "I know that look."

"No." Karina's gaze was locked on the metal ball.

"It has something to do with that day, doesn't it?"

The metal ball shifted closer. Karina didn't dare to blink.

"Tell me!" Ru shouted. "What do you know?"

Karina almost shook her head, but the metal ball hovered closer. For the life of her, she couldn't think of a spell to get out of the situation.

"It's about whoever killed my mother, isn't it?"

Karina was only vaguely aware of Kun and Rikuto, who came to stand beside Ru as the drama unfolded.

"I bet it was her," Rikuto said, his arms crossed over his chest.

"No." Karina's breath was shaky. "It wasn't me."

"But you know who it was." Ru came closer, but Karina couldn't look past the ball. "Tell me who it was."

Karina bit her lip, refusing to speak.

Ru twisted her wrist.

Faster than Karina could track, the metal ball swooped across her cheek. She hadn't even realized it had sliced her skin until the ball returned to its spot in front of her eye and the hot sting of the cut began to burn.

"Let's try that again," Ru said. "And this time, I won't miss. Who killed my mother?"

Karina let out a shuddered breath.

"You know who it is!" Ru screamed. "Tell me."

"It... It was the extremist leader. I... I don't know if he pulled the trigger, but it was his call." Karina felt like a traitor for telling her. Tears welled up in her eyes.

"He's part of the group that escaped from the camps, right?" Kun asked.

The metal ball dropped into Karina's lap as Ru turned away from her. Ru was shaking, her hands balled into fists. The dark mages and Karina flinched as Ru let out a guttural scream.

Ru charged for the door.

"Wait," Rikuto called after her. "Where are you going?"

Ru threw the door open and glared back at them. "They'll pay for this. This extremist leader and all of his followers. They'll pay. My mother will be avenged!"

The road before them seemed to blur. Darshana's breath left her for a moment. It felt as if a boulder had just barreled into her chest. She reached out with shaking hands to grasp the dashboard. She had to hold on to something for fear of tipping over, even if she was strapped in place by her seatbelt.

Shiro glanced at her from the driver's seat. "Darshana, what is it?"

"Something has happened. Something horrible. I feel… death. A lot of death."

Shiro's eyes were wide, and he visibly swallowed. He looked in the rearview mirror at Mr. Kitaro.

"Nothing's showing up on any of the news sites," Mr. Kitaro announced as he checked his Linq.

"Yet," Darshana put in. "It's only now happened."

"Do you think it's Mayhara and the others?" Shiro asked. The color seemed to be draining from his face.

"I can't be sure. I'm feeling very weak." She placed her hands on the sides of her head and tried to steady her breathing.

"Do you want me to pull over so you can get some air?" Shiro asked.

Darshana looked up at the road. Everything seemed to be swaying in her vision. The sun was setting, sprays of orange and pink streaked across the sky. It would be dark soon.

"Where are we, exactly?" she asked.

Shiro checked the navigation screen. "Just outside Sainipura."

"So far off course," Darshana remarked.

"It was the only way to avoid the roadblocks, unfortunately."

The back roads they'd been taking had slowed their progress tremendously. It shouldn't have taken more than a day to get to New Delhi, even in heavy traffic. If this was the enemy's way of keeping them from interfering with their plan to bring back Kashmeru, it seemed to be working.

"Oh my word," Mr. Kitaro suddenly said.

"What?" Shiro asked, glancing in the rearview mirror. "What is it?"

"The prison camps. News is coming in that bombs are going off everywhere."

Shiro's hands seemed to slip from the steering wheel. As he fought to get control of the car, Darshana braced herself. Not just from the movement, but from the confirmation of the deaths she felt. Such an enormous loss of mage life. She pressed a hand to her chest and fought off the ache.

"Pull over," Mr. Kitaro suggested, holding his Linq to his ear. "I'll tell the others."

Darshana's heart was still racing when they all gathered at the side of the road. Everyone was desperately checking their Linqs to see if they could find out more information.

"Not all the camps were affected," Salina said, her eyes glued to her screen. "Maybe half."

"For now," Shiro put in, pacing so much he was sure to wear a hold in the ground.

"Darshana." Loni squeezed her hands. "My parents."

"I don't see their camp listed as one of the ones that were attacked," she answered.

"But we don't know if the attacks have stopped yet, do we?" Jae tucked away his Linq and raked his fingers through his hair.

"No, we don't." Darshana glanced at the moon. Night was coming fast. "We can't worry about it here on the side of the road. We need to take shelter. I know a place not too far from here. A sanctuary where we can take rest for the night." Darshana ran her hands down the sides of her face, trying to fight off the dizziness. "We'll be safe, and I can regain my strength. We can all re-energize before tomorrow."

"Okay." Shiro readied the car key, prepared to move on. "Name the place."

Darshana nodded. "I'll type it into the navigation system. Jae, Salina, you can follow us. It's our turn to lead."

EIGHT

Salina couldn't get the recent, shocking news out of her head. The prison camps had been destroyed. Not all of them, thank the gods, but about half. Shiro had obviously freaked out at the news. She'd gotten a fright when he'd seemed to have lost control of his car.

Thankfully, it didn't take long for the news sites to put out a list of the prison camps that were not affected, and once the list was public, Darshana assured Loni both her parents as well as Mayhara's family were safe. The bad news was they weren't sure the attacks had stopped for good, and reporters on every channel were saying the authorities believed the explosions to be the work of the extremists.

The mages had known this would be coming. Jae had overheard the governor talking about it with Director Shei. It was a setup devised by the government and put into action by the Pishacha. Shiro had said Qiang and his gang were doing everything they could to deactivate the bombs, but they apparently hadn't been able to get to them all in time. Salina's heart hurt for all the lost mages and mage families massacred by such a ruthless act.

Once they were over their initial shock, Darshana had insisted they continue on their way to the sanctuary she'd told them about. The sun had already set, the sky beginning to twinkle with stars. The comet appeared to be almost directly above them. Darshana doubted they'd be able to make much progress on the unreliable back roads at night.

Now, at their destination, Salina grunted, lugging her duffle bag over the rocky terrain. They'd parked the cars near an abandoned construction site and had had to walk the whole way to what Darshana had described as a sanctuary for the night.

At first, it appeared as though they were going to be hiding out in the woods. Or perhaps in a cave. Salina shuddered at the thought. The last thing she needed was a run-in with a wolf. But then the tents appeared. It seemed like a hundred of them, in various muted colors, and each one large enough to hold a fairly large-sized family. A few caravans were set up, adorned with small flags and paper lanterns.

"Are these…" Shiro looked as though he wasn't sure how to continue. "This camp. Is it a travelers' camp?"

"Travelers?" Salina's brows scrunched up. "As in… Roma?"

"Roma?" Loni scanned the area. "You mean Romani? Like, what some people used to call 'gyp—'"

"Don't say it," Jae interrupted her. "It's considered offensive. But to your point, I thought the Romani people were from Europe."

Darshana placed her hands together. "The Roma's roots are actually Northern Indian in origin. The Punjab region, to be precise. They traveled to Europe around the eighth century. And the term used to describe them came to be because the Europeans thought the people were from Egypt."

"So we were both mistaken," Jae said. "The Europeans and me."

"There's someone coming toward us," Shiro announced.

Everyone straightened and turned toward the two men walking their way. The older of the two had hair as white as Darshana's. One would never be able to tell his age from his physique, however. From the looks of him, if he wasn't a weightlifter, he must have gotten his muscle training from pulling trees out of the ground with his bare hands. His laugh lines were deep when he smiled. The younger of the two shared most of the same features: angled cheek bones, strong, square jaw, and contagious smiles. They had to be related. His thick, dark hair hung to his earlobes in a shaggy, carefree way that was just mysterious enough to be sexy. And he looked just as built as his older counterpart.

Salina couldn't help but notice how chiseled his jawline was. When the young man met her gaze, she felt a flash of heat erupt on her cheeks and neck.

"Darshana," the older man said with a bow. "It's been many years."

"One might even say decades." Darshana appeared to be holding back a smirk.

She bowed in return, and then they both smiled as he pulled her into a hug.

"Patrin." Darshana pulled back and looked him over. "You look well. Camp life suits you. Always has."

"Says the woman who's somehow managed to slow down the effects of time." Patrin let out a low chuckle. He released her and slapped the back of the young man next to him. "This is my grandson, Vano."

Darshana touched her fingers against her mouth for a second. "What? Little Vano? Last time I saw you, you were barely cutting teeth. I remember that little wet rag you'd suck on to ease the pain. You carried it everywhere."

Vano's smile was hypnotic, his teeth perfect, and his lips accentuated by dimples on either side. "As long as you're done breaking out the embarrassing stories, welcome to the camp." When he bowed, his hair fell like a curtain of black silk across his face.

"Thank you, Vano." Darshana's eyes went to Patrin. "He reminds me of you."

"I'll take that as a compliment." Patrin's gaze traveled to the others in their group. "What brings you our way, Darshana?"

She pursed her lips and took in a long breath. "I need to be honest with you. Our presence here could be dangerous for your people."

A shadow fell over Patrin's face. "Are you being followed?"

"We haven't seen anyone, but we can't be too sure. You know of the Pishacha?"

He straightened his back. "From the prophesy. Yes, I know. The time has come, hasn't it?"

"It has." Darshana glanced beside her, gesturing to each one in the group. "These are a few of the elite mages: Jae, the sapphire elite; Salina, the golden elite; Loni, the emerald elite; and Shiro, the copper elite. And this is Satoshi Kitaro, probably the last of the remaining Sacred Keys."

Patrin bowed to them, and then he stuck out his hand to Mr. Kitaro. "It's a pleasure to meet you."

Mr. Kitaro gave him a slight bow in return and shook his hand. "Likewise, of course."

"We don't mean to cause any trouble," Darshana continued. "We are on our way to meet our fate and prevent Kashmeru's return, but we need a sanctuary for the night to regain our strength before... well, before it all transpires."

"Yes, of course. You are all welcome to stay."

"We can pitch in," Darshana added, "in return for your hospitality."

"Please, Darshana." Patrin placed a gentle hand on her shoulder. "You are about to go into battle to save the world. I'd say it is we who owe you."

"I'll get some tents prepared," Van said. He mirrored his grandfather's earlier gesture by slapping a hand on his grandfather's back. "It's nice to meet you all," he said to them. "I'll let my mother know we'll need extra servings for dinner."

Vano's eyes fell on Salina once more before he turned and ran off to do what he'd said.

"You can follow me," Patrin said. "We've just started a fire."

"Sounds lovely," Darshana said, sidling up beside him as he led the way.

Patrin rubbed one of his ears. "Darshana, I thought there were supposed to be seven elite."

"There are." Darshana wrung her hands. "The other three have turned up missing. We were all together, and some unknown events took place… I can sense they are in danger, or lost, but I have no way of knowing where they are. And I haven't exactly had the time or peace of mind to meditate and lock in on their location."

"Perhaps a hot meal and a warm fire will help."

"Perhaps."

They hiked for another minute until they reached the center of the camp. It felt more homey here, the tents bigger and more colorful. There were campers parked here and there, and people walked around, dressed in the most fascinating garb, led by small torches that were lit along paths. Word must have traveled fast about their arrival because the people gave them smiles and nods. Or maybe they all recognized Darshana.

Patrin led them to the campfire, where several people were seated. Not too far away, others were preparing food.

"Wait here," Patrin said. "I'll make sure everything is getting set up."

Darshana gave him a small bow as he backed away.

Shiro set down the bags he carried and pulled out his Linq. Off to the side, Loni and Jae seemed immersed in conversation, each of them scanning the area.

Salina untangled herself from her backpack and set it on the ground. The campfire was mesmerizing. A young teenage boy was stoking it, trying to get the flames higher. Salina held her hand out, her palm already glowing gold. In a matter of seconds, the fire crackled and roared, burning hotter and higher. The teenage boy smiled, his eyes wide with wonder.

Next to her, Darshana shot her a look, one brow raised and the hint of a smirk on her lips.

"I just wanted to help," Salina said to her.

Darshana nodded. "It's very generous of them to let us stay here tonight."

"How do you know Patrin? If you don't mind me asking."

"Believe it or not, our mothers were best friends."

"Really?"

"As children, Patrin and I were always dragged along whenever they would meet up. Our friendship went through many phases through the years growing up. From playground buddies to sworn enemies to secret conspirators—"

"To boyfriend and girlfriend?" Salina nudged her with her elbow.

Darshana let out a chuckle. "I do suspect that Patrin once had feelings for me, and I did find myself desperately longing to be in his company one summer. But I'm afraid our feelings never matched up, timewise. The opportunity was missed on both accounts, and I had to assume it was never meant to be."

"So now you're just friends."

"Old friends. Yes, of course. He moved on, married, had children, and now grandchildren. And I—" Her eyes wandered to Mr. Kitaro for a moment. "I was busy training the empire's finest army."

Salina followed Darshana's gaze, wondering if there was a chance Darshana and Mr. Kitaro would end up together. That was, once they survived the showdown with Kashmeru.

Vano suddenly appeared next to them. "Darshana, the tents are ready."

Darshana placed a hand on his bicep. "Thank you, my boy."

For a second, Salina was disappointed that she hadn't thought to thank him in the same manner.

She should have been asleep hours ago, but sleep simply wouldn't come. It wasn't because of the sleeping bag, which was surprisingly comfortable. And it wasn't because of the unusual surroundings. The tents were magnificently decorated. The hanging tapestries seemed to resemble a mixture of Bohemian and Chinese roots, a blend of vibrant colors and appealing patterns. She didn't mind the smell of earth and grass. In fact, in some ways, it reminded her of her homeland of Eritrea.

What kept her awake was the fact that they were about to fight to the death in the most important battle the world had ever seen. It made her think about how she'd landed in this position. She couldn't help but think about Huojin, her best friend. How it should have been Huojin on the front line with the other elites. But she'd been killed by a dark mage, and Salina had never even had a chance to say goodbye.

Her throat was suddenly parched. She did her best not to make any noise as she got up. She didn't want to wake Loni or Darshana, who slept not too far away from her spot. As she exited the tent, she hoped she'd be able to find some water.

The fire was still going, though significantly smaller now. Sitting alone, staring into the flames, was Vano. He looked up and her as she approached, and a friendly smile appeared on his face as he stood.

"You're still awake?" she asked quietly.

"Darshana said you were in danger. Someone should keep watch." He tilted his head. "What's kept you up?"

"Destiny, I suppose."

He smirked. "Oh?"

She couldn't help but laugh. "I mean, my destiny. As an elite mage. And how it's time to face it."

"You want to talk about it?"

"Actually, I'd really like some water."

He nodded. "Oh, sure. Of course."

He walked over to a tree stump near the tent and dipped a ladle into a bucket of water. After pouring the water into a clay cup, he handed it to her.

"Thank you."

He watched her as she drank.

She let out a small laugh. "What?"

"Sorry." He seemed to be blushing. "Was I staring?"

"A little."

"Well, at the risk of being too forward, I have to say I'm a bit mesmerized by your beauty."

Her skin grew warm. "Oh. Um, thank you. I, uh, I don't know what to say."

"I don't mean to embarrass you. But, um, look." He pulled out the thin, gold chain that hung around his neck until the pendant at the end was out of his shirt. "This belonged to my grandmother."

"Gold topaz," Salina remarked.

"Yes." He held the topaz in his palm. "That's what your eyes remind me of."

She studied his face for a moment. He was very handsome. And so kind. What was she doing?

"If you're trying to distract me from my worries, I think it might be working."

His smile lit up his face. "We can sit by the fire for a while, if you want. Until you feel tired, I mean. I could use the company."

"Sure." She cradled the cup of water in her hands. "I'd like that."

She wasn't sure how long they'd been talking for, but it must have been hours. He kept making her laugh, and she kept the fire going. They spoke about topic after topic—all the while with Vano being a perfect gentleman—until her yawns got the best of her and she decided to turn in.

She silently crept back into the tent, knowing that she probably wouldn't get much sleep before they had to get up. But in her mind, it was worth it.

As she slipped back into her sleeping bag, Loni shifted.

"Where were you?" Loni's voice was quiet and slow, as if she'd just woken up.

"I couldn't sleep. I was talking with Vano."

She couldn't be sure, but she thought Loni giggled. "Are you tired now?"

"Exhausted." Salina settled down on her pillow. "How are you?"

Loni didn't answer right away. "What do you mean?"

"I know you were struggling today."

Again, Loni took a second to answer. "I'm doing better. I'm so relieved my parents are okay. For now."

"I'm glad too. I also noticed you speaking with Jae earlier. How are things there?"

"Complicated. But… I guess I'm learning to let him go. I've fooled myself long enough. He loves Mayhara. I have to stop denying it. Besides, we'll probably all be dead tomorrow."

"Loni!"

"Too dark?" Loni let out a small laugh. "Sorry. Darkness has always been my way of dealing with things."

They were quiet for a while, and Salina thought Loni might have drifted off to sleep again.

"I don't really mean it," Loni finally said. "I don't think it's the end of us. I keep hearing my sister's voice in my head telling me that I'm here for a reason. That I'm meant to fight this battle. And that we'll win."

Salina breathed in a deep breath and slowly exhaled. "For all our sakes, I hope your sister is right."

NINE

Karina pushed around the food on her plate, her mind swirling with the words of the spell Naree had made her learn. Now that she'd spent all day reading it, she felt confident that she'd be able to perform the spell when the time came. The problem was she hated the prospect of releasing a monster.

If only she could look through the grimoire to see what else it contained. Maybe there were clues about how to stop the Pishacha, or maybe she could find information about the small scroll. She still hadn't been able to open it—back when it had been in her possession. If Mayhara and Yuki found their way back with it, she wanted to be ready.

But the grimoire was locked away. When the sun had set earlier, Naree had closed the book and used the key that hung on a necklace she wore to lock the grimoire in a cabinet in the living room. Then Bhutano had thrown Karina in one of the penthouse's guest rooms and locked her in as well. An hour later, a Pishacha soldier had stepped into the room and tossed a plate of food on the dresser for her. His eyes had only met hers for a split second before he'd turned and left the room again. The sound of the lock pad's lock engaging after he'd left still sounded in her mind.

She'd let the food sit for well over an hour now, with no intention of eating anything they gave her. Fear that they might try to drug her or poison her had crossed her mind, but eventually, she gave in. She had only eaten enough to stop her stomach from grumbling. Thoughts about the grimoire and what else it might contain kept her from finishing the meal. She needed to see what else was in the book, but in order to do that, she'd need to get out of the room.

Using a spell to disengage the lock wouldn't be a problem, but she would have to wait until no one was around. She knew they were preparing to leave in the morning to head to the Lotus temple, but she couldn't be sure anyone was still in the apartment. It had been hours, and she suspected that even the goddess Lakshmi had to get her rest before an eventful day.

A whisper touched her ears. She couldn't be sure, but she thought it might have been her grandmother's voice. And though she couldn't clearly make out the words, she was suddenly struck with the memory of a spell her grandmother had once taught her. It was a spell her grandmother had used in the swamps to avoid running into any wild animals or snakes when they were out gathering herbs and plants. A motion sensor spell. If Karina used it, she'd be able to feel if anyone was nearby. It was her best bet to getting to the cabinet unnoticed to get the book.

She paced the room, trying to decide if she should wait a bit longer. It would be easier to move through the apartment if everyone was asleep.

Her heart thumped in her chest and her palms were damp with sweat. She tried to control her breathing as she went to the door and pressed her ear against it. Not hearing any movement, she straightened her back and called to mind the words of Amalia's spell.

Her fingers tingled as the spell began to work. It was as if her fingers were inching their way under the door and down the hall, splitting up to search the different rooms. In a matter of seconds, she knew that Naree was asleep in her room and Bhutano was smoking on the balcony of his bedroom. One Pishacha soldier—probably he one who'd delivered her plate of food—stood guard outside the apartment door. She couldn't sense the dark mages anywhere and wondered briefly if their powers made it possible to dodge her sensing spell. Though she couldn't be sure if they were in the apartment or not, she couldn't wait any longer to try to get a peek at the grimoire.

Placing her hand on the lock pad, she recited a spell to disengage the lock. Within seconds, the red indicator light switched to green. She blinked in surprise. Usually, it took more effort. She hoped the small beep that sounded was quiet enough not to be heard by the others.

With her hand on the doorknob, she held her breath so she could hear more clearly. Everything was quiet.

Her steps were light as she slipped out of the room and made her way down the dark hall toward the living room. The moonlight shone in through the large windows in the living room, lighting her way in the dark.

She reached out with the sensing spell again to make sure no one was coming. Both Naree and Bhutano were still in their rooms, and the Pishacha remained at his station. Focused on the cabinet that held the grimoire, Karina crept closer.

She could practically hear the grimoire calling to her. Glancing over her shoulder, just in case, she blew out a nervous breath and then turned to focus on the keyhole of the cabinet. Though the spell to get a mechanical lock to disengage usually took a minute to work, the lock clicked open almost as soon as she touched it.

Grandmother, she thought, *your powers are amazing.*

As quietly as she could manage to be, Karina pulled open the cabinet and placed her hands on the grimoire. She might have imagined it, but it felt as if the grimoire clung to her. Like it was longing to be held by a family member. As she opened the book, she realized the moonlight wasn't enough for her to be able to read the pages. Grabbing one of the candles decorating a side table, she whispered the spell to create a flame on the wick. She held the book close and scanned the pages near the trapping spell.

A few pages after the spell, she noticed ragged parchment close to the inside spine.

Someone tore out the page, she whispered to herself.

Though she couldn't be sure, she guessed it was the spell that was rolled up in the small scroll. Someone had gone to great lengths to remove it and secure it elsewhere.

She turned back one page and read the text, her mind translating the words. She couldn't be sure, but she believed one word to translate into *poison*. Could the key to destroying Kashmeru lie in some kind of poison? Was the small scroll some kind of recipe to create a poison strong enough to destroy a god?

The sound of footsteps found her ears. It was soon followed by a low voice Karina could only assume was the Pishacha soldier standing guard outside the apartment. Closing the book, Karina blew out the candle and hurried to return the grimoire to the cabinet. She barely had time to spell the lock closed before she dropped down to hide behind a chair. It was the same chair she'd sat in all day while studying the trapping spell.

A door opened. Karina held her breath.

"How many of the camps were destroyed?"

It was Kun's voice. Karina held her hands over the sides of her neck in an attempt to quiet her heart pounding in her ears.

"About half," Ru answered, "judging from the reports coming in from the wardens."

"Half?"

"Quiet, Kun." This time it was Rikuto speaking.

"What happened to the others?" Kun asked in a quieter voice. "I thought Harish and Daiki set explosives to go off in *all* the camps."

"They did," Ru answered. "They don't know what went wrong. But half is better than none."

Karina hunkered down lower and bit on her fingertips. She knew from Shiro that Qiang and his gang had been busy dismantling the explosives in most of the camps. This discussion told her that Qiang had only managed to get to half the locations.

"I thought the bombs were supposed to be detonated tomorrow before the ceremony," Kun said.

"I convinced them to detonate them early," Ru replied. "They make me sick. The extremists. All of them. After what they did to my mother, I couldn't let them win. They got what they deserved."

Karina dropped her head into her hands. Half the mage population. Dead. A shudder ran through her body. This was her fault. If she hadn't triggered Ru into destroying the camps early, maybe Qiang and his gang would have had enough time to deactivate all the explosives.

She lowered her head, dread hanging over her like a heavy blanket, and waited until the dark mages were gone so she could sneak back to her room.

TEN

The night air felt cooler, and the ever-present mist snaked its way higher up their legs. Yuki was exhausted after their long climb down the stone steps, which had been made more difficult when the sun had set. A part of her was relieved that the concept of day and night was something that existed in the spirit realm. It gave her a small sense of normalcy in an otherwise mysterious place.

"Did you see where it landed?" Mayhara asked. "If my powers were working, I'd feel the ground so we could find it quicker."

Yuki pointed to a tree with bright red flowers hanging in a cascading, vine-like fashion. "I think it landed by that tree. I'm sure if we feel around in that fog, we'll be able to find it."

"We'll need to hurry, though." Mayhara checked behind them. "I have a feeling Avi might have found another way down the mountain."

They neared the tree and crouched down, stretching their arms out into the low, creeping fog. Yuki couldn't be sure of everything she was touching. There were definitely rocks, grass, and unfortunately prickly plants, but she didn't feel the satchel. Mayhara appeared to be having the same lack of good luck.

A sudden staccato yelp echoed around them. Yuki straightened and scanned the area. It was hard to see, but something quick and white darted toward them. Yuki let out a scream and instinctively moved toward Mayhara.

"What is that?" Mayhara asked.

The creature hopped through the mist, and Yuki grabbed Mayhara's arm.

"I don't know. It's hopping around like a rabbit, but it's quicker and much bigger."

"Just stay still. If it doesn't feel threatened by us, it won't have any reason to attack us."

Yuki did as Mayhara said, forcing herself not to move a muscle as the animal sniffed around in the fog.

A white tail emerged as it continued its search. And then another. And another. Yuki blinked in confusion.

"I think it's a fox," Mayhara whispered.

"But it's practically the size of a dog. And those tails."

Suddenly, the animal stopped. As it lifted its head, Yuki had to admit it looked like a white fox. The fox wiggled its nose as it studied them. More tails lifted from behind it in the fog.

"Nine tails," Mayhara whispered. "It's a *kitsune*."

"Whoa." A small smile formed on Yuki's face. "It's actually really cute."

As her fear dissolved, her curiosity took over and she took a step toward the kitsune.

With a flinch, the kitsune bared its teeth at them. In the next second, it ducked its head into the fog and quickly resurfaced with a strap seized in its mouth.

Mayhara gasped. "The satchel!"

As soon as she'd said it, the kitsune jumped up and scurried off through the fog.

"No!" Yuki didn't even hesitate. She chased after the kitsune, not caring where her feet landed.

"Yuki, wait!"

She was barely aware of Mayhara running behind her. The only thing that mattered was getting the satchel back. There was no telling what their chances were of escaping the spirit realm, but without the small scroll, they were doomed.

The kitsune raced into a meadow, its assemblage of furry white tails bouncing along behind it. The top tips of wildflowers in the field swayed in the fog as the kitsune made its way through. It was way too fast for Yuki, but she wasn't about to give up. The kitsune reached the end of the meadow and froze when a whistle sounded in the air. With its tails wagging, the fox trotted toward a giant oak and disappeared from view.

"Is it gone?" Mayhara asked between labored breaths.

Yuki didn't have enough air in her lungs to answer. Instead, she pointed to the oak and slowed to a walk.

Mayhara caught up and joined her as they rounded the tree. Both of them gasped at what they found.

"Kamal?"

Crouched behind the oak, looking up at them, was Kamal—the elite sapphire mage who'd been killed by the Pishacha. Yuki had forgotten how tall he was until he stood. She continued to stare in wonder as he shook his stringy, black hair out of his face. The kitsune purred and slunk around Kamal's leg.

"I don't know what's more shocking," Mayhara said. "The fact that kitsune exist or that you're standing here before us."

For a second, they simply stared at each other, and then they all let out a relieved laugh and exchanged hugs.

"How…?" Yuki shook her head. "Are you alive?"

Kamal let out a laugh. "I think you know the answer to that. We are in the spirit realm, after all. And weren't you there when I was buried?"

Yuki rubbed the back of her neck. "Yeah. Right."

Kamal eyed them. "So what happened? How did you die?"

"Oh." Mayhara shook her head. "No, we're not dead. We sort of landed here by mistake. A magic mishap. We're actually being chased by one of the dark mages."

Kamal clicked his tongue. "You just can't stay out of trouble, can you?"

Above them, the sky began to change. The comet went from black to silver, its light almost as bright as the moon.

"Oh good," Kamal said. "Our magic's coming back."

"What?" Yuki gawked at him. "Because the sun set?"

"No, it's not as simple as that." Kamal pointed to their wrists. "Our wristbands are lighting up. It comes and goes, day and night. There's no rhyme or reason to it. But what I do know is that when my powers come back, I can finally talk to this guy again." He reached down and pet the kitsune's head.

"He talks?" Yuki asked, astonished.

"Well, no. But my powers somehow let me hear him. Or his thoughts. I don't know exactly. But we can communicate." Kamal picked up the satchel from the ground and stood. "What's this?"

"That's… important," Mayhara answered, but Kamal had already removed the small scroll from the bag.

"Hey, if it's not food, how important can it be?" He smirked and replaced the scroll.

"Wait." Yuki shook her head. "You eat after you're dead?"

Kamal smirked. "We don't have to, but why should I give up my favorite pastime?"

"The scroll," Mayhara said, getting back to the vital topic. "It supposedly contains a spell that could destroy Kashmeru." She checked over her shoulder. "Which is one of the reasons the dark mage is after us."

"It's so small," Kamal remarked, balancing the scroll in one hand. "I can't imagine it's a long and difficult spell."

"Well, we don't know, to be honest." Yuki shrugged. "Karina couldn't get it open. None of us could."

"There must be some special witchy way to unroll it," Mayhara added.

"Hmm." Kamal handed Yuki the satchel. "You know who you should ask? Amalia."

Mayhara frowned. "Amalia is… dead. The poison finally took her life."

To their surprise, Kamal let out a laugh.

"Yeah, I know," he said. "She's here. Come on. I'll bring you to her."

ELEVEN

"**S**he's here?" Mayhara asked, flustered. "You've seen her?" There was a tingling warmth in her chest at the prospect.

"Sure," Kamal answered. "We've hung out. You know, discussing philosophy and stuff."

"Why am I having a hard time imagining that?" Yuki mumbled.

"Have you seen anyone else?" Mayhara asked.

"Here and there." Kamal narrowed his eyes. "You don't know, do you?"

Mayhara shook her head. Yuki looked as if she were going to say something, but then she closed her mouth and waited for Kamal to continue.

"We're all stuck here." He began to walk and waved for them to follow. "Come on. I'll explain on the way."

He led them through a forest, one so different from any Mayhara had ever seen before. The plush carpet of grass beneath their feet glistened in the light of the comet. Every tree seemed to bear some kind of fruit or flower, some of them glowing. The trunks of the trees looked like white stone, structured in a spiral design. She assumed the small floating lights fluttering around were fireflies, but she couldn't be sure. The kitsune bounded along, sometimes darting up ahead and then scurrying back to walk beside Kamal.

"As I was saying," Kamal continued. "This is sort of a holding place, and we're all trapped here. For now, anyway."

"Who's 'we'?" Mayhara struggled to keep up with the long-legged mage.

"Everyone who's died because of the war with Kashmeru. Amalia says it's not our final destination. That there's a much better place for us, and that we'll get unstuck once the war ends."

"You mean once Kashmeru is destroyed?" Yuki asked.

"Or, you know." Kamal cleared his throat. "The other outcome."

Mayhara felt as if acid were bubbling in her stomach, eating her insides. "If Kashmeru destroys the world and reigns over a new dimension, what happens then? A place worse than this?"

Kamal spared her a glance and let out a sigh as he shrugged. "Either way, we're stuck here until this unfinished business gets resolved." He reached out and plucked a glowing plum from a tree. There was a loud crunch as he bit into it.

As they continued on their way, Mayhara thought about everyone who'd lost their lives as a result of the battle against the Pishacha. Huojin, the elite golden mage who'd been killed by Avi. Riya, Mayhara's colleague and friend who'd been killed because the Pishacha had thought Riya was Mayhara.

Yuki's parents.

She didn't want to bring them up, just in case. But it would be good if Yuki could get a chance to see them before they got back to their world.

Assuming they'd be able to get back.

The trees thinned, and they came upon a clearing. Mayhara spotted a small, stone cottage up ahead, marked by a torch affixed like a sconce by the door.

"Is that where Amalia is?" she asked.

"That's her place here, yeah." Kamal whistled, and the kitsune ran up ahead. He gave Mayhara a wink. "He's letting her know company's coming."

Mayhara felt as if they couldn't get there quickly enough. Not that she wasn't appreciative of being able to see Kamal, but knowing Amalia was here and that she might be able to help them with the scroll gave Mayhara a boost of hope.

A maple-scented smoke wafted from the chimney. The house looked like something out of a fairy tale. The kitsune had jumped into an open window, and half a minute later, the front door opened. Mayhara was surprised when a muscular, middle-aged man stepped out. She slowed her pace, furrowing her brow.

"I thought this was Amalia's place," she said.

"It is." Kamal closed the distance between himself and the man, delivering a high-five that made Mayhara blink in confusion. "This is

Aiguo. He was Mr. Kitaro's bodyguard. Struck down by the Pishacha while protecting him."

Mayhara and Yuki bowed to him. He placed his feet together swiftly and returned the bow.

"Nice to meet you," Yuki said sweetly. "Are you Amalia's bodyguard now?"

Aiguo smiled. "No. Nothing to guard her from here. I'm merely her companion as we wait for the war to be resolved. Please, come in."

There was a warm glow filling the tiny house. Mayhara and Yuki exchanged glances. She was sure they were thinking the same thing: This felt like a dream.

Crouched over the fireplace, Amalia stoked the fire. She let out a grunt and a sigh as she stood and wiped her hands on her skirt.

"Amalia!" Yuki ran over to her and enveloped her in her arms.

Mayhara had tears in her eyes as she joined their hug, resting her forehead on Amalia's scraggly, gray hair. "This is incredible."

"Yes, yes. It's all very magical. Now, please, give an old woman some room."

They all took a step back, and Mayhara studied the swamp witch.

"Well, have a seat." Amalia gestured to two small couches in the tiny room. "It's a bit snug, but you can rest your haunches a bit before you continue on your journey."

"You know about our journey?" Yuki asked.

"Yes. I've been expecting you." Amalia gave her a wink.

Mayhara crinkled her brow and looked Kamal's way. He simply shrugged in response.

"You knew we were coming?" Yuki asked.

Amalia worked her way onto one of the couches. "My ancestors speak to me all the time, now that I'm here. Their voices are much clearer in the spirit realm. To be honest, sometimes I wish I could switch them off." She let out a low chuckle.

"And they told you we were here?" Mayhara was trying to wrap her mind around the information.

"Actually, they told me the scroll was coming my way. But I figured it had to be one of you bringing it to me." Amalia's expression darkened. "But first, tell me, how is Karina?"

Mayhara and Yuki exchanged a glance.

"Last we saw her," Mayhara said, "she was fighting off the enemy, protecting the scroll. And us."

"It was her magic—mixed with mine, I guess—that sent us here," Yuki added.

Amalia nodded slowly. "Yes. She may not have known it, but she was sending the scroll to someone who could help. And I'm assuming that since she's not here, she must still be alive."

This insight gave Mayhara hope. She had to assume Penny and the others were still alive as well.

Kamal cleared his throat. "Sorry to interrupt, but is there some kind of messenger or delivery reward for bringing them here?"

Amalia frowned and gave Aiguo a nod. Aiguo retrieved a jar from the counter in what Mayhara assumed was the kitchen and handed it to Kamal.

"Ooh, yeah," Kamal exclaimed. "I love these berries." He tossed one to the kitsune, who caught it in his mouth midair.

"So let's see it." Amalia held her hand out.

"Oh, right." Yuki handed her the satchel.

Amalia smiled. "This is Karina's bag."

"Yes," Yuki replied.

Amalia slowly smoothed her hand over the satchel before opening it and pulling out the scroll.

Mayhara had expected her to perform some kind of spell or recite an incantation, but all she did was flip the gold latch, and the scroll opened.

"How did you—?" Yuki's jaw hung open.

Amalia shrugged. "Maybe I've got the magic of centuries of witches on my side." She turned her attention to the words on the scroll. "Aha. Okay."

"We could leave it open," Yuki suggested to Mayhara. "So Karina doesn't have to worry about opening it when we get back."

Amalia looked up from the scroll. "I doubt it works that way. I have a feeling you two are going to have to learn the spell."

"But we're not witches," Mayhara said.

"Mages are not far off from witches. Perhaps a bit more limited in power." She winked at Kamal this time, and he rolled his eyes in response.

"But you can learn the words, memorize them, and recite them to Karina at the tomb. It might work. It *has to* work. I see no other choice."

Mayhara almost said something about not knowing where Karina might be, or if they'd even make it back and find the tomb in time, but she decided to concentrate on thinking positive.

Amalia cleared her throat, holding the scroll up, and began reading out loud.

"Abire hostem
Hoc planum es ex agro
Cum enim venenum componere
boni a Chakras
Abire hostem
Vos ultra
Per virtute divina
demoliti sunt egressi vobiscum
et non est amplius."

Mayhara tried to push down the doubt that they could learn the spell. She could barely get the first words out correctly. But the world depended on this. This would be the most important thing she could ever need to learn.

Hours later, the words of the spell swirled in Mayhara's mind. Amalia had made them repeat the incantation over and over until they got it right. It wasn't until the sun peeked its rays through the windows that Amalia finally stood and rolled up the scroll.

Even though Mayhara knew the words by heart now, seeing the scroll closed again made her cringe with worry. She hoped that between the two of them, she and Yuki would remember the spell when the time came to use it.

Aiguo escorted them to the door.

"You know where to go?" Amalia asked them.

Yuki nodded. "Yes, I do. I don't know how I do, but I do."

"Sounds perfectly logical to me." Amalia gave them hugs. "Oh. Your wristbands."

Mayhara twisted her hand and noticed her garnet stone glowing. The light had faded during the night, but now it returned. She smiled, knowing her powers would work for a while. She was unaware of what terrain they might need to cross, but she was sure her crimson mage powers would come in handy.

Amalia patted her shoulder. "You have to go. That dark mage is on his way."

"How did you—?" Yuki gaped at her. "We didn't even tell you about him."

"Amalia tapped her temple with a finger. "Ancestors."

They nodded in unison.

"Right," Mayhara said. "And if our powers are working, that means his probably are, too."

"Then we'd better hurry," Yuki added.

"There's power in numbers." Kamal was suddenly beside them. "The least I can do for my part in this war is accompany you to your destination."

"Thanks, Kamal." Mayhara placed a hand on his shoulder. "We'd be honored."

"Will you be all right, Amalia?" Yuki asked.

"Child, I'm already dead. What more could happen to me?"

Yuki let out an awkward laugh. "I guess you're right."

"Good luck," Aiguo said. "And please tell Mr. Kitaro it was a privilege working with him."

"And give Karina a big hug from me," Amalia added.

"We will." Mayhara waved as they backed away from the house. "Thank you, Amalia."

TWELVE

enny blinked as the spoon she held tapped against the side of a teacup. Everything around her began to come into view, as if she were waking from a dream. She sat at a table in a café. From all around her, the sound of cats meowing filled her ears. A little girl giggled, stroking the back of a fluffy Persian feline as her mother gossiped with a friend over tea and Japanese cheesecake.

She blinked again.

How did I get here?

There was a dull ache in her head, and her body felt as if she'd recently run a marathon. She swallowed hard, trying to remember how she'd ended up in a cat café.

As she shifted in her chair, a sharp pain in her shoulder made her wince. She moved her blouse away from her body a few inches and glanced down to find a bandage taped to her skin.

What happened to me?

Her heart sped up and her breaths grew heavier, but she forced herself to appear calm as she tried to clear her mind so she could think. She didn't want to draw attention to herself, and she didn't need anyone calling the Imperial Police about a crazy person freaking out in a cat café.

What's the last thing I can remember?

Try as she might, she couldn't get a clear image of anything she had recently done. Or seen. Or said. It was as if something was blocking her visions, her memories.

Checking to make sure no one was watching her, she set down the spoon and stood from the table. Finding no money on her, she decided to simply slip out of the café, hopefully unnoticed. She bit the inside of her cheek as she made her way toward the door. Maybe she would recognize what city she was in once she stepped outside.

The ache in her head subsided a bit as the fresh air out in the street washed over her face. A chill traveled up her spine as she took in her surroundings. Nothing on the street looked familiar at all.

After checking herself for her Linq and coming up emptyhanded, she turned to the menu displayed in the cat café's window.

Ajeetgarh. What am I doing here?

Tears threatened to spill as she realized the direness of her situation. If only she had an idea of whom to contact for help.

Darshana.

Her brow creased. She wasn't even sure if the old guru was still alive. It had been years since she'd last seen her.

Hadn't it?

She wrapped her arms around herself and started walking, unsure of where she should go. The sounds of people talking reached her ears, and she felt a strange pang in her chest at the words 'comet' and 'temple.'

Continuing down the street, the flicker of televiewers displayed in the window of an electronics shop caught her attention. Though she couldn't hear the sound from the screens, she focused on the images of the Lotus Temple displayed on the televiewers.

She didn't know why, but she was overcome with a sense of urgency. Something told her she was supposed to be there.

An Imperial Police van passed her on the street. Instinctively, she turned her head away from it. She could remember always steering clear of the police, but somehow the feeling to hide from them felt even more imperative.

What's happening? And why can't I remember?

Running her hand up her arm to stop from shivering, she scraped against a sensitive spot near her elbow. Hissing in a breath, she would have sworn she heard a voice echo in her head.

Remember.

She froze in place. There was something familiar about the voice, but she couldn't put a name or face to it. Something must have happened that had caused her memories to disappear. Not all of them, but whatever might have happened recently. And someone had known this was going to happen but wanted her to remember.

But how?

Her mind swirled, and her stomach churned. With every panicked breath, she winced at the throbbing ache in her shoulder. Had she been stabbed? Shot? Who would have done this to her? Had it been the police? But then, how had she gotten away and ended up bandaged in a cat café?

There were too many unanswerable questions, and she wasn't sure how she was going to solve the mystery. The only thing she felt certain of was that she needed to get to the Lotus Temple. And soon.

Swallowing back her fear, she picked up her pace. She didn't know how she was going to do it, but she was determined to get to that temple and get some answers, no matter what it took.

THIRTEEN

Shiro rolled up his sleeping bag and set it near one of the walls of the tent. He'd had a restless sleep, and though he would have benefited from dozing for a while longer, the sounds of the travelers beginning their day—along with the smell of something delectable cooking over a fire—gave him the needed push to get up.

Jae and Mr. Kitaro hadn't woken him when they'd gotten up. Their things were already sitting by the front of the tent, ready to go. He hoped he wasn't holding up the group from leaving. It was an important day. The *most* important day.

He gathered his bags and set them by the others, and then he let out a long breath. He'd been anxious to check his Linq, but he didn't want to face disappointment again. He'd sent a message to Qiang as soon as he'd heard about the prison camp explosions. And when the extremists had been blamed for the attacks, he'd linqed him again. But so far, he hadn't heard back. To make things worse, he'd overheard Jae telling Darshana that some arrests of extremists had already been made. To say he was worried was an understatement.

When he stepped out of the tent, Loni waved him over. The rest of the gang was gathered around Jae's Linq. As he got closer, he realized they were watching a news report.

"…has come forward with evidence that officially links the attacks to the extremists. Governor Laghari has reported that's he's received messages from the extremist leader threatening more attacks. For fear the festival at the Lotus temple this evening could be a target, acting Police Chief Kang has issued a nationwide decree, allowing Imperial Police to use brute force if any mage is found within a fifty-kilometer radius of the temple. He went as far as to say that the situation has become so extreme, if necessary, police will be permitted to shoot on sight."

Salina gasped, and Shiro rubbed his temples. He couldn't believe it had come to this.

"This is going to make it even more difficult to get to the temple," Loni said.

"They're really going to tighten security now." Jae tucked his Linq into his pocket. "We'll need to get there sooner rather than later, before it's completely locked down."

"I agree." Darshana gave them a curt nod. "We need to go."

Mr. Kitaro cleared his throat. "On that subject, there's something I need to say."

The group turned to face him.

Darshana's brows drew together. "What is it?"

"I don't believe I'm supposed to partake in this leg of the journey."

Salina stared at him, her hands coming up to her mouth.

"I would just get in the way," he continued. "And this mission is too important for you to have to worry about a third wheel… or sixth, as the case may be. I've spoken with Patrin, and he's agreed to let me stay here. For now, I mean. It's safer for you—and for me."

Darshana reached out and took his hand. "My dear Mr. Kitaro."

"If all goes well—"

"*When* all goes well. We have to think positive now."

He smiled at her. "*When* all goes well, you know where to find me."

She lifted his hand and placed a kiss upon it. "We'll come back for you, as soon as we've won the war."

Patrin and Vano approached.

Darshana turned to face them and gave them a bow. "Patrin, I owe you heartfelt thanks. You've been more than hospitable."

"It's nothing compared to what you're doing for us, Darshana." He pulled her in for a hug. "May luck be on your side."

"Salina." Vano closed the distance between them. "I want you to have this. For luck."

Her eyes widened as he placed a gold chain with a stone pendant in her hand. "I can't take this."

"Think of it as a loan. You can return it to me… after."

She smiled up at him. "Thank you. I will."

Shiro, Jae, and Loni added their thanks, and Patrin had some of the travelers help them with their bags. Shiro felt as if he were having an out-of-body experience as they loaded up the car. He couldn't believe the day of reckoning had finally come. Was he ready for this? Were any of them?

Jae clapped him on the back. "All set?"

Shiro returned the clap. "Now or never, right?"

Before his hand even touched the car door handle, his Linq buzzed. When he looked at the screen, he was surprised to see it wasn't just a return message; Qiang was calling him.

His finger almost slipped when he went to answer it. "Qiang?"

"Shiro." He sounded out of breath.

"I heard about the prison camps. I was worried about you. I mean, I still am."

"I'm okay. I'm glad to hear your voice. I'm lying low. And I'm pissed that we couldn't dismantle all the bombs."

"Don't blame yourself. The Pishacha are the bad guys here." Shiro could remember a time Qiang had said the same thing to him. "Qiang, the police have been instructed to use brute force if they find any mages near the temple."

Qiang sighed into the Linq. "I heard."

"That's why it kills me to have to ask you this."

"What is it?"

Shiro ran a hand through his hair. "If you do this, if we pull this off and stop Kashmeru, we're still going to have his followers to deal with. The police, the government… basically everyone who's going to be at the temple tonight. There's going to be chaos, and we're going to need help containing it."

"Say no more. We'll be there."

"Are you far from New Delhi?"

Qiang let a small laugh escape his lips. "Don't worry. We'll make do. And if it comes to it, I think I know a place where I can borrow a helicopter."

Shiro almost laughed, but something told him Qiang wasn't kidding.

FOURTEEN

They'd stopped by a stream and cupped their hands in the water to drink from it. Yuki had used the time when their powers had been working to keep Mayhara's mood—as well as her own—elevated. It wouldn't do to have them lose hope. But the haze reappeared around the sun, the comet turned black again, and their wristbands were no longer lit up. She hoped the couple of hours of mood-boosting had been enough to keep their spirits lifted until their powers came back into effect.

The kitsune jumped into the stream to drink, and then it rolled around in the water. When it strolled out onto the bank, it shook its body and all nine tails, practically soaking Kamal.

"Kamal, does he have a name?" Yuki asked, taking the opportunity of their short break to sit and rub her aching feet.

"Akari."

"That's cute," Mayhara said.

"It means 'bright, white jasmine.' But believe me, you spend time with him after he's had a few too many cabbages, and it's not flowers he smells like."

Akari chittered at him.

"How much farther is it, do you think, Yuki?" Mayhara flattened her hand over her eyes, looking out into the distance. "I can't help feeling we're cutting it close."

Yuki put her shoes back on and stood. "We're almost there."

Mayhara's eyes went to Kamal. "Do you know where we're headed?"

Kamal wiped drops of water from his cheek. "I'm not the spirit realm mage. The ball's in Yuki's court."

Mayhara shrugged. "I just thought because you've been here, you might have an idea of what awaits us in the direction we're headed."

"That way?" Kamal stretched his back and his neck, narrowing his eyes. "There are some caves that way."

"Yes." Yuki clapped her hands together and held her index fingers to her mouth. "That sounds right. Something was telling me I needed to find a cave."

"Okay, then." Mayhara wiped her hands on her jeans. "Let's go."

It was another hour before they could even catch a glimpse of the caves. They were nestled in the side of a hill, and farther out, the hill became a mountain.

Yuki picked up her pace, excited to finally be getting to their destination. The fog was low and covered any sight of the ground, so when her feet began to sink into what felt like sand, she let out a gasp of surprise.

"Oh, it's sand." She held out her hands to regain her balance.

From behind her, Kamal called out. "Yuki, stop!"

"What?" Mayhara froze beside him. "What is it?"

"It's quicksand!" Kamal took careful steps, his arms reaching for Yuki, but she was too far in.

Yuki scoffed. "You didn't think to mention the quicksand earlier? Don't you think that would have been an important detail to warn us about?"

"I forgot about it! Sorry!" Kamal crouched down and stretched his arm toward her, but it was of no use.

Yuki shifted her weight, trying to keep her legs from sinking deeper into the sand.

Akari let out sounds between barks and wails, running back and forth behind Kamal, probably knowing he was unable to help.

"Stop struggling," Mayhara called. "It'll only make you sink faster."

"I'm just supposed to *not* move?"

"If you die here, you'll be stuck like the rest of us. You won't be able to leave. I'll see if I can find a branch or something." Kamal ran off toward a patch of bushes.

Mayhara paced, looking up at the sun. Yuki followed her gaze. The sparkling haze went from blue to pink.

"Come on," Mayhara mumbled.

Yuki couldn't find her breath, starting to feel suffocated. She wanted to lift her legs, but that would go against Mayhara's advice.

"How's it going, Kamal?" Yuki forced her voice to remain as calm as she could manage.

Kamal ran back with a flimsy branch. "Grab hold."

Yuki wrapped her hands around the thin branch, ignoring the sting in her palm from something sharp. Kamal pulled gently, not wanting to break the branch. Mayhara wrung her hands, constantly checking the sun.

The thick, wet sand clung to Yuki's legs, which now felt as if they were made of lead.

"Don't let go," Kamal urged.

"I don't think it's working," Yuki exclaimed.

"Okay, it's happening!" Mayhara suddenly shouted.

Yuki looked up. The sparkling haze around the sun disappeared. The diamond on her wristband glowed a bright white.

Mayhara held her palms out, facing Yuki. The red glow in her palms expanded. Yuki felt her feet make contact with something hard, like rock. The rock pushed upward, lifting her. The sand at her sides hardened, creating a solid surface. She placed her hands upon it and used it as leverage to pull herself out of the sand trap. Kamal grabbed her arms and pulled her the rest of the way out.

"Okay, I don't know how long this is going to last," Mayhara said, her palms out and still glowing red. "I'm going to hold it solid as long as I can, and I say we make a run for it."

Yuki's legs were still covered in the drying wet sand, but she nodded. "Agreed. Let's go."

She had to trust that Mayhara had control over the surface and that the haze would be gone long enough for them to make their trek to the caves. She didn't want to be stuck like that ever again. Pushing down thoughts about how the lack of air to her lungs was making her chest hurt, or how heavy her legs felt with caked-on mud clinging to her, she continued to pump her legs. It helped that Akari was darting out in front of them, hightailing it, as it were, toward the caves. As long as she could concentrate on him bounding across the surface, she knew it was still safe for her to run.

At long last, and without a breath to spare, they crossed over onto a grassy knoll that stood before the caves.

"We made it," Kamal said once he could breathe again.

Mayhara looked up at the sky. "The haze is till gone. The comet's white. We should still have our powers."

"Good," Yuki said. "Because the caves look like they're blocked."

Mayhara pushed her hair away from her sweaty face to see that the entrance of the caves were indeed blocked by piles of rock and boulders. "Of course they are. Which cave do we need?"

Yuki pointed, constantly checking the sun and the comet.

Mayhara held her palm out toward the cave she'd indicated. Crimson particles traveled from her hand to the boulders blocking the cave entrance. One crack. Two. And then suddenly the whole blockage crumbled before their eyes. A heap of dirt stood at the foot of the cave entrance, dust flying off in the air. Akari was the first to hop the dirt pile and run inside.

No one spoke as they entered. They used the glow of their hands to light the way. Akari was particularly useful, his white fur reflecting the light, helping them to better see in the dark.

The entrance tunnel led to an open cavern, its walls lit up by thousands of tiny glowing crystals. Yuki skidded to a stop as two figures appeared to one side of the cavern. Her breath got stuck in her throat when she realized they were her parents, smiling back at her.

"Mama? Papa?" Her heart felt like mush. Tears flowed down her cheeks as she ran to them. "I was afraid to believe I'd see you here."

Her parents pulled her closer, snuggling her in their arms.

"Our darling," her mother said. "You've grown so much."

Yuki reveled in the feel of her mother's breath on her hair. "I'm so sorry," she said as she pulled back to look at them.

"No, dear," her father said. "You have nothing to be sorry about. You are fulfilling your destiny."

"But I didn't mean for you to die."

"You were not the one who killed us," her mother said, gently pushing back a strand of Yuki's hair. "You are not to blame. Please remember that."

Yuki hugged them again, bawling. She was barely aware that Mayhara and Kamal were patiently watching them.

"It's time for you to go," her father said, stroking her cheek.

"Already?"

Her mother pressed her forehead against Yuki's. "I'm afraid so, darling. We love you. Don't ever forget that."

Yuki kissed both their cheeks, hating that she had to let them go. She reluctantly backed away from them until she felt Mayhara's hand on her shoulder.

"Where to now?" Mayhara asked.

Yuki wiped the tears from her eyes. She turned and surveilled the cavern. It was riddled with stalagmites and stalactites. At the far end was a tunnel.

"That way," she said, leading them in that direction. She forced herself not to turn around to look at her parents. She knew, if she did, she'd never want to leave.

Mayhara and Kamal were right behind her. Though she couldn't see where Akari was, she could hear his chittering.

The tunnel forked off into two directions, but Yuki somehow knew where to go. The other two mages followed her without question. At the end of the tunnel stood large, wooden, double doors.

"This looks familiar," Mayhara said.

Yuki tried pulling on one of the cast-iron handles. "It's heavy."

Kamal snaked his hand through the handle beside Yuki's and yanked. When they managed to pull it open a crack, Mayhara grabbed the edge of the door, grunting as she helped force it open.

Suddenly, the door swung open wider, and Yuki almost screamed when she discovered two young women pushing the door from the other side.

One of them had long, black hair and glimmering, green eyes. Yuki couldn't help but think she looked like Loni. The other had even straighter black hair, which fell like a curtain of silk to her shoulders. She had big eyes and high cheekbones.

"Huojin?" Mayhara's lips curled into a smile.

The young woman she'd spoken to gave her a shy grin before Mayhara embraced her.

Mayhara tuned to Yuki and Kamal. "This is Huojin. She was the elite golden mage before Salina."

Kamal gave her a cocky, sideways smirk. "I know who she is. And this is Kanya. She's Loni's sister."

"Sorry we have to cut the reunion short," Huojin put in, "but you don't have much time. The dark mage is approaching."

"And if we wait any longer, your powers won't work." Kanya took Yuki and Mayhara by their upper arms and urged them to come farther into the room.

Only it wasn't a room; it was another cavern. But this one had an extremely high ceiling and it contained an enormous structure in its center. It was almost like a towering statue made up of seven orbs of light, connected by rock and crystal swirling in a vertical column that went from the cavern floor to its ceiling. If Yuki had to guess, she'd say it was about ten feet in diameter. She couldn't even guess how high it was.

The orbs contained moving, glowing particles. The bottom orb's particles were deep red. Above it, sparkling orange. Those were followed with spheres of yellow, then green, then blue, then purple, and finally, at the top, a brilliant white.

"It's the mage colors," Yuki said as she stared at the structure in awe.

"The same colors as the chakras," Mayhara added. "I've seen this before, at the academy. Jae showed it to me, except the spheres weren't glowing. The lights were all out.

"This is your way back," Huojin said. "You two represent both ends of the spiral. Mayhara at the base, Yuki at the top."

Kanya eyed the structure. "You need to use your powers to move the particles at each end, get the particles moving faster, until the whole thing lights up."

"It *is* lit up," Mayhara insisted.

"Oh." Huojin laughed. "That's not lit up. You wait and see."

"Think of it as unblocking the chakras." Kanya glanced toward the door. "But you have to start now. We'll hold off the dark mage as long as we can."

Yuki swallowed hard. "He's here?"

"Don't worry, he can't hurt us," Huojin said. "We're already dead. But we need to keep him away, to stop him from stopping you."

As soon as she'd finished her sentence, the wooden door creaked.

"Do it, Mayhara!" Huojin yelled. Her arms were already raised and her palms aimed at the door.

A screech echoed in the cavern as the door swung open. Avi stood in the doorway, his eyes scanning the cavern and the people within in. His shirt was now completely bloody. His eyes dropped as he stumbled into the space.

Kanya's palms glowed green, and Huojin's emanated golden light. When they pushed out their energy, a swirling shield of air and fire hovered in front of them.

Avi's brow furrowed, and Yuki wondered if he hadn't yet figured out that his powers depended on the cycle of the sparkling haze.

Huojin snarled at him. "It's payback time, you jerk."

Avi bared his teeth. He lifted his hand, and black particles flew out in a stream through the air, hitting the fire shield. Most of the particles ricocheted off the shield, but Yuki was shocked to see some of the particles breaking through.

"A little help, Kamal!" Kanya shouted.

Kamal had already been beside them, but now he used his sapphire mage powers to blast Avi back with soundwaves.

Yuki and Mayhara exchanged a glance. Without another word, they held their hands out, palms facing the structure. Yuki held hers higher, aiming her diamond energy at the top sphere. Mayhara's particles were already lighting up the red orb. Huojin was right: the spheres lit up into practically blinding, bright lights.

"He's getting through!" Kanya yelled.

Yuki snuck a glance over her shoulder. She spotted Akari in a pouncing position just before he charged Avi and knocked him down, all nine tails swaying as he swung around and bounded back to Kamal's side.

"Yuki, concentrate!" Mayhara already had the red and orange spheres fully lit.

Yuki snapped back to the task at hand and pushed out her energy harder. She had to trust that the three spirits of mages—and the kitsune— could hold off Avi.

Come on, Yuki. Everyone's counting on you.

The white sphere was now completely lit, and the purple one was getting brighter. It was exhausting, but she wouldn't let up. Mayhara had half the green sphere glowing brightly and gaining ground fast.

Yuki let out a long groan as she reached deep down inside of herself and pushed out as much energy as she could. Now, she only had to finish lighting up the blue sphere.

"Mayhara!" Huojin yelled. "Tell Loni I'm sorry!"

"Hug my sister for me!" Kanya shouted.

The lights became so bright that Yuki could only see white. She wasn't sure if the vibrating hum in her ears was coming from the structure or from Kamal's magic. It all became so intense, she was sure her head would explode.

And then suddenly there was a pop, and everything fell silent. She felt her stomach drop, and nausea overwhelmed her. Her head spun, and she feared she would fall over. The bright, white light slowly faded to black.

She blinked, spots dancing in her eyes.

"Mayhara?"

At first, there was no answer. And then…

"I'm right here." Mayhara's voice sounded weak.

The surroundings slowly came into focus. The structure with the spheres stood before her, but nothing was lit up. Everything was dark.

Yuki glanced around. The other mages—the spirits—were nowhere to be seen. She turned and focused on Mayhara, who appeared frazzled and frightened. "Are we back?"

"I think so," Mayhara said. "And I feel like I'm going to throw up."

Yuki grabbed Mayhara by the wrists. "We did it?"

Mayhara stared at her, the color slowly returning to her face. Yuki released her wrists so Mayhara could scrub her hands down her face. Yuki held her breath in anticipation.

"Okay, I'm ready. Let's go check." Mayhara took her hand and led the way.

They had to climb stone steps to reach the wooden doors, and Yuki realized they couldn't have been in the same cavern they'd been in before. The spheres had served as a portal from the spirit world.

Once they were out of the cavern and running through a hallway, Yuki began to recognize that they were in the demolished academy. The walls were rubble, and the place was covered in dirt and dust. She couldn't remember it looking so battered and broken. Though her heart wept for the place, an energy of hope ran through her.

"We're back," Mayhara whispered. "We're home."

Yuki's heart hammered in her chest. "What now?"

"Now we get to New Delhi."

FIFTEEN

Naree sat comfortably in the back of the limousine. She used breathing exercises to remain calm. Today was the day. By night's end, she would finally be reunited with her true love.

My darling, I can feel your anticipation. I, too, am overjoyed that we will soon be together.

Naree closed her eyes, reveling in Kashmeru's voice. She wanted to answer him, but a set of eyes were locked on her.

Karina sat across from her, watching her. For a moment, Naree suspected the witch might be able to hear Kashmeru's voice as well. She tilted her head and narrowed her eyes at her, wondering what she might say.

"You don't have to do this, you know?" Karina glanced over her shoulder, most likely wondering if the driver could hear her.

Our time has come at last, my love. Don't let the witch dissuade you.

"This is destiny," Naree said to Karina. Though she meant for Kashmeru to hear it as well. "Centuries in the making."

"This is a trick," Karina protested. "He's using you. That's what evil does. Why would someone who loves you make you turn against your own army?"

I have a new army for you, my love. A better, stronger army. More powerful than you can imagine. All for you.

"It is but a small sacrifice compared to what he's promised me." Naree opened her clutch and took out a compact to check her face. When she returned it, her fingers brushed against the smooth jade dragonfly Jae had carved for her. Her brow furrowed; she didn't remember putting it in her purse. Feeling Karina's stare, she snapped the clutch closed and whipped her chin up. "Every sacrifice is worth it. His love for me is all I'll ever need."

There was a pity in Karina's eyes. The sudden change of expression made Naree blanch. She ran her hand gently over her clutch, her mind on the jade dragonfly. Jae loved her too. Her brother's love for her had also filled her with joy. Her mind went to her parents, probably waiting back home for their daughter to finally come home.

What are you doing? Kashmeru's voice was full of rage.

Naree flinched. Karina shot her a questioning look.

Do not be led astray. Tonight, everything changes. No one can stop us. Or do you need a reminder of my power?

A sudden, razor-sharp pain bit into Naree's spine. She let out a cry as she arched her back, trying to make the ache stop. It felt like nails made of fire were clawing into her.

Karina sat upright, her eyes wide. "Your Highness? What's wrong?"

Do we understand each other? Or should I continue this torture to convince you?

"No! Please!"

As quickly as it had started, the pain stopped. Karina swallowed hard, sitting on the edge of her seat and appearing ready to jump to her rescue, even though she was oblivious to what had just happened. Naree tried to control her erratic breaths, shifting in her seat and pushing her hair out of her face.

"Your Highness?"

Naree's lips twisted into a snarl. "Who are you to question me? To assume to be a master of what fate has in store for me? You are nothing. You are here for one reason only, and that is to do my bidding. Anything beyond that is unacceptable."

Karina's mouth fell into a straight line as she backed up in her seat. She averted her gaze, and Naree let out a long, exasperated breath.

You will soon see, my love. It will all be worth it. We will be together, as we should be. And together, we will reign over our new, perfect world.

Penny kept her eye on the roadside. She knew she was getting closer.

"The academy is up ahead," Qiang said from the driver's seat.

"Yep." She turned to face him. "They'll be there. Trust me."

"Oh, don't worry." Qiang gave her a wink. "You're the elite amethyst mage. I trust you completely."

She flashed him a smile. It had only been a few hours since she'd found Qiang. Her visions had begun to return to her after she'd left the café. The voice that followed her had become louder as the morning went on.

Remember.

The voice made her touch a spot on her arm, a spot marked by magic. And then it had all come back to her. Piece by piece. It was Karina's voice bringing her back, restoring her memories bit by bit, until it had all fallen into place.

She'd been possessed by Bhutano, and through her, he'd manipulated the mages and stolen all the daggers. Helplessly watching it all play out through her own eyes was the worst torture she'd ever been through.

If it hadn't been for Karina, Penny would still be possessed by Kashmeru's spirit messenger—or possibly dead from the diamond bullet wound—and her memories would have been forever lost. Luckily, Karina had marked her with a spell that would help her remember everything.

Now, she was herself again, and her visions had led her first to find Qiang. Her visions were now leading her to the academy to find two important elements of the puzzle: Mayhara and Yuki.

"There they are," she called out excitedly, pointing at the two figures traveling along the road on foot.

Qiang picked up speed.

Mayhara's and Yuki's faces became more recognizable as they got closer. Penny's heart leapt with exhilaration and her head swam with relief. Both Mayhara and Yuki froze when they saw her, their jaws hanging open.

Qiang barely stopped the car before Penny jumped out. She almost knocked Mayhara over when she pounced on her for a hug.

Mayhara was a little stiff, and then Penny remembered that the last time they'd seen each other, she'd been possessed by Bhutano.

"Mayhara, it's me. It's Penny. Really."

Mayhara glanced at Yuki, shock still apparent on her face.

Yuki's palms glowed white. "By the gods, it's really you."

Penny was so thrilled, she let out a laugh as she threw her arms around Yuki.

"What are you—?" Mayhara shook her head, but a smile finally formed on her lips. "How did you find us?"

"Amethyst powers. They led me to Qiang first." She pointed to Qiang in the car, to whom they both waved. "And then to you. I can tell you more on the way. We need to hurry."

Penny signaled for them to follow and climbed back into the car.

"On the way to the temple?" Yuki asked as she buckled in.

"That's the final destination, yeah," Qiang said, swiftly turning the car around once Mayhara had closed her door.

"The other elites should be there," Penny said. "The vision's not clear. But hopefully we can find them and actually pull this thing off."

Qiang sped up the car. "But first, we've got to see if Mitty was able to get me a helicopter."

SIXTEEN

Scaffolding still stood around part of the flowerlike shape of the Bahá'i Lotus Temple. But the delay in completing the renovation of the building was apparently not going to stop the festival from taking place. The building was comprised of twenty-seven freestanding marble towers called 'petals' that were arranged in clusters of three, forming its nine sides. Nine enormous pools of water surrounded the building, set apart by stone steps and pathways that led to its nine doors. Only, tonight, the organizers of the festival had six of the doors blocked off to better control admission. One of those doors was being used by the event planners, the festival decorators, and the hired caterers.

Because of the enormous lay of land around the temple, the caterer vans were parked in one of the parking lots located about a six-minute walk from the temple. Jae used his sapphire mage powers to convince five of the caterers to go home sick, leaving their uniforms and access badges behind. The mages and Darshana used one of the vans to slip on their white, button-down shirts and maroon serving aprons. There were so many workers that evening, Jae was sure it would be hard for the event planners to keep track.

"Are we ready to do this?" Salina asked. "I can't help but feel we're ill prepared, especially because we're not a complete team."

"We don't have a choice." Jae's gaze traveled between the mages and Darshana. "We can get to the tomb and try to somehow stop the Pishacha with the limited power we've got."

"Maybe the others will show up." Shiro didn't look convinced as he said it.

"We'll do what we can." Darshana let out a slow breath. "It's all we can do."

They pushed two catering carts filled with food to the entrance being used by the waitstaff. Jae forced himself to look like he belonged there, so as not to draw suspicion from the police patrolling the area. He spotted their cyber-batons and their pistols and hoped there wouldn't be a run-in to stop them from finding the tomb. It was still hours before the festival would begin, but the place was already packed. A man dressed in a black suit with a maroon vest and bowtie held up his hand as they approached the door.

"Sorry, I don't recognize any of you." He lifted his electronic tablet and checked the screen. "Your names please?"

Jae checked the area to make sure none of the police who were patrolling the temple were watching. He then pushed out his sapphire energy, his palms glowing a brilliant blue. He hoped the comet's interference wouldn't get in the way of his powers.

"You don't need our names," Jae said. "You are happy to see us and welcome us inside."

The man blinked, and a second later, he smiled. "Glad to see you. Come in and take those carts down to the kitchen. There's a service elevator to the left."

"Perfect," Jae replied. "Thank you."

He led the others past the man, rolling the cart toward the elevator.

"Are we really going to the kitchen?" Salina asked.

"We think the tomb is under the building somewhere," Jae replied. "The kitchen is already at a lower level. I'm sure we can find access to wherever the tomb might be located down there."

There was a ding as the elevator doors opened. Two Imperial Police officers stood inside. Salina stiffened, and Loni turned her head so her hair covered her face. Darshana and Jae remained facing forward, and Shiro dropped his chin, pretending to adjust his apron strings.

Jae's white-knuckle grip on the catering cart remained tight and tense until the police exited the elevators and passed them.

Salina let out a breath of relief as they rolled the carts into the elevator.

"We're not in the clear yet," Jae whispered. "Don't look directly into the camera in the upper corner. There will probably also be cameras in the kitchen, so try not to be obvious."

His words must have jolted them, because they were silent during the ride down.

The elevator announced they'd arrived at sub-level two. Jae was trying to calculate in his head how much farther they might have to go to find the tomb. When the door opened, they rolled out the carts.

Jae led them to where the other carts were parked, and then he subtly made his way through the enormous kitchen. When one of the cooks looked their way, he noticed Shiro's palm glowing orange, and the water in the pot next to the cook began bubbling over. The cook diverted his attention to the pot and forgot about their group.

Jae checked over his shoulder to make sure the rest of the gang was following him. He spotted a door marking the stairwell. He used his powers to silence any alarm that might sound as he pushed the bar to open the door. Glad when the group was ushered through without incident, he turned to check the stairwell.

They took one flight down until they came to a door and a dead end. The door was marked with a yellow triangle sporting a black lightning bolt symbol. There was no handle. To the right of the door was a lock pad.

"Allow me," Salina said, coming forward. "When the system overrides, we'll only have a few seconds to get through, so everyone get ready." She placed her hand on the lock pad. Her palms glowed gold. In the next moment, the lock pad light went out and the door clicked open.

"Go!" she said.

They all darted through the door, almost falling over each other as Salina click the door closed.

They found themselves in some sort of utility hall. Pipes ran along one wall, and the opposite wall was filled with fuse boxes and other electrical control panels.

"Let's see what's at the end of the hall," Jae suggested.

When they got to the end, Jae let out a curse. He was about to turn around when Loni called out, "Wait!"

They all turned to her as she felt the upper and lower parts of the wall.

"I feel air," she said. "There's something on the other side."

"There must be a way to get to the other side of the wall," Darshana put in. "Or it's more likely some kind of door. Feel the bricks. Maybe one of them acts as a spring release."

Their hands were all over the wall, pushing and pressing. Jae wasn't sure which of them had found the release brick, but the door suddenly swung open.

And beyond the door: darkness.

"You think this is it?" Shiro asked.

Jae pursed his lips. "Only one way to find out."

Naree checked her reflection in the standing mirror. The dress was the purest white and the softest silk. Three thin bands of gold made up the belt that was secured around her waist. The sleeves flowed like air around her arms, and the V-cut neckline accented the gold necklace that clung to her cleavage. Her hair was swept up in a set of gold bands that matched her belt, and a few, soft, loose curls hung freely from the coiffure.

She sucked in a shuddered breath. Was this really happening? Kashmeru was near. She could feel it. Though she'd longed for this moment to come to fruition, part of her questioned if she was really ready to see him.

Lakshmi, it is time.

The door to the chamber opened, and Bhutano stepped in.

"Your Highness, we are ready."

She forced herself to steady her breathing as she followed him into the adjoining room. Six dark mages were lined up, all dressed in black. On a long side table, the seven arcane daggers were set out, each of them sitting on a red, satin cloth. Someone had gone to great lengths to polish them, because they gleamed brilliantly in the light.

Naree ran her fingers along the hilts of each one as she walked by them. They were the key to releasing her true love from the tomb in which he was imprisoned.

Yes, my love. It won't be long now.

She turned to face Bhutano. Behind him, cowering near the wall, was Karina. She had been made to change as well, and the dress she donned was almost as lovely as her own. Karina stood with one arm crossed over her waist, the light blue dress flowing loosely over her form. Someone had brushed the tangles out of her hair.

Naree moved her attention over to the mages. "It's supposed to be the Council of the Seven. We're missing one."

"Your Highness," Bhutano said. "We can only assume that Avi is dead."

"Has anyone informed his father?"

"That won't be necessary. The governor is well aware—as are all of Kashmeru's followers—of the risks that come with being invited to his kingdom. All are willing to sacrifice themselves for the reward."

"And what about the ritual? Will this even work?" A small part of her sparked with hope. Maybe she wouldn't have to go through with this at all. But that small part was quickly pushed down by fear of torture… along with a burning sadness of not being able to see Kashmeru again.

My love. I long to hold you again. I need to see you with my own eyes. Feel you. Come to me.

"I will take Avi's place in the ritual. As Kashmeru's spirit messenger, I'm the only one who can step in for a dark mage."

Naree smoothed her hands over the soft material of her dress. "Very well."

"We must go down to the tomb now, Your Highness. The comet approaches."

She gave him a nod. The dark mages each took a dagger and placed it the inside pockets of their jackets. Bhutano took the seventh and then gestured for Naree to lead them out of the room.

It is time, my love. Come set me free.

SEVENTEEN

Yuki's heart thrummed in her chest as she and Mayhara followed close behind Penny into the temple. Qiang and Mitty were gathered outside, hiding from the authorities while they assembled the extremists, waiting for the signal to make their move. Penny's palms glowed of amethyst energy, cloaking herself and Yuki and Mayhara from sight. Yuki was amazed when everyone at the party simply looked through them as if they weren't there.

Before they'd entered the building, Penny had instructed them to follow her and not to speak. She'd said she knew exactly where to go, based on visions she'd received.

As they passed through the central hall, Yuki took a moment to admire the festivities. There were thousands of people in attendance. Glittering arches of vines and flowers were spread out in various parts of the room. Paper lanterns were strung across the space. She spotted an elevated koi pond, the center of which contained a lotus-shaped fountain spouting water. Elegant standing tables draped with cream-colored silk tablecloths adorned one section of the room. The centerpieces spilled over with lilies, cherry blossoms, eucalyptus branches, and lavender. Everyone had tall flutes of pink champagne in their hands. Classical music played softly throughout the hall as people conversed.

And no one noticed them walk through it all.

Penny led them down a hall, and eventually they went through a door to a stairwell. Once they were in the clear, Penny lifted the cloaking energy.

Yuki should have been exhausted. She'd been up for two days, and traveling between two dimensions had literally knocked the wind out of her. Instead, she was filled with a strange exhilaration, a second wind made of both hope and fear. Seeing her parents had given her determination. She just hoped it was enough to defeat Kashmeru.

As they made their way through strange halls and hidden stone steps, they found themselves in an alcove of a large crypt. The ceiling must have been seven meters high. They were hidden from view by statues and tall headstones. In the center of the crypt, a large ray of light shone down onto a sarcophagus.

"Is that it?" Yuki whispered.

"It must be," Mayhara answered.

Penny was narrowing her eyes. "The others are near."

Yuki ducked her head. "You mean the Pishacha?"

"No." Penny pointed across the room.

Yuki spotted the top of someone's head behind a statue of the god Vishnu. She straightened realizing it was Jae. Before she could call out to him, Penny stopped her, holding a finger to her lips.

They traveled along the row of statues, making their way toward the other mages. Yuki was so glad they were all there and unharmed.

Jae's eyes widened as they rounded the corner. Salina slapped her hand over her mouth, and although Shiro seemed thrilled to see them, he let out a warning shush, reminding them that they were there in secret.

They kept their voices low as they ran to hug one another. The first to embrace were Jae and Mayhara. He spun her around as soon as he lifted her into his arms.

Darshana ran a hand over Yuki's hair. "We were so worried about you."

"Mayhara and I were sent to the spirit realm."

"Amalia was there," Mayhara added. "She opened the scroll."

"Where is it?" Loni asked.

"It could only be opened by her," Yuki explained. "But Mayhara and I memorized the spell."

"Karina's not with you?" Shiro asked.

"We got separated. The Pishacha have her. And the daggers," Penny said. "There's so much to tell you, but in the end, Karina made a deal with the Pishacha so they would release me. She promised them she would perform the unbinding spell."

"But we're all here now," Mayhara said. "We can stop them."

"Someone's coming," Penny said, her gaze far away.

"We've got the element of surprise on our side." Jae moved closer to the center of the crypt. "Get ready."

The others followed his lead, taking their stances. Hands lifted, palms facing forward, they were ready to fight.

EIGHTEEN

Karina couldn't slow the pounding in her ears. She was surrounded by dark mages as they made their way to the tomb. In front of her, Naree was mysteriously quiet. In her head, Karina was struggling with her options to get out of this. One thought was to recite the spell incorrectly. Would they believe her if she said it simply hadn't worked? That she'd gotten it wrong? Or would that just anger the dark god, and he'd command the dark mages to kill her?

Weighed against the destruction of the universe, it seemed a sensible sacrifice.

Yes. That was what she would do. Her death would be worth saving the world, wouldn't it?

The crypt was a dark, dank place. The surrounding statues and headstones lurked like shadows of evil spirits, ready to pounce if she made one wrong move.

Suddenly, there was so much movement, she couldn't keep track of what was happening. The dark mages took defensive stances. And in front of them, standing just beyond the sarcophagus in the center of the room, were all seven mages.

They're here! They made it!

She could barely make out Darshana's figure somewhere at the back of the room.

The pounding in her ears intensified. Palms were lit up everywhere, and Karina backed up behind a headstone for fear she'd get caught in the crossfire.

Black particles zipped across the room but were blocked by a sudden crimson shield that materialized between the dark mages and the elite. Fire then roared across the crypt in the shape of a whip, but one of the dark mages—Harish—raised his hand and syphoned the fire from the air. As another dark mage released a swarm of black energy, a harsh wind whipped toward it over the sarcophagus, blowing back the swarm and knocking two dark mages off their feet. A cloud of purple smoke seeped from Penny's palm, blinding their view.

And then Naree let out a guttural scream. Her palms glowed with all the seven chakra colors. She threw out her arms, and the bright prism of colors shot across the crypt in heavy streams that made the elite mages stumble back a few steps.

Karina had to squint to see what had happened. What she saw confused her. The seven elite mages stood frozen, their arms stiff at their sides, their heads held high as if in a vise, and their eyes wide with fright. Their feet were six inches off the ground, their bodies floating from Naree's magic. Their breathing was erratic, but otherwise, they didn't move. They'd been put into some sort of state of paralysis.

Bhutano looked pleased. The dark mages reassembled around the Lotus, smirking at their enemies.

"Your efforts are futile," Naree said, confidence in her voice. She patted her hair back into place. "You cannot stop fate. And now you must watch as Kashmeru wins his victory."

Naree approached the sarcophagus and ran her hands along the top, her fingers moving with the grooves that were carved into the stone. Ru glanced at Karina and squared her jaw. With a hard grip, she took Karina by the arm and yanked her toward the stone coffin.

Naree looked up to the light that was flooding in from the spot in the ceiling. "The comet is at its apex. It's time."

Karina followed her gaze. The light must have been coming through from above. She knew the center of the main hall of the Lotus Temple had a star-shaped window in the roof. She wondered if the window was duplicated in the floor of the hall and every sublevel of the building, all the way down to Kashmeru's tomb. If it hadn't been constructed that way before, there was no doubt the powers in charge had written it into the renovation plans, just for this purpose. The comet's energy flowing through those windows and hitting the sarcophagus was the celestial energy Naree needed to complete the ritual.

"Karina, the spell." Naree's eyes were closed as she waited. There was even a small smile formed on her face, as if she were enjoying the moment.

Karina let out a shuddered breath. She was ready to die so the binding spell couldn't be undone.

Naree's eyes popped open. "Karina."

She shook her head. "I… I won't."

Naree bared her teeth. "Maybe you haven't noticed, but I have your friends in a very vulnerable position. One snap of my fingers, and they all perish."

Karina's gaze flew to the elite mages. Jae looked like he was trying to shake his head. Tears flowed from Mayhara's eyes. Loni was blinking rapidly, her face contorted like she was in pain. Karina couldn't let them die. She knew it could mean the end of the world, but could she really just let the elite mages perish without doing anything about it? She wasn't about to let them die at her hands. She had no choice but to do the spell.

"O-Okay. Okay. I'll do it." Karina's voice was a whisper.

Naree nodded to the dark mages. They each came forward and stood in a semi-circle around Naree, daggers drawn and held parallel to their chests. Rikuto held a hand out, which Naree took to help hoist herself up onto the top of the sarcophagus. Once she was on top, she kneeled and held her arms out, bathing in the light.

Ru nudged Karina. Karina swallowed back her impending tears and began reciting the spell. All plans to mess up the incantation on purpose went out the window. As she finished the spell the second time, dark tendrils of smoke wafted up from the sarcophagus. The energy in the room felt morose and full of doom.

"The unbinding is complete," Karina said, tears flowing down her cheeks.

She expected Bhutano or one of the dark mages to strike her down, to kill her now that she'd done her part by performing the unbinding spell and was of no use to them anymore. But they didn't seem to pay her any mind. Instead, she was shocked when one of the dark mages—Rikuto— approached Naree and rammed his dagger between two of her ribs. The impact created a burst of black smoke. Naree let out a deafening shriek, her head thrown back and her arms spread at her sides. Blood quickly spread at her side, drenching her white dress and trailing down her body.

Karina gasped. Her eyes went to Jae, who was baring his teeth in frustration, his eyes filled with tears.

A bright red, glittering glow covered Naree's skin. Her eyes were aflame with a harsh, red light. As she screamed, her skin changed from flesh to hard, cracked earth. And then, the ground shook. Rubble and dirt fell from the walls as the shaking intensified. The sound of the earthquake magnified as the floor beneath them began to crack. The shaking was more violent than any earthquake Karina had ever experienced. Her teeth chattered in her head from the vibration, and she had to grab on to the nearest statue to keep her footing. She was sure all of New United Asia was suffering from the quake. It felt like forever until the rumbling stopped. The earth that had been Naree's skin cracked and disintegrated into dust, falling away until Naree's skin was exposed again.

Her blood dripped down her body, leaking into the carvings on the lid of the sarcophagus. Karina believed her blood was dripping through the grooves into the coffin, dousing Kashmeru's corpse.

Naree's breaths were hard and heavy, but there was hardly time for her to recover before the next dark mage—Kun—came forward and drove his dagger into Naree's side. Again, black smoke erupted from the impact. Her scream was louder this time. A copper glow washed over her, orange light shining from her eyes. This time, her body went liquid. It still held its form, but it was like she was made of water. She continued to scream, and water shot from her hands in continuous streams. From all ends of the crypt, water blasted in, flooding the entire room. Ice-cold water poured from the ceiling, drenching everyone. Finally, the water slipped off Naree, leaving her normal body where it should have been, and the water stopped filling the room.

Ru came forward next and stuck her dagger in Naree's collarbone. Naree immediately burst into flames. Fire erupted everywhere around the room. Karina ducked her head, wrapping her arms around herself. She felt the water that had just drenched her evaporate from the heat.

The flames covering Naree died down, leaving her intact and unscathed, but still, she heaved out heavy, labored breaths. The changes must have been doing unspeakable things to her.

The next dark mage—Harish—came forward. His jaw was squared as he jammed his dagger into her side. Her scream echoed through the crypt, and Karina swore it shook the air. The burst of black smoke blew quickly away as Naree was bathed in a deep green glow. A ferocious wind tore through the place, sending debris flying. Karina had to squint as she struggled to stand in place and not get blown back.

The elite mages seemed to be frozen in place, still floating six inches from the ground. Their expressions spoke of sorrow and anger and defeat.

When the next dark mage approached Naree and drove his dagger into her, a forceful soundwave crescendoed through the room, shattering headstones and cracking statues. Naree's body was a glowing blue vibration, barely solid at all. Her scream left a ringing in Karina's ears, even as the blue glow disappeared.

The final dark mage stepped up to the sarcophagus and stabbed his dagger into Naree's shoulder. She threw her head back as a purple glow covered her body. It looked as though she were turning into smoke. And then the entire crypt filled with purple smoke.

Karina let out a barrage of coughs as she tried to see through the haze. Just when she thought she was going to choke to death, the smoke began to disappear, revealing Naree panting on the sarcophagus, covered in blood.

It was Bhutano's turn. He used two hands as he lifted his dagger and plunged in into the center of Naree's chest. He barely let go of the hilt as a bright, white light blasting from Naree's body expanded, swallowing everything in its path in a blinding shimmer. Everything went white, and Karina was suddenly overcome with emotion. She sobbed in the lonely, white light.

Little by little, the intensity of the white light faded. As the details of the crypt became clearer, Karina found that the elite mages—as well the dark mages and Bhutano—were crumpled on the floor. The stone lid of the sarcophagus had slid open, sitting askew. Naree was on her knees beside the stone coffin, her eyes bloodshot, her face pale, and her body drenched in sweat and blood.

Nineteen

Mayhara opened her eyes. Her cheek was pressed against the hard floor of the crypt. She flexed her fingers, shocked she was finally able to move. Her body was sore. It felt like she'd been run over by a truck. And no wonder; she and the other elite mages had been doused with torrential waves of water, blasted by fire, pummeled by an explosion of elemental magic, and there'd been no escaping it. Because she'd been frozen in place and rendered helpless by Naree's powers.

She slowly lifted her head. Jae groaned beside her. She reached out and curled a finger around one of his. He twisted so he could see her. She wanted to ask if he was all right, but she couldn't find her voice just yet.

"Oh, no."

It was Darshana's voice. She'd been protecting herself behind a tall headstone during Naree's transformations, and now she was creeping out into the open, staring, pale-faced, at the sarcophagus.

Mayhara reached deep down inside herself and found the strength to sit up. The sound of stone scraping against stone echoed throughout the crypt. A dark figure loomed beneath the light filtering in from the ceiling.

Two small slivers of silver stared out beneath a black, tattered hood. The figure moved slowly, deliberately. His form was enormous, bigger than any man Mayhara had ever seen. But when the light hit his face, she could see that his snake-like skin was sunken into his skull.

The dark mages gaped at him in awe. Bhutano was the first to present himself to his lord, kneeling before him and bowing his head, his arms stretched forward and palms flat on the floor. The dark mages followed suit, falling in place beside Bhutano.

A howling wind stirred up the dust in the room as Kashmeru stepped out of his coffin. He looked down at Naree, who was still on the floor, covered with blood. She looked up at him with a combination of fear and wonder.

"It is time." His voice was deep and slow and full of power.

He extended a hand to Naree. There was a moment of hesitation before she took it and rose to her feet. There was no smile on her face as the tears began to flow.

"My love." Kashmeru pulled her into his arms. He traced her cheek with his hand and then leaned down to kiss her.

Naree let out a small moan, throwing her arms around him.

After the kiss ended, Kashmeru leaned back to look at her.

"Our destiny has arrived. And now it is time to be rid of this world and move on to our own." Kashmeru pushed back his hood, exposing his hairless head.

Mayhara could now see that the dark skin at his cheeks were made up of scales.

Kashmeru closed his eyes. A swirling black mist rose up around him. He lifted his arms, taking Naree's hand with him.

Mayhara couldn't understand the words leaving his mouth, but she could feel them. It felt as if everything inside of her and everything around her was breaking apart, crumbling and rotting, becoming void of life.

"We have to do this now," Yuki said to Mayhara, suddenly at her side. "Before he destroys the world."

Mayhara turned to Jae. "The spell." She searched his face. "It might kill your sister."

Jae's eyes darted between Mayhara and Naree. He winced, also feeling the destruction inside of him as Kashmeru worked his magic. Biting down hard on his lip, he gave Mayhara a solemn nod.

Mayhara sucked in a shuddered breath and stood. Yuki hurried to her feet and held her hand. In unison, they recited the spell.

> *"Abire hostem*
> *Hoc planum es ex agro*
> *Cum enim venenum componere*
> *boni a Chakras*
> *Abire hostem*
> *Vos ultra*
> *Per virtute divina*

demoliti sunt egressi vobiscum
et non est amplius."

She knew the spell would do nothing coming from them, but if Karina would hear them and recite the incantation herself, the spell could take effect.

Mayhara stared at Karina, hoping she would understand. Karina's jaw hung open as she listened. On their third run of the incantation, she joined in.

> *"Abire hostem*
> *Hoc planum es ex agro*
> *Cum enim venenum componere*
> *boni a Chakras*
> *Abire hostem*
> *Vos ultra*
> *Per virtute divina*
> *demoliti sunt egressi vobiscum*
> *et non est amplius."*

Mayhara thought it was another earthquake, but it was Kashmeru's low cry of anger.

With a jerk of his hand, a thick, black whip snapped in Mayhara's direction. She and Yuki were smacked back, flying through the air and slamming into stone statues.

Her vision blurred and her head throbbed from connecting with the stone. In a matter of seconds, Jae was at her side, pulling her into his arms.

She thought all was lost, but Karina was still chanting. Mayhara lifted her head. Kashmeru threw his dark magic at the witch, but she seemed to have some sort of bubble of protection around her. Nothing he did could get through. Her magic repelled his every move.

As she continued the incantation, a tiny burst of energy sparked near the ceiling. It was a bluish gaseous nebula that spread, stretching across the ceiling and getting thicker as it descended upon Kashmeru and Naree.

Harish stood and tried to syphon the cloud, but his magic didn't work.

He and the other mages began coughing, grabbing at their necks. Ru stared wide-eyed at her skin as it began to blister and bubble up into black, crusty sores. Bhutano let out a cry as his skin turned to liquid and oozed off his body.

Naree held her throat, choking on the blue gas as she doubled over. "Poison," she whispered in a raspy voice.

Kashmeru gaped at the goddess, attempting to help her, but it wasn't working. "No," he cried. "No! My love!"

She reached for him, gasping for breath. Her lips, and then her face and her neck, began to turn blue. As she fell into his arms, he let out a gruff scream.

"Kash… me… ru…"

He shook his head. "No. Lakshmi. My love. You can't die!"

She placed a hand on his jaw, her lips parted as she struggled to breathe.

He leaned down and kissed her. Together, they fell to their knees. At first, Mayhara didn't understand, but then, as the kiss continued, the blue hue slowly drained from Naree's skin. As Kashmeru syphoned the poison from her body, his lips and jaw turned blue. When the last of the poison left her body, she fell limp and passed out. She slipped from his arms when his body began to stiffen. His throat glowed blue, and his eyes rolled back in his head. The blue skin spread, then turned to gray. The gray hardened, cracked, and crumbled into powder, bit by bit carried off by the wind until Kashmeru was no more.

Jae jumped up and ran to Naree's side. He cradled her head in his lap and searched for a pulse. Her silk gown was drenched in blood. The corpses of the dark mages surrounding them began suffering the same fate as Kashmeru, the dust from their bodies blowing away in the wind.

Karina had done it. She had destroyed Kashmeru. But at what cost?

Jae felt around Naree's neck, wishing his own heart would stop pounding long enough that he could feel his sister's pulse.

"Naree, please," he whispered.

The other mages joined him, all gathered around. They crouched down, their faces full of sadness.

"Is she—" Salina couldn't even continue.

Mayhara lay her head on Jae's shoulder and reached out to take Naree's hand.

Yuki's cheeks were stained with tears. She dropped to her knees and placed her hand on Naree's shoulder. Salina sobbed, taking Naree's other hand. Shiro and Loni placed their hands upon Naree's arm. Penny stroked Naree's forehead.

Darshana stood before them, Karina at her side, and intertwined her fingers, holding her hands against her chin.

Jae suddenly felt a warmth beneath his fingers. He searched Naree's form and spotted the glow beneath the hand of each elite mage. The stones on their wristbands shone, and the different-colored lights moved over the surface of Naree's body. The red light of the garnet moved to the position of the root chakra, the orange to the sacral chakra, and so on, until all seven lights were aligned.

The lights glowed brighter and then, all at once, disappeared. Naree's eyes opened as she let out a gasp.

Jae couldn't believe his eyes. Naree slowly sat up, looking around at the elite mages as if in disbelief. She brought her hands to her lips and shook her head. "After all I did to you, you still saved me." She sniffed back tears. "I'm so sorry. So truly sorry. I... I wasn't me. I couldn't control—"

Jae wiped a tear from her cheekbone. "Of course. We know."

He pulled her close for an embrace, not wanting to let her go.

"We're here to serve you," Shiro said.

Mayhara nodded. "You have your loyal army."

Naree sniffled back her tears. "And I'm ready to lead you. And to make it all up to you."

Jae hugged her again.

"Why didn't the poison affect us?" Salina suddenly asked, looking up at Darshana.

"I wouldn't let it," Karina said with a wink.

Darshana placed an arm around Karina and smiled.

"Sorry to interrupt."

They all looked up to see Qiang and Mitty standing near the entrance of the crypt.

"You might want to come upstairs," Qiang said. "We've rounded everyone up and are holding those responsible under citizen's arrest, in the name of the Empire of the Lotus. We just need our empress to instruct us what to do with them." He bowed. "Your Highness."

Naree's gaze went around to all the elite mages. With one curt nod, she stood, looking graceful and regal despite her blood-soaked dress. She lifted her chin, a determination setting in. "Yes. Let's get started."

TWENTY

ayhara adjusted the black sash of her uniform. The red, military-style jacket was crisp and clean, the silver buttons shining. The pearled lotus pin sat near her shoulder, reminding her of the trials and tribulations she'd gone through to get to where she was now.

"Mayhara?"

She turned to find Yuki standing at the door. Her jacket—the same as Mayhara's but in white—was a stark contrast to her decorated black sash.

"Your family has arrived," Yuki said with a smile.

Mayhara ran her fingers over the braided bun of her dark hair and followed Yuki into the hall.

She was in a part of the palace that held the commanders' apartments. As elites, the mages were assigned quarters to live in, but the empress made it clear that they were free to have residences elsewhere if they pleased, as long as it didn't interfere with their duties. She made it clear that she wanted to remain fair and just in all her rulings.

The commanders' quarters—along with the empress's chambers and the throne room—had been the first of the palace to be restored. Construction would soon begin to restore the academy.

Mayhara walked swiftly down the sunlit hall to the red-carpeted stairs. She had seen her family the very day the prison camps had been abolished, but for all the years she'd been away from them, one reunion was never enough.

Yuki gave her a wink as she disappeared down the hall.

"Mama, Papa!" Mayhara found them outside the throne room, embracing them immediately. Her parents looked older, their hair grayed, and wrinkles worn into their skin. She turned to her sisters—younger spitting images of herself— and placed kisses upon their cheeks.

"Are they really going to rebuild the academy?" her youngest sister, Anjana, asked.

"Yes, and you and Kakoli will both be students. You'll be taught by the finest guru in New United Asia. And I'll be there too, just in case you get into any trouble."

"As a teacher?" Kakoli asked, she and Anjana both seemingly please with the prospect of attending the academy.

"That too. But I have a sworn duty to serve and protect the empress as well." Mayhara smiled, reveling in the fact that she shared this duty with Jae, and that they would be together always.

"We are so thrilled to have been invited to the coronation," Mayhara's mother said, smoothing out her crimson sari.

"Of course." Mayhara placed a hand on her elbow. "It's the least the empire can do for you for the terrible years you suffered. Come. Let's go inside and find your seats."

The throne room's marble floors practically sparkled in the sunlight that streamed in through the floor-to-ceiling gilded windows. The room was filled with chairs—most of them already occupied—facing a dais, upon which sat a magnificent throne.

Mayhara brought her family to their seats. "I have to finish preparing for the ceremony. But I'll see you afterward."

She left the room through the back, which connected to an adjoining preparation room. Karina stood outside the door, waiting for the ceremony to begin, and gave Mayhara a wave. As Mayhara entered the adjoining room, she ran into Shiro, almost knocking him over.

"Sorry," he told her.

She laughed. "No, it's my fault. Wait. I messed up your sash. Let me fix it."

She straightened his sash and brushed lint from his copper jacket. "Is Qiang coming?"

"You mean General Tsai?" He winked.

"Yes, of course."

Shiro smiled. "You know he wanted to be named a knight instead?" He laughed and shook his head. "Yes, I do believe the empress expects his presence."

"And will he stay for the party after?"

"I do believe that *I* expect his presence, yes."

They laughed together just as Loni entered the room. She narrowed her eyes at them.

"You talking about me?" she asked. She checked her emerald green jacket. "Did I button it wrong or something?"

Shiro raised a brow, and Mayhara bit the inside of her cheek.

"No," Mayhara said. "You look great."

Even though Loni walked past her with eyes still narrowed, Mayhara knew it was just for show. They had actually had a nice talk after the showdown with Kashmeru. Mayhara had told Loni about seeing Kanya in the spirit realm and delivered the hug Kanya had asked her to give Loni. That hug had changed things between them, and Mayhara was looking forward to building a friendship with her.

Yuki walked into the room with Penny, who looked amazing in her purple jacket and black sash.

"Hey," Penny called. "It's almost time. Has anyone seen Salina?"

"She's out front," Loni said. "Vano just got here."

"Is Patrin here too?" Shiro asked.

"Yeah," Loni answered. "He's catching up with Mr. Kitaro. Probably sulking in secret because he lost Darshana to him."

"Ooh," Yuki joked. "Love triangle."

"Yeah." Loni smirked. "Those are the worst."

The doors to the garden opened, and Jae stood in the doorway, fixing the lapels of his sapphire blue jacket. He caught Mayhara's eye and she closed the distance between them.

"Hey." Mayhara looked past Jae. "How is she?"

Sitting on the steps to the garden, Naree stared off into the distance. She looked so regal in her silver gown, hair swept up and waiting for her crown.

Naree would get this way sometimes, Mayhara discovered. When it counted, she filled the role of empress with diligence and competence. But when there weren't too many eyes on her, she would withdraw, sitting alone and staring off, as if she were waiting for something. As if she were missing someone.

Jae had said he thought she would need some time. She was heartbroken. She'd lost a love she'd had since the beginning of time. He believed she knew that the relationship had been toxic, but still, that didn't mean her soul was any less crushed.

"She's okay," Jae said. "She'll be in in a minute."

"She's the empress." Mayhara shrugged one shoulder. "She can take all the time she needs."

"In that case," Jae said, taking her hands in his, "that means I have time to do this."

He leaned closer, his gaze on her lips. She couldn't help but smile as she tipped her head up to accept his kiss.

"You promise me a dance later?" she asked when the kiss ended.

"Do I have to?"

She cupped his cheek. "You do," she joked. "I'm afraid it's simply a fate you can't escape."

About the Author

Dorothy Dreyer is a Philippine-born American living in Germany with family and two Siberian Huskies. She is an award-winning, *USA Today* Bestselling Author of young adult and new adult books that usually have some element of magic or the supernatural in them. Her repertoire also includes adult romance and thriller novels. Aside from reading, she enjoys movies, binge-watching series, chocolate, take-out, traveling, and having fun with friends and family.

You can find out more about Dorothy on her website:
http://dorothydreyer.com